I0597897

DIVINE SPARK

DIVINE SPARK

AGE OF AEON

Patrick McGorman

Divine Spark: Age of Aeon

Copyright ©2019 by Patrick McGorman
All rights reserved.

Published by Rebel Press
Austin, TX
www.RebelPress.com

ISBN: 978-1-64339-964-5

Printed in the United States of America

*To my parents and twin brother Thomas, who supported
my dream of writing for the world for my entire life.*

*To John A. Maggio, whose skill as a Dungeon Master
got my imagination rolling for over a decade.*

*To Gary Gygax and Dave Arneson, for creating Dungeons and
Dragons, one of my biggest influences and an integral part of my life.*

To every English and/or Writing teacher I have had over the years.

To those 3 AM nights working on this book. They were worth it.

DIVINE SPARK

New Morning

It was five and a half hours after midnight. The sun was beginning to rise up to greet the land with its light, and the sky changed from an endless void to a faded hue of blue. Still, the strongest light in the city street was the headlights of a jet-black automobile. As these vehicles were only invented a few decades ago, anybody would be happy to have one of these gas-guzzlers.

The man inside was unhappy with the circumstances. It meant that he had to do business fast. If he screwed up, there would be hell waiting for him. The boss of the Lefty Gang was never happy with mistakes. Nobody liked failure—just some people were less tolerant of it than others.

Seeing the sign for Porlandus Street, he took a right turn. To his relief, Porlandus Street was dead quiet at this hour. It should be; he chose this meeting spot specifically because of the lack of people. This part of Sorchos City had long been abandoned due to poor city management and faulty building construction. He sighed, remembering reading newspapers thirty years ago about how Sorchos used to be an economic gold mine. But incompetent businessmen and greedy politicians destroyed the soul of this place. Now this part of the city looked no better than a ghost town.

Although he had heard stories about how nasty of a place this was at night, he felt a little too safe. Still, he held on to the handle of the briefcase in the passenger's seat with protectiveness. He would be more than willing to die for the contents inside, but he anticipated that would not be happening tonight.

He saw not a soul as he slowly drove past each abandoned apartment, store, and office. The only sign of life he saw was a mother cat inside a shed, nursing her young. This reminded him that twelve hours ago his neighbor desired a kitten litter and asked if his cat could be the father. He was thinking about it, but he should get back to her after all this. *Why not? Little Yun would get some action for once in his lazy life.*

He found the old and abandoned glue factory that he chose for the drop-off. He parked his car in a long ignored "no parking" space. With the case in his right hand, he walked toward the buildings in his trench coat and fedora. Some of his peers said that it looked tacky on him but, with his red-tinted, templeless sunglasses resting on the bridge of his nose, he admitted to feeling pretty "hip" or "badass."

His joints had been acting up lately, so he walked with an ornate oak cane. He might be getting too old for this. Three months ago he'd reached fifty-eight and now years of physical exertion had finally begun to show their wrath. But he still walked on. It was his duty as part of the Lefty Gang. He didn't get paid to lie around complaining about aches and pains.

He forced open the door and wandered about the abandoned factory. He'd heard ominous tales about this place. He was told that when it was running, there was little in the way of safety codes. Injuries in the factory were common, and the safety regulators were bribed to keep this dump open. Rumor had it that one time somebody fell into a machine and melded into the batter. The vat of glue was still distributed around the world. Supposedly somewhere in a poor rural area, little kids in art class found that the stuff in their glue was pink rather than white.

Did the authorities arrest the factory owner? Hell no! He paid off the cops, who officially claimed that somebody put red dye in the mix as a sick prank, and filed a missing person's case for the victim. But the owner wouldn't get away with his sins in the end.

He soon received letters threatening his life, supposedly written by the son of the victim. At first, he dismissed them. But within the next few days, the notes became more visceral, speaking about cutting him up and making him eat his own entrails. After a while, family members went missing. He was soon getting mailed body parts. This all culminated in him receiving his daughter's head, driving him to hang himself in his office the same night. The killer was never caught.

Within weeks, more reasonable authorities investigated the factory and noted the flagrant health violations—the wobbly stairs, the inadequate heating system, the lack of gloves. The factory was closed down soon after. Since the factory jobs were a major part of the neighborhood's income, it eventually went to squalor as people left in search of better jobs. Within the decade, Porlandus became a shell of what it once was.

But those were just legends. Sadly, in this world, legends tend to be true.

After some wandering, he found the abandoned and dusty breakroom. There were still filthy vending machines with long-spoiled perishables inside. The smell disgusted him. But he also detected the bitter smell of store brand tea ahead of him. It could have at least been fermented.

Looking forward, he saw the man he was to do business with. A seemingly middle-aged man by the name of Mark Jonah sat at one of the tables, sipping tea he brought from home. In the honest world, Mark was an average office drone, pushed around by people higher than him on the ladder. But in the criminal underworld, he was the greatest forger on Earth.

Mark spoke up first as he took a sip. "Glad that you made it, Shèng Xià. I was almost afraid you wouldn't come with the money." He pushed a cup toward his client.

Shèng was not even in the mood to sit down. He just wanted to get this over with and go home to Little Yun and watch the crystalvision until noon and then sleep. So he spoke up, peering at Mark through his glasses in case he was trying anything funny. "I'm afraid you only have five minutes worth of my time, Mark. We'll make this quick. Do you have the fakes?"

"Quite forward, aren't you?" He skipped the formalities and placed three suitcases on the table. "Voila! Perfect copies of the Eight Relics of the Kadosh Family."

Mark slowly opened each case. Shèng counted eight fake artifacts and moved closer to get a better look. Mark stopped him. "Nuh-uh. My prize first."

Giving into the master forger's demands, he placed the briefcase on the table. Opening it up revealed more paz bills than most people see in a lifetime, fifty million to be exact. This gave Shèng permission to inspect the goods.

The first one contained armor. A breastplate was inside with the design that made any possible wearer appear as if the center of their body had a monstrous face with such lovely sights as ruby eyes and fangs encompassing the bottom of the armor. Also inside were shoulder pauldrons, that while fairly large, Shèng was pleased that at least they didn't have gratuitous spikes or anything impractical.

The second bag contained more armor, also coated in bronze. There was a mask with the appearance of a man that was portrayed to be way too calm, perfectly tranquil, or just dead inside. Also inside were iron bracers adorned with bronze skulls, which seemed unnecessarily tacky. The last item in the bag was a pair of grieves, which notably had an appearance similar to chitin.

The final bag sealed the deal. There was an amulet adorned with a bright green emerald surrounded by a golden lining. Under that was a dark cape with buttons made from onyx, adorned with an insignia of azure flames. The last piece was a bright silver war medal, which had a pure sapphire insignia of a woman with wings, a representation of Sophia herself.

He scrutinized each and every one of the forgeries. Each fake was made from the exact materials of the original, regardless of the cost and craft. Each piece was also aged to give the effect of being a few centuries older than they truly were. From what he could tell, Mark had done his work efficiently and masterfully.

"This looks legit, Mark." He began to place the forgeries back into their respective bags with the same care he would treat the originals.

He began to feel uneasy though. Outside, he heard the slightest hint of footsteps inching closer toward him. He looked toward Mark, who by all criminal logic must know when someone was approaching an operation. To no surprise, Mark just smiled as if he'd just become king of the world.

Oddly, despite realizing the setup, Shèng was not exactly scared; more curious for the reason why. "So what's the logic in having your friends outside?"

"You know why." And with those words, Mark took out a small crossbow hidden under the table. Seconds later, his associates rushed into the room, all surrounding Shèng. Each gangster wielded a crossbow in their hands, ready to shoot a bolt into him. "Your boss has a poor reputation with his clients. They tend to disappear."

But alas, Shèng's reaction was merely a dulled sense of surprise. "Well, I guess this welcome is fair." He took off his glasses, placing them in one of his coat pockets. "The Lefty Gang is having 'budget cutbacks.' Plus, there's the fact that nobody could trust you not to snitch about this deal, so my boss decided that you made yourself useful for the moment." Out of thin air, a loaded hand crossbow flashed into existence in the enforcer's left hand. "But I'm afraid that he's done with you."

Ignoring the ten assailants surrounding him, Shèng Xià made the shot at Mark's head faster than anyone could react. This would have been action movie quality…if the bolt had actually hit the target. Instead he missed by three feet to the right, the bolt sticking into the wall. Mark and his goons were awestruck that somebody could possibly miss a target five feet away.

An insincere sigh escaped Shèng's lips. "Well…I guess I'm getting a bit rust—"

Each and every gang member shot at him. The collection of bolts pierced various parts of his body. Normally, a person this shot up would be dead. But no, he just kept on standing, his cane and crossbow still in his hands. Shèng made no cries of pain or begging for his life. Instead an indigo symbol shaped like two C's back-to-back appeared on his chest.

Shèng's weapon disappeared into nothingness, granting him a free hand to rip a bolt out of his cheek. He was rather nonchalant about being all shot up. He spoke only two words in response to their ambush.

"Bad move."

The symbol on his chest flashed brighter. Within that second, long flash, his foes were hurt where he was hurt, times seven. The one who shot him in the eye had seconds to comprehend what was happening before he received a hole in his head as if skewered by a ballista. Another discovered a brand new opening in his chest that all could see through. One of the crooks that shot him in the arm found his entire arm severed from the shoulder. Another who shot him in the cheek found his jaw ripped off.

Many died within seconds from trauma and blood loss, but Mark was less lucky. Turns out he shot him in the stomach. The bolt did not go too deep into Shèng, but the backlash from his mark inflicted enough damage to the forger that he had a hole the size of a baseball through his stomach, destroying the bottom portion of his spine.

Any survivors were screaming in horror and agony. Shèng merely shook his head as his body pushed the remaining bolts out of his body, closing the wounds within seconds. As his eye healed up, he saw that there were still two uninjured enemies about ten feet away. He had to rectify that.

"You two should have hit me. You'd die quicker."

He summoned a throwing knife into his hand. Before either assailant could react or reload their weapons, Shèng threw the knife into one of their throats, piercing him through the neck. He dashed toward the two and quickly yanked the blade out of the neck, creating a fountain of blood to give the room a long overdue paintjob. The remaining attacker tried to high tail it out, but Shèng was having none of that. There could be no survivors, no witnesses. He pulled the man by the back of the collar, causing him to collapse. Then with a twirl of his weapon, he plunged the knife into his heart. There was a momentary struggle, but the body inevitably went limp.

With the nuisance over, Shèng walked over to each and every single corpse. He inspected them for signs of life. The only one left breathing was Mark, who was trying to drag himself to the exit in a vain hope it would lead him to safety. He didn't make much of a blood trail by the time Shèng pinned him down with a stomp.

Mark had the smile wiped away from his face. Rather than speak, all he could do was scream in agony and struggle in helplessness. But this was Porlandus; nobody would ever hear his cries.

"Sorry, Mark. You should've known the boss would send a psychic to do a job this important." He began to unscrew the top of his walking cane. "What the boss says, goes. That's the business." He removed the top of the cane, unsheathing a hidden sword. "Your five minutes are up."

With all of them dead, Shèng stretched back, trying to relax his tense body. But the mission wasn't completed. He took out a small crystalline device from his pocket and dialed in a number. Waiting thirty seconds, someone picked up.

"Password."

The "secretary" to the Lefty Gang always made the most demeaning weekly passwords. But without it, there was no proof that it was him calling. So he reluctantly answered. "I am a dumbass thirty-year-old bed wetter." He hoped one day his boss would hire him to kill the son of a bitch the moment he was useless to the gang.

The snickering over the phone made him want to choke that pissant. But soon the man over the phone continued to speak. "So is the deed done, Shèng Xià?"

"Yes, Ezker. Mark made himself useful for the last time. The forgeries are a masterwork. I'm on my way to deliver them now."

He hung up his crystalcell. Putting his spectacles back on and sheathing his blade back into his cane, Shèng saw light seep through the window. The sun was rising higher by the minute. He had to get the money and relics to his boss soon. He had a schedule to follow. Though the amount of bags he had to bring to his automobile would require a couple of trips, he resolved to make it on time. Stuff like this was a typical early morning for him. He'd done worse as a psychic working with the law. But with these copies of the Legendary Relics of Kadosh, he had a feeling that his boss was planning something bigger than usual.

But he wasn't the only one to have a memorable morning. Meanwhile, in the bright city of Bythos, someone else's life would soon change forever.

"Another done. That makes eight."

A teenage boy finished sharpening a twenty-five-inch metal bolt on a grinding wheel. After a close inspection with his deep purple eyes, he placed the bolt on the table alongside seven others. The various quarrel had a variety of tips—the basic steel points, rubber ends, and double-pronged as well as one that spiraled from the head all the way down the shaft like a drill bit.

"That'll do for now." He took off his goggles and looked up at the clock that appeared above his workspace and saw that it was 7:45. He had been up for two hours crafting the bolts along with making the finishing touches on his masterpiece. On top of his work desk was a sky blue arbalest the size of the upper half of his body.

He couldn't help but grin in excitement. "Took me forever, but now it's done." He lifted the freshly polished weapon onto his lap, stroking the lathe of it. "Damn, I'm good." He pulled on the windlass to check how tight the string was. The answer was very tight. "She's going to love it. I'm sure of it."

The young man then heard footsteps coming toward the workshop.

"Ercan, are you in here? Time to get ready."

As soon as Ercan put his masterpiece onto his desk, there was a knock at the door.

"Can I come in, or are you still working on more bolts?"

A yawn came through the door, indicating to him his mother had awakened not too long ago. Ercan always wondered how his work never woke any of his family members. He gave her an answer.

"Go ahead. I'm done anyway."

His mother came in through the door, her long black hair still having a case of bedhead.

"You're particularly early. How long have you been up?"

Ercan got up from the chair and covered the arbalest with a tarp. "About two and a half hours. Just finishing my gift."

"Did you shower yet?" his mother asked him, not even questioning the fact that her son was building a giant crossbow. "This room always smells of metal and wood shavings. Take one before you wake your sister up, all right? Then get ready for school. It's the first day."

Ercan tried to sniff the armpit of his striped pajamas, but didn't really smell anything. But he didn't want to disobey Rina, matriarch of the Ao'Si family. "Alright, alright." He patted his mom's shoulder and he walked past her. "But it's not my first day," he corrected her. "It's Shee'vra's."

"You know what I meant, Erky," Rina replied as her eldest child disappeared into the bathroom. "Keep her safe."

"I intend to, Mother."

"Good. I'll be making breakfast."

~ * ~

Wrapped in the deep embrace of her bed sheets, Shee'vra slumbered. The only part of her sticking out of the human burrito was her messy dark hair. But her peaceful rest would inevitably have to come to an end as the alarm clock inched closer to 8:05.

She began to wake up and saw the time. She groaned in disappointment as she saw the big hand reach the three.

But I was having such a great dream. I miss getting to wake up at nine.

She wanted to go back to the realm high above the clouds, full of dragons and licorice and licorice dragons. For a few seconds she prayed to Sophia that she had the power to turn back time but it was far from likely.

But today was a big day; she needed to get up now.

Her bedroom door abruptly opened and she heard her older brother's voice. "Upsy-Daisy, Sheev! Today's your big day!"

She could only let out an "Eep!" as she was suddenly lifted up off the bed, sheets and all. Ercan lifted her up like a log and spun her around and around. "First day at Aeon-Sophia Academy! The school where psychics become heroes!"

Shee'vra was now wide-awake but quickly getting dizzy. "I know! I know! I'm up! Just please put me down!"

Ercan complied with her request and tossed her back onto the bed, causing her to bounce and break out of the warm embrace of her blanket. She quickly came to her senses and got on her two feet to get ready.

"So are you excited for the beginning of your entire future?" her brother asked as he brushed his still wet red hair with his hand.

The words "entire future" struck Shee'vra like a mallet to the back of the head. Just because she was now a psychic, she had no choice but to stick to one destiny. No longer could she become a physician, or lawyer, or a common clerk at the supermarket. Those were the jobs of the hylic, the sparkless. Now she had no choice but to enter such positions as officer, royal guard, bounty hunter, or perhaps a mercenary for hire; only jobs that put her life at risk. Though the idea of helping the helpless appealed to her, the thought that she would most definitely meet resistance in these career paths in the form of criminals scared her. She had no idea how to fight and knew that such enemies wouldn't hold back against her.

So she decided to simply give the terse answer of "I guess."

Her elder brother ruffled her short hair. "That's the spirit. Get ready,

Sis, and I'll see you at breakfast. Mother's making waffles. I'm out." Ercan left her room, closing the door behind him.

Shee'vra went to her clothes drawer, her mind heavy with the thought of her future. As she took out her favorite pink turtleneck sweater, she contemplated how restricted her life suddenly felt. As she took out a skirt, she thought about the pressure she would go through to become—in her brother's words—"badass," which meant defeating bad guys and saving entire neighborhoods, cities, countries, and perhaps the entire world. Even her mom once in a while received a call for a faraway mission that needed her. As she took out her knee-high socks, she realized that her future now was to merely be available to the world. There would be no regularities such as sick days, monthly salary, or vacations. A psychic was only called upon when needed.

The discovery of her spark had turned her life upside down. Though her brother's spark had manifested when he began to walk, she'd only learned of hers last summer on her birthday. She blew out her candles with such force that the cake splattered all over her family and friends.

She knew the Academy would help her find out.

Her thought process was interrupted once her alarm clock rang.

By 8:30, the entire family was up and having breakfast around the table. Chocolate chip waffles with delicious syrup from the Maple Groves and a fruit salad consisting of strawberries, bananas, apples, and toast. A perfect way to start a morning.

Ercan's and Shee'vra's father glanced at his daughter through his rimmed glasses. "So is my little girl excited for her first day?"

Shee'vra had a feeling that she was going to get that question a lot today. "I… guess. I don't really know what I'm going to do there."

Her father, Ult'Tan, didn't seem to notice her hesitation and, if he did, decided against bringing it up. "I'm sure it'll all be fine. I can't say from experience, but I'm sure every new student gets scared on his or her first day—new environment, new peers, new everything." He patted his son's back. "Heck, even your brother cried during his first month before going to school when he started."

"Come on! Really, dad? I was five!" Ercan defended himself with his mouth full.

"I got scared on my first week too," Rina added in. "The idea of being in a room with other psychics that could do the craziest things terrified me to the core. But after a while it just felt natural." She placed a note on the table for Shee'vra to see. "Besides, you have been assigned to Rooster Squad, so you have your brother to protect you."

That boosted Shee'vra's confidence a bit. As she finished her meal she saw that it was time to get going. Ercan noticed as well and the two teens got up from the table. They grabbed their bags and headed toward the door.

Ercan exited first; ready to show his sister the most amazing academy ever made. "Bye, Mom. Bye, Dad."

Shee'vra followed suit. "We'll see you both tonight."

Their mother waved back to them. "Have fun, you two. I'll be here when you come back."

"I might not be," Ult'Tan stated. "I have a lot to do at the law firm today. But I'm rooting for you kids."

The two adolescents closed their apartment door behind them and headed toward the elevator. Ercan pressed the down button.

"So you're going to love it. There's going to be training and mock battles and you're going to get to learn the name of your spark…along with the basics like math, homework, and the like." The elevator doors opened and he walked forwards. "Trust me, Sheev, you'll be safe with—"

"Look out! The—"

But Shee'vra's warning did not register in time, and Ercan fell through the elevator shaft. He could barely yelp as he fell down what must have been four floors. Shee'vra looked down in horror to see her brother splayed on top of the broken elevator car.

"Are you okay?" she called out to her brother, worried, but oddly not all that worried for a girl who'd just seen her brother fall down an elevator shaft. She really didn't want to be late for her first day. What would the other students think of her?

Within ten seconds, Ercan lifted his upper body up. He winced in pain as he looked down toward his feet. Both feet were at an angle that no limb should theoretically be. Luckily his scarlet pants were not tight below the knees, so no bones would pierce the leather.

To the sight that always amazed Shee'vra no matter how many times she saw it, her brother's knees and ankles were moved back in place by her brother's will alone. Any outer wounds were completely healed up. What would have taken weeks of healing only took a brief moment.

He soon got back on his good-as-new feet and looked up to answer his sister with only mere annoyance. "So something screwed up again? Second time that's happened."

"And the second time you fell in," Shee'vra added with a cheeky grin. Ercan was luckily always the first one to discover hazards every time. Last time it was an electrical malfunction. It was as if he was the entire apartment complex's designated victim of accidents. Then again, a man with a healing factor was the best person to take the brunt of fate's abuse.

Ercan just nodded in ashamed acknowledgement, seriously considering whether or not to sue whoever was in charge of elevator repair. "Whatever. Coming back up. Stay back." Ercan looked down his jacket to check whether his platinum medallion was still around his neck. The round medallion looked like a half moon with an eye, with the pupil of the eye and the dark side of the moon a purple luster. He'd had it since birth and was unwilling to lose it. Always good to double check after getting hurt a bit.

Shee'vra followed his command and soon after, from under his loose scarlet sleeves, two iron chains with a hook on each tip appeared from the bottom of his wrists. The two chains rapidly extended toward the seventh floor, catching on a steel beam. The redheaded psychic pulled himself up and hopped back out of the shaft next to his sister.

"Well that was a waste of time," Ercan said with irritation. "Thank goodness for my Prometheus spark or we'd be late for sure, and I refuse to allow my sister to be late for her first day." He went down the flight of stairs. "Get going, Sheev."

Shee'vra followed her brother, ready to introduce herself to what her new life could be. She couldn't avoid her new destiny, so she might as well confront it head on. But she wondered what the true name of her spark would be. If Ercan's was Prometheus, what was hers?

The Disciples of Yeren

The clock struck 7:30 as Yun Xuanzang worked in his condo's kitchen. The new place had an amazing stove that he couldn't wait to use. What better time for banana pancakes than the beginning of the new school year?

He was also hyped in anticipation about the fact that Rooster Squad was getting a new member for their five-man band of warriors. He recalled Ercan saying his younger sister, Shee'vra, was going to the academy this year, so maybe it would be her. He had met her before; she was a nice girl, but maybe too nice. He wondered how she would adapt to her new lot in life.

But he decided that he should leave such thoughts for when he saw the Ao'Si siblings later. Right now, he had pancakes to make. He had a way of quickly making pancakes that no human could ever mimic. He used his left hand for holding the pan, right hand for banana tossing, his left foot for a plate to flip the pancakes onto along with his right foot for stability, and finally, his long prehensile tail for mastering a spatula. There sure were benefits to being able to turn into a monkey man.

At last the food making was finished and on the table was a stack of flapjacks, chock-full of bananas. As stereotypical as it was, bananas were Yun's favorite fruit. The softness, the texture, and how easy it was to mix into meals, especially breakfasts. There was also the idea that it took no actual effort to peel that made Yun enjoy them even more. Nevertheless, he always enjoyed a challenge, and this year would grant him more challenges than the last. He was sure of it.

Done with it for now, he deactivated his simian-based spark, though he always chose to keep his tail around. All his pants were tailored to suit a need for an extra limb. Satisfied with his work, he called for the others.

"Hey guys! Wakey, wakey! I got pancakes for the entire gang!" He sat on one of the kitchen stools, swiveling around. "If you don't hurry, it'll all be gone!"

"Pipe down, Yun! I need to focus right now!" Xiu Lang yelled back in irritation. She then continued to hum to herself the newest hit song on the radio as she admired herself in her mirror. She brushed her long, smooth hair as she sat on the flowery cover of her neatly made bed. She'd been up for an hour to get ready for the first day of the year at Aeon Sophia Academy, though she always tended to get up early to get ready. Just because she was a psychic who was expected to devote her life to battle and rescues didn't mean she couldn't look her best every day.

She was done blow-drying her hair and put on her favorite casual wear. She had put on her eye shadow and was now just about done with straightening her hair. She hoped that all the other girls' eyes would go green with unbridled envy as she passed down the halls, that the guys would trample over one another to get into her good graces. She bet that if she were a Squad Captain, she'd be the queen of the academy.

But she came crashing down with the realization that she had just been transferred to a new squad. No longer was she on Rooster Squad, but now Heron Squad. After the squad's utter blunder at the last Aeon Sophia Games, the faculty analyzed the problems with the squad in depth. They deduced that Xiu Lang hardly ever listened to Ercan, always butted heads with him, and made too many rash mistakes—unfit for the type of squad Rooster was. Her emerald eyes looked down from the mirror in a scowl.

How is it entirely my fault that we sucked? Xiu thought, grimacing. *The entire team screws up and I'm the only one punished for it. Typical. Shouldn't the entire team sucking be blamed on the leader? Have they considered that maybe Ercan isn't all that good at leading and telling people what to do?*

She put down her hairbrush, finished with it. *All he did was point us where to go as he did his own thing, just swinging his little chains around in his stupid little red jacket…that is so tight you can see his lean and muscular physique. Hell, with that tight leather, there's hardly anything left to the imagination.*

She began to blush a bit. *His deep red hair, not too short to be indistinguishable and not too long to be a stupid mullet, perfectly matches that jacket. And damn, those purple eyes. Those eyes should be utterly impossible to have, but nature just went "screw it" and blessed him with them anyway.*

She finally realized she was getting way too lost in her mind. She shook the thoughts out of her head.

~ * ~

The call for pancakes awoke Caradoc Albain from his deep slumber. The boy abruptly jumped high up out of his bed, landing feet first on the ground. He half-assedly brushed his brown hair and put on his favorite *Mechalaxy Saga* T-shirt along with a pair of jeans. And no, he didn't change the underwear he wore to bed before putting on his clothes.

But before he dashed toward the door, he realized he'd almost forgotten something. He moved toward his shelf full of sci-fi stories and franchises such as *Princess of Mercury, 1001 Cycles, Mechalaxy Saga*, and *CyberRaptor 1099*. Next to the shelf, tacked onto the wall, was a *1001 Cycles* calendar he'd gotten for the year 567 A.D. (After Demiurge).

Opening it five months ahead to February, not only was there a picture of a Mecha Ifrit with a magma cannon, but also the 17th day was circled. That day was the annual Aeon Sophia Games, a tournament for all the squads at the academy to enter. February 17th was also *Talk Like A Robot Day* but that wasn't important to anyone else but him. His team, Eagle Squad, came in silver last time, but this time they would be working toward the gold. That day he would need to be at his best.

But there was no point in thinking about the future. The present was what was important right now. Caradoc couldn't wait to figure out the fastest path to get to school. The four of them had just moved to Little Tian, an area in Bythos City with a large Qian Ye population. Yun had checked out the real estate and the rent was really fair there, so they moved during the summer. He liked the extra space, but the neighbors occasionally looked at him funny, as if he didn't belong. He'd like to think it was because of the dorky shirts he wore, but he knew it was because he didn't appear to be of Qian heritage. In fact, the only reason he didn't stick out more was because Hong Hai Long resembled a walking salamander.

But who cared? He had pancakes to gobble up. Out the door he went.

~ * ~

"So…first day of Senior Year," Hong spoke up as he bathed in the tub. His navy blue skin became smooth and slimy as he allowed the water to hydrate his body. "Last year at Aeon Sophia Academy. They're going to work my tail off."

He flopped his tail out of the tub, soaking the tile floor. "I'll be drowning in papers and training simulations. I wonder how my friends will act when they're in my nonexistent and non-necessary shoes."

Hong was the oldest of the four disciples of Master Yeren at seventeen. Xiu and Yun were both sixteen with Xiu a few months older, and Caradoc was fifteen and thus the baby of the bunch. Their master sent them to Enotita to be at the Academy for Psychics.

He sat up and twirled his open webbed hand a bit. "Well not literally mind you, 'cause I can breathe underwater. But they will break my balls with work. Which, come to think of it, is impossible, as I seem to lack mammalian genitalia. Salamanders reproduce through the male releasing their seed onto the female's eggs to fertilize them."

He tried to focus himself once again on the topic of conversation. "But that's not what is important right now. Like what do you think about the world beyond my Academy? Will it tolerate one such as myself? Should I stay with the others? Perhaps I could find a niche in keeping truths no one else wants to know. Then again, in order to learn such a truth, somebody else must already know it, thus making such a job moot." He was following his stream of thought to a tee, no matter how odd it sounded. "Oh, job stuff is hard and dumb."

He took a breath as he tried to formulate what he would say next. Hong looked up directly at his target of conversation with his glowing red eyes. His conversation mate was a six-by-six-foot eye on the red fleshy ceiling. The walls around him were covered in eyes of various colors and sizes along with mouths with tongues and various teeth. The tub's water seemed as pink as a human brain and created ripples as Hong moved about. Outside of the frosted window were a blood sky and three black suns. Most people wouldn't exactly be comfortable in such an environment, but Hong felt at home.

The big eye above had no idea what the salamander person was talking about, even with the ear holes scattered on the floor. So the flesh on the ceiling just simply crinkled its wrinkles upwards as if to give a shrug.

Hong had a feeling he hadn't explained clearly enough. He began to try and elaborate. "Well you see, from what I heard—"

There was a sudden knock on the bile-covered door. It was Caradoc. "Hey Hong, who are you talking to in there?"

He told the plain truth. "Just having a conversation with the eye on the ceiling."

There was a brief pause from his peer. "…so anyway, are you finished hydrating yet? Yun has breakfast ready. Snooze you lose, up to you."

When Hong thought about it, he was quite hungry. He slithered out of the tub. "Alright, I must feed now. We'll continue this conversation tonight."

He waved the eye goodbye. The eye above moved its pupil up and down as if to wave back. Hong deactivated his Tsathoggua spark, replacing his glowing eyes with humanoid ones. What was once a visceral bathroom was now natural and porcelain to his vision. The salamander scurried out of the door on all fours, startling Xiu.

"Dammit, Hong! You got the floor all soaked again." Xiu scowled at him. But she was ignored. The teenage girl sighed, then walked down the hall. Someone was going to slip on the floor.

What is wrong with him? Do I want to know? Probably not.

The four residents sat on the kitchen stools. The boys ate the banana pancakes covered in syrup while Xiu had some bran flakes cereal with grapes in it and skim milk.

"You sure you don't want some?" Yun asked with his mouth full, to her disgust.

"Yes," she answered tiredly for the third time. "I'm not eating such messy crap. And if any of you get any syrup in my hair or on my clothes…" purple wisps of energy appeared around her hands, "…you'll regret it."

Yun was unfazed by her threat. "Well *somebody* woke up on the wrong side of her queen sized bed." He swallowed his food. "But anyway, what's your new squad?"

Xiu grimaced in disgust. "Heron Squad. *Freaking* Heron Squad. *The* most obnoxious squad of them all."

Caradoc chimed in. "They're not that bad."

She huffed. "How can you call a yappy toilet-tongued rabbit, a giant armored fish person that rambles on and on about the most stupid things, and the academy's class clown all lead by the biggest pervert in school not obnoxious?"

"Well that depends…" Caradoc answered plainly. "Do you have any nonhuman traits like bat wings, dog ears, cat tails, fish gills, bull horns, feathers, or the lower body of anything non-human?"

Xiu became less irritated and more puzzled. "No." She really didn't want to ask why, but she couldn't resist. "Why?"

"Then Desiderio wouldn't hit on you even if you were the last lady on Earth," Caradoc bluntly stated. He recalled that during the summer, Desiderio texted his buddy Basil that after a squad mission, he managed to hook up with some snake girl. As in upper half human, lower half snake. Caradoc was less jealous and more confused about how hooking up with a snake girl was even physically possible.

"Heron Squad sounds fun," Hong added as he stared into space, mostly just talking to himself. "Sounds like wacky hijinks every day." He looked down at his last remaining pancake in contemplation, scratching on the back of his wetsuit. "I wish Kingfisher Squad was as wacky."

The others didn't pay attention to him. Xiu just finished her cereal and got up from the stool. "Whatever. If Heron Squad is all for wacky hijinks, that might be even lamer." She put her bowl and spoon into the dishwasher. "Besides, what I want to know is who the hell is replacing *me*."

The boys stopped eating to acknowledge her question. They knew that she would not relent until she got an answer. So Hong spoke up first with his mouth full.

"You mean on Rooster Squad?"

Xiu just sighed in disbelief. "Yes, Hong. On Rooster Squad."

"Well," Yun answered his peer, "this isn't one hundred percent certain. But I think it might be Shee'vra."

There was a moment of silence as Xiu contemplated who that could possibly be, but soon relented. "Who's Shee'vra?" This Shee'vra had better not be some kind of…gorgeous Kruschtyan assassin-in-training or something.

Caradoc shook his head in disbelief. "She's Ercan's younger sister."

The ex-Rooster simmered down a bit, surprised. "Wait a minute. Since when did Ercan have a sister?" She didn't recall him even mentioning having a sibling.

Yun was just incredulous. "Really?! He texted you about this! Check your cell."

Xiu took her deep red crystalcell out from her pocket to check her texts. As she scrolled down the screen, she noticed that most of them were from her circle of friends like Sabelle, Vasanti, and Shiro about hanging out, new clothes, other students, the grapevine of gossip, and other things of interest. At the bottom of an ocean of texts, there was an unopened one from Ercan. It read: *my baby sister just became a psychic! Isn't that awesome? Hope she kicks ass.*

Xiu turned her cell off and admitted defeat. "Alright, fine. I didn't know he had told me already. I was busy."

Yun finished his meal and placed his plate and silverware in the dishwasher. "Strange. I thought you would pay more attention to his texts."

Her eyes narrowed but did not initiate contact with anyone. "What's that supposed to mean?"

"That it's strange that you don't speak to your old team that much," Hong added, swallowing the last half of his meal whole. "Duh."

She was fine with accepting such an answer. It was true. Xiu Lang never really hung out with the rest of Rooster Squad. The most contact she had with them after school or missions was with Yun, but that was only because they lived together. She preferred being in the company of her girl posse. There, she was the true leader and she liked it like that. Besides, the rest of Rooster Squad didn't really share her tastes in hobbies. What exactly was so dull about malls and gossip anyway? Xiu would never understand.

Hong was still hungry and there were still plenty of pancakes on a plate. He licked his lips and raised his open hand above the counter. A small black blob no bigger than a baseball appeared from under it. The amorphous mass moved toward the stack of food.

"Eeugh! That's sick!" Xiu cried out in disgust, looking away as the mass created several pseudopods that reached for the pancakes.

Caradoc pushed his meal away, losing his appetite as the slime absorbed its meal within itself, growing in size. "Really? I *was* eating here, man."

Yun resisted the need to hurl as the goop slithered toward its master. "Did you have to use the formless spawn?"

To their horror, the formless spawn crawled up Hong's body and slid down his gullet. The salamander licked the edges of his mouth in satisfaction, oblivious to the nauseated look of his housemates. He closed the washer, letting out a loud belch.

"My apologies," Hong said bashfully as he covered his mouth. "Better coming out one end than the other."

He then grabbed his book bag and walked toward the window. His eyes once again began to glow. Opening the window, he crawled out like a lizard. Unlike most people who would fall three stories down, Hong was moving on an unseen force that, to onlookers, must have been a bridge of some sort or even a hill. Hong stood up on his two feet and began to run on the invisible trail above the buildings, occasionally jumping from one unseen platform to another.

The concept of walking on nothing would have been at least a marvel of nature for an average person, a sign of godhood for others. But in a world of psychics, it was only unusual. Everyone in the world knew what psychics were and that each one had powers that defied the laws of reality, each in their own unique way. So, the reaction of the people in the town seeing a humanoid amphibian was less "Holy crap! A slimy thing is running on air!" and more like "Looks like the salamander kid that talks to himself in the alleyway is off to school."

Yun, Xiu, and Caradoc watched for a bit as Hong disappeared from view. They all thought that Hong was odd, but he was nevertheless family to them. Yun then put his shoes in his backpack and transformed back into his monkey form.

"I'll see you guys later. I've got a new teammate to meet." Yun jumped out the window and climbed onto a power line, running on the line on all fours. *I'm sure the new member will be Shee'vra, but a part of me is hoping for a hot Eastern Tirnan assassin with stealth powers and tight catsuits.*

Caradoc soon followed suit with his backpack on. "Well, I'm off to school too. See ya later, Xiu." He then turned back toward her for a second. "By the way, I suggest you don't worry about all this squad crap. I'm feeling that this year is going to be a new experience for all of us." He then jumped out of the window forty feet up into the air as if he were on the moon.

Xiu locked the window as the last of her fellow disciples left for the Academy. Sometimes they could be such showoffs. Just because they had sparks that gave them extra locomotion didn't mean that they should just ignore doors. She sighed and prayed for this school year to be better than the last. As she walked toward her room to grab her bag, she perseverated on who this Shee'vra girl was. The fact that she had no idea that Ercan had a sister said a lot about how close she was to her old squad. Maybe with Shee'vra, they'd be better. But for now, she wondered how she'd adapt to Heron Squad.

These thoughts prevented her from noticing that the floor was still wet. She slipped and fell on her back. The profanities she spewed could be heard throughout the entire building.

Heirs to the Future

"Goooood Morning Bythos City!" The sound of a rooster crowing its distinctive cocka-doodle-doo resounds on the radio speakers in the corner of the ceiling. *"It just turned eight…you know what that means…"*

A pair of eyes opened up for another day and reactively winced at the morning radio channel. Devon Deran was always irritating to wake up to. She missed Mitchell Morkick. He at least had something resembling charisma and taste.

"…MORNING MUSIC MARATHON! Staaaarting with Serin Seriyah's superb single 'Sharing Souls with Someone' in stores soon!"

"Radio off." The woman in bed spoke out to no one in particular. Before the song she had heard a dozen times yesterday could start, the radio speakers on her ceiling turned silent.

With a sigh of reluctance, she got out of her royalty-sized bed and the embrace of her velvet sheets.

Why couldn't the first day of school be next week? she thought as she walked across her dimly lit room toward her wardrobe. *Or better yet, next year or even next decade?*

As she was plodding toward the closet, the candlestick-like crystalline communication device on her night table began to scream. Knowing who the caller would most likely be, the sleepyhead decided that picking up the phone would be too much of a chore right now. So thus, she simply pressed the speaker button. With a little bit of static, the speakers on the ceiling now had the voice of a man roughly in his fifties. It was, to no surprise, her father. Ready to speak words of encouragement no doubt for the new year.

She was met with a delightful greeting. "Morning, Jules."

"Julia," she bluntly stated as she took a gray hoodie out of her closet.

Her correction was ignored. "So, are you excited for the new year?"

"Not really."

"And why is that, my dear?" He sounded a bit concerned. "You also sound a bit tired. Have you gotten enough sleep?"

"Yes, Dad." What Julia didn't tell him was that she spent her time last night reading just about any book that came to mind.

He didn't exactly sound convinced. "If you say so, Jules. But anyway, why is it that today feels so draining on you?"

He was prying into her life more than she appreciated. But being her father, she felt like she had to answer. "Well, I've told you about the academics. That's one part of it."

She waited for a minute for an answer as she left her bedroom, with the lights going out by themselves. Finally, there was an answer out of the speaker in the living room ceiling.

"Well yes, my dear. You have told me about that. Though I must admit, getting A+'s in every academic course is quite a feat that even our ancestors would have a hard time doing. Heck, I recall that you're the number one student in the Academy."

It was true; hanging on the living room wall in a fancy-looking frame was an honor certificate. In a nutshell, the certificate congratulated her for having the highest academic grades in the thirty-year-long history of Aeon Sophia Academy. But despite the honor, Julia felt as if something was wrong.

"I know, Dad. It's just that…" She sighed as she opened her fridge for leftovers. "It's just that even with those grades, they don't even mean anything in the long run. I'm sure you know why."

Her dad did know exactly why. "I understand, Julia. I'm sure that you must feel trapped in one path. I will be the first to admit that I'll never understand how it feels to be a psychic, but I too feel that it is unfair to be denied other futures just because you have magical powers."

She put her pepperoni pizza in the microwave. "It just sucks that I'm the daughter of one of the most powerful men in the world, who runs a ninety-year-old company that is single handedly responsible for a technological boom." She was punching the buttons way too hard but kept her voice low but vitriolic. "And just because I have a piece of soul inside me named Thoth that gives me superpowers, I get denied from ever inheriting your position as CEO."

Aeontech Industries was the most powerful corporation in the entire country of Odandir as well as the world. They had many branches that each focused on different fields, such as one branch focusing on crystalline technology and another on automobiles and aircraft. To think that just a century ago, the world was lacking in public electricity, medicine, and modernized transportation.

The sad thing was that Aeontech was founded by a psychic. So, to Julia, she felt more than a little cheated about the hypocrisy of such a universal law banning psychics from any occupation but guards, warriors, and bounty hunters. So rather than have her future be focused on bettering the world with greater and greater technology, she was now probably going to live the rest of her life fighting dangerous foes, until one day, some person got a lucky shot on her and ended her life.

But even then, that was old news for her. She tried to take a deep breath to calm herself down. "But that isn't the main concern today. It's about Rooster Squad."

Her father was all ears. "Is this about last year's games? I'm sure you and your squad did the best you could."

Julia stood and waited patiently for her eats. She scowled a bit. Last game, they had earned only thirteen points. Second to last had at least received twenty-eight. It was a complete wipe out and it was all because Xiu would never listen to Ercan's advice, thinking her way was the right way. Though Ercan wasn't spotless either, as his strategies to gain points weren't exactly well thought out or gave little leeway to improvising. Because of the actions of those two, the entire team lost miserably.

"It's not just about the game, Dad. It's about the team."

Her father seemed confused. "I thought you were glad Xiu was changing teams."

There was a twinge of relief in her voice as the microwave went *ding*. "Oh, yeah, of course. She's a bitch to deal with. The real problem right now is Ercan. Of the ten Squad Captains in the Academy, he is the lowest by far after his performance. I just feel like the other captains are going to dissect the team even more if he doesn't shape up."

Even though she would never admit it, she'd never really had that many friends. Most people found her too blunt, bookish, and standoffish to be near her. Girls thought of her as a nerd and she never recalled any boy having an interest in her, ever. In fact, because of her demeanor, she recalled in the early years in school, she'd frequently sat alone at lunch with no company but a few books.

The first company she had was Rooster Squad after being selected into it at age fourteen. During those three years, they were the only people she hung out with—barring Xiu, who hung out with her own friends—and even then, a part of her somewhat missed her.

"Well don't let it get to you. I'm sure Ercan and the others, including you, have been training during the summer," her father reassured her once more. "Besides, who knows what the new guy will be like?"

Julia had a feeling about who it was. She'd heard from Ercan that his sister had discovered her spark. So, chances were, she would be Xiu's replacement. Shee'vra was nice enough. Julia tolerated her. She hung out with Rooster Squad frequently anyway, so they all knew her, though she never recalled Xiu ever seeing her.

Her billionaire CEO of a father continued to speak to her as she sat down to eat. "And if things don't go your way, remember the Themelia/ Aeontech motto." He paused a bit for dramatic effect. "To Aeontech Industries…"

"…We make our own present, we make our own future," Julia responded as she put on her glasses. She'd heard it a million times. Well, not literally, but might as well have.

As she ate her feast, she overheard from the speakers one of her father's assistants calling for him. She knew that this conversation would end soon.

"Sorry, Jules. I've got a meeting now." Back in Odandir, it was about 5 p.m. "Just remember, keep a positive attitude, stay safe, and I'm here if you need me—hundreds of miles away, but here. Love you."

"Love you too, Dad." She heard the phone hang up and she finished off her breakfast.

Maybe he's right. Maybe this year will be better than the last…should I shower? She smelled herself. *Nah.*

⌐ ✳ ⌐

At the other end of the Uptown District in a luxurious condo, a broom swept the white tiled floor on its own accord. A dustpan assisted it by scooping up all the dust and floating toward the trash to dump it. The sponges cleaned the marble table and counters, vacuums sucked up all the dirt off the ornate rugs and carpets. The mop dunked itself into the bucket and cleaned the bathroom floor. Squeegees wiped down the windows.

Finally, a strawberry blonde teen sprayed cleaning fluid on a coat-of-arms. As she wiped down the fluid, she peacefully hummed to herself. The coat-of-arms was a shield with the insignia of a brown rooster on top of a mountain with a green viper in one of its claws. Two long-dulled sabers crossed behind the symbol of the DeRoche legacy.

The DeRoches were amongst the most prestigious noble families in the world and the wealthiest in Tirnanog. Their stamp on history began during the year 352 A.D. when they opened their businesses to hylic consumers when other businesses absolutely refused to. Such historical men and women of the lineage included Javert Francois DeRoche who founded the Tirnan Parliament and Chantal Coralie DeRoche who was the second and most successful Padma and a powerful psychic in her own right. Any DeRoche worth their salt had always made an impact in the history books, whether through business, politics, or battle.

Zivot herself was from the Dech family, a lesser noble house from Central Tirnanog under the DeRoche's wing. Since she was seven, her parents had sent her to live in Rooster Ridge, the estate of the DeRoche patriarch, Emile Hugo DeRoche. But her stay there was not merely a vacation. In exchange for the best tutors money could buy, noble children under the DeRoche wing were taught to loyally serve the family name.

Though to loyally serve Emile, meant to be a playmate for his son, Cyrille Coq DeRoche. She followed through with her orders as best as she could, despite Cyrille being one year her senior and having very different tastes than her. At age ten, she discovered her spark, Tsukumogami. From then on, she, along with Cyrille, was sent to Aeon Sophia to gain worldly experience and become part of a squad. After six years of moving to Enotita, she was assigned to become Cyrille's bodyguard. Out of loyalty to the DeRoche house, she'd complied without complaint.

Now that the proud symbol of the DeRoche family was sparkling clean, she clapped her hands for a tray to float toward her to take the spray can away. She then tossed the wipe in the trash, which gobbled it up of its own volition. With the housework done, she sat at the table along with fellow bodyguard/housekeeper, Mayil Seval.

Mayil had the same backstory as her, give or take a few minute differences. Just replace the Dech family with the Seval family, the country of Tirnanog with Naya Jivana, and her Tsukumogami spark with his Kartikeya. He sat at the table eating breakfast with his eyes closed in thought as he chewed. A plate of eggs benedict and pomegranate juice floated and was placed in front of her on a silver platter.

"Thank you, Trey." She politely dismissed the quasi-sentient platter and it went back on the shelf, becoming inert until needed again.

The two had breakfast in silence as the piano in the living room played on its own to perform a relaxing sonata for the morning.

Though his two guardians were downstairs already, Cyrille had yet to come down.

"It is the first day of school," Zivot spoke up to Mayil.

"We all know that," was the matter-of-fact answer she got from him as he didn't even look up at her.

She sighed, rephrasing what she meant. "What I mean is that Cyrille still isn't down. It is 8:30 already; I just don't want him, and by extension us, to be late for school."

Mayil finished his eggs and wiped his mouth with his napkin. "Zivot, to each person, time appears to move differently. What feels like a day for one is a week for another."

She didn't get what he just said. "Are you trying to say, 'slow and steady wins the race' just in your own words?"

"More or less."

"Just get him."

Mayil got up without argument and walked up the marble staircase covered with a segmented rug adorned with intricate serpentine patterns. As he approached his lord's entrance and was about to open the doors to the master bedroom, they opened themselves.

Out came a man in the snazziest tuxedo money can buy—the kind that Cyrille's father paid a psychic a fortune to make so that it never became dirty and regenerated itself upon tearing. The suit and pants were white and the trimming and bowtie were golden. It would seem he wanted to look his best for the first day of school, but those who were around long enough knew that it had been worn nearly every day since it was made.

But the tuxedo would not be the first thing most people noticed about Cyrille. There was also the fact that he looked like a reptilian rooster. He had a large beak with ridges that made him look as if he had small sharp teeth. Rather than feathers, he had green scales covering his entire body. His feet were that of a chicken's and his hands each had three long clawed fingers and a thumb. This was not their master's true form, but it had been a quite a while since they had last seen him turn back into human form.

His chameleon-like eyes checked his surroundings and his left eye locked onto Mayil. "Morning, my friends," Cyrille spoke up with enthusiasm. "Forgive me for my lateness for I have a very important reason."

"And that is?" Zivot questioned from downstairs.

The ends of Cyrille's beak curved into a smile as he answered. "It is Mayil's second cousin Chandra's birthday. I wished to order her a gift." He patted Mayil's back, to his mild discomfort. It was his duty to remember every friend and relative's birthday—as long as they were not jerks or bad guys.

Mayil had actually totally forgotten who Chandra was, yet alone knew that it was her birthday. But he decided to ask anyway, "And what did you get her exactly?"

"A swimming pool," Cyrille answered as if he had just simply got her a gift card. "Now when we go on vacation in Naya Jivana, we can visit her *and* swim. I made sure to also include a waterslide."

Cyrille went back into his room for a second and came back with three green presents neatly wrapped with a yellow bow. "Which reminds me, I got us this amazing new invention."

Mayil and Zivot perked up a bit in curiosity. Knowing times like these and what their master could afford, it could be anything. It could be a new piece of crystaltech, a multi-purpose gadget watch, a robot, or even a laser sword like the ones in those flicks. Both of them received their gifts and the three opened their respective presents with the semi-sentient garbage and recycling bin catching all the thrown-out cardboard and paper.

What they got was a bit more underwhelming than what Mayil and Zivot expected. In each of their hands was a blanket with sleeves. Cyrille's was green, Zivot's was indigo, and Mayil's was yellow.

"These are the new thing," Cyrille explained. "Co-Z's. It allows you to use your hands to read and stuff *while* being completely under the covers." He put his on to give the two a visual. "See? Really soft. Playing games shall now be a more magnificent experience."

He took off his Co-Z and gave it to Zivot, and Mayil did the same. "Best of all, you can use your Soo-Koo-Me-Gah-Me spark on them."

Zivot had long given up on trying to correct the pronunciation. She kept the three blankets close and activated her Tsukumogami spark. She exhaled silvery air that circled around the Co-Z's. It began with the blankets twitching a bit, but not long after, the three Co-Z's began to fly around the condo. They then flew down to Zivot and each raised an arm to salute their life giver.

The power to create life, Mayil thought in amazement, despite this not being a new sight. *To think Sophia herself would grant a mortal such a spark.*

"Splendid, Zivot," the rooster man said. "Now all our neighbors can think we have ghosts. They shall be the best security ever."

She didn't have the heart to tell him that their neighbors already thought their place was haunted by poltergeists. In fact, she recalled Ercan nearly fainting at the sight of the chairs walking slowly toward him once. So she clapped her hands three times. "Octohanger come." A clothes hanger with eight "arms" walked on its tiny wooden legs to the three students. It carried their pre-prepared backpacks.

"Thanks, Octy." Cyrille gave the hanger a high four. He then pointed toward the toaster on the kitchen counter. "You know what to do, Toasty."

The toasty tipped upwards toward the group and shot a hot strawberry strudel at the DeRoche. In no time, Cyrille used his long, sticky tongue to grab his breakfast in mid-air and ate it in one gulp. Belching in satisfaction, he slid open the door to his large balcony. The other two followed.

He pointed toward Mayil. "You know what to do, bud."

Mayil nodded in understanding and activated the spark Sophia gave him. *Activate Kartikeya.*

Within ten seconds, a gigantic, majestic peacock appeared on the edge of the building, preening its feathers. The three then hopped onto the avian's saddle, with Mayil at the reins.

Cyrille pointed toward the horizon. "To Aeon Sophia Academy!"

And with that, the peacock mount flew off, swerving through the skyscrapers like it had done hundreds of times before.

~ * ~

Julia walked on the busy street to school, playing Gemhunter on her crystalcell. She was on level ninety-six and she wanted to make it to triple digits by the end of the day. Luckily the morning rush was over, so she wasn't in as much risk of bumping into anyone as people came in and out of the buildings.

She got a text message and saw that it was Cyrille. It read *do you need a ride to school?* accompanied by a smiley face icon. Julia just shrugged and texted a thumbs-up.

Suddenly, a fly zoomed around her face. As she swatted at the shiny winged insect, she felt something reach into her pocket. Before she could turn around and react, whatever it was wasn't around anymore. It might have been nothing, but her pocket felt somewhat soggy for reasons that couldn't be explained.

She heard the flapping of wings and looked up, seeing the huge peacock that she frequently hitched rides on. The civilians were awestruck to see such a magnificent bird that was so large, but Julia, acting as if this was normal, just hopped on the twenty-five-foot peacock and the four continued on.

~ * ~

In a nearby alleyway, a wet, scraggly fish-like being turned off his invisibility. In his teal scaled hands was the wallet of some teenage sap. A shiny winged fly perched on top of the large fin on his head.

"I knew we'd be able to get some chump's cash." The fly asked him impatiently in a feminine voice, "So how much money we got in it?"

"Checking now." He opened the wallet, expecting big bucks. The uptown yuppies' wallets were always filled to the brim with paz bills of the highest caliber.

To their mutual horror, there were only three things. One was a single-paz coin, a twenty-paz gift card for a Bar and Grill, and a small note. The pickpocket read the note out loud to his fly friend.

"Here's a paz coin for your troubles. Try someone else next time." Accompanying the words was a crudely drawn picture of a hand flipping the bird at the readers.

The fishman angrily crumpled the note in his webbed hands and tossed it into a dumpster.

The fly just shook her tiny head. "At this rate, we'll never get that three thousand paz."

As disappointed as he was, money was money. One paz was better than none. Besides, that gift card could come in handy today.

Yummy, yummy, YUMMY GRILLED CHEEEEESE! Yummy, yummy, YUMMY GRILLED CHEEEEESE!

His crystalcell was blaring the number one kid's hip-hop song of the month. When he took it out of his pocket to answer, his scales turned paler. But he had no choice but to answer it.

"Hello this is Vinstri…Yeah Kushoto's here too." As he listened to what his superior had to say, his jaw nearly dropped. "Wh-what do you mean we need the three grand within one week?" The next answer he received made Vinstri feel even worse. "IT'S THIRTY GRAND?!…I-I mean, sure thing. Thirty grand won't be a problem at all…See you in a week."

"Who was that, Sharlie?" Kushoto questioned, not bothering with her partner's codename. It couldn't have been the boss. First of all, if it were, the whole conversation would have taken longer and been much harsher. Second of all, the boss was always too busy, especially to bother coming to Bythos. Thanks to Aeon Sophia Academy, criminals working in Bythos had to be either very careful or very stupid. This city had too many psychics to afford carelessness.

"It was Shèng Xià" he answered with his spine still at sub-zero. "He and the big leagues are coming next Wednesday. Shit's going to go down."

Welcome to Aeon Sophia Academy

Ercan and Shee'vra walked down the street toward their destination. Shee'vra was still curious what the academy was all about. She'd heard smatterings about it in her old school, but never anything substantial. What she'd heard was stuff like "Each student is a psychic in training," "All the students were picked from around the world," "I'm super jealous. I wish I had a spark," and "Some of them are really friggin weird" among other statements. Nothing solid. As they made a right turn on the sidewalk corner, Shee'vra spoke up.

"So is this place like regular school but with…" she tried to find a fitting word as they walked. "…superpowers?"

Ercan contemplated for a bit before he answered. "Well, define 'regular,' Sis."

She didn't think about that at the moment. Aeon Sophia was the only school he had ever been to. Of course he wouldn't understand the hylic education system. But she tried to explain. "Well, you know… stuff like math, science, sports, and woodworking. School stuff."

He got the picture. "Well, we do have academics, though no wood working and sports."

"Why not?"

"Well for wood work, it was deemed a waste of time if the student couldn't even use the skill as a career."

"But then how do you make all that stuff in the workshop?" his sister questioned. He had done such stuff for three years, though only now had they been anything of actual merit and quality (not that she ever told him that). She had previously seen him make bows, arrows, crossbows, and javelins. She had even seen him work on some kind of weird shark teeth club.

"Well, I learned myself. I realized how many students used weaponry and thought, 'Hey, I can make good money out of that,'" Ercan admitted, acknowledging his greed. "So I read a few books on the subject and then, congrats to me, I now handle a sharp seventy percent of all the students' ammunition and ninety percent of their wood-based weaponry."

That answered Shee'vra's question partially. "But what about sports and stuff?"

"None of that," her brother bluntly stated. "We train our bodies and reflexes through fitness and combat training alone." He didn't want to tell her, but he still had no grasp on how basketball, football, and other sports even worked. He once asked Yun, but he had no clue either. "And besides, when have you ever seen a psychic become a sports star?"

Shee'vra pondered that as they took another turn toward Aeon Park. There was that one football player from the Dorado Toucans who scored the winning goal three years ago. But she realized he was disqualified *because* he had a spark, getting stripped of all his awards. She found that she had no proper examples to give him.

She got distracted when she saw what looked like a tapestry of flowers that were shaped in a way that matched the insignia of the Academy, a sword on top of a wooden wheel with celestial wings. The sword, the left and right of the wheel, and both wings had runes that she couldn't understand. In all her time seeing those symbols, she could never understand what they meant. She was sure she'd asked either Ercan or Julia about it, but forgot. She tried to keep her mind on track for psychic athletes, but it was no use.

"Alright, I guess not." She turned her head away from the floral patterns and toward her brother. "But doesn't it bother you at all that our futures are limited to duties that will more often than not risk our lives?"

Shee'vra saw her brother tense up as he turned away to look at the winged sword in the flower patch. He suddenly spoke to her more seriously than usual.

"Do you remember what the Academy's symbol means?"

"Not really, sorry," she admitted, unsure where he was going with this.

Her brother took a breath as he began to explain. "Each piece of our insignia stands for the most important parts of being a psychic. The symbols on the sword stand for courage, which is basic enough." He twirled a hand around. "You know—because weapons equal combat and you need guts to stand up for those who can't stand up for themselves. The symbol on the left side stands for loyalty, which tells us to always serve the hylics as atonement for our past sins and repay them for our previous atrocities. The right side is wisdom, which pretty much tells us to use common sense. The whole wheel part is supposed to represent an infinite cycle. The left wing means mercy, which tells us to use self-control and to minimize casualties in our missions. And the final one says unity, which is about not only teamwork between squads, but also solidarity between the psychics and hylics."

The two took one final turn. The redhead turned toward his sister with a smile that seemed a little too wide for her taste. "So those are the words we have to live by from now on. You, me, Yun, Julia, Cyrille, Xiu—every person here. A life of kicking ass and taking names, striking fear in evil 'till we drop. That's the psychic way." He patted her back. "*Plus,* I hear the pay is amazing for some of the hardcore missions."

His younger sister didn't really feel her question was answered, but decided not to prod him. Soon enough, the two came toward a fifteen-foot tall gate that shined like platinum, connected to a stone wall that circled the entire area within. The center of the gate had the same symbol as the one in the flowers. On each side were statues of naked androgynous angels, each on one knee in genuflection.

The security guard in the booth reading a newspaper saw Ercan and buzzed him in. Within a second the gateway opened, splitting the school insignia directly in half. Shee'vra had been within these walls many times before, but the morning sun and her newfound future made it feel like she was now at square one of her game of life.

She looked around to see a large open field with various trees, a pond, pathways, and a running track. There were five rectangular buildings, each ranging from two to four stories high.

She observed little psychics, some sleepy and some energetic, following what seemed to be a skeleton in a robe using a ruby-tipped staff as a walking stick. She recalled that the building closest to the center was for very young psychics. There was also the elementary/middle grade building close as well.

The building closest to the entrance was where she knew for a fact was the high school area. It seemed to be the smallest and barely stood out compared to the large training arena right next to it.

But on the other hand, the teenagers were the only ones to have their own building for living quarters. She saw teens from across all eight nations go outside for the first time today. Most of them looked just like any human, but others took on inhuman looks. Some were subtle like pointy ears, sharp teeth, or metallic skin, but others were quite visible like a scorpion tail, a crocodilian appearance, and what appeared to be a mermaid. While most of the students walked about, others were showing off their sparks to their peers. She saw one girl flying on a winged horse, one guy dashing off at speeds impossible for a human, and even a person with a squid-like head lifting off from the ground surrounded by a green aura.

Everybody was heading toward the largest building at the very back of the campus, the Sacred Arena of Inner Spirit, or SAIS for short. The seven story stone castle/coliseum was one of the most important parts of the entire academy and one of the most famous monuments of the nation. It was where the Aeon Sophia Games took place.

Shee'vra looked up at the gigantic circular stained glass window above the entrance. In the center was the symbol of the academy. Encircling the sword, wheel, and wings were eight other symbols, each representing one of the eight nations. Clockwise from the top they were the Victory Banner of Enotita, the Wheel of Law of Odandir, the Jeweled Parasol of Sirochko, the Lotus Flower of Tirnanog, the Treasure Vase of Qian Ye, the Twin Golden Fish of Seichi, the Endless Knot of Titlacuan, and the White Conch of Naya Jivana. The architecture demonstrated that this academy wasn't made for just the benefit of Enotita, but the entire world.

As they approached one of the many doors, Shee'vra saw something out of the corner of her eye. As she turned, she squeaked as an unknown thing hovered near her face. Reflexively, she smacked it away, thinking it was an insect.

Ercan noticed her creeped out expression. "What the…" He looked toward the ground and saw what looked like an eyeball a meter away from her, "…oh."

His sister looked down at the grass. Initially squeamish, she noticed that the little eyeball with a yellow pupil was teary and shaking. Somehow, it even made light whimpers.

She hurriedly scooped up the tiny ocular creature. "I'm so sorry, little guy! I just thought you were a bug or something." She gently petted it with her index finger. "There, there. Please stop crying."

To their surprise, the eyeball stopped crying. It even made a joyful whistling sound. It then looked upward toward one of the towers of the SAIS. Shee'vra's and Ercan's eyes followed suit.

Out of a window, a teenager flew out. On his back were wings, each twice his size. Despite the noise such a wingspan should make, they emitted no sound as they flapped. The man swooped down toward the two, making no noise.

Shee'vra could not help but be in awe in this person's presence. The winged psychic was odd looking. It wasn't that he was ugly or anything, far from it. It wasn't his clothes; they appeared to look just like anybody his age, if not a bit formal. But something about his appearance was… off. Anyone could see that. His eyes were pure blue, without any hint of white. His skin tone was almost a dead gray, like a corpse in a morgue. But most creepy of all were his dark wings. They were feathery, just like those of most media portrayals of angels. But hidden within the feathers, were hundreds of little bright blue eyes that peered all around.

This angelic being slowly lifted a hand, beckoning the eye in her palm. The little eye looked toward her, then to its master. It began to float into the air once more toward a wing. Joining the other eyes, it looked like a sun over the ocean. The wings then suddenly disappeared into thin air, leaving only a few raven feathers to slowly fall to the earth.

The two waited for him to greet them. It took time for the angelic being to speak, as if it was unsure of what to say. So he just stared at them both for a bit, to their discomfort. Shee'vra looked toward her brother. He was unusually nervous. This man didn't seem like he would threaten them, but she had a hunch as to why Ercan was on edge.

Finally, it seemed like the angel figured out what he wanted to say. "Fear not. I am merely here to…introduce myself to the new one." He was only barely audible to them, but his voice had enough conviction to make them feel that whatever he was going to say was of upmost importance. He turned toward the new girl with the same stoic look on his face. "My name is—"

"Mastema Mattatron," Shee'vra finished. "I know already." For some reason, he seemed vaguely surprised, so she elaborated. "I mean, who in Bythos City wouldn't know the leader of Sparrow Squad, none other than The Angel of Silence? The squad that managed to win the Aeon Sophia Games three times in a row, ahead by at least five points each time. Not to mention that you're part of the legendary Mattatron family, a family in which one man per generation was part of the Ashtamangala as the Victory Banner."

"Dhvaja…" Mastema interrupted with a straight face, "…actually." He noticed she had no idea what that meant. "Dhvaja is the more formal term for the Victory Banner position in the Ashtamangala." He took out a wrinkled piece of paper from his pocket as he spoke to her. "But I appreciate that you know that much already…" He handed the paper to Ercan as he looked at the red haired youth straight in the eyes. "…You will do well." He turned away from the two and headed toward the entrance. "Auditorium meeting soon…do not…fail to show up."

He took one last look at Ercan through his bright cobalt eyes before going inside. Shee'vra glanced at her brother, who was reading the paper Mastema gave him. His pupils shrunk inside his violet irises as he read it. His legs shivered and his arms trembled.

She was reluctant to ask but felt obligated. "Is everything okay?"

Ercan pulled himself together. "Yeah, yeah!" He took a breath and addressed his sister in an indoor voice. "Just surprised me, that's all. Nothing to worry about at all." He moved forward. "Come on. I've got to show you something before the meeting."

Shee'vra was far from convinced. Her brother was as bad of a liar as a Saturday morning villain. But she knew better than to question him about it. She had a feeling what was on the note anyway. She'd let him handle it himself.

Following him inside, she saw how the light of the morning sun shone through the stained glass, making a round rainbow reflection on the floor. She'd been here before for the games, recognizing what would be the pathways to the stadium seats and the ticket booths.

She never knew that there was an auditorium before, though. Ercan guided her toward a large, long hallway she had occasionally been to with her mother. The walls were adorned with pictures and names of various alumni that came and went over the years. Most of these names they were unaware of, but others were either familiar to them like their mother or considered legendary. Many of these people were still around, hopefully making the world a better place. Other pictures had flowers under them, left there by loved ones and others wanting to pay tribute.

Ercan guided her through another hallway. This led the two to a large, octagon shaped room with a high ceiling. On the ceiling was an elaborate and highly detailed painting of the night sky. In the starry sky was a sapphire three-eyed woman wrapped in cloth battling a ferocious four-armed leonine abomination. A beam of light emitted out of the woman's hand as the monster tried in vain to cover its face. As the two looked up at the divine beings, a voice was heard behind them.

"S'up, you two! Seen the sights yet?"

Shee'vra turned behind her to see Yun addressing them. Behind him were Julia and Cyrille. The chicken man in the tux dismissed his two bodyguards to go ahead and came up to her.

"So I've heard you've gained powers." Cyrille inquired, "What can you do? Super strength? Speed? Lasers out of your fingertips?" He began to point his index fingers in various directions, making "pew pew" sounds.

Julia shook her head and yawned. "No way. She seems to be the kind of person to possess telepathic abilities. Who knows, maybe she can blow up heads with her mind."

Yun blew a raspberry at his friends. "Hells to the no! She can probably summon…" he hesitated to think of something, "…meteors and stuff. Along with being able to create black holes and singularities that can fell entire cities."

"Do you even know what a singularity is?" Julia questioned the monkey man, focusing her drooping eyes on him.

Ercan intervened, "You guys do remember Sheev's birthday, right? Well she—"

"I remember everyone's birthday," Cyrille interjected, proud of himself.

Yun thought about it for a second, then remembered her blowing a splatter of cake onto their faces. His black hole hunch was out the window, but so were the telepathy and laser finger guesses.

Shee'vra felt the need to clarify for the three. "Sorry guys. No meteors or anything fancy. I honestly didn't really look into it at all, but I think it's some kind of weather-based phenomena."

"Really? I guess that makes sense," Cyrille said to her. He then noticed his old teammate nearby. "Hey, Xiu!" the tuxedo chicken called out, waving a hand high up. "How's life?!"

But she didn't even glance at the five as she walked by them, talking to her group of friends about who-knows-what and entering the auditorium. Shee'vra noticed that her brother was looking away from the girls. But it didn't seem to be the look of bashful attraction on his face.

"Only in Aeon Sophia do the two richest kids get ignored," Julia sourly stated to Cyrille.

"Come on, Julia. She's probably in a stressful time in her life." He wrapped an arm around her shoulders with his beak uncomfortably close to her. "Think about it." He pointed to the lower right of the ceiling mural. "See those four naked human beings battling nasty monsters?"

"What are you getting at?" Julia took his hand off her shoulder.

"Well you see, at the bottom left there's a sole pointy-eared warrior woman slaying five beasts at once," Cyrille explained. "Xiu is that warrior lady with the sharp ears. She must be super sad for not being able to fight alongside her four closest friends."

"Do you listen to yourself?" Julia questioned him, too tired of making sense of his crap. It was too early for this.

"I do."

Ercan ignored those two and spoke to Yun nervously. "So…is she still mad at me?"

"Yup."

"Crap."

Shee'vra had little idea what the two boys were talking about, other than it was about that Qian girl. Now that she thought about it, seeing her last year in the games, she seemed to have been part of Rooster Squad before her. Why didn't the rest of the squad ever talk about this Xiu character to her?

She decided to speak up about it. "So, who's that girl? What does she have against you guys?"

"Which girl?" Ercan answered, trying to dodge the question.

"You know which one. Your old squadmate." She slyly smiled a bit. "Who is she, your ex-girlfriend or something?"

"No," he quickly stated, ignoring teasing question and moving forward. "Come on. We have a minute to get in."

Yun patted her head. "Don't worry. It's complicated for all of us. Believe me, I live with her."

He walked into the auditorium too. The others soon followed suit. As they went in, Cyrille had a revelation.

"Wait, Lady Shee'vra. You said you had a wind-based spark, right?"

"I'm pretty sure its air based, yes."

"So…does that mean you can do mega farts?"

She honestly had no idea how to reply to that other than pray to Sophia above that her spark would not become a complete joke. Julia had a reply, though.

"Cyrille."

"Yes?"

"Shut up."

~ * ~

The five found seats in the auditorium. They all sat down together. Shee'vra looked at the seat next to her to see that Julia took the opportunity to take a nap hidden behind an eight-foot, armored fish person sitting in front of her. Ercan and Cyrille seemed excited for what they were going to see.

"What's getting them so pumped up?" she whispered to Yun.

"There's a little opening movie that they show every year."

"Wouldn't they have gotten bored seeing that constantly?"

"The effects at the beginning are really good. But me personally, I think Julia has the right idea. This is nothing you can't get from a history class."

Just then, the lights dimmed and the curtains opened. All whispering came to an end as the audience saw the big crystalvision lighting up. The screen counted down to 3…2…1. Then all of a sudden, the screen went dark and a booming voice came from the darkness of it.

Before recorded time, a being from another world oppressed mankind. That oppressor was known as…ABRAXAS, THE DEMIURGE!!!

Lightning bolts appeared on screen, slowly revealing the silhouette of a monstrous creature. When Abraxas was revealed with another thunderous sound, Shee'vra recognized it as the monster from the painting on the ceiling. But the appearance here added multiple threatening spikes, an extra pair of arms, and several more rows of teeth. Text on the top of the screen read "artist's interpretation."

The Demiurge, along with its dark spawn known as the Archons, sowed discord and despair across earth for two thousand years.

The screen showed various creatures of alien origin made from what appeared to be hokey puppetry attacking pictures of humans wearing ragged clothing. Somebody was making growling sounds for the monsters. This also had "artist's interpretation" on the screen.

But The Demiurge's greatest Archon rebelled against its creator. This unknown paragon empowered humanity to rise up against the Archon threat. Humanity named the gentle being…Sophia.

The movie created the effect of sparkling stars, revealing the blue woman from the painting, though the feminine being did not have three eyes as per the "artist's interpretation."

Sophia chose a tribe of humans from what is now Tirnanog and empowered them with parts of her essence known as sparks. These children of Sophia became the Pneumatics, the precursors to the spark users of now.

A picture showed Sophia's glowing fingers touching the forehead of a one of many followers with others awaiting their blessings. The scene then transitioned to a moving scene of various actors battling the archon menace.

The war against the Demiurge's forces was long and arduous. The archons refused to back down against the Pneumatics, still seeing them as mere toys and food. But humanity's fight was not the most difficult battle. Sophia had to battle her progenitor.

The scene cut to a portrait of Sophia and Abraxas facing off in a rocky area with a crimson sky. Sophia was inside a blue force field while Abraxas was throwing javelins of pure energy. A mighty "NOOOO!" was heard and the next picture transitioned to the Demiurge clawing at the ground in panic as it was getting sucked into a hole of light in the ground.

After an uphill battle, Sophia sealed The Demiurge in an unknown location, never to be a threat to humanity again.

The next picture was not so optimistic. It showed the savior of mankind kneeling on the floor in pain, hand covering silvery blood coming from its stomach. Sad piano music accompanied the visual alongside the visual of a dying heroic goddess.

But alas, Sophia was mortally wounded during the fight. But Our Savior refused to simply die like a mortal.

The next scene showed the blue being breaking itself apart into hundreds of thousands of pieces. A blank figure in the shape of a person developed a bright blue aura inside it.

Thus, she broke her soul into fragments and placed them into each man, woman, and child. Some of these fragments developed into Sparks. These people came to be known as Psychics.

Another human being appeared, this time with a much tinier blue aura.

Though some had less of her essence than others and possessed no sparks. These people became known as the Hylics. But the two terms mattered not to the victorious human race. Humanity's triumph took the form of the Protogenoi Empire.

A picture of a long abandoned palace appeared on screen. Shee'vra recognized the palace was in Western Qian Ye in the Al-Shadiid district.

The Protogenoi Empire remained for almost five centuries. But the relationship between psychic and hylic gradually changed over the years.

The scene changed to actors in ancient armor enslaving people in chains, marching toward an unknown destination. Other atrocities were also shown.

The Psychics soon began to think that the Hylics were inferior due to their lack of spark. It was considered evidence of being unfavored by Sophia and they were persecuted. The Psychics at the time named themselves Pleroma (Full souls) and viewed it as their right to rule over the Kenoma (Empty Souls). The Kenoma were treated as second-class citizens at best and garbage at worst.

After pictures of more scenes of oppression and needless slaughter, the music for some reason became hopeful again as the scene transitioned to a battle between the Protogenoi army and the rebel resistance.

But in the year 480 A.D., a rebellion emerged, consisting of both oppressed Hylics alongside Psychics who sympathized with their cause. The psychics that led the movement consisted of…Camael Mattatron, Angel of Balance, of Barachiel…

A picture of a tall, armored, muscular angel with three heads appeared on screen. Holy light shone over his halos as if favored by someone up above. Camael held in his hands a blue banner with stars on it.

…Kwaku, Of Many Arms, of Anansi…

The picture changed to an eight-limbed dark skinned man. Along with several weapons, one hand held a parasol that appeared to be made of webbing.

…Omikami Ohirume, Keeper of the Sun Relics, of Amaterasu…

A Seichin woman appeared, wearing the finest yellow and white robes, wielding a sword made from fire, a shining mirror, and a necklace with jewels shaped like jade commas. Encircling the background were two golden fish.

…Naranbaatar, The Dragon King, of…Dragon King…

The picture changed to a longhaired man in a black, high collared suit surrounded by eastern dragons. In Naranbaatar's hands was a vase made from garnet.

…Gugu Kucu, Rainbow Serpent, of Quetzalcoatl…

The flick showed a woman whose arms were rainbow-feathered wings. Behind her was a brightly colored feathered serpent with a rope in its mouth weaved in an infinite knot.

…Shakyamuni, The Awakened One, of Gautama…

The screen displayed a middle-aged man in a meditative position. He was wearing the bare minimum of clothing, but his relaxed expression showed that the elements never bothered him. In his left hand rested a white conch shell.

…Meinrad von Morgen, The Machine Sage, of Merlin…

Next up was a picture of an old man in a hooded robe. Meinrad looked more machine than human, having replaced most of his body with metal with the only bits of his flesh left being withered and gray. On his back was a breathing apparatus that sustained him through his mouth. In one of his artificial hands was a steel staff that ended in a blue orb that emitted electricity. In the other was a white lotus with eight petals, which stood completely out of place among the cogs and gears of the limb.

…And last, but most certainly not least, the leader of the rebellion… Merle Themelia, The Liberator of Mankind. Wielder of the Spark of Monad. SOPHIA'S CHOSEN!

A moving picture of a man in a suit of form-fitting steel stood on the high point of a battlefield. His cybernetic armor covered all but his face, revealing the most glorious mustache ever seen. Behind him was a floating, ever turning wheel that shone down on Merle like the sun.

Shee'vra looked at the sleeping Julia and realized just how amazing her great-grandfather must have been. In her old school she'd been taught about him, but they focused more on his business legacy.

Together, these brave souls overthrew the Protogenoi Empire and freed the Hylics from their oppression after a two-year-long war. But without the Empire, the world was without any structure of government.

A map of the world showing each nation popped up. Each country had their national symbol on it.

So, it was decided that the world be divided into eight nations who chose their own form of government. To help the rebuilding of Earth, the eight leaders formed the Ashtamangala. With this system, each of the eight decided they choose one country to watch over. Each of these positions became represented by a name and symbol depending on the nation. The representative of Enotita was known as the Dhvaja, Sirochko was known as Chatraratna, Seichi the Gaur-Matsya…

When each nation was named, its respective symbol lit up such as Sirochko's parasol and Seichi's golden fish.

…Qian Ye the Bumpa, Titlacuan the Shrivatsa, Naya Jivana the Sankha, Tirnanog the Padma and Odandir the Dharmachakra. While some nations elected to be ruled by one of the eight such as Titlacuan and Seichi, others chose to have hylic rulers such as Enotita and Tirnanog. But the fact was that each Ashtamangala played a major role in each nation.

The screen began to fade out.

Over the years, the eight honorifics were passed on to the next generation of psychics when a former Ashtamangala died or retired. These chosen were entrusted with maintaining balance within the world for the foreseeable future. Maybe you can become one of the Ashtamangala and make the world a better place for both psychic and hylic kind! Who knows?

As the end credits scrolled, various teachers and students applauded.

Shee'vra clapped a little too, but perceived the video as more of an exposition of where sparks came from and how the present world came to be. She thought, in all honesty, they could have just taught this in class.

The applauding grew louder as a man stepped up to the podium. He was in his twilight years, but his physique made him seem twenty years younger. Everyone knew this man as Raziel Mattatron, son of Camael and the second Dhvaja. Though the Dhvaja usually had nothing to do with Enotitan politics due to refusing to return to the days of the Empire, Raziel was still the most important psychic today.

He signaled the audience to stop clapping and spoke up. "I would like to announce that this year is officially the thirtieth anniversary of Aeon Sophia Academy!" He looked around at the audience, recognizing old faces and seeing many new ones. "Each year, I am still surprised and overjoyed to see new psychics take their first steps into learning their true potential. Seeing the sheer diversity of our future makes me feel at ease about how connected this world truly is." He opened a journal and began to read. "But even though you will all be trained in mastering your sparks, you all should know by now that this is also a school. So here's a schedule of this year's events."

For about twenty minutes, Raziel talked about fairly mundane stuff that any other school would have, including changes to the cafeteria menu, library schedules, extracurricular activities, renovations, etc. Shee'vra looked toward her friends and saw that they, even Cyrille, thought that this was extremely dull. But eventually, the superintendent was finished with the boring crap.

"And, with all that done, I wish you all a great year full of wonder and knowledge! And remember the five words we live by…" The audience spoke with him the creed the psychics lived by. "…COURAGE! LOYALTY! WISDOM! MERCY! UNITY!"

Raziel felt proud about how all the students knew the words and wrapped his speech up. "And now you all can leave. But don't forget to pick up this year's agenda on your way out."

As the students and staff got up, Shee'vra nudged Julia awake. Though still drowsy, she stood up as well. As the five left, each picked up a blue agenda from a box. Cyrille was quick to begin reading the random trivia on each weekly page.

Ercan turned toward his sister. "So, after school I have a reservation for The Stage. You should watch and see what we learned over the summer."

"I hardly learned a thing," stated Julia. The rest of the team ignored her remark.

Shee'vra knew what The Stage was. Other than being used for the Aeon Sophia Games, it was used to sharpen the skills of psychics as a training space of sorts. She nodded in agreement, wanting to make him happy.

"Perfect," Ercan stated, overjoyed as he walked ahead. "See you then and I'm glad you were chosen for Rooster Squad. So welcome."

Yun patted her shoulder as he went ahead too. "Have fun and good luck getting used to it."

Julia sighed. "Hope we don't disappoint you." She then took a turn, going deeper into the building toward The Stage.

Cyrille waved goodbye and followed Julia and the other seniors to The Stage, still looking at fun facts. "Hm? I did not know deer sometimes ate birds."

As Shee'vra exited the castle and felt the sunlight once again, she now became much more curious of what was to come next.

~ * ~

"Shèng Xià."

A young brunette woman bowed down to him. She had entered his apartment with the key under his rug. The aging assassin was busy at the moment feeding his cat.

"Please, Jakaire," he told her as he poured cat food into Little Yun's bowl, "call me Zuo. We're off duty right now."

Jakaire begrudgingly followed his request, however unprofessional it was. "Our boss has given us information for our mission." She handed him a folder of papers.

Skimming the documented plans, he saw what they were going to steal, the extent of security that night, and which members of the gang were assigned for the job. From what he could see, the boss was really going all out with this heist. He put the documents on his kitchen table to analyze later.

"You know what's special about this morning?"

Jakaire paused for a moment, and then answered honestly. "I do not know, sir."

Zuo looked out his window toward the horizon. "My nephew begins his junior year at the Academy."

Jakaire hesitated to ask but felt that she had no choice for the sake of courtesy. "Do you intend to visit him while we're in Bythos?" He had better not. It would be far from professional and would possibly compromise the mission.

She could not help but feel a surge of relief when he shook his head. "I'm afraid not. I doubt Yun would want to see me again after all I have done."

First Class

Yun sat in the back of the classroom. Every year, he favored the back; it gave him the least attention, so he could always try to get away with lazing about there. But he had a feeling this year was different.

On both sides of him were Cyrille's two bodyguards/servants. Zivot was on the left and Mayil was right of him. In contrast to his already disheveled desk with a crinkled journal and unorganized folders that still contained last year's work, both of their desks were clean and clear for learning. Yun knew that both of these guys were second-row-seaters, so he decided to ask why they were bothering to sit with him.

"So? Why am I in between you guys like this? Are you guarding me from assassins or something?" He knew he could handle a few assassins himself, not that he was paranoid of them. But sometimes Cyrille gave them such orders, such as that time last year when he told them to keep an eye on Shee'vra during one of her old school's dances. Though in that case, it turned out that her date's father cooked and dealt Rubyrice and they busted his ass.

Mayil was first to respond to his question in his usual calm fashion. "Well you see…Master Cyrille cares about each member of his squad. He noticed that your grades were slipping from C's to D's last semester."

That surprised him a bit. "How the heck does he know about my report card?"

It was Zivot's turn to answer. "He requested me to turn an action figure to life, have it infiltrate your house, and steal it. He read it and decided that you needed our help."

His tail lashed about in annoyance. "You broke into my home?"

"Yes." She continued, "And because of your poor learning skills, he assigned us to keep an eye on your education."

"We're getting paid for this job," Mayil added as he lightly glared at him. "Just make it worth it." He knew that this would be an uphill battle.

Yun felt like he had no choice but to accept the fact that now he had two new tutors. He took out a pencil from his case and noticed that it had a broken tip.

"Aw, crap. I forgot to sharpen my pencils."

Without a word, Mayil grabbed all of his writing utensils off his desk, sharpening each and every one of them with his own sharpener. Voila—all three of his pencils were good as new.

But he now had another first world problem. "Aw, man. All the erasers on these things are so tiny. I must've—" Before he could finish, Zivot tossed a purple eraser onto his desk. *Boy, these two sure are prepared. Hope they don't butt in every two seconds.*

~ * ~

Terrible thoughts raced about in his skull as Ercan took a seat in the third row of class, the spot he always preferred each year. It was not too close to be called on all the time and not too far back to be considered a lazy student by the teacher. Then again, since the classroom had all twenty junior year psychics, he would be in the very middle of the class. So he specifically chose to sit one seat away from the center, hopefully to blend in with the crowd.

But which seat he was going to place his ass on for the year was far from his worst dilemma. He must have read Mastema's note to him five times by now and each time it made his blood freeze more. The worst part seemed to him that it was a very simple note.

Ercan Ao'Si,

Based on your and your squad's performance on last year's Aeon Sophia Games, we have begun to question your skills as a squad leader. You are to meet us during the lunch hour. Failure to comply will result in your rank as leader of Rooster Squad being stripped from you.

Luck be with you,
Mastema

Ercan really didn't want to dwell more on this meeting right now and tried to distract himself with something to do. He looked toward his right and saw the large, bipedal fish man sitting right next to him in a desk too small. Though if he recalled, Dunkeen Terrelli called himself a "humanoid Dunkleosteus," some kind of armor-plated ancient fish that once was the top predator of the seas. Though he knew Dunkeen was known to babble on and on, he needed something to get his mind off the note.

He turned toward the living fossil fish, unsure of himself. "Soooo… Dunkeen?" Dunkeen turned his bone-plated head to look down at his shorter classmate, acknowledging his existence. "…How was your summer?"

There was a bit of a pause as the armored fish thought for a bit of the events of his summer break. But soon enough, he spoke up in a blustering but surprisingly human-like voice, his transformation obviously not affecting his vocal cords.

"Well I'm glad you asked, Ercan Ao'Si. Because you see, me and the rest of Heron Squad did a lot of high paying missions all across the world. How did we manage to land all these gigs from all across the wide world, you ask?"

Ercan never asked that.

"Well, with the influences of our squad leader, Desiderio Garza. His dad is a noble from Titlacuan's capital of Kanalea, meaning that he is by default very well connected. So, with his connections, me, Desiderio Garza, Petra Leonidaz, and Draghignazzo Calcabrina trekked the world, taking missions from important people and saving the lives and livelihoods of many. Though sadly, our old compatriot, Enitharmon Loz, graduated last year and left. We only hear from her very sporadically. I am worried for her safety as are the rest of the squad, though Petra denies it. She denies caring about a lot of people, but do not be fooled, she's just one of those people that acts fiery and icy, yet deep down her heart is as fluffy as a bunny rabbit."

"Why the hell are you talking about me, Dunkeen?!" Petra yelled from the other side of class to the discomfort of everyone but Dunkeen. "You better not be saying shit about me!"

Her squad mate paid her no heed. "See what I mean, Ercan? She deeply cares for the absence of Enith. They may not have been particularly close, but they were comrades in arms and, without her, our squad is probably way weaker. For you see, Enitharmon had the spark Urthona that could manipulate reality as long as she was touching solid ground. She could never really control it too well, but it was still amazing, nonetheless, and got us to fourth place in the last Aeon Sophia Games. I sincerely miss her most. Even though she was as demure as a baby deer, she had the spirit of a wild boar. She has yet to answer any of our texts and calls in any meaningful way. We called the Sorchos Psychic Police Department and they clarified that she is working with them and she seemed well, but they don't know why she burned her bridges. So that problem is at least halfway handled, and thus I am able to sleep a little better. But as I was saying about our summer…"

Ercan listened as Dunkeen went on and on and on about random events that kept going off topic to rant about some other thing. When he began to talk about things such as the soft sands on the beaches in Titlacuan and the delicious sausages of Tirnanog, Ercan tuned out.

Great Sophia! Ercan thought. *He just doesn't stop! Now what's everyone else doing? Let's see…*

He turned his head to the right. He saw Dunkeen's squadmate lounging with her feet on the desk, chewing gum. *Petra still has those twin tails. Has anyone ever told her that it makes her look like one of those droopy-eared rabbits?*

Moving his head down, he saw another familiar face deeply focused on a game. *Ah sweet! George seems to have gotten himself the new crystalgame handheld system. Lucky bastard. I hear the new Megaplay+ has sixteen bits. He seems to like it. I wonder what he's playing? Fighting Rage, Beastly Baseball, Silversteel Tactics Advanced? Gotta get one of those.*

He looked ahead of him and saw a crocodilian person in a black trench coat. *Holy crap! Gustave is STILL growing? I could have sworn that he was already nine feet. Did he grow a foot? How big can crocodiles get? More tellingly how does Gustave even find clothes? Who makes his snazzy jackets? I must know.*

Turning his head to the left, he noticed that one of the most beautiful girls in the eleventh grade sat two desks away from him. The gorgeous outdoorsy gal spoke with another girl who sat in front of her. He looked back onto his desk, not wanting to stare at anybody anymore. Mom said it was rude and would make him look like a total creep. But his mind was still running.

Kickass! Two desks away from Sabelle herself. She looks better than ever. The perfect mix of trendy and tomboyish. Her friend Shiro is looking really hot too; her long ponytail looks amazing, going all the way to her…yeah. I bet like half the student body would do their homework for the rest of their school days just to date either one.

He accidently made himself sad as he saw the note still face up on his desk. *But a loser like me would never have a chance with Sabelle. She's street smart, quick, charismatic. She'd never even look twice at the worst squad leader ever. Well…former worst squad leader ever.* He tried to regain his confidence. *Whatever. I should be focusing on mastering Prometheus as best I can for the betterment of humanity anyway. I have no time to think about stupid high school drama subplots that never go anywhere and when they do it's completely underwhelming and…Hm? I'm ranting a lot about stuff. I'm no different than Dunkeen.*

He tuned back to the Dunkleosteus person who was still rambling on.

"So then after we beat up One-Eyed Mike, me, Petra, and Draghignazzo went to this nice Dustland Steakhouse. Desiderio, you ask?"

Once again, Ercan hadn't asked anything. But the answer surprised him anyway.

"Desiderio stayed at the snake woman's home to engange in lovemaking."

Ercan couldn't help but speak up in incredulity. "Wait, what? How?"

This got Sabelle's attention too. She called out to the armored fish, "Really? Desiderio hooked up with a snake girl? Wow, what a surprise." Ercan could smell the sarcasm coming from her tongue. "Probably not as entertaining as the tale that he did it with a spider woman after slaying The Underground Dragon of the Nocturne Pits?"

Ercan noticed Shiro's, Ercan's, Gustave's, Yun's, and just about everybody's face showing surprise. Petra and Dunkeen nodded in a way that said "Yeah. He did that" and shrugged. George was too deep into his game to notice or care what was going on.

Sabelle shook her head and chuckled a bit. "You're all honestly surprised? We all should know by now that our friend Desi is a total manwhore."

Ercan was the first to answer her. "I think it's more that we're curious…" he fiddled with his hands a bit as if he was a father teaching his son reproduction, "how somebody could…mate with a spider woman…or a snake woman for that matter."

Great. First time talking to her this year, and it's about spider woman sex. And did I just seriously say mate?

Shiro, luckily, agreed with him. "Yeah. I honestly have no idea either. Do you have any idea, Dunkeen?"

Dunkeen moved his bony incisors upwards. His eyes brightened in the light at being able to speak more about stuff, especially to someone as popular as Shiro and Sabelle. "Well, lucky for you two. Here we were, in an inn. I had just gotten up to go to the bathroom when I heard a scream. Me and Drag got into battle mode and went toward the sound and barged through the door." The entire class minus George and Petra were enthralled, waiting for an answer. "And here we saw the room was covered in webbing. Though not like black widow spider-like webbing, more like the tarantula webbing, for this spiderwoman had the lower body of a red-kneed tarantula. And here Desiderio and the spiderwoman were in full action. We'd known her for about a week and she was a nice person despite her arachnid appearance. The snake woman last summer was too. This one time while on our mission she made us these nice sweaters that—"

The classroom door opened slowly. Dunkeen shut up, not wanting to speak of such improper subjects around a teacher. But instead of a teacher, in came Xiu. She seemed to have run to class based on her breathing pattern.

"Sorry I'm late! I was just…" She looked around the class to not see a single adult. Her worried expression soon turned to smug satisfaction. She'd heard that her new teacher was notorious for being late, but never more than five minutes.

Xiu was glad that two of her besties, Sabelle and Shiro, had a seat reserved just for her. She walked with pride as everyone looked on. Some looked amorously, others with jealousy, and still others just looked irritated. But to hell with the irritated ones, attraction and envy proved just how good she really looked.

She waved to her two friends as she sat down next to them. "Hey Sabelle, hey Shiro! Anything happen without me?"

"Well Dunkeen was just telling us all a story," Shiro answered with an odd amount of innocence, considering the subject manner.

"More like telling a novel, but you get the idea," Sabelle added her two cents in. "Stuff about Desi's illustrious love life."

That piqued her interest enough, especially since she was now officially part of Heron squad whether she liked it or not. Why not get to know more about the juicy crap her new leader had gone through.

"That sounds intriguing. Do tell, Dunkeen, about our new and amazing…" But as Xiu turned toward Dunkeen, she noticed that there was a certain purple-eyed redhead in between them. Her good mood immediately turned sour. "…Oh, no no no! Not you. Sabelle, switch desks with me."

Though Ercan should feel offended, the idea of sitting next to a hot redhead like Sabelle seemed like a great proposition.

"Nah," Sabelle retorted. "Don't feel like it."

Xiu was shocked by her bluntness. "Are you really doing this to me?"

"Yup."

She let out an annoyed groan and then asked her other friend next. "How about you Shiro? Are you willing?"

Ercan would not mind sitting next to Shiro either. Sadly, it was another refusal.

"Sorry, Xiu. I already put all my stuff away and it's all in the right spot and everything. Soooo…"

"No?"

"Yeah."

"Yes?"

"No I mean yeah to your no. All organized already and stuff. Sorry."

The fishy behemoth pitched in. "Good morning, Xiu. I heard that you're now part of Heron squad along with me and Petra—"

"She better not make our team suck ass!" Petra felt the need to add. If it weren't for her friends glaring daggers at her and her relaxation meditation sessions, Xiu would've taken her foot for good luck then and there.

Dunkeen continued to speak. "But anyway, as the new member of Heron Squad, and by that logic our new friend, I'm willing to switch places with you."

Xiu refused to state why such a statement was stupid. So, she just merely shook her head in refusal. Pouting, the former member of Rooster Squad got her books out, trying her best to ignore the boy to the right of her. Ercan felt a need to talk to her, to at least try to patch things up. Or at least make being near one another bearable for the rest of the class.

But he could only mutter, "Still mad?" He wasn't prepared for her wrath. He should have been, but other things were on his mind.

"Yes, still mad," Xiu bluntly stated to his face, pointing an accusing finger at him. "That's what happens when you blame somebody else for your failures."

Her words stung him more deeply than most stabs, and he had taken a lot of stabs and survived. He felt the need to defend himself. "What was I supposed to do? In real life, your actions would have gotten not only you killed but also everyone else." He was trying to keep his voice down.

"And you're any better?" Xiu retorted. "Do you know how many times the rest of us had to save you from yourself? Yes, you can heal! Woopty-doo! That doesn't mean you can't die! So the rest of us had to put ourselves in danger to save you from your dumbass decisions!"

"…You were simply better off on a different squad." Ercan had no better comeback.

"Is that all you have to say?" Xiu expected at least a bit more from him. This was just pathetic. It made her question why this guy even qualified to be in a captain position anyway when she'd never had the chance. It made her blood boil.

"…Do you want me to say more?" Ercan avoided her gaze. "You were simply better off."

"Anybody's better off—"

The entire class went silent before Xiu could even finish her sentence. Even George pulled his face away from his game to look toward the argument. Not even Dunkeen had anything to say on the matter. She saw a look of shame in Ercan's violet eyes as if she was merely just piling onto his current mountain of misery. He didn't even seem to have anything left to say to her.

She simply let out a deep sigh and looked away from him. "Whatever. I'm not in the mood to argue anyway." She sat down at her desk and took out her work binder. "Just don't talk to me unless I tell you to."

A voice that reeked of fake politeness came from the back of the class. "Well, well, well. Somebody still has an attitude problem."

A woman in all black walked in between Xiu and Ercan. She kept a necklace of crow feathers around her neck and had two bracelets with various charms that neither of the two ever understood or asked her about. What was striking about her, though, was not just the fact that her eyes were inky dark with no sclera in sight, but that rather than having hair like most human beings she had dark feathers covering her scalp. Both of them paid full attention to their classmate, for she was none other than Winona Samhain.

Everyone in class knew what Winona was fully capable of. As the captain of Crow Squad, she was amongst the strongest students in the academy. People hardly even knew how her spark worked, even after seeing her battle so many times at The Stage. She always had some new and odd trick up her sleeve. So, when she spoke up, everybody was all ears.

"Though I am disappointed, Xiu. You must have lost some of that fiery spirit of yours over the summer." The crow girl crouched down and got into her face, reveling in the fact that she made her nervous. "The old you would've finished verbally castrating someone you perceived as trash."

Winona now turned toward Ercan. "Would you like to hear what she was going to say?" She waited for an answer from him but there was none, only him trying to remain stoic. "You look brave. I'm sure you can handle it."

Ercan felt a ghastly chill run up his spine as her black lips whispered into his ear. Her voice sounded like the last breath of a nighttime breeze.

"Anybody is better off on a different squad than yours."

Gustave got up from his seat and looked down toward her. "That's enough out of you, witch!" He bared his teeth toward her. He did not care that she was a captain. She was being rude. The crocodilian would much rather have had Xiu speak such words; at least she had some reason to be mad at him. Winona was just mocking someone she perceived as weak.

Despite looking up toward lots of scales and teeth, she was far from intimidated. She let out a little chuckle as she stood up with her hands half raised. "Calm down. Don't act so cold blooded." Though she smiled, her eyes glared at him. "Besides, you shouldn't mess with those stronger than you."

Gustave was not as fazed as she would have expected. Maybe it was his reptilian instincts; maybe it was her superior attitude pissing him off. But he got to her level and spoke to her face. "You and I both know this whole Squad Captain thing is crap."

She shook her head in incredulity at what she perceived was a stupid statement. "Keep telling yourself that. Maybe it'll come true." She swiped Mastema's note from Ercan's desk. "Besides, Mastema has some news we'd all like to hear."

"The hell? Give it back!"

But before Ercan could grab the note back, pitch black energy emanated from her hands. The paper floated into the air and broke apart into twenty fragments. Each fragment then became whole, creating twenty copies of the original. Each piece flew down toward each and every student's desk. Slowly, some read the contents of the note. Most reactions were of surprise or irritation. The prospect of Ercan, The Unbreakable, possibly being booted off his position was news for the whole Academy.

Xiu's reaction was that feeling as if she just accidently kicked a kitten. She would have tolerated him at least being reprimanded for incompetence, but demotion was just too harsh. Knowing what was going on now, she realized she was unknowingly kicking him while he was down. Ercan must have thought she was a total bitch now for saying those things to him. *Damn it, I'm such an asshole.*

Yun was having none of it. "Damned witch!" He would have charged in and most likely have gotten his posterior kicked if it wasn't for Cyrille's retainers holding him down.

Gustave didn't even bother to look at whatever Winona placed on his desk. He merely grabbed the paper in his claws, crumpled it up, and tossed it into his gullet. "I'm not interested in your little squad politics, witch."

The leader of Crow Squad merely turned away from the towering reptilian. "Suit yourself, Gustave." She began to slowly walk back to her desk, secretly in her heart hoping for somebody to fight back. "But anyway, that's the news for the week, folks. Let's see how Ercan gets himself out of this predicament."

Ercan finally decided that he wouldn't take this lying down. Mustering up any remaining confidence from his soul, he got up from his desk. "Do not discount me just yet." He stared into Winona's midnight eyes when she turned back to acknowledge what he was saying. "I may not be the best leader or have the strongest spark, but I sure as hell am not going to just keel over and let the title get taken from me." He pointed his finger toward her. "No, you guys are going to have to pry the position out of me. When my sister learns about her spark, Rooster Squad will come back from the bottom. We may not be the top, probably not even second best, or hell even third. But I swear to Sophia, we will never be the bottom squad again."

Winona seemed less than impressed at his little boast. She smirked and shook her head. "Say that stuff all you want." She sat back down at her desk. "It just makes it more satisfying when you fail." She then snapped her fingers and every single copy of the note vaporized in black energy.

"We'll see about that." And with those words, Ercan sat back at his desk, satisfied with his retort. He felt a surge of confidence deep within his heart, ready to fight for his rightful title.

George looked up once again from his game system, his eyes already apathetic about school. "Alright, is everyone done making a scene already? It's starting to get annoying."

Shiro glanced at her peers. To the girl in white, it seemed that they were done with their little spat. She nodded to him. "I think so. For now."

~ * ~

In the back of class, Yun growled, showing sharp canines. His tail lashed about like a hairy whip. He had to be held down by both of Cyrille's retainers, with each one placing a firm hand on either shoulder. At first, he was willing to let his two longtime compatriots argue amongst one another, but the moment Winona started being petty, he was going to let her have it.

"Please try to keep a cool head," Mayil said in his usual composed manner. "I wouldn't want to tell Cyrille one of his best friends got suspended on the first day."

Zivot used a different method to calm him down. "Look, Yun." She removed her hand. "I understand that you're unhappy at the moment." She took out a copy of her master's schedule, which had "watch friends duel" at three o'clock. "But I have overheard that Winona will be using The Stage at about the same time as you and Ercan."

This doused his temper a bit as he thought about it. He thought about relaxation mediation sessions, took a breath and spoke to the lady in black. "Are you using The Stage after school at three?"

"I am. See you then," was all the answer he got from her. It was all he needed.

But something else had been troubling him. Where the hell was the teacher? As much as class bored him, this was just ridiculous.

The door opened once again. In came a lime green man wrapped from the neck down in tattered bandages. He put down his stack of textbooks, loosened his necktie and grabbed a piece of chalk. He wrote on the blackboard "Hello, my name is Mr. Jahikah." And as if he assumed the entire class was blind, he said. "Hello, my name is Mr. Jahikah."

He did a quick headcount and confirmed full attendance. Satisfied, he continued to speak to his students. "Forgive me for being late by..." He checked his wristwatch. "...dear gods, ten minutes? Seriously, students, I'm sorry for keeping you all waiting. But when you got to go...especially when you have to unwrap then rewrap, you know."

Sabelle grimaced. "I wish I didn't." Many agreed with her. Except George. He was paying more attention to strategically placing his in-game army.

The teacher looked toward his direction and pointed toward him with conviction. "Mr. Leeroi. Class has started. Are you done playing?"

Begrudgingly, the Sirokhan boy had no choice but to put his game on pause and slide it into his desk. With that, the mummy continued his introductions.

"As you can guess, I'm your teacher for your entire Junior Year.

Unless I die. In which case you would get a substitute. I'm here to teach you math, history, science, you name it. I'm also in charge of training each and every one of you, allowing your sparks to bloom into the next generation of legends." He twirled a loose wrapping around his wrist. "The only thing that I do not teach is P.E. That is Mr. Terrelli's job, whose son is with you all today." He pointed toward Dunkeen, who waved to the class.

The next thing Mr. Jahikah took out of…somewhere was a pile of stickers. He walked past each and every desk, placing a sticker onto each student's desk as he walked by. "Where you are sitting will from now on be the center of your universe…for learning. Your desk is now your sanctuary. It is—"

"Hey. Excuse me, sir." The crocodilian raised his hand. "Mine says 'Sobek' for some reason."

The green mummy seemed confused. "Is that not your name?"

"No sir. It's Gustave. Gustave Garvile."

"Strange. It's just when I think crocodile I think 'Sobek.' Must be an old habit."

Gustave must have told this to people a hundred times, but he was sure he would say it a hundred times more. "I'm not a crocodile. I'm a False Gharial."

He still didn't get it. "Soooo…you're not a Gharial?"

Gustave nearly facepalmed. "No sir. I'm a FALSE GHARIAL. It's a species of crocodilian from Southeast Jivana."

The teacher seemed to have gotten it. "Well then, I guess we all learned something new today. Anybody else have problems with their sticker labels?"

Xiu raised her hand. "Yeah. You spelled my named wrong. You wrote She-yoo. It is spelled X-I-U." It was a more common mistake than she would like. In fact, for a while, everybody called her "Zoo." It was either spelling it wrong or pronouncing it wrong.

Ercan was next to raise his hand. "Yeah. Mine says Eric Ow-See. As in O-W hyphen and see as in sight."

Sabelle spoke after. "Yeah and you switched me and Shiro's names around."

Mr. Jahikah felt like he'd wasted too much time already, that dealing with this would have to wait. "Leave complaints until the end of class."

He opened his book. "Now let us begin. Open up your history textbooks to chapter one, the Emperors of the Protogenoi Empire."

Ercan had a feeling that this year was going to be an uphill one.

The Squad Captains

For Julia, the beginning of senior year was as dull as expected. She, Cyrille, and the rest of the seniors had Monoceros McDooley for a teacher. Everyone knew he would rather focus all of his efforts on training rather than do more productive stuff, such as actual class. But alas, her one-eyed teacher had other plans as he spoke to all eighteen of his new apprentices who stood side-by-side in the preparations room for The Stage.

"So you all came back to school in one piece, eh? Was summer vacation too easy on you?" He walked by each student one by one, inspecting each and every one of them for fear. "Well, no more! Now that you had your little piña coladas and R&R, it's time for me to break you." He pounded his chest. "I am your final obstacle in this Academy! I have the power to deny you your destiny!"

The over six-foot-tall mass of muscle looked down toward the skinny salamander person who seemed to be lost in his own little world. McDooley got into Hong's face. "Without my teachings, you will never master your hidden potential." He still felt ignored, judging by the amphibian's blank expression, who licked his own eyes without a care in the world. "Without my teachings, you will not last *one year* out there as a psychic."

Hong finally noticed him, tilting his head in confusion as to why his personal space had been invaded. "Hello there. Just thinking about if destiny is a real concept and not an illusion to make ourselves feel special. Don't mind me."

Acknowledging that Hong had been paying attention in his own little way, Monoceros stepped back to continue his impassioned speech. "I swear to my soul that I will go to the greatest of pains to help you discover your positions as born warriors." He raised one finger. "But I feel I must warn you of one thing."

"Ooh, interesting. What is it?" Cyrille interrupted, genuinely curious. He seemed to be the only student that seemed excited about what the teacher was saying. A glare from the cyclops got him to pipe down though.

"As I was saying, never, ever expect that you will die of old age in a comfy bed. Even now, each of you already knows the dangers of our dutiful existence. We can get stabbed, bludgeoned, sliced, burned, drowned, eaten, or driven to the point of insanity, among other unfortunate fates." He cleared his throat. "Now to tell you about some of my experiences."

For what must have been an entire class period, Mr. McDooley felt the need to explain his history as a psychic. How he did his part for society as a psychic, giving the beat down on anyone who brought danger. Julia's tired mind tried to pay attention for about twenty minutes about the time he and his squad did…stuff she lost interest in. This man could somehow make things that should be exciting boring.

Maybe it was just her opinion, though. She was never good with lectures, preferring to learn through books or experiments rather than just somebody droning it out to her. So rather than listening to her new teacher, she closed her eyes and spoke the name of her spark in her head. *Thoth.*

Immediately within her mind, various words, glyphs, and scriptures appeared inside her head. Some of the texts she could read, others indecipherable, and more in languages lost to time. She narrowed her mind to search for "Monoceros McDooley" and got immediate results. She had his files, magazine articles, newspapers, official documents, even his war diary. She then further simplified the texts by compressing them into one abbreviated document. She began to analyze the facts.

All right, let's see here. Name: Monoceros McDooley. Age: Forty-five. Place of Birth: Albion Hills, Tirnanog. Spark: Polyphemus. Academy Squad: Dove. That's interesting. Moniker: The One-Eye Guy. What other stuff? She looked deeper into the documents within her mind. *Well he's vegan, father of two hylic boys. One just graduated high school, the other in middle school. Okay, scroll down a bit. What else you got?*

She nearly physically gasped as she looked through his battle records. *Holy shit! So this guy isn't just blowing hot air! This guy's been busy with the world. The War of Nergal, the Battle against the Dragon Duke of the Deep Darkness, fought in the Manticore-Ifrit War, and stopped the Blood Shower Show fights. Shit! This guy did everything! Now if only he could make it interesting to listen to.*

"JULIA THEMELIA!"

She got out of her research trance and realized that her teacher towered over her, his one brown eye staring down at her, his hands behind his back.

"So who gave you permission to take a nap standing up like a mare in the spring time breeze?"

She had no time to comprehend what he'd just said to her, but assumed it was about her eyes being closed. So she stood up as straight as possible and answered him. "Sorry, sir! I'm a very poor listener, sir! I was just using my spark to look into your personal history, sir! You were talking about your life for a bit so I thought I might as well take a closer look!"

This got his attention, so she continued to prove it. "At age fifteen, you participated in the War of Nergal, protecting a major chokepoint from the undead. One year later, the Academy was founded and you were placed on Dove Squad. Your squad mates were Aluja Jahikah and Georgia Tennisi and were led by Raphael Mattatron. You also worked with my squad leader Ercan's mother, Rina Ao'Si, though she still had her maiden name of Seed'Hii at the time."

She saw that Monoceros was not glaring anymore, so she took a breath and continued. "You and the rest of Dove Squad had a lot of action and adventure stories back in the day. You all had enough action for a lifetime."

"Two lifetimes perhaps," Mr. McDooley added, narrowing his eye in thought. Some of the things he and his squad saw during those three decades were so utterly horrid that he prayed to Sophia every night that his family or any other would never witness what he experienced. But that was why he and other psychics had to go out to fight. There was always someone out there willing to hurt others, whether for greed, cruelty, or a god complex. It was his duty to make warriors suited for taking such bastards out.

"So you prefer to read instead of listen?" he questioned her. "I have no problem with that." He then walked away from her, down the line of students. "But I'm not sure your teammates would like that."

Julia was at a loss for words. "Wha—?"

But she was interrupted. "I looked through the records of last year's Aeon Sophia Games. Your team was the lowest, though you managed to score the highest amount of points for the whole squad." Julia flinched at those words. "A whole *five* points."

Monoceros was right; she and the rest of Rooster Squad had challenges in The Stage ill fitting for each of them. Ercan and the other squad leaders got "Tundra Hunter," a hunting mission with the ten contestants tracking down a specific caribou each. They would get maximum points for catching the animal, though they would still get points if they killed the buck or caught/killed a different one. Turns out, making chains and a healing factor did not help at tracking. As the time ran out, Ercan was still at square one, as were many others. Each failure granted zero points.

Xiu had one of those "attack or don't attack" challenges known simply as "When to Show Mercy." Simple in premise, hit the bad guy who looks utterly monstrous and avoid hitting the surrendering foes who have their hands in the air. She ended up blasting nearly every mannequin, too, in the zone to distinguish "DIE VERMIN!" to "HAVE MERCY!" which resulted in a total score of two. Though to be fair, the one she didn't blast had its hands halfway up…but also had a crossbow taped to its shoulders, though having it call her a "sucker" when she lost, resulted in it getting smashed to bits and splinters.

Yun had a "defend the civilians mission" challenge known as "Night of the Lupines." The theme was werewolves, not unlike the ones from the books or flicks. The catch was that one of the pedestrians in each group was also secretly a lycanthrope. So as Yun did his thing of beating up creatures of the night, one of the villagers turned and started attacking from inside the house. When Yun finally heard the "HELP ME!" it was too late. He only managed to save two out of five by the time it was over, netting four points.

Cyrille was next in line. His challenge, "Trip to Deadwyrm Canyon," was essentially a scavenger hunt inside a canyon filled with dragon bones; the worst challenge for the guy. He got none of the riddles right. She still couldn't understand how he thought the answer to "Within the ancient wyrm's skull lies the treasure for the ages" would get him to wander into the lair of a monstrous maggot queen. Then again, he actually did slay that maggot queen and took the monster's brain with him. The giant worm beast was actually the answer to "Under the caverns lies the mother of a thousand young," so he scored two points on accident at least.

But to her, the worst challenge of all was hers; the "Open Ocean Tempest" challenge. Even today that challenge is considered controversial by the news and society in general. Basically, the ten contestants are dropped in the middle of an ocean, whether or not they could swim, fly, grow gills, etc. The goal was to make it to an island half a kilometer away as a storm raged on behind them, getting closer and closer. So here she was, desperately trying to stay afloat amid the restless sea, struggling to make it to land. She used to scoff at the thought of a stage simulation causing actual harm, but now she knew better than to mock The Stage. Struggling for breath, she began to notice that some of her luckier peers flew out, became a sea animal, or enlisted the aid of them. The less lucky ones were either also swimming for their lives or already sunk into the abyss below.

The only reason she even got a score was the fact that one of her peers whose name slipped her mind was a mermaid and took pity on her and several others. She summoned tuna, made them grow twice their size, and had them escorted to land. She was the fifth person to make it onto the beach, so thus five points, five points practically given out of sympathy. Though it was impossible to die on The Stage, that didn't quell the nightmares.

The final challenge was a free-for-all battle between the ten squads. Rooster Squad scored no victories, as they were ambushed and decimated by Eagle Squad. Though on the bright side, watching Yun on the receiving end of a spinning pile driver was pretty amusing. But overall, if it hadn't been established yet, last year they were terrible.

Mr. McDooley continued to speak, sounding almost sadistic. "That is why I'm volunteering you into the first Stage Battle of the year." That was the exact opposite of what she wanted to do today. "Along with your fellow squad mate."

He grinned maliciously at the reptilian rooster. "You too, Cyrille Coq DeRoche. Your family name depends on you learning actual skill."

Cyrille was less demoralized than McDooley thought he would be. He expected a fragile noble who would fear that his tux would be ripped. But the chicken was no chicken. Cyrille saluted his teacher, the sides of his toothy beak forming a smile.

"You're right, sir. I should always improve myself for the betterment of the DeRoche name. And the world."

Not the reaction he expected, but the cyclops appreciated the sincere enthusiasm, though it was a bit hard to portray the drill sergeant he was. He preferred fear for first day students. Instead, Cyrille marched toward the boys' locker room, ready to make his family proud. Julia just halfheartedly went to the girls' locker room.

But he felt for a first class, these two would not be enough. But he had a plan. He then pointed to the spacey salamander. "Hong Hai Long, you're going to be joining these two!"

Hong revealed his small, needle-like teeth. "Play fight session on the first day?" He licked his lips in anticipation as he scurried on all fours to the locker room. "I hope we don't hit each other too hard."

He pointed toward a six foot, heavily muscled student with red tinted sunglasses. "You too, Basil Bartleby!"

Basil punched his fists together in excitement. "Oh hell yeah! This is gonna be mental!" He then dashed out the room, chanting about how "The Giver of Pain will rock their world."

What he had in mind would still utterly stomp these four, so they needed a crutch. He looked toward the seven Squad Captains in his class. Mastema stood up straight and expressionless, assuming that he would be granted the honor of showing his skills to his new master. But McDooley didn't want the angel to carry the whole team with no effort on his part. The leader of Sparrow Squad deserved better. The second best, Bianca Narkissos was also an option. The pale, white haired woman stood still, hands behind her back. Her pink eyes pierced ahead of her, awaiting the order for her to fight on The Stage. But alas, the leader of Eagle Squad was also way too much of a cushion for victory. She'd make things too easy. But then again, pitting either of the two best students in the Academy would make the challenge nigh impossible. So tragically, the two must merely warm the bench for the day.

But to his luck, the ninth ranked Squad Captain was in class today. The short statured, Seichin girl stood amongst the other students. With her long hair covering half of her face, her arms crossed together, and her eyes looking toward the ground, she did seem to be a bit on the socially awkward side. But as Monoceros learned, the quickest way to friendship was battle. She must have learned it by now, she just needed a little prodding. But a soft teacher was a vulnerable one. He resolved to treat this shy young maiden as he would treat any other student, especially since this was the captain of Rhea Squad, despite her appearance.

"Hanako Nanaringu!" Shouting her name made her squeak and jump up. She anxiously looked toward him, waiting to see what he would say. It was as if it was her first day on The Stage. Made him wonder how she even became a Squad Captain. "You're with them! Lockers you go! Get to it!"

She scrambled out of line and bowed to him. "I-I'll try my best, s-sir." Hanako quickly walked out of the room, shivering in nervousness.

Now that he had selected the first team, the second team was next. He knew for a fact that he wanted to see the Squad Captains shine. All he needed was four of them. He had all but three Squad Captains in his class and he planned to take full advantage of it. He first pointed to the eighth-ranked of Penguin Squad, a guy whose head and arms were covered in intricate tattoos shaped like waves.

"Gaizka Pantopoda!" The tattooed teen turned his attention to his teacher, his webbed fingers clenched into a fist. "You're going against them! Lockers you go!"

Gaizka's lips curled into a grin, revealing sharp teeth not unlike those seen on tiger sharks. "Zero complaints." He went to the lockers as quick as a beast that smelled blood in the water.

Next on his list was the sixth-ranked captain of Falcon Squad, a young woman who looked like she could bench press four-fifty. "Ludmila Lamya, you too!"

"Pleasure before work." Ludmila hit her fists together. "I like that." And off she went, her icy expression hardly suppressing her excitement for battle.

Skipping over Winona from eleventh grade, he directed his attention toward the fourth-ranked captain of Heron Squad. "Desiderio Garza, you too! With shark boy and dragon girl!"

The Titlacua boy with slicked back hair and delicate, almost feminine features nodded in acknowledgement. "It is an honor, sir." He bowed down like the gentleman he was before going.

Suck up. Monceros then searched his formation for number three in the ranks, the captain of Kingfisher Squad. He'd heard and seen things about the one known as Alexandru von Coagula. Though Mastema and Bianca were more powerful than Alex by quite a bit, the bastard child of House Coagula was the most dangerous contestant on The Stage. Being a simulation, nobody could be physically harmed in The Stage, but Alexandru's spark had abilities that attacked the mind rather than the body.

Three years ago, he saw this boy drive somebody into a coma just by staring into his eyes. Upon waking up, the patient told the doctors he'd seen three moons in the sky, placed around Earth in a triangle formation. Alexandru had pointed this out. That was when gravity suddenly distorted, the oceans turned chaotic, and the world began to tear into pieces. The last thing he remembered was how Alexandru just watched from under the sea of illusions as he drowned in the flooded world. Monoceros shuddered at the thought of what a viler character could do with such a spark.

But alas, he knew that Alexandru was no monster. If anyone knew how to use a spark as dangerous as Lord Ruthven, it was the captain of Kingfisher Squad.

Monoceros finally called the last person's name. "And finally, Alexandru von Coagula!"

The aforementioned Alexandru walked out of the line, his wardrobe all royal purple. He was a pale man, but his pupils were blood red. In his hands was an unopened violet umbrella. He nodded to his teacher. "Fine by me."

Seeing the squad captain's unusually long fangs, McDooley felt the need to speak up. "Don't get too crazy out there. Not on the first day."

"Fine by me," Alexandru repeated himself, this time with more force. He walked off, twirling his umbrella by the handle.

With all of the participants chosen, Mr. McDooley turned to the rest of the class. "Take a seat guys and enjoy the show! I've already got the whole stage set up!" He grabbed a remote control from his back pocket and turned on each crystalvision in the room. Today the stage he chose was a rainforest, not unlike the Floresta Rainforest in Titlacuan. There were large trees, bright colorful orchids, dead leaves littering the floor, and even various micro-and-mega-fauna lurking about in the forest.

Monoceros grabbed a chair, sitting in a reverse position. Other students sat around the room, selecting which screens to watch. But Bianca didn't just want to sit down in some dull, wooden chair. So instead she activated her spark behind her. The result was a large obsidian throne manifesting itself behind her. Taking a seat, she crossed and lifted her legs up to create a leg rest. Slouching on her royal throne, she watched a few of the many screens, waiting for the action to start.

"Let's see if at least a few of Rooster Squad learned new tricks," she said to Mastema. She had one elbow on her armrest, her hand neatly under her chin.

Mastema dragged a spindly wooden chair from the corner next to her throne. He felt quite inadequate in comparison. "Yes…this shall help us judge Ercan's future."

⁓ ✳ ⁓

"…And she was super hot! Like, you wouldn't believe it hot—short spikey black hair, nice waist that led down to her gorgeous yellow and black scales, the whole deal!"

Nobody was really paying much attention to Desiderio as they got ready in the boys' locker room. It wasn't that they didn't believe him. They just didn't care. They were too busy putting on armor and grabbing any weapons they stored there. There was also the fact that after a while, Desi reciting tales of his conquests just blurred together. They were more surprised about how many animal/human hybrids in the world there were than that their peer had a sex life. But even that got old after the fifth tale.

"Quit moving your lips," Gaizka stated to him as he grabbed his three-pronged stingray spear with his back turned to him, "before I rip them off."

"You're just jealous, sharptooth," Desiderio passively answered back as he unbuttoned the top two buttons of his padded leather armor that emphasized his body. He then took his rapier from his locker, checking it before sheathing it into his scabbard. "She was *nice*."

Gaizka just grumbled but let it be. He never understood why other human beings appreciated the art of fornication. The violence of battle stimulated him more than any woman ever could. Why think of breasts when you can imagine stomping some criminal's head in?

Cyrille decided to add his two cents into the conversation. "Why, this mysterious maiden sounds absolutely pleasant."

Desiderio put on a pure white mask that covered his eyes and shrugged, unsure of why he was making this comment. "Well…I guess she was a pretty decent person. Got along with the others just fine."

"Good for you, Desi," Cyrille complimented. "Snake girl seems great! I wish for the best with you two."

The man in the masquerade mask questioned whether or not to correct him that it was more of a one-night-stand/friends with benefits thing, but decided against correcting him. *He's much too innocent for his age.*

When Cyrille was done putting on his gambeson armor with his family crest on the back, he took his sword out of his locker. He unsheathed the weapon to admire the quality of his longsword.

The blade was encrusted with diamonds at the edges and in the middle of the blade. The cross guard was in the shape of twin serpent tongues tasting the air. The hilt had green scales that enabled maximum grip. The pommel was silver in the shape of a rooster with emeralds for eyes.

"You sure you should be keeping a sword that wicked in a locker room?" Basil questioned the chicken man as he finished putting on his bright red wrestling singlet. "Seems like it should be locked up in your dad's office or a museum or something."

It was true. Being a DeRoche family heirloom, it was odd that such a fine blade would find itself in a locker room. But Cyrille replied courteously.

"It is fine, Basil. Cockatrice has been in battle for seven generations. She has shed her share of blood on the battlefield already." He gently stroked the edge with two fingers. "She has an undying loyalty to the DeRoche name and I will be damned by Sophia herself if I am the cause of her death."

Gaizka spoke up as he slammed his locker shut. "Yeah. But what if some jackass tries to steal…'her'?" Basil nodded in agreement to the shark man.

Cyrille quickly answered with no hesitation. "Why worry? I trust you guys." Sheathing Cockatrice into her jeweled scabbard, he tossed her to Basil without warning. The wrestler almost fumbled, but caught her in his large arms.

Holy shite! This baby must cost more than a castle in a cul-de-sac, Basil thought as he admired the craft, despite knowing nothing of swords.

"Now please pass her around," Cyrille instructed.

Though confused about his reasoning, Basil did what he was told. He gave Cockatrice to Desiderio, who partly drew it out to admire the diamond encrusting.

"Well I give you this, Cyrille," the lithe teenager admitted. "Your family sure has taste in their weaponry." He shook his head. "My family focuses more on what they wear than what they wield." He passed the blade toward Gaizka. "In fact, I'm almost jealous." He drew out his steel rapier in comparison. "My father merely had my blades forged for me, changing them as I grew older." He twirled his blade in his hands, then stabbed it back into his scabbard. "I wish my family had some meaningful tradition like passing down your old arms for the new generation." He stared toward his fellow noble with confidence. "That is why when I have children of my own, I'll pass my arms down to them…when I figure out a name for them of course."

"Well you better figure out quick," Gaizka mockingly scoffed at him. "You might have kids already knowing you."

Desi became indignant. "Hey, I use protection!"

Cyrille tilted his head quizzically. "Protection from what?" He then gasped in horror. "Have assassins been sent to kill you and people you know and love?"

The three stared at him, not knowing what to think. Each thought the exact same thing.

Is this guy serious? He cannot be that innocent.

Gaizka shook his head. He admired the craft of Cockatrice. With the diamond edges, he theorized that she could cut through flesh more effectively than a regular blade. Made him almost jealous. But he had better ways to off a foe. Ways that would scare off any other attackers.

And with that, he put the blade away, tossing it to back to her owner.

"Catch!"

Surprisingly to the shark man, the reptilian rooster moved quicker than expected. Not quick enough to be the result of some kind of spark, but quick enough that it was obvious he was keeping up with physical training. With one hand, Cockatrice was back in her owner's possession.

"Are you four done touching each other's swords?" a voice teasingly called out to them. Alexandru appeared from the next row of lockers over, clad in scarlet plate armor that made it appear as if he had been flayed. "We don't have all morning. Come along, Hong."

With that he was off, twirling his blood red umbrella. Coming behind him was Hong, reading a thick book as big as his upper body. He seemed almost entranced as he wobbled toward the exit with his eyes glowing, his mouth wide open and drooling a waterfall of saliva. On his back was a Moon Tooth Spade with a blade on each end.

"Face out of that book, Hong." A slight nudge from his superior's crimson parasol brought him back to his senses and scurrying to The Stage.

The four boys decided that it was time to move out, lest they face Mr. McDooley's wrath. As he passed by, Gaizka whispered these words to Cyrille.

"You may be safe and surrounded by trustworthy folks here. But outside these walls, I recommend you don't go around trusting strangers." He then marched on. "There're a lot of bad people out there waiting to prey on gullible folks."

Cyrille noticeably shivered at the statement but followed him. He got a good look at Gaizka's bare back. It was adorned with a black ink pattern of a spider with four limbs reaching his shoulders and four wrapping around his waist. Around the tattoos, however, were noticeable healed up scars which seemed to have come from all sorts of injuries from slashes and stabs from some kind of berserk animal.

He had an odd feeling that Gaizka knew a thing or two about the world out there.

~ * ~

A fight against four of the ten Squad Captains. Well this is going to suck. Really gets me excited for the school year. Not.

Julia frowned as she sat on the locker room bench, having just finished putting on her gray Odandin body armor. Her gear covered her entire body except her head and her fingers. Any part that was not flexible was reinforced with half an inch of plating for maximum protection and maximum mobility. On the right side of the chest area was the logo *ÆT*, the symbol of her father's company.

On the plus side, this new Armorsuit makes me look like some kind of action figure. Kinda badass.

She then reminded herself that her spark made her squishy in a fight.

But then again, I don't feel like I'm the greatest candidate for this armor. Some super strength spark person would be better off with it. But if it's to keep me alive so be it.

"Never seen such armor," Julia heard Ludmila Lamya speaking to her in her Eastern Tirnan accent. "It interests me."

"It's a prototype Armorsuit. My dad designed it for war," Julia tersely replied, not even looking at the woman in the sleeveless chainmail.

The well-toned captain nodded, intrigued. "What does this Armorsuit have that other forms of protection cannot hope to achieve?"

"Titanium alloy," Julia flatly stated. "That's what it's made out of. Also a couple of storage compartments here and there."

Ludmila lightly knocked on the armor with a finger, barely noticing Julia's flinching at her personal space being invaded. "I had no idea your father worked on gear for warfare."

Julia spoke a little more firmly. "He claims they're to be shields, not swords. Take that what you will."

Ludmila had heard how hard it could be to speak to Julia. She was acting very impersonal to her. Then again, she seemed to be impersonal to most from what she'd seen and heard of her. Perhaps Julia just hated small talk? So for now, she decided to end the conversation before Julia got more uncomfortable.

"Well then, sounds strong enough to give me something resembling a challenge."

"Probably not," Julia bluntly stated. "You know your way around armor more than me." Julia began to get up. "Well, I'm done getting ready. I'm off."

The captain of Falcon Squad honestly had little idea whether she was complimenting her on her skills and strength or merely just downplaying her own skills. She shook her head in dissatisfaction.

Seems her morale is in the latrine. Tragic. Without willpower, she'll never reach her spark's greatest potential. She had a possible conclusion. *Mayhaps the weakness of her captain has shattered her will to fight.*

Just then, Hanako stepped out of the locker room's mirror. The Seichin maiden was finished changing in private, dressed in a graceful silk red and white kimono that concealed her arms. It hardly seemed like she was dressed to fight, but anyone who'd seen her in action would have known better.

Not seeing one another before it was too late, Julia accidentally bumped into her.

"S-sorry, Julia." She bowed her head in apology. Julia could see a thin mirror strapped to her back.

Julia sighed. "It's…it's fine. My fault." She walked past her. "Let's just get going."

As Julia exited, Hanako turned to her fellow Squad Captain. She bowed once again in respect. "I wish you luck today."

Ludmila put on a mask with the appearance of a dragon's toothy maw that covered her entire lower face. She replied to her peer. "As to you, comrade."

‍ * ‍

With all parties done changing, the girls and boys headed toward The Stage. Entering one of the rooms of The Stage, they saw the devices that would allow them to fight each other to their fullest potential.

In order for aspiring psychics to fight to their maximum ability while not being in significant danger, The Stage had been created. It was widely known that various sparks could risk inflicting serious injuries. But at the same time, telling the students to hold back also risked stunting their growth and harming them in the long run. So the decision was made to create a safe stage, free to practice.

While The Stage…had an actual stage arena, students went into the arena rarely in person, only for introducing that year's Aeon Sophia Games at most. Instead, The Stage created a specific non-existent terrain that the audience watched from various screens. In order to mentally enter the battlegrounds, there were fancy looking chairs, sort of like the ones you would see in the dentist's workroom. Each seat had a dome which you inserted your head inside to enter the arena.

With ten of these seating devices in this room alone, the nine of them chose where to sit.

"Let us wish for a good fight," Cyrille said, offering one of his clawed hands to shake.

Alexandru took him up on the offer of fair play and firmly shook. "Best to you five."

The Squad Captains were the first to sit down, place the domes on their heads and enter the non-existent realm. Cyrille decided to give his little group a pep talk.

"So today shall be an uphill battle for all of us."

"You think?" Julia deadpanned.

"I know, Jules. Fighting four captains at once might be a nightmare and a half for most of us." The four listeners nodded in agreement. "But it's not a hopeless fight."

Hong tilted his head quizzically. "How so exactly?"

"Well, I'm glad you asked, Hong. You see...." He patted Hanako's shoulder, causing her to stiffen up a bit. "We have a captain of our own."

Hanako tried to search for the right words. "I-I don't know if I would be of much use, Lord DeRoche. I mean I am only ninth place."

"Please, please, Lady Hanako. Do not beat yourself up over a little tournament. We're all skilled in our own ways."

"But they're a lot more s—" Hong was interrupted by Basil closing his mouth with a hand.

Cyrille continued on. "All we truly need to do is believe in ourselves." Julia almost felt nauseous. "With that, we can do anything as a team."

"Even fly?"

"I don't know," Cyrille answered the salamander. "Can your spark do that?"

Hong dipped his head in shame. "No. Tsathoggua just gives me a visceral overlapping realm only I can see, a formless spawn, and a tome containing universal secrets no other mind can comprehend."

Basil added in, actually feeling important, "Well my Santa Claus spark can make stuff fly into the air."

Julia felt compelled to answer. "I've been working on some Thoth runes that allow for floating."

The bipedal rooster lizard felt hope and glory seep into his very soul.

"Well then, friends. We have an answer. We *can* fly. We fly as a team." He brought his hand out.

Are we seriously doing this? Julia thought in disbelief. *The thing where the team puts their hands together?*

"Hell yeah! The GIVER OF PAIN shall show them a new kind of…" he hesitated for a second to find a different word, but gave up, "…pain." He slapped his large hand on top of Cyrille's, making him wince a bit.

Hong was next in line. "Though wary, not trying would be worse. May we crush them—physically and spiritually." Hong placed his wet, slimy, webbed hand on top of Basil's, causing the muscleman's spine to crawl a bit. "But not literally for that is mean to do."

Hanako was next to speak. "Y-you guys believing in me drives me to do my best." She took out a silk handkerchief and laid it on top of Hong's hand, then gently placed her petite hand on the pile.

Ah, what the Hell. Julia decided to go along with it. "Let's at least give them a fight they'll remember for at least a week." Her armorsuit's hand slowly came on top of the entire hill of hands.

The five then threw their hands into the air, ready to kick ass. As they took their seats to The Stage, Cyrille said one last thing.

"Now let us give them a worthy battle or kind of sort of die trying." He closed his eyes as he entered The Stage for the first time this year.

Basilisk

Cyrille, Julia, Basil, Hong, and Hanako found themselves in a massive jungle. The temperature was humid, and fauna could be found all about the area if you just looked. It was dark under the forest, but the bright sunlight trickled down through the gaps of the canopy. The five took a brief look around.

"Nobody's around yet," Julia said to the group as she began writing a bright blue glyph on her right forearm with a finger.

Hanako grabbed the lightweight 3x5 mirror off of her back. Using the stake, she pierced the compact mirror into the earth. Grabbing Cyrille's wrist, she activated her spark, *Bloody Mary.*

Her eyes, hidden by her hair, turned bright red as she lightly pulled the reptilian rooster into the mirror. Soon enough, the other three were also brought into her mirror world. After glaring around the area to check for opponents, she too entered.

Desiderio, hiding behind a tree, was more than sure he saw her enter the mirror, the mirror disappearing seconds after. Above him a jaguar prepared to strike.

"So they're preparing for something. An ambush, perhaps?" He took out a rock shaped like a conch and spoke into it. "Desiderio to Gaizka. The prey is hiding in the world of mirrors near the stream with the big tree, east of our starting point."

An irritated voice came from the stone shell. "Seriously? You got to be more freaking specific."

Just then, the jaguar leaped from the tree to attack its new prey from above. The big cat didn't even see him take out his rapier. In less than a second, Desi vertically bisected the big cat with little effort, hardly even bothering to look. Stepping away from the two halves of the carcass, blood shot out from the beast seconds later.

Messy. Once again, he called on the conch as he created a deep slice at the base of the thick tree. "Now there is a fallen tree and two halves of a jaguar. Is that enough for you?"

"That'll do, Desi. I'll alert the others. We'll surround them."

"Good." He tossed the conch over his shoulder and began to push the tree over with his foot, a feat that he really should not have been able to do. "As the lumberjack says, *Timber.*"

The tree fell over and landed onto where the mirror once was.

"What are they up to?" Monoceros questioned from his seat, his one eye staring intently for where the five might be. "They can't hide forever."

Bianca was kind enough to reply from her obsidian throne, not even looking back. "They're not hiding, sir. They're preparing."

Mastema turned toward his teacher. "They're planning…I would recommend that the opposition watch out."

"Holy crap!" Julia just barely dodged the falling tree. "They seem to have found us."

Even in the mirror world, they were not perfectly safe. None of the four or any animals may have existed in this realm, but the environment could still inflict harm. Not helping the fact that even though this world seemed normal, it was reversed from the real one. The violet orchids in the east were now in the west, the stream in the north was now south. Even the logo on her armor was now written backwards.

Double checking the outside world through the mirror she was holding, Hanako saw the young nobleman sitting on the trunk, waiting for them. "It's only Desiderio so far. But I'm sure he and the others have something planned."

Cyrille seemed as relaxed as ever, Cockatrice in his hand. "Worry not." He tasted the humid air with his long tongue. "Jules has a plan."

Put on the spot, Julia tried to come up with an idea for the five of them. She had just finished creating the correct glyphs on her gear. Now she had to figure out what to do with the rest of them. Hanako had the mirrors, Hong had that weird other world he could see, Cyrille was… Cyrille, but she had a eureka moment when she thought about what Basil could do.

"Basil. I've got an idea."

"Well speak away, toots," Basil replied, anticipating his usefulness.

"I want four large-sized glass vials and four mirrors just like Hanako's."

He looked at her through his red-tinted sunglasses with a smile. "You gotta say please."

She was flabbergasted. "Seriously? You're actually saying that now? We're in a—"

He momentarily glowered. "I'm serious. Santa Claus doesn't work unless you say please."

"Alright, alright." She honestly wasn't used to saying this. "*Please* give me four large-sized glass vials and four mirrors just like Hanako's."

"YOU GOT IT!" He summoned a large brown sack from nowhere and reached into it. He took out four vials and four mirrors. "ASK AND YOU SHALL RECEIVE!"

"Yeah, whatever. Sure." Julia took the vials from him and gave them to her fellow Rooster Squad member. "Cyrille, use Basilisk."

"I'm always using it," he replied. "I know just what to do with these." With that, he drooled and spat into each and every single one, filling each vial with his saliva.

Basil felt uneasy at that disgusting sight. "So we have to take these around with us?"

"Definitely," Hong answered him. "Why wouldn't we need these? Poison makes everything easier."

"Wait a second." Basil realized something before pointing at Cyrille. "You're toxic?"

"Yes, I am," Cyrille said casually. "My Basilisk spark allows me to create poison from any of my body fluids. I'm also venomous. Yes, there is a difference."

Basil shivered a bit. *I sat next to him last year. I almost feel like I'm next to a pit viper.*

Julia took the four vials from Cyrille. She activated a yellow glyph that was shaped like an arrow plus a cloud in the palm of her armor's right hand. The glyph glowed and evaporated any saliva that missed the inside of the vial, which was, not surprisingly, a lot.

When she was finished, she gave a vial to Basil, Hanako, and Hong, keeping one for herself. "The moment you get any opportunity, use the poison. Then get them while they're weak."

Basil did not exactly feel comfortable. "I don't know. It just feels… craven."

Julia was having none of that. "Deal with it. There's no honor in real battle."

"I feel like being on her side," Hong added in. "Besides, how is poisoning someone more painful than breaking somebody's spine, beating them to death, or slicing them up?"

The muscular man in sunglasses could hardly answer. "I…guess I can't argue with that?" He accepted the vial, but still felt uneasy.

Hanako grabbed the four mirrors and placed each one behind a bush or tree. She then gave Julia a thumbs-up. "I-I feel we're ready. I have an idea too."

～ * ～

"Well this is boring so far," Bianca mused to herself. "All they're doing is wasting time at this point."

Mastema had other thoughts. Due to creating several floating eyes to watch each screen, he more or less had a perfect idea what was going on. Gaizka, Ludmila, and Alexandru were closing in from the west end of the area. What he saw amused him as he lightly stroked the top of his yellow-pupiled ocular familiar with his index finger. Aureolin watched just as closely as its master, ready to see what would happen next.

Suddenly on several of the screens, the audience watched as the mirror reappeared in front of Desiderio. Out of the mirror came Julia, Cyrille, Hong, and Basil. All four were ready to fight against one guy.

"Those aren't…the real ones coming out," he commented to his peer on her throne.

"Of course not. She's not foolish enough to go against him head on, five against one."

Mastema pondered. "So, are they…planning an ambush then?"

Bianca shook her head in doubt. "Not a chance. Outnumbering Desi is a huge mistake. A suicidal tactic." She pointed toward the other mirrors hidden away from the swashbuckler's vision. "Besides, I'm sure they've already come up with a game plan."

The audience watched the four extra mirrors as Basil, Cyrille, Hong, and Julia each came out of one. Basil dashed away to go his own direction, going at a speed three times faster than any track star. Hong's eyes glowed as he ran on nothing near the top of the canopy. Julia ran on the ground with Cyrille close behind her.

Well, until Cyrille slipped on some mud and fell over. It would have been not too big of a deal if it wasn't for the fact that he ended up tumbling down a nearby hill and dropping ten feet down into the stream. Worse still, he landed into the mating grounds of fer de lance snakes, which bared their fangs at the intruder. Much of the audience could not resist laughing as the overgrown chicken flailed about as he was bitten by multiple serpents at once. Even Bianca could not help but cover her mouth and chuckle a bit.

But Mastema's expression remained cool and collected. *Now what has Rooster Squad learned over the summer? Or anybody for that matter?*

~ * ~

Desiderio found that the odds were against him. With rapier in hand, he prepared to battle. Watching intently, he saw the captain of Rhea Squad slowly crawl out of her mirror in a manner that made it appear as if her limbs were dislocated. He could see her eyes glowing under her long black hair. She slowly got up on her two legs, her bones crackling as she stood upright. He looked toward her large sleeves, detecting a shiny object hidden within.

On the defensive, he waited for their first move. Hanako twisted her head around and screamed to the heavens. Her mouth was grossly stretched open and revealed sharp teeth. She might have been scary if he didn't know who she was. The creepy kimono girl then pointed at Desiderio with her butcher knife, signaling the others to rush and overwhelm him.

All five foes charged directly at him. Keeping a right head on his shoulders, he defended himself.

It was a poor idea to come up to me, five against one. Nobody's ever won against me doing that. Nobody ever will.

Basil was first in line, rushing him down in order to get him into a grapple. Desiderio's response was to slice his left arm off. Before the wrestler could react, he used his blade to slit his throat. Desiderio wished he could be at least a little surprised when he saw that Basil broke apart into reflective shards.

Typical. She made reflective copies. It can never be simple, can it?

The copy of Cyrille attacked him with Cockatrice next, going for an overhead to split his skull open. The swashbuckler cut the blade in half with a swipe and, with a second swipe, he turned the copy into a headless chicken. Before Julia's mirror clone could attack, he swiftly stabbed through her head, heart, lungs, and throat, making the construct break down into pieces. Hong's copy tried to pounce on him, not even bothering to use his moon tooth spade staff. He decided to sidestep and cut him in half at the waist, taking him out of the picture too.

Finally, it was captain against captain. Hanako lunged toward him, ready to tackle and stab him to death. The knife did go through his armor, but not enough to make anything more than a slight cut. His reply was to grab her head and knee her in the face, knocking her over. Stepping onto her knife wielding hand, he finished her off by stabbing her through her eye.

I'm sure you could do better than that. I'm disappointed. To his slight surprise, Hanako's body also broke down into thousands of shards. *No longer as disappointed.* He noticed that he was standing in front of her mirror, showing his reflection. He couldn't help but admire his body. *Damn, I look good.*

But he had no time to relax. His very own reflection jumped out, slashing at him. Desiderio parried the attack and thrust his blade at himself. His copy dodged and swiped at him again. Desiderio blocked, but his copy moved forward to lock their blades together. Each one pushed against the other, trying to get their foe off balance.

"Is that you, Hanako?" Desiderio casually asked as he pushed his rapier against his clone. "When have you been taking sword fighting lessons?"

He got no vocal response from his more serious looking copy. The only reply was the eyes of his clone turning bright red. The two hopped away from each other and then unleashed a flurry of attacks against one another.

~ * ~

Julia jogged through the jungle in order to conserve her energy. As she moved, the red circular zigzag-shaped glyph on the back of her left hand blinked. The dot in the center of the glyph flashed and beeped every few seconds. The more frequent the beeps, the closer she was to an enemy.

I'm so glad I learned to create this glyph last month. Feel way safer with it.

She was prepared to at least go down with a fight. Not win. Just at least show that she was worth a damn. She was a realist like that.

As she moved forward, she noticed that the beeps began to occur every second. Someone was close. She looked back. "Somebody's close! Keep an—" She saw that Cyrille was not behind her. Due to her foe detector, she was sure that he wasn't just ambushed without her noticing. He must have lagged behind.

Dammit, now I'm alone. I'm super screwed sideways.

The beeps came faster and faster. She quickly opened a compartment in her suit's forearm and grabbed a device. Pressing a button, the device quickly extended outward and became a tonfa. She then quickly scribbled blue and yellow bolts onto her weapon with her finger.

By this time, the beeping had gone into overdrive. As she was done writing on her weapon, a light blue ray shot out at her from the foliage. A warning shot, as it missed by a few feet, freezing the base of a tree in ice.

Pushing aside large leaves, a woman appeared clad in large bright silver armor adorned with pauldrons shaped like dragon heads. Her helm was shaped like a dragon's skull. Her shield was big enough to cover her entire forearm and then some and had a row of spikes with dragon eyes and a wide-open mouth at the bottom. Even her sword was curved and shaped like a draconic wing. There was a whole lot of dragon in this outfit. The wearer spoke in a familiar voice.

"Would you mind turning off that blasted thing?" Ludmila requested. "It will drive us both mad."

Honestly agreeing with her, Julia deactivated her detector, the glyph fading away. "So, we're doing this, huh?"

Ludmila pointed her five-foot sword toward her. It was a marvel how she could hold such a weapon in one hand. "This begins now."

Ludmila shot a second ray of cold at her from the opening of her facemask. The ray hit her directly in the chest. Strangely, she didn't even catch frostbite, didn't even slow down a bit. Ludmila noticed a red and blue snowflake-shaped sigil on her left shoulder. It was easy to assume that it made her cold resistant.

That's a new one from her.

Julia grabbed a small metal disk from a side compartment and threw it toward her opponent. Ludmila used her common sense to block it with her shield. Upon impact, the disk lit up and exploded, causing her to stagger back.

Julia used this opportunity to activate the glyph on her tonfa, channeling an electrical current around her weapon. Swinging at the armored woman, she managed to hit her at her side…and didn't even leave a dent in her armor. Ludmila didn't even seem to feel the electrical current that should be running through her entire body.

"Nice try," Ludmila commented. "But thinking that a little electricity can hurt a dragon is foolish." She attacked with her large sword in a downward strike.

Julia activated the white glyph on her left forearm, creating a see-through shield to block the attack. She stopped the blade from tasting her flesh, but the force was still strong enough to knock her down. Struggling to get back, Julia blocked another swipe at her side, causing her to roll over. As the implacable woman trudged in her armor toward her, Julia tossed another disk with an explosive glyph on it to slow her down. Ludmila merely swatted the projectile aside with her shield. It exploded twenty feet away.

As Julia struggled to get up, Ludmila pointed the maw of her dragon shield toward her. Out of the shield's mouth shot out a large ball of ice as big as someone's head. Julia blocked it with her shield glyph, but the projectile still sent her flying back on impact, causing her to drop her weapon. Julia crawled behind a nearby tree for cover.

Crap. I can't even hurt her a bit. But I do have one more plan. Luckily, she seems to be as slow as molasses. I can use that to my—"Shit!" She just managed to dodge another ice ball coming her way, denting the tree she was hiding behind.

"I'm impressed by your little tricks," Ludmila complimented her as she slowly approached. "But now this battle is over. Time to—" She stared in disbelief as Julia ran away from her in a serpentine pattern. "Are you really doing this?!" She attempted to shoot a third ice ball, but missed. Soon enough, Julia was out of range of her attacks. *This armor is weighing me down. I must now use Zmeu's greatest ability.*

She stuck her blade into the ground and spread her arms out, roaring into the air. Her spark's armor burst into hundreds of small ice needles that pierced the surrounding forest, even impaling several birds, insects, and monkeys onto trees and rocks. Now protected just by her light chainmail, she began to transform. Her skin became green scales, her nails became claws, and wings grew on her back. She ripped off the facemask covering her mouth, revealing sharp teeth made to tear flesh. Grabbing her sword, she expanded her huge wings and flew to the emergent layer of the forest, ready to hunt down her prey.

~ * ~

Cyrille waded through the shallow stream with a few snakes still wrapped around and biting at him. He felt lucky to be immune to poisons and venoms of all kinds. If he wasn't, he would be dead. Except not really, more like "out of the match." Honestly, come to think of it, the stakes weren't exactly that high to win. But to impress his peers and McDooley, he decided to bring his A-game to the table.

But his morale was beginning to take a hit. He was soaked and covered in mud, none of his allies were around, none of his enemies were present, and this one fer de lance was wrapped around his neck and wouldn't let go. The annoying bugs in this humid place only made it worse. It was enough to make him mildly miffed.

Up ahead near the shoreline was a large, oddly shaped rock. The top of it was pointed up to the sky and was covered in sharp…barnacles perhaps?

Why would a rock near a stream have barnacles? Is this salt water? Cyrille dipped his long tongue into the stream. *No. It tastes fresh.* He looked around at the sand surrounding the odd rock. *Why are the rocks around it so well organized?* Out of habit, he unsheathed his sword, ignoring the snakebite of the serpent wrapped around his scabbard.

As he slowly advanced forward, the rock began to shift around and move out of the sand and mud. As it escaped the earth, the six smaller stones turned out to have been the upper legs of some sort of arthropod. It turned around to reveal a giant claw hidden under the ground, accompanied by a much smaller left claw. Cyrille recognized it as a fiddler crab made from stone. He remembered seeing them at the DeRoche vacation home at Soliset Harbor. They weren't harmful at all. Though he had a gut feeling this one was, as even the serpents embracing his body let go of him and swam away as if to say "Screw that thing! We choose life!" leaving him to face the rock crab himself.

That turned out to be a wise move, as the fiddler crab was four feet tall, six feet wide and with a giant claw as big as his body. It was also advancing toward him, gurgling bubbles and brine with its remarkably complex mouthparts, looking at him with bright blue eyestalks. Cyrille got ready for whatever would happen. He realized that this thing was the work of Gaizka's spark and he knew for a fact that Basilisk had no effect on a rock monster.

How am I getting out of this predicament? I'm out of my natural element with no help in sight.

He tried to quickly slosh around the rock monster, but it sidestepped quicker than he could evade. It shot a line of bubbly brine twenty feet away, hitting his midsection and causing him to fall over, his head submerging under the three-foot stream. Looking under the water's surface, he saw the crab's sharp, rocky legs advancing toward him. In a rush, Cyrille got up, grabbed Cockatrice out of the water and advanced toward the giant fiddler crab, ready to strike. He knew that the weakness of a crab's armor were the eyes and joints. He hoped his sword was strong enough to damage those parts.

Now within striking distance of one another, the crab attempted to use its big claw to grab him and crush the life out of the scaly bird man. Cyrille managed to strike the big claw downwards with Cockatrice, her diamond edges gashing it. With the crab off balance, Cyrille used his sword to cut at the stony joint. Turns out, segmented stone joints are not quite as durable. As the crab had nothing inside the stones to keep its limbs attached, a single chop declawed it, making its greatest weapon useless.

But it was still dangerous. It smacked him away with its small claw, making him fall over once again, creating rippling waves throughout the stream and alerting all the wildlife to steer clear. Trying to trample him to death with its sharp feet, it moved sideways toward him. Gripping his blade once again, Cyrille got ready to attack. The most dangerous part was over, now he had to finish it off.

He quickly scrambled back up and slashed at one of its legs, lopping it off. This disrupted its balance once again, causing it to fall over on its face. Cyrille used this chance to slice off one of its eyestalks, further staggering it and creating an opening. His final blow was a stab through the hole of the cut off eye, piercing what he assumed would be the vital area of the crab.

He was right. The rock fiddler crab violently shook as a blue light shot out of its cracks. With a twist of Cockatrice, it broke apart, becoming nothing but a bunch of stones like it initially was. The threat defeated, Cyrille rushed toward the shore. He *seriously* needed to get out the water now. Who knew if Gaizka was nearby?

~ * ~

Hong Hai Long ran on top of the canopy, just under the emergent layer. Even on The Stage, he could see what others could not. The leaves of the trees were overlapped by fingers, its bark with scabby flesh, its holes were things that would nauseate an average person. And that was just what changed with the world. He could see and feel fallen pillars covered in runes describing dark secrets and bridges of impossible geometries as well as spikes that adorned some trees.

The salamander jumped from branches and spikes and slid down zip lines of wet sinew. He searched about for any of the opposing Squad Captains. Hanako was handling Desiderio, so he had three others to watch out for. As he advanced forward, he whispered to himself.

"I choose to release you, Formless Spawn of N'Kai."

He stopped when he noticed spider webs in between the trees, obviously some kind of trap for someone like him. Hong perched on a twisting spinal cord piercing through the large mouth of a tree. He took this opportunity to regurgitate out the black inky substance into his hand. The Formless Spawn squirmed and bubbled as he whispered to it.

"Feed and grow. Then destroy our enemies." He tossed the blob away, sending it to do what it did best.

"That's really unclean of you to do that!" came a voice from behind.

Hong hopped away from the spike in the nick of time. Gaizka

lunged down to stab at where he once was. The stingray spear went through the spike, as if it did not even interact with it. Gaizka stopped his descent by impaling a spiny spider leg through the tree. The shark man had four spider-like limbs on his back, though they were thick and hard enough to appear more like a crab's limbs.

He shot out webbing from his hands, sticking itself to the tree Hong was on. He jumped to the side of the large tree, webbing in hand. He climbed toward Hong with a sharp-toothed grin.

"No running away!" He stabbed at Hong with his spear, who in response blocked the attack with his crescent spade.

Hong tried to jump away again, but a precise shot of compressed water snapped the branch he was standing on. This bungled his leap and he fell down onto one of the sticky webs. He struggled to free himself as Gaizka crawled onto the ensnarement on his four spider legs.

"I'll make this quick!" he stated as he advanced forwards, one of his sharp limbs ready to skewer him.

Hong made a desperate attempt to escape his clutches by willing his large book of knowledge into existence. It was not for reading, for that would be a stupid idea. Instead, he manifested his huge book at one of the three edges. This snapped the webbing and caused the death trap to hang about in the understory layer.

While Gaizka attempted to rebalance himself, Hong swung toward a tall, serrated spine that shot up from the earth. Using the sharp sides of the spike, he cut himself free. Grabbing his Shangrilan spade, he descended toward the forest floor, though even the bottom was unsafe. Gaizka used his spark to create many stone constructs of sea life. Surrounding him were rock creatures in the shapes of coconut crabs, sea spiders, and sea urchins with pistol shrimp on branches. The slimy martial artist wasted no time in mowing into them.

He used his dual-sided crescent staff to cut the vital limbs of the stone constructs. Kingfisher squad had practiced dueling against Penguin Squad many times, so he had a good idea what to do around the constructs of the Areop Enap spark. He twirled the weapon in his hands to deflect shots from the pistol shrimp back at them. He spun and bent around the area in ways no human ever could as he decapitated sea spiders, declawed crabs, and overturned urchins. It was almost like some kind of chaotic dance. His movements were as precise as waves during a monsoon—erratic and everywhere but exactly where the universe planned them to be.

Master Yeren always said that his abilities were the greatest among his four disciples, and he refused to ever disappoint him.

By the time Gaizka climbed back down, most of them were already destroyed. Any that remained were broken beyond any use. Gaizka seemed quite impressed as he grinned at his opponent, drool flowing from his mouth.

"Let's paint it all red!"

He charged at Hong with his stingray spear. The crescent staff blocked the first blow, and the next, and the next. Gaizka swiped with two spider limbs and swatted Hong's weapon away from him. Feeling confident of the next blow, the tattooed warrior went for a killing shot. Hong side flipped to the right, allowing him to avoid the hit. His feet landed on the side of a tree. Using the solid surface, the amphibian propelled himself off to the side, spinning about like a corkscrew as he dived toward his opponent.

The spinning attack struck Gaizka, his spear shattering on impact. He was knocked down with Hong on top of him. Only his sea spider limbs allowed him to knock the salamander off, who back flipped like a spinning wheel three yards away, picking up his weapon.

While prone, Gaizka shot webbing toward him. Hong naturally dodged the attack, though he was not the true target. Gaizka grabbed a chunk of rock from one of his fallen creations and yanked back while his foe wasn't looking. Hong only barely managed to see the heavy rock, scarcely having enough time to dodge.

This gave the Squad Captain more than enough time to get up and grab his second weapon from the rope holster at his waist. He took out a tool from his native Polytri Islands, a handheld weapon inset with shark teeth. This traditional weapon was known among his people as a Leiomano. He'd paid Ercan good money to make this thing as effective at rending flesh as possible. He licked his lips and stared toward his opponent with bloodshot eyes.

"I'LL TEAR YOU UP QUICK!" He swiped at Hong, who jumped back. "THIS MAKES ME FEEL SO ALIVE!" He jumped forward to attack again, but once again missed. "THIS INVIGORATION IS OVERWHELMING! DON'T YOU FEEL IT?!" He slashed downwards as Hong blocked the blow with his staff. With some sawing motions, he cut the staff in half and sliced at his chest, causing the salamander to bleed. "YOUR BLOOD! YOUR BLOOD! YOUR BLOOD! I SEE IT! I SMELL IT!"

As Hong stepped back, Gaizka just could not resist anymore. "I MUST TASTE IT!" Propelling himself with his extra legs, Gaizka leaped toward the salamander, baring his teeth to pierce flesh.

He was met with a tail whip to the face. It felt like a hard slap from a wet towel; it merely slowed him down by a bit. Hong capitalized on his opponent's vulnerability by jumping back and tossing the two halves of his crescent moon spade. Each half-circle blade sliced off a spider leg, making his foe grunt in pain. Gaizka shook his head a bit and seemed to almost calm down from his battle high. But not by much.

"That…hurt." He bared his teeth once again. "BUT NOT ENOUGH PAIN!"

He thrust his club at his opponent's neck. Hong bent over backwards to dodge the attack. He bent back so low that his hands touched the ground. Hong began to crawl, going under his own legs. He smacked the club out of Gaizka's hands and crawled under his legs. As a bonus, he hit the humanoid shark in the crotch with his ankle.

Gaizka suddenly felt enough pain. He keeled over, his hands covering his sensitive area. All he could do was repeat "Ow" over and over. This was an ample opportunity for Hong to finish him off.

"This is the sort-of-end-not-really," he told him as his prepared his fist for the finishing attack.

But Gaizka was having none of that. Instead, he used his razor sharp teeth to chomp at his foe's skinny ankle. Hong could not help but shriek in pain, kicking his head to get him to let go. Gaizka then head butted him in the face, knocking him back. Picking up his spear, he got ready to go for round two.

Hong had little energy to fight. Not spark energy; he had plenty of that. It was more a case of getting physically winded. So thus, he had to crawl up a pillar with a cavernous maw to hide.

"Where the hell do you think you're going!" Gaizka cried out as he saw his foe crawl inside something he couldn't see. "We're not done here! WE'RE NOT DONE HERE!" He threw his stingray spear at the salamander.

But the invisible maw closed, going right through nothing. He shot webbing, threw rocks, got a half broken stone pistol shrimp to shoot at the spot where he'd just disappeared. But to no avail. Hong was untouchable wherever he was. He was in a spot where he simply could not reach. It pissed him off.

But his temper had to be cooled down, for he heard an amorphous putty slip and slither forward behind him. Tropical birds and insects flew right past him in a hurry. Looking back, he saw a gigantic blob eating everything in its path. The black slime was the size of a tanker and was eating trees at this point. This mass was heading in his direction.

This formless abomination was one of few things that could make Gaizka feel something few could get from him—fear. He had little choice but to hightail it out of there as the blob inched closer, desolating the wildlife behind it.

In his safe space, Hong Hai Long could hear the outside world. "Bless you, Formless Spawn. You have grown bigger than I've ever seen in such short time. Truly a savior." He then exited the mouth cave and dived down into the spawn. "We shall finish this match together."

~ * ~

Bianca was honestly surprised by the outcome of that fight. "That was much less one sided than I imagined." She was upright on her throne, watching intently.

"No surprise for me," Mastema told her. "Alexandru always told me that Hong…had captain potential." He turned toward her. "You know his aeon score was four thousand and eighty-seven last time it was recorded. Third best of all of us."

"Four thousand? Are you joking? You'd better not be."

"I…do not joke, Princess."

She shook her head. "That is not human." Such a high aeon count was unnatural. Aeon was the fuel for sparks of all kinds. To use a spark, one had to expend aeon to use its abilities. If your aeon ran empty, you couldn't use your powers. But people with high aeon counts could fight for a *very* long time.

She had an aeon count of around one thousand five hundred, which was considered prodigal for her age. But to have over double that was insanity. She really should check the aeon meters more often.

But she had to ask him. "Who has the second and first highest aeon at the Academy?"

"Winona is second…Ercan is first."

Basil dashed through the jungle. He was sure that his other allies had already encountered opposition against the other captains, but he was going for the only captain that was yet to be faced—Alexandru von Coagula.

Using his Santa Claus spark, the buff redhead could detect how nice and naughty people were, judging by the aura around them. As a bonus, this gave away where everyone was. His peers all more or less had blue auras for "nice," though Gaizka's was purple for "in between." Cyrille had nearly white for "too nice," and Hong had a green aura for reasons even he did not know. Judging by the fact that there were still eight auras lurking about, he knew that nobody had lost yet. Alexandru had yet to even be encountered.

Basil increased his velocity to that of four times the speed of a human athlete. *I am so ready to deliver a smack down to Mr. Third Place. I've got his weakness covered; now all I need to do is get my hands on him.*

Basil had to slow down his velocity as he got into the deep jungle. Here the trees were so thick that the sun could hardly shine down. It looked like a perpetual dusk reigned in these parts. Basil kept advancing toward the aura and soon enough found himself in a circular area with trees far out enough that they created a makeshift arena, but big enough that it looked like the treetops all fused together to make a dark screen sky.

"Why hello, Basil. I've been waiting for you." The aura walked up into the ring. "I'm impressed you found me. I apologize for my supposed cowardice, but the sun is just *agony* here."

Basil deactivated his naughty/nice senses and saw the pale man in blood red armor twirling his umbrella toward him. "So, Basil of Eagle Squad is out to get me. You must have some nifty little tricks, right? Perhaps you got a little help from your peers."

Basil sighed and took out the vial of poisonous saliva. "Yeah, I do." But rather than use the poison, he tossed it over his shoulder. "But I don't need this shit! Real warriors don't use cheap tricks!" He pointed to his opponent, challenging him. "I'm taking you out like a real man!

This match starts NOW!"

Detecting that he was looking straight into his eyes, Alexandru seized the moment. His red eyes flashed as he spoke up. "Why are you fighting me? We're on the same side. Those bastards are pulling your strings. But you're safe now. Come back to my—"

Basil was having none of that as he rushed him down, clothes-lining him to the ground. As he tried to process what just happened, Basil grabbed and tossed him into the air. As Alex descended, he was met with two feet to his back in a dropkick that sent him spinning into a tree.

Alexandru was beginning to get annoyed as he struggled out of the dent he'd made. *Why isn't it working? Is it perhaps his sungl—?* He was interrupted again when he was suplexed into the earth. Basil picked him up and looked at the battered and befuddled captain in the eyes.

"Sorry to make this look humiliating. BUT IT'S PILEDRIVER TIME!"

But before Basil could jump up into the air with him, Alexandru took this opportunity to bite into his neck. Basil gasped as he felt fangs sink inside him. His legs wobbled and his grip loosened as blood and blue energy seeped out of the wound. As Alexandru drained his blood, his bruises and cuts faded away. When Basil tossed him off, the blood and aeon energy from his neck flowed into Alexandru's mouth. By the time he was done, Basil was on his knees.

"I give you this, Basil Bartleby." He wiped the excess blood around his mouth with a hand. "You have given, I, the Lunar Dhampyr, a worry." He strolled toward his defeated opponent, licking the blood off his fingers. "But now I must end this."

He took off Basil's tinted sunglasses and looked deep into his blue eyes. "Hey, it is I, Cyrille Coq DeRoche. You've been under the control of Alexandru for a while now. You okay?"

Basil saw a familiar chicken man as he continually and unknowingly stared into his new master's eyes. "Really? Where is that sod?"

"We took him out, no problem." Basil saw Hanako, Julia, and Hong with them. Cyrille picked up the scarlet umbrella. "We even got his umbrella."

Basil looked down in shame. "I'm sorry, guys. I didn't use your poison, Cyrille. I thought it was a sissy move to use it. But you guys must have gone through hell to fix my mistake." He got up from his knees and looked at all his comrades. "But that's the last mistake I'm making in this match." He hit his knuckles together. "Let's go bring pain to the rest of the captains!"

He saw Cyrille and the others gain a boost to their morale, ready to finish the fight. What was truly going on was much different.

Desiderio and Hanako continued to clash blades with one another. Sparks flew about each time their rapiers struck. They used thrusts, swipes, lunges, sidesteps, parries, counters, and counter parries in an attempt to strike down the other. After a while, it seemed almost like a rhythmic dance to them and their audience.

She has not been practicing swordplay in the least. Desiderio thought to himself as they clashed again. *She has merely been copying my maneuvers. It's almost like fighting my reflection. I go left, she goes right. I lunge, she lunges, I sidestep right, she sidesteps left.* He blocked another blow from his copy.

"So, Lady Hanako, I feel as though you poisoned me with your reflection's knife." Though the masked swashbuckler's reflection did not stop attacking, its red eyes widened with worry. "Do you think a little toxin could slow me down?" He parried away another attack. "Regularly this toxin should be nigh unbeatable to an immune system." He slashed at her. "But not mine! My spark is Diomedes, Defeater of Gods!"

His speed accelerated as he began an advance to overwhelm her. "I can defeat what cannot be defeated! I kill that which cannot be killed!" He repeatedly struck at her blade as he moved forward and she stumbled back toward her mirror. "Impossible odds are made possible!" He cleanly sliced his clone's blade into three pieces.

Hanako gasped as she saw her main form of defense broken. She tried to read her foe's movements but he became too fast. Before she could react, his blade sliced her throat. Gravely injured, she went back to her original form of a scared young maiden as he covered her bleeding wound with a hand. She coughed up blood from her mouth, ruining the snow-white parts of her kimono.

"Most people cannot defeat their reflection. I can." Desiderio twirled his blade to land a theatrical final blow. "Good match. See you at the captains' meeting."

But Hanako would not go gently. She grabbed his arm with all her remaining strength and fell back into her mirror portal, taking his upper body with her.

"What are you do—?" Desiderio felt his lower half get separated from him in a bloody mess as the portal to the mirror world cut off with him only partially inside. His blood from both worlds spluttered out, obscuring the mirror in red. This situation would be agony if pain receptors in The Stage were not dulled, but that didn't mean there was no pain.

As his upper body faded away from The Stage, Desiderio gave her a final thumbs-up for winning. Hanako lay on her back in the mirror world alone, coughing up blood, struggling to breathe. But she felt no despair over a double K.O. She, the Squad Captain who was only ranked ninth, managed to defeat the fourth ranked captain. Not to mention making him actually use his spark. So rather than cry from her injuries, she smiled as her body faded away from The Stage.

I wish the rest of you well in your battles. I know we have a chance. We can, as Desi would put it, "Defeat the Undefeatable."

Cyrille was beginning to feel lonely in the middle of the jungle. Nobody was around him, not even enemies. All he was doing was strolling around looking for anybody. It was honestly kind of tedious. So all he had to entertain himself were his own thoughts.

You know what must be a sad realization? That moment when a comedian realizes the fact that they are simply not all that funny. That must be the most tragic feeling. Like you just wasted your entire life on something you're terrible at.

Cyrille heard footsteps to the left of him. Turning to the side, he saw an imposing figure rushing him down. In a panic, Cyrille shot two red laser beams out of each of his eyes. Both shots hit the being, freezing it in place.

Cyrille drew out Cockatrice once more and licked the blade with his long slick tongue, getting his fluids all over her. Advancing forward, he noticed that it was Basil, paralyzed. His glasses were gone and his pupils were red.

Looking behind his companion, he saw a familiar fanged friend ten feet away, his umbrella blocking the sunlight. "Well, well, well. We finally confront one another, Lord DeRoche."

"Less talk! More fight!" Cyrille charged toward his foe, refraining from staring into his eyes.

Alexandru drew his weapon out of his umbrella's handle, tossing the rest of it at Cyrille. Cyrille's view was obscured by scarlet canopy, enough that he couldn't see what his opponent was doing. He barely had time to move his neck as Alexandru's blade pierced through the umbrella to get to his throat.

Not succeeding at giving him a surprise tracheotomy, he kicked Cyrille away from him. He then removed his thin sword from his shade as he desperately tried to maintain eye contact with him. But Cyrille's eyes were like those of a chameleon, always moving about in different directions and refusing to stay in one place.

The two clashed together, their swords in a standstill. But Cyrille had a trick. He mentally compelled the drool on his blade to move onto Alexandru's sword. The dhampyr could do little as the toxic saliva slithered up his sword and jump onto his face, forcing itself into his mouth. He choked and coughed as the poison went down his throat, falling over onto his back. Cyrille quickly stabbed him in the neck to end his suffering, his body disappearing off The Stage.

Seconds after the final blow was inflicted, Basil began to regain his movement. His red eyes turned blue once more in a single blink. He felt his face and noticed that his sunglasses were missing. If it weren't for the fact that this was merely a simulation, he would have actually been pretty miffed about losing them. Remembering that he looked into Alexandru's eyes, he searched around for the bloodsucker. All he saw was Cyrille with his sword in the ground.

Basil shook his head, feeling dizzy. "I didn't deck you in the beak, did I?" He hoped he didn't defeat the other three while under someone else's influence.

"Not at all," was the reply he got. "In fact, you hardly did anything while under his control. At least from what I saw."

Though it was a load off his shoulders, Basil at least somewhat wished he'd been more useful as a puppet. Kind of made him feel somewhat ineffectual. But he shrugged it off eventually as he activated his naughty/nice senses. He saw two auras running toward them, one flying and chasing a running person down, and somebody on top of something very big and shapeless. There seemed to have been two auras missing since before.

"Two psychics are out." He turned toward Cyrille. "You think Hanako tied against Desi?"

Cyrille merely smiled. "I'm sure she held her own against him. Though Desiderio is a very talented man, Hanako has her own pool of skills. Shame there was no clear winner." Cyrille shrugged. "If this were real life, I would be grieving her death right now. But since all this isn't real, the tension is honestly rather slim. I'll see her after this is all done anyway and congratulate her." He ripped Cockatrice out of the earth.

"True, true." Basil had to agree. "I'm not exactly afraid of dying right now. I just don't wanna get stabbed to death by spider legs or nothing. That must hurt like hell." He looked toward the auras again. "Oh, and by the way, everyone and their mother is about to come here." He put up his fists. "Get ready."

The two got into position, back-to-back, ready to defend themselves and one another. Within seconds, they heard a voice from behind them.

"Shitshitshitshitshitshitshit!"

Cyrille recognized the panicked voice. "Hey, it's Julia!" Julia was running for her life (except not really for nobody dies in The Stage). Around her, large beams of ice shot down from the sky, barely missing her but creating large spikes in her path to avoid. "Hi, Julia! I see you need some help!" Cyrille turned toward Basil. "Can you please summon your sack and take out a sled?"

"Ask and you shall receive!" Basil summoned his magical sack and pulled out a high quality sled made for two.

Julia at this point had almost reached the spot where they were. But to the right of them, another voice could be heard.

"SHITSHITSHITSHITSHITSHITSHIT!"

The moment Julia made it to them she bumped into the second person on the run. Turns out it was Gaizka on the move. Both of them fell flat on their asses. But before the shark man could get up and react to his surroundings, Cyrille stabbed two claws into his neck. Insanely toxic venom entered his bloodstream and he passed out, disappearing like the others.

Basil felt disappointed. "Well that was anti-climactic."

Cyrille frowned. "I know. But I had to take the opportunity. Reality says I should."

Julia got up, her head hurting. "The hell was he running from?" Seeing Gaizka flee was a rare sight. It must have been something huge.

She and the others saw a cone of ice energy shoot toward where Gaizka was running from. A look through the foliage revealed a gigantic black blob the size of a whale. It ate everything in its way. It increased in height to the point that it was taller than the trees themselves. Long pseudopods attempted to lash out at Ludmila. She dodged and cut her way through the attack and shot another ray of frost at the ooze. Each subzero shot slowed the formless spawn more and more over time. The humanoid ice dragon shot breath after breath after breath to slow the ooze to a complete halt.

"I feel we should capitalize on this opportunity," Julia remarked to her companions.

"That's what the sled is for," Cyrille answered.

Basil touched the red wooden sled and it floated into the air. "I have given this vehicle the GIFT OF FLIGHT! Now you can use it to get her."

She thought it was as good a plan as any. She and Cyrille got on board the flying sled. Next thing they knew, the two were flying through the air above the forest. Cyrille steered the sleigh toward the conflict.

At this point, Ludmila was nearly done with completely freezing the Formless Spawn. The blob tried to grab her with one last pseudopod in desperation, but her ice breath froze it solid. As Ludmila tried to catch her breath, a frozen black tendril began to crack at the end of it.

Hong shot out of the frozen ooze and attempted to tackle her out of the sky, the poison vial in his hand. She was having none of that and grabbed him by the neck.

"This was poor strategy," Hong mused to himself as he threw the vial at her face. But the vial didn't break. It just hurt a bit and bounced off. "I should have tried to open it before—URK!" He was cut off by Ludmila stabbing her sword through his whole midsection. She then threw him down toward the earth. "LESSON LEEEEARNED!" was the last thing he uttered as he faded away before hitting the ground.

Ludmila then turned toward the two members of Rooster Squad.

She seemed tired at this point, but she still had aeon to spare for them.

"I have an idea," Julia said to Cyrille. "Get close with your sword and I'll do the rest."

"Will do!"

Cyrille shot out two paralyzing eye rays toward her. As she deflected the rays with her blade, he accelerated the sled's speed as they rushed toward her before she could freeze them. Cyrille swiped at her with Cockatrice, but she flew a bit to the side to escape getting cut. As she tried to cut them down with her blade, Julia tossed her open vial of Basilisk poison at her. Knowing what was good for her, she dodged once more.

Ludmila began to open her mouth to suck in air for another breath attack. Julia found this as the perfect chance to use her yellow evaporation glyph to spray the poison she previously absorbed at her as a gaseous form. Ludmila inhaled all the poison in.

Immediately, she cancelled her ice beam and began to cough heavily. Her wings flapped slower and slower. Too weak to keep herself up, she fell toward the ground headfirst. With a thud and a confirmation from Basil, the battle was won.

"Hooray!" Cyrille cheered. "We survived and won!"

"Wait, what?" Julia questioned him. "You mean Alex and Desi are defeated too?"

"Yes!"

She had a feeling this upset was going to become big news around school.

~ * ~

The crowd could not help but cheer for the underdogs winning. Sure, they had assistance from one squad captain, but she'd only dealt with one of the opponents. The others, they handled themselves. It was as if four little guys took out three giants.

Monoceros stared at the screens in surprise and awe. He did not expect the five to actually win. He may have anticipated one possible loss on the Squad Captains' part, but he expected a pretty one-sided fight. This was not meant to happen, much less three of them taken out consecutively so quickly.

It was DeRoche that allowed them to win. His poison saved this entire battle.

Mastema was also surprised, but kept his stony expression. "We should use this victory…during our trial for Ercan. Cyrille could become…a handy replacement for him."

Bianca turned to him, baffled. "But he could only do these feats because of Basilisk. Without his toxins, he is nothing. Strike him in the face and he's done."

Mastema chose to leave the debate until later. "We'll speak about this with the others, including the ones he just defeated…I trust that they will take their losses with grace."

"I guess we shall." Bianca could not help but roll her eyes as Cyrille waved to the screen. *This man showed us that we can all die so easily.*

Sylph

It had just been three class periods and Shee'vra was already pooped. She had no clue who had the bright idea to have math as the first period class, followed by ancient literature. Her mind was still pulsating on how to translate *The Pearl* written by the one known as Steinbeck. But here she was, sitting in a round, soundproofed room with her new teacher and all her new classmates.

From what she could tell, this class period was less about academics and more of some kind of relaxation class or something. Everyone was sitting in a circle, legs crossed, all in some kind of meditative state. Each one radiated a hardly noticeable aura around their bodies.

She recognized a few of the students. She saw that one of Yun's peers, Caradoc, was in her class. She had never really talked to him, but he seemed nice enough. Yun did consider him a bit of a nerd but loved him like a brother. Though Yun always hyped up the skills of his peers, she had a feeling Caradoc was far from the strongest in her class.

That title definitely went to the one and only Vural Kyogeki. Known on The Stage as Hyperbug Antlion, Vural was the captain of Swan Squad. He became a squad leader at age thirteen, the youngest of any student in the history of the Academy. She recalled that though he was only seventh place at last year's Aeon Sophia Games, he was always a spectacle to watch. Even now, rather than meditating in the circle with the others, Vural stood upside down on the ceiling, arms crossed. She wondered if Vural deliberately tried to be as flashy as possible for attention.

Gushing about captains aside, she had no idea what she was supposed to do. Even though she saw all her new peers relaxed in meditation, she didn't have the knowledge to emanate wispy energy. Even seeing Ercan do this occasionally at home gave her no clues whatsoever.

"Do not worry yourself, Shee'vra." Her soft-spoken teacher reassured her. "Entering your spark is never easy the first time."

Her teacher this year was Ms. Rumi Yamauchi. According to her, it was her first year teaching here. She seemed to be a gentle soul, though Shee'vra was intuitive enough to know that she'd had her fair share of battles as well, just like any other psychic worth their salt.

"You just need to close your eyes and try to stay relaxed," Rumi calmly instructed her as she knelt down next to her, bringing with her an odd chill in the air. "Try not to think of your surroundings. Just think about your spark and desire to get to know it better, not unlike an old friend that you haven't seen in ages. You might not remember it, but your spark has known you its whole life." She closed her eyes as she herself got ready to meditate. "Just try not to be too startled by your first visit."

Following her teacher's advice the best she could, Shee'vra took a deep breath and shut her eyes. For a few minutes her mind raced about what might happen or what it would be like. Ercan had once or twice told her that it was like having a temple inside your soul. She was curious what it could possibly look like. Would all sparks look the same on the inside, or were they customized to suit the idiosyncrasies of the spark?

No more thoughts. Shee'vra shoved aside her imagination and began to relax herself. The moment she escaped the thoughts in her mind, she felt a tingling sensation. The black void in front of her flashed and flickered in a bright blue. It was almost like that one acid trip scene from a movie she once saw.

But as suddenly as it began, the blue light faded. Instead, Shee'vra found herself in a lush green field. The grass and flowers were gently blowing with the breeze. The blue sky was clear except for a couple of clouds. The trees bore perfectly fresh apples. It was about as serene as it got and nobody but her was around.

Shee'vra began to ponder to herself. *Since this is some kind of subconscious world, can I create a gigantic lake? It would look great next to those hills to the—*"It does not work that way, Shee'vra," a soothing voice above told her. It sounded like thirty angels spoke to her at once.

Naturally like any teenage girl, she was startled by the sudden voice. "W-who are you? Where are you?"

The voice above spoke on. "I am a fragment, one of many. I reside in all." It almost said those words as if it had said it a million times before and would say it a million times more. Then the feminine voice from the heavens laid down a bombshell. "I am a fragment of Sophia."

Shee'vra couldn't believe it. She was speaking to a deity. If all psychics could do that, then why was nobody learning about the universe, the afterlife, or other mysteries of life? So, she volunteered to ask those questions. For humanity.

She bowed down in reverence. "So…Great Savior Sophia…what is…the meaning of life."

"I do not have those answers," a blunter answer than imagined, "though many have asked."

Shee'vra got up from the green fields. "Alright, fair enough. So where am I then?"

"You are within your own soul. Not your mind. Your soul. Specifically, the Spark Region."

She had heard of such a place from Ercan, but never understood it. That answered why she couldn't manipulate the environment around her. She questioned the calming voice again. "Why does the inside of my soul look like an open valley? Does everybody's Spark Region look like an open field?"

Sophia's voice answered once again, "Far from it. The Spark Region is solely suited to accommodate the kind of spark you have. Seems you were lucky enough to get a relatively serene Spark Region. Your teacher's region is a snowy mountain, for example."

That final comment got Shee'vra's attention. "Wait? You can see the inside of other people's souls? Not just mine?"

"Well of course. I am the source of each and every psychic's power. My fragments live inside each and every one of them."

"Well then, how do you choose who will or will not get a spark?" Shee'vra asked the fragment of their savior once again, "is it just chance?"

The world around her was silent for a bit, but soon gave an answer. "More or less. I have no control over who can or cannot become a psychic. It is merely up to fate."

That was enough questions. Shee'vra had to get down to business. "Anyway, where do I learn about my spark?"

"This trail will lead you to the answers you seek." Some leaves blew in the wind, flying and swirling across the sky. "I wish for you fortune and prosperity."

The wind pushed the leaves over a gravel road that appeared to be neglected for a hundred years. The road went over a hill, beyond her vision. Shee'vra followed the trail to see where the leaves were taking her. She traversed the hill and earthy pathway to see what was over the horizon.

Looking down, she saw that she was on a green cliff. The wind was stronger here and the breeze became a gale. She could see that there was nothing but sea for miles and miles at the edge of this world. In honesty, she didn't really want to find out what was beyond the tranquil blue sea. There were more important sites to look at, such as the large wooden windmill at the edge of the cliff, which must have been at least three stories tall. Its four fanning blades spun around and around to the wind at a steady and consistent pace. She had seen windmills before and had a basic knowledge of what they were made to do. But she also had a feeling this was no ordinary windmill. There must have been something within it that she had to see. The leaves flowed toward the structure and the path ended there.

She proceeded to walk toward the windmill. The entrance was a large wooden door with four bright green ovals on it that reminded her of a dragonfly of sorts. With a push, the door creaked open. Shee'vra coughed as dust blew out of the building, which must have been collecting for years. When she regained her focus, she saw the worn insides of the windmill.

It honestly made her question how the thing could possibly still be working. Most of the wood was rotted and hollowed out by insects, cobwebs were everywhere, and there was no lighting other than the sunlight from the filthy windows. Even worse, there seemed to have been a gear or two missing in the mechanism, meaning the structure was not claiming energy from the wind outside.

But the shabbiness of the place was not what lured her. She knew she would discover the name of her spark within this place. Going up the creaky stairs, she came upon the long abandoned living quarters.

Despite the conditions of the rest of the place, this room seemed to be tidy enough by human standards. The closet was empty but free of dust, the bed was tidily made with a green quilt, and the windows were crystal clear. There was a door that led to a balcony, allowing for a good view of the serene blue sea. If it wasn't in the middle of nowhere, this could actually be her bedroom.

Looking at the floor, she saw the trail of leaves that she followed. Each leaf lay on the floor in one direction as if they were pointing at something. She could see that they were pointing toward a desk. Shee'vra opened one of the drawers, finding a stack of papers. She sat down and read the front page of the documents to herself.

All sparks get their names from the minds of a world long gone. Yours is no different. Your spark is based upon the fairies of the air. Among one of the four alchemical elementals, your Spark is named Sylph; may you master the winds.

Sylph. It was a quaint name. Not too hammy, not hard to pronounce, only one syllable and rolled off the tongue. She could get used to the name.

Sounds better than Prometheus at least. She'd always thought her brother's spark sounded too over-the-top and tacky. Sylph sounded nice and casual.

She flipped the paper over to see more writing.

These papers will help you learn more about Sylph. It will start off simple enough, but will end with some of the most painstaking training of your life. So, take it slow. Now look behind you.

Shee'vra quickly turned back, expecting some kind of spirit or something. But she just saw the wind somehow blow the leaves onto the bed. She then turned back to reading.

If you lie down and close your eyes, you will return to the physical world smoothly. You will also wake up in this bed every time you enter your region. Mind you, time here works the same way as time out there. It has been half an hour so class is ending, get to bed already.

Shee'vra wanted to read a bit into her powers but felt like she had time to do that later. Just learning her spark's name was enough. She had to leave her Spark Region and return to reality. So she rested herself down and closed her eyes.

Within a split second, Shee'vra found herself back in the physical world. She checked the clock in the room and just as the papers noted, it had been half an hour. Everyone else in class was also coming out of their trances. Her teacher also awoke to see Shee'vra finished.

"Well, did you see your Spark Region?" Ms. Yamauchi asked her. Shee'vra nodded in response. "So how was it? I hope it was not too terrifying to behold. I hear some students have utterly nightmarish Spark Regions."

Shee'vra shook her head. "No, quite the opposite. I encountered a peaceful meadow with a windmill by a cliff."

Her teacher seemed pleased. "Well I'm glad you have a pleasant Spark Region."

Caradoc had just come out of his trance. "Did somebody say pleasant?" He turned to Shee'vra. "Was that you, Shee'vra?"

"Yeah. I was just talking about how my Spark Region is a peaceful meadow with a windmill," she answered him before realizing something odd. "Wait? How do you know my name? We never really met before." Shee'vra was not exactly a common name in these parts. She knew him from the Games but how did he know her?

Caradoc quickly answered her question. "Yun told me about you and stuff. But anyway, learn your spark name?"

"Sylph. Yours?"

"A much more mundane named spark known as John Carter," Caradoc admitted. "Sounds like a middle aged accountant, right?"

"I don't know," Shee'vra said. "Kind of sounds more like an action hero to me. What's your Spark Region like?"

Caradoc was giddy to answer that. "Oh, it's awesome. It's a giant, red, dusty world with roughly one third of Earth's gravity. There are two moons and I also have a swanky palace."

"That sounds like Mars," Shee'vra pointed out.

"According to Sophia, it is!" Caradoc told her with pride. "I am essentially proof that space aliens exist!"

Shee'vra wouldn't exactly go that far, but chose not to contradict him.

"The name is Sylph, huh?" She turned around to see Vural speaking to her, still standing on the ceiling. He dropped down with his arms still crossed, landing on his two feet. "Well then, Sylph." He cleared his throat. "My name is Vural Kyogeki, captain of Swan Squad."

"I know who you are," Shee'vra stated. "You're the proud owner of the Myrmecoleon spark. Your team came seventh place in last year's games. But to hell with the numbers, you kick ass."

"Well, seven is the luckiest number of all," Vural said, almost matter-of-factly. "Me and my squad always love to entertain the masses. Why bother being psychics if you can't be flashy?" He did a backflip with little problem right in front of the whole class.

"Do not show off, Mr. Kyogeki," his teacher softly chided him.

He bowed to his teacher. "Forgive me. Just making an example." Turning back to Shee'vra, Vural then took out a notebook and pen. After some quick writing, he gave her his autograph. "Here you go, Sylph."

She looked at the autograph, which said, "Dare to amaze the world. Vural." In cursive. It was odd to just give signatures without others asking, but she rolled with it. "Um…thanks, Vural. By the way, the name is Shee'vra, apostrophe between the second e and the v. I'm Ercan's sister, if you know him."

Vural treated this as some sort of world altering revelation. "I do. Decent man. How foolish of me. Then who is Sylph?"

"My spark's name. Just learned it today."

Vural's eyes squinted in contemplation. "Interesting. Interesting."

The school bell rang. The teacher turned to the class. "Class, it is lunchtime. See you all in forty-five minutes."

"Yes, teacher," Vural stated with upmost respect. "I shall be off. The other captains need me." He ran out of the classroom with his body leaning forward, his arms behind him, and his scarf trailing behind him. The sight was cartoonish to Shee'vra.

"Does he always run around like that?" she asked Caradoc. It was cool on the crystalvision, but kind of silly in real life.

Caradoc nodded. "Yup. He watches too much CV for his own good." He began to walk to the door like the other students. "But who am I to criticize? I'm off to the cafeteria to feast. See you later."

As everyone was leaving the room, Shee'vra thought to herself about

Sylph. She wondered about the potential of being able to manipulate air. She knew she could make winds of various forces, but what else? She'd read in the papers that it would be very difficult to master, so there must be more than manipulating gusts.

But for now, she was just satisfied with knowing her spark's name.

Judgment Time

"Well this day just sucks," Kushoto stated as the fly perched on Vinstri's shoulder, fighting against the wind as they rode on a metallic green motorbike. Normally such a bike would stick out like a sore thumb for two crooks like them, but nobody on the road seemed to notice they even existed.

"Yeah, only three hundred and forty-seven paz," the wet scaly man commented to his peer. "Just twenty-nine thousand and something to go." He didn't care about math at the moment; he was too busy thinking about being found in a gutter next week.

Vinstri dodged a silver car and kept his space from the rest of the automobiles. "But we have one speck of brightness. That card to *Eddy's Bar and Grill* saved us some cash for lunch." He still had the warm, cheesy taste of grilled cheese on his tongue and even had more food for their compatriots.

The fly was far from convinced. "I doubt an above average lunch from a beloved restaurant chain is going to affect our luck." She just hoped the others would not take it too harshly.

Soon they found their turn and entered Seraph Park. Nobody even heard them as the two drove into the park. There was no damage to the grass as the bike crossed the lawn deep into the trees. None of the birds or squirrels even smelled the gas emitted.

The two drove deeper and deeper into the park, passing the Bass Eagle monument along with a playground or two. Soon enough, they went into an area where neither tourists nor joggers entered. Going beyond the vast collection of trees grown from across the planet, they found themselves by the park's national Lake Keter. The two got off their bike behind a grassy lump in the earth and knocked on what appeared to be a door within the small hill.

A voice came from within. "Halt stranger! Who goes there?"

"It's just us."

"And who is 'us'?"

Kushoto shook her head. "Kushoto and Vinstri. Who else?"

"A lot of people actually. All who are not invited into our lair, ever!"

"Can we just get in?" Vinstri requested with the bags of food in his hands. "I got lunch."

There was a moment of silence as the two of them heard the sound of various locks moving and unlocking. Soon, the entrance opened up for the two. They were greeted by a man clad in black spikey armor. His eyes met Vinstri's and looked deep inside them for an uncomfortable amount of time. He then spoke up.

"What's in the bags, Sharlie?" He did not seem to use codenames either. Grabbing the containers, the armored gangster grabbed the contents from inside a bag. Opening the box inside, he found spaghetti and meatballs. His scowl turned upside down as he turned toward Sharlie.

"How'd you know I was hungry for spaghetti?" he asked as he ate a cold meatball, not even minding the mediocrity of a cold pasta. He didn't even use a fork, just his spiny gauntlets.

The fly chimed in. "You eat it every day, Ewen." She flew to the ground and began to transform. Within five seconds, what was once a mere insect was now a dark-skinned woman in her early twenties. "But more important news. We got a call from Shéng."

Strands of pasta fell out of Ewen's mouth as he stopped chewing and his jaw dropped. He stood up from his chair, towering a foot over his two compatriots and guided the two into the next room.

Inside the next room were their other two fellow Lefty Gang members. One was a hulking man wearing a jean vest but no shirt with two horns on his head and large hooves instead of feet. The other guy was an average-sized Titlacua man who wore a green jersey with yellow trimmings and the number twelve on the back of it. He looked like he would've been ready to play a game of soccer in a stadium a couple of years ago. The guy in the soccer outfit was writing down the amount of money they'd been spending while the big guy was dozing off in his chair.

When the door shut behind the three, the man in the green jersey looked up toward them, already tired despite it being only 12:30. He looked at the bags from Ray's Bar-and-Grill and sighed in frustration.

"How much did that crap cost?" His voice was low and resonated the sheer frustration of his job. "We can't afford spending paz on lunch, Sharlie."

Sharlie was quick to relieve his worries. "No problem, Louiz. I got a giftcard in a wallet I stole. So it was just about sixteen paz. Great deal, right?" He took out two boxes of food for his compatriots. "Feed yourself, boss. You haven't even had breakfast."

Relieved that their budget was not completely in the toilet, Louiz slowly got up and grabbed his leafy salad. "Thanks then." He let out a high-pitched whistle through his teeth, stirring the sleeping man awake. "Asterion. Lunchtime."

Asterion got up from his chair in a cranky huff. It took a bit for the hulking behemoth of a psychic to register what his boss said. But the moment he realized he'd said "lunch," he was wide-awake and as giddy as a nine-year-old getting the latest cool video game.

"Didya get the steak, Sharlie?" the large imposing man asked, his stomach audibly rumbling. Sharlie nodded and revealed the steak to his compatriot. Unlike Ewen, he didn't like his food cold, so he placed his slab of cow meat into the microwave.

As Louiz munched on his salad, he spoke up. "So how much money did you collect today?"

Muvumo and Sharlie were reluctant to answer. Nothing they could say would make their boss feel any better about it.

Louiz swallowed his food and repeated his question. "*How much?*" He bared his teeth at the two. A growl was enough to create a chill in the spines of all four of his comrades.

Sharlie looked away from him and feebly muttered an answer. Louiz was not satisfied with that.

"HOW MUCH DID YOU TWO GET?" The fingers in his left hand were replaced with vicious claws that scratched the wooden table.

Muvumo had little choice but to answer with her head down. "Not even three fifty. We're sincerely sorry. But with all the psychics around, it's just too risky to be doing high profile robbing."

"It's true!" Sharlie chimed in to complain. "We're living in the psychic capitol of the world. Thanks to that damned academy, who knows who has a spark and who doesn't?" He turned toward Ewen and Asterion. "You guys are having problems too, right?"

Ewen put down his spaghetti in shame. "Yeah. Me and Asterion do stick out like a sore thumb. Hard to mug when we're so easy to recognize." The armored criminal turned toward his fellow bruiser. "Do you think it's the armor?"

"It's the spikes, Ewen." Asterion answered without a second thought. "Get them off and paint your armor silver and you'll be fine."

Muvumo doubted that would work, but decided to merely continue to answer her boss. "The thing is that after all these months we've been going nowhere. The rest of the Lefty Gang sees us as a joke. We literally cannot pay back any of the money we owe our superiors. It's a miracle they haven't abandoned us as a lost cause by now."

"They don't abandon," Ewen muttered a bit. "That would leave loose ends." The five knew what their superiors did to "loose ends" and were not ready to be found in a ditch.

Louiz took his claws out of the table, leaving a large gash among other gashes. He let out a sigh of anxiety. "You're right. None of us have been making any progress with getting money. I don't think that we're ever going to get that three thousand paz by the end of the week."

"Ooooooh," Sharlie awkwardly hissed. "I got a call from Shéng." Louiz already felt uneasy. "It's not three thousand we owe, it's *thirty thousand.*"

Louiz's world became gray and he could hear his heartbeat more than he could hear Ewen pigging out. A high-pitched noise invaded his mind as all he could think about was the consequences of his actions. He'd been a crap leader. He'd heard of other members of the Lefty Gangs in other towns having enough money to live in luxury. Those gangs had millions to spare, enough to support themselves, treat themselves, pay off their debts, and to pay off both the police and any psychics willing to take a bribe.

But for them, they could hardly make a living under a hill like a freaking Halfling in those books Ewen liked to read. No way could they rob a liquor store or mug a businessman or break into a house. Any one of them could call a psychic, the strongest ones available. Knowing his skill, they would get creamed, maybe killed if the psychic was in a bad mood.

But there was an argument to this conundrum. Why not just kill your victims, leaving no witnesses? Well Louiz may be a crook, but he had standards. Those people might have families and friends who would grieve for them. Pragmatically, it would be better to avoid such a thing, as grief frequently could lead to revenge and he'd heard stories of psychics on vengeful killing sprees. The five of them would be wiped off the face of the earth. Empathetically, he was sure that none of them would be able to forget what they did to a completely innocent bystander. Even most of the other gangs from the other cities at least kept the body count to a minimum. Attracted too much attention otherwise.

His thoughts were interrupted by Sharlie. "Well, boss. We do have…that stuff."

That stuff. Louiz looked toward the side room where they kept the stuff, long untouched. Stuff they could sell for a lot of money and ruin a lot of lives with. Stuff such as Ghouldrool, Goodnite Powder, Nosefood, among other drugs—such drugs the other Lefty Gang members freely sold without any remorse.

But he was having none of it. He got up from his seat and grabbed the sea serpent man by the fleshy, leafy protrusion under his chin with his claws.

"Listen here, Vinstri! Under no conditions will any of us *ever* sell that crap!" He yanked harder at the barbel/goatee, looking straight into Sharlie's eyes with his bright yellow pupils. "That garbage will get us caught and ruin a bunch of lives!"

Sharlie tried to fit a word in edgewise. "But the other gangs do—"

"I KNOW THEY DO IT!" Louiz shouted straight to his face. The room was dead quiet for a while, to the point that you could hear a pin drop from the table. Louiz slowly let go of Sharlie and began to walk back to his seat, a hand on his face. "But those cities are not Bythos. You can't get away with that crap here. Maybe it's because of the dangers or maybe the morals of the people. But after two years here, we've made no dent in this city whatsoever." He sadly chuckled a bit. "It's almost beautiful how incorruptible it is."

Sharlie comforted his poor barbel beard and asked his boss a simple question. "Then what do you plan we do?"

Muvumo cut in. "What we're trying isn't working. So what do you propose?"

Louiz contemplated a game plan for what to do next. This would have to involve both getting the money and keeping his group safe from any harm—whether that harm was from the authorities or from their bosses.

Suddenly the microwave went *ding* and Asterion's steak was ready. At that same moment, an idea popped into his mind.

Louiz turned toward the large horned man. "Aster, pass my cell." Asterion did as he was told and tossed his crystalcell as he dug into his steak. Dialing a few numbers, he brought the phone to his ear and waited.

"Password?" the man at the phone requested.

Louiz sighed, knowing what was coming next. "I am a dumbass thirty-year-old bed wetter." *God dammit, Ezker.*

Ewen couldn't help but chuckle a bit before receiving a glare from Muvumo.

"Correct password," Ezker replied, trying to contain laughter. "What do you want, Izquierda? Does Clé need a new set of armor? Those don't come cheap."

He looked at Ewen, who had just finished his meal of cold pasta. Though stained in tomato sauce, the armor looked fine. "No, nothing of the sort," Izquierda insisted. "I was just here to relay that I've gotten Shéng Xià's message about the money we owe. I've got a plan to cover that predicament."

"Call me amused. You guys, the disgraces of the entire Lefty Gang, have a plan?" The man on the phone had zero faith in them. "Humble me, what is it?"

"If you must know, I know this bank in the Chokmall that is totally vulnerable to a bunch of psychics such as ourselves. We get the money, pay you guys back with interest, and you get us out of this town."

"And why should I do that?"

"Because there is pretty much nothing here for the Lefty Gang. We have tried everything, but money will not rake in. This city will never be in our grasp."

The man on the other side of the phone didn't speak for a while. The entire gang wondered what he was about to say. Would it be a "yes," "no," or "you have outlived your usefulness, goodbye"?

They almost felt relief when Ezker spoke up again. "Have you tried to sell the drugs, Izquierda? Those would give you quite a pretty penny."

Louiz knew he couldn't say they hadn't even tried. Feeling nauseous, Louiz told him a lie. "Yes, but no buyers. Almost got caught by a couple of psychics last time we tried. It's too easy to get caught in this place."

There was another tense pause before Ezker spoke up again. "Well, I guess you'll have to talk to somebody higher than me about this. Maybe Shèng could put in a good word for you. He's coming in about a week. As am I. Later."

"Oh, okay. Thanks for the heads up. Bye." Louiz hung up his cell. He grumbled a bit, not quite satisfied with the answer he received.

"So what did he say?" Muvumo asked him as she leaned on a wall, arms crossed.

Louiz put down his crystalcell and addressed the group. "We spoke about leaving and we'll see if Shèng Xià can help us with our situation." His eyes widened at the realization. "Holy shit." His jaw would have fallen on the floor if it could. "Shèng is coming. He only shows up when the gang is doing something *really* big." He began pacing around the room. "We're so screwed, so freaking SCREWED!" he groaned as he signaled the entire group to huddle together. "Alright, everybody. Today we're robbing Chokmall blind. So to prepare, here's what we're gonna do…"

~ * ~

"So I heard you've been talking shit lately, witch." Gaizka was right in Winona's face. She didn't exactly seem intimidated by his sharp teeth being bared inches from her face.

"Don't make such a big deal out of it." Her crow feather earrings swung about as she turned away from him. "I just called Gustave cold blooded. Silly pun, that's it." A smirk appeared on her face. "Maybe you should grow a thicker skin."

Gaizka didn't let it go just yet. "I'm not talking about Gustave here. He doesn't give a crap about that. He just told me what you said to the whole junior class."

Winona feigned surprised, "Wouldn't take the walking luggage to be a snitch." Black liquid with orange specks emerged from her fingers as she poured it into a vial for later. "Besides, people would've learned sooner or later."

Gaizka had little idea what Winona could do with such a potion. Perhaps it enhanced strength or speed, maybe it exploded into thousands of black ice shards, or perhaps it drained the aeon of anyone who was exposed to it. It could possibly even be for something not battle related like ink that wrote itself onto paper, a drink that could allow her to stay awake for days without end. Maybe even Winona had no idea what the substance was meant to be and was merely fiddling around with her spark. That or she was deliberately doing this as an excuse not to focus on him. But nevertheless, the sight of the inky substance somehow calmed his nerves.

"If I may interrupt…" The shark man and the witch turned to the right of the long semicircle table to see Alexandru sitting at the end of the table in an upright and proper position. "What Gaizka is trying to say is that he is angry that you blatantly disregarded somebody's private note for the sake of humiliating him in front of his peers."

"More or less, dhampyr," Gaizka replied to him, slowly moving away from Winona's personal space and sitting in his seat next to Hanako, who sat quietly eating today's lunch with plastic cutlery.

During squad leader meetings, Mastema would bring the best five-foot sandwich subs ever. This time it was a hero sandwich with meatballs and mozzarella. Gaizka also decided to chomp into his piece of the hoagie, watching the feather-haired girl as he chewed.

Winona was not fazed by the words of the third strongest squad leader. "As I said, they would've figured it out anyway. Crap like this does not just remain behind closed doors. I merely just hastened the process."

Ludmila added in her two cents from her own seat right next to Winona. "Perhaps so, but this is a trial of one of our peers. The least you could do is act professionally." She looked to the left toward their youngest member with derision. "That goes for you too, ninja."

Vural was hardly paying attention. He was too busy leaning back on his chair, feet on the table, reading a light novel. He only barely heard what his peers were saying, but he nonetheless somehow acknowledged the muscular woman next to him. "Come on, Lud, the trial hasn't even started yet." He flipped to the next page of *Guitar Maniaxe*, engrossed in the lore. "Aw snap! Tinpenny did what? It just went down."

"What could possibly be more important than waiting to determine the fate of one of our very own?" Ludmila asked the captain of Swan Squad, visibly annoyed by his lack of professionalism.

Vural placed his *Hyperbug Force Go!* bookmark at his stopping place and put down his literature. "Well if you must know, an amazing plot twist had just occurred. It's more intriguing than anything we're doing right now."

She was reluctant to ask, but the captain of Falcon Squad could not help but ask. "What could possibly be more important than what will be happening in..." she checked her crystalcell for the time, "...two minutes?"

The youngest psychic in the room wrapped his arms across his chest. "Well you might not understand what I'm saying, but spoilers. So these five musicians form a band and use the power of music to fight giant monsters and stuff. Then it really goes down when..."

Desiderio also seemed to roll his eyes at Vural's summary of a mediocre story. *Why does he seem so compelled to tell us the story of an entire book series? There's not even cat girls from what I'm hearing right now. Hope this dumb trial moves quicker.*

Bianca sighed to herself as Vural went on a pointless tangent about some stupid dime-a-dozen book. *Why couldn't we all be more mature about this?* She turned toward Mastema, who sat next to her silently like a statue, waiting for Ercan to appear. "Will you get them back in order?"

Without an utterance, Mastema rose up from his seat in the middle of the table. With the spontaneous creation of his wings, everyone stopped what they were doing or saying. All they could do was look at the strongest student in school and stare in awe. They knew from the moment they saw his thousand-eyed wings, he expected silence and order. None of the other captains were willing to challenge him on that.

"Thank you...for listening." Mastema sat back down, allowing his wings to disappear. "Now sooner or later Ercan will appear..." he heard footsteps coming from outside the room, "...right about now."

The rest of the class got ready for the trial to begin as their weakest link entered the room. Ercan quietly closed the door behind him, then turned and awkwardly waved to his judges.

"Hey guys. I'm not late, am I?"

Mastema checked his watch, and shook his head. "No…we begin."

Ercan took a seat in the chair in front of the whole group. Clearing his throat, Mastema was the first to speak.

"Ercan Ao'Si, squad leader of Rooster Squad, you are summoned in front of this court to determine whether or not you are worthy of being among us." The Angel of Silence took out a list from his bag. "While we are here to determine your capabilities, we would like to reassure you that you are far from weak, judging by the last aeon test everybody took."

He passed last year's aeon test results to Bianca, who began to read it more clearly than Mastema ever could. "I'm beginning to read the last year's aeon score results of everybody in this room." She started at the bottom. "Desiderio Garza (Diomedes): 40."

Desiderio shrugged in indifference as some of his peers looked on in astonishment at how low he scored despite his skill. "Skill matters more than size I say."

"Vural Kyogeki (Myrmecoleon): 352."

That was a respectable aeon level, but nothing special. Vural must not have seen it before, as he fist-pumped with pride. "Awesome! A whole twelve points higher than eighth grade!"

Bianca glared at him with her pinkish-red eyes, silencing him. "Keep an indoor voice, please. Hanako Nanaringu (Bloody Mary): 666."

The Seichin maiden looked down with a whimper, almost as if she was trying to hide in shame. "Why does it never change?" was all she mumbled to herself.

Gaizka turned to her. "Don't kick yourself over it. Maybe this year's different." He patted her on the back, perhaps a little too hard, as she squeaked in surprise.

Bianca ignored the sharkman and continued on. "Gaizka Pantopoda (Areop Enap): 684."

Gaizka grimaced in disappointment. *Same as sophomore year. Gotta try harder.* He turned to Hanako once again. "At least you're not alone in stagnation."

"Alexandru von Coagula (Lord Ruthven): 843."

The sharply dressed man accepted such an above average rank. "Mother wouldn't lie about my levels to me." He spoke to the muscular woman from the other side of the table. "It seems you've made it ahead of me—"

He was cut off by Bianca. "Ludmila Lamya (Zmeu): 844."

"Just by that much, huh?" Ludmila questioned as she turned to the dhampyr. "So this year I assume is anyone's game."

Alexandru gave a smug grin. "Twenty paz, it's me this year."

"You're on."

Bianca read on, the golden circlet around her head reflecting the light from the ceiling. "Now it is, I, Bianca Narkissos (Tezcatlipoca): 1551."

Most of the room already knew she was strong so they made no big deal of it. Desiderio still lightly clapped for her. "Outstanding results, Princess. It is proven I could not do better myself."

Bianca halfheartedly accepted his praise. "Thank you, I guess. But next is none other than the highest ranked captain among all of us. Mastema Mattatron (Dumah): 1849."

"Really? Just one thousand, eight hundred and forty-nine?" Vural publically wondered. "I expected five thousand at the very least."

Mastema took a breath to address his naïve friend who never bothered to really read the lists. "Nobody in this school has five thousand... though several are close." He gestured for Bianca to continue.

Winona never paid much attention to the charts. She had better things to do and concoct. Words on paper meant nothing in the big picture. But she admittedly was tempted to know who had more aeon. Was it her, or was it that failure, Ercan? She would have to wait until that pale diva was done gawking at the sheer size of their aeon levels.

Bianca could hardly comprehend what she was seeing. These two were easily academy records. But she straightened herself out and spoke up. "Winona Samhain (The Morrigan): 4263."

Though it was a known fact of how high the aeon levels were of Winona and Ercan, it was still hard to believe how insane it truly was. Sure, aeon levels meant nothing in how strong a spark or psychic was, but it sure meant they could use their spark for long hours at a time and still have energy for more. Nobody truly knew how strong somebody like Camael, Naranbaatar, or even Merle were, as the device to measure aeon was not invented, but they sure imagined it was close to that level.

Winona did not seem satisfied, though. She could not comprehend how such a disgraceful psychic could have more aeon than her. But she merely brushed it off. *It doesn't matter how much aeon we have. It's the powers. You can swing around on chains and heal from your wounds all you want. But I will eventually snap your bonds and take you out before you can even register that you need to heal.* But she admittedly was fidgety about how his aeon level was higher.

Bianca then got to the last one. Smoothing her white ponytail with her dainty fingers and tightening her blue bow that kept her hairstyle together, she made it to the last member on the list. "Alright, final one. Ercan Ao'Si (Prometheus): 4799." She crumpled the paper and tossed it into the recycling bin. "And now that our aeon measurements are established for comparison, we will continue onto the trial."

Mastema nodded toward her and then spoke up in this usual soft way. "Thank you…Bianca. It would take too much time for me to explain all that." He turned toward Ercan. "But anyway, we can see that you have a huge…" he checked the notes in front of him, "…supply of aeon at your disposal. Such potential." He gestured to Hanako to turn on the crystalvision in the room.

When it activated, Ercan found it to be a recording of last year's Aeon Sophia Games. Hanako fast-forwarded it to the final game, the free for all. The entire room saw how Ercan and the rest of Rooster Squad performed. It seemed Xiu and Yun got quite impatient with the pace they were going and Julia's morale seemed quite low. Only Cyrille seemed any bit content. But Ercan didn't take charge. In fact, he seemed very tired and broken himself, already accepting loss.

So when Xiu brashly ran ahead, not listening to his warnings, it all went to hell. Xiu was the first to be defeated, skewered by a blizzard of glass and obsidian shards. Yun was next, grappled and pile-drivered by Basil, who admittedly had a pretty amusing scream of terror like a scared little tamarin monkey. Julia was cut into three pieces by Caradoc's blades. Cyrille was shot with light arrows by Mayil and cut down by Zivot's self-aware swords but congratulated his two servants with a thumbs-up. Ercan tried to fight off his foes, but he was outnumbered five-to-one. Bianca inflicted the final blow, a reflective dagger thrown into his skull. Eagle Squad annihilated his squad in the span of a half-assed tooth brushing session. It was embarrassing how pathetic it was.

"Oooh," Desiderio winced. "That looked painful. But on the other hand, it is Eagle Squad. The only squad better is Sparrow Squad. And see what they did to me." He pointed to Hanako. "Please fast forward a bit, Hana."

She did as she was told and after a bit, she got to the part of the raw footage where Desiderio faced off against Mastema. Though Desi's lips moved to speak, nothing came out. In fact, the entire battle was eerily silent, not a sound from anything, from anyone. All twenty seconds of the battle. Turns out being really good with a rapier is not very useful when floating eyes can shoot lasers into your back. Mastema wordlessly inflicted the final blow with a halberd made of dark red fiery light.

"Pro tip: Lasers sting like hornets on fire," Desiderio advised the class. "But thank you, Hana. I think we're done with the CV."

Hanako nodded and turned off the crystalvision after that, returning to her seat at the right end of the table.

"Thank you…Hanako." Mastema said before once again turning toward Ercan. "Now Ercan…what did you do wrong?"

Ercan struggled to maintain eye contact like a scolded toddler. "I-I didn't take initiative and my squad got defeated because of it?" Ercan felt uneasy as Mastema's azure eyes stared him down. "So Xiu ran on ahead when I told her not to and Yun followed and…you know…it didn't work out."

Mastema took a deep breath before speaking up. "Ercan Ao'Si…do you believe you are at fault for your failures as a captain?"

"Well…partially? But Xiu never listened even when I tried to tell her that—" Ercan stopped the moment his judge gestured to him with an open palm.

"Enough…it seems that you are blaming one person for your inadequacies as a leader…unacceptable." He did raise an index finger, though, as he took out a batch of documents. "Though judging by your post-mission reports, she always knew how to get into trouble." Mastema began passing documents to Bianca and Ludmila, who likewise passed them down. "From what I read, she comes across as…volatile to say the least."

"That is a way to put it." Ercan groaned to himself. "She was a handful when it came to authority."

Ludmila spoke up. "From what I read here, it seemed she was far from dead weight."

Ercan nodded and shrugged. "Well…she knew how to fight damn well. Score one for her, I guess."

"Martial prowess is not what I am talking about," Ludmila added in. "I am speaking about working on missions as a whole. Take this one titled 'Mystery of the Missing Orca.' She managed to track down the missing Orca from Blueseas Theme Park using just her spark. Turns out, there was no orca. It was actually a pirate psychic undercover that could turn into cetaceans."

Ercan's memory began jogging back to the second half of freshman year. "Oh yeah! That one was weird. He was stealing money from the park and had framed the owner for embezzlement." He then sighed. "But the son of a bitch got away."

"Truly tragic," Ludmila commented. "The report seemed to be going so well until then. Though you used your chains to vainly attempt to keep this orca imposter from swimming out to sea, Xiu Lang cut the chains before the man could drag you with him." She put down the report. "From what I can tell, it seems Xiu Lang saved your life."

Ercan remembered getting pulled back to shore by her, as he was much too exhausted to do so by himself. Despite everything else about her, he would always remember her doing that for him.

"Though in contrast, Yun, Julia, and Cyrille seemed to have done very little during this mission," she continued. "Were they busy with other things? Or did you not give them orders."

Ercan scratched the back of his head, thinking of an answer from the vaults of his memories. "Wellll…they tried, buuuut…Cyrille was at the bathroom, Yun couldn't swim, and Julia stood back. Must have thought that she'd be of no use or something. I dunno."

"Perhaps if you'd given her an order of sorts, she could have been of help," Alexandru chimed in.

Ercan winced. "I couldn't think of anything at the time. Sorry."

It was Winona's turn. "Why did you think it was a remotely good idea to let Cyrille take a bathroom break in the middle of hunting a criminal?"

Ercan smiled. "Well, funny story. You see, Cyrille actually got lost and—"

"Enough." Bianca stood with a stoic expression on her face, but her eyes seemed passionate, like rubies shining in the moonlight. "It sounds like there's a lack of discipline throughout the whole squad. You seem to allow them to do whatever they want." She pointed a finger in accusation. "That's not how real squads are supposed to work. Your life and their lives are on the line. Such undisciplined actions are unacceptable." She sat back down softly and gracefully, hands in lap. "It is a miracle you are all still alive. Be grateful for that or this trial would be over before it began."

There was a long silence within the room. Not many people really ever saw Bianca get worked up like that. It couldn't even be from experience from her team, as actual losses in academy squads were actually very rare thanks to never being selected for the highest jobs. So nobody knew what hit a nerve. But The Angel of Silence ironically ended the silence.

"Anyway…from what I've read from these missions, you and Xiu both have a roughly equal amount of moments where you…perform in less than a stellar manner. Your other teammates occasionally are to blame, but you two are the primary ones. But…none of you have been killed, and technically every mission has been completed, even with less than the desired results. So, I…personally feel like we should give you one last chance to…redeem yourself." He turned toward the rest of his fellow captains. "Do we agree?"

Each of the members began to raise their hands. Some were quick to agree such as Vural and Desiderio, others were more reluctant such as Alexandru and Winona. But sooner than later, each man and woman's right arm was raised.

Mastema seemed satisfied with the results. "…Perfect. Though this will not prevent us from analyzing the rest of your team for a possible replacement."

Alexandru cut in. "Yes. Cyrille did very well for himself only a few hours ago."

Ercan had little idea what they were talking about. "What did he do exactly?"

Hanako piped up this time, rather excitedly. "Cyrille actually was a big help at defeating Alexandru, Gaizka, and Ludmila at the same time!" She then looked toward the three people she mentioned and tried to compose herself in front of them. "B-but it was far from one-sided and he wasn't alone."

"Indeed, DeRoche was grossly underestimated," Ludmila agreed with her assessment. "But I feel this might be a one-time thing." She turned to Vural. "How is the newest member of Rooster Squad doing?"

"Wait, you mean Shee'vra?" Vural replied. "Oh yeah! She learned her spark's name."

That got Ercan's attention real quick. For a good while, he had wondered what his sister's spark would be named. And with the learning of the name, the real training began. "What is it then?"

"Sylph."

"Sylph?" He expected a grander name. He had Prometheus and his mother had Titania. Sylph just didn't sound as larger-than-life as his own. But he knew from experience that discrediting a spark for its name was a terrible idea.

Vural kicked back in his seat. "Yes-siree! Now she can master the art of being a psychic. Something about wind powers, too, and windmill stuff. But she is officially ready to get to work on your squad."

"Who knows? Maybe she'll replace you," Winona mockingly remarked.

"Mayhaps," Mastema quietly stated to the group. "But…we need to find a way to pass judgment upon you." He looked upon the documents of past judgments since the Academy's beginning days. "Well…according to the papers, to resolve such situations we use a…" he unnecessarily stood up for effect, "…trial by battle—your squad against another. Pick a squad. We will pass final judgment based on your performance."

Ercan looked about the room. *Who can I challenge? I can't choose the lower ranked, that just seems cowardly. Mastema is a death wish. But there is one squad I can go against that would bring me back to their good graces for sure.* He decided. "I choose Eagle Squad."

A gasp emerged from Hanako and Desiderio. The rest looked shocked, except for the two strongest captains. Bianca merely took a deep breath and replied.

"Are you sure about this? I will not hold back, not even against your sister. Novice or not, she will experience what I can do firsthand."

"Yes, I am. Though it will be an uphill battle, I have been exploring my Spark Region lately." He allowed himself to smirk a bit. "And I found a few new tricks. Besides, I have full faith that in the end, it will be just you and me this time."

Bianca rolled her eyes, but accepted his naivety. "Fine. We battle next Wednesday. One week. Train your sister, train your friends, but most of all train yourself."

"I intend to, Princess," Ercan answered with upmost respect. "I promise you will not be disappointed."

Mastema began to tidy up his papers. "That about clears it up for today…I thank you all for coming." He directed his eyes at Ercan. "And I wish you luck for next week…you will need it."

Winona was the first to leave. She brushed past Ercan, her odd concoction in hand. She spoke very dryly as she walked past. "See you at The Stage. Toodles."

Soon enough each member of the squad captains left the room. Gaizka even took the remains of the meatball sub for himself. All that was left was Ercan, Mastema, and Bianca.

"So I'd better get going. We have fifteen minute until class starts again. Trigonometry will be a nightmare, I'm sure of it." Ercan stood there for a moment, as if waiting for permission to leave. "Well anyway, later." And off he went to tell his squad the news.

Alone in the room, Bianca spoke up to the one student stronger than her. "So do you think he has what it takes to beat Winona?" Her arms were crossed in front of her chest, still contemplating why he would he be crazy enough to choose her for the trial.

"…Of course. We all have a chance to defeat one another. The Archons were not invincible…we're not invincible," Mastema answered without even looking at her. "Besides…judging one another by rankings is foolish. They take account of the whole squad, not just the captain. If only more of us…saw it that way."

Bianca couldn't help but chuckle a bit, "Would not expect that from you."

They began to walk out the door together, documents in hand. "I merely state the truth, princess. Us captains…"

Witch of Summer's End

Finally, the first day of school was done. Shee'vra left the school building and walked toward the Sacred Arena of Inner Spirit. She noticed that other students were heading that way too, though some were just going back to their dorms. Looking up, she noticed Vural backflip off the side of the building next to her.

"Hey there!" he greeted her. "You going to watch the after-school match? I hear The Stage is looking good today!" His red scarf blew in the wind like a flag of freedom.

"Yeah. My brother signed up today. It would be a shame if I didn't show up," she said, "though I just realized that I have no idea where the students watch the events. Can you show me the way?"

He gave her a thumbs-up. "No problem at all! Just follow me!"

Entering the SAIS, Vural led her down a hallway she'd never entered before. As he guided her down a flight of stairs, she noticed that she could have just simply followed the other students down here, but better safe than sorry. Vural stopped at an entrance where others, including fellow classmates, entered.

"After you, Shee'vra." He opened the door for her, revealing a room with almost theater-like seats and many screens to watch from. "Hope you enjoy the show."

Shee'vra stepped inside graciously. When she entered, she realized he was not following her. "Are you coming in too?"

Vural shook his head. "I'm afraid not. The captains have their own

VIP room. We have massaging recliner seats and a vending machine." He looked away from her. "Besides, I don't like the movie theater atmosphere."

Shee'vra had an inkling of knowledge of what he was talking about. She'd read in a magazine that when Vural was seven years old, he was in a film adaption of the hit Seichin CV series, *Hyperbug Force Go!* The series starred his father, CV icon Takuya Kyogeki. It was an innocent show about guys in bug-based battle armor known as the Hyperbug Force that fought evil bird aliens known as The Avions. Fight scenes, giant robot battles, and campy acting ensued.

But the movie was a tragedy. Critics panned it as well as the audience. Even fans of the franchise despised it for "destroying canon." Thus, the movie bombed in the box office. All movie watchers blamed the little psychic Vural for hogging the spotlight and making the story revolve around an annoying kid hero known as Hyperbug Antlion. The special effects and writing were also criticized for being lackluster compared to other films. Because of all these events, the franchise was ruined for good. She could understand his dislike of theaters. She saw *Hyperbug Force Go! The Motion Picture* herself once while channel hopping, and even she changed the channel within minutes. Must have been tough for a kid.

She managed to speak up finally. "Yeah. I get it. Enjoy the show in your massage chair."

"I shall," he said. "Wall running and wall jumping does strain the muscles." He began to slowly close the entrance when a voice came from the hallway.

"Hey, Sis!" Ercan dashed over to the two, giving Shee'vra a gigantic hug, spinning her around. "Congrats on Sylph!" He was wearing his usual red leather jacket and pants, but with the words "for battle purposes" on the back of it. "You're here to watch me duke it out?"

She did not even bother to answer such an obvious question. Two others were with him. One was Yun who was wearing his best fighting wear, a green silk martial arts suit with a gold sun and some tree branches embroidered on it like the ones you see in Qian Kung Fu movies. The other was the girl Shee'vra replaced on Rooster Squad.

She was also wearing her best clothes for battle. She wore a silk yellow top with puffy short sleeves with long black fingerless gloves to cover most of the rest of her arms. Her top had a black inky pattern of a tiger starting from the back and ending in the front, its claws just under her fairly well-developed breasts. She wore a matching colored skirt and black thigh-high socks, complete with a lovely pair of Qian slipper-like shoes This Xiu woman would make most boys at her old school drool. Maybe even some girls too.

But rather than staring, Shee'vra got back to speaking to the three. "Yeah, bro. Vural here was just helping me find the way here." She turned to Vural, who was admiring Xiu's outfit. Stealthily, like a true ninja.

He stopped checking Xiu out and got back to his senses upon being spoken to. "Oh, why yes, Ercan! Just helping the new girl out! It would be a shame if she got lost and missed your bout with the Witch of Summer's End." He saluted the three competitors. "I bid you three good luck!" He dashed off into the next-door room, presumably the VIP section.

Xiu shook her head. "What a dork." She then turned her attention toward Shee'vra, trying to recognize her. "So, you're Ercan's little sister, right?" She seemed a little too docile to be a psychic, much less her replacement.

"Right," Shee'vra replied with a smile. "Just finished my first day of class. Learned my spark name and everything."

Xiu inspected her former squad leader's little sister, but found no malice within her. No passive aggression of any sort. She couldn't think of a time she'd met her before. The other members of Rooster Squad had all seen this Shee'vra character before and said nothing but good things about her. It was almost too perfect to be true. Perhaps she was just that pleasant to hang around with.

Seems like not a bitch, Xiu thought. *But she doesn't feel ready to be a psychic either. The shit we go through is going to slaughter her.* She looked toward Ercan, patting his sister on the back. *And I can't trust him to exactly lead her to victory either. And if she kicks the bucket because of him, Ercan would just shut down. What can a lady like me do about this?* She remembered something her master once said to her and the other disciples.

"You must help even the smallest seed grow. The smallest of seeds can become the biggest of trees, though if it remains in the shadows of other trees, it will never reach its potential. But if the trees share the light with the seed, it will slowly grow just as high as the others. Remember, a forest sharing light is better than a cluster of trees fighting to see which can become the tallest."

So, Master wanted me to help somebody who needs to learn their full potential to become a great psychic, right? She looked at Shee'vra and thought of the innocent girl trying to fight a psychic that turned into a lizard monster. She imagined her getting ripped to shreds within seconds and eaten. Ercan would never stop grieving and would plunge into deep despair.

She resolved to follow her master's teachings (or at least how she interpreted them). *Okay its official, after school I must show her the ropes of my fighting style. For her own good.* She now imagined Shee'vra grappling the lizard mutant's wrist, throwing him over her shoulder and punching him in the throat while he was down. *Yeah. With my help, Ercan's sister shall become a fighting machine. Tripling her survival chance is the least I can do for him.*

"Xiu?"

"What, Yun?" Xiu replied a little snappily. She abandoned her inner monologue for later. "I was just thinking of strategies to take out the witch. I was planning this even before you or Ercan. I signed up for The Stage first, you know."

"Well, we got to get going. The battle's about to start," Yun replied. "Don't want people to think we forfeited. We'd never live down being branded as cowards." He grabbed Ercan's shoulder. "Come on, Ercan. You congratulated your sister enough." He began to drag him away, with Xiu following. "Congrats, Shee'vra, on learning your spark name. Big step."

She waved the three away and went inside the theater. Shee'vra found Cyrille sitting with his two bodyguards/servants. Julia was not there, probably in the library or something.

Cyrille acknowledged her, "Hey, Sheev. People are talking about me today for some reason."

Shee'vra took a seat next to Zivot. She whispered to her. "What are people saying about Cyrille?"

"He took out three Squad Captains during practice this morning,"

Zivot stated to her. "Rumor has it the captains are considering making Master the new captain of Rooster Squad." She sounded proud of him. "His father would approve very much of this. I honestly cannot wait to send a letter."

Shee'vra was surprised by this turn of events. She did respect Cyrille and his skills, but she also wanted her brother to stay leader. It would make him happy. The room then got dark and the show began.

~ * ~

Ercan, Yun, and Xiu found themselves in an abandoned city borough. Not abandoned as in nobody was around but otherwise normal but like some cataclysm had destroyed the entire town. It seemed like the place had been neglected for at least a hundred years. Buildings were covered in vines, wild animals roamed the streets, and wooden structures were on the brink of decay. It was as if humans had just abandoned the world, leaving their structures behind.

"This place reminds me of a horror movie I once saw," Yun remarked to the others. He activated his spark; his body grew hairier, his hands and feet elongated and morphed, his canines became more pronounced, and his tail grew longer. The monkey man then climbed up the highest square building nearby. He looked at the others. "How about you?"

"A bit familiar." Twin metal chains emerged from under Ercan's sleeves. With his powers, he latched them around a pipe on the roof of the same three-story building. Retracting the chains back inside him, he pulled himself upwards. Once he was at the top, he lowered another chain for Xiu.

"Why are we even getting up here anyway?" she asked, grabbing the metal links, yanking it so he could pull upwards.

Ercan assisted her. "Well maybe Winona and the others would attempt to get to higher ground and ambush us. But now they can't."

"I just wanted to climb up a vine building," Yun answered. Receiving stares, he quickly gave a better reason. "Well, what Ercan was thinking, I was thinking too."

Xiu looked out in the distance for a bit. "Okay, we're dealing with the witch and who else exactly?"

Ercan shook his head, expecting her to have read who signed up for today. "The other two are Gustave and Dunkeen."

A sly grin appeared on her face. "Perfect. She has two teammates who she has no idea how to work with, the surly croc and the blabbermouth fish." Her hands emanated blue wispy energy. With a wave of her hands, she created a jackal made from the pure aeon. It barked to her, ready for orders. "Anubis! Search around for the highest aeon energy in the city."

The ghost dog did as it was told and ran to Ercan, pointing at him. Xiu was both annoyed and impressed. Ercan half-shrugged. "Sorry."

"Whatever," Xiu replied dismissively. She tried again. "Anubis! Find the *second* highest aeon energy source in the city."

The aeon jackal barked and ran off, moving across the buildings and leaving an indigo trail to follow. The cube buildings were all attached to one another, so all three could follow, no problem. As they ran, Yun could have sworn he heard something squawking from a tree but ignored it. Big mistake.

~ * ~

Shee'vra intently watched a screen with Winona on it. The woman in black wore a dark, feathery cape and had a bow in her hands and a quiver and spear on her back. With her were a humanoid crocodilian man and a large fish guy with armor plating on his head, shoulders, and part of his back. She recognized the woman as Winona Samhain, captain of Crow Squad. Throughout the years she had seen her perform many tricks with her spark. *What would she do this time?*

A crow perched onto Winona's finger. Looking at the other screens, she saw many other crows looking at Ercan, Xiu, and Yun run across the plaza complex. She turned back to Winona and heard her softly utter, "Nemain."

The crow on her hand flew away, though the rest of the birds around the arena disappeared completely. Shee'vra saw her grow wolf-like fangs and her nails become sharp claws. She then created a black mist. Out of the mist came six wolf men, each one looking ready to rip someone apart.

Grabbing an arrow from her quiver, she signaled the werewolves to charge toward where she was pointing. Shee'vra checked the other screens and saw that they were entering a tall brown building at least twenty-five stories tall. The gator guy followed suit. The armored fish stayed behind but used his spark to stick his hands into the earth and grab a boulder with no problems. Winona hid inside a building, her arrows ready to taste blood. She paid no heed to the energy jackal trying to attack her, merely shooting it in the head, its body dispersing into nothingness. Winona then seemed to set her watch for a specific time.

Shee'vra felt nervous about how Ercan and the others would get out of this one.

~ * ~

The three of them followed the trail into the business district of the city with skyscrapers covered in vines. When they made it to the other side of the building complex, they noticed that the trail went up to the top of the nearest structure, which was, in fact, the tallest building in the lost city.

When they made it to the edge of the buildings, Ercan created a chain tipped with a grappling hook and shot it upwards to the top. Pulling on it, it felt very tight. "Alright guys, it's sturdy! Up we go!"

"With pleasure." Yun dashed on all fours, balancing on the chain to the top of the building with great agility, keeping his speed even while climbing. He quickly made it to the top.

Xiu was a little bit shaky about the height she had to traverse. "You honestly don't expect me to climb that, right? We'd have better luck—" She felt an arm wrap around her waist. "What the hell are you— AAAAAAAAAH!"

She wrapped her arms around Ercan's neck as he pulled the two of them upwards at great speed. She saw the trees and animals below her become tiny as they went higher and higher up. Within twenty seconds, Ercan got them both up to the top of the building.

"You see anything, Yun?" Ercan asked him. Yun had a bird's eye view of the whole city. Though he didn't have any super sight or anything, any movement would warrant caution here. He tried to move up to him but noticed Xiu's arms were still wrapped around his neck as tight as a lock without a key. She seemed to be shaking heavily. "Um? Xiu? It's over now." Ercan tried to pry himself out, weakly trying not to beg. "You can let go now." He continued to struggle out of her iron grip. She only got tighter the more he tried to escape. "Please. I beg you! Yun… help me."

Hearing Ercan's choking and gagging, Yun strolled toward them and lightly tapped Xiu on the top of her head. She quickly got out of her trance and back to reality. She noticed her arms around Ercan, crushing his throat. She managed to get herself to let go when she felt she was on solid ground, stopping herself from choking him to death (a tempting idea).

When Ercan was free to breathe, she shoved him away from her. "Dammit, Ercan! The least you could do is warn me when you get into my personal space!" She used her foot to draw a line in the gravel, about a foot and a half away from her. "This line, you do not cross! ESPECIALLY WHEN IT INVOLVES ROCKETING ME UP INTO THE AIR!"

The redhead had his hands in front of him, backing away from her. "S-sorry. I just got into the moment. Saw it in a movie and thought it'd be a cool trick to do. Don't get too mad at me."

Xiu seriously considered it but had more important things at hand. She took a deep breath like Master Yeren had taught her and turned away from him. "Whatever. I'm checking the trail. Keep an eye on the door or something." Walking next to Yun, she saw that the trail went over the building and into the smaller one below. "Did not know Anubis had such hops." As she inspected further, she noticed that there was no more trail to follow up on. That meant only one thing. "Oh crap. They know we're coming!"

As they got ready for a confrontation, she saw a gigantic rock coming right at them. Yun and Xiu had plenty of time to dodge, but the boulder broke off a chunk of the building where they had just been. Ercan created two chains, one ending in a spear point and the other ending in a meat hook. Wrapping the excess length around his forearms, he was ready for them. Xiu focused on her aeon and her hands and feet radiated blue energy. She and Yun got into a defensive position, just like their master had taught them. When another boulder just missed them, they knew it was far from safe on the roof and entered the building.

Running down the stairs and through the hallway, they tried to make their way toward the main staircase. Large rocks smashed through the walls, decimating the long forgotten offices. Feral cats ran off in different directions as well to escape the bombardment. At the end of the hallway was a door that said "stairway," which meant "stairs during times when elevators are not to be used." Ercan opened the door for the other two to run in and shut the door just when another boulder was coming at him.

"Who knew Dunkeen could become a one-man siege engine?" Yun commented as he ran on the railing on all fours.

"I had a feeling," Ercan answered, trying to be aware of his surroundings. "His spark is called Gnome, an earth spirit back in the old days."

"I just thought a gnome was a little person who you put on your lawn," Yun took a sharp turn, "right next to the flamingo."

Ercan also took the turn down the nineteenth-floor stairs. "I guess you were wrong." He looked up to see boulders bombarding the higher floors. Some were rolling down the stairs after them, breaking the staircases and rails. "Aw, crud! The rocks are coming down after us!"

Xiu was in the front of the group. "What are you two talking about?! What do you mean by rocks following—" A boulder shot though the wall, decimating the stairway she was just about to run down. "—CRAP!" She looked up to see more rocks coming down to crush them and then looked down to see the rest of the stairway utterly ruined ahead to entrap them. "New plan. Use the hallway, find a new exit."

The three of them ran through the door, hearing the rocks behind them avalanche downwards. All were relieved that they made it out just in time. That is until another huge rock smashed through a window.

Xiu was getting fed up with this real quick. "Okay! How in the hell does he know where we're going to be?"

"I don't know…" Ercan stopped when he had a realization. Looking at the other side of the office building, he saw a crow looking at them. "Winona's been spying on us!"

He quickly changed his meat hook into a steel weight and shot in out toward the window. The window was smashed apart, leaving no barrier between metal and familiar. Concentrating on the chain, he willed it to wrap around the bird to ensnare it. Retracting the chain back to him, Ercan caught the bird in his hand.

Ercan showed the helpless and struggling avian to his two allies with a sense of triumph. "Got it, guys. Now no more—" A boulder smashed through the building as fast as a cannonball, which ripped and crushed his entire arm right off, along with the crow. It took him a bit to process the entire situation before reeling in agony.

"GAAAAAH! FREAKING SOPHIA! IT'S GONE!" He flailed around, blood pouring out of his lost limb. It happened to most people when it came to losing an arm or leg, even if it wasn't the first time it had happened to him.

It took Yun smacking him across the face to get him back. "Keep it together, Ercan. Just heal it up. Just heal it up."

"Okay, okay," he whimpered weakly. Ercan tried his best to concentrate on using his healing factor. Soon enough the bleeding and the pain was gone and Ercan could move on as he recreated his limb, minus a sleeve. "Alright, let's get moving to the exit again!"

Nobody needed to be reminded twice, as Dunkeen still blindly threw boulders at them. Finding another stairway, they quickly got inside, ran down two stories, scurried across the abandoned office, and entered the first stairway they entered—all to prevent Dunkeen from having any idea where they were. Though on the other hand, this stairway was all wrecked to bits and covered in broken boulders.

"How do we get down these? It's ruined!" Xiu stated to the others. At least she didn't have any way to get down without risking injury.

"Well this is nothing Hanuman can't handle," Yun told her as he began to jump and climb down the stairs without issues. "I'm going to the fourth floor if anybody needs me."

When he was gone, she turned to Ercan. "And what's your big plan to get out of here?"

He pondered for a moment, looking upwards and looking downwards. He created a weighted chain and let it drop downward until it hit the lower floors. He then wrapped it around the rail, supporting the rest of the weight with his own arms to keep it stable.

"Alright, climb down," Ercan instructed her. "I'll get down after you."

The green-eyed Qian maiden nodded in agreement, jumped the rail and grabbed the chain. "Alright. Just don't get smashed by a rock before you actually get a fight." She smirked at him. "That'd just be embarrassing."

As she began to slide downwards, she used the blue energy to keep a firm grip and not suffer the metal equivalent of rope burn. But when she made it to the fifth floor, she looked up to see a bright blue tusk shoot out at Ercan, barely missing him. Unfortunately, it also broke the rail holding the chain. As she fell, she just barely managed to grab onto the rail of the third floor. Climbing to safety, she wondered who could have possibly attacked him. But then she heard the howls.

Ercan turned back to see a familiar false gavial advancing toward him. Gustave wore his usual trench coat, though underneath was leather armor. He wielded two hook swords shaped like the head of elephants, with one part of the blade the curled trunk and the tusk as an additional blade to help with catching swords.

But his physical weaponry was not the main point. All around him was a blue aura of aeon. Around his head was a light blue emanation of crocodile jaws, strangely with a trunk at the end of it. His feet were surrounded by an aura that gave them the appearance of elephant feet and his tail had a fish-like fin made from aeon. Below a forearm was a bright blue tusk with another one reappearing under the other arm.

"I'm here to judge you on orders of Gaizka," Gustave told him with a straight face. "He has determined if you can't beat me, you have no hopes of ever becoming captain again." The trunk pointed directly at him. "Do not hold back. I will not."

Water shot out of the trunk and hit Ercan like a strong hose. He was knocked into the stairway, down to the floor below. The trunk trumpeted, and Gustave stomped on the floor, smashing his way down to the next floor.

"Ah, so you had the same idea, too?" Desiderio asked Gaizka as he was being massaged by his chair. "Dunkeen has that exact same mission."

Gaizka went back to his seat with a glass of water and sausage sandwich in hand. "Yep. Figured that if he couldn't take out Gustave, there's no hope for him." He took a chomp at the sandwich, speaking as he chewed. "Not that Gus is weak or anything, just using him to measure strength. The Makara Spark seemed like a good measuring stick."

"We think alike," the dashing swashbuckler commented. "I like that."

"Ditto, pretty boy," the shark man stated back with his mouth full. The two reclined back in their chairs, hoping to see what events would unfold.

All the other Squad Captains were relaxing and watching the show. They were meant to be analyzing Ercan's actions, though only Mastema and Bianca seemed to prioritize that.

Bianca counted the people in the VIP room, only seeing seven other heads. She turned toward Mastema. "Have you seen Ludmila? She's missing the event."

"Don't worry about her," he replied. "She's testing Ercan's qualifications in her own way."

She shrugged and took a sip of her seltzer water. "If you say so."

Winona looked on, frustrated. She had yet to do anything other than send a few wolves into the building and guide where Dunkeen should throw his boulders. It was embarrassing.

"Why so glum, Winona?" Dunkeen asked her, levitating a boulder just above his hand. "Due to the panic you've seen on the faces of our three opponents, I have a feeling that we're easily on the winning side— that and the fact that we have six lycanthrope and Gustave up there. You're strong, so the wolves are strong, and Gustave is strong. We're all strong and the strongest team wins these battles."

Winona looked toward him. "I'm *not* worried about losing, Dunkeen. I just want a real fight. But those idiots just had to trap themselves in a building."

The armored fish man could sense that she was itching for a blood battle, probably with the Squad Captain on the opposing side. He spoke to her again. "Well, Winona. They got themselves into this situation. We're merely being pragmatic enough to take advantage of the situation of being able to bombard them without getting into harm's way. Gustave just volunteered to pick out any who have separated. We still have the home field advantage. In fact, your wolves have probably taken out at least one of them by now."

Just when he said that, a wolfman smashed through the window of the fourth floor. It died upon hitting the concrete. A familiar monkey man climbed down the wall of vines and faced the two, giving a sly grin.

"Well, good thing I learned a thing or two about taking down werewolves last year or that might have been a struggle!" He pretended to just notice them and playfully waved with a werewolf's severed arm. "Hey, you two!" He tossed the arm over his shoulder. "I promised you a fight, witch! Bring it on!"

Dunkeen mentally pushed his boulder at him, but Yun dodged to the side and it smashed a power line to bits. He was about to create another big rock, but Winona grabbed his wrist.

"I don't need you here, Dunkeen," she bluntly stated, her eyes not leaving Yun. "Go inside and look for the other two. Kill on sight." She aimed with her bow and shot at Yun, with him just barely dodging it.

"Sure thing, if you say so. I'm here to test out Xiu Lang for her skills and abilities on orders of Desiderio anyway. He wanted to see if she would be a good addition for Heron Squad. So now off I will go to try to kill Xiu except not really since we are in a simulation." At the sight of Winona's glare, he began to run to the entrance, but not before shaking the ground, causing Yun to lose balance for a moment. "I AM COMING TO JUDGE YOU, XIU! FOR THE BETTERMENT OF HERON SQUAD!"

Winona took this opportunity to shoot at him again. She was this close to hitting him, but he somehow managed to roll to the side. He then charged right at her. Grabbing an arrow from her quiver, she got ready to hit him point blank. But rather than tackle her, he flipped right over her.

"What did you just do?" She turned back, bow at the ready. She looked on in shock when he smiled, arrows wrapped around his tail. She checked her quiver and found that he had taken all of them but the one in her hand.

He snapped the arrows with a squeeze of his fifth limb and took a stance, ready to fight for real. Winona likewise put down her bow and arrow and got her claws at the ready.

"If you want a real fight, you got it." She charged toward him, ready to tear him apart.

⁓ * ⁓

Xiu softly walked through the hallway, ready for werewolves. It was obviously werewolves. What else would howl like that? Therefore, she expected werewolves. She kept the bright blue radiance around her hands and feet, ready for what might happen—most likely a tackle with claws from a werewolf.

As she moved, she felt like she stepped on something hard, though not hard enough to make it snap. Looking down, she saw that she walked on a half-eaten cat, ribs showing and all. Its face was the face cats made when they realized that there was no escape and their lives ended here—utter horror and hopelessness.

Sons of bitches ate a cat. She shook cat guts off her shoe. *They're not leaving this building alive.*

Going around an office corner, she saw three werewolves. They were huddled around in a small circle, eating more wild cats. One had a struggling feline in hand and chomped down, creating an explosion of blood like a fruit snack. Another wolfman was eating baby kittens by the mouthful, three at a time. A third was defecating on a pile of bloody feline bones.

This disrespect of felid life struck a chord in her. She was fond of cats, would even have one if it wasn't for the massive responsibilities and Yun's allergies. Such cruelty to cats was unforgivable, even if it was technically "the circle of life."

She did not even care when she heard breathing down her neck. Without looking, she grabbed the fourth werewolf by the wrist before it could slash at her, crushing it with a mere squeeze.

Eagle Claw Style.

The wolf yelped as she flipped it over her shoulder, using an Eagle Style maneuver. While it was on its back, she smashed her foot on his chest, crushing several ribs.

The other wolves detected her presence and began to attack. She made her fingers appear like a pair of claws.

Tiger Fist Style.

She rammed her hand into one's stomach. She focused her aeon to create a blast of soul energy right through it and out of the beast's back, creating a second-long azure light show.

One werewolf got behind her and tried to trip her with its claws. She elbowed it in the face, causing it to stagger. Focusing her attention on the enemy in front, she kicked its kneecap and bashed it in the face with the back of her fist, knocking some teeth out. Bringing her attention back to the other one, she ducked a slash from a pair of claws.

One of the wolves managed to trip her, though, and she fell on her back. As they were prepared to finish her off and rip her to pieces, she tripped one of them.

Cornered Dog Style.

She spun on the ground, gaining momentum and inflicted a surprise roundhouse kick in the standing wolf's face. She then crushed the prone wolf's skull with one hand. Getting up, she confronted the last wolf, going back to Eagle Claw. As the beast charged, she grabbed the attacker's wrist in one hand and its throat in the other. With a tight squeeze, the lycanthrope's throat was crushed into paste.

Finished and panting, she took a deep breath and began to concentrate on recharging her aeon supply. She deactivated the glowing energy around her limbs, closed her eyes, and counted.

One…two…three…four…five…six…seven.

Seven seconds of recharging should do the trick. She was far from running on empty, but it was better to have more aeon than less. Many famous and infamous psychics had been killed from running out at the worst time. She would not end up like one of them.

She summoned her spirit jackal once again. "Bring me to the nearest psychic around." The jackal complied and ran through the hall and down the next staircase. She followed it without question.

Ercan rolled to the side, avoiding another energy tusk getting shot at him. He shot a spear chain at Gustave, who caught it with a hooksword. With a yank, Gustave pulled Ercan toward him. With Ercan face down before him, Gustave took this opportunity to try to stomp the redhead's head open, but Ercan rolled to the side just before his head became pasta sauce on the floor.

The elephantine stomp broke the floor they were standing on, causing them to fall to the next floor. Ercan used this chance to move back, two hook chains ready. Ercan dodged a tusk getting shot at him, which speared into the wall and disappeared. Dodging a second tusk, he got up close and personal.

The two of them fought hook to hook, trying to disarm the other. As they locked weapons, Ercan was much too close to the reptile for him to shoot water from his trunk or skewer him with a tusk. Gustave readied to bite his face off with his enhanced jaws. Rather than chomping into a skull, he winced in pain as he received a metal weight for a snack. He opened his eyes to see Ercan with a chain coming out of his mouth.

Ercan tugged at the weighted chain, causing Gustave to stumble forward. Ercan lashed at the croc once more, wrapping around the crocodilian's left arm. Spitting out the metal in his mouth, he then charged forward, hook at the ready. Rather than go for the throat, he slid under Gustave's legs, causing him to flip over onto his back as the chain around his arm pulled at him. He dropped the weapon in his left hand, and Ercan grabbed it from a distance before he could get it back.

"How am I doing so far?" Ercan asked with confidence, tossing a hook sword out the window. He used a spear chain to launch a finishing move at the prone croc, but he was sent back by the oddly soothing waters of Makara's trunk.

Gustave used the chain around his arm to yank Ercan back, impaling him through a tusk.

"You have a ways to go, Ercan Ao'Si." Gustave coldly remarked before launching the tusk into a wall, pinning Ercan in place like a preserved butterfly. He shook his head in disappointment as Ercan desperately tried to wriggle out, aiming his second tusk at him.

But before Gustave could make the shot to his head, Ercan shot a chain link net out of his hands. Hitting his upper body, Gustave became entrapped in the net. His trunk, his jaws, his sword, and his tusk made it so much harder to free himself. As Gustave flailed around, Ercan slowly slid himself off the tusk.

Healing the grievous wound, Ercan got ready to go again. "There's a reason I am known as The Unbreakable. I'd like to at least try to live up to that title today."

Gustave knew he had a ways to go. But he, too, was far from finished.

~ * ~

Winona launched two dark purple wolf heads from her hands. The blast howled as it tracked Yun's movements. The monkey man ran about the abandoned hardware store to outmaneuver them. He swung on lights, went between shelves, and jumped off walls. But nothing he did would stop the wolf heads.

Luckily, Winona had summoned more wolves to ambush and flank him. Without slowing down, he grabbed a garden hoe and struck it through a wolfman's jaw. Using two hands, he lifted and tossed the wolf and hoe behind him. As the wolfman was struck by one of the homing blasts, it began to shrivel and collapse.

Oh crap! Don't want! Don't want! Yun ran faster, grabbing a green hose with his tail. Running in a circle, he wrapped the hose around a wolfman's legs, causing him to fall over. Landing on its back, Yun waited a bit before dodging, allowing the last head to hit the werewolf.

Done with the homing shots, he maneuvered himself back to Winona. They exchanged blows, fist to claw. Though they matched in speed, Yun had far more agility, dodging blows going for his chest, head, and throat. He struck at her with his hands, feet, and tail. He felt that though Winona was a danger at long range, she folded once you got too close. That was until another werewolf came up behind him and slashed at his back, causing a bleeding gash and tearing his clothes. Turning back, he decked the wolfman in the face three times and gave it a knee to the stomach.

This was ample time for Winona to jump on his back. Grabbing his arms, she sunk her jaws into his neck, trying to rip his throat out. Though the agony was brutal, Yun did didn't her dig into his flesh. Grabbing a screwdriver with his tail, he jabbed it into her side. She let go with a pained howl, holding onto her stomach. Yun took his chance to kick her away.

Both opponents stared one another down, panting. As they stared, Winona's wristwatch beeped.

Winona's face went from a pained scowl to a smile of satisfaction. "Perfect. It's been six minutes." She ripped the screwdriver out of her, ignoring the bleeding. "Macha."

When she said that word, her lupine features disappeared completely. In their place, her muscles grew and her feet became hooves. She even replaced her head feathers with a red horse mane. The wound at her side and any other bruises washed away and vanished as if they were merely stains in need of washing. She grabbed the black spear on her back.

"I recommend that you pray for your allies," Winona remarked, twirling her spear in her hands. "You won't get an answer."

Yun could only gulp. *What have I gotten myself into?*

~ * ~

Xiu ran down the stairs to the first floor. "Okay, as long as I don't encounter the witch alone, I'm safe. But I am done if she's in here." As she went down to the second floor, she saw her jackal faithfully waiting at the door. Inside she heard Dunkeen yapping on as usual.

"Xiu! Xiu? Xiu Lang? Where are you? It is I! Dunkeen Terrelli! The Land Leviathan! I'm here to challenge you on the basis that our new squad leader, Desiderio, wanted me to fight you to prove your worth to Heron Squad! If you're dead but not really, I'm sorry I messed this up without giving you a fighting chance! But if you come down here and challenge me, you'll be considered very awesome! Everyone in the audience will think you're awesome too!"

That was enough drive to go down and encounter him. She peered through the door window and saw the Dunkleosteus person waving and pacing about, waiting for her. Occasionally, he would use his earth powers to toss a boulder directly upwards. She looked around and saw he only had two boulders left.

Now's my chance. I can handle him in this condition. She pushed the door and entered. "Looking for me, big boy?"

Dunkeen almost seemed to be surprised she was still in the battle. "Ah, Xiu Lang, we now finally meet upon the battlefield. I hear you're quite skilled in various martial arts."

She chuckled. "No need to praise me, Dunkeen. I'm just here to beat you up as part of Desi's little test."

"Ah, so you heard me then?" Dunkeen interrupted. "Thus, you already know that I'm the one who was chosen to help determine how strong you are for Desiderio's sake. He could have chosen either Petra or Draghignazzo." He looked behind at one of several Stagecams. "Hey, you two!" He waved at his two watching compatriots, who most definitely cringed in embarrassment. "But anyway, your reputation for recklessness and being a lone wolf precedes you. That will not fly." His face turned into a fishy grimace as he touched both boulders, melding his hands into them like mud. Smashing his two rock fists he got ready to fight. "Show me what you've learned."

But before the two could confront, they heard a rumbling sound. It was soft at first, but it grew steadily louder and louder. It got to the point that the debris on the floor began to rattle about. They both began to hear sharp neighs and whinnies outside. Both silently declared a temporary truce to see what was going on.

To their mutual horror, they saw an entire stampede consisting of hundreds of horses. The wild horses didn't even flinch as they smashed through windows and doors, moving straight forward. They were just across the street. Both parties realized in panic that they were at risk of being trampled and quickly ran up opposite staircases to the second floor. Dunkeen smashed through the door with his boulder hands while the aeon jackal followed Xiu up the stairs. They barely made it out in time, only seconds away from being trapped in a river of equine bodies.

On the second floor, both took deep breaths, glad they weren't trampled to death. Xiu was the first to get her nerves back. "The shit Winona can do, am I right?"

Dunkeen nodded wearily. "The aeon maneuvers she can perform with her spark exceed most I've seen in my life. It's as if she's not even fully human." He straightened himself out, ready. "Now are you ready to duke it—" Her aeon jackal bit him in the leg. "AAAHHHYYEEEEOOOOOOWW!!"

"Good girl." Xiu took this chance to charge in. *This is still an uphill battle. But we're not going down like punks, dammit.*

Julia was in the academy library doing her history homework. It was on the history of the Artifacts of Kadosh. Items created by many of the earlier emperors of the Protogenoi Empire. Each country had one of the eight artifacts, kept safe and preserved. Though the Empire had fallen, the world had vowed never to forget them. It was refreshing to read an actual physical book once in a while. Felt good in her hands. Way better than watching a stupid fight.

As she read on, Ludmila sat down two seats from her. She seemed to have something to say to her.

"What do you want?" Julia bluntly asked, not even looking away from the pages. Captain or no, she felt like this would be a waste of her time. She didn't like time wasters.

Ludmila was a bit taken aback but remained calm. "Well, I'm here on behalf of the Squad Captains to say that you and the rest of your squad will be fighting Eagle Squad in a week. Just reminding you."

"I heard. We're gonna lose."

"Well don't be so negative," the captain told her. "But if you lose and Ercan is stripped of his title, would you want to replace him?"

Julia looked up and closed her book. She got up from her seat. "No."

Ludmila was shocked and appalled by her answer. "Why would you not want such a privilege?"

Julia gave a simple answer. "I don't want to do the paperwork after every mission. See you tomorrow." She walked right past her, leaving the Ice Dragon with nobody else in the room but a squid-headed guy deeply engrossed in cosmic horror literature.

Flames of Prometheus

"By Sophia." Alexandru looked on in awe at the stampede of wild mares and stallions. "How can one psychic create so much life?"

Everyone in school learned that when it came to summoning creatures as a spark ability, it was a rule that quality beat quantity. You could either have one powerful monster, or many weaker ones. But all these horses seemed to be just as strong as your average horse and Winona wasn't even tired yet. In fact, when Yun was too distracted with escaping from being trampled into the concrete, Winona spent that time meditating to recharge her Aeon. So not only did Winona have so much more Aeon than the average person, she had a spark that provided plenty of opportunities to recharge it.

"I'm beginning to wonder why she's only five in our itty-bitty pecking order," Vural commented. "She keeps on surprising us with this stuff."

Hanako shivered in her seat, dreading the next Aeon Sophia Games. "She's scary."

Mastema stared at the screens intently. *She's learning more and more about what she can do. I've reached my limits. What are hers?* He let out a sigh. *Has everybody else here reached their limits? We're so young still; everyone is bound to learn more tricks and maneuvers.*

"Something the matter?" Bianca asked him, concerned. "You seem to be brooding than usual."

Mastema looked away from her. "I am, Princess Bianca. Just

thinking, that's all."

Bianca was far from convinced but chose not to intrude.

~ * ~

Gustave kept stomping and stomping, falling down floor after floor. He struggled to remove the net from his body. He'd already lost his second hook sword during the fight and his only plausible line of defense was his trunk. Whenever Ercan closed the gap between them, he would blast him away with his sacred healing water as hard as he could. It was very counterproductive for taking him out, but it was the only option he had. His arms were too tangled to aim his tusks effectively and the metal net prevented him from using his jaws.

After smashing through who knows how many floors, Gustave was getting tired of stomping. Ercan closed in once again with two hooked chains, twirling them around and ready to lash at him. The false gavial managed to catch the chain around his tusk.

Gustave got ready to stomp down once more. *Alright. If I recall, this is currently the fifth floor. For one reason or another, the floor below us has a pool. If I can land in the pool, I might just be able to gain the upper hand again. Here goes nothing.* Gustave smashed the floor below him and fell to the next floor.

Luckily, his guess was correct. He landed right in the pool. The chlorine would have been an irritation to his eyes, but the solid animalistic aura around his head was suitable protection, not unlike a pair of goggles. Ercan was dragged down with him and he, too, fell into the water. Feeling confident enough of this opportunity, Gustave got rid of his two arm tusks and elephant feet. This allowed him to escape the chain net and swim in the water. The aeon fins on his tail made him much faster than a regular crocodilian.

Ercan harshly fell into the pool. He let go of the chain and splashed to the surface. To his relief, the water was shallow enough to stand in. The bad news was that just under the surface, he saw an angry crocodile swimming right at him.

He cried out in agony as Gustave's enhanced jaws bit into his leg. He did not even have time to take a breath as his head was dragged under. Trying to hold his breath as best as he could, he saw Gustave through the stinging chlorine, performing the death roll. He spun around and around under the water, twisting and tearing his leg apart. His vision began to fail as his blood invaded the water like a red mist. He felt the horrid ripping off of his left leg.

Creating a chain from the stump of his limb, he began to thrash up to the surface and into shallower water. Hopefully the spiked chain was chomped into along with the rest of his leg. Wrapping one chain around his forearm with the hook in his right hand and loosening the chain in his left, he waited for Gustave to come again and adrenaline to kick in.

Inevitably, the reptilian swam in, ready for another chomp. Ercan was ready this time and submerged into the three-foot water. From watching The Animal Channel, he learned that though crocodilians had a strong bite force, they have little strength when opening their mouth. Ercan grabbed Gustave's jaws and began to wrestle with him. He was no pro at alligator wrestling, but Gustave seemed to be struggling.

As he tried to pin the croc down, Gustave managed to escape his grip for a second to chomp his hand down on Ercan's left arm. But as the redhead was on top of him, he was unable to do the death roll. Even when he tried smacking him with his aeon trunk, the teen would not get off him.

Little did he know, Ercan planned to have his arm chomped down. The chain around his left limb moved around and around Gustave's mouth, sealing it for good. Unable to open his mouth, he lost his greatest advantage.

Ercan lifted his opponent's head with his entrapped left arm, revealing the crocodilian's throat. With the hook in his right hand, he did what he must do. "Thank you for your test." With a swift motion, Gustave's throat was sliced open.

As the false gavial's body faded away, his mangled arm was freed. Ercan clung to the side of the pool, panting. He began to heal his severed left leg and mutilated arm along with any other injuries. He looked at his clothing and how he was missing half a pant leg and a sleeve.

He groaned to himself. *Why do my clothes always get ruined like this?* He got out of the pool and headed for the stairway. *Oh, crap I forgot.* He jumped back in to look for his severed foot. Finding it, he removed his sneaker and placed it on his current foot. Tossing his old foot into a trashcan, he then headed downward in search of the others.

~ * ~

Yun hung onto the wall on the second floor. He barely managed to avoid the stampede Winona seemed to have created out of thin air. He found himself in a crystaltech shop. There were phones, gaming accessories, and CVs, among other things, all dusty from decades of neglect.

Winona refused to give him breathing room, thrusting with her spear. Yun managed to dodge and grab the weapon. Both tugged for the armament, but both were roughly equal in strength.

"You're strong for a monkey," She begrudgingly complimented him.

"Thanks. But Hanuman makes me no Monkey." He snapped the spear in half. "It makes me a Monkey Prince!"

Winona kicked him in the stomach, knocking him back down to the bottom floor. The entire place had been utterly wrecked from the stampede. In the distance, he could see the straggling horses leaving through the previous building. Behind him, he heard more galloping and wheels turning. Looking back, he saw a tall humanoid horse in bronze armor steering a chariot of ordinary warhorses. The horseman threw a javelin at him, but he sidestepped it.

Yun ran up to the horse person and got ready for a flying kick. But the hulking brute merely grabbed his leg. Yun kicked his arm for him to let go, but he still managed to grab his tail. He punched Yun in the stomach and then smashed him into the ground. The beastman then tossed him away. Yun barely had time to crawl away as the horse warrior tried to stomp on his spine, only having a second to roll away. But he was not fast enough, getting a kick to the ribs.

Yun was grabbed by the neck and was smashed through a wall. In fact, Yun could almost see a sadistic smile on his long face. Right next to him on the highest shelf out of children's reach, there was a machete. Yun snagged the blade and sliced at his assailant's neck. It neighed in pain and anger and threw Yun away. Though the attack was painful, the horseman's neck was much too thick and muscular for him to inflict a critical wound.

As Yun once again got ready for another slice, he felt a strong hoof to his side. Falling, he saw Winona looking down at him. The monster she summoned soon followed forth, both ready to give a beating.

Oh crap.

~ * ~

Xiu and Dunkeen had been duking it out for a while now. Dunkeen had constantly tried to smash her with his rock fists but was too cumbersome to land a hit. She kept dodging this way and that. Xiu, on the other hand, could hardly hit him. Due to his size, extending his reach and entering his space would allow him to attack her easier. Her aeon powered attacks may have made her stronger, but she was still a human when it came to durability. One hit from him and she was a goner.

Just got to bide my time a little bit more. Got to show Heron Squad I mean business. I haven't even used my new trick yet.

The spirit jackal she had was doing a little bit of work. It was currently biting at the armored fishman's right leg. Though it wasn't hurting too much, it seemed to be irritating the big guy.

It was also blatant that with every failed punch, the rocks around his hands broke off chunk by chunk. By this point, the boulders were now less boulders and more very big stones.

"You've lasted this long, huh?" Dunkeen commented, lifting his leg to look at the jackal nibbling at it, shaking it off. "But other than your jackal buddy, what else do you have to show me? Sure, your energy fist attacks are strong, but what good are they when you can't come close to me?" He used his spark to shoot out a chunk of pebbles at her, grazing her side. "I have more tricks in my bag and I'm sure you do too." He began to shoot more rocks at her, his new ammunition encircling himself. "For the sake of Heron Squad, the audience, and yourself, show me something new."

Xiu ran around in circles, evading the tiny stones. As he was ready to shoot out the huge chunks of rocks in his hands like cannonballs, her aeon jackal leaped onto Dunkeen's arm, biting at it. This caused Dunkeen to miss with both chunks of earth, shooting one into the ceiling and the other out the window. With the big problem out of the way, she was ready to make her move.

"Alright, chatterbox!" Her right hand emanated more blue energy. "You want to see a new trick! Here's one!"

Out of her hand, she shot out a ball of pure aeon. Since Dunkeen was too preoccupied throwing the jackal off him, the ball hit him straight in the chest, causing him to stagger back. The rocks around him fell, signaling to her that he lost concentration. This was her opportunity to lay a beat down.

She started with a simple punch to the face. For a normal person, this would break a hand due to the armored plating. But for her, the armor plating cracked from the punch. She hit him again with her other fist, breaking off a toothy bone-plate. She followed that up with a roundhouse kick to the face along with a spinning kick with the other leg.

Dunkeen moved back more, stunned from the assault. Xiu prepared a Tiger Fist attack and thrust her hand onto his forehead. The armored plating around the area completely shattered. Flowing more aeon into her hand, she shot out a cone of energy. Dunkeen was sent flying back from the force of the attack and straight out of a window. The moment she heard a thud, she looked down to see him disappear.

She sat down on the ground, tired, petting her spirit jackal. She looked toward where anyone may have been watching the fight. "So, Desi, did I pass?" She felt quite relieved. For these last few months, she had been questioning her true abilities compared to everybody else, especially among her peers. She felt satisfied knowing she still had the skills to win.

She heard the door open and saw Ercan enter. She addressed him without looking. "So? Still alive?" Seeing him all wet and his clothes torn made her wonder what he had been up against.

Ercan walked toward her. "Yeah. Gustave was testing me to see how strong I was. I passed. But what sort of building has a swimming pool on the fourth floor?" Sitting down next to her, he also patted the jackal's head. "But anyway, what were you doing while I was gone?"

"Just passing another test Dunkeen was tasked with enforcing." She put her hand on her side to cover her wound. "I passed too."

The two sat down for a bit, neither of them speaking to one another, recharging their aeon in silence. After roughly half a minute, Xiu turned to him.

"You wanna kick the witch's ass together?" She got up and signaled her pet. "Track down the second largest aeon source around." The jackal dashed behind them, into the neighboring building.

"Yeah I'm itching to give Winona a slice of humble pie," Ercan said, also getting back to his feet. "Better three than one against someone like her right?"

The two of them headed down to the next building. Though neither of them told the other, each considered this battle the last time they'd be fighting on the same squad.

~ * ~

"Whoah." Shee'vra couldn't help herself. "They actually beat those guys." She knew those two as the Land Leviathan and the Sacred Croc. From other fights she saw with them over the years, they were not pushovers.

But still, Shee'vra felt that Winona still had an upper hand. She'd been watching her thrashing Yun alongside her summoned horse man for a few minutes now. She knew that Winona's Morrigan Spark worked in a way that she could change into a different incarnation every six minutes. Nemain was for the wolves, Macha for the horses, and Badb was for the crows. Each form also had different properties, but she didn't remember them too well. All she remembered was that Nemain was the most destructive, Macha was the hardiest, and Badb allowed her the greatest movement.

She wondered how somebody could have a spark so powerful at merely sixteen years old. Shee'vra hoped they would find some way to overcome the Witch of Summer's End.

~ * ~

Yun could barely stand up. Though he was faster and more agile than the opposition, it was still two against one. They were also both significantly stronger than him. Their basic strategy to take him out was to essentially play catch with him. One would pummel him for a bit and then throw him to the other for another beating. After a while, even his durability wore down. So here he stood, trying to stand up with cuts and bruises and broken bones. He just hoped that Ercan or Xiu had at least taken out the other two.

Winona kicked him in his side, sending him tumbling away. Her hooves clopped on the broken floor as she slowly stepped toward the struggling simian. Her horseman assistant tossed her his javelin, which she caught in one hand.

"I'm beginning to wonder where everyone else is." She mused to her summon as well as to Yun. "They couldn't possibly all be defeated. You were here and they were in there. So at least one of them should've survived. Unless at least one or both parties were spiteful enough to take them down with them." She twirled her javelin. "But enough what-ifs, time to end this skirmish."

Just as she was about to inflict the finishing blow, a spiked chain wrapped around the humanoid horse's neck. He gagged and choked as he was quickly pulled away with a single tug. When Winona and Yun looked back, they saw Xiu and Ercan ready to fight. Xiu quickly removed her hand from the dead horseman's back and let go of Ercan's chain. The aeon jackal tried to attack the witch once again, but Winona just simply backhanded it out of existence and focused her attention on Yun's two teammates.

"Better brace yourself, Winona," Ercan said to her. "It's—"

"Two against one," Winona finished his sentence, stabbing the javelin through Yun. Yun disappeared from The Stage.

If this were a real battle, Ercan would've lost one of his closest allies. No captain should have to see one of their own squad members die so helplessly. With tranquil anger, he created a large chain with both hands tipped with an anchor. And not the kind of anchor you'd use for a paddleboat, the kind of anchor you use for a yacht. Though the attack damaged the building greatly, Winona sidestepped it. Summoning an anchor may have been able to inflict maximum damage, but it was clunky and left him very open.

Winona charged forwards with the speed of a galloping horse, javelin at the ready. But before she could stab into his skull, Xiu aeon-blasted her in the face, knocking her back. Before Winona could react, Xiu kicked her in the jaw. Putting her dislocated jaw back in place and healing her broken nose, Winona gave a smile.

"You hit a lot harder than last year, Xiu." The blood on her face washed away without any visible water. "New tricks, I see."

She threw a punch at her, but Xiu moved to the side. With both hands, she grabbed the witch's arm and dislocated it from the shoulder. Rather than a cry of pain, Xiu received a chuckle and a smack to the back of the head with the wooden end of a javelin.

"However," Winona continued as she popped her arm bone back into place, "I will not let a fallen captain and the dumb bimbo he kicked out make a fool out of me." She readied her spear to impale Xiu's neck. "So, you first."

"Dodge!"

Xiu looked behind Winona and jumped to the side. Winona had no idea what she was doing. But before the witch could realize it, she saw the sharp end of an anchor impaled through her back. Shrieking in agony, she felt herself getting pulled toward Ercan.

"Need a hand?" Xiu ran back to Ercan and grabbed the chain with her aeon powered hands. Together, she and Ercan lifted the anchor and the witch up into the air. They both then slammed her down into the road behind them. As the anchor met concrete, there was a clanging sound mixed with bones breaking. Ercan patted Xiu's back as he tried to look through the dust.

"Kudos," Ercan complimented her. "Without you, I'd be bucked and beaten by horses." They and the rest of Rooster Squad were at their best when dealing with a straightforward strong foe. After years of having a healing factor, he knew the limits of other fast healers. After a while, you just can't concentrate on healing your wounds and succumb to them.

Tired, Xiu answered him. "It was a basic fight." She shrugged with bravado. "Winona just got unlucky. Her horse form may be tough but has little in the tricks department." She stretched her arms lazily as she deactivated the aeon energy from her limbs. "Better miss me after this." *I just brought your rep up. Better be thankful.*

"Yeah. I will I guess," Ercan admitted, strolling closer to the anchor. "You're a handful, but the squad just won't be the same without you." He admittedly felt uneasy. The Stage simulation should be over by now. It wasn't.

Xiu looked at him, indignant. "Handful? What's that supposed to—?"

"Xiu, we're not done yet!" Ercan warned her. He got out his chains and Xiu surrounded her limbs with aeon energy again.

~ * ~

Yun got out of the simulation chair. He passed by Ercan's, Xiu's, and Winona's chairs and went to look at the screen in the "loser's quarters" along with Dunkeen and Gustave.

"Is it still going on?" Yun questioned the two as he sat down next to Dunkeen.

"Why yes, it is, Yun Xuanzang," Dunkeen replied. "You see after you were slain, the two of them killed the horse man. Then Ercan threw this anchor at her. He missed, of course, but Xiu did this spirit aeon blast attack that I didn't know she could do until today and then kicked her in the face. But Winona's healing factor got to work, and nothing was really fazing her. After some trash talk on Winona's part, she realized too late that Ercan was quickly retracting the anchor back to him, impaling her through the anchor's fluke. With Xiu's help, they lifted the chain up into the air and slammed it and Winona into the ground. But it seems that she isn't ready to be defeated just yet."

It was a yes or no question, but Yun was intrigued. On one of the screens, the dust began to clear up. Out of the dust was a fully healed and very pissed off Winona. Rather than play around with her prey like she mostly did with them, she seemed ready to annihilate them on the spot.

"Holy Sophia." Gustave began to cover his ears. Yun and Dunkeen followed suit.

Shee'vra saw that Cyrille, Zivot, Mayil, and pretty much everyone else in the room began to cover their ears. She figured out that it would be dumb not to also. In fact, some students just straight up ran out of the room.

With her fingers in her ears, she saw Xiu and Ercan look on in fear as Winona said something. She couldn't hear what, but by reading her lips and using the process of elimination, she must have uttered "Badb," her final incarnation. Winona's muscles decreased back to their normal size, her normal feathery hair returned to her head, and crows began to flock around her out of nowhere. But most jarring of all, her pure black eyes (normally unsettling on their own) now had small yellow dots within them like a flame in the darkness. Those eyes radiated with fury.

As Xiu made the first move to charge at her, it began. Winona opened her jaw to unnatural lengths and screamed. It was so loud it sounded like the audio of the screens was brought to maximum volume. If it wasn't for the soundproofing of the floors and rooms, she was sure the whole building would have heard it. Everyone in the room, including her, tried as hard as they could to muffle the wail. Cyrille and his two servants seemed to have brought earplugs just for this occasion, and even they seemed uncomfortable. If it was bad for those in the room, how must it feel to Ercan and Xiu?

From what she could see, not good at all. Ercan and Xiu were on the floor, writhing in agony. Both tried in vain to cover their ears, but it was obviously not working. Neither of them could remotely concentrate on anything around them. The buildings' windows shattered and fell onto the street like sharp raindrops. Though Xiu was safe from the shards, Ercan was bombarded and cut with glass and could do little about it. Looking closer, she could see that both of their ears were bleeding profusely. It was obvious their eardrums must have burst, but she knew that hardly helped in situations such as this.

The scream just kept going. Shee'vra had seen Winona wail like this before last year. In fact, this maneuver had led to her decisive victory against all of Rhea Squad. Falcon Squad defeated her own team, so she had little to lose. The implication of someone like her using such an ability in real life was horrifying to say the least (well at least for everyone but the hearing aid manufacturers). It was nothing short of relief when the shrieking ceased. Shee'vra was sure half the audience had a headache.

Ercan's ears rang like a demon as he slowly got up. He staggered in pain and confusion and felt something wet on the side of his neck, the blood from his shattered eardrums. As he looked forward in a daze, he saw Winona approach Xiu.

"Look out!" he cried out in vain. But Xiu couldn't hear him as she got up.

Winona was uninterested in playing around anymore. Instead, pure distilled darkness enveloped her fingers and turned into long talons. With a thrust of her shadow claws, the Witch of Summer's End ripped out the throat of her opposition. Xiu fell on her knees and collapsed, her body disappearing off The Stage.

Seeing all of this, Ercan realized that he had let two of his allies die to one woman. Real Squad Captains might have to brace themselves for losing one member, but two in one day was unforgivable on their part. It showed how terrible and weak they truly were. Maybe Winona was correct; maybe he wasn't captain material. But this was a world where being a psychic led you to a limited future. You were either a great psychic or you were weak. A weak psychic was of no worth to anyone, especially one who couldn't rescue anybody, even during a simulation. In real life, you had to prepare for anything. Failing against someone he prepared himself against made him feel even worse about it.

But like any good ally, he braced himself to avenge both of his friends. Healing his wounds, he lashed at her with a spiked chain with a weight at the end of it. But Winona merely turned into a murder of crows and flew around him, clawing and pecking at him. He tried to swat them away, but it was futile. When he lashed at a couple of them, they would just fly away and come back to pecking.

He felt beaks and claws rip apart his shirt and dig into his flesh. They bit into blood vessels like worms, claws raked into his sinew, and he felt an eye get plucked out the moment they were pried open. If Winona could even speak as a bunch of birds, she obviously had nothing to say. She only seemed to be focused on finishing him off, but Badb was doing a poor job at doing it quick.

As Ercan was on one knee, he knew what he must do. He must use his secret weapon. It was the most opportune time. He'd been saving it for a while now.

⌐ ✳ ⌐

Eight Months Ago

The Aeon Sophia Games were over and Ercan was wandering his Spark Region in a rampage. He hit the sides of the mountain with his fists as a downpour drenched the land. *So few points, and no wins, whatsoever. How could they do so horribly? Was it the challenges being unsuitable, was it Xiu charging into danger, or was it…him?*

Day after day, he trained until his joints ached. He labored and toiled and worked hard on the limits of his healing factor. He clawed his way to captain. But it was not enough. Was he being weighed down, or was he simply not cut out to be on top?

He felt fortunate that nobody could see him. He felt pathetic that he would cry and rage over losing a tournament. He liked to think that he was crying over something more complex that he was not currently acknowledging, but chances were that was just denial.

He approached the top of the mountain of his Spark Region. On the pinnacle was the statue of a forty-foot tall man lying down embedded into the mountain. Stone chains wrapped around the stone man's wrists and ankles. On the stone man's stomach was a statue of an eagle with its wings spread out. Underneath the eagle were glyphs that explained the powers Prometheus offered. Chains and healing. That was it.

But that wasn't enough. He was not strong enough. If he was to become a psychic worth a damn in this world, he would need more. He needed to be at the level of the elite psychics or die trying. Why did Sophia bless him with such aeon if he wasn't good enough to be of use to anyone?

In fact, he'd never heard the voice of Sophia. He heard about how every other person could hear her. But why not him? Did she abandon him? She spoke to every psychic, good or evil. So why not him? What did he do to not be guided by her?

He went to his knees and pounded at the stone. "I need more power! I need to learn more! I want to be worthwhile!" The rain fell harder, and the winds blew stronger. "I want to be on Bianca's level! I want to be on Mastema's level! I want to be on mom's level!" he screamed to the heavens. "Come on! I've got no other future!" He took a breath as pain set into his fists. "None...none of us do!" He checked his broken and bleeding hands. "I mean…is it just my destiny to fail at the one thing you brought me here for?" He took out his medallion. He'd had it since birth. What did it mean? Did it mean anything or was it just a mere trinket?

As he contemplated, he received no answer as usual. That was the last straw. If she refused to notice him, he would make her notice. He got up and screamed harder to the heavens than ever before. "WHY WON'T YOU LISTEN TO ME, DAMN YOU?! WHAT HAVE I DONE TO YOU FOR YOU TO SCORN ME?! He yelled at the top of his lungs. "SEEEEEE MEEEEEEEEEEEE!"

Lightning struck him down. But for some reason, the volts of electricity didn't knock him unconscious. But it did hurt like divine retribution should.

But as he looked down, he saw two chains coming out of his wrists.

But this was not his usual metal links. No, over the metal was fire. The flames licked every link of it, even the parts that went into his body. The rain didn't put it out either. He looked at the flames in awe, wondering why they didn't burn him. He even twirled them around a bit to create an infernal wheel. The flames dried his tears and cooled his temper.

As he turned around, he saw lightning strike the head of the giant stone man. With that, the statue's mouth began to slowly open. He felt obliged to enter, and using the flames as light, he read the first words. "The Flames of Prometheus" He must study up on this. And tell no one. He must surprise them all with what he could do.

After a while, he left his Spark Region and went back to the reality that was his bedroom. Shee'vra popped in cautiously. "Are you okay, brother?"

He made himself smile. "Of course. Just thinking about stuff."

~ * ~

Ignoring the pain, he showed the academy what he practiced for many months. As the crows tore at him, his chains lit up. The sudden heat halted the crows' assault. Before they knew it, Ercan was healed enough to lash out at the murder, taking several of them out as their bodies broke and feathers burnt.

The crows had little idea what to do, as they had never expected this to happen. Some of the crows tried to blindside him, but Ercan took them out with a twirl of his weapon. Ercan then began to spin his chains around him almost like the dance of two burning wheels. Before Winona and the audience knew it, there was only one crow untouched by the fiery tongues.

Damn it! The hell is this? the final crow thought. *I can't take him out in this condition, but I still must wait four minutes to get into Nemain mode.* She began to fly away. *I must retreat for now.*

But Ercan was having none of that. As Winona tried to make a tactical retreat up into the air, Ercan shot out his burning chains onto the top of a building, launching himself into the air. Winona looked on with shock as she saw the redhead she mocked following her, swinging from building to building. She tried to make a sharp turn around another skyscraper, but Ercan made the turn also by swinging into a semicircle. She flew lower to the ground, but he swung lower too. She flew as high as she could, but he could still reach her.

After three minutes, her wings tired of flapping at speeds greater than crows should. Winona stopped her escape on the top of a building. *I can't escape him like this. Got to make a last stand.*

As she perched on a rail, Ercan landed right in front of her. As he readied a flaming whip, she made a shrieking sound. Out of her beak came a dark purple energy beam. It hit Ercan's shoulder, but it wasn't enough to deter him. A shot from one crow was too weak to seriously hurt him.

"I've been practicing, too, Winona," Ercan said. "Just like you and the rest of them." With a swipe, he wrapped his burning metal links around the bird. "Good game."

Winona had nothing to say as she was embraced by heat. She just was too shocked to see this occurring. It seemed cliché in a way for her to go out like this. The burning chains squeezed harder, crushing her into a fried poultry not even fit for a fast food menu.

Ercan put out the fires with but a thought and retracted the metal back into his wrists. He waited on the second highest building in the simulation to go back to reality

The VIP room was speechless. Sure, most expected him to actually learn a new trick or two—but to win? That was a surprise.

"I'm beginning to think we completely underestimated Ercan," Alexandru admitted to the group. He picked up his umbrella and prepared to leave.

"I feel like us captains underestimate…everyone around here these days," Mastema softly stated to the rest of the group. "Let this day be a message that as captains, we may be strong, but we are…far from invincible."

"Well that's kind of obvious really," Vural spoke up. "I mean seriously, all of us have a weak point. Like getting crushed by rocks or lasers and—"

Mastema raised a hand for him to stop. "Please…we understand." *Don't undermine me. It took me two hours to come up with that phrase.*

"But anyway, nice to see the witch get humbled like that," Gaizka commented to the group. "Dunkeen was good, too, despite his loss.

Maybe Xiu is fit for Heron Squad after all."

Desiderio smiled. "Perhaps so, my sharp toothed compatriot. Gustave also had Ercan on the ropes for a bit. The pool part had me worried for a bit. Like something out of Animal Channel."

Gaizka pounded his chest. "Well, me and Gus have been working on a new routine lately."

"I hope Winona won't take the loss too hard," Hanako said to herself, shivering. "I hear she can be really scary after losing."

"I will make sure she's not too angered," Bianca replied to her. She then addressed the whole group. "Even though Ercan has won, keep in mind he still lost both partners. In real life, that is inexcusable for any captain. No matter what new tricks you learn, in the real world, his friends would have still stayed dead." She began to walk out. "He still has a lot to prove in my eyes."

The rest of the six thought about it and silently agreed that she had a point. On The Stage, you could treat losing an ally like losing a buddy in a game of *Blastertag*. But in real life, there was no thirty-second timer until they were back in. In the real world, an "out" ally was gone for good.

~ * ~

The audience cheered. They applauded and clapped as the screens turned off. Shee'vra was one of the many cheering, though when she looked down, she saw this redheaded girl, a Seichin girl with a long ponytail, and a sophomore girl in overly sparkly clothing. They looked like they were expecting a bad time as the trio left the theatre.

She turned to Zivot. "What's the matter with those three? They have the look of dread in them."

"Oh, you mean Sabelle, Shiro, and Vasanti?" Zivot replied without really looking. "They're from Crow Squad with Winona. Seeing her lose must mean they're bracing themselves for the witch's temper. She's a bit of a sore loser so to say."

"Well that must stink," was all Shee'vra could comment.

Cyrille was still cheering, shaking a stoic Mayil around. "Wooohoo! Did you see that, Mayil?"

"Yes."

"Who knew Ercan was holding out on us?" Cyrille continued. "It's like he was saving a fiery chain attack for eight months for the sake of surprising us all!" Cyrille suddenly felt a wave of exhaustion fall upon him. He opened his beak wide and yawned loudly. "But anyway, I am tired. Goodbye, Shee'vra, and I wish you a better tomorrow."

He and his two bodyguards/servants left to go home for Cyrille's two-hour nap. Shee'vra also had no reason to stay and decided to leave too. She would congratulate her brother next time she saw him.

~ * ~

When Ercan was brought back to the real world, the first thing he heard was the door slamming shut. Getting out of the chair and stretching, he saw Dunkeen, Gustave, Xiu, and Yun waiting for him.

Yun was first to speak. "You never told us you could do that—the whole fire thing."

"Yeah. Were you holding back against me?" Gustave asked, bemused.

Ercan answered them, "I've been hiding it for almost a year now. Wanted to make it a surprise for everyone."

"That's stupid, Ercan." Xiu told him to his face. "Fire whips are not exactly first-class surprise attacks in the first place. But you could have used it for missions and crap. Maybe they would have helped you and the rest of the squad." *About a year? Did he learn it just after the games? Did he double down on exploring his Spark Region? Did he blame me?*

Dunkeen was next to talk. "Well the one thing that matters is you won fair and square. This battle proved that, despite you being the lowest tiered captain, it doesn't make you weak at all. So now you can finally rest easy about that predicament due to your new confidence boost." He also patted Xiu's back harder than he meant. "And our new Heron Squad member is now most definitely Heron material after beating me up. But I'm sure that somewhere in her heart, she will always be part roost—"

"That's nice and all, Dunkeen, but I have to go," Xiu told him, embarrassed about what he was saying. She quickly exited the room. *Okay, now I must change and go find Shee'vra.*

Ercan wondered why she left. "What was that about?"

Dunkeen had a hunch and began to speak once again. "Well, I do have an assumption. You see the young maiden that is Xiu Lang might have—"

The fishman's mouth was closed shut by Gustave. "Meh. Time of the month."

Ercan wasn't sure if he bought that answer, but whatever. Yun didn't buy it at all but declined to contradict the crocodilian.

~ * ~

Zuo found himself in the hellish landscape of a razed village. He watched in horror as he saw shadowy figures shaped like people getting slaughtered by his old compatriots with demonic smiles. Some of his fellow soldiers were psychics; most were hylics. Horses ran about, and huts were burning. No shadowy figure was being spared, be they man, woman, or child. He felt compelled to slice and stab at many of the shadows, noticing that they had no features except for green eyes.

He was beckoned to move to the same hut he did many times during these dreams. A shadowy figure assumed to be the father struck him with a hammer to the face. The father's head burst immediately upon impacting him. He healed his head wound and proceeded through. He encountered a woman screaming in terror, huddled in a corner. He grabbed her and as she begged for her life, slitting the shadow's throat with a knife, creating a waterfall of darkness.

As he breathed heavily, he heard the crying of a little girl no older than seven. The noise came from behind a door. He creaked it open and saw a young child embraced by shadow. Her green eyes were filled with terror and despair from the chaos surrounding her. He gripped his dagger and was prepared to fulfill his duty. But by seeing her huddle back in fear, he found himself unable to do it.

He turned around and left the weeping girl. As he exited the room, a Sirokhan man wrapped in bandages spoke to him.

"Did you finish it?" the mummy asked him without a hint of emotion in his tone.

He paused for a minute, not knowing what to say. Every time he had this dream, he was never able to speak. Not once. So, his fellow psychic spoke once again.

"Good."

As the two went to the next house, he saw his old master fly down with his large bat-like wings. This ten-foot monstrosity was the former Bumpa of Qian Ye, Tai Xun. The man was currently more beast than man, looking more like an upright tiger than a human. He ripped with his claws, stung with a tail with five long stingers, and chomped down on shadowy figures with his multiple rows of razor sharp teeth. As it finished killing another shadow who desperately tried to fight back with a spear, he called toward Zuo in a manner which seemed like he saw this carnage as an utter necessity for Qian Ye.

"DO NOT LET ANY ESCAPE! NOBODY MUST KNOW WHERE THE SEAL IS!"

⁓ * ⁓

Zuo woke up in his bed, sweating. "That damn dream again. When will it end?" That cursed day was the moment he realized that if your government would force you to inflict that on a peaceful village, you might as well be a crook. A day did not go by that he didn't feel remorse for what he did to the Altahn people that night. The most disgusting part of it was that deep inside him, he knew there was an actual reason, however minute, that they had to die.

But he would dwell on his sins another time. He checked his clock and saw that it said 3:45. He hated sleeping in late, but his job forced him to more often than not. But enough oversleeping, he went to make himself a sandwich and check the documents Jakaire gave him.

He read the document as he ate, his cat on his lap napping. "Okay, let's see here. Go to the Sephirot Museum of Bythos. Steal the Pauldrons of Kadosh and replace it with the forgery. Kill any opposition." He had that part down. Not too hard to remember.

He turned to the next few pages. They detailed all who would accompany him on the heist. First on the list was a familiar guy known as Ezker. Everyone in the organization hated Ezker. He was an obnoxious prick of a person. Hell, he hated the picture of that asshole with his smug grin and wearing nothing but striped pajamas and a nightcap. The gang also trusted Zuo enough to give him Ezker's real name and the name of his spark, just in case any of them "went rogue."

"Patrick Jay 'P.J' Porrige." He was unimpressed with the name. "Spark: Little Nemo." He was even less impressed by the name of his spark. Sounded like the kind of name of a kid with way too vivid of an imagination. But then again, P.J here would not be in these papers if he did not have skills to back it up. He'd heard of the crap Ezker could do, how his marks all died in their beds without a single injury on them. Their hearts just stopped beating and their brain shut off.

Going to the next member on the list, he saw that Jakaire Mara, AKA, Kairieji was to accompany him also. He enjoyed her company, having entered the Gang alongside him. She was almost like the daughter he would never have. He knew her name and her spark already, so he skimmed her page.

As he ate his sandwich, he looked at the next page. He felt a drop of dread as he saw him. That man in the hunting vest with the duck caller in his mouth was the most utterly insane member of the gang. A psychic only used at the most desperate of moments, but a gang member who always succeeded in getting his mark, whether psychic, policeman, or politician with the power of the Fontus Spark.

Seeing the one known as Roy Aven Mallard, codename Sinister, on the list made him think that his superiors didn't want a set of pricy pauldrons just for money or decoration. They must have wanted it for something deeper, more meaningful. These artifacts must have meant something more to them. *I'm going to the library after I take my paycheck for last night to the bank.*

Flipping the pages again, he saw pictures of the members from Bythos. There were instructions on how to handle these members. "These five members are becoming a liability in the financial department. They're bringing us only a fraction of their expected earnings. They either have no idea how to run things or they don't want to. If any are left by the time you get to Bythos, recruit them as meat shields for the important members. Resistance is going to be expected. Any who makes it out alive or free, kill them. They are no longer useful to us." Zuo shivered a bit. *Boss is as cold-blooded as always.*

Turning to the next member's page, he first saw a picture of a young woman no older than eighteen. She had short brown hair, bright green pupils, and wore a blue hoodie that covered most of her head. She had a stoic frown on her face. Reading her file, he saw her name as Balra, real name Enitharmon Loz. He was unfamiliar with this one, but it said that she recently graduated from the Academy and worked as a member of the guard in this very city.

How did a promising young kid get into a place like this?

As he read her file some more, it mentioned her spark's name being

Urthona. Unlike other files, Urthona had more to say about it. He took a sip of his coffee.

Warning: This Spark is unlike any spark we have seen before. Urthona is exceptionally unstable and its power seems to be based on the mood of the user. This means Balra could range from utterly worthless to catastrophic enough to kill the entire team (or city block) if she is not careful. To circumvent this, we have given her a headband that stabilizes her aeon into a median number of roughly seven thousand.

Zuo spat the coffee right out, soaking his cat. Little Yun hissed and ran right off. "Holy shit! Seven thousand? And that's her spark being moderated?" He read much deeper into this.

But mind you, the headband only works because we convinced her it works. Do not—I REPEAT—DO NOT make her think the headband does nothing. At her worst, she has zero aeon and at her best, she blew up the measuring machine. She is to warp reality in a way that makes the museum appear undisturbed and cut all cell lines. If you can, do not allow her to do anything else. This mission relies on her being mentally stable enough to do her job. The rest of them are backup and shields to escape if things go south.

Taking a breath to process all the information, he looked at the young woman's page with utter terror. "T-this young lady. This one girl is strong enough to make even Roy an afterthought." He imagined what Enitharmon could do with the ability to change the world around her with but a thought. If she willed it, she could just give him a heart attack and he wouldn't be able to do a thing about it. The boss was using all these forces for a piece of armor? To him, it was not worth the danger this one girl brought to her team members, civilians, or even to herself.

He got out of his seat his went into his room, skipping his shower. "Forget after the bank. I'm going to the library right now. I *need* to know more about those relics."

Xiu's Posse

In the hallway of the high school building, Shee'vra grabbed her books and closed her locker. When she turned to the right, she saw Xiu Lang leaning against a nearby locker, arms folded.

Xiu gave the new kid a smile and a wave. "What's up, new kid? Enjoy your first day?"

Shee'vra wondered why a girl that should be way more popular than her was speaking to the lowly new kid. But she replied, "Pretty good, I guess. My teacher is nice, and the campus is great. Along with—"

"Yeah, yeah, that's great and all," Xiu interrupted, "but I'm going to cut to the chase here. You know who I am, right?"

The girl nodded, unsure where this was going. "Yeah. Xiu Lang. Formerly of Rooster Squad, now in Heron Squad. Spark Anubis. Junior ye—"

She signaled her to stop talking. "I get it. You know who I am. Can't shame you for that, but that's beside the point." Xiu's face went serious suddenly, her green eyes staring down at her. "You're my replacement for Rooster Squad as well as new to this whole psychic thing, are you not?"

Shee'vra couldn't help but feel a little intimidated. "Well, yeah actually." She was beginning to remind her of Kaitlin Joles back in middle school. She was always so mean to her, calling her names and copying her schoolwork. "But why are you telling me about this?" She prayed she wasn't somehow offended by getting replaced by an inexperienced psychic such as herself.

Xiu saw her shaking a bit. *Oh crap. Is she scared of me? I know I'm stronger and prettier than her, but am I really scaring her? Like I'm going to beat the crap out of her or something?* She swiftly cut to the chase. "But anyway, I wanted to meet up with you. One Rooster to another." *By Sophia, that sounded dumb.*

"Huh?" Shee'vra felt a lot less scared now. "Oh, okay, sure thing. Where are we going?"

Relieved that her amazing diplomacy skills had gained her trust, Xiu answered her. "Well to the mall, of course." She grabbed Shee'vra's arm and began to walk. "To the Chokmall, the greatest place in all of Bythos."

Though it was not Shee'vra's idea of the "greatest place in Bythos," she did enjoy that place. The clothes were lovely and extravagant; there was a great theatre, amazing jewelry, and a great food court. Though she had little reason to say no, she felt she had little choice anyway, getting pulled along. "Okay, but I have to text my brother."

Xiu stopped in her tracks just as they went outside. That fabulous new dress could wait thirty seconds. But she must not let Ercan know of her plans, lest he viewed her intentions as malicious. As the younger lady texted on her green crystalcell, Xiu grabbed her hand.

"I've got to come clean, Shee'vra," Xiu admitted to her. "Me and Ercan are not on the best of terms."

Shee'vra had no idea what she was talking about. "But you two seemed fine at The Stage. You seemed to work together well enough."

She wasn't wrong, but Xiu had to contradict that. "Well, you see, people put those things aside during dire times. We both wanted to beat the stuffing out of Winona, so we worked together. Besides, Yun mediated between us all the time."

Shee'vra still didn't exactly see a problem but complied to her wishes nonetheless. She texted on her cell. *Going to hang out at Chokmall with new friends. See you back at home.*

"Okay, done," she told Xiu. "Just said new friends. No names."

Friends, Xiu thought. *Is it possible to be friends with a pupil? Debate for later.* "Thank you." She pointed to the mall's general direction over the horizon. "Now to the Chokmall!"

⁓ * ⁓

Ercan waited at the front for his sister. Cyrille and his two bodyguards had already flown away, leaving him with only Yun and Julia.

"So, you actually beat Winona with fire chains?" Julia questioned him half-heartedly, her face still in a book. "Whatevs. I buy it."

Yun was aghast at her lack of caring. "Whatevs? Ercan just kicked the ass of the captain of Crow Squad, the fifth best squad in the school. With the fact that you and Cyrille were integral for beating three captains, captains are falling from grace like fruit from a tree."

Julia took a moment to reply. "What did you say? I wasn't paying attention. Something, something, fruit falling? Captain stuff. Please. That stuff is BS anyway." She closed her textbook. "You know, Ludmila came to me as you two were punching stuff."

That got her two friends' attention. "Really? About what?" Ercan asked.

"She wanted to see if I was interested in being a Squad Captain should you fail next week," she told them with honesty. "I refused. Too much paperwork. How do you put up with it?"

Ercan considered that question. How did he constantly write after-action reports without boring himself to tears? "Well, I guess I just treated it as homework or something. But it's never as fun as the mission."

Yun chimed in. "Speaking of missions. I found us a nice and easy one for Saturday." He showed them a flyer he ripped from the wall where squads could get little missions for training and finance. "This weekend, we're going to Seraph Park. The park rangers have had complaints about stuff being stolen there but can't find the perpetrators. I feel that something like this will be a cinch. We catch a thief, we all get money, and Shee'vra gets experience on the field. Win, win, and win."

The other two saw nothing wrong with this proposition. Ercan nodded. "That sounds good for Sheev. Though I do wonder where she is." His crystalcell vibrated, so he took the silver phone out. *Going to hang out at Chokmall with new friends. See you back at home.*

"Making new friends so quickly? Classic Sheev," Ercan commented to himself, happy that his sister was integrating into her new life so quickly. He turned to the others. "Alright guys, Sis is going to the Chokmall with some new friends."

"That sounds boring and dull," Julia added in just because. "I don't know why people even go there. The clothes are expensive and all the girls there are giggling morons with their little posse of friends”

"I like the Chokmall," Ercan weakly said to her. "Where do you think I get my clothes?" He and Julia began to walk home, with Ercan yapping on about the values of chic clothes like his. Julia phased him out within the first sentence.

Yun thought, *the Chokmall, huh? Xiu loves that place to death. Is she with Xiu? What would Xiu want with Shee'vra...Probably just trying to show her the ropes or something.* He quickly caught up with his friends.

～ * ～

The Chokmall—one of Bythos's most popular locations and an architectural marvel. The inside was made of white marble, pillars lined the hallways, and the most popular clothing brands of the world fought one another for open spots. The entire building was three stories tall and as long as five blocks.

Another remarkable part of the shopping heaven was a large greenway. This railway trail was once an ambitious train track meant to unify the entire city. It was deemed impractical and the project was cancelled, leaving a gigantic railroad two stories high in the middle of Bythos. But thanks to hearty donations from the one and only Emile DeRoche, the tracks were renovated into a garden full of plants from across the world.

The destination was called the Skygarden by the community. In fact, the Chokmall was built just next to the garden a few years later, even having a door on the second floor leading to the greenway. Together both sites were one of the most popular attractions in the city for both tourists and residents. The tourists enjoyed the view and attractions along the way, and the residents could avoid the busy streets and relax.

Shee'vra and Xiu were taking a break from browsing and shopping to have a bite at the Greenhouse Café. The small café was on the greenway just outside of the shopping center. Shee'vra was eating a turkey club while Xiu had a salad.

Shee'vra swallowed what was in her mouth. "I like the new dress you got."

Xiu kept the bag close to her as if it was her own baby. "I know, right! I saw it last week and said to myself it looked like it was made for me. I asked the store clerk and she said that the line was made by Qian designer, Jade-B. JADE-B! Can you believe it? He's the greatest designer in the history of ever!"

Shee'vra had little idea who this person was and honestly didn't care, but she was glad Xiu got what she wanted, though she was surprised that psychics could have that much money to throw around. "It's a very pretty dress. Do you know when you're going to wear it?"

Xiu went silent for a moment before speaking up. "Well, duh. Course I know the perfect time to wear it. What girl doesn't?" Shee'vra was not exactly convinced but did not question it. "The Jade-B brand is the greatest thing to ever come out of Qian Ye."

The greatest thing? Shee'vra didn't expect a native of the eastern country to consider a mere fashion brand to be the best part of their nation. Sure, some people had issues with their countries, but none had really considered a mere consumer brand to be the best part of it. Usually the most important part of a country to someone was freedom, independence, culture, etc. She might regret it, but she just had to ask.

"Is this designer guy *really* the best thing Qian Ye has? Or are you just exaggerating?"

The fashionista's smile faded away and she seemed lost in thought. A shiver crept up her spine as she shook her head. But she tried to give a legitimate answer. "Well…I guess Master Yeren is cool. He taught me and the other guys how to defend ourselves and stuff. Doing well for himself, last time I heard. Old, but staying strong in the mountains as always."

The only mountain region she knew of in that country was the Shangrilan Mountains. "Oh, so you're from the Shangrilan region? I hear that place is beautiful. I hope to go there myself one day."

Xiu took a light sip of water. "Well, yeah. The view is nice, I guess." She was avoiding eye contact.

Shee'vra felt something was wrong with her. "You seem…out of it right now. Did I ask something personal by accident?"

Xiu waved dismissively. "No, no. It was a perfectly normal question. I just…don't really like that place. Maybe I just stayed in Enotita for too long. I dunno."

"Oh, alright," Shee'vra said to her, choosing not to prod about it further. "You seem like a decent person. Why haven't we ever met before this?"

Damn, she's nosy, Xiu thought as she composed an answer. "Well, to be honest…I never really knew you existed until today."

Shee'vra seemed surprised. "Really? To be honest, I find that hard to believe. Ercan never mentioned me *once*? Not even in passing?"

Xiu took a deep sigh. "Okay, maybe he did. I honestly never hung out with Rooster Squad during free time. I have my own little group of friends," she checked the time on her cell, "who you should have met two hours ago, but Winona must be keeping them."

Something was troubling the fifteen-year-old that she had to get off her chest. She didn't care how Xiu would react, but she had to know, for Xiu's sake as much as hers. "Are you and my brother…?" That caught Xiu's attention really quick. "Not on speaking terms?"

Xiu looked as if she was dreading this question. She crossed her arms with a frown. "Well, until the foreseeable future, yes!"

She felt a bit stumped. "But you two seemed to work fine against Winona."

"Well, relationships during battle and peacetime are two different things. I had to work with him. Besides, I wanted a piece of the witch too. You know, working together against a bigger foe. And I was about to win until Winona cheated anyway." She still had a headache from that damned scream.

Shee'vra didn't see it that way. Ercan explicitly tried to stop her before Winona screamed. But Xiu did not listen. They also seemed to be quite civil after their respective fights as they recharged their Aeon. If it weren't for her brother's words, she might be convinced the two were dating. In fact, she wouldn't exactly be surprised if the two had been secretly dating but had a nasty breakup. Xiu seemed to be a girl Ercan would go for—long black hair, fighting skills, and an overall exotic Qian appeal to her. According to how she understood the opposite sex, she was a boy's definition of "hot."

She honestly had to know. "So, this might be personal…" Shee'vra began to talk once again.

Xiu cringed, knowing for sure what she would say. "Oh dear, no, plea—"

"…But did you and my brother have…'something' going on together?" The sight of Xiu's beet colored cheeks might have given her an answer. "Did you two have a nasty breakup or something?" She prayed to Sophia herself that her brother didn't cheat on her or anything serious. That would change her view of him forever.

Xiu shivered a bit but pounded her open hand on the table. "No," Xiu told her as honestly as possible. As exciting and sensual as she imagined it would be to have secret two-person "missions" together, none of that had happened. "We have not been having a secret affair together. I'm sorry if I disappoint you, but we have *never* been an item. Besides, if he did something worth breaking up about, you would have been at his funeral by now."

At this point, Xiu might as well tell her the truth. "The real reason we're not on speaking terms is that I'm more than convinced Ercan got me kicked out of Rooster Squad. Not that I'm mad at you or anything. You seem like a good kid, if a bit too curious. But I feel that after that damn game last year, I'm more than convinced he got me transferred. Maybe he let me stay until the end of the year. But the moment summer began, he got me on a different squad behind my back." Xiu spoke about it as if the event was a betrayal as she got up from her seat. "I mean, why is it my fault we lost horribly?! Has he even considered that maybe that rich twit, Cyrille, might screw up every so often? Or what about negative asshat Julia? Or even Yun? I've been living with that Monkey for years and I know firsthand he can get into a lot of trouble! Or why not himself!? Has he considered that maybe he's not that good of a captain?! Maybe he sucks at it! Maybe he shouldn't be captain! But does he blame himself for our shit job at missions?! No! He takes it out on me! Not Cyrille, not Julia, not Yun, not the entire squad, and *especially* not himself! ME!"

Xiu took a deep breath, trying as hard as she could to control her temper and not smash something. She saw aeon energy forming around her hands and everyone in the café looking at her. Shee'vra also looked quite stunned at her little outburst. Realizing that she was making a scene, Xiu got back into her seat. "Anyway, until he genuinely apologizes to me and admits the crap he pulled, I'm not going to talk to him."

Shee'vra finished her sandwich quietly. When she finally gulped the rest of it, she began to speak. "Well, I guess that makes sense. I'm sorry my brother can be like that. He's always been super competitive. If it makes you feel better, he did isolate himself in his room after the games for a week."

As pathetic as that was, Xiu was not one to speak. She had done that too. In fact, Hong thought she was sick for the first three days. "I guess." She decided to get to business since it was as good a time as any since the atmosphere had become much more serious. "But talking about your brother or going shopping was not the main point of me bringing you here. I brought you here for a more important reason."

Her crystalcell vibrated and she paused to check the message. It read *behind you*. Looking over her shoulder, she began to feel a good bit better. Her other friends were here.

"Hey girls!" Xiu got up to greet the three newcomers. Hugging the three, she pointed to Shee'vra. "I'd like you all to meet Shee'vra!"

The first one to greet her was a Jivanan girl she recognized from class. Shee'vra seemed to recall that her name was Vasanti. Vasanti was quick to shake her hand with both of hers.

"Hey there! It's me! The Great, Multitalented Vasanti Kavita herself! From class, remember?"

"Yeah," was all Shee'vra could say.

"So glad you do! Who wouldn't know me? You know, before you, I was the new girl in school," she huffed in indignant anger. "Being a psychic cost me my singing career. Bastard agent got rid of my contract the moment he found out." She stopped perseverating on her broken dreams when she had a realization. Letting go of the newcomer's hand, she reached into her purse. "I forgot to give you this when you first came to class. Here." She handed her one of her CDs back when she was a child singer in Naya Jivana, titled *Vasanti: Young Goddess of Music*.

Shee'vra inspected the case and looked at the back. She recognized none of the songs. They were probably a big deal where Vasanti was from, but she honestly had little clue who she was. Though she promised herself she would try to listen to it in her free time, she was not sure when that would be. But she managed to show gratefulness.

"You are most welcome, Sheev!" Vasanti told her. "I'm sure it will bring you great nostalgia."

The girl with red-tinted sunglasses on top of her head walked up to them. "I question whether you know what the word nostalgia means, Vasanti." She focused her eyes on the new kid. "You must be the new kid, right? If you aren't, I'm going to assume you can turn invisible or something because I've never seen you before." She gave a playful grin.

"My name is Sabelle Frech, yours?"

Shee'vra seemed to recall that name from somewhere. She recalled hearing that name come from Ercan's mouth once or twice to his friends, always fondly. But she could hardly blame her brother. She was quite pretty. In fact, these girls began to make her feel super inadequate in comparison.

As Shee'vra mentally sulked to herself, a demon in pure white, bony samurai armor walked up to her. Its face was an eternally still canine with red eyes, large brows, horns, and a snarling, smug, smiling mouth with sharp teeth. She should have been scared as the look intended, but she recognized it as armor and not some kind of evil spirit. Shee'vra saw a large ponytail on the back of the stranger's head. No warrior demon would have time to keep their hair so well maintained. The girl behind the mask waved to her, speaking in an upbeat voice, "Hello, Sheev."

"I didn't want to say anything, Shiro." Sabelle said to her armored friend, questioning her logic. "But you do realize that you're still in armor, right?"

Shiro looked at her hand and saw that it was encased in samurai armor, complete with claws at the end of her fingers. Hastily grabbing her mask, she yanked it off. With that, the hannya and her scale armor turned into bright orange sand, disappearing before it could get into anybody's eyes. Inside the armor was a svelte young lady in pure white clothes. It might just be a hunch, but Shee'vra was pretty sure that white was her favorite color (or at least shade).

Shiro apologized. "Sorry about that. It's like a second skin to me at this point." She formally bowed to Shee'vra. "My name is Shiro. Pleasure to make your acquaintance."

The others mentioned their last names, except her. "Shiro…what?" Shee'vra asked, puzzled. She expected at least a last name or something.

"Shiro," she repeated gladly to her. "Just Shiro. Well if you want to get technical like on a driver's license or something, it would be Shiro. But there is truly just one Shiro." She gave a playful shrug. "Bastards in Seichi get no last name."

Shee'vra was speechless. *How could someone say something like that so casually? Is such treatment normal in Seichi?*

"I don't recall many people being so casual about such issues, Shiro," Sabelle told her friend, shaking her head. "Not exactly a fun topic. Hush

hush about it,' kay?"

Content with having given her answer, Shiro silenced herself. Each girl then took a seat around the table. Shee'vra enjoyed the company of Xiu's girl posse. She honestly just expected a bunch of jerks, even more arrogant than regular queen bees due to their powers. But she was glad she was wrong. Whether it was due to life experiences or just being naturally good-natured, they all seemed pleasant enough, though a bit odd.

"Sorry we got here late," Vasanti apologized to Xiu. "Winona does *not* take losing well."

"Big surprise." Xiu rolled her eyes, refusing to acknowledge the fact that a couple of hours ago, Winona tore her throat out. "So how much hell did she put you girls through?" Xiu had a feeling that it must have been a nightmare. It was common fact that Winona was the most demanding of the ten captains, requiring utmost responsibility and discipline from each member. Say what you want about Ercan's leadership skills, but at least he gave his squad mates space.

"Well she was making us fight her werebeasts for about forty-five minutes," Shiro added. "But her heart wasn't really in it and she just gave up and went to her room, telling us to do whatever we wanted. So here we are."

"Well we were here for two hours. I texted you guys when we got here," Xiu told her friends, pointing to Shee'vra. "What were you three doing then?"

Sabelle raised her hand, twirling a keychain with a picture of a dog. "Sorry, *boss*." Her blue eyes gleamed as she gushed. "But they have this new pet store and they had the CUTEST puppies ever! Beagles, labs, Pitbulls, Dachshund, collies, you name it! ALL ADORBS! I even saw this one Doberman that looked just like Midnight back home." She showed Shee'vra the picture on her keychain. It was a strong hunting dog with a forest in the background. In its mouth was a pheasant. "If the Academy didn't have that stupid 'no pets' rule, I would totally have brought Midnight here. He's the biggest sweetie ever."

As her little group of girls huddled around the new kid, Xiu spoke up. "Now as nice as it was for you all to come here today, I have a special proposition for Shee'vra."

"That's interesting. What is it?" Vasanti asked, not wanting to wait.

"Be patient," she reprimanded. "As I was saying, I am going to have Shee'vra…" Xiu imagined a quick drumroll "…become my very own pupil."

The four other girls went silent. Shiro was the first to speak up. Looking at Xiu, she said, "Are you sure you're ready for this?"

"Of course she is," Xiu answered matter-of-factly. "Everybody has to start sometime. Why not now?" Shiro tried to correct her about who she was addressing, but Sabelle patted her shoulder.

"That sounds fun actually," Vasanti said to Shee'vra. "You get to learn how to kick ass and take names just like her."

"Yeah…sounds fun," Shee'vra replied nervously. She doubted she could do what Xiu could by the time she had to face Eagle Squad. "When do we start?"

Xiu patted her new apprentice's head affectionately. "Tomorrow I'll give you a firsthand introduction to the ways of the Chin Na martial style." She also went into her shopping bag and showed her a book called *Up Close and Personal: The History of Chin Na*. "I even got this for you while you weren't looking. Study up." She placed the book into her hand. *Better read it. Spent forty paz on this thing.*

"Thank you very much," Shee'vra said as she placed the book into her backpack. "I'll be sure to read it when I get home."

Sabelle sat back, thinking to herself. *Now how is someone like Xiu going to handle having an apprentice? She isn't exactly leader material. Hell, I'm pretty sure she brought us all together as if we were her own little squad to feel a bit better about herself.* She scratched the back of her head as she watched the others talk amongst themselves. *This will either end really well or really like crap. Either-or. Kinda curious how this is going to go down.*

~ * ~

Louiz was at the back of the line, waiting to make his move. He himself was well dressed in a business suit, as if he was going to cash in his monthly salary. But little did everyone know, Vinstri and Kushoto were already behind the counter. He looked up to see his fly compatriot on the ceiling, draining the heat from the lights.

Good. Within one minute, Kushoto will absorb enough energy to turn out the lights. Vinstri has hopefully looked over security's shoulder for the vault passcode and the other two are ready to charge right in. He looked around and saw no children in the bank. *Nobody has to get maimed. We take the amount we need, and we split. Then we leave this city for good.*

He bent his fingers, sweat on his brow. This would be the first time he had done a robbery as big as this. He looked up again and saw the fly's wings begin to glow. With that, the lights suddenly turned off. Most were confused, some felt a sense of dread, and others knew that today was going to be a tough day.

Within five seconds, Louiz strengthened his will to become Izquierda. In the darkness, he began to transform. His suit, too tight and weak to handle the increase in muscle, tore apart. His legs became like those of a wildebeest, his arms ending in badger-like claws, and he grew a lion's tail. His head deformed into a snarling hyena beast with sharp, saw-like bone instead of teeth. Even in the darkness, people could see his crystalline eyes sparkle. This beast was the result of the Crocotta Spark.

Izquierda ripped off the tatters of his suit and emitted a sound that was a sick bastardization between a hyena's laugh and a dolphin's clicking, his tongue covered in slobber. In that moment, Aristera and Clé entered the scene. By the time the emergency power turned on, the bystanders saw that there were two brutes barricading the exit. Aristera was a beefy, bipedal bull towering at ten feet tall. Clé, decked in his armor and armed with a claymore in one hand, rode on a pitch-black warhorse adorned with spikes.

The robbery began the moment a woman screamed at seeing the three gang members. Kushoto used the energy she absorbed to unleash a laser of pure heat to decimate the counters. With that, nobody would be able to press that tiny little button under the desk.

"Everybody—hands up and knees on the ground!" Izquierda shouted to the crowd. "This is a robbery! Now everybody behave or things will get violent!" He pointed for Aristera to head to the vault as he and Clé kept a sharp eye on the front entrance. Psychics would arrive. He just knew it. His crystal eyes were never wrong.

~ * ~

As the girls were chatting, Sabelle picked up a peculiar sound. If she didn't know better, it seemed to have been a scream. Looking behind her at the Chokmall, she noticed an armored dark knight on a pitch-black featureless warhorse. They seemed to have been robbing the bank connected to the mall. She could not help but smile—*finally, something to alleviate her boredom.*

She tapped Xiu's arm to get her attention and pointed down below. Xiu and the others took a few moments to realize what was going on and began to grin. Shee'vra had a bad feeling about what was going on.

"W-we should call somebody," Shee'vra recommended to the group. "They'll know what to do."

"No can do," Xiu told her. She pointed to the other café goers, who were already calling police. "Besides, people are already doing that. But who will stall for time? Answer: us." The blue aeon radiated from her limbs as she turned toward the other psychics in her posse. "You girls ready?!"

Sabelle, Vasanti, and Shiro did not even bother to answer. Shiro swiped her hand in front of her face, recreating her coyote hannya mask. The orange sand reappeared around her, recreating her skeletal armor and two katanas. She twirled her blades around, ready to fight.

Vasanti opened her hand to Shiro. "I left my sword back at the academy. Can you make one for me?" The orange sand floated into her hand and formed a large, wavy kris blade. Grabbing the sword in two hands, she was ready. "Thanks."

"Hm," Sabelle mused. "It seems that I left my daggers back home." She shrugged. "Well no matter. Don't need them." Her eyes turned yellow and cat-like as she nudged her tinted shades over her eyes. "Bagheera." Speaking the name of her spark, she crouched down and quickly transformed into a black leopard, yowling in anticipation.

With the four all ready, Xiu turned to Shee'vra. "Wait here and keep an eye on our stuff! We'll be back!"

With that, Vasanti ran right off the side of the Skygarden at unnatural speed. Behind her trailed a rainbow, which left behind a prismatic bridge when she jumped off the side. Xiu followed suit by running on the rainbow down to the ground. Shiro slid down next and Sabelle dashed right after. Shee'vra stayed put, unsure of what was going to happen.

~ * ~

"Hey, Mom! I'm home!" Ercan closed the door behind him. He was initially going to come straight home, but Julia had the new Crystal Game System, the Powercell 3. He, Yun, and Julia were having too much fun shooting aliens together.

His mother was sitting at the dining table, reading a book. She looked up at him. "So how was your first day, Erky?"

Ercan had a lot to say. "Well, at first not so great. I'm in the middle of a trial to determine whether or not I will remain captain of Rooster Squad."

She looked at her son sympathetically. "I'm sorry to hear that. The good news?"

Her son was glad to answer her. "Well you see, I signed up for The Stage yesterday. Turns out that smug captain of Crow Squad, Winona, also signed up. And guess what?"

"What?" Rina asked curiously. Perhaps he got close to beating her or it ended in a draw or something. She loved her son and all, but Winona was Winona. All the kids' parents knew that. She should be proud of him for just confronting the scary young lady.

"I beat her," Ercan expressed with pride. "I first took out Gustave. You know, the gator guy. Then Xiu defeated Dunkeen, the armored fish chatterbox. And Yun took on Winona all by himself." He created a chain under his wrist. "And as a finale, I finished her off with my new trick."

"Please don't set your chain on fire," Rina requested nonchalantly. "You'll set the alarms off."

Ercan was surprised. He had not told anyone about his fire chains. He retracted the metal links back inside him. "H-how do know about them? I never told you. Or anyone."

Rina took a sip of tea. "I know everything about my children, Erky." She did not tell him that her spark could see into other people's Spark Regions but had little reason to tell him. In her opinion, her sister's spark was much more accommodating. She did question why she never heard Sophia's voice inside Prometheus though.

"Well I guess that makes sense," Ercan said. "So yeah, we won and such. Winona lost. All good."

Rina was not as impressed as she should have been. "Did Xiu and Yun survive the simulation?" His expression went glum. "Is that a no?"

"Yeah. Winona took them both out."

His mother got up from her seat. "I'm sorry to hear that. It's not that I want you kids to be perfect on The Stage or anything. It's just that I want you and your friends to stay safe in the real world." She hugged her child. "I have faith that you'll live a long life, but you have to realize that your friends do not have healing factors as well. They cannot take as much punishment as you can. In actual life, when they die, they die for good. The last thing I want you to see is any of your peers dying."

That thought came back to him again, the idea that while he may have aced it on The Stage, it was a pyrrhic victory. "Dang it, you're right, Mom. I just must play more defensively, I guess. Try to minimize the casualties." He softly left the embrace. "I have to use Prometheus to protect the less durable, so they can deliver the final blow. Sheev is in my squad, I can't let her suffer because of my incompetence."

That got Rina thinking a bit. Looking around, she did not see her daughter anywhere. "Ercan, where is your sister?"

Ercan took his cell. "She said she's hanging out with some new friends at the academy. I'm sure she's fine. Probably back before dinner."

"I hope so," her mother remarked, proud of her daughter for quickly making friends. "Unfortunately, your father will not be. He has a massive court case coming up, so he's preparing all his paperwork for tomorrow." As much as she loved her husband, Ult'Tan was always working late. He did say that working in law was a lot less entertaining than in the movies. He once showed her the massive pile of papers on a lawsuit about a mere fender bender that was as big as a dictionary. Perhaps being restricted to few jobs had its perks as a psychic. The hylic ones seemed really boring.

"Well anyway. I'll be in my workshop finishing Sheev's present," Ercan said as he walked away. "Just making sure it all works. Love you, Mom."

As Ercan closed the door to his workshop, Rina thought about her child. He had red hair, as opposed to the black hair of his mother, father, and sister. That was not even getting into his bright purple irises. No human around had such eyes and she had a feeling his spark was not responsible for it. *Did Ercan really not know that she was not his true mother? He might not be a genius, but her son was not stupid. Maybe he just chose not to speak about it.*

Rina did remember when she and her husband found the infant on their doorstep. He was roughly three months old, wrapped in brown cloth and had a medallion around his neck that seemed like a half moon and an eye. Looking around, the couple did not see anybody clearly who could have left the child, though Rina could have sworn somebody or something slipped through an alleyway. There was a little note with the infant, which read *His name is Ercan. Treat him well.* The two felt that they must raise this infant themselves. Just one year later, Shee'vra came onto the scene and the family was whole.

She had been looking into Ercan for a while now. During a doctor's checkup, the doctor called her in private about the boy's body. Turns out he had two hearts instead of just one, the second working as a backup of sorts. Since he was only a baby at the time, she and Ult'Tan decided not to make a big deal of it. It just seemed so random.

Since then, in her free time she had been looking into psychics born with inhuman features. Many psychics gain such features as the result of their spark; others choose to be genetically altered by another psychic. Still others have no rhyme or reason to be born with alien features. People such as Hong and Winona were among these kinds of people. There were even more subtle examples, such as Enitharmon bleeding green blood. Those three and her son all had extraordinary aeon levels as well, which could be normal for these kinds of people.

She had read books about such cases. They were few and far between, but each case was the same: Inhuman features, spark and a high amount of aeon. Scholars even gave these kinds of people a name. Not hylic, not psychic, but a new type: Pneumatic. In each case, one or both of the pneumatic's parents were unknown or missing. She read a prevailing theory about this. Some stated that pneumatics had the blood of archons inside them. Sophia's chosen had been frequently called pneumatics by historians, some even referring to them as her own children, which was comforting enough for her. Who would not be proud that their child had Sophia's blood in their veins?

But there was a darker theory too, which she prayed was not true. That the pneumatics were not descended from Sophia, but from a different archon—one that escaped being either killed or sealed away. One that that still walked among us, breeding with human beings to create perfect warriors—biding its time to awaken its siblings to once again conquer humanity.

It was best not to think about such things, though. But Rina had asked her husband when they should tell him where he came from. Though he gave her no straight answer, he did say sooner or later Ercan would need to know.

Cloudstabber

Izquierda knew what was coming. Through his crystal eyes, he predicted a teenager running at him with a rainbow trailing behind her, her violet sword ready to slice him. Turning around, he was right. He did, in fact, see the rainbow girl dashing at him. Predicting her move, he blocked her attack with a claw, swatting the blade away. Staggering back, Vasanti pointed her kris at him.

"What nice eyes you have," Vasanti remarked, her sword now radiating a blue color. "Shame the rest of you is ugly, though." She lunged at him, swiping and slashing. A blue light followed just behind her wavy blade like a glow stick at night.

Izquierda saw every moment just before it happened, dodging and weaving before the blade could graze his hide. *Plucky young lady. But still inexperienced. What a shame.* He slashed with his left hand, using only his index and middle claws. Though he wasn't exactly trying, she dodged to the side at unnatural speeds, the rainbow catching up a second after her.

"Are you playing around or something?" Vasanti scolded. "At least try!" She cut at him, but a claw deflected the blow, making her move back.

She asked for it. The crocotta lunged toward her, his natural weapons ready to feel flesh. But as he moved, he saw a vision of his jaw being smashed by the back of a blue glowing fist. Abruptly stopping, he put his arm up to defend himself, just managing to block the attack. Though his arm took the brunt of the damage, he was still sent tumbling back into a wall.

"Is this guy bothering you?" Xiu playfully asked Vasanti, cracking her knuckles. From what she could see, she had badly sprained the robber's wrist.

"I had it under control," Vasanti claimed, stomping her foot down. "There should be more of them at the vault. I'll handle this guy."

Xiu shrugged dismissively. "Alright. If you say so." She then ran toward the back of the bank.

Always treats me like a baby. Vasanti shook her head and quickly dashed to the downed beast man. Before Izquierda could stand back up, she had him at sword point. "Ready to give it up?" She aimed her blade at his shoulder.

"Are you?" The crook slowly got up, nursing his wrist. Vasanti stabbed at his shoulder. She looked in shock as the blade did not even pierce him. "Surprised, are we?" Determined to keep him from getting up, Vasanti used her Iris spark to change the color of her blade from blue to green, her most balanced color. Made her attacks decently fast but also made her blade quite strong at the same time. She unleashed a quick barrage of slices and strikes upon the criminal.

"That's rude." Izquierda grabbed the green kris in his mouth. "But human weapons will not work on me." He bit down on the sword, crushing it to shards.

Vasanti just couldn't believe it. How could a common crook be this strong? But then again, Ms. Yamauchi did tell her that no matter how strong a spark is, there will always be another that was the perfect counter.

Izquierda spat out the sharp pieces in his mouth and spoke up once again. "Me and my buddies are in a rush today. You and your friends are making us late." He stepped closer to her, tending his injured arm. "But I don't like hurting kids like you. You have your whole life ahead of you. So I'll give you a warning." He placed his index claw under her throat. "Leave, or this will get messy."

Too preoccupied with Vasanti, he didn't notice a panther with red shades tackling him from his side. He found himself getting scratched and bitten all over, though he could tell that the cat was holding back from biting into any major arteries.

Feeling that she would be of no use, Vasanti hesitantly took this opportunity to help somebody else as Sabelle attacked what she assumed to be the leader. As the fight went on, the bystanders began running out of the bank, giving everyone more space.

Shiro and Clé clashed their blades together. The horseman was surprised that the white demon could block attacks from his claymore with just two katanas. His steed got up on its hind legs and tried to crush her, but she stepped back from the hooves.

"I respect your skill, fellow warrior," Clé commended. "It's not easy to dual wield two weapons of that size." He tried to attack her again, but she caught his sword between her blades like a pair of scissors.

"My blades feel as light as soft sand." She pulled at her blades and disarmed him. "But they're just as strong as any steel." She cut through the air with both weapons, manifesting her sand in an X shape.

The hot sand got into his armor, making him itch and spasm, causing his horse to go temporarily wild. Shiro took this opportunity. Smacking her katanas together, they began to meld. The particles floated into the air and combined to create a naginata in her two hands. She used her polearm weapon to jab into the featureless horse's throat. A semicircle swipe and she cut his mount's front legs off. The horse didn't even make a sound as it faded away into black shadows.

This had the side effect of making the armored knight fall flat on his ass. "OOF! MY GLORIOUS REAR!" Clé cried out. "You have dismounted me, demon." He pointed at her. "Tell me m' lady, what is your spark that has got me on the ropes?"

Shiro was waiting until he was done speaking, pointing her weapon at him. It would not be honorable if she attacked him then and there. She also found little reason not to answer him, though she kept her guard up. "My spark is Coyote, Trickster of the Sands. But my name is Shiro. And you are?"

The knight answered her without hesitation. "I am Clé, true name Ewen. I am of the Lefty Gang." He grabbed his head with his left hand. "And my spark is…" To Shiro's surprise and horror, he ripped his head and neck right off his own shoulders. "…IS DULLAHAN, the Headless Horseman of the Night!" His decapitated head smiled at her, as if trying to freak her out. His neck oozed his own blood, staining the floor. "Now for round two."

Vasanti dashed to Shiro's side, ready to fight alongside her. Shiro made her a second two-handed kris but shook her head. "This is not your place, Vasanti. This is one-on-one. Go help Xiu out back."

Vasanti tried to question her. "But—"

"Go to Xiu," Shiro reiterated, tranquil but firm. "She might need your help more than me."

Though reluctant, Vasanti complied. She sped off toward the back vault, her blade now glowing red.

"I respect your honor." The bank-robbing criminal told her. He reached into his bloody stump and pulled out his spinal cord, which he cracked like a whip.

Shiro charged at him with her naginata, using the weapon's reach to her advantage. Clé entwined the weapon around his spine and yanked it away from her. Shiro shot out hot sand from her hand, going for the head held under his left arm. He cried out in pain but tossed his head into the air like a shot put. As the head spun in the air, Shiro dodged a swipe from his boney whip. She created an iron club from the sands of her naginata and got ready to swing. But before she could smash his armor, the body disappeared.

Looking up at the high ceiling, she saw the spikey armored knight in the air with his head on his shoulders. His limbs were spread out and he was ready to body slam her. Well, he would have if he could see. Instead, he just fell flat on his face.

"OOCHIES!"

Shiro just winced. *Beyond the headless thing, this guy is too silly to be scary.* But she prepared her club to strike him, though because of honor and a dose of pity, she didn't strike when he was prone.

The knight got the sand out of his eyes and quickly crawled away. Making it to his giant sword, he hastily grabbed it in his free hand. Getting up, he put on a menacing face as he wielded both his blade and his whip.

"HAHAHAHA!" he gloated. "Two weapons against one. What shall you do now?" Clé feebly claimed as he cracked his spine whip and smashed his blade on the ground.

Though he could never see it through her mask, she was rolling her eyes.

~ * ~

Aristera hastily made it to the vault. Two security guards tried in vain to stop him, armed with electrified batons. Before either could even shout "Freeze," he'd already knocked them both out with bops to their heads. Charging ahead, the Minotaur saw that the vault was open. *So, Sharlie got the code just as planned.*

Entering the vault, he saw more cash than most witnessed in a lifetime. So much paz just made him want to cry. All organized into giant money-blocks. But it was no time to ogle money; it was time to steal it. He grabbed his sack and started stuffing as much money in it as possible. As he was at work, he noticed Kushoto still stuffing money into her bag, not even caring what kind of bills she was grabbing. He assumed Vinstri was there too but couldn't see him, though he did see cash suddenly disappearing.

"Pick up the pace, Aristera!" Kushoto instructed him. "Psychic pigs are sure to show up any second now!"

"I'm going as fast as I can, Muv-Kushoto!" Aristera answered back as he grabbed chunks of cash in his large hands, filling his bag up sloppily but quickly.

"Looks like we got company!" their invisible ally warned.

They all looked toward the door of the vault and saw a teenage Qian girl. She brushed her long black hair with a glowing blue hand and began to address the three.

"As tempting as all this money is, it isn't yours." She got into Tiger Fist Style, ready for anything. "In fact, you're messing with my favorite mall. That is not okay."

With the formalities done, she shot out a blast of aeon from her hand at the bull's face. Aristera managed to block the projectile with the palm of his left hand. He grunted in pain but took it like a champ. Though he felt a bit reluctant, he raised his right fist to strike her. It was either his gang behind bars or a young woman in a coma. *Sorry miss. Just business*

As he threw the punch, he was surprised to see her catch his fist with both hands. Her nails sunk into his skin as she was pushed back by his sheer strength, her feet sliding on the smooth floor.

"She's open! Take her out!" Aristera ordered his two peers. There was a brief pause as he saw a familiar fly dash out of the room and wet tiles appearing on the floor.

Xiu held onto his fist, expecting an ambush, though nothing showed up. She used this opportunity to taunt him. "No honor among thieves, huh?" She pushed his arm away with great force, causing him to lose balance. "What a shame." She then gave him a foot to his stomach.

Aristera's eyes widened with pain as the wind was knocked out of him. *She packs a surprising wallop for a teen. But can she take a wallop?* He stood his ground and got ready to punch her lights out.

But before his gigantic fist could meet her everything, brilliant lights dashed toward him. Before he could see what it was, the red flash went right past his head. Looking back, he saw another girl with a weird wavy sword in both hands. He then heard one of his horns falling right off, causing both girls to giggle a bit. But he cared little about that.

What he did care about was that Vasanti's sword radiated a red aura around it. He could do little but focus on the red. He hated red. But more than that, he feared it. He felt like a young weak kid again. He began to remember his grandfather. He and his sister had lived with the bastard since their parents' accident. He remembered how he would strike them with his belt whenever they got out of line. Whether that be breaking a vase by accident or not doing the dishes correctly. He would even do it in front of their friends, threatening them not to tell anyone lest they feel his wrath. It was especially bad when he was already drunk on booze.

He always wore this red shirt of his favorite soccer team. Whenever his team lost, he always took it out on him. When his older sister ran away, the abuse got worse. He dropped the belt and began to use his fists to discipline him. Any resistance would only encourage him to hit harder. None of the teachers in school even cared about the bruises and black eyes he would come in with. To them, he was just a poor troublemaker getting into scraps outside of school.

When his Minotaur spark manifested, his grandpa only got crueller. Feeling weak now, he refused to let him learn how his spark worked, for he would no longer be the man of the house if he did. He threatened to hurt his friends if Asterion told anyone he was a psychic. Even when he tried to make his grades better in a desperate attempt to make him proud, his grandpa resented him.

When he was a teenager, Asterion and his friends were hanging out as normal. But then his grandpa, who was completely wasted and furious, attacked them with a club and crossbow. His grandpa ranted and raved about how much of a "damned burden" he was and wanted to just get him out of his life already. He managed to shoot one friend in the head and smashed the other friend's skull in. Asterion backed away into a corner, terrified as he moved closer, red blood soaking his face.

But no strike came. When he heard a pained cry, only then he looked up. His grandfather's lower body was somehow transformed into that of an anaconda. The giant snake hissed as its jaws opened wide to devour him headfirst. He witnessed in horror his "guardian" getting his head enveloped in a visual that reminded him of a sick parody of an ouroboros.

As he watched, shaking and teary eyed, he saw someone or something. This being looked almost like a chimera between a human, a dragon, a serpent, and a demon. He claimed to have been watching him for a while now and knew that he was a psychic. He offered him a position in an organization of psychics. The Lefty Gang. Lost, scared, and unsure of his future, Asterion accepted the offer of the being. This unnatural man offered to teach him the ways of the spark as they left his grandfather to be digested by his own lower body.

"GET AWAY FROM MEEEEEE!" Aristera cried out in absolute terror. He quickly tossed a surprised Xiu at the threat and ran off without the money. "STAY AWAAAAY!"

But before either of the two could follow him, a stone wall rose up from the floor and crashed into the ceiling. To entrap the two further, the Minotaur slammed the vault shut.

Xiu was in a daze, getting off Vasanti. "The hell just happened?"

"I-I don't know," Vasanti replied befuddled.

The panther and the monster circled around one another, never letting one's eyes stray. Izquierda was on all fours, snarling at the big cat in front of him. Sabelle likewise hissed at him as she pounced.

The leopard inflicted quite a number on him. Natural attacks such as claws and teeth worked better than steel ever could on him and since he was pinned, he had little way of seeing what she would do next. It took kicking her off to escape her claws. Even then, this cat stared him down, her yellow eyes peering through her red shades.

When he saw the cat make what seemed to be a smirk, he used his crystal eyes. What he saw through his eyes shocked him. It was yet another panther just behind him, yowling as it pounced on him from behind. He quickly bucked the beast behind him but gave an opening to the initial panther. Sabelle quickly took this opportunity to jump him again, biting the nape of his neck. The second cat got back up and bit at his good arm. Though the attacks stung like a demon, he could tell that the bites and scratches were gentle enough not to allow him to bleed to death. He would use their mercy as an advantage.

Struggling to escape the two, he looked at Clé's duel. He was using both of his weapons at once without a degree of finesse. Izquierda always did tell him that duel wielding both weapons would get him nowhere. And he was right. Clé tried to wrap his spine around Shiro but missed due to using his off hand. The white demon swung her club like a whiffle ball bat and hit his side, cracking the armor. While he was stunned, Shiro used her weapon to swipe his feet from under him.

But as Clé fell back, he had just enough time to toss his head over his shoulder. Flying through the air, his falling body disappeared and reappeared upright reattached to his head.

But Izquierda had to focus on his problem. The sharp bone plating in his mouth would take care of one pest. He yanked his hand from the cat without the shades, bringing it closer to his jaws. When it was close enough, he bit straight into the panther's face. It howled in agony as his jaws ripped into its flesh and crushed its skull. Izquierda felt nauseous as he tasted feline brain matter.

Spitting out skull pieces and brain fluid, he got up with Sabelle still on his back. He jumped and deliberately landed on his back to get her off. As the panther released her grip, he sprung up. Before the cat could roll back up though, he decided to see if he still had it in him.

Let's see if my kick is as good as ever. Bringing his leg back for extra force, his hoof struck her side and sent her toward the wall. As she went unconscious, the black cat changed back into a normal human girl.

Goal. Izquierda still had it in him after all these years. Looking back at Clé, he called out to him. "I'm open."

The knight immediately got the message. He addressed his opponent one last time. "It's been a fun duel. But it ends now."

Without a second thought, Clé threw his head at his leader. Thanks to his abnormally hard skull, Clé had no problem with getting his head kicked with the force of five men. As the head spun around in the air at high velocity, he teleported his spiky armored body back to him and rolled into a ball. Shiro barely had time to meld her weapon into a large shield with a red and black symbol of a coyote's face. But even with the defense, she was sent flying into a wall by the sheer weight of the human cannonball.

Though the shield took the brunt of the damage and spikes, the force of the attack was enough to take her out of the fight. Shiro slumped down into a sitting position and lost consciousness.

Both Lefty Gang members took a brief breath of relief. But it could not last for long. Izquierda sensed not only police sirens but also Aristera running and howling in terror. The Minotaur had the right idea. It was time to book it.

~ * ~

Shee'vra was worried about them. She couldn't get a good view from where she was, but she could hear that the fighting inside had stopped. She looked behind her to see police vehicles at the ready. The cops made her feel a little more comfortable.

But she gasped as she saw a giant bull man run out of the building and up Vasanti's rainbow bridge. She reflexively stepped back as far as she could, but she was still in his way. When he was just in front of her, she tried to think about what Sylph could do. The first thing she could remember was wind. So instinctively, she made a pushing motion, thinking as hard as she could about moving the air.

And she did it. She felt the force of air move toward the bull in a condensed line. Maybe she wouldn't be so useless after all.

Sadly, all it did was ruffle his brown fur a bit, though it did bring him back to his senses. Looking down, the bull man saw a scared teenage girl trying to crawl away from him. She cried out in terror as he grabbed her with one hand.

But to her surprise, he merely put her down just behind him. He hardly even seemed mad that she'd tried to attack him in self-defense. "Stay out of my way." The bull then continued to run across the greenway to make an escape.

Shee'vra was stunned at why a criminal would show such mercy to her. There was a possibility that he just didn't register her as a threat (she would not blame him). But there was a possibility he just simply didn't want to hurt her. It made sense in her mind. Thieves are not necessarily murderers.

She looked back at the bank to see a hybrid of many animals run off on all fours. Though this person looked ferocious, there was a chance that maybe the gang had a no-kill policy and Xiu and the others would be alive. The gigantic bull guy might have been proof of that theory.

The next person to exit pretty much clarified that the four girls lost rather than that the gang simply retreated. A knight in black spikey armor rode on a horse. Shee'vra almost found herself shrieking when she saw that he had his own head in his hand, which displayed a confident grin. When she looked beyond the decapitation, she noticed that his large sword had no blood on it and the crook's armor looked completely battered. The armor was dented in several spots and it seemed that many of the spikes were missing.

Then she realized he was galloping toward her up the rainbow slide. "Out of the way, lady! I am making a geta—"

She saw a fist meet Clé's side, shattering the leftmost part of the armor to bits. His grin was gone and was replaced by a wide-open mouth that barely registered what had just happened. His eyes bulged as his muscular assailant grabbed his body *and* his horse, smashing both into the road. Clé's head was left in the air, spinning about for a bit before hitting the ground. His head tumbled down the rainbow. His body teleported away from his assailant and reattached to his head and was sprawled on the cement unconscious.

Shee'vra turned her head to see who just punched that guy out. Looking down, she saw a familiar one-eyed warrior. "Mr. McDooley?"

The cyclops looked up to see his goddaughter. "Sheev?" He was surprised to see that she didn't run away. "What are you doing here?"

"I'm waiting for my friends," Shee'vra replied straightforwardly. "They're still in there."

"Right away, Sheev." Monoceros quickly ran inside. Behind him, some cops cuffed Ewen's hands together.

~ * ~

Twenty minutes later, the manager of the bank managed to open the vault. With him were Monoceros and Shee'vra as well as the beat up Sabelle and Shiro. The four had been outside for quite a bit, hearing the sound of smashing and breaking. It took Sabelle finding him hiding under his desk to get him to help.

Inside, they saw two teenaged girls panting in exhaustion after having just smashed through a stone wall that was most definitely not there before. Vasanti at least had a sword, but it was apparent that's Xiu's shoes were a mess.

Xiu grumbled as she looked down at her feet. "Well shit. These are ruined." She walked toward the vault and spoke to Sabelle and Shiro with urgency. "Did either of you two take down a giant bull guy? Son of a bitch freaked and trapped us!" She showed them her filthy and dented shoes, ignoring the fact that blood could be seen seeping out of the stockings. "I mean, look what he made me do to my shoes!" She stomped an aeon enhanced foot down, cracking the floor. "I'll turn him to steak! Where is he?"

Shee'vra was the one to answer her. "He…got away. Sorry."

"Is that so?" Xiu almost seemed to tear up a bit. She cradled her footwear in her arms. "I loved these shoes like my own baby!"

Vasanti ignored the drama queen and had her head down in shame. She noticed that Sabelle was putting pressure on her side and Shiro had an icepack on the back of her head. She addressed her two injured comrades in sorrow. "I'm sorry, you two. I was useless this whole time. If I hadn't run to help Xiu, you two wouldn't be hurt."

The redhead shook her head. "I refuse to hear any apologies from you. You did the right thing, helping her at the vault. Who knew how many others there could have been?"

The lady in white slowly disintegrated the copy of Vasanti's sword into sand. "If anyone should be blamed, I should be. I told you to leave just so I could have a duel against one of them. It was naïve and pigheaded of me." She solemnly bowed. "I am sorry."

Mr. McDooley patted Vasanti's head. "No need to feel down on yourself. Everyone is alive, thanks to you girls. They might have just all gotten away if it wasn't for you four."

Those words made them feel a whole lot better. To hear those words come from the Academy's most notorious hard-ass made them feel like they did something right.

But the cyclops continued. "But sadly, only one of them has been captured." He became somewhat sterner as he showed the group a small emblem. The emblem had a red left hand on it, with marks representing the lines on the palm. "This emblem is the symbol of the one and only Lefty Gang." He had no idea they even had a base in Bythos, but they were getting much too ambitious for his taste. "These guys are not to be trifled with. They are the most dangerous crime syndicate in the underworld. These people are devoted to robbery, assassinations, drugs, you name it." He stared down at the four girls with his one big eye. "These parasites are in our city now. I recommend you girls watch your backs. They might come back to finish the job."

The girls shivered after hearing how big of a deal these crooks were. They heard from the news that all the important members of the group were psychics. Psychics could do a lot of things and most blended into the crowd. Nobody knew how large the group truly was. In fact, not one of them had heard of any of these members. Who knew how many members there truly were? They could be an entire army of psychics for all they knew.

Xiu was the only one who even said anything about the matter. "Wow…shit."

The bank manager did not listen to any of that whatsoever. He was utterly dumbfounded about the conditions of his beloved vault. "What have you two done to my vault?" he cried out with his hands on his toupee. Bits of stone were everywhere, once-fresh bills wrinkled and torn. He pointed his finger at Xiu and Vasanti. "This money is filthy! You ruined it all! Do you know how much this sets us back? The costs?"

Vasanti looked away in guilt, but Xiu was indignant. "Hey, wait a minute now! Without us—"

"Without them, you would have lost much more," Mr. McDooley bluntly stated to the manager. "The Lefty Gang is a ruthless bunch. Who knows how much would be lost? The money can be replaced, but who knows what would have happened if they'd had time to take hostages. So instead of yelling at these young ladies who risked their lives, for free mind you, why don't you thank them?"

He was glaring a dagger at the manager. In terror, the manager dropped the issue immediately. "Thank you for your help. Without you four, the authorities would not have made it in time."

"You're damn right," Xiu told him, not impressed by his forced gratitude. "This day cost me my best shoes."

"Um…Xiu?" Shee'vra grabbed a shoebox out of Xiu's bag and gave it to her. "You bought some really nice shoes today. Maybe you can wear these instead?"

Xiu just remembered she bought a pair of the greatest shoes on instinct. Black, shiny, slightly raised heels, amazing material, they were made to kick ass with style. Caradoc was going to be quite miffed at the compulsive spender. She was excited to try them on. "Thanks for reminding me!" She tossed her old pair into the vault and quickly put the new ones on. "Like a friggin' glove!"

Shee'vra gave Xiu her bag back and the five psychics left the bank. When they were outside the Chokmall, Shee'vra noticed the condition of Sabelle and Shiro.

"Are you two going to be okay?" Shee'vra asked, concerned for them. She hadn't seen much of the fight, but for all she knew they could have internal bleeding.

Shiro merely nodded, but the other answered her. "Don't worry about us. We'll just go to Winona." Sabelle looked up to see a crow perched on a small maple tree in the sky garden, peering at the five. "She'll be waiting for us."

"Shee'vra," Monoceros chimed in abruptly. "I feel that it's time to say goodbye to your friends for now." He nodded at Xiu and her posse for keeping her out of the battle. "Your mother would be worried if she realized you were here." He signaled a cab.

Not wanting to say no to her godfather, Shee'vra waved goodbye to Xiu and the others. "Thanks, Mr. McDooley. Alright. Bye, guys. See you for training, Xiu." She entered the cab and soon she was on her way back home.

Monoceros focused his attention on the other girls. "I suggest the rest of you go home too." He pointed at Sabelle and Shiro. "You and you should see your squad leader for healing."

"Fully intend to, sir," Shiro replied, the back of her head aching.

Sabelle felt that was an obvious course of action. "Don't have to tell me twice."

"Good." Monoceros directed his voice at Vasanti. "You, get rid of the rainbow bridge slide thing. It's a safety hazard." As Vasanti quickly willed the prismatic construct out of existence, he addressed Xiu. "And you, train her as well as you can. You better." His one eye stared her down. "Or I will make your senior year hell."

Xiu could not help but shiver. "Yes sir. I'll try as hard as I can," though she did feel that turning a gentle girl like Ercan's sister into a paragon of power was going to be an uphill battle. She hoped she wouldn't regret this.

~ * ~

Louiz and Asterion rode on their motorbikes back to their base within the park. Louiz's bike was yellow, whereas Asterion's was purple. The two had changed back to their human forms the moment they were out of sight from anybody. This, along with the fact neither had any money on them, meant the escape back was smooth sailing. But still neither bothered to look behind them.

As they parked their bikes at the base, they noticed that only two bikes ad come back; Sharlie's green one and Muvumo's blue one. Neither could see Ewen's black bike. Entering the base, they saw that Sharlie and Muvumo had just finished counting the money.

The walking seadrake greeted them with a smile and wave. "Do we have some good news for you!" He tossed a bundle of cash at Louiz. Looking through the paz, he could see that they were all hundred paz bills. They had two whole bags of them.

"Thanks to our heist, we got the three hundred thousand!" Muvumo told the two upfront. "Plus, another thirty-five grand just for us! We should do this kind of stuff more often!"

Louiz ignored the good news and looked around the room. The big knight wannabe was not inside either. He asked the two straight up, "Where is Ewen?"

Both of their smiles faded. Sharlie was the one to speak. "I-I thought he was with you guys."

That was all the confirmation he needed. Ewen may not have been as sharp as his blade, but even he would know to get here as fast as possible. He waited for a minute, standing completely still. Ewen still did not come. Lashing out, Louiz turned his right foot into a hoof and kicked one of the walls in, not even saying anything. The other three jumped at the leader's temper.

"Hey, cool it down!" Muvumo barked at him, not even caring that he was her superior. "It's not a hundred percent certain that Ewen was caught! Chill out already!"

Heeding her advice, Louiz merely sat down on the chair he usually sat on. "I doubt it, Muvumo. Those girls wasted a lot of our time. Asterion and I saw the cops outside. Chances are a psychic managed to take him out." He tapped his finger on the table anxiously. "If they break Ewen, it's only a matter of time until we're found."

Asterion came to Ewen's defense. "He would never do that. He's much too loyal to the gang. I have faith in him."

"Let us hope so," Louiz replied. "Let's just hope next week comes fast."

~ * ~

Shee'vra opened the door to her home. Her mother was waiting for her on the couch, reading a mystery novel. Dinner was almost ready, and it smelled good.

Rina got up and hugged her daughter. "So how was your first day, honey?"

"Well, it was interesting," Shee'vra answered. "I learned a lot of stuff about psychics, I found out my spark's name is Sylph, and I saw my brother actually win." She took a seat on the sofa. "And finally, I managed to make friends and become an apprentice to one of the students."

Rina had never heard of any apprenticeship programs when she was at school. Maybe it was a new system the Academy was trying out. "That must be an interesting experience, dear. Tell me, who is it?" She began to consider students that might sign up for such a program. "Is it…Cyrille perhaps? He is such a nice young man."

Shee'vra enjoyed the chicken man's company but could not really see him being anyone's master. "No. Not Cyrille."

Not wanting to list every student in the academy, Rina quickly relented. "Alright then. Who is it?"

She prepared to answer her mom. "I'll tell you. But she told me that Ercan can't know."

That sounded strange, but Rina went with it. "Odd request. But I won't tell your brother."

Making sure her brother wasn't around to hear, Shee'vra told her mom. "It's Xiu Lang. She volunteered to help me learn her fighting craft to be of more use to Rooster Squad."

Rina did not expect that girl to be the one to assist Shee'vra. If anything, she thought Xiu would have resented her daughter for replacing her. Though she never did really see the girl that much, she knew of Xiu's temperament from her son. Hopefully, her daughter could mellow out her attitude problems as they trained together, though she could see why she might not want Ercan to be in the know. Those two never really saw eye to eye.

"Xiu, huh? Well hopefully she'll be adequate." Rina then remembered that her son had a present for his sister. "I almost forgot to tell you. Go to your brother's workshop. He has a gift for you."

"Sure thing." She scurried over to the workshop and opened the door. "Hey, Erca—Whoah." Her eyes widened.

Waiting for her was Ercan, who had just finished sharpening a foot-long bolt. He put it down and acknowledged her. "Hey, Sis. How was hanging out with badass psychics?"

"Not a new experience." She wasn't technically lying.

"Good to hear." Ercan grabbed the cloth on the table. "Now that you're a psychic, you're going to be expected to put your life on the line for the betterment of humanity. I could not in good conscious allow you to enter that life without a bit of defense. So thus, I have created your new best friend." He pulled the cloth off the desk, revealing a large crossbow that was almost as big as her upper body and painted the color of the sky. "TA-DAAA!"

Shee'vra stared at her brother's creation, unsure of how to feel. He was essentially giving her a weapon of war in the same manner one would give a birthday gift. She picked it up to see how it felt in her arms. It was predictably hefty, but she could get used to it, though it might restrict some movement. She did always have a good eye for seeing long distance, since her eyesight was 20/20. She suspected her brother wanted her to be out of range of most bad guys and shoot them. Though the idea of shooting somebody with a bolt the size of her head did make her feel uneasy, sometimes it was just for the better. Besides, Sylph was a wind-based spark. If she could learn how to fly, she'd be untouchable to most.

This style of fighting would contradict Xiu's training. But then again, who's to say you can't have two styles to work with, one for up close and the other for distance? It made sense to her. She aimed the empty weapon at the wall, trying to feel the experience of what using the thing would actually be like. She imagined shooting down a demon from the skies, which spiraled downward back to earth. She then imagined inflicting a tiger claw jab on another demon, sending it flying with a burst of air.

"Shee'vra?"

She returned to planet earth. "Yeah?"

"You were spacing out for a minute there." He smugly smiled. "That must mean my present ruled."

"It did," she answered truthfully. "I was just thinking what I could do with it. Thank you, Ercan."

"Perfect. But now you must name it." His voice went eerie. "It's bad luck to not give it a name."

"That's true." She thought long and hard for what to call it. She thought about the sky and what was in the sky: Clouds. She then thought about what bolts did— stabbed through things. So thus, she figured out a name.

"Cloudstabber," she told him. "This arbalest shall be known as Cloudstabber."

"Neat name," her brother commended, "though I would have gone with Deathbolt or Pointblanco. But anyway, Cloudstabber *was* my third idea." He picked up some of the weirdly shaped crossbow bolts. "You want me to teach you about your ammo?"

Shee'vra felt she had other stuff to do. She still needed to read a bit of that book Xiu gave her to get a head start in training. She also needed to explore her Spark Region a bit more. She had things to read there too. Plus homework. A lot of reading, overall.

"Not now. I have a lot of studying to do. Maybe later." She opened the door to leave with her new toy. "Thanks again."

Going into her room, she put her weapon down on top of her shelf. Sitting on her bed, she took off her backpack, got into a comfy upright position, and closed her eyes to visit the windmill again.

~ * ~

Xiu Lang unlocked the door to the apartment. Going in, she saw that her peers had made it back home before her. Hong was asleep on the couch with a towel under his moist body, lightly snoring as his arm hung off the side. Yun was in the kitchen making a dinner of shrimp and noodles. Caradoc was watching the crystalvision.

"Hey, Xiu," Caradoc called to her, his eyes on the CV. "Did you hear about this?"

"What is it?" She sat down on the airchair, unsure whether it was important or mundane but entertained solely Caradoc, like they discovered a new planetoid or something. As she watched the CV, she saw that it was about the attempted robbery she sort of foiled. The balding newscaster talked about how four brave young ladies fought hard against members of the Lefty Gang at the Chokmall an hour ago. The News was fast when it came to getting recent events.

"Do you know about this?" Caradoc asked her. "You go there a lot and you just got back."

"Oh yeah, that was me." Xiu was quick to admit. "Nobody messes with any part of my favorite mall. I was a worthy opponent against such bastards." She clenched her hands in mock fisticuffs. "Gave them a *real* tussle."

Two of the girls were found trapped in the vault twenty minutes after the fight. The other two survived their battles with minor injuries. Sadly, only one of the members was captured with the help of Monoceros McDooley, Eye of Judgment. A picture was put up showing the cyclop's scowling face. *This man is the hero this city deserves. Without him, the robbery would have most definitely been much worse. Sadly, three hundred and thirty-five thousand paz was stolen. But that is small cookies compared to what could have been.*

She called out to the screen. "Wait, what?" But then she recalled the fly woman and some invisible guy or something. "Dammit."

"What's the matter?" Yun called from the kitchen. "Did you forget anything at the mall?"

Xiu kept her bag in hand. "No, Yun. I just realized a few mess-ups I had today."

Yun was nonchalant, as if that was normal for her or something. "Oh, okay! Dinner in ten, guys!"

The two watched the news for a bit. One was about how a few dead bodies were found in an abandoned factory in Sorchos. As they watched, Caradoc asked her a bombshell of a question.

"So how was hanging with Shee'vra?"

Xiu turned to him quicker than a bullwhip. "What do you mean?"

"Yun said that before the match with Winona, you spaced out when you were introduced to Shee'vra. Then after that, Ercan got a text about how Shee'vra was hanging out with new friends with no names mentioned. I just felt that it was obviously you who asked her to keep your meeting on the down low." Caradoc shrugged. "It was just simple deduction."

That made enough sense to Xiu. Though she loathed admitting it, the youngest of their group was the one with the most common sense out of the four. "Whatever. It was not like I invited her to go along to haze her or anything." She crossed her arms together. "If you must know, I'm taking her on as my pupil."

Both Caradoc and Yun looked at her like she was crazy or something, though Yun actually had the gall to laugh. Caradoc merely looked worried.

Xiu felt quite slighted. With a dirty look, Yun shut up. "And what's wrong with my plans? We all must spread Master Yeren's teachings *sometime*. Why not now for me? Besides, somebody needs to help her out and I doubt Ercan could."

"Sorry, sorry," Yun answered her, trying not to chuckle still. "It's just that…" He tried to find the right words that wouldn't set her off. "… Of all of us. I don't think any of us…expected you to be the first to try." He quickly added some more words in order to not sound offensive to his peer. "I mean if you really set your heart to it, I'm sure you'll help Shee'vra in the long run. She'll become as tough as us in no time."

It was Caradoc's turn. "Though I do agree with him on how beneficial this is to Shee'vra, I feel that I must warn you." He got more serious. "Shee'vra is new to this whole world. Chances are, she's not going to learn everything first try. You can't just get frustrated at her for her failures, even when she makes one, two, even twenty of them on the same maneuver. Just think about how much time it took you to learn three styles."

Xiu did remember her training in the art of Chin Na with Master Yeren. He was very patient with her over the years. But even now, though she was naturally talented in Eagle Claw, Tiger Fist, and Cornered Dog Styles, she still had much to learn about them. Yun was smart enough to only choose Monkey Style Kung Fu to focus on. Caradoc chose how to master swordplay and Hong…she would like to say something similar to Drunken Boxing but it seemed to be something else along with that weird crescent blade staff thing. Yeren made sure to teach them all as equally as possible.

As their legal guardian, she wondered what her master was doing now. He had yet to get a crystalcell (not that it mattered) and there was no mail service up where they used to live. The Shangrilan Mountains was an extremely isolated area in Qian Ye. She could almost miss it if not for the rest of the country.

As she reminisced about home, the salamander man woke up in a daze. "You guys are making a lot of noise about this Shee'vra stuff." He didn't explain how he could possibly have known what they were saying if he was asleep. Instead he droned on. "It's not going to be easy teaching her fancy tricks like we learned as kids. She has a lot less time to learn how to fight against baddies. She needs to learn quickly but not skip anything in the process." His eyes began to glow. "That might just spell doom for our young heroine."

He then went back to his nap. The other three were always creeped out when he acted like this. But they'd all known since childhood that Hong's advice was never to be ignored. He could not precisely see the future, but he always seemed to be one step ahead of what was going on. He would sometimes tell them odd dreams that would become true. For example, when they were children, he had a dream about a red sword with many wings surrounded by a burning wheel. A year later, they were all sent to Aeon Sophia Academy, which had a similar symbol. He once dreamt of Xiu and Yun riding on a giant rooster as it waded in a green corrosive substance. Xiu fell in but Yun held on. It sounded stupid then but, looking at the present, there was sense to it. Sometimes he would be just rambling. But just in case, they always made sure to pay attention to him. Xiu had a feeling Hong had many more dreams like that. He just refused to tell them for one reason or another.

But right now, Xiu had to make sure that she wouldn't fail as a mentor. She needed to be seen as somebody worthy to be a master. She would make Shee'vra a warrior even if it were the last thing she did—for herself, for Shee'vra, for Master Yeren, and for Ercan.

A Single Day

It was the second day of school and a pleasant Thursday. Shee'vra was sent to the nurse's office during first period to get her aeon measured. She took a seat as the nurse strapped a metal device around her forearm. It tightened around and a little light glowed blue for roughly a minute. The device was attached to a bigger machine that was to determine her aeon score.

Shee'vra was kind of pumped to see what her score was. She was not able to take the test the first day due to the calling list going down in alphabetical order by first name. But she spent a bit of time wondering how much aeon she would have. She never knew much about aeon levels but her brother did have over four thousand. Maybe she'd have five thousand or higher. She began to wonder how high of an aeon score someone like Mastema must have, thinking that he may be over the ten thousand threshold.

The nurse, named Ionela judging from her nametag, looked at the screen out of Shee'vra's view. "Let us see here. According to the Aeon Scale, your score is about…" Shee'vra braced herself, kicking her feet on the chair. The machine beeped, signaling that it was done processing. "Five hundred and eighty-two."

That deflated her dreams. That number sounded terrible. "Really? That's it?"

"Whatever do you mean by 'that's it'?" The nurse replied to her. "That is actually around an average aeon score for psychics."

Shee'vra thought she just said that to make her feel better. "Are you sure? Because my brother has about a four thousand and something aeon score and, between you and me, he seems to have a lot to learn."

The school nurse thought for a moment and then found herself chuckling. "Oh. You must be Ercan's sister then." She could hardly see a family resemblance as she wrote down the results with a pen. "But don't worry yourself. You aren't a weakling or anything. In fact, I've seen students with aeon scores in the double digits before and they are still fruitful psychics." She put her clipboard away. "It's just that Ercan has a very high level of aeon inside his spark."

That caught her interest. "Really? I honestly thought he was exaggerating it."

"Your brother is no liar," she reassured Shee'vra. "In fact, he was not even the highest-scored student."

"Who was that?" Shee'vra wondered who it could be. That student must have been able to use his or her spark for days on end—a deity in human form.

The nurse took the device off of the patient's arm as she spoke. "Well, I don't like to give out names. But there was a girl who actually broke the machine." She then remembered something odd. "But when we brought out another Aeon Scale, she scored a straight zero." Ionela wondered how that was even possible. "But when we tried again, she scored a sharp ten thousand, which still did heat up the scale but it set a school record."

Shee'vra got out of the seat. "That's a strange spark she must have had." She picked up her backpack. "But I got to get back to class now. Bye."

"Come over if you get sick." Ionela waved the girl away.

Her next patient was a teenage boy whose skin shined like a steel sword. He looked tired and his eyes were baggy. He took the same seat he always sat on during these frequent visits.

Ionela grabbed a thermometer. "Is your temperature acting up again, Amund?"

The boy weakly nodded before covering his mouth to cough.

"Sorry to hear that, dear. It's never any fun feeling that way." She placed the thermometer into his mouth.

As she was waiting to get the temperature, her son entered the room. Alexandru bowed to his mother. "Greetings, mother. Greetings, Amund." Amund weakly saluted his captain back.

"Morning, dear," Ionela Coagula said to her child. "Do you need anything? If so make it quick. Amund needs my attention."

The dhampyr strolled to her clipboard and picked it up. "Nothing really, just need to check Ercan's new aeon score to help judge him for next week."

He checked the board and his eyes nearly popped out of his eyes. It improved to a whopping five thousand and sixty-six. His mom and squadmate had to catch him as he nearly fainted.

~ * ~

Second period for Cyrille was science class. He had a feeling that it would be so much fun. Mr. McDooley said that they were to learn about chemical reactions and such. Cyrille wondered if his beaker would explode by accident. Each member was assigned a lab partner. His for today was Hanako. The two put on their lab coats and goggles. Despite being immune to poisons, Cyrille was very strict about lab protocol. It just ruined the experience if he wasn't.

He tried to handle each test tube as gently as possible under his chicken claws, trying not to scratch the glass. Hanako wrote the notes about the results and what colors the beakers turned into. As they tried to make the liquids get all bubbly and fizzy with different reactions, Hanako began to open her mouth.

"So…Cyrille," she quietly talked to the reptilian rooster, focusing on the experiment rather than looking at him. "Me and the other captains have been talking about things."

"About what?" Cyrille asked, stopping what he was doing.

Hanako continued. "W-well you see. You're from a big, prestigious family. Have you thought that your father…" She took a deep breath. "D-don't you think that perhaps…your p-parents would be proud of you if you became a Squad Captain?"

Cyrille saw where this was going. Though his father, Emile, and his mother, Izolda, always supported his position in the Academy, his more distant family members were less enthused. More than once they had remarked on how embarrassing it was for a DeRoche to be an inferior, especially when his superior wasn't of noble blood. They acted as if him working under a lowborn was an insult to the entire bloodline. But he didn't care. Being captain made Ercan happy and that was what mattered to Cyrille.

He opened his beak to speak. "I'm honestly not sure, Lady Hanako." He poured some element with two letters on the tube into a beaker. "I am not sure that I'm worthy of such a position."

"But you are a DeRoche," Hanako felt the need to remind him. "You becoming a captain would make your family so proud."

That would be correct. The insults about being a commoner's servant would die down, but that was the least of his worries. "I should not become a captain just because of my heritage." He pointed his index finger at her. "I need to earn such a position just as you did. You did not become captain because of your family tree, I'm sure of it."

It was true. The Nanaringu family was one of the most influential families in Seichi. Though the bloodline had humble roots, they were given an important task by the first Gaur-Matsya, Empress Omikami. When she was at death's door, the Ashtamangala of Seichi tasked the family with guarding three holy relics. A holy sword of light, a brilliant mirror with eight corners, and a piece of jade said to contain the aeon of all the psychics who had died in the past, present, and future. The family was honored to guard the three artifacts with their lives, storing them away deep inside their temple shrine, never to be seen again. On the empress's deathbed, she named Hanako's uncle and loyal guardian, Hinode, to be the next Gaur-Matsya. But such a history was nothing compared to the DeRoche's monopoly on the world.

Still, she hadn't just been given her position. She had to fight tooth and nail for the title of captain. Even then, she felt she hardly deserved the credit for her feats. It was thanks to her time in Eagle Squad under Bianca that gave her the drive to better herself. But alas, maybe she should have stayed in Bianca's shadow. Though Rooster Squad performed worse, Rhea Squad was not exactly stellar, as George would be quick to remind her.

But Hanako did choose to remind him of something. "But you performed so well yesterday."

Cyrille performed the last part of their little experiment, making the beaker fizzle up. "We all performed well yesterday. But the truth is that I don't really feel that I'm powerful enough to become one. Ercan is more durable, Julia is smarter, Yun is stronger, and Shee'vra…" He pondered for a second. "I'm honestly not sure about her, but I am sure she would last longer than me. I mean, imagine me against someone like Bianca, Desiderio, Winona, Gaizka. It would be a closed coffin funeral I assure you."

"But if you use your poison, their fate is sealed," Hanako retorted, feeling a bit more confident about this debate. "Even Mastema cannot handle your toxins."

Many people in Seichin had told her how cowardly and vile the use of poison in combat was. But she never thought of it as any worse than beating somebody to death. It was just another form of survival in this world. The animals were not afraid to use it, so why did humanity feel above it? In fact, she felt that Cyrille was proof that poison use did not equal cowardice. Maybe his way was considered dishonorable to some, but not to her. She felt he had more compassion than most people on this planet.

Cyrille wrote down the results of the test while looking at her with one of his eyes. "Perhaps you're correct. But alas, I wish for Ercan to remain a captain. It would make him happy. I know you're not trying to get me to backstab him or anything of the sort, but he might feel slighted if you voted against him just to get me promoted in his place. But if on the unfortunate scenario that Ercan is booted off, I volunteer as his replacement. I make no promises on my results though." He took off his uncomfortable five fingered rubber gloves and offered his hand to shake. "Do we have a deal then?"

Hanako did not hesitate to shake his chicken feet-like hands. She nodded. "Deal." She would vote for Ercan on his account. Judging from yesterday's battle against Winona, he had gotten much stronger than last time. Maybe all of them would vote for Ercan.

The two turned in their experiment results to a half-asleep Mr. McDooley, hoping they actually did it right.

~ * ~

It was fifth period and the one and only Vural Kyogeki was trying to concentrate in class. It was training time at The Stage, and Ms. Yamauchi was testing out the skills of her students. He was partnered up with Caradoc, Vasanti, and Draghignazzo. They were up against the rest of the sophomore class except for Shee'vra, who was sent to the gym to train her body. So that left seven students that needed an ass kicking.

When the battle started, Vural back flipped into the air, to the bewilderment of his allies. "GO ANTLION FORM!" When he landed on his two feet, he was no longer a human being. He was now a mix between an ant and a lion. He had the light brown exoskeleton and head like an ant but a bristly mane that was similar to a lion. Inside his mandibles were sharp teeth; his hands had two fingers and a thumb that ended in sharp claws and he walked upright like a human being.

He stood there with his arms crossed, waiting for his prey as his red scarf blew in the wind. Though he was to be fighting today, he felt the need to think about whether to elect Ercan in or out. But the horned boy, Draghignazzo, interrupted his thoughts.

The red demon in a colorful patchwork costume spoke up with a smile. "You seem to be at a loss for words, Vural." He flicked his tail that ended in a sharp blade. "I pray you keep your head within this game. Squad Captains are being squashed like flies nowadays. You becoming another fly would be sad." He twirled his two-pronged hook staff around, the bells on the opposite end jingling. "It might just break the hearts of the people."

Caradoc summoned two golden scimitars out of thin air. He had both blades in a reverse grip for a defensive stance. His eyes wandered the open countryside. "They could be anywhere about now. They might begin trying to ambush the strongest one of us first. So keep an eye out, Vural. You sorta die now and this is over really quick."

Vasanti's kris glowed orange for defense. She looked beyond the field of unfertilized farmland and saw something in the sky. She signaled Vural. "Hey buggy! I think Jorun is scouting us! Get ready for the onslaught!"

Vural got ready to dash like a mad ant, crouching down with his hands near the ground. "A ninja is always ready, Vasanti." He took out three shuriken from his pack.

Nobody seemed to care about how ninjas were always ready or whatever. The other three just looked straight at where they saw the girl on the flying horse. As they looked on, they saw roughly two hundred swords flying down toward them like a rain of arrows. Behind the sword onslaught was a red-and-yellow-feathered therapod dinosaur, whose roar could be heard loud and clear from a hundred feet away. Just behind the dinosaur was the girl on the horse, carrying a lance. But as the four saw, this was only three out of seven of them—Amund, Alberto and Jorun.

"Drag, Vasanti! Get to shelter!" Vural ordered them as he tossed his throwing stars at the flying swords to absolutely no effect other than sparks igniting out on impact. "Me and Caradoc got this."

The two listened and Vasanti dashed off while Draghignazzo flew to the farmhouse on his bat-like wings. Caradoc in turn jumped high into the air, some of the blades trailing him. As Vural dodged the swords, the dinosaur got closer. But Vural saw no problem with a thirty-foot Allosaur stomping his way toward him. Instead, he dived into the ground as if it was merely a chunky pool. The swords stuck into the earth in an attempt to catch the antlion.

As Vural was traversing underground as if it was water, Caradoc jumped toward the dinosaur. Alberto roared as he tried to chomp into him with his dagger-sized teeth. But Caradoc just landed on his snout and used him as a stepping-stone, though the Allosaur did accidently bite into several of Amund's flying blades, cutting his mouth and tongue.

But the dinosaur was not his target. The girl on the winged horse was. Jorun prepared her lance to dive down and skewer the boy in the Mars-red armor jumping toward them. "Come on, Pegasus! Let's show this guy how the Valgard Tribe does battle!"

She charged downwards with her lance, but Caradoc was too quick. It was almost as if the rules of Earth's gravity did not apply to him, as if he was an alien from a world with heavier gravity and Earth's gravity was nothing. He sliced the lance tip off with a mere slash. With the other sword, he cut her horse's chest. Pegasus let out a weak snort as both rider and mount fell from the sky.

Pegasus disappeared into nothingness, but Jorun landed cleanly on her own two feet. This was despite the fact that she fell down almost forty feet. She drew out her broadsword and got ready for her next move. She could use her Bellerophon spark to summon her mount again, but that would take time that she didn't have. So as Caradoc landed back on the ground, she charged him. He blocked and dodged her strikes, but had little choice but be on the defensive. Along with Jorun slashing at him, he also had to deal with deflecting the flying swords coming for him, and then deal with the dinosaur charging for him.

As Jorun continued her assault, he found one second's worth of breathing room from the aerial swords. He used this opportunity to go on the offensive with the warrior girl. He readied his Blades of Barsoom and jumped at her. She dived to the right and narrowly avoided the human cannonball, getting her wolf skin cape covered in dust. As she got up, Jorun smiled as she noticed fellow Rhea Squad member, Alberto, behind her. With fellow Valguard tribe member, Amund, supporting her as a storm of swords, she felt unstoppable. She raised her sword in the air and let out a war cry, "FOR FUN AND GLORY, TEAM!" She summoned a unicorn and got onto the saddle, the golden bridle in her hand.

Alberto roared out in reply for his squad mate. Caradoc took his eyes off the floating swords and saw a dinosaur and a horned horse charging straight for him. He knew this was bad news, even as he felt his arm get cut by a sword.

But neither the therapod nor the unicorn reached him. The two found themselves in some sort of quicksand trap, courtesy of Vural, no doubt.

And he was right. The antlion jumped out of the sand like a dolphin ready for action. As he flipped in the air, his first move was to kick the Allosaurus in the back of the head with his heel. Usually this would have no effect on something that big, but Vural had the strength of ten ninja warriors. The collapsing dinosaur made a splash in the quicksand.

As the Burrunjor spark deactivated, the dinosaur turned back into a human boy. Alberto's last words before losing consciousness were "So cool." If he was to lose to anyone, might as well be his idol.

Jorun stood on her unicorn with her blade ready for him. But Vural tossed a sharp kunai at her skull, which she deflected. He then ran on the quicksand as if it was perfectly solid. Jorun tried to cut his head off, but he quickly smacked the sword away and hit her with his open palm. Caradoc watched as Jorun got sent flying back twenty feet. As her body hit the ground, she tumbled out of control as she disappeared.

Vural called out to the blades. "Come and face me, Amund! I know you can!"

Swords from all around The Stage began to home in on the most dangerous enemy like a shining silver river in the sun. Vural dived back underground, entrapping some of the blades. The ninja then popped up to toss up chunks of mud, entrapping the majority of the blades in earth. With a chunk of the blades weighed down or broken, the rest of the weapons flew to one another, combining into a skinny silver boy with a foxskin cape.

"How can one man…." Amund panted and coughed, "…take out a dinosaur so easily?"

He turned his fingers into daggers and slashed at Vural in exhaustion. Vural easily dodged and kicked him into the air. Jumping up after him, he got Amund into his claws. He then turned them both upside down and began to spin in a corkscrew motion.

"ANTLION SPIRALING PILE—" Before he could finish calling out his attack, they had already hit the ground. Amund, The Body of Blades was defeated.

Caradoc didn't even really do anything during all of that. He just had a front seat ticket to an ass kicking. *He just beat three opponents just like that? Including a freaking dinosaur? I'm not sure if even Mastema or Bianca could be so quick. How is Swan Squad not higher up in the ranks?* Though admittedly, Caradoc did feel that his thunder was stolen.

Vural waved to the audience outside The Stage, basking in his glory as he struck a pose under the red sun. "That is the power of MYRMECOLEON! Now who is next to challenge the Master Ninja Vur—?"

A surge of lighting struck the ground. Though rather than from the sky, the electricity came from behind him. Hyperbug Antlion tried to see where the blast came from and saw that it must have come from the farmhouse. He then felt a pain in his chest. Looking down, he found a new hole. Black blood seeped from the near cauterized wound.

Vural could only sigh as he fell to his knees. "Guess I have more to learn." Hyperbug Antlion collapsed onto the now solid dirt.

So I guess another captain falls. But it was no time to think of quips. Caradoc had barely any time to start moving when another line of lighting shot out at him. He started zigzagging to avoid the shots as he approached the farmhouse. He knew who the attacker must have been.

As he dived away from a shot aiming for his head, he saw one of the house's windows shatter. Coming out were two figures. One was Draghignazzo and in his hook was a cloaked man with artificial yellow eyes that wore a helmet with a single spike on top. Lightning surged through the opposition's body as well as his odd scoped thin-barreled lightning cannon. Though the demon boy's hook latched on through the electric man's stomach, there were no sounds of pain. In fact, the electric sniper made no sounds whatsoever. Caradoc recognized him as Hilbert.

The demon tossed Hilbert off of his hook with a heave. Hilbert landed on the ground with a loud clank. The helmeted man's metal eyelids lowered to show irritation. He threw off his tar-covered cloak, exposing his metal body of cogs and electricity. Hilbert engulfed the bayonet of his cannon with electrical energy and stabbed at the fiendish jester, though he caught the attack with his hook. The bells on his costume jingled as Draghignazzo struggled against the machine man.

"May we take it easy for a wee bit?" he playfully asked Hilbert, a black substance preventing the lightning from conducting through his metal weapon. "My stomach has suddenly turned queasy."

Hilbert's only response was using Jupiter to create two metal tendrils from his back. Both tendrils conducted electricity. But before he could strike down the devil, Draghignazzo shot out black tar from his mouth, making an exaggerated "BUUULEEEEEEEH" as he puked it out all over his mechanical classmate. Though such a hot substance would normally leave a man in agony, a machine didn't have nerves. It merely obscured his sensors and irritated him.

"You annoy me, clown," Hilbert said in a monotone voice as he lashed at him with his tendrils. But he detected no impact. The fiend flew backwards out of reach. All he heard was the loud clanging of swords from inside the house.

But what Hilbert did not detect was Caradoc coming from behind him. With a slash from both blades, he was done for. His torso separated from his legs and his head fell from his body. Hilbert's spiked helmet fell off on impact, revealing a human brain protected by thick glass. He was no robot, but a cyborg. Caradoc remembered that Hilbert always did lecture his peers about the difference. It was probably one of the few things that annoyed him. That and Draghignazzo; but Drag annoyed everybody

Caradoc prepared to inflict the finishing blow on him, but was stopped by an electromagnetic field around Hilbert's head. Draghignazzo could not get through it either with his tail-blade. They even had barely any time to escape the shocking tendrils from the torso. All they could do was watch as Hilbert magnified his body back together. When he was finished, Hilbert let out a noticeable shot of steam from a hole that would normally be somebody's mouth.

But before he could aim his weapon at them, a huge blade cut the entire farmhouse in half. Seconds later, a rainbow streak dashed right next to her two allies. Vasanti's glowing red blade cut the brain in the dome right in half, ignoring the electric field around the head just with overwhelming force alone. Hilbert did not even have time to react as he disappeared from the battle.

"Did you boys miss me?" Vasanti asked, expecting gratitude. She frowned upon getting a "meh" from Draghignazzo.

A swordfish with arms and legs exited the door. He had a slender sword in his hands and he shivered upon seeing the three ready for him.

"Oh phooey," Saif said to himself, panicked. "They're all after me now." He got into a defensive position as his sword increased in length and width. "I hope I'm not the last one."

All three of them attacked him at the same time. The swordfish was surprisingly agile for being on land. He blocked the attacks as if his sword only weighed as much as a feather. When they got too close for comfort and his back was to the barn's door, his blade extended by thirty feet to sweep the area. Vasanti hopped over it, Drag flapped his wings, but Caradoc chose to make a huge leap.

Saif felt that Draghignazzo was vulnerable up in the air. He moved back and slapped Vasanti away with his tailfin. He looked up to see that the demon was preparing to inflict pain from above with his hot tar. Saif didn't want that. It would hurt, but it would not kill him. He knew that the demon would go for merely his feet. But being trapped in the sludge would doom him.

So he retracted his sword, pointed it at the jester and quickly extended it. The blade shot out and impaled through Drag's shoulder. The sword kept on extending until he was almost out of sight. He then retracted his blade within a second, with only blood remaining.

But Saif was still worried. He still had two tough students to deal with. One was very fast and the other was very agile. Both were also good with swords. But he held his ground as the barnyard doors opened.

First thing to come out of the barn was a large stream of blood, which covered and disturbed both Vasanti and Saif. Forcing her eyes back open, she saw someone swimming inside the puddle deep blood. As Caradoc came down back to earth, he tried to slice down the shivering swordfish like a spinning twister. But a hand quickly pulled Saif away from the attack. In his place, Caradoc sliced at Sanjay.

All he did was scratch the surface of the skin of the seven-foot tall, bulky man in the metal mask. Sanjay wore a crude imitation of Jivanan Kshatriya armor of chainmail and padded cloth. In his hand was a short, semi-rectangular sword. Sparks flew as the Blades of Barsoom failed to even dent Sanjay's metal skin. The towering brute only shook his head.

Though Sanjay was known to be quite sluggish walking, his reflexes were awfully sharp. When Caradoc tried to aim for his eyes, he found that Sanjay's fingers were around his neck. He lifted him up to eye level and readied his khanda sword to stab him in the stomach. Caradoc still tried to stab at him, but Sanjay merely swatted his swords away. Caradoc kicked the blade out of his hands, but Sanjay just decided to use both hands to suffocate him. He was totally helpless against the masked behemoth as he struggled to breathe. The scene felt like a slasher flick.

Vasanti was unable to help him. She was too busy dueling against Saif, with her on the offensive. Though her blade glowed red, it was still not making any dents in his sword. She wasn't looking down to see that the blood on the ground was spreading quickly toward her. Too late though.

From under her, a bloody skinless hand grabbed her heel. Its nails were as sharp as needles, which dug into her. Vasanti cried out in pain and tried to dash away, dragging him out of the blood pool. The blood boy was completely skinless head to toe, had razor sharp teeth, and only wore a pair of shorts. Vasanti fell over and Tommy jumped on top of her, hissing at her.

"I win! I win!" the skinless weirdo cried out to her with a gross smile. He then turned to Saif and nodded. "Swordnose do good keeping rainbow lady unaware." He would not have been able to grab her if she had kept moving all around. So, credit where credit is due.

"You're welcome, Tommy," Saif replied, not really knowing what to do now. He had nobody to really finish off, so he just took a seat on the ground to wait the simulation out.

So thus, the final two were helpless. Vasanti was about to be skewered by Tommy's claws, and Caradoc's windpipe was being crushed. But when all seemed hopeless, a ball of cooled tar splatted onto Sanjay's face like a pie in a dumb comedy movie. The big guy loosened his grip enough that Caradoc kicked off from his broad chest to escape, crashing into Tommy.

But before Tommy could get up, a two-toed exoskeleton foot met his back. The skinless psychic was sent crashing onto the broad side of the barn, creating a blood print as he collapsed. Vasanti looked back to see Vural was still up and running.

"Hyperbug Antlion is not done yet!" Vural weakly stated to his allies, his enemies, and the audience. He covered his wound as he dashed toward Saif. Behind him was a wounded Draghignazzo.

Saif had barely any time to ready himself as Vural kicked the back of his legs, causing him to flop onto the earth. Caradoc then stabbed the swordfish with both blades while he was prone.

Sanjay was the final opponent. It was four against one, though. But he had no intention of surrendering. He was of Sparrow Squad; he would not disgrace Mastema by showing fear. A slender sword shot out from his gauntlet and he braced himself for four foes.

None of the four's attacks remotely hurt him. No pain registered to him. Not from any of their weapons or even Vural's strikes and Drag's tail-blade. But Sanjay felt his feet sink into the earth. He kept fighting them off, but all of them defended one another. Within two minutes, Sanjay was up to his neck in quicksand. Though none of them could hurt him, Sanjay was not able to fight anymore. Thus, he disappeared from The Stage.

The four celebrated their victory with a quadruple jumping high five.

"Hey, Vural," Caradoc asked him. "Hilbert blasted a hole through you? How are you alive?"

"Yeah, you should be howling in agony," Vasanti stated, kind of creeped out.

Vural puffed out his opened chest, his hands at his hips. "Sheer willpower, my friends," he told them as if it was no problem, "that and the fact that my Antlion form has primitive nerve cells like an insect."

Just as he was finished explaining, he collapsed face first, the final casualty of the fight. It was as if he only got up to steal the scene and then died when finished.

"And here I thought no more captains would know loss," Draghignazzo joyfully mourned as he threw a daisy onto where he had vanished. "Here begins the true downfall of the captains. No longer shall they ever be called kings. The gods falling back down to earth. Tragic." He cried crocodile tears.

Though the demon was just being deliberately melodramatic, Caradoc and Vasanti knew he had a point. Captains did not feel so unreachable in power anymore. How long would it take for the princess to be dethroned or the angel to fall from grace?

~ * ~

It was lunch period and Ercan and Yun were in the library after eating. Yun was working with Mayil on history while Zivot was having a business discussion with Ercan at the opposite end of the table.

"I am going to need you to sign a few papers for me, Ercan," Zivot told him in a professional manner. "You know, as always."

"But we're only going to look for a thief in the park this weekend."

"Doesn't matter. Sign the papers or he's not coming," Zivot flat out replied, not even changing her inflection. "You of all people should know that missions can be more than they seem."

"Alright, fine." Ercan had gotten used to this. Whenever Rooster Squad had a mission, he always had to sign a few contracts. Emile DeRoche must have been quite overprotective of Cyrille because even his own mother always groaned when he told her what he had to do to get Cyrille into a mission. But Ercan scribbled down his signature on the contracts in mediocre cursive. He then passed the papers back to Zivot.

She took a look through each signature and then straightened out the papers before putting them away in a folder. "Thank you very much, Ercan. Master Cyrille's life is now in your hands for the mission. You are responsible for any harm that comes to him, and I'm sure that you will guard him with your life."

Zivot said those same words every time they were done doing this. In fact, he had yet to ever see her not doing some kind of work. She and Mayil were either doing housework, being bodyguards, at school, or training, or doing missions with Eagle Squad, and now getting paid to help Yun with Academics. It occasionally made him wonder if the two ever slept.

Two years ago during a dinner party at Cyrille's, he noticed that while the other partygoers were having fun, those two were still at work. It made him feel bad for them. They were always so alert and uptight all the time. So during the party, he found the courage to ask Zivot out on a date. Though the primary motivation was to get her to look happy for once, he did also find her to be quite cute. The medium-length, strawberry blonde hair and the hips really appealed to him. Plus, she had the whole maid/bodyguard thing going on that he found captivating.

But she quickly shot him down, saying that dating her master's business associate would be "unprofessional." He was disappointed, but he got over it like a normal teenager. He never took it personally against her. It must have been stressful doing her job and he would just be in the way. His infatuation with her faded away, but he never stopped respecting her or Mayil for their service to their master.

But he did feel the need to ask an important question. "How long is Cyrille supposed to be signed off to me like this?" She had once told him that Cyrille was not allowed to watch rated R movies and any horror flicks were out of the question.

She sighed, having a feeling that he would say this. "Until he becomes eighteen, which would be in about five months and fourteen days." She placed the folder neatly into her bag. "Unless Cyrille somehow manages to prove that he can handle responsibility such as becoming a Squa—" She stopped herself, but Ercan got the message. "A strong contributor to the psychic cause." She feigned a cough. "That is what I meant."

"Don't beat yourself up over it," Ercan insisted. He changed to a less professional topic. "So I wonder how Yun is doing on that HW of his."

Zivot showed little interest in the monkey learning about the previous empire, but changed her mind when her partner made an outburst.

"BY SOPHIA'S BLUE REAR END, YOU ARE DIM!" Mayil got out of his seat. "How can you not know that Emperor Barbar Kadosh was the *sixth* emperor of the Kadosh Empire?! Not *second*! Sixth! SIIIXTH!" He stormed past Zivot. "It is *your* turn to teach the banana brain. This is ridiculous!"

He stepped to the exit in a huff. As he left, a squid-headed senior student changed colors from white to green as he made a shushing sound at the disturbance. He then changed his pigment back to white as he focused once again on the book that he lifted with his mind.

Since she was contractually obligated, Zivot took a seat next to the hurt Yun. She looked at his answer and saw a reason for why he had said that Barbar was the second emperor of the Protogenoi Empire. "Don't beat yourself up over such an answer. You're half-right on this one."

"How?" Yun doubted himself.

"Well you see, Barbar the Queller was the second in something. He was the second emperor to create an artifact of Kadosh, after his mother named…" She waited for him to answer.

"Beatrice?" Yun asked hesitantly.

Zivot nodded. "That's correct. And what relic did Barbar create?"

Yun scrunched his mind like dough and gave an answer. "The pauldrons?"

His tutor gave him a smile. "See? You're getting it bit by bit. Now, onto the next question." She turned the page of a textbook titled *Rise And Fall Of The Protogenoi Empire: A Look Back At The First Empire.*

Feeling like he was finished with the library for now, Ercan bid the two farewell. "I'll be going now. Later."

"Going to skewer you on Wednesday," Zivot replied in the most casual way without even looking back.

"Not if I take you down first," Ercan answered back with no trace of spite. It was simply The Stage. No need to take such threats personally.

Ercan did hope that Shee'vra would be ready to fight by then. If not, his sister wouldn't last against Eagle Squad. Bianca would show no mercy. Ercan knew that firsthand.

~ * ~

After school, Shiro and Vasanti were playing a game of cards while Sabelle was playing *Gemhunter* on her crystalcell on the bleachers in the gymnasium. All three seemed quite bored. They were only there to see how Xiu's training would go. They expected some amusing screw-ups from either the master or the pupil. But it was overall kind of mediocre to watch. Turns out the first day would be a slow one. Last time they looked back at them, Shee'vra was being taught the Tiger Fist stance. The sophomore's stance looked quite silly with her fingers tucked into her hands like a tomcat. The fact that the spinning training dummy was more than a match for her was also somewhat amusing, but they got bored watching monotonous training exercises.

"Do you have any fives?" Shiro asked, lacking interest. The one who was losing by a wide margin was always the most bored.

"Go fish," Vasanti answered her, not interested as well. She looked down to the redhead two rows below her. "I'm bored, Sabe. Can't we help with training or something?"

"No, Vas," Sabelle replied without removing her eyes from her game. "This is something Xiu has to do herself. We have no part in this." Word on the street was that Julia was the highest-level gem hunter. She must exceed her and become the Gem Master. But she had twelve more levels to go until then. "Just entertain yourselves with gossip or something."

Shiro tried to think of something interesting that happened to her today. Finding a silly moment in her head, she told the anecdote. "So Vasanti, today Sabe and Dunkeen got in trouble."

The former idol was intrigued. "What could they possibly do to irritate Mr. Jahikah?"

"Well it was less irritating and more confusing to him," Shiro explained. "You see, Dunkeen passed a note to her. The teacher caught him red handed and took it. He then read it aloud."

Vasanti wondered how juicy such a letter could possibly be. She looked at Sabelle, who appeared uncomfortable. Shiro then satisfied her curiosity.

"So, the teacher said 'Spider Vagina' out loud." Shiro smiled. "The end."

She had no idea what the heck that had to do with anything. Vasanti had zero context of what it meant. What did the genitals of an arachnid have to do with anything? And why would Dunkeen give that to her? But alas, it was her turn to tell a story.

"Well today the entire tenth grade class minus Shee'vra went to The Stage. Me, Caradoc, Drag, and Vural were on one team with everybody else on the other team. So while I was dueling against Saif—"

"Who?" Shiro interrupted.

She stopped to jog her friend's memory. "The walking swordfish, Zulfiqar's brother, Falcon Squad, nervous wreck. Ringing a bell?"

The girl in white began to recall. "Oh, yeah. I faced him at the last games. It made me feel bad because he was so jittery as we fought. But then his brother was taken out and then his sword cut an entire mountain in half, killing all three of us."

It was true. Saif Shamshir was stronger than he thought he was. But she continued her story. "As I was saying, as we dueled, Vural took out Alberto, Jorun, and Amund all within about a minute."

"So what?" Shiro cut into the story again. "He's a Squad Captain. Of course he'd win." She said this knowing full well that Alberto could turn into a dinosaur.

Vasanti was beginning to get annoyed. "Can you let me finish?"

"Okay."

"Good. Well after stealing Caradoc's spotlight like the attention whore he is, he was shot through the back by Hilbert."

"That's not amusing at all," Shiro chided her friend with a stern look. "I, for one, find nothing fun about someone getting mortally wounded."

"I never said this was supposed to be amusing," she told her, hoping for no more interruptions. "I was just saying another captain has gone down just like that." She made her hand make a diving motion. "Well, he didn't 'die' until he took everybody else out, but you know what I mean."

"Maybe?" Shiro had no idea what the message of this story was.

"You don't, do you?" Vasanti questioned.

"No," she admitted. "All I got was fight scene and Vural getting horribly wounded."

"Well what I mean is that another captain has fallen." Vasanti put up seven fingers to emphasize her point. "That means in the last two days, *seven* captains were defeated. And here we thought they were all way out of our league."

Shiro got the gist of what she was saying now. "Well, of course the power gap is changing. We are getting older now, more mature, and thus stronger. The captains are early bloomers with already powerful sparks. But now that we know so much more about our sparks, chances are we and the other non-captains are beginning to catch up to their level. I mean, it just makes sense."

Vasanti could not really argue with that logic. But it did leave an argument that even the captains had yet to find out how much they could do. They focused their attention on the gym mats to see Xiu sparring with Shee'vra. Though Xiu was not even trying at all, Shee'vra still couldn't even touch her. After a few attempts, the master just simply grabbed her apprentice's forearm and threw her over her shoulder. No fancy spark tricks, just simple technique.

"You have a lot to learn," Xiu told the prone girl as she encircled her like a predator. "But that's only natural. It took me about three years to get to where I am now at just one style."

"Three years?" Shee'vra questioned, distraught at how long it would take to even be remotely good at it. Perhaps it was true that the later your spark awakens, the harder it is to learn how to fight.

"Yes, three years," Xiu repeated to her. "And Master always told me I was a fast learner. So the question is…" She brought her face down to her pupil's level. "…Are you?"

An alarm went off right inside her bag. Xiu was reminded of something she had to do. She went to check her cell and saw that in five minutes she was due to meet her new captain.

"What's it today, great master?" Sabelle dryly asked, hardly looking at her. "Are you done with today's training montage?"

She ignored the fact that Sabelle was sassing her. "I have a meeting with Desiderio and the rest of Heron Squad," Xiu replied, grabbing her stuff to leave.

"That's nice I guess," Sabelle feigned interest. Though inside, she did feel quite jealous that Xiu managed to be in the same squad as the hottest guy in Aeon Sophia.

Xiu quickly helped Shee'vra back up. "That's all for today. Now go eat something healthy, remember what I taught you, and read that book I got you." She was out the door.

This is going to take forever. Shee'vra panted in exhaustion. She thought sports like soccer and volleyball were arduous, but this was a whole new level. But at least she seemed to have the Tiger hand down a bit. She wondered how she would make use of this with air powers.

The other three girls of Xiu's little clique also got ready to leave.

"Later, Sheev," Sabelle told her with a bit of unease. "It's almost 4:30 and Winona is going to train us and break us like horses."

"This is going to blow," Vasanti added in fear of what their captain would sic on them to get them alert and ready. Shiro opened the door and they were gone, leaving Shee'vra in the gym with only a few others.

The new girl looked around to see Sanjay still with his metal mask on lifting a hundred pound weights in each hand as a warm-up, Tommy (with skin over his flesh) climbing a rope with no knots to keep his feet steady, Jorun and Alberto sparring as they disputed whether *Pony Paradise* was better than *Hyperbug Force Go!* or not, and Ludmila dueling with Saif to train her youngest squad member in the art of swordplay.

But Shee'vra had had enough training for today. She sweated heavily, her joints were achy, and she really needed a drink of water. So she decided to get ready to go home. The bright side of the Academy was that there was no school on Fridays. That day along with Saturday and Sunday were meant to be for missions. Each Squad had to complete at least one per week.

~ * ~

Xiu traversed the student's dorm building. She had rarely been in here other than to occasionally meet Sabelle and the others. Coincidently, all the members of Rooster Squad lived off campus so she usually had little reason for going. As she traversed the halls, she looked for the third floor public quarters. She soon found her destination.

The room had the appearance of a living room—couches, CV, tables, etc. Waiting for her as promised was her new leader lying back on a couch half asleep. Xiu could not help but notice that his top was mostly unbuttoned to show most of his chest. At the table, Dunkeen, Petra, and Draghignazzo were having an early dinner of Qian food— pork dumplings, steam cooked noodles, shrimp, the works. They even had fortune cookies, which Xiu could say for a fact was an Enotitan thing. Dunkeen was looking at his numbers.

"So Petra, what are your lucky numbers?" he asked the still chewing girl with the long pigtails. "I got myself here 4, 10, 23, 54, and 69." Drag could not help but snicker at the last one as he ate his noodles. "But since none of those numbers are my age or anything, I don't think my fortune applies. I have the saddest feeling success is not going to come to me."

"I honestly don't care," was really the only thing Petra said as she chewed on her duck sauce chicken with sharp teeth. She looked to her left to see the new recruit. "Hey, it's the girl who kicked your ass yesterday."

Petra was giving Xiu a scowl already. Maybe she didn't trust new recruits. Maybe she was too fond of the old member to just deal with a replacement. Or maybe she was just jealous that puberty was nicer to Xiu. With her D's compared to Petra's A-cup, who could honestly blame her?

Draghignazzo was first to greet her with an open hand. "Welcome to Heron Squad! Put her there, pal!"

Out of courtesy, she shook the demon boy's hand. Feeling a strong buzzing sensation on her hand, she reflexively pulled away. Draghignazzo fell onto the floor laughing. Xiu glared, just now seeing the joy buzzer in his hand. Petra and Dunkeen more or less ignored him too.

"I'm so sorry, you must forgive me, miss. I honestly wasn't able to resist," Drag insisted, still the only one laughing in the room. He pulled a chair for her. "But let's have a seat and enjoy the feast. You won't be able to resist in the least."

Xiu immediately saw a Whoopee cushion on the chair. She grabbed it and pressed it right on demon's face. Drag still felt a compulsion to laugh as it made a fake fart.

Petra just shook her head. "That's enough, Drag. It's pissing everyone off," She told him as she swallowed her food.

"I must agree with Petra here," Dunkeen said as he tossed some shrimp into his gullet. "It wouldn't be a smart idea to scare off our brand new Heron Squad member within thirty seconds. Desiderio would not like that. He summoned her for the sake of a professional conversation and doesn't want to miss it. So please, enough with the pranks."

"Alright, alright, fine. I shall stop for now," The prankster conceded. "Hey Desi! Get up! The new girl is here!"

Desiderio slowly got up from the couch and put his expensive footwear back on. Lying around wasn't something most other captains would be doing if they were expecting to meet someone soon. "Evening, Xiu." He took her hand and gently kissed it. "I'm sure you're ready to discuss important matters."

She had little idea what they were going to talk about. She was not part animal, so she was pretty sure he wasn't trying to hit on her. Maybe kissing someone's hand was an upper class Titlacua thing. She took her hand back. "So what is it that we're discussing?"

Desiderio buttoned his shirt up and took a seat at a nearby table.

His voice got more businesslike. "We're going to have a professional discussion. I insist you take a seat." A pen and paper were already in front of him.

She had no reason to refuse. She sat down opposite him. She looked around awkwardly and was the first to speak. "Sooo? What is this about exactly?"

"I'm sure that you know why I brought you here today," he told her, acting more like Bianca than himself. "But on the off chance you do not, I will jog your memory." He picked up his pen and began to write. "We're going to discuss your former leader, Ercan Ao'Si, and your experiences with him. It's to determine how I shall vote next week. Believe me when I say I intend to take this whole discussion very seriously."

Xiu's heart sunk. Her new captain was essentially telling her to say everything wrong with her old one. After two years of mediocre missions and poor stage performances, she would no doubt have a lot to say about him. But at the same time, what she would honestly have to say would definitely make Desi vote against him. But lying would also hurt Ercan and the others in the long run too. Besides, she had a feeling that he would know if she was lying.

"So I insist that you tell me all the pros and cons of Ercan Ao'Si's position as captain of Rooster Squad," Desiderio prompted. "I promise I will make no biases one way or the other. My opinion is solely based on your word. So what do we start with? The good or the bad?"

"The bright side first, I guess," Xiu told him. "Ercan is…" she tried to find the right word, "…enthusiastic about his position. He gets up early for missions and is always the first to enter dangerous places. He's cooperative with his squad mates, even with people like Julia…" her eyes began to look down, "…or me. Maybe he's just naturally forgiving, I don't know. So he has the spirit of leadership down."

Desiderio made sure to write it all down. "And his negative attributes as captain?"

Xiu scrambled around in her head on what to say. When she was ready, she softly spoke up. "Well ironically, for a guy that makes chains come out of his body, he kept the rest of us on a very loose leash." She remembered blowing off meetings to hang out with her friends and he wouldn't even lecture her. "He didn't really berate us very much if we just ran into the fray. He was kind of a doormat of a leader. Then there was the fact that more often than not, the bad guy of the week would get away. Though it was honestly less that we were weak and more that we had bitten off more than we could chew. His investigation skills aren't exactly up to snuff either, though I admit I'm not one to be talking." She forced a giggle. "But the fact is, maybe Ercan was just not up to snuff compared to captains like you. You, Alexandru, Bianca, Mastema—most of us stand no chance comparing to any of you. We work our asses off and we're still not at your level."

Desiderio stopped writing and looked up to her. "I, for one, do not believe I am worthy to be compared to the others. They always say top three instead of top four, do they not? But those three have struggled all their lives to be where they are now." He began to lament. "In fact, I feel that most students in this place have conflict in their lives they wish to forget. The path us psychics tred is never easy, and I assure you it never will be."

His words got her lost deep inside her head. Thinking about conflicts made her remember. They showed up so suddenly, attacked out of nowhere, swore to leave no survivors. Fires were set around the whole town. Her friends, neighbors, and horses all slaughtered indiscriminately. Her parents killed by this one man with a wide brimmed hat and glasses that reflected the chaos. If Yeren had not come, the Manticore would have finished the job.

"Xiu. Xiu! Are you well?"

She shook her head and saw Desiderio looking concerned. She had been staring into nothingness for a quite a bit of time. "Are you okay? You seem to be uncomfortable. If you want, we can continue this later."

"NO! NO!" Xiu quickly stated, causing him to flinch back. She steadily composed herself. "I mean no. Sorry. I was just remembering something totally not relevant to the moment. Please continue." She locked that memory away back where it came from.

Desiderio was skeptical but went on with what he needed to say. "If you feel you can. So next question, how personally involved are you with Ercan Ao'Si?"

"Not as personally as your meaning of *personal*." Xiu forced herself to make a quip to lighten her mood.

He was far from offended by mere facts. "Touché. It seems Ercan doesn't know what he missed. What a shame. Though you're not exactly my type, you are a very lovely woman."

She couldn't help but turn a bit red, but she tried to retain a professional demeanor, and he better keep his. "But in all seriousness, to be honest, I never really hung out with them."

That got his attention. "And why is that? Are you too good for them?"

Xiu did not want that to be the answer. She quickly tried to explain herself. "W-well it's not like I hate them or I think they smell or something. It's just that I find Julia to be an insufferable nerd who thinks she knows everything. I live with Yun and I can tell you he drives me up the wall. Cyrille's actually one of the most pleasant people I've met but it's sort of embarrassing to be seen around a giant chicken lizard. Ercan…well." She got lost in thought.

"Ercan what?" Desiderio asked, smiling, picking up on something. "Don't tell me. Are you nervous around 'Ercan the Unbreakable'? Are you just scared to show how you feel around him? But you cannot just hold a charade ranging from indifference to ambivalence forever. So you keep away from him in order to not get lost in his deep lazuli eyes?"

Xiu got redder as she tried to look away. "W-what's lazuli exactly?"

"Oh, you know. That deep purple color. The color of royals. Everyone wants to be royal or be with a royal. So is Ercan your prince?"

"What?"

Desiderio made it simpler for her to understand. "Are you attracted to your former captain?"

"And why would I tell you?" Xiu said, her temper flaring up. "So you can make rumors? Rumors that are, of course, *false*?"

That did nothing to convince him. "So your answer is yes then?"

Xiu could not fool him no matter how hard she tried. She gave in. "Maybe."

Desiderio could see why Ercan would've never tried to date the spirited young lady. Ercan must have been put off by her more vitriolic traits and thought she hated him. Vural told him about this kind of character trait once or twice and he had met girls like that before. But he knew firsthand that underneath that entire facade was a woman who was dynamite to romance.

"Well then, what do you see in your scarlet savior?" Desi pressed on playfully, putting down his writing utensil. "I'm sure it isn't just his personality. I can tell these things."

"By Sophia, you're an ass," Xiu snapped at him. "You're right. The personality is not the big draw. If I wanted to date a guy with a 'wonderful personality,' I'd be seeing Cyrille." She tried to see the things she saw in him. "Though his non-judgmental attitude probably helps a bit. And maybe his sheer willingness to follow the psychic way to the letter. Or maybe the fact that he has absolutely no air of mystery to him. He was born to a psychic, raised, and that's it. It's just so upfront it hurts. Let's face it—you and I have had difficulty in our lives that changed us into who we are." Those uncomfortable thoughts tried to crawl back into her head. "But his life is just so mundane it's almost refreshing."

Desi faked dismissiveness and looked at the clock. "Eh. Sounds boring to me."

Xiu pounded the table. "Hey, screw you, man! I'm here trying to tell someone how I feel about a guy and you just—" She realized he was messing with her. The bastard. "But yeah, maybe it's also because I find him hot and stuff."

"It's the clothes, right?" He hoped she agreed with him.

"Hell yes, it's those tight clothes!" she told him bluntly to his face. "It's like a friggin second skin!"

Desi prayed she'd answer this one with as much gusto. "And the whole chain thing is pretty damn kinky? The shit you two can do alone, huh?"

Xiu covered her burning red face. "T-that's just weird. You made it weird." Those thoughts were definitely not first date thoughts.

"Perhaps so" Desiderio replied, content with her answer. "But from what I can gather, you love him." He made a heart out of his two hands.

That struck a chord but felt not exactly true. "To be honest, I doubt it's actually love." She'd read about love in sappy romance stories and flicks. How undying those couples were and how they would die without one another. She had rationalized that she could live without him. At least tried to.

"Lust then?" Desiderio was being obnoxious on purpose; she just knew it.

But he was not wrong either. She had occasionally thought about him late at night when she was bored. But what teenager doesn't have that feeling once in a while? In fact, she was sure that if she offered herself to Ercan straight up, he would accept it wholeheartedly.

"It's a little bit of both, you could say. I guess." She chose the road in the middle of the two feelings.

"Ah, so lost then? The in-between of love and lust but stronger than like." Desiderio shook his head in pity. "Such an emotional limbo." He never personally had to deal with such things. Every girl he was with was told straight up that he was non-committal. It was also why he explicitly made a rule that he not see any girls from the academy. It would be too awkward and could lead to unprofessional actions on his part.

Xiu groaned at the portmanteau of words. "That sounds stupid."

"Perhaps so." He shrugged. "But it's not my problem." He then changed back to his more serious tone. "But as you have just proven to me, you cannot be trusted to give an unbiased view of your old captain." He put his writings away. "But that is of no matter. I've made my choice either way. If you're telling the truth, I find him to be not adequate enough for the job. Though he is powerful, his role in Rooster Squad at this point could have been filled by anyone. He seems to be nothing out of the ordinary. But if you're telling white lies to make your dreamboat look better, I might as well just vote against him," he gave a tired sigh, "which I intend to do."

Xiu's green eyes shrunk in worry. She totally screwed this up for him. The worst part, she was completely honest. She felt she had no choice but to speak the truth. But now she could assume at least two people would be against him. Winona was probably still butthurt about losing against him and would vote him off out of spite, and now Desiderio questioned his competence as leader.

"Sorry I had to make that choice," Desiderio apologized. "And sorry for making you tell all. But it's for the sake of people's lives, psychic and hylic alike. And from experience, they'll always blame the Squad Captain, no matter how well he or she performs. You may resent me now, but I'll be saving you and him more pain in the long run." He got up and put his hand on her shoulder. "If it makes you feel better, I promise to not tell a soul about your true feelings." He looked toward the other three members, who had just seen and heard everything. "That includes you three. If I hear that what was said in this room has spread, I 'll be sure to punish all three of you in the most brutal nonviolent way possible." He then playfully shrugged. "Or I'll just sic our newest member on you three." Petra, Dunkeen, and Draghignazzo all knew better than to disobey him. Though he was a very fair leader, deliberately disobey him and your punishment would be swift and brutal. They all quickly started speaking up.

"I didn't hear shit!" Petra exclaimed, shaking her head. "Not a damn thing! No!"

"Though it may be somewhat tempting to cry out," the jester stated, "I value my tongue more than temptation."

"I already knew all that romantic stuff," Dunkeen admitted. "It's probably like one of those romantic subplots in a movie or a book series where they act like they don't like one another. But in secret they are gaga for their soul mate. But it takes an ungodly long time for them to just spit it out, to the point that fans only into the series for the romance start getting really pissed off about it. Soon enough the writer is in what some people call a Catch 22. That means that a person is trapped between two choices with no perfect answer. If you just get them together really quickly like that, viewers get satisfied and either drop the series or only want to read specifically about their love life. But if you leave them hanging, the audience starts to get even more impatient. And let's not get into the idea if one or both of the potential couple have other potential romantic interests. Then it gets very ugly. When that happens—"

"Shut up, Dunkeen!" Petra elbowed him. He was rambling again.

Desiderio then turned to Xiu. "See? Our secret."

Feeling grateful for such loyalty, she managed to mumble her gratitude as quickly as she could. "Thankyouiguess."

Desi clapped his hands together. "Perfect. Now it's been a long school day for us all and I'm sure you are hungry." Xiu's grumbling stomach gave it away. "And since two of our fellow squad members have insatiable appetites," he looked at Dunkeen and Petra, who both shrugged sheepishly, their plates once full completely devoured to the morsel, "I made sure to order more Qian food. Are you fine with that?"

"Yeah, sure, of course. Qian food sounds fine," Xiu told him, glad to have a meal after the hassle of being a trainer. Just then, the takeout guy was at the entrance. Desi gave him the money plus a tip, and the five feasted together as one big happy squad.

~ * ~

It was 11:30 and Mastema was still in his personal gym surrounded by mirrors. He lived on top of the SAIS with his grandfather. At this point his elder was asleep, but he had been awake for the last few hours doing nothing but honing his strength, skill, and reflexes. With his halberd of red light in hand, he maneuvered against imaginary enemies. Floating eyes surrounded the entire room, shooting down at him with their lasers. Mastema moved about the room, deflecting the shots and twirling his polearm to shield himself. To prevent his family from waking up, he made the whole room go silent—no footsteps, no blast sounds, so grunts of pain, not a sound.

Sweat covered his entire body. It was as if it had rained inside and the drops were trickling from his head and shoulders down his chiseled chest and abs. His shoulder-length hair stuck to him like a poor quality adhesive. He felt himself hit by an eye blast on the shoulder. Though the eyes were set to their weakest power, it still felt like a bee sting.

As he kept going on and on, he was hit more and more times. Eventually, the yellow eye in the swarm of blue saw its master being overwhelmed with shots and made a bright flash. Immediately, the dozens of eyes stopped their barrages.

Mastema fell onto one knee. With a wave of his hand, sound came back. He could finally hear his own panting as he was on the verge of collapsing from exhaustion. Creating his dark wings, the floating eyes went back into the horde of blue lights. Hearing footsteps behind him, he clenched his halberd as tight as possible.

Looking back, he saw the captain of Eagle Squad within the mirror. Though she remained stone-faced, her voiced had a tint of concern. "You're overworking yourself more than usual, Mastema. I implore you to stop." She exited the mirror and entered the real world.

The angel willed his weapon out of existence, feeling safe. "I feel a need to do this. I feel…vulnerable." The eyes blinked under his wings.

Bianca took a deep breath. "Alright, what got you so distressed?" Mastema was hesitant to answer her. "Just let it out. I'm not going to criticize you."

Feeling safe, Mastema answered her. "I heard Vural was also defeated on The Stage. Though it's true that he defeated his foes before that…he succumbed to his wounds soon after."

"And why does this concern you?" she questioned him, leaning on the mirror. "Vural's impulsive, that was bound to happen eventually."

"Perhaps…but I worry because many captains have been losing their edge lately." He visibly frowned. "It got me thinking that perhaps…I'm not good enough."

Bianca hated when he got like this. Always talking about the accomplishments of his family—never about his own. It was almost irritating if not for the fact that as a Mattatron, he truly did have a ton to live up to. Camael overthrew an Empire, Raziel slayed Egil, The Duke of Undeath in the War of Nergal, Raphael killed Jalil in the Manticore-Ifrit War—all feats that made the history books, though if you looked at it in a more cynical direction, each descendant's feat was less glorious than the last. Maybe Mastema had caught on to that and intended to break the cycle. But his health would only get worse at this rate. She had to stop him.

"And why do you say that?" Bianca questioned. "You are number one in the Academy, and your father, grandfather, and great-grandfather were all Ashtamangala. Your skill is fine, just rest for now."

Mastema shook his head. "That gives me all the more reason to work harder. Those three left great legacies behind them. I feel a drive to strive higher than them."

"You're still a student. They accomplished what they did after graduation. Just focus on the now."

"But, Princess—"

A loud slap echoed within the square room. He put a hand on his stinging cheek. His eyes were wide as she glared directly into them. She was not having any of this. It was for his own good.

"Don't you dare ever hope about one-upping your family. You should not ever dream of trumping their actions. They had no choice but to fight insurmountable odds for the sake of order. But at the same time, each one made the world a better place because of their actions. Hoping to outdo your family just means that you're hoping for someone or something bigger than anything the world has ever seen. The world does not need such an event. It does not deserve it."

Mastema thought long and hard on what she said. Her father was the Shrivatsa of Titlacuan and king of the entire country. She had a lot to live up to as well. But she either did not let it bother her or she hid it well. He shook his head as he had his wings disappear.

"I am…sorry, Princess. I was pigheaded…again." He looked down at the floor, ashamed of his perceived selfishness.

Her expression softened as she felt relief. "It's alright. To be honest, I feel a slight bit of concern as well. But it's not that we are stagnating. It is just that the others are catching up to us." She clasped his chin in her fingers. "This is a good thing. We've already learned nearly every trick in our sparks. The others are just learning more and more. With hope, these next few years will have the strongest graduates ever seen in the Academy."

Mastema gently removed her hand. "I understand. But please…try to refrain from entering my quarters. If you're caught, the others will have…ideas."

It was true. As the Princess of Titlacuan and him from the exalted Mattatron line, a rumor about the two in an illicit affair would risk damaging the relations between their nations. "I'm sorry. I didn't mean for my words to come off that way."

Mastema cracked a small smile. "Don't worry…you are forgiven." He put on his shirt hanging on the rail, covering his upper body. "I'm going to sleep now. I recommend you do too." He turned toward the door. "Goodnight…Bianca."

"Sleep well," she replied quietly but warmly.

Mastema heard her phase back into the mirror. Though he was loath to admit it to others, he felt at his most comfortable around her. In fact, if his grandfather forced him into marriage, she would be his first choice. For the longest time, he imagined what events such a union would lead to. *Would they stay in Enotita? Would he become King of Titlacuan? Would one not be able to become an Ashtamangala?* He had no idea. Such a union had never occurred before. But if he were a braver man, he would be willing to learn.

Hopefully, both would live long enough to have a chance. A psychic's lifespan was always unpredictable. As he thought of these emotions that made his heart beat, the bright yellow-gold eye trailed behind him.

He delicately held the yellow light in his hands. "Come, Aureolin. We need our rest for tomorrow." The eyeball rocked back and forth in response, whistling a happy tune.

Sacred Texts

He did not like the orange clothes one bit. He had been wearing them since early this Saturday morning. Just today, Ewen had been transported to none other than Prisoner's Perch. An island in the middle of the Atlin Ocean, Prisoner's Perch was predictably a maximum-security prison dedicated to detaining psychic criminals.

It seemed like no easy feat, but there were ways to keep them in line. For starters, a collar was put around Ewen's neck. It was lined with a material known as sarkic, a rare metal that locked his aeon down. Without being able to use his aeon, he might as well not have a spark. Sarkic stone was integral to the uprising against the Protogenoi Empire. When eight in ten psychics sided with the empire, hylics needed all the support they could get and sarkic was the greatest equalizer they got. More than a few powerful Protogenoi generals lost their lives due to a sarkic-laced arrow. Nowadays it's more often used to help detain psychics. Just touching the material shut down the flow of aeon.

A tiny bright side was that every psychic had their own cell. He had a toilet, a sink, a cold shower, a desk, and a bed. Rather than jail bars, he was trapped behind a giant steel door. The only kind of opening on the door was a spot where the guards slid in a food tray three times a day. Each hour from 8 a.m. to 10 p.m., a horn blew, signifying an hour had passed. He would have an hour and a half to be outside in cuffs each day. It was a privilege that he had no intention of losing. But overall, his superiors were right. It was going to be a boring five to ten years. He just prayed there would be more to do if he behaved.

But he still had reasons to feel proud of himself. Ewen had plenty of chances to tell the cops all he knew about the Lefty Gang in exchange for a smaller sentence. But he was no snitch. First, the wrath of his boss would descend down upon him like a meteor. But second, it would put the others in danger—Louiz, Asterion, Sharlie, and Muvumo. They would be annihilated if the hideout were ever found. Not to mention that the reason he was in this place would be all for naught. Even if his four comrades in crime escaped, they would lose the money. Without the money, Boss Reliquit would throw them away for not being useful to anyone.

But that was enough of thinking about his predicament. Ewen had all the time in the world to think about that. He heard that Saturday was spaghetti night at the very least. He lay back on his bed and waited for his favorite meal.

~ * ~

Zuo found building 22 on Longoos street. It was a five-story high brick apartment complex. He was told to meet an associate here. He had to figure out more about the Artifacts of Kadosh and the library was a waste of time. All he learned was the history of the Emperors and Empresses who made the artifacts in the first place. Nothing deeper than that, and he knew his superiors knew something he didn't.

So he called an associate of the Gang who knew where to find things. Zuo was admittedly unsure about this guy, but he felt it was better than just letting his bosses use him as a tool for their own gain. He was going to figure out what the damn things did even if it killed him.

He opened the door to the rooftop of the building. Wary of a possibly trap, he entered slowly, the symbol on his chest lit up for anyone to see. He looked about, ready to draw his weapon out of his cane in case this was an ambush. A snakelike voice came from behind him.

"Nice fedora, dork."

He swiftly spun around. What Zuo saw was some sort of humanoid serpent dragon demon. He had coal black scales, large fangs, two horns, bright yellow irises, and a long purple forked tongue. This creature was standing exactly where he had just entered and Zuo had not even heard him.

The old man did not take any chances. He decided to warn him upfront. "You attack me, and you die without me even lifting a finger."

The mysterious creature merely held his hands up with a smile that showed many more fangs inside its maw. "I don't intend to hurt you, Zuo Xuanzang." He had never given his name during the call. "I merely intend to asssssissst you." His tongue leaked a slushy liquid every time he said a word with an *s* in it.

Zuo kept his nerves in check. "Well, if you know my name, I need to know yours. We need more trust in this world and it's damn hard to trust anything looking like a serpent from Hell." He stared him down through his tinted glasses.

The serpent dragon man answered without a second thought. "Fair enough. My name issssss…Cianfa."

Zuo had heard of such a name before. That name originated during Protogenoi times but had lived on as an uncommon name in parts of Titlacuan, particularly the Florentino region. He thought about it for a bit but rejected the idea. There was no chance *that* Cianfa could ever be still alive.

"Sssssspeechlesssss?" Cianfa playfully tilted his head. "I'm ssssurprisssed. Most enforcersssss of the Lefty Gang would have tried to kill me by now. But you're sssssmart. They were not and paid dearly for it."

Now he started to feel uneasy. This Cianfa guy had all but admitted to killing members of the Lefty Gang. And for some reason, he was still associated with them. His bosses were unforgiving of such slights. *How is this bastard still alive?* His bosses should be sending droves of goons at him. He was either extremely strong, his superiors didn't care, or this Cianfa guy was extremely valuable to the gang. Zuo assumed all of the above.

Cianfa tapped his foot, almost bored. "You know. You could at leasssst make a little ssssound. It'ssss rude, you know."

Zuo snapped out of his daze and replied in a cordial manner. "Apologies for my rudeness. Let's get to business."

"With pleasssssure," he hissed with a grin. Zuo smelled some odd yet distinct odor coming from him. His nose was not as strong as it used to be, but this guy must have released one strong pheromone or something.

A rattling sound came from someplace close. Out of the corner of Zuo's eye, he saw a large python come out of one of the many nooks and crannies on the roof. Zuo was no herpetologist, but he didn't recall hearing about any pythons with a rattle or hood. The snake slithered slowly to what he assumed to be its master. Balanced on the top of its head was what appeared to be a very old worn out book. Cianfa took the tome from it and gently patted it on the head.

"Thank you, Kiji." Cianfa blew some dust off in Zuo's general direction and showed the book to him. On the cover was a bright blue glowing sapphire of sorts, shaped like a crescent moon. The snake master stretched out his hand, tempting Zuo to grab it from him. "Go ahead. Take it. It won't bite." He flickered his tongue.

Zuo reached out and gently took it from him. Looking closer, he saw how old it was. The pages were ripped up, the ink wearing out, the spine broken. There wasn't even a name on it. But he knew better than to ask questions. Though he was always told by his mother to never trust snakes, he felt odd sincerity within this Cianfa fellow. But then again, the truth might just be worse than the lie in this case.

"How old is this book?" Zuo asked, skimming through the pages, "two hundred years or something?"

"Three hundred," Cianfa corrected him almost immediately. "I recommend you keep it sssssssafe. It isss the only one I could find." Zuo watched as the python wrapped around its master's leg. "It would be a ssssshame if it went misssssing."

Zuo looked on in shock as the snake began to enter inside Cianfa's stomach. There really shouldn't have been room for it, but it fit inside completely and without leaving any trace.

"I recommend you start reading sssssoon." Cianfa began to walk away. "Your mind will be blown at what some pssssychics can pull off."

Cianfa stopped smiling for a moment when he heard a sound. Zuo heard it too. It came from behind the building in the alleyway. It sounded like something was trying to be forced open. Both decided to look down to see the commotion. The two saw five crooks trying to break inside with a crowbar. No doubt they intended to steal from the innocent residents.

"Look at thosssse kenoma bastardsssss," Cianfa commented with contempt, using an archaic insult for hylics. "Like vermin, they only prey on the weak and defenssselesssss. In the ssssunlight, they all flee from our eyesss." He opened his hand to create a floating orb of green liquid. "What filth. There are too many in thisssss world." The orb grew to become as big and wide as a car and floated just above the crooks. "Thesssse kenoma really sssshould learn their place."

Before Zuo could say anything about it, the sphere dropped down on the unsuspecting petty thugs. The ball exploded on impact, covering the thieves in green toxins. Immediately, the five fell to the ground, screaming in agony. Their bodies racked and twisted as the liquid seeped into their skin, melting them layer-by-layer. The poison atrophied their muscles, preventing any escape and forced them to wallow within the sickly green pool.

Cianfa was getting a kick out it as if he was watching his favorite sports team. His chin rested upon his hand as he leaned down to watch the carnage. "You really sssshould watch. I esssspecially like it when they try to crawl away like a baby."

Though Zuo refused to look, he still felt like he was about to vomit. He could hear their cries for help and he was able to hear the burning toxins melting their skin off. And here this snake freak was just looking at it with the amusement of a circus spectator. If he wasn't convinced before, he now knew he was bargaining with a complete sociopath.

Within thirty seconds, the screams ended. Zuo found the courage to look down and did not like what he saw. The bodies were half melted, most of the remaining flesh looking like wet dough. He saw many bones, such as rib cages and fingers and jaws and eyes were still melting on the ground. Worst of all, this demonic psychic now just appeared bored.

Cianfa shook his head, disappointed that it was over. "Well that'ssss that. They're dead and nobody will misssss them."

Though it seemed almost suicidal, Zuo felt the need to at least say something. "Why did you do it?"

"They were just random burglarssss," he replied without remorse. "Probably jusssst a bunch of sssssickos trying to get money for their next drug fix." His fang-filled grin was amongst the most disturbing he had witnessed. "If anything, I did them a favor. It's like putting down a sssssssick dog to end itssss missssssery."

"But to die like that?" Zuo argued. "Can you say they deserved to become a fleshy puddle?"

Cianfa still gave zero damns. "Well this is Ssssorchos the city with the highesssst crime rate in all of Enotita. If anything, I'm doing thissss city a favor. The police sure won't." He began to contemplate. "That doesss give me an idea what to do thissss week."

He got what he meant, and Zuo didn't like the sound of it. "How can you just not care about such actions?" he angrily called him out. "What makes you think you can just go around killing people left and right?"

Cianfa merely tsk-tsked and placed a hand on his shoulder. He didn't even care that touching Zuo made it feel as if his own shoulder was in a vise. He didn't seem to even flinch.

"Tell me, Zuo?" he tightened his grip, "do you honessssstly care about thossse kenoma?"

Though their demise was awful, the grizzled veteran could not find it in himself to actually have an emotional connection about the deaths he just saw. "No."

Cianfa seemed almost confused by the reply. "Then why are you making ssssuch a big deal out of it, drama queen?" He spat a green lob of poison off the edge of the building. "There are too many kenoma in this world anyway. Trimming a few won't hurt them too much. Sssssso why not get rid of a few crookssss that many will be glad are gone?" He gave an uncaring shrug. "Pleroma like ussss sssshouldn't care about getting rid of a few. The ratsss will just mate and reproduce quicker than we can poissssson them."

Though he had a wide fanged grin, Zuo saw how empty and void his eyes truly were. He just knew this reptile would be cold-blooded even if he were human. But at this point, there was no use in debating with this psycho and fighting him just sounded like a death wish. Zuo merely stepped back and bowed, book in hand.

"I thank you for the text, Cianfa. I have much reading to do today." Zuo wanted to leave as quickly as possible.

Cianfa waved him off. "Good, good. Don't forget to read chapter two. It hasss the info you are looking for. All about Emperor Barbar and the pauldronssss." He looked at the symbol on Zuo's chest. "Nice sssspark you got there. I hurt you, but you hurt me back far more. Loving it." He moved his shoulder a bit after so much discomfort. "From one Pleroma to another, what's your sssspark's name?"

He would probably not allow him to refuse, so he allowed him to know. "My spark is called Cain. Yours?"

Cianfa suddenly sprouted black dragon wings with a bright green membrane. "The form you ssssee in front of you issss Azi Dahaka." He began to flap his wings. "I bid you farewell."

As Cianfa flew into the distance, Zuo had the feeling he was off to the underbelly of Sorchos, specifically to find more prey. He probably didn't even care that he would be killing crooks, just that they were hylics, and being criminals just gave him an excuse.

Clutching the old book in his hands, Zuo decided to get out of there as soon as possible. By the time he was driving away, he heard a woman scream out, no doubt having found the melted burglars.

241

Labyrinth

Rooster Squad was on the road to Seraph Park. They were all in Julia's shiny silver Puma brand car. Julia was driving while Cyrille was in the passenger's seat. In the back were Yun, Ercan, and Shee'vra. Ercan was in the middle, an undignified seat for squad leader.

Shee'vra found herself in one of her mom's old chain shirts. On her lap was Cloudstabber and she had the ammo on a bandolier. She felt safe, but a bit overdressed for such a simple mission.

"Are you sure I need to bring all this stuff, guys?" Shee'vra asked everyone in the car. "Aren't we just hunting for a simple pickpocket in the park?"

"Yes," Julia replied, her eyes on the road. "Most missions we end up taking have the astronomical luck of being more than meets the eye." Julia was wearing her ÆT power armor. The only one who was holding back in the gear was Cyrille, who only brought a normal longsword; Cockatrice was deemed unnecessary for today.

Soon enough, Julia took a turn into Seraph Park. Once parked, they all got out and started formulating a plan.

Julia took out five empty wallets and gave each member one.

"Why are you giving us money?" Cyrille questioned. He honestly did not need any donations for pretty much his entire life.

Julia groaned. "Check the cover, cockadile." All four checked the wallets given to them and saw a lightning bolt symbol on each of them. "These are decoy wallets just in case the thief gets any ideas. Touching the glyph will give them a nasty couple of watts."

Cyrille had another question. "But why would a thief want to try to steal from people who are armed and ready with swords, armor, and a giant crossbow?" He glimpsed at her powerarmor. "I don't even see pockets on your armor."

Julia had no way to argue about that. Her idea failed before it even started. She looked to the side to see Ercan and Yun grabbing the wallet at the wrong end. Ercan received several volts of electricity while it did not even affect Yun. She grumbled in irritation. "Fine. It was a moronic idea anyway. But what's your plan, Captain?"

As he healed his left hand, Ercan answered her. "Well, I think we would cover the most ground if we split up." He desperately tried to make it sound more intricate, his captain position on the line. "Cyrille and Julia search the west part, me and Sheev will check the east, and sorry, Yun, you're on your own to check the forests in the middle. And if any of us get results, we use the alarm that connects our cells together."

"Alright, fine." Julia mockingly saluted. She did not want to be walking around a park at ten in the morning. Who knew how long she was going to be here?

Cyrille had no problems with the orders. "Yes, Captain." The two richest members were off together.

"Alright, fine. I'll be off by myself," Yun told his superior. He understood that with squads being an odd number, it was his turn to be by himself. Cyrille was not to be trusted alone much of the time due to his tendency to trust strangers so quickly, Julia needed a partner to motivate her to do work, and Shee'vra was the newest member, so it made sense that her brother would keep an eye on her. So he turned into his simian form and went into the forest.

Shee'vra turned toward her older brother. "So where do we start?"

He pointed the way, a map in his hand. "We begin at the statue of The White Wolfhound of Winter and go from there."

~ * ~

Cyrille and Julia walked past the gate to the Seraph Zoo for the third time. It had been four hours and no progress had been made whatsoever. Julia had texted the others and they were in the same predicament. Overall, Julia was bored out of her mind, and evidently so was Cyrille.

"I wish that thief could just show up and turn himself in," Cyrille complained, looking back at the zoo. "We could be watching the tigers and the crocodiles or even the seals being fed fish." His voice was full of lament. He looked at everyone around them, but nobody was stealing anything.

"Well that's life, Cyrille," Julia told him apathetically. "Such is the life of a psychic. Or so we're told." The teachers always warned them about the dangers out there, but never said a thing about the tedious minor missions.

"I know, I know," Cyrille said as checked about in different directions. He looked around as people kept their distance from the two. "Hey, Julia."

She sighed, expecting something dumb to come out of his beak. "What is it, Cyrille?"

"I made sure to shower this morning. Did you?"

Where did that come from? But she decided to answer him. "I guess, for a bit." She began to scold him. "You know that most people, especially women, don't like being questioned like that right?"

"Well that does make sense," the reptilian rooster replied. "My apologies. But do you have any other idea why people are stepping away from us so quickly." A jogger looked at him and dashed out of their way. "Like that?"

Julia had no idea why he had yet to figure out that most people, psychic or hylic, would be intimidated by a green humanoid scaly chicken that is highly poisonous *and* venomous with an unnaturally long tongue. People at the academy might be used to it, but very few others. Cyrille was about to take a right in the forked pathway, but Julia pulled him to the left. No point in scaring the children at the playground again.

She then made up a white lie. "They're just scared 'cause we're armed and ready. Probably makes them think something's about to go down." She looked at a purple glyph that was shaped like a clock on her wrist. "Which at this rate, won't be happening." *Best. Saturday. Ever.*

Cyrille bought it. "That does make a lot of sense." He took a sip of water out of his thermos. But when he closed the lid, he failed to notice a shiny winged fly being trapped inside. It was an expert bug catch and he failed to even notice.

The DeRoche went on to make small talk to pass the time. "I went to a movie premiere yesterday."

"And are you going to tell me what you watched?" Julia expected a silly kids' movie or something lame.

Cyrille's eyes brightened. "I am so glad you asked. You see, George Leeroi of junior year class has a cousin who's a producer. This cousin helped make a movie known as *Inhuman Rights*. And George invited me and the rest of Rhea Squad to see it. I managed to squeeze in because my third cousin's uncle is the director."

Julia could not help but wonder what the flick was about. She let him continue to speak. He explained how it was about an alien from a distant galaxy that landed on Earth. Some "meanies" want it experimented on, but a majority of the Enotitan population wanted to keep him safe, whether out of kindness or to not risk angering its race. Some "meanie" general tried to claim that the alien had no human rights because it was never human. Therefore, a lawyer volunteered to go to the Enotitan Supreme Court to grant the alien his civil rights as a citizen of Enotita, facing many obstacles on the way. At first the lawyer was defending the alien for the publicity, but eventually developed a close kinship with the alien. Cyrille did not explain the rest for fear of spoiling the movie for her but did promise that it was Critic's Award material.

Meanwhile, as the two conversed, Muvumo struggled to escape from her entrapment.

Shee'vra was more than tired. She was tired two hours ago, now she was just exhausted. She called over to Ercan, who was scanning the area on top of a rock. "Did you find anything yet?" To think her first mission would be so dull. They had been doing this for forever now and nothing productive had occurred. "Is work usually this boring?"

"Not usually," he replied as he looked on. "It's just that this biznatch refuses to show their face around here." He jumped off the rock. "I guess he or she is hiding within the forest." He went through the trees, ignoring the "Do Not Go into the Forest" sign. "Let's see if Yun has found anything."

"Alright, fine." She reluctantly followed. Hours of walking around doing absolutely squat was tiring.

Going deeper into the woods, the siblings walked up a strange hill in the front of Lake Keter. Ercan absorbed the view of the lake on a bright sunny day. The light reflected on the clear water, making it look like gold was just an inch under the surface.

"Don't you just love it?" Ercan commented. "The view is remarkable." He then took out his cell and texted to the others. "But on the other hand, I'm more than sure this has all been a waste of our time."

Shee'vra sighed in a mixture of relief and disappointment. On one hand, they would finally go home. But on the other hand, her first mission was a massive waste of everyone's time. Bored and dejected, she desperately called their contact's missing cell number. She didn't expect anything, but she could at least say she tried…six times.

To their surprise, they heard a noise. A ring tone.

Yummy, yummy, YUMMY GRILLED CHEEEEESE! Yummy, yummy, YUMMY GRILLED CHEEEEESE!

Shee'vra followed the jingle and found a red cell vibrating on the ground. She immediately reached for it, enjoying her luck and success. But as she picked it up, something odd occurred.

Some mysterious force was pulling on the other end of the crystalcell, trying to rip it out of her hands. But she wouldn't let go. She wouldn't make this mission go on any longer. She yanked the phone as hard as she could, but the mysterious force yanked back their way.

"Let go, missy!" the unseen being told her in a strained voice. "It's mine!"

"Nuh-uh!" Shee'vra answered back as she kept on tugging. "This crystalcell is the property of one Mike Gorden." She remembered her spark training from yesterday and decided to make use of her new skill. "So, let GO!"

She quickly used an open hand to create a gale of wind. Whoever was giving resistance let go. As she put the crystalcell away, she saw something weird. The mysterious force's invisibility fully wore off. It looked a lot like a weird scaly fishy guy face down in the grass, though he seemed quite dry for a fish. Having the ability to turn invisible, she presumed that this was the thief who had been stealing from people in the park for so long. Though since he smelled like old seafood, she wondered why she couldn't smell him before or why she couldn't see his footprints in the grass until after he appeared.

Sharlie got up in an angry daze. "So, you wanna play it like that?" He put up his fists. "How about you and I duke it—" He noticed Ercan just behind her, chains out. "Never mind." He put his hands up in defeat. Despite the fact he was dealing with youngsters, he refused to take chances. Even the youngest of psychics could kill swiftly.

Ercan had a smile of satisfaction on his face. "Are you, invisible man with a stolen crystalcell, the pickpocket of Seraph Park?" It was mostly rhetorical on his part, but he wanted proof.

For some reason, Sharlie felt the need to answer. "…Maybe?" Out of his pockets, fell several trinkets—a stopwatch, a pair of glasses, and even the wallet that Julia gave them. Ercan checked his pocket to see it gone. This was more than enough proof for him.

As Shee'vra dialed for the other squadmates, her brother spoke up. "Well we're taking you in kelpy…beard guy." Ercan couldn't think of any other way to name him. He readied his chains.

"You'll never take me alive!" the crook blurted out. He picked up his ill-gotten gains and began to book it. But upon his skin touching the lightning glyph on Julia's wallet, he was introduced to several volts of electricity. He fell to the ground, convulsing with his tongue out. "GugGLAHAHAHAHAHah!"

As Sharlie convulsed on the ground, losing control of his muscles, Ercan walked up to him. But before he could create a pair of cuffs, somebody called out to them.

"What the hell are two kids doing here?!"

Ercan and Shee'vra turned around to see two angry looking animalistic people. Only Shee'vra had any idea who they were. Izquierda and Aristera of the Lefty Gang. It turned out there was a hidden door to a secret base behind them. They both were in deep water now.

The big bull even seemed like he was trying to recognize her from somewhere. He pointed at her. "Hey, haven't I seen you somewhere, little girl?" He strained his memory. The chain shirt and the arbalest threw him off.

But she remembered him, though she did recall that he was missing a horn before. He seemed to have grown it back somehow.

"It is no matter," Izquierda remarked to Aristera. "Vinstri, come over here!" Before Ercan could prevent the thief from running toward his allies, the Crocotta quickly sidestepped to block his way. "We in the Lefty Gang have very little patience for opposing psychics. Normally, I would just give you two a warning, maybe a slight beating if you insisted on fighting back," he snarled, the sharp bone plates in his mouth covered in slobber. "But now that you two just saw our base, I cannot let you two go."

The redhead was having none of that. He created a spiked chain and lashed at what he assumed to be the leader's chest. It did nothing, not even pierce his soccer jersey. Izquierda seemed disappointed. "Nice try I guess, punk." He kicked the teenager right in the stomach, knocking the wind out of him. He was holding back by about half of his strength. Didn't want to rupture his stomach.

"ERCAN!" Shee'vra tried to run to her brother, but Aristera grabbed her in one hand. "Let go!"

"No can do," the bull regretfully told her.

Vinstri mockingly waved to the two from behind his boss. "Yeah, sorry, no can do!"

He received a back slap across the face from Izquierda's left hand. "Shut up, Vinstri! It's your fault they found us in the first place. Bringing two kids here," he growled in disgust. "Their parents are now going to be worried sick." He turned back to Ercan, who he had in his other hand by the collar. "I'm sorry, but you two are coming with us for a few days. You'll be treated as humanely as possible, I promise. You'll be freed eventually, but you're not going anywhere until we get to leave this damn city."

Ercan had no time to ask why he would want to leave the city. Izquierda was too busy suddenly getting a monkey foot to the face, getting knocked to the ground. Asterion heard a noise from behind him and saw a girl in body armor and a chicken guy in a spiffy tux. The girl in glasses dropped a weird glowing purple disc next to her and threw another at Shee'vra. Before either captor or captive could realize it, Shee'vra was teleported right next to Julia, Yun, and Cyrille.

"So glad you guys showed up," Julia passively commented to the gang. "Proof that looking for you wasn't a waste of time."

Yun pumped himself up and pointed at Asterion. "We doing this, beefcake?" He remembered Xiu mentioning something about a bull guy. He might as well finish the job.

"Come quietly or today shall be a bad one." Cyrille took out his sword. But he felt his empty water thermos heat up quickly. "Ow! Ow! What on earth?" He quickly tossed it in front of Vinstri in a panic. The thermos exploded in a flash of light.

"There's no air in those things," Kushoto said to herself, finally free from the clutches of a bottle. She'd been blasting at it for forever, but steel is hard to burn through without a heat source to absorb from. Looking around, she saw a confrontation was about to go down. "Are we doing this? These are just a bunch of kids."

"A bunch of kids who somehow managed to capture you without even thinking about it," Izquierda snidely commented.

"Sorry," Cyrille told her sympathetically. "I didn't even see her, I promise. I'm sure you folks are great people deep down inside, only living the way you live to get by in an unforgiving world. If it makes you feel better, I forgive you for your lives of theft. I hear a lot of the time about people in precarious positions resorting to desperate measures to have an income. I'm sure you guys weren't just born and decided 'Hey, I feel like becoming a criminal when I grow up.' But if you guys just turn yourselves in, I'm sure the court will also sympathize with your plight."

Izquierda was stupefied by the scaly fowl. He honestly had no idea if the chicken was being patronizing or honestly thought that such a little speech would just magically have them decide to turn themselves in. This idiot may let them off easy, but not the cops, and *especially* not their superiors.

"Chicken guy, *shut up*. None of us are turning ourselves in." He threw a kick at Yun, who blocked it with his arm. Even Ercan could hear the impact of the blow, but Yun still stood on his two feet, hardly hurt at all. *Damn, this monkey's going to be a tough one.* He resorted to emergency measures. He shouted to the bull man. "Aristera! Labyrinth!"

Without even replying, Aristera activated his Minotaur spark's greatest trick. Stomping on the ground, stone walls shot up from the earth. As Rooster Squad and the Lefty Gang looked around, they found themselves separated and many paths to go through. But they all knew an enemy could be just around the corner.

All of them (except Sharlie) were ready to battle. Shee'vra placed a bolt into her Arbalest and took the left pathway.

I hope I don't have to use this. But I will if I must. Now which way should I go? She then had a realization. *Wait a minute. Air is high up. What am I, stupid?* She remembered training in her Spark Region last night and reading about being able to fly, which in hindsight sounded like an obvious result of having wind powers. But what did she know?

She stood in place and focused on the air around her. *Come on. Come on. Fly, Sylph, fly.* Her aeon radiated from her body and she began to float an inch off the ground. Though pathetic by psychic standards, it still felt cool. She tried to concentrate harder and, soon after, the aeon stayed back inside her soul and she elevated. She was learning how to fly, but she had to learn fast.

⁓ * ⁓

"NONE HAVE ESCAPED THE UTTER CONFUSION AND CHAOS OF THE LABYRINTH!" Asterion shouted in triumph. "DO YOU KNOW WHERE YOU ARE? NO! FOR YOU HAVE ALL BEEN SCATTERED ACROSS THESE WALLS OF STONE! BUT I KNOW WHERE EACH AND EVERYONE OF YOU LURK AS WELL AS THE GATEWAY TO FREE—"

He stopped his big speech as he saw in the Minotaur radar of his mind that somebody was flying upwards, two others were running on top of the walls, and somehow someone was teleporting around the maze. Disappointment swelled deep inside his heart.

"Aw come on, you guys!" he complained. "That's against the rules!"

"I'm still in the maze!" He recognized that voice calling out to him to be the rooster guy. "This power is pretty cool for those who move around normally! Reminds me of the hedge maze back home!"

Asterion knew he was trying to be nice and all, but he was just rubbing salt into the wound, which was why he planned to capture him first. Charging his way through the maze, he went closer and closer toward the bird in the tux.

But he stumbled and tripped. Getting up, he saw a steel chain around his hoof. Snapping the chain, he got up to see the red head…in red clothes. With a flick of his wrists, those chains became red flames. Too much red.

Ercan gave a sly smile. "So, if I beat you into steak, will the walls come down?"

As he approached him, Asterion was not seeing a teenage kid

with fire chains. He saw his grandfather ready to whip him with two different belts—the buckle side. He must have forgotten to buy him his cigarettes again after school. The shop owner refused to sell him any because of his harassing of the other customers, so he used Asterion to get what he needed. But consequences would be dire if he ever forgot. His grandfather's eyes glowed purple as he started making a dash toward him.

"GET AWAY!" Asterion bolted off deeper into the maze to get as far away as possible.

Ercan followed suit, trailing behind the easily heard stomps. He had no idea what had just happened. *The hell was that about? He was confident enough before.*

~ * ~

Yun ran across the top of the maze walls, looking down occasionally to see if he could find any friends. Though he had yet to see any, he did find the occasional glyph and a few small trails of saliva across the walls and floor. Hearing light hooves and weird laughing, the weird hyena thing attacked him again. Izquierda was running on top of the walls as well, ready to give a huge kick to the neck.

He ducked under the attack and hit him in the chest with both fists, knocking the crocotta back. He then prepared to inflict a blow to the jaw, but his hand was caught within Izqueirda's palm. But before Izquierda could sink his claws into his flesh, Yun tripped him with his tail.

Izquierda took his time to check through his crystal eyes. He saw that the monkey martial artist was intending to jump into to air and land on his chest with as much weight as possible. To avert this, he swatted the airborne Yun's feet, sending him onto the maze floor. He followed him down there to finish their skirmish. Louiz had a hunch that out of all these kids, this Qian boy was the most physically dangerous one to him. He was strong enough to fight him evenly without any cheap magic tricks or anything and was fast enough to be able to move out of the way of his attacks. The others, he felt would be dead in one kick if he went all out, but not this kid.

Izquierda kicked at Yun once again, who quickly dodged. The rock wall cracked from the impact of the hoof. He predicted a Monkey Style kick about to come his way, so he blocked it. But that was what Yun wanted. The intention was not a simple kick. Izquierda was now open for a counter attack with his other foot.

Grabbing him by the throat with his foot, Yun used his momentum and gravity to land both hands on the ground. He then used his strength to do what was almost a cartwheel, lifting Izquierda into the air. Eventually, the cartwheels ended and Yun was back upright while his foe was prone on the ground with him on top.

"Surrender yet?" Yun questioned him.

The only answer he got was a snarl. The crocotta swiped at him with his claws and used his enemy's brief retreat to get back up. Louiz saw the teen's next action and simply tanked a fist to the face. Ignoring the pain, he tackled the monkey to the ground.

But primates are agile. Yun merely punched his side and tumbled them over with him on top. But Louiz found an opportunity to kick him off with both hooves, sending him flying through a wall.

With Yun stunned, he took his chance to pounce, his claws and mouth aiming for non-vital areas. Though he had no intentions of killing a mere student, he was willing to at least disable him. A few broken bones would hopefully keep him compliant enough. But he had another vision. He saw just above Yun, a glowing pinkish glyph shaped like spiral inside a sphere. Popping out was a tonfa crackling with electricity. Though immune to weaponry, elemental attacks would do just fine against him.

He stopped his advance and stepped back. As predicted, an electric baton did come for him from a glyph he should have noticed earlier. The girl with glasses came out of the portal not long after.

"Get up, Yun." she plainly told her squad mate. "I need a meatshield."

He looked away without a care in the world. "When I feel like it, Jules," he quickly back flipped onto the wall, "which I do right now!"

He sprang from the wall to launch himself at Izquierda. Spinning in the air, he tried to kick him with his heel. But the attack was already predicted and sidestepped. What was *not* predicted was a gigantic crossbow bolt that flew just inches from hitting the crook's neck. The shot stuck deep into the stone wall. Not that it would have hurt him, but it did distract him from seeing what was about to happen next.

Before he could react, he found himself smacked across the face with a shock tonfa. Though being bludgeoned didn't hurt at all, the electrical current going into his body stunned him. Yun took this chance to unleash a barrage of punches.

As he was being pummeled, Izquierda managed to get control of his body. The electricity was made to disable a human being, his spark made him tougher than that. He predicted Yun's next move and then quickly bit into his forearm. The monkey boy screeched in pain as his bones crushed under the intense bite pressure. He tried to yank his arm out of his jaws, but the beast just refused to let go.

Julia had to do something fast. She could heal a broken arm, but regenerating a lost limb was something beyond most psychic healers. Upping the dose on the electricity would also not help, as the surge could risk making the jaws clamp down hard enough that they would have to be pried off.

She needed to make a plan fast. She used her spark to erase the electric glyph on her weapon and then quickly scribbled a gate glyph in its place. Dropping a disc with a green up-arrow glyph on the ground, she sprang into action.

She attacked the Lefty Gang member on the head with her tonfa. Thinking that it wouldn't hurt at all, he didn't even bother to dodge. But when his head made contact with that glyph, he suddenly found himself not biting down on anyone. Instead, he found himself flat on his back in front of the portal gate. He turned his head to see both kids were just a few feet to the right of him. But he also felt something funny underneath him.

Before he could react though, he was catapulted into the air by a sudden kinetic force. He yelped and flailed about as he soared into the sky and even more so when he began to descend back down into the labyrinth. Julia and Yun watched the whole thing.

Before Yun could climb up the wall to trail him, he was stopped by Julia who had a firm grip on his tail. "Aw, come on! Let me go!"

"No," she firmly stated, pulling him back to the ground. "Your arm is a mess."

Yun looked at his bleeding and mangled left forearm. It looked like a dog with saws for teeth had clamped down on him. Rather than be horrified and in utter agony, he seemed to be enduring it. "It's fine. I've had worse on The Stage."

He tried to climb back up again, but she pulled him down once more. "This. Is not. The Stage." She gave him a deep glare from behind her glasses. "It's fine in there because everyone always comes out of it just fine. But this is reality. If I don't patch this mess up, you're going to suffer the effects of blood loss." She shook her head. "And heaven help us if you actually died. I'd have to sit around at your funeral for hours." She drew golden plus signs on the palms of her hands. "I'm too lazy to write a eulogy that *doesn't* include the stupid way you died."

She didn't mean that, right? Yun thought as he reluctantly sat down. She tended to say many things she never meant when she was upset. But she could at least be a little bit kinder on the snappy remarks. He presented his arm to her, trying to ignore the pain. When he thought about it, real life wounds hurt a lot more than the ones on The Stage. Perhaps it was the actual risk of serious injury that made it feel worse.

Julia immediately began mending his wounds. Though the most life-threatening injury was the arm bite, he was also covered in bruises and minor scratches from duking it out with that guy. This was going to take a while to heal as good as new.

~ * ~

Shee'vra missed her shot against the guy attacking Yun and Julia. Perhaps it was the lack of proficiency with the weapon that did it. Though it was also likely, because no matter how hard she tried, she just did not have it in her to kill him. These crooks may have tried to capture them, but at the same time they should offer them mercy. It also seemed that the hoofed hyena guy was holding back during the fight, at least by a little. It would feel wrong to go against him full force for some reason.

She looked around for her brother and saw him chasing down the bull guy. But as she looked around the air, she saw that the woman had turned into the shiny winged fly again. The fly seemed to be gathering heat from the sun as a large bright ball appeared in front of it. Seeing as she was aiming for Ercan, she knew what she must do.

She unleashed a small gust of wind against her foe. Though it was pathetic by regular standards, a fly didn't exactly weigh all that much. It was more than enough to make Kushoto lose her aim just as she was about to fire. A large beam of solar energy mowed through the maze and into the lake, even evaporating a bit of the water. The beam looked like what happens when you put a magnifying glass under the sun.

Kushoto turned around to see a flying teenage girl with a big crossbow. She turned back into a winged human form. "You made me miss." She began to absorb more sunlight. "I won't miss again."

Shee'vra quickly flew diagonally upwards to avoid her. But before Kushoto could take a shot, a laser hit her arm. Her wings stopped flapping and she fell fifteen feet down into some mud in the maze, unable to move.

Looking around to see who saved her, she saw Cyrille just under her. He waved at her, a long trail of saliva behind him.

"Good work, Shee'vra." Cyrille gave her thumbs-up. "Can you tell me which way Ercan is?"

Ercan was still chasing down the Minotaur. He wasn't even close to Cyrille. "He's very far away from you."

"Then can you please pick me up and bring me to him?" Cyrille politely asked. "He may need my assistance."

Shee'vra could not exactly say no to somebody who had just saved her life. Therefore, she put Cloudstabber away and flew down behind him.

"It must be so great to be able to fly," Cyrille commented as he spread out his arms. "I wonder how it feels."

"I'm sure with practice I'll be as free as a bird." She tried picking him up by lifting him from under his arms. But after some heaving, she concluded that he was too heavy. Not that Cyrille was fat or anything, she just didn't have the upper body strength. "Sorry. You seem to be too heavy for me," she panted.

"It's okay," Cyrille told her. "I have an idea."

"And what is it?" Shee'vra asked, slightly skeptical. She prayed to Sophia that it did not involve him dangling under her by her legs. The weight would probably stretch them out so much it would look like she was walking on stilts.

"Perhaps you fly by moving the air around you to lift you up," he theorized to her. "If you use your aeon to let the air around me move, perhaps you can lift me."

Whatever he just said, it was worth a shot.

~ * ~

"Where is it? Where is it?" Vinstri desperately looked for the exit. He knew what psychics were capable of and he was having none of it.

Luckily, he found a puddle to get himself wet again. The contact with water activated his Ogopogo spark. Now he was unable to be seen, heard, or smelled, though he could still be touched, and he did not really want to know if he could be tasted. When he moved while invisible, the environment around him didn't change. The ground didn't leave tracks, branches didn't appear to move, and water didn't ripple. It was almost as if he didn't exist. As a bonus, the spark turned him into this sea serpent guy and now he could swim and breathe underwater. Score!

Sadly, there was little use in it for fighting. He didn't have any enhanced physical abilities or even any combat training. He had discovered his spark after high school, and thus, never went to the academy. In fact, he never really told anyone about his spark. Why would you tell your neighborhood that your spark is a perfect fit to be the greatest thief in Kruschtya?

But somehow, The Lefty Gang discovered his existence and he was strong-armed into working under them. So here he was, trapped in a labyrinth looking for the exit. He needed to go grab the money fast. Even if he got away, he just knew that the organization would find him and punish him for his failures. But even if the others were arrested, if he had the money, he'd be safe.

He took a right and found Kushoto lying in mud. He initially ran right past her but forced himself to return. She was a fellow thief and thieves never leave thieves. They only leave thugs behind. It was a form of criminal natural selection—at least that was how he rationalized it.

As he was ready to drag her to safety, she got up by herself.

"What just happened?" she questioned, looking around to see herself in the mud. "I'm so getting back at that chicken." She was about to fly upwards but bumped into Vinstri. "Sharlie? What are you doing here?"

"I'm going to grab the money and split to the emergency hideout!" Sharlie frantically told her. She couldn't see it, but he was waving his hands about in a panic.

It was five against four, and the two of them were without anyone to fight against for the moment. That meant that unless Louiz and Asterion had taken out a couple of them already, they were grossly outnumbered.

Though she could create great beams of heat, that took time and those kids would not give her that time. Their boss also really wanted that money. They needed to keep that money safe, and fast. Their necks were on the line.

She swiftly turned into an insect. "Okay! Let's grab the cash and take a bike!" She flew off toward the base. Sharlie followed suit.

Ercan was gaining on him. The bull man was only a sharp turn away. For some reason this guy insisted on blubbering to him to stay away, but he just took it as fear of being overpowered by a youngster like him. He had taken out a few big thugs in his life. Each one thought they could kick the skinny punk's ass, but he had kicked their ass instead. This guy might just have been all show but no skill.

Eventually, he got him into a dead end. Asterion was trying to climb over the wall, but it was too high. As he drew closer, the bull huddled into a corner. From what he could tell, the crook seemed to have urinated. Feeling no need to beat him up, Ercan turned off his flames and created a big pair of handcuffs fit for a Minotaur.

He twirled the cuffs on his wrist and slowly approached. "Alright, chase over. Now show me your hands. This will only take a second."

This will only take a second. His grandfather's words violated his mind. Asterion could not escape him. Even in death he haunted him. Red was meant to symbolize bravery, love, passion, and leadership. But to him it represented fear. As his grandfather came closer to putting his cuffs on him as punishment for poor grades, he felt something surge within him. Like a cornered animal, Asterion remembered that red represented a primal emotion—anger.

"I SAID GEEET AWAAAAAAY!" He abruptly charged straight into an unprepared Ercan with tears in his eyes. He managed to skewer his grandfather by the horn.

But he did not stop there. He jerked his head upwards and threw him off his horn. He saw his grandfather lying on the ground like a ragdoll. But to his shock, he got up, his stomach fully healed. Asterion snorted steam out of his snout and scooped up dirt with his hoof. This just meant that he would have to try harder.

He charged at him as fast as he could, but his grandpa was more agile than he remembered. He slid under him and used two chains to trip him over. Before he could get up, he was on his back like a rodeo clown. He tried to throw him off, but he just wrapped chains around his arms.

Asterion tried as hard as he could to get him off. He ran about through the maze in a panic. As he ran about, he walked through a field of bright glyphs. They shocked and burned him and even warped him to an unfamiliar part of the maze. But his grandfather held on to him. He tried to smash him into the wall, but he persisted. It was hopeless. Even as Asterion tired, he would not let go. He just made more chains to hold on.

He made a turn to see Izquierda. He would help him. "GET GRAMPA OFF ME!!"

Izquierda looked confused for a second, but he complied. Though he was injured, he would try as hard as he could to save him.

But gramps had friends. For some odd reason, a black haired teenage girl flew in holding a weird rooster guy by the foot. They looked so light in the air. The chicken chameleon man drooled down onto his leader. At first, Louiz felt disgust, but within seconds began to lose his balance. He went down in a sickly daze, struggling to get up.

Then it hit him. This was the girl at the mall. She was a psychic too. Grandpa would never befriend a teenager. Grandpa also wouldn't have any weird healing factor or chain abilities. He was dead and in Hell. But if he was dead, who was the red guy on him?

He smashed into the wall, loosening the chains. Asterion then reached onto his back and, rather than seeing an old decrepit nightmare, he saw a youth in red. His purple eyes gave away that he was far from giving up.

"Get out of here, Louiz!" Asterion smacked the toxic fowl to the ground. "I'll hold them off!"

Louiz was reluctant but complied with his wishes. Though he was moving at far from full speed and was quite wobbly, it was still quicker than any normal human. As Louiz jumped into the maze and disappeared, Asterion was ready to buy time.

Shee'vra concentrated on her spark and, pushing with both hands, created a large gust that knocked both her brother and her target back.

Getting up, Ercan created eight skinny bike chains, one from each knuckle. Each one had a small weight at the end of it. He wrapped them around the horns of Asterion. As he dodged the counterattacks, he ran around the Minotaur. The chains began extending longer and longer around him, binding his body up. Eventually, it was too hard to move.

So I guess it's time for Prisoner's Perch? Asterion thought. *Well, goodbye freedom.* He fell onto his back, bonded as tight as a clam. Soon after, he slowly began to transform back into a man.

Cyrille got up from the floor. "I-is it time for the zoo?" He slurred his speech as he saw itty-bitty chickens flying around his head. "I w-wanna see them feed the antelopes."

The other two were convinced he had a concussion. Shee'vra held onto him to prevent him from falling flat on his beak. Around them, the maze sunk back into the earth as if it was never there. Looking around them, they saw Julia healing Yun's arm. But all the other crooks were gone. None of them had any idea where they went. Hopefully they wouldn't come back.

Twenty minutes later, the police arrived. In the front of the park, the cops were taking in Asterion. Turns out there were many drugs kept inside the base. Obviously, this would affect the sentence. Though on their search, they saw dust on, but not in, the boxes.

The five watched as he was stuffed into the cop car. Each one of them noticed his large frown. It would be a chore being in Prisoner's Perch. Every psychic knew that place. It was like a bogeyman to a five-year-old, and if you misbehaved you would be dragged there.

Ercan couldn't even be satisfied with his victory over him. Asterion had run for most of it and only fought back when cornered and seemed to be more frightened than angry. Like an animal escaping a predator. The fact that he stalled them long enough to allow the others to escape made him feel that if life had given him a better hand, this Asterion guy would have been a great alumnus of Aeon Sophia Academy.

"To think that The Lefty Gang has guys like that," Ercan said to nobody in particular, "feels bad to see someone so scared of prison."

"It must bite being a Lefty Member," Yun commented. "Live in fear of your boss, then either wait to be arrested or killed. Who would choose to live that life?"

Julia brushed her hand through her partially blue dyed hair. "It's not that simple, Yun. Chances are he had nowhere else to go. We're the fortunate ones."

Still a bit dizzy, Cyrille wore a paper bag to conceal his face. "It hurts to see how there are people in the world that just use people and then just throw them away when they're no longer useful." He knew for a fact that, chances were, Asterion's superiors would not be there to bail him out of trouble. They must have so much money that bailing out a big lug like him would be pocket change. But no, they wanted it all for themselves, giving their minions scraps.

Shee'vra didn't say anything. She didn't even point out why Cyrille would even use a paper bag. Judging by his currently human hands, he must have simply strained his Aeon supply and needed to get out of his Basilisk form. Why would he need to hide his face though? Did he just not trust being seen in public as a human?

But she had bigger priorities. She slowly walked to the cop car. A policeman stopped her with an open hand.

"Hold on, young lady. Keep away from the perp."

She was nervous, but she could not stand to see such a miserable guy go to prison for twenty years. Both times she had seen him, he'd had perfect opportunities to turn her into paste. But he hadn't hurt a hair on her head. She decided to speak up.

"Officer. I want you to give him this." She handed out one of her dad's law firm's business cards. "I feel that this man deserves a good lawyer. From the evidence we saw, none of the members had sold any of their drugs, the bank robbery seemed to come from desperation rather than greed, and this man allowed himself to get captured in place of his friends. This is an honorable man, and I believe he deserves an honorable trial." Hopefully the *Lawful and Good* firm would help him.

The big guy in the back of the police car was stunned that the girl who helped capture him was sticking up for his rights. He nodded in thanks to her as the policeman gave him the card through the window.

Shee'vra then walked back to her brother and friends as they watched the cop car drive away. "Let's hope he's treated well." She turned to Ercan. "Let's hope dad's law firm will volunteer to be his lawyer."

Ercan felt shame in his heart. He didn't have the initiative to show open compassion for a victim of desperate circumstance. He felt disgusted at how unaccomplished he felt today. Though the squad got paid a hundred and fifty paz each, it just felt empty. Even the fact that they were applauded for finding a Lefty Gang base in Bythos helped little to quell that fact. Maybe Winona was right about him. He sure didn't feel like a true leader today.

He turned to his squad. "What do you guys want to do for the rest of the day?" He needed to take his mind off things.

The paper bag on Cyrille's head ripped apart, revealing his usual lizard chicken face, though even his beak seemed to frown. "Well…the zoo is still open, I guess. I'll buy tickets if you want."

Julia patted his back. "Sounds just fine. Maybe monkeys flinging shit would raise my mood."

The others had no reason to refuse. They all put their stuff in Julia's Puma and decided to spend the rest of the day relaxing. Ercan knew that after this day, he was going to train the crap out of them for the rest of the week.

In the secondary hideout, Muvumo and Sharlie were counting the cash they managed to hastily grab. Luckily, they had managed to take exactly the money they needed to keep their heads. But this hangout smelled like dead rats and garlic. The fact that they must hang out in this dump until Wednesday was irritating, but small potatoes compared to Prisoner's Perch.

"You think the others are coming?" Sharlie asked nervously. If the others came, he prayed they weren't being tracked down. They had nowhere else to run.

Muvumo shook her head to get rid of the worst-case scenario from hijacking her brain. "I'm not sure, Sharlie. Just give me a moment to think."

"But what if some other psychic finds—"

She tossed a bundle of bills at his face. "I'm not sure! We must wait until Shèng Xià and the others get here. We give them what we owe and then they'll get us out of town when they're done with whatever they need to do." The Sirokhan shook in terror. These next five nights were going to be unpleasant to say the least.

As they wordlessly continued to organize the key to their survival, they heard a crash from up above. A few minutes of silence later, the door abruptly opened to reveal Louiz. He staggered toward the two in utter exhaustion and pain. His green soccer jersey that had the name "Agudo" on it was full of holes after all the fighting today. Sweat covered his shaved head and dripped off him as if he had just come out of the sauna. He was cut and bruised and even a bit singed. But he still stumbled toward them. His eyes stared them down sharper than his claws ever could.

Before they could react, Izquierda had his hands around both of their necks. He seemed to almost hurl as he spoke. "You cowards! W-why did—" He gagged on his words, but didn't loosen his grip. "Did you abandon us as we—" he vomited out what was once a little bit of his lunch, "w-were overwhelmed?"

Sharlie was panicking as he struggled to breathe, his scales turning from green gradually to a shade of purple. Though the rooster guy's poison took a toll on his health big time, he really wanted to wring their necks right about now. But Muvumo didn't struggle. She just glared with her deep brown eyes.

"We needed to keep that paz safe," she told her leader with a stone-cold expression. "It's the only reason we will be alive by next Saturday. If sacrifices had to be made, then fine. Ewen and Asterion knew the risks. Now they've paid for it."

Louiz had no time to argue with her. He was much too sick for that kind of crap. "Whatever helps you thieves sleep at night." He let go of his grip to go to the toilet to vomit some more.

Now the gang was reduced from five to three, and Sharlie had the gut feeling that it was soon to shrink again. Judging by how strong those kids seemed, maybe even some of the elite gang members should watch out.

~ * ~

It was 8:23 p.m. in Sorchos. Zuo knocked on his neighbor's apartment door. On his shoulders was Little Yun. Within fifteen seconds, his neighbor, Mrs. Cratil, answered the door.

"Why, hello there, Zuo," she said warmly. "What can I do for you?"

He propped his cane on the outside wall. "I'll be gone for a while, and I was hoping you would look after Little Yun for a bit." He stretched his arm to grab his cat. It hurt a bit as his joints rubbed together.

The middle-aged woman saw him struggling for a bit to reach for his pet. "Do you need help getting him off you?"

"I'm fine. I got him." He reached as far as he could and took his tabby cat off his back and into his arms. He made no sound, but his shoulder blades were not happy with him and made it apparent to his nerve cells. He handed her Little Yun. "Here you go." He began to walk back and leave.

"Why are you leaving so suddenly?" She petted the striped cat gently with her fingers. The cat relaxed in her arms, "business?"

Zuo looked over her shoulder. "Yeah, business in Bythos. Maybe even bump into my nephew."

"I didn't know you had a nephew. Is he a bright boy?"

"Not sure. Haven't seen him in years." He waved as he walked off. "Goodbye, Dana, and do what you want with Little Yun. You always did want kittens."

He went down the stairs and out the back door. Outside, a black van awaited him. Inside the automobile was Jakaire ready to take him to the hideout. The heist was in a few days and the boss wanted everyone gathered and ready.

"You're late, sir," she told him, conveying little emotion.

"Sorry, had to take my cat to the neighbor."

She rolled her hazel eyes. "Pets…such a hassle. Just get in quick."

He had little reason to argue. He got into the passenger's seat as she started the car. Shèng Xià took out that ancient book he got this morning and continued reading it. Though his portrait had him looking like a long-bearded savage posing as a mockery of a king, Emperor Barbar was in fact a tough but fair ruler. He treated his loyal subjects with upmost respect, but any rebellions were quashed thoroughly. Any dissidents were considered traitors of Protogenoi and were killed by a man with him on the front lines.

Barbar was the second Emperor to create an artifact of Kadosh. Zuo thought that these artifacts were mere props to show the power of the current emperor. As he continued researching into the lost book, he saw that he and most of the world were wrong about what they truly were for.

"What're you reading?" the driver asked as her eyes kept to the nighttime road. "Looks old and smells bad."

"It is an old one," Shèng Xià answered his younger gang member. "It's about these artifacts and such." His eyes were glued to the worn pages. "Makes me wonder what our boss truly wants with these things."

Jakaire was not too fazed. "What are they, magic or something?"

"More or less."

She was a bit dismissive about the answer. "So, what? Do you see what we psychics can do?"

"This is not average spark stuff," Zuo told her, deadly serious. "This is something different, something that does not follow our rules."

Roosters and Eagles

In the VIP room, the remaining eight captains held a discussion with one another before the fight began. Some of the captains even had votes ready.

"I don't care what anyone says," Gaizka told Vural as he chomped his teeth into some steak. "I'm voting for Ercan no matter what. You have to admire the bloodbaths that guy gets into and survives."

"I'm voting for him too," Vural replied as he stood on the ceiling, peering down on the shark man. "I have come to a revelation. The other students are catching up to us early bloomers. He's no stronger or weaker than any of us, barring Mastema and Bianca, of course."

"I believe it's less that they are catching up and more that some sparks have advantages over others," Alexandru explained to the two from the seat behind them. "For example, Hilbert's Jupiter spark allows him to shoot lightning from a long distance rifle, allowing him to take Vural out unnoticed." He ignored Vural wincing in shame as he praised his squad mate. "But unless the results of today's fight are absolutely disastrous, I feel that my vote goes to Ercan staying."

"And why is that?" Winona got into the conversation as she slouched on her massage chair, bored.

"Because, Winona." The dhampyr showed her the updated list of the top three aeon levels of the student body. "Ercan just hit the five thousand mark." He tossed the list onto her lap. "Besides, at least my vote is without bias."

The witch huffed in indignation. "Well it isn't just because he beat me! Make sure you know that!"

"Entertain us with your reasoning then," Desiderio playfully replied, just next to her, holding some fancy sparkling in between his fingers.

Winona decided to humble them with a legitimate reason for voting no. "It's because of his sister. She has only been around for one week and still has a lot to learn." With a wave of her hand, she created small apparitions of Yun and Xiu, specifically the moments she defeated them one week ago. "I stabbed Yun with a spear and ripped Xiu's throat out. Keep in mind those two were trained by a master martial artist. Shee'vra has only been doing this for a week at most and I can bet that there are psychics out there that are more aggressive than me and won't hold back against a young girl like herself." She dissipated the illusions. "So if Ercan couldn't keep those two alive against me, what chance does Shee'vra have to live under his authority?"

Desi took a sip and nodded. "I can see what you mean, Winny. I voted against him too." He crossed his legs. "A while ago I spoke with ex-rooster, Xiu, and asked her about his leadership skills. I wasn't impressed."

"I also voted nay," Ludmila butted in from behind Gaizka. It was three-to-three at this point. "I find Julia or Cyrille to be better alternatives. More mature than the current one."

"More mature?" Alexandru questioned her. "I don't doubt either's potential but mature is not the word I would us to define someone like Cyrille. Or even Julia for that matter."

"More mature than some of us here," the brawny woman answered back, looking up at Vural. She got the quiet Seichin girl into the discussion. "Hanako, what's your opinion on the matter?"

Hanako quickly looked around at the group, not expecting to be called upon. She brushed her long hair out of her face. "W-well I initially wanted Cyrille to replace him. But he wanted Ercan to keep the position because it makes him happy. So I guess I choose Ercan staying."

Gaizka gobbled the rest of his steak. "Yeah, so that makes it four-to-three with Ercan staying in the lead." He licked his lips and sharp teeth. "And does Mr. Number One have an opinion on the matter?"

Mastema looked toward the group with a dour expression. He seemed really concentrated on the upcoming event. The others could not help but shiver a bit as he stared them all down, Aureolin in his hand. "I shall determine my vote…depending on today's victor."

~ * ~

"Alright, Eagle Squad! Me and the rest of Rooster Squad have been training all week! From six to nine p.m. on weekdays and four to seven p.m. on weekends!" Ercan boasted to Bianca, pointing at her. "We won't go down so easily this time, I promise you that! We will prove to the entirety of Aeon Sophia Academy that Rooster Squad is the greatest squad of all!" He outstretched his arms to make his speech seem more grandiose and less like empty trash talk.

Bianca Narkissos hardly even emoted as she intently listened to what he just said. She wasn't exactly impressed. "You do understand that each and every squad trains, right? You're far from abnormal."

Ercan ignored her remark. "Well, oh yeah? Me and the rest of the squad found the Lefty Gang hideout last Saturday."

She still looked at him with staid expression. "That was nice, I guess. But you let three of them get away." She twirled a shard of obsidian in her fingers. "Besides, last Saturday, we went up to Ville-Mary and took out a different Lefty Base."

"Yeah, it was awesome!" Basil added in with enthusiasm. "The boss there was some guy who could control bears! I managed to get one into a headlock!"

Ercan was feeling very upstaged right about now. Ville-Mary was such a peaceful countryside in the southern part of Enotita. They must have searched far and wide to find evidence of the gang's whereabouts. But Ercan had one last tactic. "Well then, Bianca. This is your last chance to surrender. I'll understand if you—"

"No." She and the rest of her squad quickly shot down that tactic. "We're going inside The Stage now. I recommend you hurry up and do the same." She, Caradoc, Basil, Zivot, and Mayil all went inside the simulation room. On the back of the princess's tight padded armor was a symbol of a purple narcissus.

"They seemed *real* scared of you, boss," Julia flatly commented as she followed suit.

Cyrille followed her in. "I sincerely hope Zivot and Mayil perform impressively."

"I swear that I'm going to take at least one of them out," Yun promised Ercan. "At least then we could say we accomplished something."

Ercan tried to put on a brave face. But in hindsight, this was a terrible idea. Going against Bianca was a death sentence. They were in for an uphill battle in the best-case scenario. He should have picked somebody like Gaizka, Ludmila, or maybe even Alexandru. But he should have shoved his bravado back into his corn-hole last Wednesday.

"Don't worry too much. It's trying that counts," Shee'vra tried to reassure her big brother. "Maybe even if you lose, they'll still keep you if we do well enough."

That was a possibility. But Ercan had another concern on his mind as well. "Are you sure you're ready for this? When you lose, it sort of feels like dying. Never exactly the most fun thing to do after school."

Though she felt a sudden shiver, she kept a smile on her face. "Well, I have to do this sooner or later. Besides, I probably got the most training of all of us this week." Not only had Ercan been training her like a racehorse, but so was Xiu. Though not an expert in the field of shooting bolts, Tiger Fist, or wind powers, she hoped the variety of techniques wouldn't make her dead weight.

"If you insist." Ercan did not question her answer. "Just try to leave Bianca to me." Him defeating the second strongest squad leader would make it guaranteed that he remains a captain.

"No promises," she remarked as the siblings then entered the room. They took the last two remaining seats. "So what are these things and how do they work exactly?"

"That's easy. Meinrad von Morgen invented these Bühne Seats back when the Academy was first founded. It allows us to enter The Stage, which is sort of like an artificial, customizable Spark Region without a psychic." He pulled down some weird device over his head. "All you do is put this dome thing over your head." His finger hovered over a red button on the armrest. "And then press this button." He pushed the button and with a surge of power, the chair brought his mind into The Stage.

Shee'vra got the point. She placed the device over her head and, after taking a deep breath, pressed the button to take her to another world.

~ * ~

Meanwhile, in the regular theater for the non-captains or staff, Xiu waited for the match to start. Judging from the screens, today's stage seemed surreal. The entire area seemed to be composed of black and white squares, almost like that ancient yet timeless game known as chess. Looking into the arena deep enough, she could swear she could see cubic structures hidden around the area, both on the ground, on the walls, and even on the ceiling.

"What the hell is this shit I'm looking at?" Petra called out from the seat behind her, her eyes hurting just looking at the spectacle.

Dunkeen scooted by Draghignazzo. "Well I think it's meant to be one of those optical illusions, except as an entire arena. You know, just like the ones in those books the student psychologist has in her waiting room." As he sat down, a loud fart was heard around the room. The students were at first disgusted, but when the demon kid started laughing, everyone knew no fart had actually happened. And true to form, the armored fishman pulled a woopie cushion from underneath him. "That's very mediocre of you, Draghignazzo. You tried to use this exact same prank on Xiu last Thursday. Have you any better pranks to work—"

Shiro gently shushed him from next to Xiu, "The battle is starting."

Everyone looked on as the contestants manifested into the black and white world. The squads seemed just as perplexed by their surroundings as the watchers. The fact that Cyrille started on the side of the walls and Mayil was on the ceiling did nothing to help anyone understand what was up and what was down.

Looking at the five members of Rooster Squad, Xiu noticed something peculiar. There was a giant crossbow on Shee'vra's back. She turned to Vasanti. "What the hell is on her back?" Shee'vra had never told her that she had a weapon. It risked putting her off balance.

"Oh, that there? That's a big crossbow," Vasanti explained to her as if she thought she had no idea what a crossbow is. "You shoot people with it."

"Actually, it's an arbalest," Shiro corrected her.

Sabelle shrugged dismissively. "Her brother must have got it for her." She turned to the supposed leader of their little posse. "Who would have thought that Sheev's older brother, who's on the same team as her, would give her a weapon to defend herself with, right? Especially when said sister was explicitly told by her master *not* to tell her brother that she was being trained by somebody else?"

Xiu rolled her eyes at her friend's dry tone. She just pouted and crossed her arms. "Whatever, she just better show what I've taught her."

~ * ~

Rooster Squad stuck close to one another on Ercan's orders and explicitly on the same gravitational field. The aeon detecting glyph was all but useless on Julia since she had all her squadmates around setting it off. They all knew that Bianca was known to create mirrors out of the ground and strike at any time. Though unlike Hanako, she had no way to bring anybody into the mirror world.

But that was little comfort. Basil and Caradoc were strong, fast, and able to leap great distances; Zivot could grant sentience to items, including weapons; and Mayil could summon a giant peacock and rain down on them with his bow and javelin. They agreed that the two most dangerous would be Bianca and Basil. Basil could detect how naughty or nice they were from long distances and then quickly rush in to quickly take one of them out. Bianca was a whole different story altogether. People at the academy said that she could flay a man with her spark in twenty seconds. Some of her victories did not make them doubt that at all.

"So, what?" Yun piped up, his tail flicking about in anxiety, "do we just wait for them to come to us?"

Ercan nodded his head as he twirled two chains around. "We wait here together. If they want to fight us, they don't get a chicken drumstick. They get the whole rooster." He was oblivious to how half the spectators were laughing at him. He thought it was clever.

"Whoa! Careful, Eagles," Julia commented as she looked upwards, "we got a real deep fried badass over here. Be wary, he might give you food poisoning."

Cyrille didn't get it. "But why would Eagle Squad want to eat us? Neither Alberto nor Gustave are on the team to get all bitey on any of us." He kept Cockatrice at the ready, his eyes looking in different directions.

Ercan felt a little sad inside. "It was a spur of the moment one-liner—lay off, Jules." That was a lie. He'd thought of it last night at two in the morning.

Shee'vra gently placed one of the winding screw bolts into her arbalest. She remembered how her brother told her to use her wind to enhance the power of them. From how he explained it, one hit from a twisty bolt would take most people out of the game.

But as they all walked together, they had a sense of dread. Even in a place that looked the exact same for several hundred feet, something didn't feel right.

Ercan knew they were in enemy territory. He whispered to the other four. "Do you hear that?"

As they focused their ears, they heard the light sound of flapping. No doubt that it was from the giant peacock they were expecting to fight. Despite their graceful yet narcissistic appearance, all of them knew how vicious a peacock could be when you got too close.

As they got into battle positions, they saw both Basil and Caradoc rushing toward them. As Caradoc and Basil jumped down from above, their gravity shifted midway from ceiling to ground. They set their eyes on Cyrille, possibly perceiving him as the most dangerous.

Ercan was having none of that. He needed Cyrille right now. Losing him would put them at a strict disadvantage. He lengthened his chains and set them alight. But before he could grab them both, he heard a faint noise, the noise of many small fibers flying through the air, occasionally bumping into one another. He feared the worst.

As Ercan was distracted, Cyrille shot a laser from both eyes. The two brawlers of the Eagle Squad were prudent enough to dodge them at the cost of their death-from-above strategy. As they turned around, they saw Bianca's first maneuver for the fight.

A winding storm of mirror shards shot toward Rooster Squad like a shimmering tidal wave. Though it would need his undivided attention, Ercan had a strategy specifically devoted to thousands of reflective daggers.

"Cover me!" He called out as he began to spin both chains around like propellers. As he spun faster and faster, the metal links of fire looked like an inferno wall. The shards smashed and melted into nothingness upon contact by the hundreds.

Julia placed a green up-glyph on the ground for Yun to hop on. The force sent him flying upwards, tackling into Basil. The gravity sent them onto the ceiling. Shee'vra used a gust of wind to knock Caradoc to the side of a cubic structure, with Cyrille moving in for a finishing blow, coating Cockatrice in poison.

With the two speedy bruisers out of the way, more attacks came to compensate. Once the storm of reflective knives was finished, Ercan found himself hit in the shoulder with an arrow of pure light. They looked up to see that giant peacock flying a fair distance away, with Zivot hopping off the bird to confront them.

Zivot wielded two daggers in her hands, but from the four scabbards on her back came four blades that danced in the air behind her. A sword shot toward Shee'vra, but Julia stepped in front of it blocking the attack with her shield glyph. Zivot entered the fray, her autonomous blades in front of her.

"Shee'vra! Get the archer!" Julia told her as she hit one of the swords away. "I'll take care of her."

Shee'vra had no reason to not listen to her and flew up toward the peacock. She moved in a serpentine pattern to avoid the arrows coming for her.

The light arrow dissipated from Ercan's body and he healed his shoulder with little effort. But in the distance, he saw the one he was truly aiming for. Bianca. She beckoned for him to come closer, a mirror shard in both hands ready to bleed him out. Though it may have been foolish to do this, Ercan had an idea.

"I'm coming for you!" he cried out as he charged toward her, two spear points in his hands. Bianca said nothing as she coldly waited to strike.

Just when he was within reach of her, she quickly threw both knives at him. He deflected one of them, but the other scratched the side of his neck. Instantaneously, she created two more from her wrists. The two got into close combat as one tried to outdo the other. Dagger or chain? Who would win?

~ * ~

Caradoc came to his senses as he was pinned to the wall. Turns out each cubic monolith had its own sense of gravity and it treated him as if he was sprawled on the ground. Looking forward, he saw the venomous chicken coming for him. He knew one clean hit from him and he was finished. He also knew to watch out for his eye beams. If those petrifying blasts touched his skin, he was a sitting duck. Luckily, he knew that the beams only worked if they hit flesh, and he only had his hands, upper arms, and head open to the eye rays. Though when he thought about it, that was plenty of vulnerable areas.

He placed his feet on the side of the structure and made use of his John Carter spark to ignore the world's gravity for his own. He jumped off at high speeds toward Cyrille, feet first. Cyrille barely had time to fall onto his back to avoid his feet meeting his beak. He spat a wad of saliva as he was prone, which began squirming toward its target.

Caradoc looked up to see Yun and Basil duking it out, trying to out-grapple one another. He knew that Hanuman made Yun stronger than he looked. The agility was also doing favors. Though Basil was faster than Yun, the monkey was quicker to dodge and roll away. He was also stronger than Basil, knocking him around the arena.

Cyrille could wait for later. Though the rooster was deadly on contact, one clean hit would take him out. If he could just overwhelm and take out Yun now, Rooster Squad would have to go on without their physically strongest member. It would be like cutting off a limb.

He summoned his two blades and prepared to jump up. Cyrille tried to stop him with Cockatrice, but the dual wielder merely parried the sword away and kicked him back. With a deep breath, Caradoc defied gravity and launched himself into the air. He flipped the moment he felt the gravitational pull reverse and landed on both feet, making a dash toward his fellow disciple of Master Yeren.

As he dodged another of Basil's tackles, Yun jumped on top of the muscular teen's head to avoid Caradoc's blades. Kicking himself off of his skull, Yun launched back a safe distance. He could not help but feel a bit cocky. If Caradoc was here for him for a two-against-one battle that meant they both thought he was that much of a danger to them.

He signaled the two to try to come closer with his whole hand. "If you two want me so badly, come get some." He made sure to smile as smugly as he knew how.

Basil straightened his glasses with a finger. "Oh, you getting cocky now, huh?" He ran at great speeds to wipe that smile off his face with his fist.

Yun caught the punch. He tried to make the feat seem like a breeze, but his palm hurt quite a bit. Basil might have been as strong as a hylic wrestler but, with his great speed, it felt like he had just caught a car. But ignoring the pain, he kicked him straight in the chin, followed by a second kick with the back of his heel into his side.

As Basil was knocked away, Caradoc charged in with a flurry of cuts. Yun rolled and dodged the attacks. Fists and feet he could handle, but everyone knew that grabbing a sword just was not worth it. Finding an opening, Yun managed to jab him in the stomach, followed by a knee to the chin. With Caradoc staggering back, Yun hit him with a roundhouse to the face, knocking him down. Feeling proud of his skills, he failed to notice what was behind him.

"I got you, buddy!" Basil got Yun in an arm lock, getting the monkey ready to be finished off. "Caradoc go!"

But Yun would not go down so easily. He hopped back, getting Basil on the ground. He hit the wrestler in the face with the back of his head. Caradoc got up and tried to take advantage of the opening, but Yun grabbed his wrist with a foot.

But this was only a temporary setback for the two. Basil still held on with all his might and there was a second scimitar to deal with. Yun tried to struggle out, but Caradoc kicked him in the face to pacify him.

"Nothing personal. Just a game." Caradoc raised his second blade to strike him down. There was no shame in killing a pinned foe like this. In the real world, there is no such thing as a fair fight. So why fight fair in the fake world, especially to save your struggling comrade?

But just before a sword could reach his heart, all three could hear a splatting sound. Caradoc's hand began to shiver. Dropping both of the Blades of Barsoom, he went down to his knees. Feeling the back of his head, he felt something wet. But as he looked back at his hand, he saw it was covered in bubbling drool that stung to the touch. He sighed, knowing exactly what this meant as his body weakened by the second. Looking back, he saw Cyrille with Cockatrice in one hand and a disc with an up-arrow glyph in the other. *I hardly even did anything. Sorry, Captain.* He collapsed to the floor.

Basil knew what was up and immediately threw Yun away from him to rush the new threat down with a fist. But Cyrille merely shot him with both eye beams, stopping him right in his tracks. With a wave of his fingers, he maneuvered the spittle on Caradoc's head onto his blade.

With one small cut from Cockatrice, Basil was finished.

"Good game," were the last words Basil muttered as he fell onto his back.

Yun came to his senses to see the two warriors of Eagle Squad disappear into nothingness. He stood up to see that Cyrille did this without even breaking a sweat.

His ally turned to see him upright. "Why, hello there, Yun. You okay, friend?"

He cringed as he felt his bloody nose. "Not as okay as I want to be." Yun hesitated for a moment, but he just had to ask. "Since when did you get so strong to take two psychics out just like that?" He snapped his fingers to emphasize his point.

Cyrille slightly frowned and shook his head. "I'm not strong, Yun. I merely had the advantage in both surprise and spark." He coughed a bit. "To be honest, creating and moving around such a deadly toxin has taken a bit of a toll on me." He pointed toward Julia, who was still defending herself from four swords surrounding her as Zivot waited for an opening. "Can you help her? I'll give you a boost."

Yun nodded his head and Cyrille aimed Julia's glyph toward the two girls. Yun hopped on and was boosted into the fray. He somersaulted before he hit the ground. Zivot barely moved aside.

"Heya, tutor!" He saluted his opponent. "I'm ready for some extra credit."

Zivot had a gut feeling that if Yun was in front of her, Mayil was confronting the new girl, the captain was dealing with their captain, and that both Basil and Caradoc were defeated, though they had seemed to injure him a little bit. "You had help from my master, didn't you?" She pointed both of her daggers at him.

"Maybe I did. Maybe I didn't," he bluffed to her. From the corner of his eye he saw three swords start coming for him. He did the smart thing and ran.

Finally having some breathing room, Julia went more on the offensive. She swatted the weapon away from her and quickly took out a disk. But as she tried to scribe a glyph onto it, the quasi-sentient sword unleashed its secret maneuver. The handle began to unscrew to reveal a stiletto. The thin dagger levitated into the air and darted toward her.

Though her shield deflected the attack on time, the other swords seemed to act as if they saw what their fellow weapon did. They took the cue and released their stilettos. The swords and stilettos focused all of their attention on Yun. The Monkey frantically ran about in an attempt to gain distance from eight different weapons.

I must stop just standing around. Zivot made the decision to go for Julia. Her living blades would handle him for now, but she could not leave Julia with any breathing room. She ran toward her with daggers ready, forcing Julia to drop her silver glyph once again. Julia tried to block with her energy shield. Upon impact Zivot threw her other dagger into the air, which began to curve around her defenses. It dodged her electric tonfa and went for her throat. Only the timely intervention of her hand prevented her from getting a knife in her esophagus.

The dagger squirmed in her hand, struggling to get free. Her fingers were getting more cut by the second and Zivot was moving in once again. In desperation, she dropped her weapon and turned off her shield to lighten her load. As Cyrille's maid/bodyguard went in for the kill, Julia dived toward her unfinished glyph.

Zivot saw what she was doing and had a backup plan. She jumped on top of her and used Tsukumogami to breathe out silver air onto her powersuit. The full body armor just stopped moving.

Julia tried as hard as she could to budge, but nothing came of it. "Come on! What's going on?" She found that her suit was getting up all by itself. "You didn't…"

"I did," she told Julia with a straight face, "your suit is no longer your own. It's mine."

Her powersuit's arm began to move on its own. The dagger in her hand quit struggling in favor of allowing itself to settle into the armor's hand. The knife came closer and closer to her throat, ready to stab into it like a pork chop. She struggled with her arm from inside the suit but its strength was too much for her.

So this is how it ends, first one down. Well this s— She sprouted an idea from her mind. *If these things are truly alive, they can see and hear. Gives me an idea. Well here goes nothing.*

She reactivated her alarm glyph. With Zivot being so close, it started blaring like crazy at full volume. Tragically, weapons given life have no way to block out sound. The dagger in her hand went nuts and bolted away like a minnow. She flailed about in her suit, which was going utterly nuts now.

Zivot covered one ear. "Turn that damn racket off!" She tried to finish her off personally, but her knife flew out of her hand away from the noise.

Though the screeching alarm pained her ears, Julia exerted enough strength and willpower to move through it. Fighting against her own armor, she fell to the floor. Crawling to the glyph, she used her fingertip to finish the final arc of a large silver magnet. She looked behind her to see Yun rushing toward her with eight weapons trailing him. Now was her chance.

Turning off her alarm glyph, she tossed the seal like a flying disc for a dog. Zivot just managed to roll to the side, breathing in relief, feeling she dodged an explosive disc. But that relief was short lived as she felt her upper body getting pulled backwards. Her breastplate armor felt as if it was being pulled toward the disc. She fell back as her body was dragged toward the silver glyph. When she saw the monkey roll back, she noticed something terrible.

Though her blades tried to continue their endless pursuit, they, too, could not resist the magnetic force and moved toward her. At high speeds. Point first.

She could only prepare for the inevitable as she closed her eyes. If she was going to "die," at least she could do it with dignity. Within seconds, she was a pincushion.

Luckily for Julia, her sentient armor was both heavy and determined enough to keep in place. But soon, the uncontrollable struggling ended and Julia had her body again. Deactivating the magnetic seal, she looked behind her. As Zivot disappeared, all of her weapons disappeared with her.

"You alright, Jules?" Yun asked, helping her up. "That was good thinking back there."

Other than having cuts on her neck and right-hand fingers, she felt all right. "I'm in just as good condition as you are." She looked toward the two captains as they dueled one-on-one. "Should we help him?"

Yun merely shook his head as he saw the clash between inferno chains and obsidian and mirror knives. "Nah. I feel he wants to do it himself. Got to prove himself or something."

"That's dumb." She shrugged. "Anyway, three down, two to go.

Now where's Shee'vra?"

~ * ~

Ercan lashed at her again and again. Bianca ducked and weaved each attempt against her. His clothes were getting all torn from the various long-healed wounds from her mirror shards. A couple of shards were pushed out of his body every once in a while.

If he could get one hit on her it would be over for her. But Bianca was not going to make this easy. In fact, her face did not even seem angry, frustrated, smug, or bored. There was a look of utter indifference in her eyes. He was having none of that.

He shortened the length and charged in with dual fire meat hooks. Taking a glass knife to the jugular, he refused to stop. As he tried to close the gap, Bianca created an obsidian sword in her hands to counter him. Their weapons clashed again and again. During a power struggle, Bianca kicked him in the stomach with a boot shard. As he lost his concentration, she sliced his neck with her blade.

Ercan swiftly healed from what would be a fatal strike and shot out both fire chains like bolas. She deflected both attacks and raised a mirror from the ground. As Ercan shot out a flaming net for her, she jumped inside to the mirrorworld. The mirror smashed as the heavy net hit into it.

Ercan took this short breather to monitor his surroundings. *Now where could she have gone?* As soon as he was finished thinking that, four more mirrors shot up to surround him.

Bianca threw shard after shard at him from the safety of the mirrorworld. She ran circles around him as she tossed mirror, glass, and obsidian at him. His right eye, left tendon, and liver were all struck. As he fell on one knee from the pain, the redhead created a gigantic chain with both hands. He spun around to shatter each mirror to pieces. Quickly healing, he waited for her next move.

To his supreme irritation she continued to do the same thing, tossing more shards at him. Ercan created a wrecking ball at the end of his chain and smashed it into the ground where he predicted she'd go. Hearing her trip on the sudden crater he made, he got out of the area.

He had watched and studied old recordings of her battles all week. He learned that though she could see the world around her without trouble in the mirror world, a living being had to be in front of a mirror for her to see or hurt them. His and other people's reflections inside the mirror were unable to be hurt by her and vice versa. Reflections were like ghosts in that manner—could be seen but could not be disturbed.

He dropped his giant chain and created three thin ones on each hand. With a spear at each end of them, he pulled himself upward toward what he was pretty sure was the ceiling. When the gravity changed for him, he fell straight on his back.

"Why does it have to be this weird stage?" He restored his fractured bones. "Wait a minute." He had a realization. *Bianca has only two ways to get me up here. Both require her to be in the real world. If she would just get out, I can get her when she's off guard. She can't just go around throwing shards forever from the mirror world. I hear it's taxing for her to bring herself and her projectiles through the mirror.* He just had to wait her out.

But would she go for him? Or would she take out his squad mates first. Ercan began to feel a sense of worry. If Julia or Shee'vra were still in the battle, maybe they could help the rest come to the ceiling. But where were they?

And why was Bianca taking so long to come out?

Shee'vra was zipping around the arena as fast as she could. Hot on her tail was Mayil, his bow at the ready. Today she learned that giant peacocks are much faster fliers than they appeared. She had been trying to keep her space against him with her air powers, but they only bought seconds at most.

No, no. What do I do? She dived up over a cubic structure. *He's not even giving me a chance to fire back at him. If I stay still too long, he'll hit me.* She squeaked as a light arrow just missed her ear. *This can't go on forever. I need an idea.*

An idea came to her. It would be risky, but it was an idea. She had seen and felt the gravitational pulls this place had. The ceiling, walls, and cubic structures all had their own gravity. When she flew up high enough, it would be like flying on her back, and when she flew close to a cube, she was dragged closer toward it. Luckily, Sylph was very forgiving with how it handled flight. The air moved along with her almost like crowd-surfing, except all around her body. But she doubted a large winged creature could handle being upside down in the sky.

She looked around to see that there were two block structures just opposite of one another above her and below her. Quickly diving down toward the floor, she took a sharp tight turn around a block. She peered from a corner to see that the big bird was going nowhere near any of the cubes. Mayil also seemed to have been expecting her to come from the top area. He would eventually start looking her way, so why not confirm his first theory?

She looked at Cloudstabber to see the windy-bolt-thingy still safe inside it. Ercan had previously talked about using her wind powers to make the projectile spin in the air like shooting out a drill. Seemed like a handy trick against a peacock, why not? "Well here goes nothing." She focused on the air to channel through the bolt like a winding tunnel. The projectile began to spin faster and faster in place as more air was rushing through it. Eventually she realized it was as if she made a javelin of wind.

When she saw Mayil turn his head toward the corner she was at, she swiftly flew out of sight. She flew up the cube, across the top and down below. When she was under the bird, she channeled her wind powers as hard as she knew how just when the peacock squawked out her presence.

The gust must have been strong enough to knock ten people back, because the peacock could not resist the sudden updraft. The windblast brought it closer toward the cube above them. She saw the surprised look on his face when he clung onto his bird for dear life as gravity flipped for him.

Now taking her opportunity, Shee'vra took the shot. The bolt spiraled through the air at alarming speeds. It ignored the abnormal gravity and hit its mark. The peacock made a pained cry as it fell onto the ceiling. From what Shee'vra could see from the blood, the shot went through the entire avian and kept on going.

This feeling was odd to her. She'd watched many battles on The Stage all through her life. She'd seen many ways a person could bite the dust. She even saw her brother do the deed a couple of times. But the sensation was different in person. It was quite an ugly feeling and would only get uglier as she got older. But she'd have to get used to it. She must.

As she loaded another shot, she flew toward the dead bird. Looking at the peacock's back, she was correct in her assumption that the bolt went straight through. But where was Mayil? Did he "die" in the crash?

As she was asking herself questions, she felt a stinging sensation in her stomach. Looking down, her pupils shrank in horror. Jutting into her stomach was an arrow of hard golden light, which disappeared in her fingers.

She staggered and struggled to breathe as she saw the archer leave his hiding place under the wing of his mount. His bow was pure gold and carved with ornate symbols, but the string was made of light.

"Forgive me, miss," Mayil softy spoke to her, "this must be your first time experiencing such a sensation—this pain." He shook his head bitterly. "But I'm afraid you must get used to it. Sophia herself found it in her to bless us with great power." He pulled the light string back. "Our penance for extraordinary power must be pain. Get used to this sensation." A golden arrow appeared in his fingers, ready to shoot. "Or you will never survive."

Shee'vra was not going down like this. She needed to prove to herself, Ercan, Xiu, and everyone else that she was psychic material. She quickly took aim with Cloudstabber, but Mayil merely shot her weapon out of her hands.

"Defiant to the end I see," he told her with a stone-faced expression. He prepared another shot, aiming for her head. "Admirable but—" He was knocked down by a gust of wind. Getting up, he saw the girl rushing toward him. Her stance seemed like one of the styles of that girl Yun lived with. He got up as fast as he could to hit her away with his bow, but she blocked the attack. Mayil's face then met her palm. Though it hurt a bit, it was far from enough to knock him out. The attack felt clumsy to say the least. Xiu had much more to teach this novice.

But he was not expecting what was to come next. Another gale burst shot out from her hand point blank. Mayil had no time to react as he was sent flying back. He went far enough to ignore the cube's gravity and fell toward what was either the floor or ceiling, which was at least a couple of stories high.

Shee'vra held her stomach as she watched him hit the ground and disappear. Her first victory felt pretty good, she guessed. But there was no time to bask in her glory. Her brother's position was on the line. And she wasn't going to disappoint him.

She looked at her wound and saw that the arrow cauterized when it pierced flesh. The sensation was not fun at all, to say the least. But she had to move forward to help the rest of them.

She picked up Cloudstabber. "Now am I on the floor or ceiling?" As she began to fly up, the world suddenly went dark. The last thing she felt was a sharp pain in the back of her head.

"What just happened?! Where am I?!" That second question was solved quickly. She recognized her surroundings and found herself in the simulation seat. Somebody must have got her from behind.

"Bianca killed you," Mayil bluntly told her as he got out of his seat. "You should check your surroundings before you relax." He walked toward the loser's room. "Good victory on me, though. Wasn't expecting it. Sophia has blessed you well."

Shee'vra shrugged and followed him into the loser's quarters. There she saw Basil, Caradoc, and Zivot as well. She must have been the only Rooster Squad out. She couldn't help but smile a bit.

"I suggest you guys shouldn't get cocky, though. Bianca's more than a match for them," Basil said to her with confidence in his captain. "They better watch out."

"I hope they keep that in mind then," Shee'vra replied as she sat next to Caradoc. "So how did I get defeated?"

"Bianca sliced your head in half with obsidian," Zivot plainly told her, her eyes not leaving the crystalvision screens. "It was as painless as she could make it."

She shivered at the visual of her skull being sliced in two. But Shee'vra watched on as she saw Cyrille walk toward Yun and Julia, waving to them. She nearly gasped as she saw a mirror rise up behind them.

⁓ ✳ ⁓

Where is she? Where are they? Ercan scrambled around the arena to look for anybody. Shee'vra, Yun, Julia, Cyrille, Bianca. Nobody was around him. He ran as fast as he could. He could bet that Bianca was picking off his squad mates without him around.

"Oh crap," he muttered to himself in awed epiphany, "that was what she wanted, wasn't it?"

He quickened his pace. Up, down, left, right, everything looked the same. All he knew was that he was on the ceiling—at least he was pretty sure about that.

Sounds began to suddenly invade his eardrums. They were sharp cries of pain that stopped as soon as they had begun. She must have found them and it was too late to save them. He shivered at the thought of what his sister felt upon her defeat. *Was she merely knocked out or was she "killed"? Did Cloudstabber help her at all? Will this fight break her spirit?* He wasn't there to protect her from Bianca. He'd failed them and failed himself. She was just too strong for him and choosing to fight her was a terrible mistake.

It wasn't that she was invincible or anything, far from it. A few hits and she would be done for. The big problem was that she was just so damn hard to hit. Bianca was not only one of the greatest gymnasts in school, but her mirror jumping was just so freaking irritating. Hanako was less of a problem because she needed to have her own mirror on her to enter that world. Bianca could just make her own out of the ground. It was not only just mirrors either—any reflective surface would do. The fact that she could create sharp objects out of glass and obsidian made her even more untouchable. They might not do much to someone like him, but he had his limits. All she needed to do was wear him down to his last point of aeon. A thousand small cuts are just as effective as one large slash, if not more so.

Worse still, not even his reflection could hurt her. Only the environment could hurt her. Anything attached to his body just went right through her.

Wait a minute. If only the environment and objects not on my person can hurt her, can't I just detach my chains midair? Would it hurt her? He might as well try. He depended on it working.

He created one short chain with a spear tip. He lit it and readied it to launch it from his wrist, just biding his time for her to show up. He waited for what felt like an hour but was only a couple of minutes. Even expecting it, he nearly jumped in surprise as a mirror shot up five feet from him.

Inside the mirror just behind him was Bianca. Though she'd taken out his entire squad, she didn't have a single drop of blood on her. Not on her form-fitting padded armor, not on her priceless boots, not on her pale skin, not on her bow that held her ponytail, and most definitely not on her golden circlet nor the purple amethyst in its center. How efficient was she to be as stainless as her weapon of choice?

But it was time to enact his theory. As she tossed a large shard through his back, he tossed his spear behind him. Looking at the reflection, he was stunned.

It actually hit her. She blocked it with her hand but she cried out in pain as it pierced and burned her. Though she said nothing, her open mouth and wide eyes proved to him that she hadn't expected it. He milked this chance to launch a large weight at her, but she rolled away from the mirror's view.

He expected some more waiting. He wouldn't need to, though. Twenty feet across from him, she came out of the mirror world to confront him in person.

Her expression gave nothing away. "You want to fight me in person, do you?"

He pulled out the shard in his body with a pained expression he tried his damnedest to suppress. "Yes?" Two spiked chains hung out of his wrists.

"Good." She created two obsidian daggers. "I do too."

Ercan rushed toward her. She dodged his vertical strike and grabbed him. Creating a reflective spike on her knee, she jabbed it into his stomach. Ercan gasped in agony as she dislodged the spike into his body, taking a few steps back from him. Vomiting blood on the floor, he went to his knees.

"If it gives you consolation, your sister didn't feel a thing."

This was not over yet. His heart pumped faster as he ripped the piece out of his body. Blood and stomach juice was all over the once clean floor. His eyes began to shut but he forced them open.

Not yet.

As he got back to his knees, the hole in his body fixed itself up until there was just his abs left. He shot out three metal links from his right hand, each ending in a cylindrical weight. Bianca merely zipped to the side and charged him with an obsidian sword. Before he could use the hook in his other hand, he was minus one limb and gained a slashed throat. He gurgled on his own blood as he tried his best to not fall over.

He was not finished, though. He repaired his throat and spat out any blood in his mouth. He forced a grin. "You're going to have to do better." He lashed at her and shattered her black stone sword.

She was far from frightened. Bianca merely created a flechette of shards that skewered him around his upper body. She shook her head as he still clumsily stumbled around on his feet in a daze.

"I am finished with you," she muttered to him. Raising an arm up, hundreds of obsidian knives manifested from thin air. The sharp volcanic rocks ascended. With a mere flick of her wrist, each and every shard dived down toward her target.

Ercan could only watch helplessly through one eye as it all rained down on him.

A Captain's Failures

"Is it truly over?" Desiderio deeply stared at the screen, expecting something more. He didn't know what it would be, but there was going to be more.

"Of course it is, Garza," Winona huffed. "None of us can survive that." Confident as she was of her own abilities, even she knew Bianca would find a way to beat her.

"Then why is he not disappearing?" he answered back to her. Desiderio had counted the time of when a beaten opponent disappears. Five seconds, maybe ten tops. "It's been almost a minute."

That caught Vural's ear. "You mean that he could get up and make some kind of insane comeback?"

Alexandru shook his head. "I sincerely doubt it. Ercan is doomed I'm afraid to say."

"That is merely fate when you mess with the likes of Bianca." Ludmila sat back in her seat.

"Whatever," Gaizka growled as he chewed on a burger. "At least he had the balls to fight her." Food dribbled out of his mouth. "More than what can be said about us."

Mastema ignored their squabbling and all his eyes were on the screens. Even as the redhead lay face down with at least sixty daggers in him, he had yet to disappear like any other fallen opponent. He and the rest of his floating eyes peered at the limp and bloody body. As he watched, he saw a finger twitch. At first, he wanted to dismiss it as rigor mortis or something, but if he were "dead," then he would be off the stage by now.

His focus was interrupted by Hanako gasping. "D-did you guys see that?" Her hands covered her mouth in shock. "H-he's moving."

The others focused their attention to the screen once again and saw that, yes, Ercan was beginning to move his hand. The arm started to shift positions to place his hand onto the tiled floor, ignoring the three shards in his palm. Bianca was watching all of this from only a couple of meters away. But she did nothing but silently look on expressionlessly.

Winona barely knew what to say. "No way. He cannot be still alive."

"But he is," Desi said to the woman in black right beside him. "Hard to deny, honestly." She had no way to dispute that.

Vural got off the ceiling and sat his butt on a chair. He threw his fists around. "Alright! Time for round two!"

"I doubt round two will last very long then," Ludmila remarked to him.

By this time, Ercan had forced himself onto his two feet that were barely able to support his weight. Shards of black glass shattered on the ground as his body began to force them out one by one.

Alexandru got up from his chair. "If I watch any longer I am going to be sick!" He marched right out and shut the door behind him.

On the screen, Ercan ripped out the shard in his eye. The agony was apparent on his face. Barely waiting to heal, he created a singled burning spiked chain. He walked toward her with his clothes shredded up and more than enough puncture wounds on his back. But if the audience expected a grand climax to this battle, they would be very disappointed.

The moment Ercan moved to attack, Bianca shot one large obsidian shard through his head. The captain of Rooster Squad fell onto his back and stopped moving for good.

Though Mastema did not enjoy doing this, he must now vote against him. He lost. Simple as that.

⁓ ＊ ⁓

Ercan was completely silent as he came back to the real world. He still felt the knives in his back, even knowing nothing was there. Nearby, Bianca got out of her chair with hardly a word. Her expression was as hard to read as usual.

"You lasted longer than last time," Bianca told him without even looking back at him as she exited the room.

That was true. But she still ran circles around him. Even after handicapping herself by staying in the regular world he still couldn't even touch her. People like her were a perfect example of how much he had yet to learn.

But the problem was not just his loss. He'd also allowed his whole crew to die. He was so focused on taking out the opposition that he didn't know where they went. The moment she had a chance, Bianca went for his squadmates instead. Julia. Yun. Cyrille. Shee'vra. All defeated just like that.

It must have been horrid for his little sister to experience. The fear she must have felt as she got a mirror shard through her neck. The nightmares she'd have to endure. The first "death" of every student was always the hardest. Hopefully she would recover soon enough.

Mustering enough strength to get out of his seat, he saw Rooster and Eagle Squad sitting together. At the very least, he knew his crew was talented enough to score victories by themselves. Maybe they were better psychics than him.

"Hey, Ercan, you alright?" Yun called out to him, concerned. "It took a hell of a lot to put you down. Must have hurt an insane crap ton."

"I'm fine, I guess." Ercan half-heartedly answered him, trying not to frown. "Sorry we lost, though."

"Well you tried your best," Cyrille comforted him. "That is what matters. You even hurt Bianca a little bit."

"Besides, we've had worse losses," Julia chimed in. "At least we kicked the rest of the squad's asses before we got slaughtered."

Mayil took offense as he sat next to his squad mates. "We're right here, you know. Try not to treat us as merely Princess Bianca's fodder."

"Now nobody said that, buddy." Basil patted his compatriot's shoulder. "They're just happy to take us all down fair and square." He stared at Cyrille through his glasses. He did not like poison, but he would be hard pressed to call it unfair to use a spark the way it was meant to be used. Besides, real battle was not fair. His wrestling wouldn't be nearly as effective in a war as toxins.

Zivot got up and turned to Rooster Squad, bowing to them. "Though ultimately Eagle squad has won, you five have proven to be worthy opponents. In another scenario, there's a possibility we wouldn't be so victorious." She turned toward their captain. "I recommend that you don't let this loss affect you so hard."

With that, Zivot quietly left the room with Basil, Mayil, and Caradoc following soon after. At least Ercan knew that today was not a complete failure. But it was like using a bandage to fix a ship. He still found himself feeling a bit empty. Shee'vra must have noticed.

"Are you sure you're okay?" his sister asked him, concerned.

Ercan did not feel like speaking about his issues. It was probably pathetic that he was so concerned about the loss of his title. It wasn't like he had much to lose. Just a title that, chances were, would be passed on to one of his friends. But he needed to answer.

"Fine. Just thinking about how painful today was. Natural reaction to being stabbed a hundred times." He wasn't exactly lying. It hurt like a bitch with a buzz saw. "But how was your first battle?"

Shee'vra felt a sense of self-respect for her skills. "Well, I defeated Mayil by myself." She quickly turned to Cyrille. "Not that he was weak or anything. I just feel that I got lucky."

"It's okay, Sheev," the lizard chicken reassured her. "Mayil will get over being beaten by the new girl."

Her victory raised his spirits another bit. Ercan gave her a brotherly hug. "That's great to hear. Good to know my sister is getting used to the psychic life really quickly."

"I wouldn't exactly say that," she replied, unsure of herself. "I still have loads to learn."

"We all do," Julia said. "That's why it's school." They ignored her comment.

Yun got up from the bench. "What now? Just go about the rest of the day normally? Maybe get a bite to eat?"

Ercan let out a sigh. "Maybe tomorrow, Yun. I honestly have a lot on my mind right now. Do you guys mind if I take a walk alone for a bit?"

Having lost his trial by combat, the crew knew he needed a bit of space. Being a captain was a high honor. Having it stripped from you must suck. The four looked around at one another to see if any of them objected to their soon-to-not-be-captain having some time to be alone.

"Sure thing, man."

"If it would make you feel at ease."

"Don't sulk too much."

"Alright," Shee'vra told him reluctantly. "Should I tell mom and dad that you won't be coming home for dinner?"

He took a few seconds to think about it. "I guess so. I'm probably going to go to the Binah Library. Mr. Jahikah is merciless with the homework." He softly strolled away from the group. "See you guys later, I guess."

As Ercan exited, there was an uncomfortable aura in the room. His teammates could tell that the loss had hit him hard. No matter how hard he tried to survive, even with every ounce of determination, he still couldn't come even close to victory. And it was all his fault he would no longer retain his position. He could have picked a duel with maybe somebody like Gaizka or Hanako. But no, his pride made him choose Bianca. And now he paid for his arrogance.

But they didn't worry for his anemic state. They felt that he would never do anything regrettable even if he felt depressed. Instead they knew that, like a hamster, he would just merely isolate himself when stressed. He would be better in no time. Hopefully.

But Julia felt like she had to bring something up to the group. "He knows that the Binah Library closes at 5:30 on Wednesdays, right?" It was currently 4:45. But he would learn eventually.

⁓ * ⁓

Xiu Lang exited the SAIS alone. She had a lot to think about and her friends would only distract her. The Ao'Si siblings were troubling her brain. First was Shee'vra. She never told her about wielding a big ass crossbow. It looked cumbersome to wield and might not mix well with her training. Chin Na required precise movements and such a weight could disrupt her balance.

But then again, she seemed to have learned something from her. Though the attack was imperfect at best, her Tiger Fist attack on Mayil worked. Shee'vra's natural wind powers were what made the attack truly effective. She would need to work with her on that. She couldn't just rely on her spark to do the heavy lifting when it came to martial arts. Overall, she would need to have a talk with her as soon as possible.

Then there was the issue with Ercan. She knew about how this whole duel was about him retaining his place as one of the ten captains.

She had to admit that she was somewhat impressed that he managed to make some kind of weird spinning firewall. Without that trick, the fight would have been over much quicker.

But he picked a fight with Bianca. It was bound to not end well. Hell, she was pretty sure that The Razor Sharp Reflection herself was holding back against him to see what he could do. Though Ercan did something resembling damage against her, it was far from enough.

But overall, the fight was not embarrassing. Ercan stood up longer than expected. His endurance against pain was also quite impressive. Xiu would be reeling on the floor with a glass shard stabbed into her. Not to mention a hundred. Or a slit throat. Or impaled. If anything, this fight showed his determination. She'd known he had it inside him somewhere, but damn, she was glad to see it every so often.

But she knew that he was going to be pretty torn up about losing. Should she talk to him? Comfort him? What could she do about his inevitable sulking? *Honestly, when things go wrong for him he could be such as baby.*

But speak of the Demiurge. Just as she was exiting the school grounds, she saw one Ercan Ao'Si. As expected, he wasn't in the best of moods, but it felt like a crime to just not say anything. She approached him. "Ercan."

"Xiu." He acknowledged her existence, though he thought they were on non-speaking terms.

She had the idea to play dumb, just so he might be a bit more talkative. "I was busy with the HW and such, so I missed your big day." She playfully punched his arm. "So how'd it go?"

"Well actually—"

"I bet you're just all mopey because you feel bad about hitting a princess, right?" Xiu told him. "Don't worry. Bianca's not going to have you hanged for it."

"That's not it." Ercan tried to correct her, a frown still on his face.

"Then what is it?" She acted oblivious.

Ercan hesitated for a moment before answering her. "I…lost."

She knew that already but pressed the issue, feigning surprise. "Oh. Well how badly?"

"We took out four…she took out five," Ercan told her honestly, "by herself."

"Well, she is number two for a reason," she comforted him. "Seriously, the fact that you guys managed to take out her crew before she annihilated you all says something about your skill, right?"

"Well, I guess." He looked directly at her. "But there was a little more at stake."

That was obvious to her, though she decided to play along. "And what could that be?"

"This was supposed to be a…Trial by Battle." He seemed quite ashamed of himself. "The fact I lost means that unless the stars align for me or pigs fly, then I'm no longer captain of Rooster Squad."

Xiu tried to be surprised about the reason for his mood. "Well, that is an issue, I guess. Can't say from experience, but it must suck, losing such status and getting privileges taken away from you."

"Yeah, it's going to suck hard." Ercan sighed. "I guess you're right about me then."

That stumped her. "About what exactly?" She had no idea what he was talking about.

"That 'anybody is better off on a different squad than yours'," he reminded her. "But now that I think about it, maybe you're right. I might just be a glorified punching bag."

Xiu could tell what was going to happen next. "Hey, now. Don't just suddenly have a pity party."

"I might actually be holding the others back. Yun is stronger than me, Julia is smarter, and Cyrille is…Cyrille." Ercan felt a sense of worry inside. "But Shee'vra could do better than just me. She isn't safe under my care. None of them are. Today proved that."

Damn, he has a lot to say. Xiu was questioning to herself if Ercan was just talking to her to vent his frustrations. "That is some heavy shit right there. But damn, are you done flogging yourself yet?"

Ercan was taken aback by her comment. "S-sorry I didn't mean to talk about all my life problems. But I do need you for something." He found inside himself a surge of confidence. "Will you help train Shee'vra?"

Xiu was not exactly expecting him to say that. "Why me and not Yun or Caradoc or even Hong? Why all this trust suddenly?"

"Weeeell…" Ercan tried to explain. "Yun's style has very steep requirements and he—"

"What's *that* supposed to mean?" Were her combat methods considered simpler or less complex or something? She worked just as hard as her peers to hone her skills.

He backtracked really quickly. "Sorry! Sorry! Didn't mean to insult your technique!" He waited a bit for her to cool down. "What I really meant is that Yun fights mostly as a monkey man. Shee'vra cannot catch up with a monkey in training, she knows nothing about sword wielding, and I'm more than sure it's impossible for a regular human to do most of the stuff Hong does."

Xiu rolled her eyes and huffed. "So, what? I'm chosen by process of elimination?"

"No, not that!" Ercan waved his hands. "The truth is that I've been watching old videos of our past battles and checking you out…in the videos. Your style of course." He felt a need to make that clear. "I feel like your Tiger Fist Style would do wonders for her." He jabbed his open palm at nothing. "Imagine her hitting someone's face and then shooting out a blast of air. Pretty cool, right?"

"Yeah…pretty cool, I guess." It was blatantly obvious to her that he'd had yet to see a recording or anything of the battle.

"I know it might be tough on you, but can you please train Sheev in your way of battle?" He clasped his hands as if he was desperate for her to say yes.

She decided to milk her former captain's pleas for all it was worth. She looked away, appearing unsure and contemplating her options. "Well, I don't know. Admittedly it might be a bit hard."

Ercan bore an expression of disappointment, as if he'd bet his house that she would comply. "I do understand that it will be very tedious work. But I promise you she's a quick learner." He quickly made a last-ditch effort to persuade her. "If it would help your answer, I'd be willing to give you half of my mission payments."

She rolled her eyes, almost tempted to take him up on his offer. The goods she could buy with extra allowance aside, it would be a pathetic attempt to entice her to say yes if it wasn't for the fact that a potential life could be on the line. She finally dropped the charade. "No need. I'm already training her."

His violet eyes widened with surprise. "Really? Since when?"

"Since last week," she replied with gusto. "And yes, we are focusing on Tiger Fist Style. And if it makes you feel better, she did that tiger paw wind thing you were talking about. Though the stance and strike were pretty damn botched, it worked against Mayil."

He seemed genuinely grateful to her. "Well that's a load off my mind. Thank you." But then shame swept up on his face. "But I don't deserve your kindness."

"Why not?" Xiu didn't like where this was going. They were making so much progress, too.

Ercan took a deep breath. It was time to throw a massive weight off his shoulders. "I'm sorry, Xiu Lang."

"Foooor what, exactly?"

He was about to feel like the school dumbass. "For having you removed from Rooster Squad." This was happening. "I was angry and a sore loser after the last games. I recommended to the board that you be transferred to a different squad. It was short sighted and petty, and I have only myself to blame for our troubles. If I knew how to be a better captain, we would never have been at the bottom. I just really wanted to stay captain. It's fine if you're mad at me, just don't take it out of Sheev."

He was right. She was mad. But not for the reasons he assumed. "Is being a captain that important to you?" He didn't reply, only looked away from her glare. "Before I verbally rip you a new one, I have to say one thing. I'm not mad that you had me transferred to Heron Squad. I admit I made my share of mistakes. Dammit, I'm hardly even mad about your reasoning. If I was captain and you were screwing everything up, I'd kick you out too."

She roughly grabbed him by the collar. "You look at me as I talk you! What is pissing me off is that you treat this whole captain crap as the biggest issue of your life! If keeping your semi-privileged position is the main problem in your life, then dammit I want your life! Millions would want it!" She tightened her grip. "You don't know how good you got it! You have doting parents, a not-bratty little sister, food, money, friends, and a spark! You've hit the lottery of life! But you still insist on bitching and moaning about this 'oh my captain position is at risk' crap! Just shut up and deal with what comes next like a real man! Maybe you'll keep it, maybe you won't. Just deal with whatever the world gives you! It's not a big deal!"

She paused to breathe and calm herself. "A lot of us other students envy your quaint simple life. The rest of us have memories we'd rather like to keep *deep* inside us. You know, *real* problems—like being kidnapped, suffering from disease, living in a hostile environment, being part of a cult." He could see her green eyes well up with a liquid. "Or losing your parents, your village, maybe even the whole world you once knew. Those are problems the rest of us face. Be appreciative for what you have." She shoved him out of her personal space.

Ercan had not once seen her act like this. What must have happened to her to make her snap like that? He softly began to reply to her. "I'm... I'm sorry. I had no idea. A-are you okay?" As he walked closer to her, she stepped back.

"I'm fine, I'm fine," she insisted to him.

He was far from convinced. "But—"

She shook her head and covered her eyes. "Just...go off and sulk or whatever you were planning to do. Just remember that there are worse things than a demotion."

Xiu briskly walked away back to the Academy, ignoring his pleas to come back. She'd brought up all those memories again, including that monster. By Sophia, she could not get his roaring out of her head. It was the kind of sound a tiger from Hell would produce as it hurled up screaming souls of the damned. That wasn't even getting into the claws covered in blood, multiple rows of fangs as sharp as knives, or the long tail ending in sharp stingers that oozed venom. The body might have looked like that of a hideously muscled big cat, but the face of the bastard looked too human.

She kept out of sight and slipped into the girl's bathroom. She went into a stall and took a seat. As she heard the cries of the monster's victims, she softly let the waterworks go. She felt grief over her loss and envy for those who'd lost no one. If only Ercan could know how fortunate he was to not experience her life. But she kicked herself, knowing that if she would just tell him or anyone about it, they would comfort her. Even Ercan.

Why was she so scared about telling anyone then? Was it to seem tough? Not wanting to be pitied? Other insecurities? She had no idea why she could never say what she wanted to say as she quietly sobbed.

Damn Qian Ye. Why would a country do this? What have we ever done to them?

She reminisced what her old life could have been like before it was ripped away from her. What would she be like? Would she be a renowned horseback rider? Would she still live with her parents? Would she even have a spark? Even have been sent to the Academy? She had pondered those questions and more too many times to count.

~ * ~

Shèng Xià was at the wheel. He'd been driving for three hours. Jakaire/Kairieji had been driving for the other four hours of their journey and was currently asleep in the passenger's seat. How she could sleep comfortably in a car was a mystery to him. The drive from Sorchos to Bythos was in total almost three days' worth of driving. They'd spent last night in the town of Coopstone and just now they made it to Bythos.

Bythos was nothing like home. It was clean, stable, prosperous and not bankrupt. The mayor must have been ten times the man than the one in Sorchos. In fact, little girls were more man than his city's mayor. He never really heard about much crime in this town. Other than last week's desperate bank robbery that made it to the news, crime kept a low profile. They had to in "The City of Psychics."

Meanwhile, back in Sorchos, a string of mysterious disappearances was currently occurring. Those that didn't disappear were found dead from poison or had parts of their bodies turned to live snakes.

He wished some of the other members could catch some rest before the heist, especially the one already in pajamas.

"So, Shèng?" Ezker played with the little ball on his nightcap. "Word on the street is you have a cat lady neighbor?" He refused to feed him information, but he didn't shut up. "Soooo…you putting your dick in her, or what?"

Shèng was so tempted to murder him on the spot, but reined in his impulses. Unfortunately, this only encouraged him.

"I take that as a no. You obviously seem much too stressed to have been getting any lately." He jokingly gagged, "But no big deal, the thought of your wrinkly winky ramming into a cave of cobwebs is too much even for me."

From the rearview mirror, he could see his smug grin. The kind of smile that you wanted erased from the world. The kind that would be wiped off the moment he met resistance—easier said than done, though.

So instead, he gave him as witty a comeback as he could conceive at the moment. "Well you're peppy enough for a man in jammies. Have you been going to sleep without your clothes on lately?"

To his disappointment, he got a quick, joking reply with his loud city voice. "Why should I bother boning? It's boring and strenuous. Besides, my job gives me much more fun than your average broad. Ain't that right, Sinister?"

The man that sat two seats away didn't reply in a way a normal human would. Sinister merely made a small quacking sound with his duck caller as he nodded while he looked out at the skyscrapers of Bythos just out the window. On his lap was a bright blue and yellow rifle with a scope on top. None of them knew what the thing was until it was explained to them on paper. Supposedly it came from his spark and shot out water quick and powerful enough to kill a man. No doubt several had perished because of the garish thing.

But the jackass in PJs kept on talking. "At least try to lighten up, Shèng, and talk to good old Ezker here. I'm better at conversation than Duckman and the kid in the back."

He pointed with his thumb to Balra alone in the backseat. The teenager wore a large blue hoodie and a Sarkic collar around her neck. She wore a bright green headband to match her eyes. She stared at nothing with an expressionless face as she shut out her surroundings with her headphones.

"You don't get points for actually speaking," Shèng told him, hiding his impatience. "Fact is, most people don't appreciate your conversational skills."

The pajama man brushed him off. "Whatever. I'm endearing to all you guys." Sinister rolled his eyes and quacked at him. "We Lefties are one big happy family and you know it." Everyone just knew that Ezker must have thought that his ideas for phone passwords were total knee-slappers to nobody but him.

The driver parked the car and got out. Shèng Xià walked right into a nearby alley. Crouching down, he saw a sewer gate. A conspicuous pebble was right next to the lid. Pushing the pebble made a ringing sound like a doorbell.

It took a minute, but soon the Bythos faction of the Lefty Gang climbed out of their little hideout. There were only three of them, though: Izquierda, Kushoto, and Vinstri. Shèng kept both hands on his cane just in case they failed to get the paz needed. All three looked intimidated by an old guy like him, especially the scaly one hiding behind the dark-skinned lady.

"Where are Aristera and Clé?" Judging by the fact that they met them in the backup hideout, he already had a feeling for what happened.

Izquierda spoke for the group, though he appeared a bit sickly. "They got sent to Prisoner's Perch last week. We're all that's left." He threw a bag of money at his feet with a snarl. "But you guys probably just care about the damn paz. Am I wrong?" He coughed loudly into his hand.

The veteran gang member shook his head. "Not exactly, I must admit." He whistled for his crew. Almost instantly, the rest of the crew got out of the automobile. Even Kairieji who was just asleep a few moments ago was just as quick as the others to come to him.

Zuo must admit his crew did not look too intimidating. Jakaire looked fine, being a woman in her twenties, wearing a black chain shirt with a thrush symbol on it. But the others looked somewhat ridiculous. PJ wore PJs and held a body pillow with some Seichin light novel character on it. Enitharmon was a teen just out of high school and her more inhuman traits were not exactly scary compared to what most psychics saw. Roy was dressed the silliest of all. His top consisted of a hunting vest and checkered shirt, but he also wore swim trunks and flippers. The duck caller in his mouth that quacked every once in a while made him look like a waterfowl had somehow managed to become a member of the Lefty Gang. Even a silver-haired vet with arthritis like him was not exactly terrifying. But any smart psychic would know that appearances could be deceiving.

Sinister waddled over to the bag of cash and checked the bills. After an inspection, he turned to his comrades to quack in approval.

"Hm. You guys actually did it?" Ezker asked the three, surprised. "I was sure we would have to kill you." He chuckled to himself as Vinstri shivered in his presence.

The Titlacua leader of the Bythos Lefty Gang coughed once again into his hand. "You guys are going to get us out of this place, right? Just as promised?"

"Yes, of course," Shèng replied with honesty. "But first, you three need to help on tonight's heist. But not in your current condition." He patted Balra's back. "Heal him."

The youngest of the group looked up at her superior, her headphones off. "Yes sir, whatever you wish sir."

Removing her collar, Balra approached Louiz and touched his chest with an open hand. Her eyes shined and the land under her feet glowed bright green. Suddenly, sickening poisoned bile came right out of his mouth and floated in the air in front of her. With a thought, the toxins faded away into nothingness.

Izquierda now felt much better with that chicken man's poison completely out of his system. "You have my gratitude, young lady."

Balra gave a small bow. "Not a problem, sir. Whatever you wish, sir."

Now that eight gang members were part of the heist, what could possibly go wrong? Shèng Xià began to stroll back to the van. "You guys following? We still have some time to prepare." The other seven were quick to follow, some slower than others.

Zuo pondered about the text he had been reading from the book he had hidden in the compartment. He memorized that there were words that, when spoken, would reveal the true purpose of The Pauldrons of Kadosh.

By Barbar's broad shoulders these pauldrons stay. Quell the rebellions until all shall obey. Within these pauldrons lie the Divine Spark Odin. His spear, his power, his ravens, and his eye that can foretell any omen. Gugnir, Huginn, Muninn, Wuotan. I summon the power that shall last till Ragnarok.

If Cianfa was telling the truth, saying those words would reveal the real reason his boss wanted those artifacts. From what he could theorize about what this all meant, he couldn't blame them. Such power they must give! To think the emperors of old could make such items. He needed to try it for himself the moment he got his hands on those bronze shoulder pads.

A Man in Green

It had been about two and a half hours since Ercan left to be on his own. He wasn't answering his texts or calls and the rest of the squad were getting worried about him.

"I do hope our captain's okay," Cyrille stated to the other three, ignoring the pedestrians keeping their space from him. "He could be just about anywhere in this big city." He sent Zivot and Mayil back home to get dinner ready while he searched for his captain along with the rest of the group.

"Well, we already know where he is," Julia told him, annoyed at his forgetfulness. "The Sephirot Museum of Bythos. He goes there all the time when he's feeling down because he keeps forgetting that the library closes really early on Wednesdays and Mondays."

This seemed to be new news to the DeRoche. "Really? I guess I just never remember his sad days, just his happy ones." His beak frowned and his eyes got teary. "Am I a horrible friend?"

Julia begrudgingly comforted him. "No you're not, Cockadile. It's just rare to see him act like this." The last time Ercan had done this was the day after the Aeon Sophia Games. Ercan's despair was oddly predictable in a way. Whenever teenage angst hit him, it was either the library or museum he would be at.

Cyrille's noxious tears dried as quickly as they had started. "That's true. Our captain has usually been upstanding in the emotional department." One of his eyes looked at Shee'vra. "Has Ercan been

"

acting stressed lately?"

"I don't think he has," Shee'vra told him. "I assumed he might not take losing so well with his title on the line, but I thought he, along with the rest of us, did great today."

"Yeah," Yun agreed with her. "We did kick our fair share of ass today, and against Eagle Squad to boot. He should at least be proud of that." He scratched the stubble on his chin. "Something else must be troubling him. But what?"

"We're being followed." Cyrille stopped in his tracks and looked back with both his chameleon-esque eyes. "Just around the corner."

The rest also stopped walking and looked toward the street corner. It could be anyone—a friend, a parent, or, worst case scenario, a Lefty Gang member looking for revenge. The sidewalk was quite empty, so it would be the perfect time to strike. Yun took no chances and stepped in front of the others, transforming into his monkey form.

"Whoever it is, come out without giving us any trouble." Popping out of the corner was one of his fellow disciples of Master Yeren. "Xiu?"

Xiu looked embarrassed to be seen by them. "Yeah, it's me. I've been following you guys since you left the Academy." She wasn't lying. During the bathroom cry-time, she began to feel guilty about dismissing Ercan's problems just because they weren't as big a deal as her issues. She decided to stalk the group as they left to search for him half an hour ago.

"But why?" Julia questioned her. "And since when did you care so much about our squad problems?" She had never forgotten how Xiu never came to squad meetings and hangouts. Did she think she was too cool to be seen around with them or something?

Xiu had no answer for that. She just looked away with a guilty expression. Shee'vra decided to defend her.

"Cut it out, Julia. Without her training, I would have been a giant target for all of Eagle Squad during the duel. I trust that she's here to help us."

Yun jogged his memory. "Yeah, I did hear about that training stuff last week." He patted his fellow disciple on the back, to her discomfort. "Thanks for not backing out first day, Xiu. Master Yeren will be proud." A small smile crept across her face.

"Then why do you need to see Ercan so badly?" Julia questioned with less hostility.

Xiu frowned yet again as she answered without eye contact. "Wellllll…I might have yelled at him earlier." The group was surprised, but not as surprised as she expected. "He was really down about losing after going through so much pain. He was also musing about how he might not even deserve to be captain since he couldn't protect you guys. Then he asked me to train Shee'vra, and I said that I already was. Then he felt that he didn't deserve my sympathy after getting me transferred to Heron Squad." She hissed in pain as she continued to speak. "Then I got mad about how much of a big issue he made of his captain position and I told him off. I yelled at him about how much worse off a lot of us other students had it, and if not being captain was the worst thing to happen to him, then he was just pathetic." She crossed her arms. "So that's why I'm following you guys. To apologize for yelling at him and whatever."

There was a silent pause between the five psychics. That silence was broken by Cyrille, who went to give her a big platonic hug. "I knew you were our friend! I just knew it! Once a Rooster, always a Rooster!"

Xiu was completely stiff, in fear of being accidently poisoned and there was a small dose of embarrassment with her personal bubble being invaded. Yun eventually got him off of her. "Thanks for the sappy feelings. But honestly, where are we going?"

"To the Sephirot Museum," Shee'vra told her. "It's his sad place."

"Sad place?" A museum was not exactly the first place Xiu would think about going if she were moping, though maybe she shouldn't be the one to talk after just crying in the girl's bathroom. But still—kind of a dorky place to feel depressed.

"A place where you go when you're feeling down," her pupil informed her as if it was common knowledge. "But that's not important. The important part is that we find my brother and make him feel better." She fist-pumped with energy. "Now let's get going." None of the others had any objections as they walked a few more blocks to their destination.

~ * ~

It turned out the library was closed. So instead, Ercan sat in the museum's food court. In front of him were three sodas and a geometry textbook. But his mind wasn't on math. It wasn't even on being a captain. Xiu's words were still echoing in his head and no amount of soft drinks could drown them out. What could have possibly happened to her to make her snap like that?

As he perseverated today's problems while he did math homework, a man came up to him. "Hurry up with the numbers. The museum shall be closing in five."

Looking around his surroundings for a moment, he realized the food court was completely empty. All except for the tall guard with a winged sword wheel badge on his chest. This guy was a graduate from Aeon Sophia Academy, at least a ten-year alumnus.

The guard noticed that he was staring at his badge. "You're zoning out a bit, kid."

"My bad. Sorry!" Ercan opened his mouth for the first time in a while, "but by chance? Are you a psychic?"

The man nodded with pride. "Yes. None other than Jacque Jax Jackson, The Master of Jacks and user of the Jack spark." He put his hands on his hips. "Back at the Academy, I was a Quail. Ever heard of them?"

Ercan squeezed his brain cells for information about a Quail Squad. He'd heard the occasional smattering of them from the school faculty, but nothing solid. Eventually he had to admit that. "Not too much, sorry."

Jacque wasn't offended one bit. "I'm not slighted." The man in green took a seat in front of him. "So what's troubling you, kid?"

"A couple of things, actually." His senior braced himself for a long spiel. "Well first of all, I feel like I should mention that I'm a fellow psychic. Prometheus spark. But to get into my…problems, I've got roughly, more or less, three."

"Do tell," Jacque compassionately said to him, expecting quite the troubles.

Ercan began to list his current woes. "Well first of all, I'm captain of Rooster Squad, but at the last games, me and my squad scored thirteen points total."

"That is quite awful."

"Thanks," the boy dryly replied. "So last week I got a notice from Mastema, the strongest captain in school, about how my position as Squad Captain was at risk. The group as a whole decided that I must do a Trial by Battle. Wanting to redeem my image, I chose Bianca Narkissos to fight against."

"You mean the Princess of Titlacuan?"

"Yeah, her. I recommend you never challenge her. She's kicked my ass twice now and I'm sure it won't be the last." He could swear that he could still feel shards in his back. "But, yeah, I lost miserably and, chances are, I'm now an ex-captain." He let out a sigh. "Worst of all, I could not protect any of my squad mates, not even my younger sister. I mean, what kind of captain can't keep their own friends from dying like flies?" He drank up the last of his cola. "Maybe I just wasn't cut out to be a captain."

The man twirled his thin mustache in contemplation. "Hmmmm. This feels all too familiar to me, I hate to admit. You see, back in the day when I was your age, I, too, was a captain. Quail Squad was never really that great either and consistently was last place in the games. Eventually, the other captains told me to either shape up as a captain or renounce the title. I volunteered for Trail by Battle—bad idea." He shook his head in regret. "The Jack spark can do a lot of things—enhanced jumping, magic beans, cryokinesis, the ability to get powers based on monster masks—a bunch of wonderful tricks. But a platter of powers doesn't automatically mean skill. My squad and I were completely out our league that day. It wasn't that the opposition was that much stronger—it was that I was much too arrogant to come up with strategy and tactics." He balled up a passionate fist. "That day I realized something. I was much too rash in the battlefield and I couldn't defend my allies. But at the same time, my allies couldn't defend me. Protecting a squad is not a one-way street. Though you must protect them, they must protect you in turn. They only failed because I made it hard for them and didn't protect them in kind. So I deliberately got rid of my title and gave it to a member who deserved it." He looked away to reminisce about his former compatriots. "Being a captain is not about how powerful you are compared to the next psychic, it is about how efficient you are and being able to make hard decisions." He turned back to the attentive Ercan. "So does that answer your problems?"

"I guess that makes sense," he replied to his senior, "but to be honest, my captain position is the least of my problems."

"Then what is, youngling?"

Ercan ignored being called youngling. "It's about what a girl said to me."

"Is she your mate?" Jacque asked straightforwardly, "because you seem a bit young to settle down."

Ercan was utterly flabbergasted. "Who says that? But no we are not dating. She's just an ex-squadmate and I think maybe a friend. I honestly have no idea about the friend part. She tends to act temperamental around me and belittle me a lot. But then sometimes she greets me nicely and other times either insults or ignores me. To be honest, I find it off-putting and confusing."

"So what did this maiden say, exactly?" the green shirt asked him, wanting him to get to the point.

Xiu's words were lodged in his mind as he talked. "She spoke about how I was lucky that being scared about losing my title was my biggest problem. She spoke about how many of my peers would give anything to have my life right now because their pasts are so much more stained than mine is." Ercan pondered the potential histories of his classmates and realized that many preferred to have dodged that question, even Yun. "You get what I mean, Jacque?"

He got what he meant. "I see. It's true that we psychics are destined to have harder lives than most. Oftentimes the difficulty comes before even becoming one. Have you read about how sparks tend to awaken during moments of high emotional levels?"

Ercan had learned a bit about such things last year. "Yeah, most commonly fear, sadness, and anger were the triggers. But I've actually had Prometheus for as long as I can remember."

Jacque raised an eyebrow. "Honestly? That's most unusual."

"Yeah, I get that sometimes." Ercan scratched the back of his head. "But what I think she's saying is that this whole captain stuff is not so important in the long run. Is it?"

The older psychic shook his head. "I'm afraid not. Though Quail Squad was still our squad, eventually we began to separate as we got older. Though a peer of mine works at Aeon Sophia Academy, I chose to get a job working security at this prestigious museum. The rest... moved on."

Ercan got the message quick. "Sorry to hear that. I'm sure they were great."

"Glad to hear that, child," Jacque replied, forcing a smile. "Eventually the Missus insisted I take a safer job than in the field, so here I am. We're due for child soon and she wants to be sure the infant has a father."

"Congratulations, man."

"So polite," Jacque praised the kid. "Now how about you pack up, use the lavatory and go back to your friends?"

"Alright." Ercan nodded his head. He did start feeling a sensation in his gut. Those sodas wanted out of him. "Definitely. Bye." He got his things and rushed to the bathroom.

As the teenager left, Jacque thought about how he reminded him of himself when he was younger. Of course Jacque was way more badass, but still, the kid would hopefully have a long time to learn to play with the big boys and girls of the psychic world. The life of a psychic was a limited one; sooner or later they all hit a power glass ceiling. He knew he had hit his and, as a result, had resigned himself as head of security for one of the most famous museums in the world, which was not half bad. But maybe this kid had more potential than him. Who knew?

Jacque then heard the metal detector go off. Swiftly heading toward the entrance, he saw eight people strolling in. From the looks of some of them, they seemed to be psychics. "Sorry, guys. It's closing time. Come back tomorrow." He knew these guys were up to no good, but would rather not have this end in bloodshed. Luckily, the museum had officially been closed at this point, so no civilians were around.

An old Qian man with a fancy oak cane moved forward. "No can do, sir. We need something from here and we're not leaving empty handed." He glared at him through his red glasses. "So I recommend you go home before you get hurt."

Jacque manifested a plastic green mask with stiches on its face. "Are we going to do this the hard way?" He pressed the button on his walky-talky two times for backup. Once meant help, twice meant get out as fast as possible. But as he pushed, no sound was made. How could they have tampered with it without him seeing?

"You won't be calling backup," their leader told him before turning toward a young girl in a hoodie. "Thanks, Balra."

With her aeon-restricting collar in her hand, Balra pointed toward Jacque's communication device, getting it off his belt with her mind alone. With but a thought, she crushed it into a ball.

Shèng asked him once and only once. "Where do you keep the Pauldrons of Kadosh?"

They would get no answers from him. "If you're looking for a fight, I shall grant your wish." Jacque placed the mask onto his face. Upon putting it on, his body began to change. His body turned green as his muscle mass grew to twice its regular size. He became covered in stitches and two metal bolts appeared on his neck. The bolts conducted electricity through his body. The plastic mask on his face was tacky, though.

Watching Shèng fumbling with his cane, Izquierda protected his leader by transforming and pouncing claws first at the guard. Jacque merely shot a blue ray out of a finger, entrapping him in ice mid jump. Vinstri trembled at the hulking opposition, but the other Lefty members kept their heads. Kushoto even kept a hand on his shoulder to prevent him from running off.

"Well that's inconvenient," Shèng mused to himself as he looked at the living ice sculpture. With a forceful tug, he got his sword out of his cane. "There it—"

He had no time to finish as Jacque's electric-charged fist met his chest. He was sent flying into the door, shattering glass. Her master being hurt didn't faze Kairieji. He had his symbol on his chest, the same indigo C symbol she had on hers.

The rest of the gang (including the one in the ice) saw a massive bloody hole erupt from Jacque's chest, around the exact same spot where he hit Shèng Xià. The green guard spat out blood from under his mask as he fell over onto his back. After one last desperate breath for air, the guard passed away.

"Damn, that stung," Shèng exclaimed to the group in surprise as he healed his broken ribs. Kairieji went to help Sheng up without a word, but he would have none of it. "Your symbol, Kai. It won't end well for either of us if you touch me with that thing on." He cracked his sore neck and got up. "Balra, unfreeze him, will you?"

"Whatever you wish, sir." The girl with eyes of lime stared at the ice and, as the floor under her feet turned green, the ice began to melt away to free the beast.

"I owe you once again," the crocotta told her in gratitude. He received no reply; Just a blank stare. *Creepy girl.*

Sheng stored his unused blade into his cane once more. "Alright, Lefty Gang, listen up. Izquierda and Kushoto, find the guards in the east wing, Ezker, north wing. Vinstri, check the bathrooms for anybody, and then go with Ezker. Sinister and Kairieji, west wing. Balra, stay here and use Urthona to make the museum appear undisturbed and cut off cell service."

"Whatever you wish, sir." Balra turned to the entrance and put on her headphones. The green around her feet emanated brighter than before.

With their orders, the Lefty Gang got to work. Zuo, himself, slowly took his time to walk to wherever those damn pauldrons were. *I should have asked for a map before killing him.*

~ * ~

Ercan finished draining the lizard. As he hummed the latest hit single, he heard a noise from the entranceway. It sounded just like Jacque confronting the footsteps of several other people. They spoke in a hostile manner and then something about pauldrons. Crackles of electricity and the sound of blowing ice followed soon after. Then there was an audible punching sound, following by an explosive violent mulch.

Getting a chain ready, he heard somebody's voice. It was saying something about separating and finding any remaining guards. He recognized the name Vinstri, recalling it to be that weird invisible sea serpent looking guy from the Lefty Gang. *Crap, the Lefty Gang is here.*

Hearing somebody coming toward the bathrooms, Ercan had to think fast. If he was caught, he was doomed. If he took the guy out, they would suspect something and check it out, then he was doomed. He looked up to see that the bathroom had a slanted roof with large wooden beams supporting the foundation. Using his chain to grab a beam, he quickly hoisted himself up and hid on top.

As he peered down, he saw that familiar sea serpent guy barge in, trying to look intimidating. "Alright, you chumps! This is a heist!" He got no response. "Hiding, are we?" Vinstri kicked open each stall one by one. Finally he barged into Ercan's stall. "Now what do we have here?" Vinstri gagged. "Some gross jackass that didn't flush. Think they're entitled to have someone else do it." He flushed the toilet with his foot.

Ercan waited until the exit door opened and closed before he even thought about moving a muscle. Once he was sure the coast was clear, he grabbed his crystalcell to call the police. There was no service. Not one bar. *Why now, why now?* He then recalled hearing somebody named Balra was ordered to cut cell service, probably with a spark or something. But that was just cell service. He had one other way to contact help—the alarm for his squad. He hoped they were looking for him and were close at the moment. Those guards and curators were in trouble and, at this rate, some could even be dead. He wasted no time pressing the big red button on his touch screen.

Getting down, he checked the map on his cell. According to the red dot, they were actually only a block away. Very convenient of them, but he would not complain about Sophia's blessings right now. Creeping out of the bathroom, he saw this girl in a hoodie with headphones just staring at the entrance. The floor under her feet radiated green, so he had a feeling that it might be a bad idea to confront her.

He slowly snuck toward the window and looked out. To his relief, he saw Rooster Squad approaching. But they were heading toward the entrance. That girl was at the entrance. If she saw them, this Balra person could call the other seven on them. They'd be screwed.

But he had an idea. He got down from the window, leaving it a bit open and grabbed the chandelier with a chain. With a strong yank, he committed horrible property damage for the safety of his friends. Releasing the chain from his wrist, he bolted away as the chandelier crashed to the floor in a thousand pieces.

It was a success. As he hid behind the door, the Lefty member slowly and near lifelessly, headed toward the noise. As she passed by the door, Ercan sneaked away toward the entrance. Looking down, he saw Jacque's corpse with a giant hole through his chest. What could have possibly killed him so quickly?

Keeping an eye on the hooded girl, he made a hushing motion as his allies rushed toward the door. Getting the message, they slowly went through the revolving door while making as little noise as possible. All five of them nearly jumped as they saw the corpse face down on the floor. They then followed Ercan into the Hall of Sirokhan Mammals as Balra looked out the open window. Feeling safe from Balra's line of hearing, he whispered to the group as they stood around the Stuffed Sirokhan Elephants.

"Thank you so much for coming, guys." He saw that everyone was here. Shee'vra, Yun, Julia, Cyrille, and…Xiu?"

Xiu looked away from him with a frown on her face. "I'm only here because I pity you. Don't look into it." She took a deep breath. "So why are we avoiding one guard? We could overwhelm her six-to-one."

Ercan signaled for her to keep her voice down. "Because there are seven other Lefty Gang Members all around this place. And yet the leader found it fitting for only her to keep an eye out. Doesn't that seem suspicious?"

Xiu couldn't argue against that logic. "Fine. So what do we do? We're six unarmed teens going in to stop a heist. Shee'vra doesn't have the crossbow, Julia doesn't have her battlesuit thing, and Cyrille—"

"I actually have Cockatrice with me." Cyrille showed her his sword with a smile. "Gaizka told me last week that I shouldn't be keeping an expensive family heirloom in my locker. So after training, I've been taking Cockatrice back home with me."

"Very convenient," Julia deadpanned. "But if it makes you guys feel better…" She took out a few small blank metal disks from her jacket pocket. "I come somewhat prepared."

Ercan had complete faith that those two would be able to handle themselves well enough. But what about Shee'vra? What would she be able to do? Would Xiu's training even be enough?

"Don't worry." His sister put a hand on his shoulder. "I'll stick around Yun. He's the strongest and most durable of us."

The monkey nodded his head. "Sheev will be safe with me. I'll be sure to fall to the floor before her, which will not happen by the way."

"So we're splitting up then?" Cyrille asked the group. "In that case, me and Jules will scout the west wing." He pointed to Shee'vra and Yun with two talons. "Then you two can scour the east for bad guys. And then that leaves Ercan and Xiu to save the day in the north wing or whatnot." Cyrille pressed his alarm button on his super expensive looking crystalcell that made the others except Julia feel inadequate in comparison. "I have also set an alarm for my two bodyguards and they'll know what to do."

"Fair enough," Ercan replied. He had stuff to talk to her about anyway. "I heard somebody mention pauldrons—"

"So with my substandard detective skills, I deduce they are after the Pauldrons of Kadosh. Northmost wing in the Empire, under Barbar section," Julia informed the group.

"I had a feeling about that too," Ercan claimed to everyone as if he wanted to impress them or something. "But, yeah, that thing must be worth a fortune. Let's take them out, save any bystanders, and not let anybody get their hands on that artifact.

With everybody knowing what he or she would be doing, each member took a different exit. Yun and Shee'vra exited through the doors next to the rhinos and hippos toward the Ancient Aliens exhibit. Cyrille and Julia went past the buffalo and oryx taxidermy and into the Tirnan Sculpture Galleria. Finally, Xiu and Ercan ran down the entire hall to go through the doors in between the quagga and atlas bear.

As they ran through the Great Hall of Reptiles, Xiu felt like she had to talk. "Look, if it makes you feel any better, I'm sorry for yelling at you or whatever."

Though he was surprised that she was doing this now, he answered back. "No, it's fine. I deserved to get yelled at. I was just thinking about my own tiny problems. And even then I was feeling sorry for myself until somebody made me see a slightly bigger picture on my position in life."

"Who gave you a pep talk?" She and the rest of the Rooster Squad members were supposed to be the ones who did that.

Ercan looked ahead as they passed models on how crocodiles bred. "We stepped over his body at the entranceway." She felt really awkward now. "They'll not get away with this, though. I can promise that much." He might not be a captain anymore, but he would be damned by Sophia herself if he was going to just let them do whatever they wanted. This wasn't just for him or his squad. It was for Jacque and his family. He would be avenged.

Calling all the Captains

Yun and Shee'vra found themselves at the Space and the Universe wing. Keeping their guard up, they quickly moved through the exhibit. They passed models of planets, meteorites, and a theater demonstrating the big bang, among other cosmic concepts. The lights were completely off, making the area that much creepier.

Shee'vra was unnerved. "It just feels so quiet." This feeling of fear was much more pronounced than Saturday.

"I don't like it any more than you," Yun remarked warily. "I just feel that somebody is watching us."

"Because somebody is!" Both teenagers looked upwards to see a familiar woman sitting on a model of the sun, legs crossed. She had fly wings on her back, fully shining. "What if I told you that this room used to have all the lights on a minute ago?"

"We wouldn't care!" Yun activated Hanuman and began to scale the walls as well as the planar structures to get to her.

Kushoto merely gave a smug grin. "Bad move, hairy." She extended her hands and shot out the largest beam of heat she had ever shot out. It was almost blinding to her, but she was sure he was down for good. Probably only enough of him was left to dump in an ashtray.

"Yun!" his companion shouted out in terror. Such a blast was utterly destroying the wall and the floor. Such force from the heat ray was more than any human being could handle.

But he was no mere human being. Once the beam stopped, Yun

was sprawled on the ground. Though the fall hurt a bit, he wasn't even singed by the attack. He just jumped up and got ready to attack again.

"By the way, I'm immune to fire and electricity," he remarked. Another blast came his way but he just dodged it. Climbing upwards, he hopped onto planet Venus, then Mercury, and leaped over another beam as he got ready to strike her down.

"S-shit!" Kushoto quickly transformed into a fly to dodge the kick. But Yun's tail swatted the insect into a wall.

Kushoto turned human once again as she lay unconscious on the floor.

Shee'vra, on her part, was relieved that he didn't just disintegrate in front of her eyes. She forgot about the immunities Hanuman gave Yun. Everyone mostly just saw the monkey part of it and just assumed that was all it could do, though she had a feeling that there was more to it than even Yun knew.

Yun bent some metal and pinned them into the floor around Kushoto's limbs to prevent escape. "One down already. You ready to move ahead?"

A surge of confidence came to Shee'vra. "Yes!" If the rest were as simple as that fight, this would be a breeze. The two ran out of the damaged space center.

Vinstri was at the Gemstones exhibit and contemplated what he should steal. All these stones were so shiny and priceless; he had no idea which ones he should pick. Should he snag the rubies, the emeralds, the sapphires, diamonds? So many different precious rocks to select from. He didn't even know half of their names, but they all looked like they would set him up for life. It was a shame he forgot his burgling bag at the old base.

He settled this issue with a simple solution. "Eeny, meeny, miny, mo! Catch the tiger by the toe! If he hollers let him go! Eeny, meanie, miny, mo!" His finger landed upon an amethyst that must be millions of years old and bright purple. But there were better gems. "My mother says to pick the very best one and you are it!" He landed on a gigantic chunk of topaz the shape of a dinosaur. "Roses are red, violets are blue, and I choose you!"

He nearly cried tears of joy as he saw a beautiful sapphire as bright as a twinkling star. He smacked his soggy palms on the glass. "I need you so much, baby." He looked at the name on the exhibit. "Star of Jivana." He looked at the description again and drooled. "Five hundred and sixty-three carats. Fricking beautiful."

He took his switchblade and got ready to carve a circular hole around the glass. He didn't care about any alarm lasers going off; Balra had that covered. All he needed was to grab the golf ball sized gem and then he would be as rich as a DeRoche.

But before he could even put a dent in the glass, he heard footsteps quickly coming from the entrance. *Probably just a couple of guards feeling brave.* All he needed to do was knock them out and tie them up somewhere.

But as he turned around to face his opposition, his green scales turned much paler. It was that red head with the chains from last Saturday. "Oh shit, not you!" He was with some far eastern girl that he had never seen before but was probably also a psychic. So he did what he thought was the smart thing—ran to pull the emergency sprinkler switch. Upon pulling the alarm, the sprinklers shot water down on everybody. This was perfect as getting wet allowed him to use his Ogopogo spark. Ogopogo made him perfectly invisible. Sight, hearing, and smell were now useless at finding him.

Ercan slammed a chain down where Vinstri just was. "Where'd he go?" He couldn't see him anywhere. He had seen invisibility based sparks before, but this guy was not leaving any trace of his existence. No puddles of water were getting stepped on and the sprinklers were not leaving a visible outline to find.

As Ercan continued to lash at thin air, Xiu instead got on the defensive and summoned her spirit jackal. "Anubis, find the unseen force."

The blue canine barked and ran about as the water rained down on the group. As Ercan still tried looking for Vinstri, he felt an arm reach around him from behind.

"You're getting annoying, kid." Ercan felt he was at knifepoint from an unseen blade. "Now you're a hostage. Feeling smart—?" Anubis bit his ass. "—noOOOOOW!"

Vinstri dropped his weapon, which became visible upon impacting the floor. Ercan hit his face with the back of his head. As the invisible man staggered, he saw an open hand glowing, radiating blue energy coming toward him. Xiu felt the back of her hand hit someone's face and seconds later, saw a new hole in the wall vaguely shaped like a person. Anubis barked at the hole and disappeared for now.

"I owe you one," Ercan told her, seeing not only a knife on the ground, but a few sharp teeth. "It would suck getting my throat slit."

"I'm sure suck might be an understatement for most," Xiu told him with a scowl. "Just be thankful I saved you some pain from that fishy creep."

As they left the room, they could both see how soaked they were. Their clothes stuck to their bodies closer than before. Ercan's leather clothing was ruined and Xiu's long black hair stuck to her back and shoulders.

"Well I'm sure we could agree that that guy was more annoying than dangerous," Ercan commented, trying not to look at her as her clothes clung to her figure. "Crap. Ruined my favorite shirt." His loose sleeves felt as if they had turned into flippers.

"Easy for you to say," Xiu snapped at him. "You have like ten more of the same outfits in your closet." She felt her soggy hair with a bit of sadness, but mostly anger. "Do you know how long it takes to blow-dry my hair? Very, and now I'm super pissed!" She was incensed enough that she completely ignored the lovely botany around her.

But they had little time to just wait to dry up. They had more Lefty Gang members to take out. Feeling that they had wasted enough time, both teens dashed through the Life of Plants exhibit.

The two wealthiest members of Rooster Squad went up the stairs and wandered into the Tirnan-sponsored History of The Round Table Knights exhibit. These items had been around for at least a good few centuries. In fact, being a member of The Round Table was still one of the most prestigious psychic positions one could ask for short of Ashtamangala. There were beautiful tapestries with house sigils, old family weapons, and many suits of armor from various members. Neither Julia nor Cyrille could deny that they shared blood with Round Table Knights from centuries ago.

But this was not the time to take a tour. There was danger afoot and they could not get careless. They had already found the bodies of security guards cut up or riddled with holes. Cyrille had Cockatrice out, and Julia drew a few glyphs on her clothes and disks. As they scanned the area, they found an open door to what should be a professor's office. Slowly, Julia checked inside with her shield glyph up while Cyrille looked behind her in case of an ambush.

"Just typical," She commented to herself as she saw a couple of scholars tied up in their chairs with tape over their mouths. In front of them was a woman in black armor that had just finished tying up an innocent bystander. "This won't be pleasant, will it?"

The woman in black did not seem amused. "A dry one, aren't you?" Kairieji shook her head as she created a black sword out of shadows. "You are not to hinder the goals of the Lefty Gang."

Julia was pretty meh about being threatened. "So is the gang name political, geographical, hand based, or something else entirely?"

"That doesn't matter." The woman stepped out of the cramped room and formed shadowy bird wings on her back. "You're at a disadvantage of two-to-one. Do it, Sinister."

Before she could retort, she heard the sound of a weapon cocking and pointed at the back of her head. The assailant behind her for some reason made a quacking sound; the most threatening quack she'd ever heard in her life.

"Courageous attack from behind!" Julia felt somewhat relieved when Cyrille popped up out of nowhere to ambush the duck guy behind her.

Julia turned around to see Cyrille clash his blade with some hunter guy in shorts and flippers with a duck caller in his mouth. She couldn't help but smirk at the stupid looking five foot four-inch Gang member. "So that's Sinister, huh?" She focused her attention back on Kairieji. "Not exactly impressed. What's the name of your other partners? Super-Scary or Boo-Man-Choo?" Sinister quacked in anger as he struggled against Cyrille's sword with the bayonet of his rifle. "Seriously, your names are dumb."

"Do not mock our syndicate!" The winged woman lunged at her with her dark blade. Julia merely activated her shield glyph with no problem. Kairieji, in turn, received a kick to her shin. Just as planned.

Just as Julia was getting confident, she felt a sharp pain in her own shin. Looking down, she saw that nothing actually touched her as her pants were undisturbed. *Wait? If I kicked the birdbrain in the left shin, and my left shin now hurts like a monster... Then...*

"So you figured it out that quick?" Kairieji inquired. "Smart girl. Now you know that you can never hurt me or you take double my damage, thanks to my Camio spark." She drew attention to the back-to-back C's symbol on her chest. "Master Shèng Xià's Cain spark has the exact same ability but even stronger." She pointed her curved dark sword at her once again. "To get to Shèng, you must get through me."

"Fine, then." Julia tried to ignore her bruised shin. "Cyrille! Take care of the duck guy!" She took out a disk and braced herself for an actual fight. "I'll handle her."

"Got it, Jules!" Cyrille shot his elastic tongue at the elevator button. When the doors opened, he shoved the duck guy inside, pressed the fourth floor button and spat out poisonous saliva. He then exited the elevator and rolled away before Sinister could actually get a clean shot as the doors closed. "You need help with the other bird?"

"Go ahead to the third floor and save those pauldrons!" Julia shouted to him as she blocked attack after attack. "You're no use here!"

Though always reluctant, he knew Julia was smarter than him. He found the stairs and started running up them. As Cyrille went up, he manipulated the saliva inside the elevator. Hopefully the duck guy was knocked out by now.

As he found himself inside the Birds of The World exhibit, the elevator bell rang. Quickly spinning around, he only barely managed to dodge a shot of concentrated water, the attack hitting a stuffed macaw instead. Cyrille stared in surprise as the duck guy softly quacked, yellow eyes piercing through the rooster as if he was his prey. Around him the poison just floated above his head as if it was covering the surface of a pond. No matter how hard he tried, the toxins would not dive down toward the mallard man. The poison eventually just dissipated into nothingness.

Sinister readied a shot, but Cyrille struck his rifle with Cockatrice and sliced the weapon's barrel in two. The blade felt like it cut through a body of water and made Cyrille lose his balance. With the remaining half of his rifle, the duck man shot out a fountain's worth of H20 in a spread-shot. Cyrille was sent flying back across the wet floor from the pressure right next to a model of an Emu. Though unharmed, his white tuxedo was now soaking wet and Sinister had every intention to stain it red.

With quacks that emulated the symphony of laughter, Sinister used Fontus to repair his rifle, adding a scope and removing the bayonet. To the DeRoche's bewilderment, he didn't just shoot him while he was down. Instead he began to float into the air, paddling his flippers as if he waded on the surface of a lake. He shot a window and then "swam" his way out of the building, perching onto one of the museum's many roofs. Cyrille watched, wondering why he would not take an opportunity to finish him.

The reason became very clear soon after. As Cyrille tried to get up, a shot of water struck him in the shoulder. The pressure of the liquid stung like nothing he had felt before. The hit only grazed him, but he could see the blood pour off of his clean suit, the tears stitching themselves up. If only the tuxedo was also bulletproof. Having no way to defend himself, the only option he had remaining was to get out of his sight.

Sinister reveled in the very idea that the son of Emile DeRoche would run away from him. The rich were all the same. Cowards. Each and every single one of them. They talked a big ambitious game but, once the tables were turned, they fled, pleaded, even bribed their way out. They were all selfish bastards to the very end. Aristocrats deserved to die under folks like him. Their money couldn't save them from his rifle.

Sinister licked the tip of his duck caller as he made a sensual quack. Following the chicken by wading in his invisible floating pond, he searched for his prey through the many windows. His prey was hiding just behind a tree full of fake birds, and he wanted to play with the boy a bit. Taking a shot at a cock-of-the-rock, he startled the disgusting fowl lizard. Roy was a patient man. Cyrille would die. But he needed to suffer first.

As Cyrille ran toward the stairs in an attempt to get back to his friend, Sinister shot through the calf of his leg. The duck then deliberately missed as the chicken limped away from the staircase. The rich wouldn't get away this time. Roy wanted the little bastard alive. That would teach the upper echelons a lesson they would foolishly ignore. Why would they care if one of their own died? They wouldn't care if this abomination died by his hand. They were only out for themselves. But damn, it was fun to stick it to them. Roy softly quacked as he aimed through his scope for another shot, not caring for his real mission in the least.

~ * ~

Zivot took another smoke out of her blunt as she laid back on a couch fit for ten people. When the master was away, it was time to chill out all by herself, the crystalvision, and her stash of Titlacua Sevenstar. Her reddened eyes watched on as the frumpy guy on the CV farted in the car during the college road trip. It was the funniest frigging thing she'd ever seen in her life. She didn't care what critics said about *On The Road Again*, it was utterly gut busting. Why didn't Emile allow his son to watch this comedic gold? Then again, she was paying more attention to the bright backgrounds.

She reached out her hand to the bowl of salty chips and it skedaddled over to her hand. Grabbing a handful, she satiated her munchies. Best damn food in the universe. She needed this after this last week. School was stressing her out, Bianca was busting everyone's ass, and Yun was just so damn hard to teach. Why did the cute guys always have to be such dumbasses? Working under the son of one of the most powerful men on earth really did take it out of her. But right now, she was just chilling for a change. No duty, just relaxing for the rest of the night. Not even Sophia could take this from her.

But Mayil could. That party pooper marched up to her in a huff. "Heyo, Mayil? How's it hanging, my bro from another mom?"

Mr. Poutyface still scowled at her. He showed her some weird blinky light on his crystalcell. She looked at it in utter fascination. "What is this, buddy? Some krunk ass new game app?" She lazily poked the red light. "Boopy," she grumbled as nothing happened. "This game sucks! I hate it!" She rolled over and pouted, arms crossed. As she hid her face toward the sofa, she began to feel really sleepy. The sounds of drunken idiots laughing at glorious hijinks made her want to relax her eyes. But that wasn't going to happen. "OH SHIT!" She jolted up as ice-cold wetness embraced her entire upper body. Looking up, she saw a floating bucket above her. She threw a pillow at the bucket in indignation. "Why'd you do that, asshole? You ruin everything!"

"Zivot, turn around, damn you!" She did as she was told and saw a furious Mayil with his cell still out. It was rapidly beeping an alarm. The alarm was sent by Cyrille.

Her high just puffed out of existence and her senses came right back to her like a speeding train. "Oh shit oh shit oh shit!" She whistled for her swords and daggers. "How long's that been going off?" If Cyrille died because of her tardiness, who knew what Emile would do? She would never be invited to polite society ever again.

She jammed her shoes on and snatched her cell, rushing out the door with her blades and daggers strapped on to her. She didn't at all look like a dignified guardian of a DeRoche in her pajama pants and chip-covered tank top, reeking of sevenstar.

The peacock was already waiting on the balcony. "Hop on quick!" Mayil instructed her forcefully. "Master's life could be over if we falter any longer." With her on, he flew the bird into the night sky. *Please Sophia may you forgive my partner's indiscretions. She is young. She knows not what it truly means to devote oneself to a master. Just please let us save him in time.* He repeated a prayer within his head. *You are within us all. You have blessed me. I must repay.*

"Are you feeling okay?" Hanako asked her friend, concerned. "You seem to be really focused on something."

She and Bianca shared a dorm room. Since her family guarded the Seichin Holy Relics, she was considered to be worthy enough to share a luxury room with royalty, funded by the current Shrivatsa Kiara. Currently Bianca was writing in a notebook while Hanako was drawing a lovely crane with her ink brush.

"I'm contemplating at the moment," Bianca replied, not even looking back from her desk. "I'm determining whether to vote for or against Ercan Ao'Si."

The Seichin girl brushed her hair out of her face. "T-that makes sense. I guess. I just thought you would have decided by now."

Bianca wrote in the last sentence of her history homework. Nothing short of an A would be satisfactory to her. "It's not that easy, Hana. We all have different skills and sparks. Some of them have an advantage over one another. If Ercan actually managed to land a clean blow on me, I would be finished. He also has the strongest healing factor I've ever witnessed. You saw how much punishment was needed to keep him down." Today Ercan managed to bring her down to merely a quarter of her aeon. "He is strong, but just not as ready for the real world as some of us." She swiveled in her chair to look at her roommate. "You understand where I'm coming from, right?"

"I know what you mean," Hanako answered truthfully. Alberto also has that problem. He can turn into a terrible dinosaur, strong enough to smash cars and crush bones like toothpaste. But he always had terrible luck with his match ups when it came to fights. It turned out for some psychics; turning into a dinosaur just made you a bigger target. "But if you do vote against him, who do you recommend replace him?"

Bianca had already made her decision a few days ago. "I don't mean to sound classist, but I would recommend Cyrille." If he was inducted into being a captain, the majority of them would be coming from privileged backgrounds, though by privileged she meant "from wealth" not "spoiled rotten."

Hanako's smile was thin. "Oh wow. I also chose him as a replacement. Such a sweet guy like him would be a wonderful figurehead. Besides, I find it fitting for someone of his looks to lead Rooster Squad." She softly giggled into her hand, but quickly stopped as she had heard it was impolite to laugh at your own funnies.

Bianca's cell suddenly began to vibrate. Picking it up, she saw that it was from Zivot. After a quick read, she immediately stood up and got herself ready.

"W-what's going on?" Hanako asked anxiously.

"There's trouble at the Sephirot Museum!" Bianca explained hastily as she pressed buttons on her cell. "Chances are, all of Rooster Squad is out there!"

Hanako felt a twinge of fear, but decided to grab her knife and yumi. "I'm coming too. We need as many of us as possible."

"I thought about that." Bianca sent a text message. "I sent a message to my squad and to Mastema. They should be on their way too."

Both maidens swiftly jumped into their opposing mirrors and trekked the mirror world. If they hurried, they could make it there within twenty minutes thanks to the lack of people within the world of the mirror.

~ * ~

At home, Caradoc was reading the latest novel of the action-adventure-romance series, *Cosmic like You*. It was not as good as the third book, but better than the seventh. So, overall, mediocre. Hong meanwhile was reading his giant tome of eldritch thingies in the bathtub. From what Caradoc heard from him, that book contained many things man wasn't meant to know. Seemed like a fun read to him but the definite chance of delving deeper into insanity made him pass on skimming it.

The apartment sure was quiet without Xiu and Yun. It felt so peaceful with just the two of them. No roughhousing, no snappy remarks, nothing chaotic, though he did begin to wonder where they were. It was striking eight o'clock and they still weren't back. Caradoc just assumed that Yun was trying to cheer Ercan up from his inevitable slump after losing and Xiu was just hanging out with her BFFs or something girly like that.

In the middle of reading about the resolution of a romantic subplot, his crystalcell vibrated. Checking it, he saw it was a text from his captain. It read *Museum now.*

Caradoc put his book on the coffee table and bolted out of his seat. He opened the window as he called to the bathroom. "Hong! I have important business at the museum! I'll be back soon!" He then used John Carter to spring from building to building.

Now alone in the house, the salamander man closed his tome and crawled out of the tub. He had a dream last night about Enitharmon Loz lost in a museum, three large eyes watching down on her. A one eyed man with bronze armor and pronounced pauldrons with a large gray beard threw an ornate iron spear that went through many walls and pierced her heart.

He considered going along to the battle that would ensue, but no need. The tome had said nothing of the fate of his peers. Not yet at least. He waved the eyeball on the ceiling goodbye and turned off his supernatural vision. Upon that, his surroundings once again became inorganic, and the pages of his tome turned blank. Draining the tub, he put on a towel and decided to have an early bedtime.

~ * ~

In the school rec room, Basil and Gustave were arm wrestling to prove who was the stronger. Man or False Gharial? They stared into one another's eyes in a tactical effort to break the spirit of their opponent. But neither one was relenting.

"I'm honestly impressed you lasted this long," the crocodilian complimented him. "But now you're done." He exerted more force onto his scaly hand, trying to force his opponent's arm onto the table.

But Basil kept his cool underneath his sunglasses. "You are also mighty. But man has one advantage over beast." He lowered his voice to sound cooler. "Stamina."

With that one word, he used the energy he had been saving up since the beginning of their bout. Like how man conquered nature, Basil gained traction in the bout. Using the maximum amount of muscle power, he made Gustave's hand hit the table. Basil was victorious. Gustave, on his part took his loss with dignity.

"Not too bad, Basil." The croc massaged his losing hand. "What's your secret?"

"A perfect fusion between power and willpower, buddy!" Basil answered proudly. Suddenly, Basil's cell went off. He raised his sunglasses in surprise to double check what he'd just read. "Round two tomorrow! I gotta get to the museum!"

As the wrestler dashed off, Gustave shrugged to himself. "Eh, why the hell not? I'll text boss." So he took out his scale-themed crystalcell and began to message Gaizka.

~ * ~

"Thanks for all the support! See you Friday!" Gaizka exited the school therapist. She was always so understanding of his issues.

"See you then," Ms. Yamauchi answered him back. "And if you see Xiu tomorrow, can you remind her that our appointment tomorrow is going to be at 3:45 instead of 5:30?"

"Sure thing!" The tattooed shark man left the building and was on his way to get some grub in the food court. If his teeth weren't so sharp, he'd whistle like a happy sailor.

On his way to the food court, he got a message from Gustave. "Now what can this be?" Analyzing his friend's message, he figured out that something must be going on at the museum. Though those kinds of places usually bored him, he was in the mood to skewer someone who was deserving of it. "OHHHHH YES! TIME FOR BLOOD AND GUTS TO COVER THE STREETS!" The Sea Spider knew it was wrong, but he couldn't resist a violent bout. It just felt so right to him to end the lives of the cruel and arrogant in ways that struck fear to any other criminals—pissing on the corpses, optional.

As she was grabbing a late night meal, Shiro watched as the blood hungry sharkman dashed off campus grounds. She heard him speak about something going on in the museum. *Maybe it was a party.* She texted Sabelle with the good news.

Sabelle lay on her bed, playing around on her cell. The new app *Doggie 4 Adoption* was so much fun. The app gave her all the options to groom and train the puppy of her choice. It reminded her of raising Midnight when he was a little puppy back home in Firebird, Odandir.

On the other side of the room, Winona had been at her desk since this afternoon. She was working on some sort of weird starry black fluid in a vial. "So, Winny, what's with the black gunk you got there?"

The Witch of Summer's End addressed her roommate as she placed various herbs into the liquid. "This 'black gunk' is for my cousin back with the River Mink Tribe. She got married last year but they're having problems conceiving."

"You mean Chumani?" Sabelle asked rhetorically. She had known Winona's cousin for a while now. Used to babysit her when she was younger.

"Yes, her." She shook the vial, which made it glow a bright blue. "I heard how much she wanted a child and her tears were starting to… unsettle me." The concoction was complete. "But once I send this to her, it is assured that her fertility will increase."

The redhead seemed a bit skeptic. "Are you sure there won't be any drawbacks or anything? If she hypothetically gets the nerve to drink that stuff, nothing bad will happen, right? No septuplets or mutant babies or anything?"

"Of course not," Winona answered back, kind of annoyed that one of her only friends didn't have full faith in her skills. "I made sure to plan for every worst case scenario, though if I added the blood of a still living squirrel, she would give birth to a squirrel baby. Any animal's blood added would have similar results."

"You could seriously do that?" That honestly sounded hardcore for a spark to do.

"Yes." Winona put away the glowing vial into a box to package later. "But I doubt Chumani would want that."

The Doberman on Sabelle's app gave its owner an envelope. "Oh that is just precious. The puppy gives you your messages." She took the envelope and got her text message and read it aloud. *From Shiro. Gaizka is on his way to the museum. Basil too. Do you think there's a party there?*

That piqued Winona's interest. A wide smile lit her face as she grabbed her bow and quiver. "That sounds worth my time." The woman in black opened a window. "Badb." She became a murder of crows and flew out with almost a hundred wings.

Sabelle was not exactly interested in going with. She texted Shiro back with *I don't think it's a party. Winny 2 excited.* She got a sad face as a reply. Sabelle then decided to text Vasanti. *Winona's off to the museum. No training at 10.* With those messages sent, she laid back once again to play with her new app.

~ * ~

"Zombies in the next room!" Vural warned his companions as he destroyed the undead with an AOE Holy Light attack.

Vasanti went into the fray with her dual sabers, cutting everything in her path in half. Draghignazzo cast Fireball to inflict burn damage while Sanjay tanked the necromancer's attacks with his Superior Shield. This latest sequel to *Necrowarp* ruled, and all four players dominated the game with their respective character classes. The new crystalsystem, Diamondgamez, was revolutionary in gameplay.

"I sense a dark evil within the treasure," Draghignazzo warned Sanjay before he opened the chest. When the large man in the metal mask carefully controlled his level seven sentinel to attack it, the treasure grew fifteen times its size and revealed sharp fangs and six beefy arms.

"That is one big mimic," Vasanti commented as she realized that this must have been the dungeon's bonus boss. "Alright, everyone focus on the mimic king!" Bonus bosses were always stronger than regular ones, but reaped more rewards.

Vural's hierophant, Vasanti's assassin, Draghignazzo's elementalist, and Sanjay's sentinel dueled against the Mimic King of The Forty Treasures. They were overall doing well, except for Vural. Turns out, most enemies were programmed to aim for the medic over all other players. Before he knew it, Vural's high priest, Valuhar the Pious, was eaten alive. The others did not last much longer. Sanjay couldn't help but grumble as they realized that they hadn't even chipped away a fifth of the giant treasure chest's HP.

"Curses! This game is a nightmarish conquest," the demon looking teen remarked to the others. "Mayhaps we should grind ourselves a bit more. I doubt we're of adequate level to challenge these overleveled dark ones."

"Well at least until we get strong enough to beat that chest monster," Vural reluctantly agreed. Sadly the video game world wasn't like real life. It was impossible to use willpower and just ignore the odds if your opponent was much too high leveled for you. Why must video game logic be so cruel?

Vasanti was unfazed. "Whatevs, we'll just level grind." Her cell got a message.

"What is it?" Drag asked her skeptically. "Did Winona push your training schedule to earlier?" Sanjay shivered at the idea of being forced to train under the witch's command. Must be brutal.

Vasanti couldn't help but smile at the news she got. "Hell no, even better! Sabelle said that there's no training tonight. Winona's going to the museum for some reason." Sanjay scrunched his face under his mask as he sounded stumped. "Yeah, I dunno why either, Sanjay."

But Vural knew and he felt the need to tell them all. He deepened his voice and squinted his eyes. "For one reason only. There's a battle occurring there at the moment!" Before anyone could question his logic, Vural put down his controller and back flipped into the air. When his feet hit the ground, he was Hyperbug Antlion, his arms and legs spread to form an H. "I, Vural, shall assist her!" He began to run out of the room. "Go on without me, friends, for I must conquer against evil."

The other three just shrugged and continued playing the game as if he wasn't there. None of them wanted to say it to his face, but he was their weakest link anyway.

As Vural dashed through the halls, he passed by the captain of

Kingfisher Squad. To the antlion's surprise, Alexandru managed to keep up with him in speed.

"Evening stroll, Vural?" he asked, knowing that wasn't the answer. They both jumped over the wall of the school.

Vural was stunned to see that the normally squishy dhampyr could move as fast as him. "How are you keeping up with me?"

"New trick I learned over the summer," Alexandru replied to him as he pointed toward the full moon. "I discovered that the Lord Ruthven spark grants me enhanced physical abilities during the night. With it being a full moon out, I'm at my peak. So where are you off to?"

Vural answered him as he rushed along the sidewalk. "To the Sephirot! I hear a big confrontation's going on there!"

"Well color me intrigued then," Alex said, contemplating what could possibly be occurring. "I must use the skill of multitasking to write a text as I run."

"Sure thing! Take your time, vamp! I sure won't."

Vural bolted off at speeds Alexandru couldn't hope to accomplish. Now learning how fast he was compared to Vural, the dhampyr decided to just focus on texting Ludmila about what he had just learned. She might find showing up a good workout.

⁓ * ⁓

Ludmila was at the table with her adoptive family, the Terrellis. The family consisted of her, her new dad, Riazzo, and Dunkeen. Her new mom was off at a business meeting in Qian Ye. For most people, it was hard to tell that all three lived under the same roof, especially when one of them looked like a prehistoric fish. She occasionally wondered why Riazzo would ever allow Dunkeen to be morphed into a fishman. But she guessed if Dunkeen didn't mind, then no big deal. Riazzo was speaking about his day.

"So you see, son, as coach of Aeon Sophia Academy, I play an important role in shaping up the new generation of psychics. Those little simulations on The Stage aren't the real training; you get no muscle from sitting in a chair in La-La Land. The true way to become a great psychic is time in the gym. No use fighting with flabby limbs after spending your training in a fantasy world." The muscular paternal guardian stuffed his mouth with more potato salad. "Coach Kren was merciless to me back in my day, and I used to hate him for it. But now, seeing my long streak of accomplishments in life, if he were still alive I'd kiss him right on the mouth and thank him for all he's done for me." He had a moment of silence for the late Kren.

Ludmila honestly zoned out to eat her meal after a while. It was nothing she hadn't heard before. Just what went on during PE classes and stuff—rope climbing, Basil's prowess, how that George kid cared more about them crystalgames than being fit—random stuff like that. She felt relief when she received a message on her cell. It was from Alexandru and it was mentioning something going on at the museum. From how it was written, it seemed like a fight. She was in the mood for a brawl. She got up from her seat, her food done. "Father, may I be excused? Something is occurring at the museum and I want to see what it is."

Riazzo paused from mid-rant then continued. "So something is occurring at the great Sephirot Museum of Bythos? That sounds interesting. Why would it be open at this hour? Unless something terrible is occurring under the city's noses." He nodded his approval. "You can fly to the city. I feel you're needed with the others. I bid you good luck. Just don't get hurt. My wife will kill me if anything happens to you."

As Ludmila flew out the window, Dunkeen swallowed his steak in two bites. "You know, dad, I feel my captain, Desiderio, should know about this." He took out a blue cell that was much too small for his hands. "As the fourth greatest captain, I feel he's entitled to know of the going-ons of this city. I know you don't like how he looks at Ludmila when she's in ice dragon mode, but I trust him enough to let him give Ludmila a hand. He always knows how to turn the tide of battle." The armored fish began to send a message. "Though it is sad you can't join her in battle. Stinks that the mayor deemed Bahamut to be 'too destructive.' Shame, an earth dragon in the fray is always super cool. But the least we could do is just call the authorities."

~ * ~

Desiderio dueled against Mastema one on one. There was no audience for the two and the entire stage was silent—just the two of them in the SAIS arena testing one another's skills. The Killer of Gods wielded his rapier with swift efficiency against the Angel of Silence. Mastema was only using his hard light halberd to parry his attacks. One fought as if it was all a performance whilst the other kept on the defensive, waiting to inflict the perfect strike the moment an opening was found.

Mastema seemed to have found himself a chance to finish the duel. But as he was about to trip the swordsman, the rapier cleaved his weapon in two. An ordinary blade cut light in half? How was that even possible? Next thing he knew, he found himself on the floor in front of the wrong end of a rapier.

Resigned to his defeat, Mastema deactivated Dumah's sphere of silence. With that, they could hear the world once again.

"I told you Diomedes defeats the undefeatable," the man in the masquerade mask told him as he twirled his weapon before sheathing it. "That which is invincible is not exempt from my steel." Desi helped him up. "That was a nice fun duel." He was aware that his opponent was holding back as he summoned no laser eyes or anything.

Mastema had always acknowledged Desiderio as the greatest swordsman in the academy, so did not fret too much about his loss. "It…sure was…thank you for your time." He bowed and began to walk away. "I must be on my way now…for supper."

Desiderio stopped him from leaving. "Are you sure, Grey? Because you know you and I could most definitely go off campus and grab a bite to eat—maybe even score a date for you." He wrapped an arm around Mastema's neck to his discomfort. "Do you realize how popular a champ like you is with the maidens of this shining city?"

"…No?"

"I honestly don't know either. But that could change with the help of me, the world's greatest wingman." Desi wanted his friend's imagination to soar. "Just imagine how many girls in this city would beg to be your first with my assistance."

"First…what?" He wasn't feeling comfortable about where this was going.

"Don't play dumb with me, Mr. Broody. I mean about how—"

As if it were a miracle, both of their crystalcells hollered. Mastema thanked Sophia for reducing the awkwardness as he rushed toward his cell.

"Who's it from?" Desi asked as he picked up his cell.

Reading the contents of the message, Mastema's face became much more serious. "It's from Bianca."

The Titlacua made a cheeky grin. "That's veeeery interesting. Since when did you have the princess's number?"

Mastema kept a straight face. "I felt the need to request every captain's number…in case of emergency."

"And what does she want with you at such a late hour?" The sheer sauciness of two emotionally repressed teenagers entwined in sheer passion was too much for his imagination. But the angel's answer ruined the thoughts of possible forbidden romances going on under his nose.

"There's an alert coming from the Sephirot." Mastema glared at him, not in the mood for his teasing. "I must assist. Farewell." His dark wings formed on his back and he flew up out of the empty stadium.

Desiderio checked his message. It was from Dunkeen, more or less saying the same thing. He mused to himself. "Must he insist on texting entire paragraphs?" At this point, he began to wonder why Dunkeen didn't just write a novel or search for a future career in politics.

But Desiderio wasn't going to just let them steal the entire spotlight. Though it was going to be quite a journey to get there, even he was going to go to the museum. Hopefully he wouldn't be too late.

The Beautiful Game

Zuo was officially lost. He found himself wandering through the Protogenoi Arts exhibit on the second floor. Paintings made by artists were on every wall and it seemed like the kind of place somebody could just sit on a bench and relax for a while. If only, if only…

Tragically, he still needed to find those damn pauldrons. Where were they? He needed a map badly or he would be here until daybreak and the boss would not appreciate that. This was not going well. Chances were, Roy and P.J spared no witnesses whenever possible and a trail of bodies was going to be inevitable.

But to his luck, he saw a familiar folded glossy paper lying on a bench. He strolled toward what he assumed to be the item to guide him to his goal, hissing in pain as his bones rubbed together. His doctor had told him something about his arthritis getting worse earlier this year, but he didn't think it would be this irritating.

Grabbing the map, he analyzed the whereabouts of the artifact. It was in the Empire under Barbar section. Which made sense, the pauldrons were his. Turns out it was a floor above him in the east wing. Finally, he could actually make some progress.

As he began to head that way, he noticed a giant painting more wide than tall. It was from some hylic known as Mikael back during the empire days, maybe a couple hundred years old. The picture seemed to have reveled in religious imagery, judging by its visual portrayals of Heaven and Hell. The Heavens appeared on the top of the portrait as a peaceful paradise with a blue sky and clouds as fluffy as cotton balls. In fact, it just looked like an average summer morning, far from anything special. The pious deceased appeared as doves as white as virginal snow, each radiating a bright blue glow. Sophia radiated very much within them.

As he looked down, the worlds were divided by a crust of stone meant to possibly represent Earth. Further down, he saw a visual of what the artist's interpretation of Hell was. Rather than the classic fire and brimstone or the less popular but widely considered icy wasteland, Hell was a cavern almost completely dark. The outlines of the damned were hardly visible, but their forms looked utterly mangled and twisted as if The Demiurge itself birthed them. Each one seemed to be wallowing in hopeless despair, their reward for their sins on Earth being lost forever in the blackness. But still, a faint blue light shone on the very top of the underground, out of reach from every soul trapped within, tantalizing them for eternity.

But there were a few visible entities in the darkness. A good bit under the light, were some flying…things. These spirits of the dead looked like blobby bald human heads that looked half melted. Tiny dots were used for their eyes, and their mouths had forced toothless smiles. They all seemed to be trying to fly toward the light on stubby little bird wings on the sides of their heads. Looking closer, Zuo saw one or two feathers upon the heads of each flying thing. It dawned on him. These things thought they were doves and that light was none other than Sophia, and were endlessly trying to reach her. Each one's face seemed to say, "Look at us, savior! We are one of your chosen! Everything we did was for you!" as if none of them knew why they were in Hell. All of them looked to be in utter denial of their damnation.

Zuo admired the picture, knowing this was possibly one of the places he would end up in upon his death, but hopefully not as one of the flying blobs. He knew that form was meant to be for those who committed atrocities for reasons they believed were in the name of Sophia. He never questioned what he did was wrong that night or any other, but he still did it out of loyalty to Qian Ye. Even after nearly a decade, the screams of terror were still fresh in his mind, never letting him forget. He felt cleaner today as Shèng Xià than as a psychic under Tai Xun. If a ruler could order you to end the lives of those who have done nothing to you, why not just become a common crook? One path was no better than the other. But he had no time for reminiscing on regrets and his eventual fate. He had an artifact to grab and a theory to test.

~ * ~

Ercan and Xiu were now on the second floor. They noticed that they were in the East Qian exhibit showing the important cultural objects, arts, and artifacts before and after Qian Ye became a nation—golden statues of spiritual guardians with big curved teeth, jade dragons, and imperial crowns of former Protogenoi nobles of the region, among other items of great value.

Ercan looked around a bit, interested in what the exhibit offered around him whilst Xiu felt apathy at best. But a tour would have to wait, as they needed to get to the pauldrons. As they ran through the area, they heard somebody make a loud yawn as if they'd just awakened. Both stopped in their tracks.

"How the hell was somebody napping at a time like this?" Xiu questioned both herself and her companion as she tried to detect the source of the sound.

"Beats me," Ercan replied with a shrug. "Some people are just heavy sleepers."

As their eyes wandered around, they saw a man in his pajamas with a very risqué body pillow under his arm. The man yawned once again. "Hey, kids. It's a bit late for a date here, don't you think?" He pointed at their wet clothes. "Though by the looks of it, you already got one another wet. You scored big time, red." He gave Ercan a thumbs-up.

Neither of them was particularly amused. Ercan was in no mood for any jokes. "Sir, this isn't a time to be funny. The Lefty Gang is here and is after the pauldrons of Kadosh. We have to get you out of here." He opened a window, making a grappling hook at the end of a chain to form a makeshift emergency exit.

The man's eyes almost popped out. "Oh, shit, really?" He turned and shook his head to Xiu. "This is what a lowly janitor gets when he decides to take a nap on the job." He also began to speak for his body pillow in a high-pitched voice. "You're such a bad man! Very naughty! Punish later!" He rushed toward a professor's office. "There's really valuable but heavy shit here that I just know those douchebags are going to steal no matter what, and my good professor friend…" He quickly read the name on the door. "…Professor Cheung's career would be in utter ruins if his fancy stuff was robbed."

Ercan was about to follow him in, but Xiu firmly grabbed his shoulder. "Ercan, stop. I don't trust him."

The man in his sleeping clothes froze up just after the door creaked open. "And why is that, young lady?"

She got ready to punch his lights out. "Well first, how about the fact that a janitor managed to bring his nightwear to work? Or maybe the fact that a museum this prestigious wouldn't have already booted your ass onto the curb for being a lazy bum?"

The sleepyhead slowly turned his head back to the two. "Smart little bitch, aren't you? You got me. Name's Patrick Jay Porrige, or P.J for short. Unsubtle isn't it? But my codename is Ezker."

Ercan felt uneasy as he readied himself to tie his opposition down. "Why are you telling us this?"

P.J gave a small soulless smile before nudging the door open. Inside the room was a gray corpse whose eyes were closed, but its mouth was wide open as if to scream. "Because you two won't be alive much longer." He dropped his pillow onto the ground.

Both teens were having none of this trash talk from a murderer. They went on the offensive. But P.J fell onto his pillow fast asleep before they could even land a blow.

"So, what? He just talks shit and then goes to bed?" Xiu pondered angrily as she kicked Ezker's side. He did not wake up.

Ercan was very wary at the moment. "I think a Lefty member has a damn good reason to do this." He pointed at the corpse in the room. "He's probably here to—" He yawned loudly as his eyelids became heavy.

She turned to him more slothfully than she would have liked. "Why are you yawning at—" She also felt utterly exhausted all of a sudden. *Oh no. No.* Before either could get away, they both collapsed onto the floor in deep slumber.

～ * ～

"Where are we now?" Yun asked Shee'vra, looking around a room with a bunch of humanoid skeletons. They'd taken a detour to free some tied up guards and professors and they'd gone a little off course. At least he thought they did.

"According to the map, we're at The Evolution of Mankind exhibit," she answered, trying to be quiet. At any moment they could be ambushed by a Lefty Gang member. "If I remember from a field trip two years ago, the stairs to the third floor should be a few rooms away."

"It was a simpler time back then." Somebody was in the room with them. "All these Neanderthals worried about were food, shelter, and a mate. Damn, times today are just so much more complicated, especially for us psychics, huh?"

Both of their eyes scanned around the room until they came across a familiar face. It was Izquierda who called to them right next to the most controversial exhibit in the museum—the chart of human evolution from cell to man. The Crocotta stood at the end of the chart before jumping down to them. "You guys are seriously getting on my nerves."

Despite being here, Izquierda didn't look to be in much condition to fight. Shee'vra saw this week's worth of injuries on his body. Scars from Sabelle's claws and teeth, bruises from his last fight with Yun, a wrist injury from Xiu, and he looked a good bit skinnier than before, as if he'd had trouble eating the last few days. But still he stood against them, claws and jaws at the ready.

Yun didn't feel comfortable fighting a guy in this condition. "Are you sure you want to do this?"

"You will not get in our way," Izquierda growled at them. "Just one more mission and I get to leave this place for good." He pounced at the monkey and got easily countered and sent across the room. But he got up. "You kids must think that being a psychic is the greatest thing on earth." An attack with his claws completely whiffed. "You brats got your sparks at the perfect time." Yun ducked a mighty kick from him that took out a chunk of the wall. Yun countered and held him down onto the floor, but Izquierda refused to feel any pain. "Ever thought about what happens when an adult develops a spark?"

Neither of them had a proper answer for that question. But Shee'vra had the nerve to decide to ask him. "What *does* happen to an adult who becomes a psychic?"

The gang member momentarily stopped struggling and decided to answer. "Well, would you two like to hear a story?"

Yun was wary but decided to humor him. "Alright, fine." *This had better not be in order to stall time for his boss.*

Shee'vra felt the need to want to know his backstory. How could a psychic just choose to become a criminal? "Yes, tell us."

Having an audience, Louiz begun. "Well then, it all began three years ago."

~ * ~

Three Years Ago

It was WoFoL (World Football League) Cup, and most of the cities in all the nations competed for the gold. Today was the final round between the Dorado Toucans and the San Michel Sapphires. Louiz Agudo, player number twelve of Dorado (but player number one in Titlacuan) was having the game of his life. It was his duty to protect his city's honor as the number one team on planet Earth.

But, by Sophia, it was an uphill game. The score was 3-3 with only thirty seconds on the clock. If they tied, there was a heavy chance that they would lose. San Michel had Bobby Paliposey, the greatest penalty kicker in the league. His goalie was already exhausted from overexerting himself. There was no way he could block a kick from Bobby. A loss in its own stadium would smash the morale of the entire city.

But Louiz's muscles felt like they were about to boil and burst. He was working his ass off, but still those guys in purple were scoring goals. But he needed desperately to break the tie and score another year of victory for Dorado.

He saw a familiar number three in a green jersey as its wearer passed the ball to him. Louiz received the black and white ball and ran as he kicked it around. Just in front of him were three Sapphires as well as two behind him. To the detriment of the entire team, there was nobody open to pass to. He dreaded giving a stain of silver for Dorado.

As he struggled with what to do, he felt something. His fatigue was completely gone. His will to win surpassed his body. He ran faster and faster and, with the strongest kick he could muster, got that ball into the visitor's goal.

It was moments like this that made football the most beautiful game of all. The home crowd cheered and chanted his name over and over.

"LOUIZ THE BEAST! LOUIZ THE BEAST!" His fellow players picked him up into the air, giving him the giant trophy to hold. Even the opposition took their loss gracefully, nodding to him in begrudging respect.

Once again Dorado was the champion of football. He wished this moment would last forever. But this was not the happy ending of an inspirational sports movie. It was reality and the story did not just end with him as a champion.

After a week of parties and celebration, Louiz was called to the WoFoL Court. He had absolutely no idea why they would want him. Judging by their faces though, the administrators and even his coach were far from happy.

They showed him a video of last week's game. It focused on him making the winning goal. He was so fast, faster than he'd ever been in his life. They paused the video to show him why they'd brought him here. The screen froze to show a tint of blue aeon energy emerging from his body that the naked eye could barely see. He had absolutely no idea what it was.

The higher ups shouted at him not to play dumb with the WoFoL and that the organization had no tolerance for cheaters. Having a spark gave you an advantage and they wouldn't tolerate such foul play. Louiz tried to claim that he had no idea about any spark and was forced to take an aeon test. An average hylic would have a score of about ten aeon at most. Louiz had a number ranging at around three-fifty.

He tried as best as he could to claim that he wasn't lying about hiding his spark. But just now his fame as a soccer champion backfired against him. He was so good that they refused to believe anyone could ever do what he did without a spark. They'd heard of secret psychics messing around in hylic positions. They'd heard about golfers who subtlety moved their golf balls with their minds, stockbrokers who could foresee events, and poker players that read minds. It was people like that who used their powers for an unfair edge that stained the psychic's reputation for most jobs and competitive events.

Thus, by the end of the trial, Louiz was stripped of his medals and banned from sports for good. His reputation was in tatters, and Dorado's golden streak was hastily destroyed. Within the next six months, Louiz's life had gone to hell. His entire town thought he was a fraud, his former teammates blamed him for their wrecked reputation, and his fiancé left him due to the pressure.

Getting up from his bed, he wandered around his filthy apartment. More mail was at the door; no doubt all hate mail. Louiz grabbed a bottle of tequila and took a massive swig. As he drank it all down, he began to think that the letters sometimes made good points. He was useless and dead to people. Maybe he *should* just end it all. Not like anyone in town would miss a fraud like him.

Smashing his drink into the wall, he staggered toward his balcony. He took a long look down. It was twenty-five stories, so unless his spark made him immortal too, it would all be over within the next minute. Taking a deep breath, he closed his eyes and stood up onto the edge. With a leg that inspired many, he began to step off the side.

He felt himself fall, but he also felt as if somebody stopped him. Daring to open his eyes, he saw the being that would define his future.

~ * ~

"And on that day, I was inducted into the Lefty Gang and was taught how to use my spark," Louiz told the two. "Though I regret many of my decisions, the Demon Dragon gave me a second shot at life, brought out my true potential." He sighed and shook his head. "It's a lot harder getting a spark as an adult. You lose whatever you had before, and you have to grasp at straws to find another lot in life. So here I am—a man who is no longer allowed to play a game of football without being called a cheater."

Though he sympathized with his plight, Yun did have a few questions. "Then why didn't you just join a psychic guard? You could've been really useful in such a position."

Louiz cringed. "I ask myself that a lot nowadays. If only I was in the right emotional state at the time, my life could be going a lot better. But let's face it—it's too late for me to be forgiven. I've robbed and hurt a lot of people over the years and I'm more than sure I'm not just going to get a slap on the wrist."

"But you can help us now," Shee'vra said to him. "The Lefty Gang wants the artifacts for Sophie-knows-what. You have an opportunity to help us underdogs keep a national treasure safe." Her face radiated sheer determination to make it out of here alive.

"You do realize you're asking me to work with the kids who are responsible for giving me hell this last week, right?" Louiz said, more than suspicious of this alliance. "Chances are the cops are just going to lock me up the moment it's all over."

That was true. Cops were not really known to forgive bank robberies. But Shee'vra continued to try to convince him. "Possibly...probably. But at least you get to go to prison with a clear conscience. In fact, chances are, you'll get a few years shaved off your jail time."

The hoofed hyena beast man slowly changed back to his original form. Yun let go of him to allow him to get up, seeing him as no longer a threat. Louiz counted the possibilities of what could possibly happen to him depending on his next actions. The boss was going to be livid if it was discovered that he had aided them in botching the mission. Chances were, he might not even be able to survive prison if he slighted the gang. Then again, he would be much safer in jail than free. Even if he chose to be an ungrateful little shit and knocked both of them out, chances were another psychic was going to get him.

So Louiz rubbed the back of his shaved head and gave the two an answer. "Fine. I can work something out with you. But I want to be able to see Ewen and Asterion in Prisoner's Perch. They're my friends." *Screw Sharlie and Muvumo. Those two are spineless cowards anyway.*

Shee'vra offered a hand to shake with. "Perfect. So, we have a deal?" Louiz hesitated a little bit but grasped her hand and shook.

Though relieved they had more help for now, Yun still felt uneasy about their chances. Recalling Louiz's story, there was mention of a man that had the appearance of a dragon, a demon, and a snake combined. He also remembered the Venomous Helldrake from experience and dreaded the thought that he was potentially still out there searching for more psychics to corrupt. Some of those psychics might revel in the opportunity to become criminals, though others were probably the desperate type who had no other choices. Chances were, that snake probably reveled in corrupting all of them. Who knew how many unregistered psychics he'd visited within these last few years? Such thoughts had to be put on hold as the three found the stairs to the third floor.

Manticore

Ercan's eyes slowly opened themselves as if he'd slept for hours. Hastily getting up to confront P.J, his purple irises focused on his surroundings. He couldn't see the pajama clad criminal or Xiu anywhere. Looking about a bit more, he found that he was definitely not in the museum anymore and most likely not even on Earth.

"Xiu? Xiu?"

He wandered the unknown area. The sky above him was bright purple with large stars (as in the shape, not the hot balls of gas) plastered into the sky as if it was a five-year-old's art project. Around him were various small buildings that almost gave the appearance that the place was an odd mix of a small town and a circus. Each one had a sign on them such as *Prometheu, Weaponcrafting, Guilty Pleasure Cinema,* and *My toys are alive but don't move when I'm around.*

Ercan wasn't an idiot, he knew what this meant. *So that guy trapped us in our minds? No, no our dreams. That's why he wears pajamas and carries a pillow around, so he can feel comfy when he uses his spark. Chances are, Xiu is in her own dreamscape or something, right? Or are they connected together?* He couldn't help but frown as he saw a huge neon sign that read "Ercan's Greatest Phails" accompanied by a cartoonish picture of Bianca sticking her tongue out. *Ow. My self-esteem.*

As he looked around, calling for his ally, he noticed how empty the place was. Perhaps everyone was just indoors? But maybe he didn't want to see anybody. However, walking around was getting him nowhere. He found a building called *I Can Fly!* that seemed safe enough. It seemed like a good enough start. Not only would being able to fly give him a bird's eye view of the place, it would also keep him on duty. Buildings like *Mega Videogames* and *Shiro's Amazing Bod* would distract him way too much. Plus, they might be traps.

Then again, an enemy spark put him here. Everything could be a trap. But he had no choice. Xiu could be in trouble. Making a weighted chain, he hastily opened the door to *I Can Fly!* ready to find P.J. Though it was pitch black inside, he braved on.

Wandering into the silent darkness, he saw a light. Praying to Sophia it wouldn't lead to his death, he pursued the light. To his unlimited relief, he saw that he was at the edge of a snowy mountain range. It was also as cold as any high-altitude area and he was woefully underdressed for this. So Ercan used his wits to come up with the idea of creating a warm jacket for himself.

Ten seconds later…absolutely nothing. No warm gear. Just wasting his time, freezing his ass off. "Dammit."

But this was supposed to be an area where he could fly. Defying all logic like most dreams do, he jumped up and flapped his arms. And it was working. He was going higher and higher up into the air. *This must be how Shee'vra feels. It's beautiful.*

He soon began to soar across the landscape like a mighty condor, flapping his arms whenever he needed to gain altitude. He could almost feel tears of joy welling up inside his eyes. The real world felt so far away from him. Was today all just a dream? Or was this his true world? It was just so intoxicating he couldn't stand to contemplate what seemed to be reality.

But just as he was gliding around, the sky turned sickly green. Tops of the mountains morphed into grimacing faces that puked red liquid and roared at him. A sickening cackle invaded his mind. No longer was this bliss. This truly became a nightmare.

"YOU CHOSE THE FLYING, REALLY?" a voice called to him. "CALL ME DISSAPOINTED! I WOULD THINK A TEEN LIKE YOU WOULD CHOOSE A MORE RISQUE DREAM BEFORE YOU BIT THE DUST!" it cruelly laughed, "AT LEAST YOU WOULDN'T HAVE DIED A VIRGIN!"

He heard loud shrills coming from behind him. Bright red condors as big as a horse were just behind him. He knew the birds of prey saw him as just another meal. Worse still, his flapping was failing him. Ercan began losing altitude by the second and the canyon just turned into a maw full of teeth waiting to swallow him up.

He needed to think quickly to get out of this. Shooting a chain around a condor's leg, he hung high into the air. Ercan shot out a metal net from his free hand and entrapped one of the birds, allowing it to fall into the toothy canyon. A condor swooped down at him, talons at the ready. He swung from his chain and jumped onto the bird's back.

The demonic avian hissed as it tried to shake him off. At the same time, the bird with the chain on its leg began to target him from above. Even the one he was on turned its head around 180 degrees and tried to peck at him with a beak as sharp as a dagger. Ercan took a hit to the shoulder but found an opening to slit the condor's throat with a spear point.

Needing to get off the dying bird, he wrapped a chain around the last condor's other leg. Ercan now had two chains to hold onto. He hoped this would save him. He tugged on the left leg and the condor went left toward a snowy mountain. *Holy crap that actually worked! Now as long as I don't look down I should make it.*

He thought too soon. Out of the demon bird's anus came a trickle of lava. In a panic, Ercan swung to the right chain to avoid the burning bird crap, causing the condor to veer to the right. So close to the ledge, he needed to get it closer. Reluctantly shooting a chain up the bird's ass, he heard a horrible agonizing cry.

With the lava clogged for now, Ercan went back onto the left chain to get the bird back on course. But the turn had to be much sharper or they would miss the edge. He shot another chain to wrap around the bird's beak and pulled harder. The bird squawked in pain as it sharply turned to the side of the cliff. With land now below him, the redhead dropped off the bird and landed onto the snowy peak.

Taking a moment to breathe, he looked up to see the condor crash into the mountainside and fall right in front of him. The bird got up and shrieked at him, wanting to tear him to pieces. But at this point, Ercan just used both hands to shoot an anchor at the bird's face. With that problem solved, Ercan saw that he was in the mouth of a cave. Above him, the blood from the top of the mountain was sliding downwards like an avalanche. With no other choices, he jumped into the cavern.

In the darkness, Ercan lit two small links on fire to provide light and warmth. Icicles were above and below him, though against all logic they decreased in frequency as he went deeper and deeper into the cave. He was just about ready to wring P.J's neck the moment he could find him.

"Kudos for making it this far! Thought you'd be mush by now!" The voice echoed around the cave. "Neat S&M chains you got there!" The voice grew quieter than he was comfortable with. "But now that you made it this far without my permission, I'll have to punish you."

Just then, P.J appeared right in front of him with a smug smile on his face. Ercan was quick to attack. "Where's Xiu?" He lashed at him, but P.J just poofed away.

"You mean that Qian chick you were with?" He was now right behind Ercan. "Last I saw her she was trapped inside her own dream world. Though between you and me, you were much more difficult to concoct a nightmare for." He poofed away from another attack and just continued to talk. "Her nightmare was a cinch to make, so I decided to give you a couple of options. Heck you took so long I had a visit in your land of wet dreams. Yes, I can interact with that world. Lost my virginity in one too back in the day." He avoided another chain. "Though I do admit I'm very disappointed in you. All the ladies there were around your age. Now I might not be what you traditionally call a good man, but I'm not into teens. Got to have one line you don't ever cross."

Ercan was in no mood for this spiel. "JUST SHUT UP ALREADY!" He slashed his burning whip at a greater velocity. P.J teleported away, but his body pillow had been hit. The chain broke and singed the fabric, making it look as if the scantily dressed woman on it had just been cut in half.

Patrick Jay Porrige checked the damage on his beloved Kazuko-Chan Pillow and was far from amused. He looked back at the purple-eyed psychic with a lazy glare. "You do not hurt a man's waifu. Congrats *Erky*, you get to die first." He kicked off his slippers and tossed his nightcap over his shoulder.

Right before Ercan's eyes, P.J began to transform. His muscles tore his pajamas off as he grew in size and mass. Bat wings formed onto his back, claws replaced his nails, his head became that of a hairless tiger/

human with a maw containing a legion of sharp fangs, and a long tail grew containing five stingers as thin and sharp as needles. Ercan knew what P.J had become: Tai Xun, Corrosive Tiger of Qian Ye and wielder of the Manticore spark.

Ercan had heard of this man from history class. The Fourth Bumpa of Qian Ye, trained by Master Yeren himself. His actions, along with Sirohko's Chatraratna Jalil Afritan, were the very cause of the last war. Even today, nobody truly knew why this had all started. The interrogated claimed it was due to the initial massacre victims associating with disgusting cultists of the Demiurge. Some of those victims were tourists from other nations, so it quickly devolved into a war that ended up taking both Ashtamangala's lives along with so many others. His mother fought in the war and killed many psychics that she went to school with. Even now she refused to speak about it.

But now the one and only Tai Xun was right in front of him, his rows of teeth dripping with saliva. Ercan quivered more than all the times he ever had in his life combined. Knowing Tai Xun's reputation just made it worse as his piercing gaze loomed over him, ready to tear him in half. "H-how could you become…him?"

"Are you about to piss you pants yet?" P.J gave a low playful purr that did not suit the reputation of Tai Xun. "Well you see—your girlfriend had this guy in her memories." He checked out his new body with curiosity. "Whoever he is. I mean where the heck is this dude's dick? Did this guy just walk around not having a dick as a giant ass tiger scorpion thing?" With a shrug, he decided to just get to business. "No biggie. Time to die shitting yourself, punk."

Tai Xun roared so loudly, the icicles behind them rattled in place like wind chimes. Ercan needed to do something. If he was dead, Xiu would be next in line. But, where was she?

Then a plan hit him. It was going to be utter agony and maybe Ercan would be too mutilated for it to even work. But hopefully, *hopefully*, this P.J guy was enough of a sadist to do what Ercan was predicting. So, he readied his burning chains once more and charged at the overwhelming odds.

P.J could not help but laugh. "Oho! We really doing this, huh? Now pray and die, bitch!" He jabbed with his spiked tail, hitting flesh.

～ * ～

Xiu had been wandering down a dark tunnel for a while now. With no idea where she was, where P.J was, or where Ercan was, she just moved forward. Step by step, she began to hear sounds grow louder and louder. The fires, the screams, the violence, everything made her just want to turn back. The darkness was so much safer than what would be ahead.

As she trudged on against common sense, she began to see a line up ahead that leaked out a burning light. It was that moment she knew for sure precisely where she was. Xiu was back there, back in her old family's home—back in the time where they showed up out of nowhere. Back when her old life was lost.

As soon as she was only a few feet from the door, she listened to it happen once again—the death of her parents. Her father tried to fight back but made a disgusting gurgling sound as his head only remained attached to his body by just some skin. Her mother was next. Her scream suddenly silenced as a sword pierced her heart.

Overwhelmed by her senses, Xiu stumbled over, her back hitting some sort of wall. Felt like wood. Hastily detecting her surroundings, she felt her mother's clothes all around her. She could barely move upon realizing this was the exact spot her mother hid her on that very night. It was cramped back then and even more cramped now.

She had no idea how long she stayed inside, watching that little line of light and praying that it was all just a dream. But it never happened, even when seconds felt like hours. She hated the idea of crying. Made her feel helpless and weak. She never shed tears in front of anyone to keep her image up, not even to her closest peers. But just perseverating about the loss of the Altahn was more than enough for her to let it all out.

As she began to sob, she heard a creaking sound as the door opened wider, bringing in more light. She looked up with her green eyes to see peeking through was the man with the red glasses. Behind him, lights from an inferno could be seen. He did nothing but stare at her through those lenses, which made him impossible to read. There seemed to be no bloodlust, or joy, no violent hatred or sadness—just a pure blank slate of a face. All she could tell was that he must have pitied the seven-year-old girl back then, and he still did now. He just let her live, closing the wardrobe on her.

The moment she heard him dragging her parents out to add them to the pile of bodies, her terror and despair were replaced by sheer fury. No chance in hell would she allow that man to grant her cruel mercy. This time she would kill him. She'd dreamed of this moment for years and now here was her chance. She emitted her blue aura on her fists and kicked open the door.

"GET AWAY FROM THEM!" She jumped out and attacked the man in the glasses as he stood over her family. She was in no mind to consider technique, merely flailing her fists about, trying to bash his brains in. But she couldn't even touch him. Every blow she inflicted just went right through him as if she was hitting thin air. She tried again and again as he went out her hut with her slain family in tow.

"I'LL KILL YOU! I'LL KILL YOU! I'LL BASH YOUR BRAINS IN!" She was borderline berserk at this point. "WHY WON'T YOU DIIIIE!?"

As she began to tire herself out, she saw that now she was not even attacking anything. The man just up and disappeared, leaving her alone with her parents at her feet. All around her, shadowy figures slaughtered the rest of the Altahn Tribe, ignoring her as if she was just a ghost. With all hope lost, she fell onto her knees as the shadows continued to incinerate her home and kill her former neighbors. She placed her hands upon the still warm bodies of Jiahao and Xinyi Lang as her despair returned twofold.

"What did we do to deserve this?"

"Ooooh! You seem to be having quite the nasty dream," a voice called out around her without a lick of sympathy. "I mean, I just assumed that these guys and gals slaughtering everyone you knew were just bandits or some shit." A red cloth with a long green dragon peeking out from within a lovely golden vase fell onto her lap. "But turns out, all of Qian Ye had it in for you hicks for who knows what? Even Sirochko was in on it. Who would have thought?" P.J laughed it up. "Can't even trust your own government not to kill you. I actually sort of wonder what you nomads did to deserve being genocided the living shit out of?"

Xiu trembled as she continued to gaze upon the bloody bodies of her parents. "I…don't know." It was all she could whisper out at the moment.

P.J merely tsk-tsked at her answer. "That just does not seem right. I might not like politics and that sort of shit, but I hear they don't usually just spontaneously slaughter an entire population. *Surely* you savages must have offended them first."

She punched a hole into the earth as she gritted her teeth to reply. "We. Did. Nothing." Footsteps came from behind her. Xiu's very soul felt an even greater unease as she saw *him* looming over her. The man who ordered everything: Tai Xun.

"Well then believe what you want, little missy," the manticore told her in P.J's voice. He seemed to notice her shivering as he grinned from ear to ear, showing every tooth in his mouth. "You seem a little tense right now. These two your mom and dad?" He swatted her away and ripped her father's head off to examine it. "Pity. Your dad here really should have thought A HEAD in life and maybe he'd be still alive." He tossed the corpse away like an empty beer can at Xiu's feet, who reflexively shrieked in terror. He then checked out her mother's body. "Well, well, well. Your mom was quite the babe. How old was she when she kicked the bucket? 'Bout twenty-four?" He shook his head in feigned pity. "Bit young for popping kids. You mountain ladies are just soooo irresponsible. You know when I think about it, your mom and dad look a lot alike. You inbred?" He tore Xinyi in half and tossed her over his shoulders and then crushed Jiahao's skull with his foot as Xiu looked on, feeling powerless.

"Why are you even bothering to be all gaspy and stuff?" The monstrous winged tiger man questioned her. "Your parents were already dead. And there is no spark that will ever bring them back. They're already long gone, burned in a pile like the rest of your people." He grabbed her father's body and tossed it onto a pile of corpses as a malicious shadowy figure lit the corpses on fire. "Besides, I have someone else who you'd miss that's a *little* more recently deceased."

Xiu's heart grew heavier, knowing it was Ercan he was talking about. She got up slowly as she tried to confront Tai Xun. "What did you do to him, you bastard?"

P.J playfully clapped for her. "Congrats, congrats. You freeze up when I tear your family apart, but you get on your feet the moment I mention that your man *might* just be dead. What a bitch. You bring feminism back twenty years." His laugh grew more malicious. "So here he is." He showed her his long tail, expecting to show her the dangling corpse impaled on his stingers.

But instead, all that was there was some fresh blood. Xiu could not resist breathing a sigh of relief, knowing Ercan was okay. As P.J looked at his tail in confusion, familiar burning chains wrapped around his neck and pulled back. Knowing that the real Tai Xun would never have been so dumb as to turn his back to an enemy, Xiu covered her fists in aeon again and went in to give the bastard a well-deserved beating as he choked. Xiu struck him repeatingly, each attack for her family and the Altahni legacy. Knowing that the manticore was feeling every hit was so cathartic to her only made her attacks faster and stronger.

With a final kick, she knocked the monster over. As she paused to take a breather, she could not help but feel slightly more at ease as Ercan rushed to her side. "Ercan. What took you so long?"

Ercan seemed very regretful as his eyes absorbed his surroundings. "I'm sorry…I didn't know. I'm sorry you had to go through this. All of this." He wished he had managed to rip himself from those spikes earlier so P.J would not have the chance to rip those two bodies apart. He had a good idea who they were.

Xiu brushed it off for the moment. "Not right now. Let's just finish this and wake up." She could see that the manticore was rising back up.

Ercan did not complain. The jammy-wearing dickhead needed to be taught a lesson. The two readied themselves side by side as an angered P.J roared and got his claws ready to tear them to pieces.

P.J attacked first with a swipe at Xiu, who swiftly caught his hand and broke two of his fingers. Ercan followed up by hitting the opposition directly in the throat with a weighted chain. Xiu hit P.J's arm away and shattered his kneecap while Ercan entwined the manticore's tail. Running around him, he managed to get the tail entrapped within P.J's maw of teeth. With a strong jab to the crouching tiger-man's jaw, Xiu got him to bite his own tail off. Ercan then chained up P.J's good leg to topple him over. P.J may have looked like Tai Xun, but he didn't have his skills at all.

Ercan lassoed the manticore's neck and tugged with both arms. His small yellow pupils emphasized his terror as he was at the mercy of two students. "Please let me go! I'll free you all I promise! Just don't hurt me anymore!"

Neither Xiu nor Ercan bought it for a moment. Ercan held him down as Xiu readied herself for the finishing blow. Her satisfaction was now gone, what was left was anger at P.J's very existence. With one last punch through his skull, P.J began to disappear. That particular attack was from the Tiger Fist Style, the style Tai Xun himself was widely known to be the master of. Karma's a bitch.

"NOOOOOOO! WHHHHHHY!?" The dream weaver's body began to melt away as he grasped for the last straws of life before becoming nothing more than a puddle.

After that confrontation, Ercan immediately checked his surroundings. As they utterly stomped P.J, nothing in the background stopped slaughtering her tribe members. In fact, it seemed that the dream looped around constantly from beginning to end.

"Did this actually…I am so sorry." Ercan immediately began to apologize to her once again. "If I had known, I never would have—"

"It's fine," Xiu hastily replied, not even looking at him. "There was no way you could have known about this." She was focusing more on everything in the village being burnt to a crisp. "The worst thing is that I still don't know why this happened."

Ercan had no idea either. In none of the history textbooks did they mention the reason for the desolation of an entire Qian settlement. In fact, judging by some of the figures burning all the books and papers, they seemed to have wanted that sort of information to be kept secret from the world. He did not have much to say as well. "I don't know either." At this point, they both just wanted to wake up.

All of a sudden, the fires turned bright blue as P.J's voice came back full force. "JUST KIDDING!"

Patrick Jay Porrige reformed himself out of sight of either of those brats. He had been playing with them this whole time, but perhaps it was necessary to finally just kill them already. He already got the girl to relive her worst memories and the guy had little material to work off of without repeating the same clichés. Chances were, Ercan would not have fallen for them anyway at this point in the game.

It was a shame he didn't know martial arts or anything about the Manticore spark for that matter. If he did, this Tai Xun body would have been perfect for killing them. But that never stopped him from improvising with some new adjustments. He increased his muscle mass even more and grew to fifteen feet high. He formed two extra tails and each tip was now covered in three times as many needle stingers as before. He formed twice as many rows of uneven teeth and grew out a putrid black mane. His eyes developed black scleras that were ready to find and murder those two.

With his colossal wings, he flew into the sky just for the sake of dropping down right in front of them. Xiu and Ercan could not help but jump at the very sight of him. Just what he wanted.

"Did you two honestly fall for my acting? You're both dumber than I thought!" He licked his teeth with a long inky tongue. "I'm honestly impressed you both lasted this long, though. But the only bright side is that neither of you will die alone. You Lucky guys." He let out a low chuckle as he crossed his arms.

Xiu was incensed that this monster was still alive and shot a ball of aeon at him. The blast didn't even reach P.J, dissipating just in front of her.

"That might have hurt if I wasn't me."

"You son of a—" Xiu failed to speak any more as she suddenly could barely keep her own balance. Her movements became sluggish as her surroundings became blurry.

Seeing her suddenly become in no condition to fight, Ercan rushed to her side. But somehow, he moved about as slow as a sloth, falling over. Not being able to get up, he began to attempt to crawl toward her. P.J took his time and looked on for a bit, thick saliva covering his teeth.

"Now you two seem really confused. Have you ever realized that in dreams, you really SUCK BALLS at anything you do? You may be hot shit in the real world but the moment you go to sleep, you're never in control of anything. Not even your own body. For example, this can happen to you." P.J willed that all of Ercan's teeth would fall out and Xiu's legs would melt under her. "Are either of you particularly vivid dreamers?" The only answer he got were their barely audible yells as their mouths suddenly stopped working properly. "No? Well then, this will be too easy."

The abomination of Tai Xun decided to go for the boy first. As he picked him up with one hand, Xiu tried to attack him. At best, she could only give a groggy slap to his shin. "Not so tough now, you dumb inbred whore." He kicked her onto her back. Trapped in his clutches, Ercan desperately tried to create a chain, but could only form a tiny one that limped on top of his index finger. At this point, their determination was beginning to annoy P.J. "Well of course you can't use your spark correctly. My Little Nemo spark created this world around us. Here, I'm invincible." The monster's mouth dislocated and opened wider. "HERE, I AM GREATER THAN ANY ARCHON! HELL, EVEN SOPHIA IS WORTHLESS IN THIS REALM! I COULD BEND HER OVER AND MAKE HER MY BITCH HERE! WHAT CHANCE DO YOU THINK YOU WHELPS HAVE!?"

P.J began to bite into Ercan's stomach, feeding on his entrails. He reveled in his screams of unbearable agony as he began to eat him alive. But he didn't intend to just munch him up and be done with it. No, he wanted to savor this meal—the flavor of a boy who had lost all hope in surviving against him. He'd experienced this taste many times against cops, politicians, psychics, even his noisy neighbors. The fact that they all struggled just got him so hard. Using so many teeth just made the feeling seem surreal in its enjoyment. He just could not wait to chomp into him again.

But before he could slurp up more of Ercan's guts like spaghetti, something weird happened that he couldn't have possibly expected. He dropped the struggling boy against his own will. He then began to transform back into the less monstrous manticore form for some reason. P.J tried to see if the girl was somehow responsible for this, but he wasn't able to control his movements.

Some outside force made him move away from Ercan and to begin killing villagers with speed and technique P.J never really realized he had. He looked down to see Shèng Xià, of all people, participating in the massacre, though he looked like he wanted to be as far away from here as possible. There were also other psychics running about exterminating any villagers in sight, such as this mummy looking guy, a mandrill killing people with coins and gold, and a woman with wings parachuting down baskets that had dangerous baby dinosaurs inside them. But his body kept moving toward a hut Shèng had just came out of.

Inside the hut, he noticed a young girl running out of the back entrance. Involuntarily roaring with fury, P.J began to pursue her. He was not stupid. He'd read that girls memory. It was her as a scared seven-year-old. P.J also knew how this would end and tried to will himself to not pursue. *No no no no NO! Keep away from her! Just leave her alone! I DON'T WANNA DIE!*

But his body refused to listen. With a mighty roar, Tai Xun smashed through the hut and began his pursuit down a grassy hill. Little Xiu quickly ran away twice as fast the moment she saw the manticore coming for her. The village became more and more distant as Xiu entered a small cave. Tai Xun's body forced him to reach a claw into the crevasse in an attempt to drag her out, making long deep claw marks on the walls that would last for years to come. Pounding the mountainside in frustration, P.J was made to fly upwards for a bird's eye view.

Finding a big enough opening, he entered the cavern complex. His feline eyes were strong enough to see within the dark and his nose was strong enough to detect her scent. Tai Xun quickly wandered deep inside the caverns, growling and drooling as he crawled about looking for one child. At this point, P.J began to wonder why a Bumpa would want to kill a little girl so badly.

Trekking deeper into the chilly cavern, he seemed to have gotten an answer. Deep inside the cave was something P.J never thought he would ever see in his life. On the cavern walls, shining in a bright green light, was some sort of glowing ancient painting. It was shaped oddly, like an egg with horns complete with two tails. Tai Xun seemed to focus a lot on this seal as P.J was compelled to hiss in disgust at the very sight of it. Around the cavern floor were some scrolls and a bowl of incense that smelled as if it had been used within the last day. Tai Xun seemed to have picked up a scroll, skimmed it, and tore all the papers to pieces in a fit. P.J had no time to see what was on those scrolls but they must have been important enough to cause this frenzy.

His mouth was forced to move and say what Tai Xun said years ago. "How long did the Altahn know this seal was here? How many souls did you corrupt?" He made four long scratches on the seal with a roar. "Those Archon-worshippers cannot be allowed to live!" P.J detected a slight bit of genuine worry within the manticore's voice. It was as if he was killing them, not out of xenophobic hatred, but as if they were a threat to the entire world. P.J had heard about people worshipping Archons before. Hell, he even worked with a couple of them once in a while. Some seemed pretty normal, even a bit prudent. But others…he would rather not be trapped alone with.

As Tai Xun looked around, P.J was able to see that among the objects on the floor was a small statue of the Blue Lady Sophia. The manticore didn't seem to notice as he ran deeper into the caverns. As he wandered the narrow pathways, he heard small footsteps and crying. No doubt it was the girl. P.J struggled for control of his body, but Tai Xun climbed up to pursue her.

The young Xiu shrieked the moment she heard him coming. The only reason she hadn't been butchered already was thanks to the low ceiling and stalagmites forcing him to crawl and they got in the way of using his natural weapons to their maximum ability. Eventually, he chased her out into the snowy mountains. Xiu had problems running thanks to both fatigue and being thigh-deep in snow in nightwear. In the distance, Altahn was completely engulfed in flames. The exhausted girl fell over, realizing that the view of her home burning would be the last thing she would ever see. Her face fell into the snow, too tired to continue her escape.

With more room to move, the Fourth Bumpa quickly caught up with her. He must have felt little reason to scare her one last time, as he did not roar or growl. Tai Xun just got his long tail ready to sting straight into her back—a quick, painless death.

But before P.J could watch her get skewered, a strong arm covered in white hair grasped the tail just inches away from her. "What have you done, Tai Xun?"

The manticore turned around to see none other than his old master, Yeren, Man of The Mountain. P.J hadn't even seen the old hairy geezer coming. Yeren looked like he was roughly six decades old and, judging from his strong muscles and straight posture, he was going to live many more. He seemed to be revered enough that Tai Xun went on his knees to bow to him.

"Master Yeren," he formally addressed him with his head down. "Qian Ye has found evidence of cultist activity within the Altahn tribe."

The ape-man with long white hair had a look of horror and disappointment on his face. "I see your intentions for your country, but what you did will never be forgiven." Feeling safe around him, Xiu hastily scurried behind the master.

His former pupil seemed to nod in agreement. "I understand the consequences of my actions, master." Tai Xun got up, to P.J's dread. "But to protect billions, many must die. I will be damned for my actions, but the safety of Qian Ye is worth any torture in Hell." His eyes focused on the frightened girl hiding behind his master.

Yeren stayed where he was, not moving a muscle. "I implore you to let this girl live. Whatever happened in Altahn, she is not responsible for it."

"And what if she knows what's in those caves?" Tai Xun argued, suppressing a growl. "If she tells anyone, who's to say knowledge that what's inside those caves won't spread like wildfire? Are you aware of how many men would want to free it?"

Yeren remained calm as he spoke to his irrational pupil. "If you say whoever knows what is within these caves should be killed, what about you? Do you intend to keep the secret to yourself until you pass on?"

Tai Xun snarled in indignation. "How can you accuse me of such blasphemy, master? Before the sun rises, I shall take my own life. The secret will die with me."

Yeren felt an ounce of pity for his former pupil, seeming remorseful that he hadn't taught him well enough to keep him from wickedness. "I…understand, Tai Xun. I give you one last chance. Leave and give this girl the mercy you have denied her tribe or kill her after you have killed me."

P.J had an idea how this was going to end and begged to Sophia herself that he would gain control before he could commit suicide. What was controlling him anyway? Tai Xun seemed to contemplate his decision for a while. It was either give the girl the benefit of the doubt and leave, putting the whole world at risk or attack and most likely die by his master's hands. Either way, he would not see morning.

Tai Xun seemed to have been ready to pick the latter. "If anyone is worthy to send me to Hell, it is you." P.J panicked as he was compelled to pounce at Master Yeren.

In the blink of an eye, The Old Man of The Mountain punched a hole right through his chest. Tai Xun/P.J struggled to breathe as he still reached for the frightened young girl. If he was destined for damnation, it was better to finish the job. P.J tried to resist aiming a stinger at the young girl. Maybe if he regained control now, he could recover.

But nothing would allow him to move by his own will. Before Tai Xun could even kill his target, his tail disappeared, his body shrank, and he became a normal human being. Tai Xun spoke his last words. "Block that…cave…no one must…see the seals of Afor…" His lungs gave out and he fell into the snow on his back.

It was official; Patrick Jay Porrige was going to die here, of all places. As his and Tai Xun's vision went dark, he tried to curse whoever did this to him but could not even make a noise of his own. All his body did was gurgle a bit as Yeren carried the girl in his arms to take her away from here. Looking through the last moments of Tai Xun, he saw something right above him, looking down on him. It seemed to be some kind of large multicolored crystalline spider that descended from some rainbow web. It said no words as it went closer and closer to his body. If only he could scream as it all went dark.

~ * ~

Ercan screamed as he awoke. Hyperventilating, he looked down at his stomach. It was just fine, as if he had not just been disemboweled. Feeling the inside of his mouth, he felt that all his teeth were in the proper positions. Checking around, he saw that he was surrounded by Qian artifacts. To his relief, he was still alive and still in the museum.

But was Xiu? Ercan needed to check. Last thing he saw was P.J turning back into regular Tai Xun and running off. Hopefully that demon didn't get to her. He shook her awake, praying to Sophia that she would wake up.

Luckily, his prayers were answered as her eyelids opened, her emerald eyes seeing the world once again. She abruptly sat upright to look around. "Where am I?" She saw Ercan kneeling over her and began to regain her composure, knowing that he was safe and not half eaten. "You're alive! Are you alright?" She hastily checked to see if his stomach was closed.

"Yeah, I'm okay for now," Ercan answered her, helping her get up. "Luckily, damage during a nightmare doesn't transfer over to reality." It would have been horrible but tolerable for him to lose his teeth and have his stomach chomped open, but for Xiu to lose her legs would risk ending her career as a psychic. "But we need—"

Xiu's face became more serious than he had ever see it. She seemed almost completely calm other than the fact that her glare was as sharp as a spear. She rushed to the resting P.J. Before Ercan could do anything, she had him by the neck.

"You sicko. You made me see it all over again. Feel it all over again." She tried to refrain from shedding tears as she got an aeon fist ready. "People like you don't deserve to live."

Ercan despised the guy too, but he didn't want her to kill someone at her mercy. Sure, they never held back on The Stage, but that wasn't real life. "Wait Xiu! Stop!" He grabbed her wrist, ignoring the aeon flowing around her hand.

"Let go, Ercan." Xiu gave him a single warning. "Think of the things he did to us and many others. Give me a reason for why he deserves our mercy."

"Please! I don't want you to just murder a helpless man in cold blood!" Ercan knew that if he let this slide, they would risk being at the edge of a very slippery slope.

"And what do you want us to do?" Xiu pushed him away from her.

Ercan hastily thought about what to say. "Don't you remember the most important qualities of a psychic? Courage, Loyalty, Wisdom, Unity, *Mercy*. And if the Academy's agenda won't convince you, think about what master Yeren would want?"

Though she grumbled about it, his words seemed to cool her down enough. Xiu dropped P.J., whose body slumped over. Xiu kicked his body as hard as she could without her powers, but the guy still would not wake up, though he still had a look of horror upon his face. Upon thinking about it, neither of them had heard the chatterbox utter a word since they woke up. Ercan went to the body and looked for a pulse. He could find none.

"I don't think you need to kill him anymore," Ercan told her. "He's already dead."

"Good." Xiu almost spat out her answer. "Monster deserved more than that."

Ercan couldn't exactly disagree with her. "That's true. But what happened to him?" Being the second one to wake up, maybe she had an idea of how he was killed.

Xiu didn't want to say much. Never did. But at this point, why bother keeping it all a secret from Ercan about what happened that night anyway? "That night repeated." She did not look at him as she spoke. "But before I tell you, I suggest you keep this to yourself."

This sounded personal, definitely personal. "You have my word. I will not tell anyone about that village, not even Yun."

"To be honest, Yun, Hong, and Caradoc know bits and pieces," Xiu explained to him. "He knows I came from a lost village, but I just said that it was the fault of a rogue psychic. But those shadowy figures were not just bandits looking for money." She took a deep breath as she explained her story. "In the Eversnow Mountains of Qian Ye, there are many nomadic groups that wander across the mountain range their whole lives. We hunt, we gather, we move when there is nothing left for us. I came from a group of nomads known as the Altahn tribe. To be precise, they stopped wandering the land before I was born. But only because they found the perfect valley." She started to get quite vivid. "This Golden Valley, as we called it, was like heaven on earth. It had plenty of animals to hunt or use as livestock, clean water, fertile ground, cool temperature, isolated by the surrounding mountains—it was amazing. So, the Altahn settled down and it became almost like a town of sorts. My elders said that the valley was blessed thanks to magic within the caverns."

Every word seemed to be a needle in her neck. "Inevitably, others began to find the Golden Valley and took an interest. They used new technology to check the fertility of the land around the area and deduced that the ground should have been completely infertile. They began to question us, wondering if one of us were a psychic able to fertilize land. Lame spark power to be honest, but can't say it wouldn't be practical. We denied it and told them that some magic in the caverns made all this happen." Her voice became grimmer. "We shouldn't have told them shit. When I was seven, archeologists representing Qian Ye's government came to visit in order to explore the caverns. The Altahn's best mountaineers and cavern explorers gave them a long tour of the caves and cliffs of the area. I don't know the details, but the archeologists looked stunned when they left the caves."

Ercan didn't want to admit it to himself until he heard it from a firsthand witness, but he had a feeling who perpetrated the massacre of his friend's people. P.J didn't just turn into Tai Xun just because he thought he was cool or something.

"Eventually, our guests left to report to Tai Xun." Her voice became more somber as she began to walk ahead. Ercan followed soon after, leaving the body behind. "I never remembered their names, but I never heard of any news about what was in those mountains. Rumor has it that Tai Xun killed them himself to keep the secret." The next few sentences were amongst the most difficult she had ever spoken. "Two nights later, they came without warning. Most of us were asleep when they began slaughtering us. Soldiers from Sirochko and Qian Ye set out to destroy every scrap of the Altahn tribe. We had no possible way to defend ourselves and we were completely surrounded by both psychics and hylics alike. My mother and father tried to hide me, but they were killed…and t-this man with bright red glasses found my hiding place… and just left me."

Memories of the hellish dream P.J gave her made the memories all the more real. "That monster made me experience it all over again somehow. He turned me back into that scared little girl to relive the exact same moment twice. I felt the need to run away, my hiding place found. None other than Tai Xun pursued me. He's like a savage beast when he hunts. He followed me through the mountain cavern, not stopping until I was dead just because I existed." Her voice got less dour. "The only reason I'm not dead is because of Master Yeren. He killed Tai Xun and took me in. For that I am forever grateful to him." Her fists shook. "But even now, the Altahni genocide has not even been acknowledged by Qian Ye, dismissed as a bunch of Archon cultists. Damn, it pisses me off how an entire nation can just throw away their own citizens like that when it's convenient to them rather than accept that they screwed up."

He didn't recall ever feeling so much sympathy for one person as he did now. No child should ever have to endure what Xiu suffered. But, by Sophia, was she strong for being able to not have her past define her. Hearing what happened within the nightmare, Ercan had a crazy realization. "If you re-experienced that memory so precisely, is it possible that your memory is the reason we're still alive? Is it possible that your vivid memory of Tai Xun might have just overridden P.J's control."

"I guess." Xiu had no idea why P.J would do and say the exact same things Tai Xun did. He may have been a smug asshole, but surely, he knew better than to recreate a memory that would get him killed, right?

"I guess we'll just leave it to luck then. Now let's just make sure we didn't oversleep."

But before she could go up the stairs, Ercan put a hand on her shoulder. She stopped nigh-instantaneously.

"Thank you for being so honest with me. If I had known, I would have supported you sooner."

"I don't need your pity."

"It's not that," Ercan insisted to her with a straight face. "I'm just reminding you that you're not alone. Never were and never will be. You have all of Rooster Squad supporting you—me, Shee'vra, Cyrille, Yun, even Julia. And that's not even getting into the other students. And I can promise you that this atrocity will never happen to anyone else as long as we live."

It wasn't a bad pep talk despite it obviously being improvised. Xiu Lang looked back at him with a bittersweet smile. People like Ercan gave her the will to move on and have more faith in humanity. Today she resolved to never lose her family ever again. "Thank you Ercan. Now let's save that dumb artifact and get out of this nerd headquarters."

Rooster, Duck, Thrush, Peacock

Thirty Years Ago

Roy heard his uncle speak to his mother from the staircase. The boy, no older than thirteen, listened intently as his father's brother told her the horrible news. While working in the glue factory, his father had fallen into the vat and was mulched to bits. Uncle's voice was furious when his boss told him that they were still going to distribute the now pink glue.

His mother demanded that they find a way to sue the company, but his uncle just shook his head. There was no chance a couple of lowly Sorchan workers would ever win anything over an entire corporation. Roy heard his mother sob, questioning why the rich treated the poor as mere tools to be replaced. It was annoying when his mom cried, but tonight it was especially loud.

But he, too, wished his dad was still alive. They were going to go on another duck hunting trip next week to curb his "antisocial" tendencies in school. He'd been getting into fights lately, and the principal was at his limit with him. One more fistfight and he was out. They never did much about Horace Delry or any other guy or girl that messed with him. Though then again, they tended to be worse for wear.

Duck hunting was strangely relaxing. His dad always saved up what little they had so they could take a train and just shoot ducks with crossbows. They would have duck to eat for weeks. He loved duck.

But now with his dad dead, his temper would probably just be a burden to his family. Mom didn't deserve to be known as the woman who couldn't control her child, so he decided to find a way to rid her of her burden. He had ways to make it out there.

Last hunting session, he found that he could make a thin-barreled weapon, that when you pulled the trigger, highly concentrated water shot out. It was perfect for hunting. He'd heard of this new place known as Aeon Sophia Academy and, with his new spark, maybe he could start a new life. His dad had simply recommended keeping it a secret. His temper might cause trouble there. But Roy didn't give up. He even prevented himself from using Fontus during his fights just to prove that he had restraint, though it was always tempting to blow those jackasses' brains out who thought he was fair game to be messed with.

So he did what he thought was best for his family. Roy Aven Mallard left to find a new home. He wandered the streets, scrounging for his next meal, using his water rifle to shoot rats to eat if there was nothing to find. It was a hard life, but he had an edge over any hylic. It also helped that water could have high enough pressure to shoot the scum of the city when he needed to feel some satisfaction.

One night he saw a familiar face. His father's boss was laughing it up in a snazzy restaurant with his family. They were telling stories and making japes. How could these upper-class bastards even have the nerve to laugh when they knew they'd just covered up the death of his dad? It made him furious. But this rage was not the kind that caused him to pick a fight. No, this was more personal. They needed to be punished, and Roy was going to be the one to inflict it. Hell, the whole family was going to go down. The upper class in Sorchos needed to learn a lesson, and he would become the perfect teacher.

When the family was done with dinner, Roy followed an old fart that looked to be either the father or uncle of the boss. No point in starting with his main target. Save the best for last, though giving him foreshadowing of his fate might be nice. For the first few days, he decided to just simply send letters threatening the boss's life. The next week, Roy sniped the corporate dickhole's old relative as he strolled through the streets at night, cutting off a toe and hiding the body in a dumpster. Using the postal service, he gave his dad's boss the body part he scavenged.

A few days later, Enotitan newspapers had the uncle's death on the front page. Roy spat in disgust. Why didn't his dad get to be on the front page when he became glue? Such blatant favoritism for the rich drove him to commit more pain. He tested how to inflict pain on petty thugs, learning what the body could and could not endure until either the body or mind broke down.

Within the next month, he targeted each and every family member he could get his hands on. Each time, security got thicker and thicker, and he honed his skills to capture his target alive to break them. When he was done with their begging, crying, and screaming, he killed them and snuck various body parts in front of the boss's gate. He also took their wallets. Always full.

It all culminated when he decided to target the boss's daughter, no older than him. She had her whole future ahead of her, but he didn't give a damn about it. She was probably going to make the life of a blue-collar worker worse anyway. The moment he had the chance, he killed her bodyguards and shot pressurized water through her head. Taking out his saw, he gave his father's old boss a final gift—his own child's head.

By this point, the boss was a paranoid wreck. Receiving his own daughter's head with the words "You're Next" on it drove him straight over the edge. The boss hung himself with his own belt in his office soon after. Upon receiving the news, Roy felt a sense of satisfaction—like he'd done the world a favor. A favor no one would ever appreciate but was necessary, like bitter medicine. But the cops were picking up on his tracks. He needed a way out of the city of Sorchos.

As he was about to be cornered by the cops, the teen was approached by a serpentine abomination. Most definitely some kind of psychic he didn't want to mess with. But the black-scaled man offered him the chance of a lifetime.

"I've been keeping track of you for a while now. You're very skilled for a child. The Lefty Gang could really use people like you. What do you say?"

Roy took his offer in an instant. Few years later, he took the codename of Sinister.

～ * ～

Sinister hunted down the chicken boy through his scope. Perched upon one of the roofs, he found Cyrille within the Ancient Islands

Exhibit. The rich punk was hiding behind a large stone head. It would take more than that for him to be safe. Just above the brat was a dangling raft that natives used to use hundreds of years ago to travel from island to island. Roy quickly shot through the glass window to cut several ropes supporting the boat, forcing Cyrille to dive away in order to not be crushed.

The sniper took this opportunity to shoot him in the arm. That made four clean shots and seven scrapes. The teen in the tux could barely get up from his knees at this point and could hardly be counted on to wield his expensive looking sword. At this point, it was safe to say he was ready to be taken alive.

Roy began to imagine the pain and humiliation he would inflict upon the wealthy pig. He'd start by putting a Sarkic collar around his neck and use it as a leash to make him walk on all fours and eat his scraps. Then he'd start cutting off body parts, starting with the pinky, and send them to the DeRoche household, one body part per day. He pondered to himself about how long Cyrille would last. First, he'd try using bribery for his freedom. When that didn't work, he would just beg for the torment to stop. Eventually, he might even try to kill himself to make the pain end. Within a week or two, resigned that this would be the rest of his life, the chicken would just lie there catatonic. At that point Roy might as well just put him down. He fully intended to keep the sword, though, as a souvenir.

He wondered how the world would react to seeing the son of one of the most affluent families on the planet found dead on the side of the road. The upper caste from all eight nations would learn to fear him. They may find other psychics to hunt him down but, with the help of his bosses, they wouldn't even touch him. With every elite he slayed, blue-collared workers from around the world would cheer for him. The very thought of billions chanting his name brought a bright smile to his face. Roy bit down on his duck caller so hard that he managed to snap it in two.

As his oral fixation hit the ground, Sinister saw two bright red rays come for him. Roy didn't have time to wade away into the air. The beams went through his invisible water layer, with one hitting him directly on the chest and the other impacting the arm he used to cover his face. Sinister had absolutely no idea what was going to happen to him. Was he going to explode or burn up? What was with the delay?

But the sight of Cyrille's head drooping down and acknowledging failure was more than enough evidence that the beams did nothing. Perhaps they just needed to touch flesh to take an effect and not just clothing. As the reptilian rooster panted and struggled to defend himself, Roy waded closer and closer, like a mallard finding a tiny fish to devour.

But behind him came a flapping noise. Probably just Kairieji flying over to him, done with her own opponent. With his shit luck the nag would probably not let him keep the boy for torture, say that it would leave "An impractical bullseye on our backs" or something of the sort—one of many reasons why he preferred to work alone.

Upon turning back, he barely found the proper sounds to gasp. Breaking through the green energy of Balra's mundane illusions, a giant peacock swooped down to him. Roy quickly noticed two more teens mounted on the majestic bird. Though a bit surprised, they were much too late. He would shoot this big game out of the sky just like any other bird.

Before he could pull the trigger though, an arrow of light entered the hole of his rifle. With a squeeze of the trigger, his weapon burst in a wet explosion. As he was knocked back by the pressure, the young woman in nightwear jumped off the bird.

"Get to the Master!" Zivot called back to the peacock. "I'll handle this weirdo." The girl stared at Sinister with as cold a glare as she could muster while her co-worker entered through the window. She seemed to notice Roy's prey's condition. "What have you done with Lord Cyrille?"

Sinister didn't reply to who he assumed to be a bodyguard for his prey to hide behind when the coward was in a corner. With a crack of his neck, he once again began to reactivate Fontus to blast her into oblivion. But a rifle would not do. No, he needed something bigger. Creating a makeshift stand to support his new weapon, he manifested a crank-powered Gatling turret.

Seeing a weapon that shot who-knew-what caused Zivot's eyes to widen a bit. But her devotion to the DeRoche line trumped any thoughts of running away. Once she drew one of her sabers, the other three slid out by themselves into the air directly toward the threat.

She slid down the side of the roof as Sinister began to rapidly fire pressurized water at her, barely missing her as he turned the crank handle of his weapon. His attention was diverted as the other blades flew toward him. Shooting at the living steel, the swords deflected most of the shots with skill that would drive many a swordsman green with envy. But inanimate objects could only deflect so much, and one of the sabers shattered when overwhelmed.

Sinister winced when one of the swords managed to cut through his unseen aquatic sphere and slice his leg. To counteract the swords, he began to will his hydrosphere to swirl round and round like a whirlpool to entrap the weapons. Looking to the side, he witnessed the girl using roof tiles as stepping stones around him. After stepping off each tile, it shot out at the gangster. They had more force and weight than the swords and the ones that made contact with him inflicted enough pain to knock him on his back. The remaining tiles either were blasted to bits or whirled around him.

Zivot jumped off the final tile and breathed out silver air that phased through the unseen hydrosphere and entered the turret. She then hastily moved back to keep her distance. Sinister thought that it was stupid to give him so much space to riddle her with more holes than cheese. But when he tried to crank his weapon, it felt as if his own turret was resisting him. Trying to pull harder only made it worse.

"My Tsukumogami spark gives life to inanimate objects," Zivot told him, not once dropping her guard. "I also give those I grant life to loyalty. Not just to me, but to my master." His turret began to turn around to point back at the gangster. "Now pay for the pain you brought onto Lord Cyrille." She refused to let him off easy.

With six barrels aiming for his chest, Sinister felt something foreign—fear. He'd always accounted for the upper crust to have bodyguards, even psychic ones. But he always thought they would hire those with sheer destructive power, ones that brought death to anyone who opposed them.

But this girl created life rather than specializing in ending it. Got his own gun to become autonomous and betray him. That would not be forgiven. Cyrille's young maid had to die. And he had only one trick left to try it.

~ * ~

As Mayil healed and closed his master's wounds with Kartikeya, he watched the fight between the flipper-wearing freak and Zivot. She seemed to have the advantage by breathing life into his weapon, but he was sure this wasn't over.

He had taken off Cyrille's top and used his healing hands to close his many wounds. Kartikeya was supposedly a war god, but even the worst of wars had medics dedicated to keeping soldiers alive. Cyrille used to be so clumsy when he was younger. Always tripping and slipping. Mayil had had lots of practice healing the cuts and scrapes he would get. But even then, master would refuse to be cautious. He and Zivot were always so busy dealing with him. But at this point, Mayil could not imagine a different life.

Luckily Cyrille was still conscious, though it seemed that even breathing took genuine effort. Mayil always felt chills whenever Cyrille would have his beaky smile wiped off his face. At moments like this, he could never read him.

"Mayil…" his master told him between hefty breaths. "…Leave… me. Go help…Zivot."

The healing was far from over. "But sir—"

"Now!" Cyrille tried as hard as he could to bark out an order. "He's just letting me live. But the moment he gets the chance, he's going to try to kill her."

If his master willed it, so be it. As Mayil reformed his bow, he saw that the man with the flippers willed his turret to disappear. I guess he could see why, but what was he planning? Definitely not surrendering.

He got an answer soon after when he saw that all the objects whirling around him shot out in all directions. Everyone took cover as water soaked the building, blades clanged on stone, and roof tiles smashed to dust. When the barrage was over, he saw that Zivot had been hit in the leg and shoulder. She seemed to be trying to stand there and act tough, but it was obvious she was hurting. Worse still, her saber was "killed" when it was shattered in half by another tile. If only she'd found time to properly prepare before.

The crook took off his flippers and rushed her down. Before Mayil could land a shot, Sinister had already tackled her. They both tumbled to the edge of the roof, about to fall three stories down. The butler/bodyguard sprung into action as quickly as possible, hoping his master would stay where he was.

Ever since he had manifested a spark, Mayil's family told him how blessed he was. All other members of the Seval bloodline were hylics. His elders took this as a sign of Sophia's blessing and instructed him to follow three rules in life. First, pray to Our Savior every day and always keep a symbol of her on him. Second, focus on making the world a safer place for psychic and hylic alike. Finally, put your duty above your own health, for few else can do what you do. Mayil had all three covered.

He witnessed Zivot getting strangled by the Lefty member. Mayil could not see the murderous glare on Roy's face but he had no need to. His colleague was in trouble. That was all he needed to butt in.

As Zivot tried to reach for her broken blade, Sinister created a handheld version of his rifle. Pressing down tighter on her throat, he made sure she wouldn't be able to breathe on his weapon again. Soon she would not be breathing ever again.

Mayil shot a light arrow into Roy's back. It was the first time he heard the man actually vocalize. Sinister cried out in pain as he reached for the arrow. Zivot took her chance to grab what remained of her sword and give him a rough cut across the cheek before kicking him off.

In response, Sinister shot Mayil's shoulder without so much as looking at him. He then smacked Zivot across the face and pushed her off the edge. The only reason Zivot didn't lose her life was because she managed to grab onto a hanging gargoyle. But the duck man was having none of that. To stop him from shooting her off, Mayil launched another arrow. But since he was struck in the shoulder of all places, his aim was off and the arrow swished by Sinister's head.

Roy did not appreciate being a few inches away from being killed. He was supposed to do the killing. Ignoring the dangling girl, he turned his entire focus on the insolent archer. Shooting the teen in the chest, Mayil toppled over with a loud gasp. Not satisfied with Mayil trying to stand back up like a baby giraffe trying to learn to walk, Sinister pinned the boy down with a bare foot.

It was checkmate. All Roy had to do now was shoot the archer in the head until he got bored and shoot the lady that could animate things to life and let her fall and break her skull. With no one left to hide behind, Cyrille Coq DeRoche was now his toy. The only problem was that, chances were, the coward probably had run off. It would be a pain to search for him, but *so* worth the effort.

But before he could pull the trigger, he felt a sharp pain in his stomach. Getting off his murderous high, Roy began to sense his surroundings. Looking down, he saw that his vest was torn and his stomach was cut. But it wasn't as if it was deep enough to see his entrails or anything, just a little more than a scratch. He couldn't see too much blood. Then why did it hurt so bad?

"You're lucky," a voice told him without a hint of warmth. "Lucky that I know what mercy is." Roy refused to believe who was speaking to him.

Standing right in front of him and shielding Mayil from the water pistol, was the rooster. His injuries were still in the process of healing and some had even opened again from exertion. Sinister was absolutely agape as he saw the determination in Cyrille's unmoving eyes, ignoring whatever wounds he'd had inflicted onto him. His sword was covered in more blood than possible for such a small slash.

But there was another pressing question running in Roy's head. Those two were his social inferiors. Why on earth would Cyrille protect his own bodyguards from an assailant? Why was he not hiding or begging to survive another day? Why did he risk taking another shot just to spare a mere servant? Why was this craven aristocrat playing the hero?

"Do not move a muscle," Cyrille ordered him, pointing his sword at him. "My blood is inside your system now. You'll lose consciousness in about thirty seconds. But you'll live and face a fair trial like any other criminal."

Sinister could not and would not believe him. This must have been some kind of act to make the chicken look good in front of his servants. He was sure that the moment he woke up, he'd find himself on the rack ready to be tormented by his entire family. The upper echelons must get off on torturing those who disobeyed their authority and cause them trouble, and they would make sure he lived for days if not months. Any mercy was bullshit for a greater scheme.

Noticing Sinister's glare, Cyrille stood his ground as well as he could in his condition. "I implore you to drop your weapon now. Failure to listen, and I'll be forced to kill you." Cyrille really did not want it to end this way. Taking someone out of The Stage was one thing, but he was unsure if he could simply remove somebody from the world. He could tell that this man must have had some kind of grudge against him, but he had never seen him before. Why would he hate him so much?

Nevertheless, he moved Cockatrice toward his throat. His father always did tell him to never make promises you couldn't keep, even if they were threats. "You have three more seconds to listen. One…"

Roy might never have despised a rich man more than this freak in his life. At least the others were openly cruel and uncaring. This monster just had the sheer gall to mask his true intentions. His body grew weaker and weaker as the poison in his system got to him. He was not going to last.

"Two…"

He had come to terms long ago that one day the rich would eventually win the war against him. And damn it, he refused to live with the shame of surrendering to a chicken-hearted rooster. In another life, he would do this all again.

"Three…" Cyrille slowly got ready for the coup de grace.

"Never," Roy spoke up with more venom than a basilisk, "never take me alive." He swiftly readied his shooting hand. "See you in Hell."

Before Cyrille could stop him, Roy shot his final target—himself. Condensed water shot straight through his skull and out the other end. Roy Mallard then fell off the side of the building, his corpse being impaled upon the fountain statue of a three-headed angel's sword. The water would run red for the rest of the night.

Zivot managed to climb back up with the help of the now sentient gargoyle and rushed to her master's side. Before Mayil stood back up, he felt his chest. No problems other than that his gold shirt was torn and wet. The emblem of Sophia in his front pocket stopped the shot from reaching his heart. Sophia's miracles always came unexpectedly.

But with his master in critical condition, Mayil checked his wounds. His wounds once again were bleeding profusely. How Cyrille was still standing was amazing. "My Lord, I implore you to lie down for the moment as I heal your wounds."

"Will do." Cyrille slumped over as he was told, his legs giving up. Zivot supported him and slowly got him onto his back. Looking down at the museum courtyard, he bemoaned the fact that someone would prefer death to mercy. But perhaps it was for the best. He needed a second opinion. "Do you…think he could have changed?"

Zivot refused to sugarcoat facts from her master, at least for tonight.

"I'm afraid not, master Cyrille. He was a high-ranking member of the Lefty Gang. He must have done worse and gotten away with it." She looked at the Lefty Gang emblem dripping in gastric fluid and blood that dangled just above the fountain water. "He was much too far gone."

"Please, Lord Cyrille," Mayil implored. "You're much too injured to speak."

Cyrille found the power within him to let out a sigh. "Lord. Master. Why must you two always refer to me as such? You are not mere servants and never will be." He made the same goofy chicken smile he had every day since the two could remember. "You two are my friends. My family. Always shall be."

Mayil tried as hard as he could to keep his composure. He thanked Sophia that he was not stuck guarding a spoiled brat but instead one of the purest souls he would ever have the privilege of knowing. Once he stabilized his friend's wounds, Cyrille grabbed his arm.

"That is enough. Julia is one floor down in the Round Table Exhibit." His injuries were still very apparent. "Find her and make sure she survives."

If he willed it, Mayil would do what he could. "If you wish, sir."

Zivot was the one to keep an eye on the master. She sat on the roof and placed her tired and worn out lord's head onto her lap. "Rest easy now. We alerted the others." She gently petted his rooster comb. "You shall not be losing anyone tonight. That is a promise we intend to keep and will keep as long as you are under our service."

Some days, she wondered how Cyrille would take it if one of them or someone in his squad were to be killed. Chances were he would not be able to sleep soundly for years. She was even questioning how he was feeling about watching a criminal kill himself rather than choose imprisonment.

Cyrille opened his beak once again to softly speak, almost oblivious to his current surroundings. "I feel that I used up my aeon again. If only I had some more…like Ercan or Winona." His eyes began to gently shut to rest for now. His job was done. It was up to the rest of Rooster Squad.

As he began to doze from a mixture of exhaustion and half-healed wounds, Cyrille's form began to change. No longer was he a weird poisonous chameleon chicken, but a human teenager. In fact, if he were to walk around as a human around school, he would most definitely gain many admirers. With his golden blonde hair, eyes as blue as artic lakes, and his slim and well-toned figure, even Zivot had to admit that he was much prettier than her.

She sometimes questioned to herself why he decided to look like a mutant chicken. Maybe he didn't want people to see him for stealth missions. Perhaps it was so people would like him for his personality rather than his appearance. Or it could be that it was just tiring to change forms all the time. Then again, she would not put it past him that he just liked looking like that.

As his breathing slowed and he began to softly doze off, Zivot gave her master a soft lullaby. A lullaby she was taught to sing to him when she began to work under the DeRoches. One about the snakes and the chickens settling their differences and learning to understand one another to become friends. She knew that she was a mediocre singer, but he never complained. Mayil was never as kind, though. As her master dozed off, she hoped to herself that the promise she made was not completely empty. If one Lefty Member was that dangerous, how deadly were the others?

Kairieji was overwhelming Julia by a long shot. Not only was she more physically fit, but Kairieji also had the edge in sheer experience. Years of working with the Lefty Gang had trained her to the bone in order to never fail at her missions.

But still Julia defended herself. Her shield glyph was the only thing preventing her from being cut to ribbons and left on the floor to bleed out. Despite that, she still had shallow cuts and bruises. At this rate, she was not making any progress at all. Not only did the winged woman have a sword, Kairieji also flew up the moment she got a little bit tired. But even still, Julia was forming a plan.

I can't take this for much longer. If she hits me, I'm done. If I hit her, I take twice as much damage as her. And then I'm done. Now how could I hurt her without hurting me? Her opposition flapped her dark wings and flew upwards. *Bingo. The wings.*

Using this opening, she inscribed a fire rune onto a disc. Perhaps she had better options, but it was the quickest glyph she could make, and she didn't have much free time. Through her glasses, she aimed for the right wing. There could not possibly be any physical backlash for hitting a wing—she had none of her own.

With haste, Julia tossed the disc at the criminal. Luckily her aim seemed to not be as rusty as she thought. The disc turned in the air and aimed for the wing. Best-case scenario it would light the wing on fire and she could use this chance to escape. Maybe get Ercan here. He could handle someone like this much better than she ever could.

But hope was not a thing she should ever get used to believing in. Kairieji noticed the direction of the attack and without any hesitation, abruptly grabbed the fire glyph with her off hand. She hissed out in pain as her hand lit up in flames, but the burning was nothing compared to Julia's pain. Though she was not lit on fire or anything, the teenage girl saw and felt all the agony of getting her hand charred and burned. The sensation was enough to bring her down to her knees and lose concentration on her shield.

But still Kairieji refused to put out the flames. She could live with a few burns and all she needed was one good hand. It was a pity that she had to kill someone who had her whole life ahead of her, but orders were orders. No witnesses.

"You've stolen precious time from me and the rest of the gang." She flew down toward the young woman and lowered her sword to strike her down. "I offer you one last sentence to speak. Use it wisely."

She expected a cry for mercy or for help. But Julia did neither. Instead, she hastily inscribed something on her arm. With that done, Julia got up in defiance. *What is she trying to pull? Some kind of last resort?*

"This hand hurts like a bitch. But not for long. It's funny really. In other worlds, I'm sure second-degree burns are a thing that you can have for years if not your whole life. But here, medical sparks abound. I'm rich; I can get a psychic to heal up anything you inflict on me. Even if I get a little scarring, who cares? I was never prom material anyway." She glared at the criminal with black wings. "Now do your worst."

Kairieji was not an idiot. She flew back and waited to see what Julia was up to. Staring one another down, both waited to see what the other would do, though the younger of the two fighters seemed to be a lot more zoned out.

Suddenly, she found out that Julia's plan was to just run away.

Seeing her darting for the exit, Kairieji wasn't going to just let her just exit this place. She might alert the outside world and then this whole heist would turn to shit. The boss would not let such failure slide.

She flew down toward the teenager. She needed to be careful, as she still had no idea what Julia had inscribed onto her sleeve. Flying ahead, Kairieji cut off the only exit. "There's no escape. Accept defeat."

Julia spat in defiance as she nursed her injured hand. "Not happening." A small smile appeared across her face. "Slicing me will be the last thing you do. So, I give you three choices. Leave and live another day, surrender and have a vacation in Prisoner's Perch, or finish me off and see what happens. It might surprise you, Jakaire Mara."

Kairieji's eyes opened wide. "How do you know my name? WHO TOLD YOU?!" She bounced ideas around her head as to how a teenage girl could possibly know her true name. Could she read minds? Did she get information on the way here? Was it that there was a mole in the Lefty Gang who leaked information to the authorities?

Julia chuckled, looking at her angered expression born of paranoia. "You look stupid when you're irritated. Anyone ever tell you that? Or is it 'Those that have are not alive anymore' or something cliché like that? If it makes you feel better, I'll tell you my secret." She took a breath to add suspense. "As we were having our little staring contest, I looked up any file with the name Kairieji. I found one with your face on it and skimmed it a bit." She didn't tell her that the only thing she had time to find and read was a list of a bunch of names that her bosses might have written down to remind themselves on who was who. The other names made little sense to her. "And now I know the identity of each and every member in the organization and where they live along with each of their weaknesses." Julia was just making stuff up at this point. Pointing an arrogant charred finger at the thrush, she laughed again. "So whatcha gonna do about it?"

Jakaire analyzed the situation. She needed to kill this girl. She was much too dangerous for the entire organization. But why was she telling her this? In no part of their skirmish had Julia ever been in the advantage. She had a burning glyph and one that made an energy shield. What other glyphs could she make?

An overly obnoxious voice interrupted her thoughts. "Well if you're going to just stand there, then I'm out of here. Guess you really want me to blab it all out to the world. Damn, your boss is going be steaming."

She could not allow her to just walk away, especially after insulting the Lefty Gang. Kairieji needed to kill her now. Raising her pitch-black sword, she readied a strike. Julia, in defense, raised an arm. The arm's sleeve had a familiar glyph on it—an indigo glyph. One with two C's back to back.

Realizing what she was about to do, Jakaire tried to pull back her swing as hard as possible. At the same time, her mind was filled with what was going to happen if she even touched the Mark of Cain. She slowed the fall of her sword, but not by enough. Even at its slowest, she still cut at Julia right where the seal was.

A large cut spontaneously appeared on her arm. As Kairieji saw how deep the wound was, Julia's jacket began to rip more. In response, her wound became bigger and bigger and reached to her bone. Kairieji screamed in wracked agony as her arm simply fell off, the severed limb still breaking down in a bloody pulp. Julia looked on in shock as her opposition's body began to break down, hardly noticing that her sleeve was destroyed to a thread and working on destroying the entire top.

Jakaire recognized her failure and resigned herself to her fate. *I'm sorry, Zuo. I wasn't strong enough.* With the last of her strength, Kairieji slashed at her one final time. *Some student I was.*

⁓ * ⁓

Nine Years Ago

Jakaire Mara had no idea what was going on. One minute, she and her family were getting a tour of one of Qian Ye's most famous landmarks: The eighteen-mile-long Stone Lung Wall. But the next minute, Qian and Sirokhan soldiers climbed the ancient wall and surrounded the tour group.

A man who seemed to be the commander spoke up to the group. "We've had word that a runaway cultist is amongst your group!" The soldiers grabbed each and every one of them! "A psychic who worships the Demiurge has been found. He is known to shape-shift into other people. He must be executed for treason against humanity!"

The tour guide reasonably thought this was insane. "How could any of these people possibly be a cultist? They're not from here and I have been keeping an eye on them the whole time."

The commander homed in on the much scrawnier man. "That's for me to decide, not you. He had last been seen trying to escape the country and here we are at the border." He drew out his blade. "Now where are you, you Altahni cretin?"

The commander's soldiers held onto them tighter. The twelve-year-old girl had no idea what all this stuff meant, but instinctively knew they were all in danger.

Jakaire's father spoke up against this. "Leave us alone! We have international rights you are violating!"

The tour guide agreed with him. "I don't know who you are looking for, but I insist none of us are the cultist."

"We don't have time for games, Bai." The leader pointed his sword at the group of fifteen. "Show yourself or you'll have more blood on your hands."

Jakaire, along with everyone else, began to hope that one of them was the cultist. It was the only way they would ever get out of this alive. But after five minutes of silence, still nobody talked.

The commander shook his head. "That coward." He thrust his sword inside the tour guide first. The entire group immediately began screaming for mercy, begging with money, and crying for a miracle. The corpse did not change form.

The captain was getting pissed. "This is all your fault, Bai! Show yourself!" He stabbed another tourist, then another and another. None of them became the Altahn he was searching for.

Jakaire was hyperventilating and freaking out. She was at the end of the murder line and her father was coming up next.

"SHOW YOURSELF!?" The commander stabbed through an obese old lady. He needed two stabs to do the trick. Eventually, the commander got to her father. "Are you Bai?"

Her father didn't look him in the eye. "J-just…don't hurt my daughter." A sword to the throat was all he got in response.

The worst part of all this was that not a single soldier was reacting to this. No maniacal laughter or annoyed sneers. Just painful silence. Like everyone wanted to get this over with, like they had the nerve to think that the tour group was obstructing them and making everything more difficult.

Jakaire loudly cried when it was her turn. The commander placed a hand on her head and gripped her hair. "Some nerve you have for hiding as a young girl, you Altahni filth." He raised his sword. "They did not deserve to die. You made me do this."

She could not compose herself to brace for the stab as she struggled to free herself from his grip. The moment the sword pierced her body, it activated. The trauma of it all awakened her spark. Wings manifested onto her back and the Mark appeared on her chest. Before the commander could react, he puked blood as he fell over disemboweled.

None of the soldiers had any idea what had just happened. But before they could deduce anything, two long bandages wrapped around some posts. Lying on the floor in pain, she saw a mummy man and the person who would eventually become her master.

Zuo was first to speak up. "What is going on up here?" In his hand was the severed head of a man with green eyes. "We already found Bai."

The mummy spoke up next as he looked at the innocent bodies in fury. "What did you people do?" He grabbed a soldier by the collar. "Do you realize that this will bring a war to our nations?"

Jakaire did her best to try to breathe loudly to catch their attention. Zuo noticed the sound and alerted his partner.

"Aluja! This girl is still breathing!"

With upmost haste, the green man used his spark to wrap bandages around her wound. The pain stopped, and her body felt more stable. Aluja tried to help the shivering girl up but noticed the mark on her chest.

"Zuo! You should see this!"

Upon looking at one another, both Zuo and Jakaire each saw that the other had the same mark: The Mark of Cain. Any who even so much as touched anyone with the mark would receive more pain than they inflicted. This was a sign.

Zuo knelt toward the young girl and spoke to her like an uncle. "How long have you had this?"

"J-just now. When this soldier killed them." She could not stop crying as she weakly answered him. "My father too."

Neither psychic was going to let this go under wraps. Aluja decided to speak for the both of them. "We are both finished." Taking out the Altahn Tribe was one thing, but having your own military slaughter a bunch of tourists out of paranoia was another. "If our nations are going to declare war on the world, count us out."

One of the soldiers piped up. "Are you mad? That's treason!"

"Us, traitors?" Zuo took a deep breath as he created a knife out of thin air. "Maybe. But it's no worse than the crimes we already committed."

Before anyone could reply, Zuo quickly stabbed into a soldier's throat. He then summoned a crossbow to shoot another one. The soldiers tried to hurt him, but that only made their deaths quicker. Throughout the entire slaughter, Zuo did not make one peep. All Jakaire and Aluja could do was watch as soldiers went down one by one.

Once the final soldier's throat was slit, he slowly went back to Jakaire. His clothes were dyed red and his breathing became heavier. Upon removing the sword in his chest, he spoke once again. "That ought to kick us out."

Aluja could not help but feel uncomfortable at how mercilessly his colleague was at butchering his own side. But he, too, felt this entire thing was pointless and just wanted out as well. He, too, would officially be labeled a traitor the moment it was discovered that he let Zuo murder troops and desert. So he conceded. "Indeed. I'm going back to Enotita for sanctuary. I have friends there." He looked toward the traumatized child. "This girl will be sent to Aeon Sophia to learn about her spark."

"No need," Zuo told him with hardly any emotion, "I'll handle the girl. She has the same mark as me. This has got to be some sort of sign." He spoke directly to her. "What is your name?"

"Jakaire."

"Jakaire? What nation are you from?"

"Tirnanog."

"Do you have any living relatives?"

She slowly shook her head. "My mother died of sickness when I was very little."

Aluja knew where this was going. "What are you planning, Zuo?"

Zuo kneeled down to her. "Well if you have nowhere to go, I give you two options. Option one, you go with Aluja and enroll in Aeon Sophia Academy. The people there will bend over for you to help you discover your potential. Option two, you come with me and I'll teach you everything about that mark." He hit his cane onto the ground. "So, what will it be?"

On that day, Jakaire became the apprentice of Zuo Xuanzang. He taught her everything he knew. Though it turned out that her mark was weaker than his, it was still extremely powerful. He became a second father to her in a way.

Eventually, Zuo made the decision to join The Lefty Gang. They needed money to live and they were the best source of income for psychics down on their luck. They had nowhere else to go. The Qian government essentially blacklisted Zuo after he massacred his own nation's soldiers and now no country exactly trusted him, and he knew it. So thus, Zuo became Shèng Xià and Jakaire became Kairieji.

Jakaire managed to land one last blow to Julia's shoulder. After that, Jakaire's entire body burst into a fountain of blood. Julia's jacket was also destroyed. But even then the mark backlash continued. The cells of blood and the fibers of the shirt continued to inflict damage on one another until not a molecule was left of woman or clothing.

Julia was in a good bit of pain at the moment. Along with her burnt hand, she had several cuts. The two most prominent ones were the cuts under her wrist, with which she made the glyph that save her life, and the slash to her shoulder. The left side of her body was not looking very good. *How stupidly fitting. Deal with a Lefty member and all the pain is on the left side of my body.*

To rub salt in the wound, her favorite jacket was essentially vaporized. It was too cold in here to just be wearing a T-shirt. Maybe that was just the blood loss getting to her. Checking the profuse bleeding on her wrist, she saw that an artery was sliced open. *Shit.* This day just sucked. First her squad lost against Eagle Squad, then Ercan left to pity himself, then these bozos show up to steal a pair of glorified shoulder pads, then she had no choice but to kill a woman, and finally she was bleeding out. *I hate today.* She collapsed onto the floor face down.

If she had been conscious for any longer, she would have noticed Mayil entering the room. His eyes opened wide with shock to see the injured Julia. He checked her pulse and found that she was still alive.

"Thank Sophia, Master Cyrille sent me when he did." He immediately got to work healing her arm. If he had come any later, she might not have made it.

Little Monkey

Balra's lime green pupils remained completely alert. Ever since seeing Sinister's corpse skewered on the Fountain of Camael, she had her headphones off and was on edge. Her fingers lightly touched the band around her head. That headband was the only thing preventing her spark from going ballistic. She remembered accidently hurting so many people just because she lost control of her emotions, whether it was because of her spark's potential destructive force or having no force at all. She cursed herself for her accidents…whenever those were.

The Gang had found her unconscious on the streets of Sorchos. At the time, she had very few memories. She could only recall her name, Enitharmon, educational facts such as math and geography, and her spark Urthona. She had no knowledge of who she was or what she did before they found and took her in.

The organization soon found out the hard way despite her warnings that Urthona was utterly unstable. If she got too temperamental, her powers would lose control. If she got depressed, she was utterly devoid of aeon. So, a higher up known as Reliquit made a spark-enhanced headband just for her. It kept her aeon completely stable, meaning no more fluctuating aeon. How had she not found something like this sooner?

The Lefty Gang told her that she worked in the Sorchos Psychic Department (SPD). People there were her friends, so she could trust them for just about anything. She also had friends on her crystalcell who called her occasionally. They were Desiderio, Dunkeen, Petra, and Draghignazzo. She had forgotten what they looked like, but she hoped to see them again. They seemed like great people from what little she remembered about them. Supposedly they used to go on adventures. Though she was to always speak to her friends, she was never allowed to tell them about the Lefty Gang or use her codename, Balra, around them. She wondered why.

The Lefty Gang had never used her for any missions before. This museum mission was her first one. She was told how the museum stole a precious artifact from them, and the government had done nothing to help them retrieve it. They needed her to cover them to steal it back. The whole killing the security guy might have been overkill, but whatever they wished.

Balra got to work to see how the others were doing. Closing her eyes, and feet firmly planted on the ground, she looked for her allies with the third eye in her mind. She wished she hadn't bothered to look. Not only was Sinister dead, but Ezker and Kairieji too. Ezker was limp on the ground, his eyes closed but his mouth open in a silent scream, while Kairieji was nowhere to be found. Looking for the members from Bythos, she witnessed Kushoto struggling to free herself from metal bindings while Vinstri was knocked out with teeth missing near a hole in the wall suspiciously around his size.

This would not slide. With the will of Urthona, she freed Kushoto and healed Vinstri. Under both members, green light appeared and disappeared within a few seconds. Though unsure of what had happened at first, both immediately got back onto their feet and got back to their job. Feeling relieved that she was able to salvage two of them back to the mission, she began to look for the final member.

Upon seeing Izquierda, she gasped. He was with two teenage kids. They all seemed to be going to the same place. The place where Shèng Xià was going. The Pauldrons.

Balra stomped on the floor, creating a crater around her. She needed to take this traitor out before he ruined everything. But before she could do anything, she felt something on her back. It felt like a very, very strong kick.

Before she knew it, she was sent tumbling through a stone wall. Normally this would have put a person into a coma at least, but she managed to will the damage to be minimal. Getting back up, she checked her surroundings. Balra found herself outside the front of the museum. Looking at where she was kicked from, she saw something jump through the rock as if it was water, not even damaging the stone at all.

A weird chimera of an ant and a lion appeared in front of her. "Museums keep the greatest treasures man has ever made! How dare you try to steal from it! Thieving scum!" The antlion got into a battle position; at least she thought it was. His pose kind of made him look as if he was a crooked praying mantis or something. "For violating these treasures, you will face the wrath of VURAL!"

He threw three shuriken at her. Balra simply willed her skin to become as durable as steel and stood still as the throwing stars bounced off her. But when she blinked, she saw that this Vural person was gone. *Vural…sounds familiar.*

She felt sharp claws grab her foot. Looking down, she saw that Vural was under the concrete road. With a tug, he had her neck deep in earth. Balra watched him swim around in the street as if it were the sea.

Vural back flipped out of the road. "You are trapped, and thus, my prey! Surrender, fiend!" He dramatically pointed a chitinous finger at her, his scarf flowing in the wind.

Though she struggled for a bit, the street around Balra began to glow lime green. With that, she effortlessly climbed out of the earth, though her hood got caught on the gravel, revealing her face.

Vural took a good look at her in surprise. "Enith?" The antlion recalled that Enitharmon was once a part of Heron Squad who had graduated last year. No one had seen her since she left, but she supposedly kept in touch with the other Herons. Vural remembered her as a quiet soul who always wanted to help as much as possible. How could she have possibly ended up doing such dishonorable criminal acts?

"How do you know my name, insect?" Balra questioned, her eyes squinting at him. "Those that know the name of our members must be annihilated."

Balra willed a giant pair of disembodied hands behind Vural. Using his amazing ninja skills, the antlion sensed the attack and jumped away just before he got squashed. The resounding clap was strong enough to shatter windows. Failing that, Enitharmon simply used her will to make

Vural appear on the ground.

"What?!" Vural exclaimed, hamming it up. He was just in the air a second ago and now had his feet on the ground, back to where he was.

The two hands tried to smash him with balled up fists. Figuring that Enith was beyond reasoning, he decided to dig down into the earth to avoid the hands once again. If she had no idea where he was, she was powerless.

Balra needed to get him out of the ground. She had explored the vast primordial plane of earth that was her Spark Region, but found that, though Urthona could warp reality itself, it couldn't just instantly kill somebody or affect free will. But she had plenty of other ways to get to him.

Just by thinking about where the bug was, a green light began to move along the ground to indicate where Vural lurked. Balra turned the surrounding concrete into titanium to trap him in. She then imagined that he was inside a water geyser and shot him high into the air. As Vural was sent flying upwards, she willed the disembodied hands to hold a large firework the size of a car to launch at him. She wouldn't even need to aim. Just thinking about the firework hitting him would be enough to blow him up.

But before the hands could take the shot, some guy with two swords cut their fingers to pieces. The falling Vural was also caught by some buff guy with sunglasses (despite it being nighttime) and landed back on the ground safely. It was just two more, she could adapt to the situation.

"So, it seems some ruffians have been trying to break into the museum. Glad I came all this way for something." Balra turned back to see a pale man dressed in regal violet. She could see fangs hiding within his mouth. "Though I am disappointed to see you here, Enith."

"Why are you here?" A murder of crows appeared on the power line. "Don't tell me you're the cause of this trouble."

"She's a part of it," the antlion answered his older peer as he stood next to Basil. "She's with the Lefty Gang." He showed the birds the Lefty Emblem. "See?"

Enitharmon hastily checked her pockets, noticing her emblem was missing "How did you…? When did you…?"

"NINJA!"

The reality warper had had it up to here with the bug. She willed the creation of a cone of fire to fry his exoskeleton. The flames didn't even make it halfway when a beam of ice stopped the attack in its tracks, evaporating as quickly as they came. When the steam faded, Balra saw a dragon woman standing in front of Vural.

It was Ludmila's turn to speak up. "Greetings, old comrade. It sure is a shame that our first meeting after all these months is…cold." Everyone from Caradoc to Alexandru couldn't help but groan.

"Aren't *you* clever, Lud," Winona snidely remarked to the captain of Falcon Squad. "Was 'an icy reception' not witty enough for you?"

Ludmila's eyes opened wide. "I didn't think of that one!" She cursed the concept of hindsight. She needed to use that one next time she met a familiar face on the opposite end of the law.

Balra had no time for this. They all needed to die for the sake of the gang. But before she could will anything, she was snagged by what appeared to be webbing.

"Why are you all just standing around her?" Gaizka questioned his peers as he yanked his catch up the building he was perched on. "You heard Vural! She's a gangster now! Never give 'em an opening!" It didn't matter to him whether Enith was a classmate or not. He knew her power and, the moment she willed it, she could devastate them all. He did not intend to give her that chance. He remembered that as long as she didn't touch any earth, she was utterly powerless.

Hanging upside down, Enith was getting more and more frustrated as more and more people showed up. All these witnesses. And that wasn't even getting into the civilians escaping the scene. And how did they know who she was?

As the sharp-toothed warrior was pulling her up, she placed her hands on the building. Being concrete, it counted as earth. A spot on the building became green as a large pair of scissors manifested to snip the webbing. She fell onto the sidewalk legs first, breaking them upon impact.

Though the pain was nauseating, Balra found enough sense to will her legs unbroken and restore her spine to be able to get up. The shark man was deadly; she must kill him. Punching the building, she created a line of green light that trailed up the building. The line cut all in its way, even birds flying nearby, and was trailing toward Gaizka.

But yet another interruption—a guardian angel grabbed the tattooed warrior just before he could be split in half. Flying down, Mastema confronted her. "Stand down…" He struggled to think of a name.

"Enith."

"Enith." The angel must thank Basil later for helping him. Names could be just so hard to remember. But duty first. "Stand down. If you don't…there will be consequences." He summoned one hundred eyes from within his wings. He twirled his halberd and pointed it at her. "Be wise."

Balra barely could hear the guy. But it didn't matter. She knew she was surrounded. But as long as she had that headband, she was in control. Not these strangers. But upon getting ready to fight, four mirrors rose up from the ground. She could see nigh infinite reflections of herself on all sides. She was not alone.

"Enith," Bianca spoke to her, a dagger ready for the worst-case scenario. "I know what you're like. We all do. And we also know that you would never volunteer to become a member of the Lefty Gang." She tried to speak reason into Enitharmon Loz. "What do they have on you? We can help you. The authorities can help. You're in a position to put a massive dent in one of the biggest criminal empires in the world."

This was the last straw for Balra. "I have no idea who any of you are. Any!" She stomped her foot down. "Who are you people?"

That pretty much confirmed her theory. Some member of the Lefty Gang ranks must be a psychic with a mind-bending spark of some sort. How long could it have been since her mind was tampered with? And would it be fixable without the forced assistance of the culprit. There was one way to try.

"I am Bianca Narkissos," she told her upfront. "The other girl in the mirror with me is Hanako Nanaringu." The many reflections of the stringy-haired girl all awkwardly waved at her. "We are the captains of Eagle and Rhea squads, respectively. The sharp-toothed brute is Gaizka Pantopoda."

"Who you calling brute?!"

The princess paid no heed to his complaints. "The antlion 'ninja' is Vural Kyogeki, the ice dragon is Ludmila Lamya, the hivemind of crows is the witch, Winona Samhain, the pale man in purple is Alexandru von Coagula, and the champion of our academy is the silent angel, Mastema Mattatron." She also recalled seeing two of her squadmates here. "And then there's Caradoc and Basil who work under me." Her eyes narrowed down at the girl with green pupils. "Try to remember us. Try to remember the time you were in Aeon Sophia Academy. Remember your time in Heron Squad under the lewd but warm-hearted Desiderio. You must, or you'll never get your freedom back."

Desi. That was a familiar name. It was one of the names she occasionally received texts from. She scrunched her brain to remember who this Desiderio truly was. He must have been a student as well. Then by that logic she, too, must have once been a student.

The memory dawned upon her. She was part of Heron squad under him. She remembered the ramblings of the dunkleosteus man, Dunkeen, the snappy aggressiveness of Petra, the lame jokes of the demon jester, Draghignazzo. Then Desiderio came to mind. Captain of Heron squad and as graceful as the bird their squad was named after. Even working under him for two years, she had not once given any hints about how she felt about him. He probably wouldn't have been interested in her anyway. She was from his school and on his squad, and thus dating her would have been unprofessional in his book. She had no animalistic features that Desi was so weirdly attracted to. Finally, he never seemed to be the kind of guy to be interested in any form of commitment. Since losing his virginity during her junior year, he had been very "loose" when it came to partners. He probably wouldn't have been interested in dating an…underdeveloped peer one year his senior.

As she was lamenting about how she had forgotten her classmate and allies, a pain shot up inside her brain. A high-pitched noise invaded her head. Covering her ears did absolutely nothing. Deep within her mind's eye, she saw a blank white hand with three eyes inside its palm.

Wait…what was she thinking about again?

Enitharmon looked around to remember that mirrors surrounded her with some albino woman staring at her. She realized that she was still in the middle of a fight. There were at least six others she had to deal with as well. She knew that the masquerade she created of the museum being completely normal and secure was gone, the cops would be coming any minute now. But they needed those pauldrons for the boss.

Balra's eyes became completely green as she focused on her mission. She shook and spasmed between her words. "I must…finish the mission…for master…whatever he wishes I shall make reality." The ground flashed green as she glared at the women in the reflection. "I am Balra!"

So, it had come to this. Bianca regretted having to do this the hard way but, for the safety of everyone, she must. She saw from her face that she was beginning to remember, but some outside force dragged her away from her memories. She tossed a shard through the mirror to stab into Balra's shoulder. The girl cried out from the sudden pain, but it would take more than that to merely slow her down.

Hanako made the next move. Though she trembled at the might of a known reality warper, she was going to do all she could to make sure the others would be okay. She and all her reflections shot their yumis in unison. Hundreds of arrows shot right at their target within the countless layers of the mirror. But Balra was ready for the attack as she made her body as hard as steel. Her true arrow snapped in half as her reflection's arrows shattered into small particles upon impact. She did not accomplish a thing—typical for the second lowest ranked captain.

Balra's will allowed her to reach inside the mirror with both hands. But before she could blast both of them with energy rays, all four mirrors completely shattered. Looking about the street in confusion, she saw Bianca and Hanako exit from another mirror. She checked to see how many enemies she had to deal with—ten—ten psychics in total. Enitharmon couldn't help but feel a twinge of fear. Surely, she would be overwhelmed.

But she touched the headband on her forehead. With it, she would always be in control. All she needed to do was think about how to even the playing field. Her mind raced to think of something about that psychic Shèng Xià killed when they first got here. The sky was the limit with Urthona.

Focusing on this man, she willed herself to know his name: Jacque of the Jack spark. That would be more than enough. Her eyes glowed brighter as the man in green reappeared in front of her, ready for combat—and another, and another, and another. The Jacques began to either put on various monster masks, ready cryokinetic abilities, or even begin hopping around. None of these clones spoke a word and each one had a near lifeless scowl upon his face.

The ten students got into a circle for maximum defense. Caradoc twirled his blades, Basil took a cricket bat out of his magic bag, Hanako's eyes glowed as she took out another arrow from her quiver, Gaizka summoned stone crabs out of the street, Vural got more throwing stars ready, Ludmila summoned her full plate armor, sword and shield, Winona whispered "Nemain" as she drew out her bow, Alexandru's body absorbed the moonlight and made himself glow, Bianca created two obsidian shards in her hands and Mastema finished the circle by sending two floating eyes above each member. They were ready for whatever was to come at them.

Shèng Xià finally made it to The Empire under Barbar exhibit. Tossing the map aside, he searched around the large room. The impact of his cane hitting the floor echoed around as he slowly wandered about. He saw weapons, armor, scrolls, models of ravens, and the home life of both psychics and hylics of the time. He also made sure to destroy the cameras around the area with chakrams. No one should witness what he was about to do.

Finally, he found those pauldrons. They were part of a display that showed what Barbar the Queller probably looked like, a chiseled man clad in bronze armor and wolf fur with the most fantastic beard he had ever seen. In his hands were his trusty spear and shield. But Shèng Xià didn't give a crap about the rest of it. He smashed the glass with a smack of his oaken cane and snagged the pauldrons.

Taking off his trench coat, he placed the artifact upon his shoulders. He did not exactly feel any different, though. But the book did tell him that they were just below average shoulder pads until he spoke the words. Shèng Xià could feel a hint of excitement inside his heart. He was going to make history by being the first man to wield this great power, controlling the spark Barbar had hidden within the pauldrons for centuries.

With that out of the way, he took out the forged pauldrons and got ready to place them onto the display. Looking back, it was probably a bad idea to have broken the glass, but something within him said that he didn't have as much time as he thought he had. Hopefully the authorities wouldn't be able to tell what items were taken.

But before he could strap the shoulder pads onto the model, some feminine voice called out to him.

"Put that back!"

Expecting the finest psychics Bythos had to offer, Shèng created two daggers and threw them in the voice's general direction. Both weapons were caught. Looking back, he saw three assailants—some young girl, a monkey kid, and Izquierda, who caught both projectiles. It seemed that he had turned traitor. Who would have guessed? Izquierda never seemed to be so keen on doing Lefty Gang business anyway. He was far from surprised that these two teenagers talked him into joining their side, probably in exchange for a lighter sentence. If he was willing to go this far, he probably wasn't above giving all the info he knew about the gang. To Shèng Xià, no good deed should go unpunished.

But something dawned on him. The monkey looked familiar; too familiar. Either it was someone with an extremely similar spark or…

"That you, Yun?"

Yun's defensive stance faltered as he recognized his long lost relative. "Uncle Zuo? I…I thought…you were gone for so long." He swiftly got back into his Monkey Style stance, refusing to make an opening. "Why are you here?"

This was a damn shame. Zuo put down the forged artifact in his hands. "Sorry, Yun. Over these last few years, I've been under new employment." He took off his glasses, giving the group a good look at his true face, a face that displayed a mixture of shame and dissatisfaction.

"With the biggest criminal syndicate?" his own nephew called him out. "You abandoned my mom just to do shady shit?"

He might have deserved that. "I've been doing 'shady shit' before all this. Maybe I just decided to be honest about it." Though abandoning his sister-in-law was in his top five biggest regrets, he tried not to show it. Instead Zuo gave a glare at the defector. "I'm very disappointed in you, Louiz Agudo." He got no reply as he saw that Shee'vra and Louiz surrounded him. "Don't think about trying to stop me. The moment you land a solid clean hit, you're done."

A gust of wind came from the girl in the pink sweater, knocking him back. Only his sturdy cane prevented him from falling over. Zuo shook his head. "Don't try to be cheeky using wind powers. *Any* attack that hurts me goes right back to you sevenfold." He hit his cane on the ground. "You're lucky that I decided to regain my balance, or you would have to be in a wheelchair for the rest of your days."

Yun stepped closer and closer to his uncle. "You're not getting out of here, Zuo." His glare of utter loathing struck Zuo more than most fists could do.

Louiz knew exactly what he was about to do. He tried to shout some sense into the kid. "The hell are you doing?! Landing a punch on this guy is like getting hit by a sledgehammer!" His words went through one ear and straight out the other. "Seriously, if you plan on martyring yourself or something, it won't work! He heals pretty much any wound you can inflict on him!"

Nothing registered with Yun's ears. All he did was slowly move closer and closer. "We needed you to support us. You were the only one who kept us from being on the streets. You were supposed…" Zuo could see his eyes getting misty, "…to take care of us when dad couldn't."

⁓ ✳ ⁓

Nine Years Ago

A young boy by the name of Yun Xuanzang climbed back up to his apartment. With bread and fruit in his hands and teeth, he traversed the power lines and pipes to get back up to the twentieth floor. Opening a window, he jumped back into his tiny messy room. He needed to get it clean before dad came back. He hated a mess. He got mad at things he hated—when he got mad he got aggressive. Dad's aggression always translated to violence.

Luckily, dad had never known about his spark. Xing hated psychics with a passion—always thought of them as "Sophia's special little snowflakes" that only existed to make the hylics seem utterly useless in comparison. Sometimes, maybe dad had a point. They lived in the worst part of Tian City, the Winter Turtle District. Isolated from the rest of the city, it was always seen as a dumping ground for the working class who would never go anywhere in life. It was not a big surprise that only hylics lived in these parts. Psychics always had the money to afford better living spaces with how well missions paid.

Maybe if he could just manage to be able to get a mission for himself, maybe they wouldn't live in squalor anymore. But his mom always insisted that he was much too young to risk his life like that, much less actually get a mission. Though Yun accepted her answer, he also thought that it might have also been so she would not be alone, especially living with someone like Xing.

So for now, he made do with finding other ways to support them. Turned out that like any other monkey living in the city, he was very good at the art of theft. He never stole anything too valuable like jewelry. That had more worth to others and he was too young and suspicious looking to sell stuff. But the occasional loose paz and food were fair game.

Yun refused to steal within the Winter Turtle District on principle. The residents there had enough thieving problems and he didn't want to make their lives more miserable. But The Autumn Tiger district was ideal. He could always rely on the occasional tourist to have loose change or the local market to be lax with security. It was difficult at the beginning. But soon after, stealing became second nature, doubly so after awakening Hanuman.

His mother hated when he stole. But he felt that he simply had no choice. The "man of the house" was unemployed and wasted most of the savings at the bar. He was supporting the family more than his dad Xing was. It was honestly quite sad. A seven-year-old being more financially sound than his old man probably made him the village idiot. He rationalized his reasoning with his mother about his thieving ways being the only reason they were not going hungry. She unwillingly accepted it but told him that he was destined for greater things than just stealing food.

He memorized all the street signs of the two districts and knew where the best areas to steal from were. The symbols on the signs were the first words he ever learned to read due to lack of education. He knew that most other kids were literate and not just able to figure out the story through pictures and it was always a sore spot for him. He always did pray to Sophia for his dad to finally stop drinking, get a job, and take him to school. But each year, he felt that his words fell on deaf ears.

He currently had himself about sixteen paz and enough food to make a small meal for two. Dad would just have to make do, finding a meal himself. But before he was ready to eat, he heard his mother weeping. Dad must have come home early or stopped by. Must have got into another fight.

Entering the living room, he expected to see his mother with some new bruises. But when she looked at him, it looked as if dad had never even touched her. This was unusual.

"What's wrong, momma?"

She was reluctant to tell her child, but he needed to know. "Your father…he's been found dead in the river."

Yun would have been more devastated if he'd had a good father. But losing a violent, alcoholic loser of a father would not make him lose much sleep. He remembered that when it seemed they had extra money because of his stealing, dad would get furious at his mother. He would slap her around and accuse her of being a hooker, something that took years for Yun to understand the meaning of. But Yun knew that it wasn't the loss of her husband that truly devastated her.

One week later, an investigation was made for who killed Xing Xuanzang. The social services noticed his family's living conditions and declared it "unsuitable" for a young child. Mother was not employed, dad used up all the savings, and his uncle Zuo went AWOL from the military and was declared a traitor. Yun was separated from his mom and sent to an orphanage.

He hated it there. Everyone did. It was a completely miserable place run by miserable people and everyone knew that nobody cared about them and probably never would. Yun decided to escape from there at the first opportunity. In a back alley he saw the most terrifying person he believed he would ever meet. A black scaled being who wanted him for something.

"Greetingssss boy. I am Cianfa." His tongue slobbered green liquids when he hissed. "I have heard of a kid that could gain the abilitiessss of a sssssssimian. According to my amazing detective sssssskillsss, that sssssshould be you." Yun should have stayed in his regular form. Though he spoke to him politely, even a kid like him could tell there was an inner malice within the snake.

"But, to bussssssinesss." Cianfa covered his mouth to cough. "I have a proposition should you be interested." His hissing completely disappeared for some reason. Was he trying not to scare him or was he just messing around? Yun felt that it was the latter. "Would you like to hear it?" The demonic looking snake man offered an open hand.

Yun might have been young and illiterate, but he wasn't stupid. The moment he saw an escape, he took it. Strangely, this Cianfa man never even bothered to pursue him. Not that he would ever give him the chance to. Yun was leaving town as soon as possible.

Wandering the countryside either alone or with company, he made it to the city of Shangrila. There, he made a decent living as a thief for a while. He made a name there, becoming known as "The Monkey Prince." Supposedly he was able to lead all the simians in the city to steal for him. It was far from true, but he never contradicted anyone.

One year later, he found this old guy. He had a very nice straw hat, maybe worth a week's worth of food. He hung upon a tree in wait for him to pass by. Once the old man was under him, he reached down to snag his hat.

He wasn't expecting to get caught, though. The old man grabbed him by the arm in a grip stronger than any senior citizen should have. Yun trembled in fear when he saw the elder grow to almost eight feet tall and grow white hair all over.

"Please forgive me, sir!" Yun begged for his life as he dangled over the ground. "I didn't know you were a psychic! I was just hungry!"

His elder seemed to understand his plight. He asked him one question. "Are you the Monkey Prince that this city speaks of?" Yun weakly nodded. "Then I'm giving you an opportunity to better yourself and use your spark for the sake of mankind—something above theft."

Yun took this opportunity to become a disciple under this man known as Yeren. Master Yeren of the Yeti Spark, the Old Man of the Mountain. Yun had heard stories of this living legend and the great feats he had done and the heroes he trained. Yun decided to devote himself to him from then on as Yeren's fourth disciple.

No longer would he steal for food. From now on, he would use Hanuman for the betterment of Qian Ye and the world. Yeren would teach him Monkey Style Kung Fu, teach him discipline, and even help him learn how to read. His entire life was turned around over trying to snag an old man's hat.

~ * ~

"I will hate myself for saying this," Zuo told his nephew, "but I will not turn off my mark for you or anyone. If you strike me down, you'll have to suffer the same consequences as anybody else would." Yun still wasn't listening to him. *Why are you being so damn stubborn?*

"Yun, stop!" Shee'vra begged him. "Listen to him! We can find another way to stop him." She knew in her gut that the moment Yun landed a punch or kick, he was done for. "We can wait until brother comes. Just stop!"

Yun began to slow down. It was truly no use and Shee'vra was trying to keep him safe. But he wasn't going to let him just leave. "Alright, Sheev. But, uncle," his glare did not go away, "I demand you either turn yourself in or leave without those pauldrons."

"No can do," Zuo said directly to his nephew's face. "I came for the Pauldrons of Kadosh and I'm leaving with them."

"Why does he want them so badly?" Shee'vra asked Louiz, who just gave a shrug.

Zuo turned to the girl. "You know you could just have asked me. Allow me to explain. The Eight Relics of Kadosh began with Empress Beatrice the Inqusitive, the fifth in the Kadosh line. Years of researching the world and universe around her granted her a discovery. She found a way for her spark to live on even when she was long gone."

"What?" Yun could hardly imagine any way someone's spark could outlive its user. The moment a psychic died, the spark was lost forever. Was there some kind of spark that bent the universal rules or something? From the looks of it, Shee'vra and Louiz were just as stumped.

"Beatrice had been reading into texts long lost to time during her reign. Somehow, she discovered how to seal sparks into objects. When she was due to die, Beatrice sealed her spark, Ouranos, inside an amulet her husband got her for their wedding decades before. All her aeon and power lurked inside that necklace from then on. She passed down this knowledge to her child, Barbar, who passed it down to his, and you get the point."

"But why just eight relics?" Shee'vra questioned, confused. "There were many more emperors and empresses that came after her. Did something happen?"

"Every ruler after Beatrice was to keep their spark inside an object on their deathbed. But Cent the Just, the thirteenth ruler, put an end to it by defeating the previous ruler, the infamous Diabolos the Demon King." His voice went grim as he remembered the atrocities the emperor committed. "Diabolos sealed his Chernobog spark long before his death and mastered how to use the previous artifacts for his own gain and ruled the world with an iron fist. After a battle that ended with hundreds of psychics and millions of hylics dead, Kent killed Diabolos and had every text mentioning the sealing ritual burnt to be forever lost to time."

"That doesn't explain how you know this, though," Yun told his uncle. "If they were all burned, how do you know all this?"

"Someone a few hundred years ago managed to save a copy. Some guy named Cianfa was oh so kind enough to lend it to me." He saw Yun shiver a bit at the very name. "So, you know that name too? Well I just learned who this guy was only a little while ago. Something is off about him and I wish I could know why he just gave something so important to history as if he were a bored librarian." Zuo shook his head to get rid of any possible insidious plans the snake might have. "But anyway, all I have to do is speak roughly a paragraph of words and I'll get Barbar's spark and aeon all to myself. I can see why my boss would want them."

Shee'vra asked Louiz an important question. "Who's your boss?"

"I honestly don't know," Louiz told her. "Never saw him in my life. We just call him Reliquit. I just got recruited by some draconic serpent guy."

"So, you saw Cianfa too?" Zuo said to the traitor, turning his back on his own nephew. "He did not recruit me. Do the lower ranks of the gang see him often?" Louiz shook his head. "Interesting." *Just who is this Cianfa? He doesn't seem to be a Lefty member, but he's the one who recruits potential psychics. What is his allegiance?*

Yun balled his hands into fists. "What are you going to do, Zuo? You know that we aren't going to just let you walk away."

Shèng measured up the monkey. Having monkey powers probably didn't entitle him to be able to counter the Mark of Cain. But he also didn't want to just get his own nephew killed by his actions. But if it was unavoidable, so be it. He was due for Hell anyway. Therefore, if Yun was killed by his mark, just more paperwork for the devils.

"Yeah, I can." he remarked back. He began to steadily walk away, cane in his hand. "I wish you well, Yun. Stay safe and out of our business. Only warning."

As Zuo began to walk away, he heard the girl scream. Hastily turning back, he saw his own nephew spring toward him. On familial instinct, Zuo deactivated his mark. His joints grinded on one another as he hastily put an arm up to try to defend himself, but Yun still smashed his arm with a sharp blow, shattering bone. But when he went for the stomach, Zuo activated his mark once again. Though pain erupted in his gut, Yun received a hit seven times worse.

Zuo refrained from looking on in pity as he healed his broken arm. He spoke to his kin sternly. "You cannot believe how blessed you are that you are my nephew." He winced upon seeing Yun coughing up beige and red. "If you didn't have my mercy, you'd be minus a limb."

"You call that mercy?!" Shee'vra rushed toward her friend. "Your own nephew is puking up blood!"

This was all beginning to just tick him off. Zuo should be gone by now. "I KNOW THAT! His stomach and kidneys probably just burst. He has only about an hour to live!" He smashed a display case with his cane. "SO JUST LEAVE AND GET HIM MEDICAL ATTENTION!"

Putting a lid on his emotions like he was taught to, Shèng Xià began to walk away. Upon passing by Louiz, he gave him a firm warning. "Count your days, Izquierda. Soon enough, you'll wish I was the one to have killed you." Chances were Sinister and Ezker were dead. But Jakaire might not be. Maybe Cianfa worked as an executioner too?

He went toward the doors, his joints feeling more friction as he moved. But as he began to exit, he heard the running footsteps of at least two more souls. *This is insufferable.* In front of him were two more teenagers. One was a boy dressed in striking red leather, red hair, and purple eyes. The Qian girl had…jade eyes. "Shit."

He and the Altahni woman locked eyes with one another. Neither one knew the other's name, but they knew that fate would eventually have them collide.

Xiu's legs shook as she saw the man who helped commit genocide upon her people. He didn't have his glasses on, but she knew no other Qian psychics that used an oak cane to walk. Without the glasses, this monster looked just like anyone else you could meet on the street. Disgusting.

Xiu took a deep breath as she allowed her limbs to radiate aeon energy that crackled like blue flames. "Do you know who I am?" She'd imagined this one moment for years. She visualized what his reaction would be. She dreamed of him begging for mercy, asking for forgiveness, even taunting her about her loss to her face in defiance. But each time, she would punch a hole through his chest. He would then always grasp at the air as he fell down and died at her feet.

But she received none of that. Instead, the murderer just sighed and nodded. "Yeah. I do." He unscrewed the top of his cane. "Nine years ago, Bumpa Tai Xun initiated an order to kill the entire Altahn tribe. Most died that very night, but a few managed to escape. None of them were left within twenty-four hours. This whole incident got bystanders involved, creating what is known as The Manticore-Ifrit War."

Xiu moved closer and closer. "I don't need a history lesson, you bastard." She was ready to punch his face in. But his next words stopped her.

"You must be thinking 'why?' right? It was obviously not that the Altahn worshipped the Demiurge. That was only the cover. The truth was worse." He took his sword out of his cane. "I sneaked one of the Altahni books that gave me quite a clue." He had everyone's attention. "The Altahn people found a seal keeping one of the Archons at bay. When Tai Xun discovered the truth, he went ballistic and ordered the destruction of the village. But he didn't want to do it alone. For years, the nations of Sirochko had been at odds with Qian Ye. They endlessly debated and fought over what to do with the remains of the Protogenoi Capital of An-Saladin. The Sirokhans wanted to preserve it as a symbol to prevent history from repeating while the Qian wanted the place destroyed to repay the Protogenoi for good after all they'd done to the hylics."

His spine felt a chill as Zuo gave his history lesson. "Tai Xun saw this purge as an opportunity to work together with the Sirokhan Chatraratna Jalil Afritan. Not only would they have a common 'enemy,' but this would also be a chance to help mend fences with his old foe." He delivered the twisted reasoning of the whole genocide. "We killed your tribe on the off chance that anybody, outsider or native, would try to find a way to unseal whatever Archon was in there." He felt guilty for saying this, but he needed to. "Though I personally regret what I did that day, I will say that perhaps the last Bumpa had a point. There are a lot of crazies that would kill to devote themselves to something like an Archon for power. Unsealing such a being..." He tried to get the horrible thoughts out his mind—"World changing."

The entire group was silent at the forbidden news. Shee'vra could not believe that her mentor went through such a hell and hid it so well from her. This was probably why Xiu never really liked it when she asked her about Qian Ye. Louiz was appalled that a nation could just advocate an overnight genocide whenever they felt threatened. Yun had heard bits and pieces of this incident from her but vowed never to tell anyone, but the fact that Zuo was part of it disturbed him to his core, though he could now see why his uncle abandoned his nation. This information was all still too fresh inside Ercan and even now, he felt shame that a country could just kill out of paranoia like that.

Xiu couldn't believe this guy had the nerve to say that there was a chance that wiping out her people could be justified. "How dare you even imply killing everyone I knew had a justification." She did not give a damn if there was an Archon within the mountains. Nobody had a right to just casually wipe out an entire tribe.

Zuo resigned himself to what he was about to do. "If you hate me so much, why don't you just try to kill me? You must have been waiting for this chance for years." He knew one of them was going to die in this room, maybe both of them. "Strike. Me. Down." Shèng pointed his sword at her.

Ercan was suspicious of this guy. His stance was much too careless to seriously fight her. He noticed that Xiu shook as she readied herself into Eagle Claw Style. He knew this wouldn't end with satisfaction. Xiu's earlier emotional wounds inflicted by P.J had yet to heal. Shèng Xià was planning something. He wanted to see her rage.

"Well, what are you waiting for?" Zuo forced himself to taunt her. "A permission slip from your parents?" Those words tasted like piss on his tongue. "Kill me already, bitch!" His indigo symbol lit up as bright as it ever had before.

"FUCK YOU!" Xiu made a mad dash at the murderer, ready to turn him to paste. A chain wrapped around her leg and tripped her over. Suddenly Ercan was pinning her to the floor with all his might. "HE DESERVES TO DIE! I NEED TO KILL HIM!

Ercan held her down as much as he could, trying to ignore the pain of her trying to hit him off. No matter how her strikes were hurting, she was hurting much more than him. Shee'vra got in between her and Zuo while Louiz blocked the exit.

"Please, Xiu," Shee'vra begged, "calm down. I know it sucks to have to deal with this for years. But attacking will not kill him." Xiu was still struggling to get Ercan off of her. "Any pain you inflict on him will come back to you much worse. Please just calm down." This wasn't working. Shee'vra needed to get more personal. "Think about what would happen if you died here. You would be missed by all of us—me, Yun, Caradoc, Hong, Sabelle, Shiro, Vasanti, Desiderio, Cyrille, Julia, and Ercan."

Ercan doubled down on trying to restrain her when he heard what hurting the bastard would do. "Please think about how we would feel if we lost you. Think about how your parents would feel. Would they really want you to just throw it all away for one punch?" Xiu's struggling slowed down. "Please. For us."

The words finally registered within her ears. Though her tears of anger remained, she began to focus less on Zuo and more on the Ao'Si siblings. The aeon flowing around her limbs faded out as her head looked down at the floor. "I cannot just do nothing. You must understand that. This man can't just walk out of here." Ercan got off her and allowed her to get up. "So how can we do that?"

Shee'vra had little idea how they could possibly take out a psychic with such an unfair power. She sadly had absolutely no answer for her friend and she hated that. But somebody else did.

"Then I will fight in your place."

Xiu could not believe what she was hearing from Ercan. Shee'vra had just explained to him what this man could do to her. Would he be so willing to endure so much pain just so she would not have to suffer? Would he defeat the man who helped destroy her life? He hadn't even thought about it, he'd just volunteered. Perhaps it was moments like this that gave her these confusing feelings for him.

"You…really would?" she asked her redheaded companion. She might as well not have asked as he had that look in his eyes. A look she'd only seen a few times. Those violet orbs radiated no anger, despair, or joy, only a willingness to live another day and leave no one behind—a decent quality for a leader.

"Of course I would, Xiu." Ercan told her with all the honesty he had. "This guy was part of the worst day of your life. I'm not going to let that slide."

Xiu considered reminding him about who he was up against, but it probably wouldn't matter anyway. Ercan would not care. He would never be as strong as somebody like Mastema or Bianca, but he dwarfed those two in one important quality—endurance. Come to think of it, Prometheus seemed ideal to go against this foe. Binding him up wouldn't inflict massive injuries for either party, and Ercan's healing factor would be able to heal any wounds he received along the way. It was perfect.

She went and helped Yun, supporting her fellow disciple up, and before Xiu exited the exhibit, she had a few more words for Ercan. "I'm taking him to Julia, wherever she is." She firmly pointed at him with her free hand. "I'm going to hate mys—YOU if you don't make it. Don't you dare die tonight. Promise me that."

As the two passed by Louiz and left the exhibit, Shee'vra detected something in Xiu's tone. It sounded like worry. Which was natural, but it seemed that she would be less mad at her brother, but madder at herself, which was also normal. But it seemed as if she was actively trying to hide something from him—like she was trying to put a cap on her already strong emotions. *Does…does she love my brother?* Maybe even Xiu didn't know the answer.

With those two gone, it was just Ercan against Zuo. Ercan created two perfectly normal chains as Louiz and Shee'vra stood by the sidelines to make sure he would be all right. Zuo on his part was just fed up with all this.

"Really brave of you to put yourself in front of the lady," Zuo backhandedly complimented in an attempt to get under his skin, "though I cannot blame you. She's developed nicely since I saw her last."

Ercan smacked his sword out of his hand with a whip to the wrist. Though his wrist was shattered by the impact, Ercan had felt worse and quickly began to heal it back good as new. "Quit trying to piss me off any more than you already have. I don't know you very well, but you made a member of Rooster Squad cry," he spun his weapons of choice around, "and the girl whose parents you killed, her name is Xiu Lang. I'm going to make you remember it."

Zuo was unfazed by his little spiel. "Feel pretty confident, don't you? Well I'm not going to waste my time talking anymore about why I'm here. I'm now going to show you what the Artifacts of Kadosh really do." He threw his cane away as he moved back. It was time to speak those magic words.

"*By Barbar's broad shoulders, these pauldrons stay. Quell the rebellions until all shall obey.*" He sidestepped a lash. "*Within these pauldrons, lies the Divine Spark Odin. His spear, his power, his ravens, and his eye that can foretell any omen.*" Ercan grabbed him with two chains and wrapped his body around, ignoring the tightened squeeze the mark brought back to him. But Zuo kept on with the chant. "*Gugnir, Huginn, Muninn, Wuotan. I summon the power that shall last 'til Ragnarok!*"

With those final words, Barbar's pauldrons began to shine as if they were in mint condition. Within seconds, his right eye turned bright pink, emblazoned with a green rune shaped like three interlocking triangles. With this new eye, Zuo shot a thin pink laser right through Ercan's chest. As he fell over, the one who unlocked the secret of the pauldrons broke free of his restraints and summoned into his hands a large spear made of energy inscribed with more runes than anyone had time to read.

Zuo Xuanzang looked back at the three awestruck onlookers and twirled his new weapon with a confidence he had not felt in decades. "Fun fact, this spear here is Gugnir and the symbol on my eye is a Valknut. Barbar's Odin spark sure was what you young folks would call 'kickass.' I hear that this Odin guy was a big deal in legends back in the day." A harmless wave of energy swept the floor when he hit the ground with Gugnir as his new ocular upgrade stared the two remaining opposition down. "I'm sorry to say that you two will be next after this. I suggest you get to running."

"You won't even get to touch them." Zuo looked back to see Ercan getting right back up with a grin on his face. "It's going to take more than that to keep me down." Ercan knew what to do against this guy. *All I need to do is get those pauldrons off and chain the asshole down.* The only problem was how.

Zuo was not fazed. "On the contrary, I can do this now." With the flick of his wrist, he summoned two ravens at least five times the size of regular ones. Both wore bronze helmets and had a beak as sharp as a steel sword. Upon their helms was the Valknut rune. That wouldn't be so bad, but they also had that distinct indigo mark on their chests. He continued, "And give them my Mark of Cain."

The ravens' master signaled for the two birds' attention. "Huginn, Muninn, kill the girl and the traitor. And make sure their deaths are quick." Louiz and Shee'vra had no choice but to get out of there and think of a plan. Zuo got ready for a battle bigger than he wanted tonight. "Just the two of us now. You have two options. Live today and keep your little promise. Or you die right here and be the disappointment you were going to become sooner or later."

Ercan didn't even bother to think about it. He had already resolved to survive tonight. He might not be able to stop this guy, but he was going to live to see tomorrow. And he was most definitely going to give this guy the hardest time possible.

Urthona

Desiderio had many skills. Such skills included swordplay, leadership, literature, guitar, natural charm, and being precocious at the art of pleasure. Quite a gifted senior student if he could say so himself. But sadly, skills in direction were not among them. He knew he had to go to the Sephirot but didn't know the precise street. He occasionally asked for directions, but to him, they just began to contradict one another.

"Do you know where the Sephirot is, good sir?" Desi asked a businessman who seemed to be about sixty. He was beginning to run out of breath from running so much.

The old man didn't seem to have the desired answer. "Sorry son. I'm just here for business from Odandir. Ask a local if you need to be there so bad."

Once again, disappointment. But before he could drop his head and try somebody else, Desiderio began to hear a faint noise. Many faint noises. They were getting louder by the second. To his right, he saw terrified bystanders running and screaming for their lives. Looking behind the crowd, he saw a green light emanating from where he was assuming the museum was several blocks away. From this distance the pillar of energy seemed to emanate around ten, maybe twelve stories tall. But the green aura was all too familiar to him.

But that could not possibly be. Enith was back in Sorchos investigating the recent disappearances and killings of several criminals and police officers. There was no way she could cross half the country in one day, especially without alerting the rest of Heron Squad.

He picked up his pace as he headed toward what he assumed would soon become a battlefield. As the light faded away, he witnessed several cars of different brands get sent flying across the street. Some landed on top of buildings, others onto the road. Descending toward him was this highly expensive looking *Bronco*. A shame this car would have to be destroyed.

Unsheathing his rapier lightning quickly, he jumped into the air. The crowd didn't even see him cut the vehicle in half. But the next moment, the car was now four quarters. As he dropped down to the ground with serene grace, the scraps landed harmlessly all around him.

But he had no time to revel in his finesse. This confrontation involved Enitharmon somehow and he was going to get to the bottom of why she would be here. As he began to speed up, three figures jumped in front of him.

I don't have time for this nonsense. Desiderio sliced the throat of one of the foes before he could ever really notice what the guy could do. Looking at the remaining two, these men in green seemed to be wearing the sort of masks a child would wear during Prowl Night. One mask looked like an ugly old green hag with a pointy hat while the other was pale blue and had fangs, not unlike Alexandru; a witch and a vampire respectively if he was correct.

The witch cackled and threw some vial that he quickly dodged. Looking behind him, it seemed to have contained some sort of green fire. Hearing legends of witches as a kid, he immediately moved in to stab the hag straight through the heart. Seeing that both were in green clothing, he suspected that they were either from the same group or the same person. Once the witch disappeared upon death, the latter theory was all but confirmed. For some reason, it disappeared into that lime green light he had known for years.

This is Enith's light. Why? He shouldn't have taken his eye off the vampire. Desiderio felt a strong chill inside his soul. Looking back at the vampire, he saw him sucking up blue energy into his mouth like a funnel ten feet from him. This masked minion was trying to drain him of all his aeon. This monster had yet to attack, so why did it need aeon? Perhaps going to zero would mean the opposition's demise.

Desiderio was amused by this action rather than scared. He shook his head. "You realize that I have only forty, right?" The aeon vampire did not look at him. "Surely I should be dead by now." Desi gave a smug smile. "Do you know why I'm not dead?" The vampire still ignored him to his irritation. "Because I balanced out our aeon scores. Evened the odds. You had an aeon score of one thousand exactly. I took five hundred. Even as you try to suck up my energy, we are still at an equilibrium of five hundred and twenty each."

Desi stabbed his rapier through the opponent's jaw and into his brain. "You folks are not ones for conversation, are you? Pity." The man in the mask faded into green light. That light once again. *This cannot all be a coincidence. I must get to her now. If these…things are attacking anyone at random, she must be losing control of herself. I need to stop her now.*

As he ran toward the museum, he cut and pierced any of these creations in his path. He did not care whether they could jump high, were werewolves, could create ice, or even had horns with them (whatever those did). His entire focus was on Enitharmon, why she was here and why these creations were attacking him.

As he got closer, he saw a giant eight-legged creature that was a couple stories tall. No doubt Gaizka was there too. Chances were he would be the last of the captains to arrive. But he wouldn't be the last psychic to enter the fray.

～ * ～

"THAT ALL YOU GOT, WORM!?" Gaizka snapped the neck of a Jacque with a four-foot stone fiddler crab claw he attached to his arm. He didn't have time to grab his weapons, so he had to improvise. But damn, was this invigorating! He impaled a muscular Frankenstein-masked one with his giant claw right through the chest, crushing its heart. A guy in a werewolf mask tried to be smart and attack him from behind, but the berserker tore him to shreds with the spider limbs on his back.

A vampire-mask-wearing idiot tried to do what vampires do best and went close quarters. Gaizka was taking none of this. "You're neck's mine!" The shark man used his razor-sharp teeth to sink into the vampire's neck, squirting blood everywhere. Gaizka then shoved the

Jaque off of his two-story Stone Sea Spider Colossus, which was doing a pretty nice job of taking out some of the Jacques on the ground, though it was also piercing several of the cars below, almost making it appear as if the sea spider had incy-wincy shoes.

Gaizka laughed heartily as he webbed up one of the witches. "IS THIS ALL YOU HAVE TO OFFER!?"

Another four nimble Jacques tried their best to all jump him at once, each one with steel claws. Gaizka smacked two of them away with his claw and pierced through the other two with his spider legs. But a shot of ice entrapped his feet from behind. Struggling to free himself, Gaizka saw one of the Jacques create a pumpkin mask. The moment the mask touched his face, that Jacque's head became a flaming Jack-o'-lantern.

But before either the ice guy behind him or the burning pumpkin could attack him, two of his comrades came to his aid. A ball of ice smashed through the pumpkin head, squashing it. Coming up from under the frosty Jacque was a shout for the greatest of justice.

"DIVING BEETLE BREAKS THE SURFACE!" Vural leaped out of the stone spider without even harming the structure. The antlion slashed the Jacque with both sharp claws in opposite directions, taking it out in one shot. With a mighty lion's roar, Vural kicked another Jacque flying into a building.

"Was that necessary?" Ludmila questioned the two as she flew in the air, shooting an enemy down with her shield cannon. "Kicking a Frankenstein into a building is one thing. But was making a gigantic, property-destroying stone sea spider absolutely needed?"

"It is." Gaizka replied, dismissive of her criticism, blood covering his teeth. "Have you seen the results?" His creation was taking out any Jacque that was not fast enough. It also attracted many of them like a lighthouse. "They cannot resist this wonderful beast!"

"Yeah, Ludmila," Vural agreed with all his heart. "Giant spiders are cool! I approve." He tossed a shuriken at a werewolf, who deflected the attack.

Ludmila used her ice breath to take out the wolfman. "You two could at least take this somewhat seriously," she scolded the shark. "I expected as much from Vural, but not you. This is serious. Enitharmon is attacking us for Sophia knows why." She blasted a Jacque behind her with her shield cannon.

Gaizka huffed in irritation, the ice dragon ruining his blood high. "I know all that crap. I'm just not worried."

Using her brute strength, Ludmila deflected a car thrown at her. "And why is that?"

Vural was the one to answer her as he flip-kicked a Jacque into the air. "Because she's Desi's former squadmate. We all know how it will end." The antlion jabbed his hand up into the back of the falling Jacque. "Desi gets into her head and she stops being brainwashed." He threw the body into the stone spider, making a muddy splash. "Then we're all friends again."

"And how do you know this?" Ludmila questioned him skeptically.

Vural would have given a smirk of confidence if it weren't for his mandibles. "Because I read and watch CV and whenever an old buddy is attacking his/her friends, they're mind controlled."

Gaizka ripped a once cackling witch in half. "That makes a shit ton of sense, Vural."

The Ice Dragon would love to argue with them, but it was not the time or place. Besides, knowing sparks, Vural was probably right anyway. Suddenly, the Stone Sea Spider Colossus began to shake.

"The hell is going on down there?" Gaizka kept four spindly limbs lodged into the stone. He knew from instinct he had to hold on. Chances were the Jacques finally managed to wear out his baby. "The spider's going to break real soon! Brace yourselves."

But what happened next was utterly unexpected. Out of the spider came a gigantic beanstalk. The weight of the huge plant overwhelmed the spider and forced it down onto the street. The three had absolutely no idea how this could happen.

Except for Vural. "Something tells me the guy I threw inside the spider created a beanstalk somehow. How should I have known? These guys keep pulling powers out of their asses."

Whether it was with webbing, flight, or ninja jumping skills, the three captains managed to grab onto the eight-story mass of plants. The beanstalk's leaves were strong enough to support Ludmila, Gaizka, and Vural.

Gaizka's legs honestly couldn't help but tremble as he looked downward. Two stories up were just fine, but eight stories felt like a mile. "Long way down."

This was an irritation to Ludmila. She needed to get down to Enitharmon to try to stop this madness. Even now, more Jacques were appearing on other leaves, each of them with their own mask. She dismissed her shield and summoned her sword. Likewise, Gaizka took off his stone claw and beat a Jacque to death with it. Vural also readied for what was to come. Ludmila was more than sure that at this point they all had less than half of their aeon left. They had to make every point count.

But before they could go for round two, small flashing rainbow lights went into the beanstalk in different areas faster than anyone could see. Though none of the three had any idea what was going on, those weird lights began to show results.

Out of the gigantic plant, more plants began to emerge—the kind of biomes that really shouldn't exist. Gigantic flytraps gorged on victims. Beautiful flowers shot quick acting poison darts into necks. Long vines covered in thorns gave many Jacques the embrace of death. There was even this bulbous pitcher plant that regurgitated corrosive substances.

"Where'd this floral nightmare come from?" Vural wondered as he watched in shock as a guy in a zombie mask got grabbed by a plant monster's tongue to be eaten. "I hope they don't think we're food."

Just after he spoke, a large bright red flower spat out some sort of pollen on them. All three immediately felt the need to cough, but they noticed that the thorny vines were completely ignoring them along with the other floral abominations.

Though Vural might have no idea who was behind the plants, both Ludmila and Gaizka knew who this was firsthand. Flying in front of them was a woman who had huge bright orange and brown spotted butterfly wings. The user of this spark was none other than Rina Ao'Si.

"Thanks for the save, Mrs. Ao'Si," Gaizka told his elder psychic. This woman had saved his ass in the worst moments of his life. One day, he would repay her.

Rina was not exactly in a lighthearted mood, though. She looked about the area in haste. "Always a pleasure, but do any of you know where Ercan and Shee'vra are?"

Sensing that she was worried for the lives of her kids like any good mother in a battlefield, Ludmila tried to quell her concerns. "I heard that Ercan was inside the museum with the other members of Rooster Squad." She had no idea if they were alive or not, but she chose not to give an opinion.

Rina felt no relief but understood what she meant. "Thank you, Ludmila." She placed her hands upon the beanstalk. "Brace yourselves. The stalk is going to shrink now."

True to her word, the giant plant in the middle of the road descended lower and lower in height. Eventually, it was small enough for the three of them to get off safely on top of the library. As they watched for a second, they saw that the other remaining members of Dove Squad were here too. Aluja wrapped many green shirts in bandages and struck even more down with his trusty khopesh. Monoceros smashed through even the strongest of the Jacques with brutal efficiency. Even Rina had no choice but to delay her search for her children to help her squad mates with more lethal plants.

Amongst all their allies, they saw Mastema's eyes giving their support and shooting small stinging beams of energy at foes. Though weak alone, in groups, these eyeballs seriously tipped the scale. All three were more than sure that those eyes had saved their asses once or twice already, even if they hadn't noticed.

But that was enough watching. At essentially the same time, they all got back in the fray. Ludmila flew down to the ground, summoning her mighty armor and shield. Gaizka crawled down the side of the building, creating webs from his hands and rock beasts from the sidewalk. Vural dived into the street like a professional athlete, popping back up occasionally to ambush foes.

Xiu followed her aeon jackal's trail as she carried around a weakened Yun. Luckily, after being in Rooster Squad for a while, Anubis managed to memorize Thoth's "scent" and find the easiest path to Julia. Yun needed it. He had long since reverted to his baseline human form and was in a cycle of gaining and losing consciousness.

If Shee'vra was correct, that vile crook's ability was to inflict more pain back to the attacker whenever hurt. She knew more than most people that Yun was actually surprisingly strong. Most would think that when it came to a monkey man, it would have more mobility than strength. But that was simply not true. She'd heard of how primates could lift a surprising amount, depending on size. In fact, she'd heard that chimpanzees were about as strong as four humans on average. So, taking into account that a chimpanzee is about four feet tall tops while Yun was about five feet, eight inches in his monkey form, he would definitely be stronger than a chimpanzee. And that wasn't getting into human adrenaline. So whatever attack he had done to that murderous scumbag's stomach must have completely damaged several organs.

Even now, she regretted just leaving Ercan to fight her fight, but she knew she had no choice in the matter. She did not even know his name, but still she could not help but utterly despise that murderer. But as luck would have it, she would be denied a chance to get back at him for what he did to the Altahn. Life is just never fair that way. But she had faith that Ercan wouldn't let him get away after all the crap he'd pulled. Right now, she needed to focus on finding Julia and getting Yun back to health. Xiu was not going to lose another family member to that man.

The indigo trail brought her to a set of stairs that led to the Ancient Islands Exhibit. Trying to get Yun down was an uphill battle without just letting him fall down the stairs. Upon reaching the last step, she was face to face with a huge stone statue of a human head. Though she personally thought museums were "geeky," that unreadable face intrigued her. She recalled from a school trip four years ago that it was found on a faraway island untouched by man for what seemed to be several millenniums. That honestly should not have been possible, but somehow somebody made a ginormous head in the middle of nowhere.

She shook her head. "Enough distractions. Where is Anubis taking me?" Checking the trail, it seemed that Anubis was pointing out that Julia was somehow not in the building.

Before she could find a way out though, she noticed loud sounds occurring outside. It seemed like a full-scale battle was at the front of the museum and the destruction was spreading. She didn't need keen hearing to know that. Propping Yun down onto a bench, she got on the defensive as she saw green lights flickering outside the windows.

Jumping through the windows were four guys in green. Each one looked the same. In fact, Xiu recalled seeing a corpse looking just like them upon entering the museum. Having no idea what they could do, she suddenly watched as each one created a different mask in their hands. Knowing that this could only end badly, Xiu attacked the one trying to put on a witch's mask and broke most of his ribs with an open-handed jab with a Tiger Fist.

With one of them down, she focused on the other three: a vampire with metal claws, a white furred wolfman, and a muscular pumpkin-headed man with bolts on his neck. The lycanthrope created ice on the floor around her. Xiu dodged the vampire's claws, but he managed to trip her onto her back. Using Cornered Dog Style, she swept the vampire off his legs. On all four of her aeon imbued limbs, Xiu jumped toward the ice wolf before he could puff out more freezing wind, elbowing him in the face.

The pumpkin breathed flames, but she managed to dive under his legs. She then kicked him three separate times in the lower back, finishing with a spinning kick to the back of his squishy veggie head.

With the pumpkin smashed, the ice werewolf and the long-clawed vampire both tried to pounce on her from opposite sides. Channeling all her aeon into her hands, Xiu created two large spheres that shot into each foe's stomach. The white wolf smashed into a holy tomb of jade while the vampire was propelled into a glass case of exotic feather headdresses.

Xiu breathed in and out and in and out. Sweat was on her brow and her new shoes were getting soggy in a puddle that was once a layer of ice. Those four might not have given her the satisfaction of braining that murderer, but they would have to do for now. She looked around to see that Anubis's trail was still active. Regaining her composure, she went back to Yun in order to continue her mission.

Looking down at her peer, she noticed that he was struggling for air at this point and lying down was not helping him at all. The moment she propped him up, blood and stomach fluids poured out of his mouth. A disgusting sight, but she knew better than to complain to somebody dying to not be gross.

But as she began to move forward with Yun in tow, more green lights appeared. Twice as many. No, three times more. All the same guy in green. She put Yun down again and tried to fend them all off, though something inside her told her that these creations wouldn't stop appearing until the psychic making them was defeated.

Before anyone could inflict a blow, a disc came from the window and landed in the puddle. Electrical energy flowed into half of the green shirts. A stone gargoyle barged into the room and began to attack various Jacques with its fists and wings. Following that, several floating swords entered the room and sliced at the enemy. Finally, entering from the window was none other than Julia and Zivot. In Cyrille's bodyguard/maid's arms was a jackal made of aeon.

Feeling a temporary sense of relief, Xiu brought Yun to Julia. "Julia! Glad you found Anubis! Yun is hurt really badly, and if we don't do anything, he'll die!"

Guessing that this was not the time for smart-ass comments, Julia immediately took out a disk and inscribed a healing glyph on it. Without speaking, she placed the glyph upon his stomach. She had a lot of healing to do, but Yun seemed to be on his way to being physically stable.

Xiu looked around the rest of the room, even behind Zivot. "Wait, where's Cyrille?" She never really did pay attention to the chicken man much, even as a teammate. His looks and abilities always did find new ways to repulse her. But she never wanted to see him dead. "Where is he…Zivot?"

Neither of them had ever spoken to one another before, not even as classmates. Zivot always assumed that Xiu just thought she was too cool for her to talk to or something. But she felt that Xiu was entitled to an answer. "Cyrille's alive, but he's been heavily wounded by a Lefty Gang member. But luckily, he alerted us about this situation and I alerted the rest of Eagle Squad, who alerted many others it seems." Zivot felt relief that the other captains were here or else they would be in deeper trouble. "But Lord Cyrille is safe and he's being healed by Mayil as we speak."

Zivot's eyes saw that dumb monkey man in massive pain. Vomit containing blood was not far away either. "What happened to him?"

Xiu made a scowl as she looked at her injured peer. "He hit someone who…really deserved it. But that bastard had some spark that hurt him even more."

"Did you neutralize this foe?"

"I wish." Xiu's fists began to tremble. "I wished so badly to brain him, but Ercan is the only one of us that has any chance to take him down. So, I had no choice but to leave it to him." She hoped that Ercan or Shee'vra were not already dead. She would never forgive herself if either died for her sake.

Feeling that this was a tense issue, Zivot dropped the subject of this mysterious person. They had more immediate matters to focus on anyway. "We'll leave it to Ercan then. His leadership skills may be questionable but, as he proved today and many times before, his tenacity is something to be admired. Let's get Yun to a safer area."

"Sure," was all Xiu could say. But just outside, more green lights appeared.

~ * ~

Hanako was beginning to regret getting involved. The battle was getting much too intense and dangerous as it went on. She'd only come to the museum because Bianca decided to see what was going on and she just wanted to make sure she was safe. She was beginning to think that was a stupid idea. *Of course Bianca can handle herself. She's one of the strongest psychics I know. But me, I don't know why I'm even here. All these scary enemies. It's just my luck these guys all wear Prowl Night masks.* She shot her last arrow at some witch-masked guy, for they were the creepiest. *Oh no! I'm all out of arrows! Now I have to get close to them!* Hanako took her butcher knife out of her sleeve. *If only there was a mirror around. Why did I not bring my mirror?* She snuck behind a Frankenstein and her eyes flashed red the moment she jumped on his back and slit his throat.

After bleeding the apparition's throat out, she could feel that she was covered in goose bumps. Hanako knew that she was now out in the open and she could be surrounded and killed at any moment. *Where do I go now? What do I do?* She couldn't just simply transform into one of the enemy to blend in. What if one of her allies accidently killed her? That would traumatize them for life. She saw in front of her an unoccupied alley. *This is my chance! I could get out of here and nobody would know. I'm not even needed here anyway, so I might as well not have anybody worrying about me.*

She took two steps into the alley but found that she couldn't move any further. No matter what she said to herself, she could not bring herself to just run away. It simply didn't feel right for a Squad Captain to just escape when others needed her. She was The Midnight Maiden in the Mirror, for Sophia's sake. What would her family think if one of her fellow captains got seriously hurt and she could have done something, but she ran away? It would be unforgivable!

She whimpered to herself as she turned away from the one escape route. Peeking from behind a wrecked car, she saw Alexandru mowing down as many Jacques as he could with his sword. Looking up, it seemed as if the moonlight was making him stronger somehow. She watched as the dhampyr moved quicker than he usually did and his strikes more effective as he fought under the full moon. Alexandru grabbed one vampire Jacque's face and made him look directly into his eyes. Within a few seconds, Hanako watched as the guy in the scary mask began to fight alongside Alex without any issues.

But as they fought, she saw a white furred werewolf appear just in front of her but behind the dhampyr. The wolfman was about to create an icicle spear to ambush him. Hanako had to do something.

I can't believe I'm doing this. She jumped on top of the wolfman, stabbing him in whatever vitals she could find quickly. But the frost wolfman was durable and wouldn't just go down. He pinned her in between his back and a car, trying to smash her loose. But Hanako tried to hold on as much as she could. But it wasn't enough. The wolfman got her off him and he glared at her through his wolf mask. His upper body was all bloody from her cuts and stabs but adrenaline seemed to be seeping within the emanation's body. He made icy claws and prepared to strike her down. Dropping her only form of defense, she tried to brace herself from being torn apart. Even in certain death, she felt nothing more than unbearable fear. No matter how much Mr. McDooley told her about the inevitability about dying violently, she could never prepare herself for it. Could the others? Or was she just a coward?

But as she closed her eyes, those ice claws never met her neck. Reluctantly opening her natural eyes, she saw that a laser shot a hole through the wolfman's head. Flying down toward her, that little golden eye Mastema tended to hold in his hand greeted her, spinning around, happy as if it was the big hero.

She could not help but tremble as she got back to her feet. "T-thank you so much, Aureolin." Aureolin whistled happily as if to say "You're welcome." Hanako picked up her knife as she checked her surroundings. She noticed that Alexandru had come up to her, concerned for a colleague's safety, no doubt.

"Are you alright, Hanako?" he asked her as his hypnotized Jacques covered the two. "You seem shaken up." He patted his peer's shoulder and gave a weak smile that still managed to expose his fangs. "Call it a hunch, but I feel like we have bitten off much more than we can chew. Do you feel the same way?" She quickly nodded. "Good to know that at least two of us are aware of our limits. Though I do not intend to run away, I won't blame you if you try to escape. We're still students—elite ones, but still students. We're the future of psychic-kind and when one of us dies, the impact on the world will be catastrophic. I'm sure of that. So, if you at all feel that you can't handle what's going on right now, do not be ashamed to leave."

She knew that he cared about her safety, but Hanako couldn't help but think that he was only saying this because she looked weak. Maybe she was. But she couldn't help it. She was raised a shrine maiden to preserve holy relics, not go out and kill people. In fact, Bloody Mary was hardly the most optimal spark in a full-scale battlefield. To her, it was mainly for espionage. That, she could handle just fine (even though it would be shady work). But battling all these people? Crazy. Worse still, it seemed Enitharmon was deliberately altering reality in such a way as to cover each reflective surface with mud. Without reflections, she just felt so exposed. One clean hit and she was done for. But as the Lunar Dhampyr and the shiny floating eye awaited an answer, she spoke up.

"I'm not leaving." Hanako was kicking herself in the back of the head for saying this. "I might not be as strong as Ludmila, fast as Vural, versatile as Winona, vicious as Gaizka, talented as Desiderio, tough as Ercan, graceful as Bianca, magnificent as Mastema or as calm as you, and I never will be. But I'm captain of Rhea Squad and I need to act like it. If I just ditched Jorun or George, what kind of person would I be? You guys are like a second squad to me, everyone in school is." The eyes hidden by her hair glowed with determination even if she still shivered. "Even if it terrifies me, I will not run. I will stand by until this is all over. Until each and every single one of us is one hundred percent sure that nobody's in danger." She gripped her stained knife in a reverse grip, ready to see everything to the end. Hopefully when this is all over, she would think about how reckless she was being.

Aureolin shot lasers at several foes to slow them down. It seemed that some of the enemies went through Alexandru's minions. Feeling his sword was not sufficient, Alexandru put away his blade to deal with the enemy bare handed. The moon invigorated him so. Any cut he received healed almost immediately by the moonlight. Hanako followed suit with the flying eyeball covering her, slashing arteries and tendons to disable the enemy as well as she could.

As the two captains fought Jacque after Jacque, a Franken-Jacque appeared and picked up a large car. As tough as they were, neither Alexandru nor Hanako could survive getting crushed by a car. Both tried to get out of sight as efficiently as possible.

But before the muscle-bound minion could crush either one of them, ten flying blue eyes surrounded Aureolin. They each connected to one another with a tether of pure light. They seemed to form an ornate shape that looked vaguely like a hexagon. Aurelion was on top with three below him, three were to the right and three to the left with one eye at the very bottom. All their lasers combined to create one large beam that shot out and obliterated the car in midair along with the one who threw it. There was no sound made as the laser went out as quickly as it came. Both captains were in awe at just what Mastema could do even when he wasn't around.

"Acts like this is why Mastema is always ahead of us," Alexandru commented to his peer. "He could be on the other side of the battlefield and still overshadow us." As he spoke, more lights flashed to reveal at least thirty more Jacques.

But speaking of the devil, just above them was the greatest captain Aeon Sophia Academy had had in years. As the guardian angel's wings flapped, hundreds of eyes flew out from underneath. Lasers went down upon the enemy masses like holy rain. Each Jacque vainly attempted to shield himself, run away, or find cover from the silent annihilation. Neither Hanako nor Alexandru could hear the howls, screeches, cracks, or even explosions as they witnessed the sheer devastation inflicted upon their foes.

Looking at Mastema's face, they saw no trace of emotion as he wiped the summons off the face of the earth. To him, joy, despair, or rage was not to be a factor in the heart of battle. A Mattatron's duty was to merely judge the guilty and determine a punishment for transgressors, even if it meant execution—nothing more, nothing less. How much force they used was up to them, but the results would always be the same—the complete decimation of the opposition's will to fight or their life.

When the smoke subsided, one lone Jacque remained. It used the corpses of its fellow Jacques to cover itself from the attack, though not a hundred percent from the looks of it. Mastema didn't even give him a chance to do anything. The Silencing Angel merely swooped down and, with one swing of his halberd, sliced the Jacque's head clean in two. Within one minute, thirty foes were killed just like that.

Mastema's sapphire eyes glanced upon the two onlookers. "Fear not…for you are not below me." He spread out the eyes above him across the battlefield in groups of eleven. "The more that are summoned…the weaker and less intelligent they get. All of us are able to take on these foes…these creations are just mere tests for us." He extended his wings once again and flew back into the air. "I've learned all I can…have you?" He was done talking and left to help someone else. Aureolin followed its master.

Knowing that Mastema could take out so many made Hanako and Alexandru became more confident. They may not be as strong as him, but both had yet to master their respective sparks. Perhaps when they did, they would become as powerful as him. They just needed to survive tonight and then they would have all the time in the world to figure out what they could possibly do for the betterment of mankind.

The ravens pursued them no matter where they went. Shee'vra and Louiz just couldn't shake these birds off. You turned right, they turned right. You went down a floor, they followed. Close a door on them and they blasted it open with rays from their helmets. At this point of the chase, Shee'vra found herself back in the space exhibit. It had the highest ceiling in the entire museum and a glass roof.

If it weren't for the mark on the birds' bodies, they would have killed both of them long ago. But they knew that if they struck one of the ravens, all their bones might as well turn to dust. So, they had no choice but to escape and think of a plan. Shee'vra flew upwards as Louiz began to jump onto and climb up the Big Bang Globe. As the two went in separate directions, each raven began to focus on one target.

"Do you have any ideas how we can get them to stop trailing us?" Shee'vra asked Louiz desperately. When Huginn was too close for comfort, she pushed it back with a gust of wind. She had to make the attack gentle, though, and make sure the bird didn't hit any solid surface. Though she managed to get the bird off balance, Shee'vra's entire body stung as if a wet cloth harshly had slapped her whole body at once.

Louiz jumped from one sphere to another, dodging a flechette of feathers shot from under Muninn's wings. "Not really, but we need more breathing room!" The crocotta used the steel feathers as stepping-stones to jump on top of the Big Bang Globe. With his powerful leg muscles, he jumped fifteen feet into the air and used the strongest kick he could muster to break a hole in the ceiling.

Using his crystal eyes, he dodged another laser on the way down as he passed by the raven. Before Muninn could create a second beam with its helmet, chunks of the ceiling fell, enough to squish a bird upon impact.

Louiz held his breath for a sharp second, bracing himself in case he might just become victim to the Mark of Cain. Nothing. Though to be honest, he smashed the ceiling to find a way out onto the roof. He could have just tried to find an escape out a door or window, but outside looked like a warzone with constant flashes of green. He chose life, thank you very much.

But it seemed accidents with the natural environment did the trick. He yelled out to his temporary ally about the news. "If you get these guys hurt in an accident in their surroundings, you won't get hurt!"

Shee'vra glanced at Louiz as she flew about, acknowledging what he just said. "That's great and all, but we can't just make an accident out of thin air!" She dived down to avoid several feathers that missed by a hair. The projectiles shattered a stained-glass window of the galaxy. "I need to find another way!"

It took a few seconds of looking outside the broken window to figure it out. Those flashing lights they kept seeing on the way here were creating men in green clothes. They must be summoned by some other Lefty Gang Member. If she could get the raven killed by one of their attacks by accident, it would be a "two birds with one stone" situation. Though it would be throwing herself into deeper waters, she had little choice. She had yet to master aeon control, so flying was draining her aeon supply. If she continued, she could risk falling to an untimely death.

She called out to Louiz, "I'm going to get one of those masked guys to kill the bird for me! Don't wait up!" She flew upwards, leaving the former football player alone in the astrology wing. Shee'vra had a feeling he might try to just run away now, but she didn't care. Somehow, she doubted he would commit any more crimes.

As she flew through the hole in the roof, she made a sharp turn to avoid a laser beam. But as she tried to fly across the roof to get closer to the crowd of masked men in her riskiest maneuver as a psychic yet, she felt as if knives stabbed into her legs. Huginn's feathers stuck into her calves, making her cry out. The pain made her lose her focus on riding the air, causing her to fall onto the side of a roof, breaking more than a few tiles. She tumbled down the side and fell three stories down into the Topiary Garden's pond.

Gasping for air, she brought her head out of water that was rapidly turning red around her. She found herself surrounded by masked enemies on all sides. She planned to just pass through, dodge their projectiles and make sure one of them hit the bird. But now she was trapped on all sides by beings in various horror masks. Looking up through chlorine-touched eyes, she saw Huginn speeding down toward her, its beak as sharp as a knife ready to pierce her throat.

She tried to move out of the water, but it felt like as if her right leg had been crushed by a bear trap. Her left arm fared little better, not even being able to move. She didn't dare to inspect either injury, knowing she wouldn't like what she saw. In an act of desperation, she tried to move the air in a slanted angle with a swipe of her hand. Hopefully it would work. Either way she was as good as dead if she either accidently hurt the raven herself or missed with the wind.

Shee'vra did manage to get Huginn in an air current. The bird was pushed away, and the wind moved it in a curved angle right in front of some witch-masked person trying to shoot a blast of ice at her. The raven was frozen solid and shattered on impact with the ground. The witch also froze solid but shattered in a great explosion that scattered shards to all of the Jacque around him, who dematerialized in green flashes upon death. Shee'vra managed to avoid the ice by keeping her head under the water.

Bringing her head back up once again, she saw to her dismay that she was still far from safe. There were still at least nine more beings. But before a vampire-masked one could approach her, he got a fist the size of his head to his face. The being that sent the guy flying into a bush shaped like a trout was a bipedal horse. Following suit was Winona Samhain in her Macha incarnation. The captain of Crow Squad shot a yellow arrow at the strongest looking greensuit, which became hairy and grew long sharp teeth. By the time Winona and her horseman beat the rest of the masked men with either spear or fist, the Franken-Jacque became a particularly imposing looking werebeast.

Finished for now, Winona looked over her shoulder dismissively. "Hey, Ercan's sister, can you get up? Or do you need me to treat your boo-boos? Don't make me wait all night for an answer."

Shee'vra forced her body out of the shallow pool. Winona's eyes opened a bit more as she saw that the girl had a twisted leg and an arm fractured in two places. The new kid looked miserable and they had nothing wanting to kill them at the moment, so Winona took this opportunity to use the great healing skills of Macha. "Stay still, Ercan's sister. This feels weird the first time."

With a touch to Shee'vra's forehead, Macha literally washed away the wounds and pain. Her leg went back to its normal direction and her arm bent back painlessly as if it was never even broken. The nauseating agony even faded out.

Getting up, Shee'vra nodded in gratitude. "Thank you very much. Without you, I wouldn't be—"

"Don't bother," Winona cut her off rudely. "If you want to show your thanks, start by backing me up." Her voice became quieter. "I feel them coming closer."

True to her word, several more of them jumped down from the roof toward them. As if on impulse, Shee'vra counterattacked with her largest gale yet. Each Jacque was sent flying back before they hit the ground, smashing into the side of the building and piling up.

Winona and her two lackeys used this chance to finish them off. The woman with black feathers for hair spoke to her as she concentrated on stabbing and stomping the enemy while they were down. "Okay, I guess. You have a lot to learn, though." She pierced a mummy Jacque through the skull. "But I'm sure that little voice inside everyone but me will teach you juuuuust fine."

Shee'vra had only the vaguest idea of what she was talking about. Winona seemed to have been talking about Sophia's voice within all Spark Regions. *But why would she mention "everyone but her" then? Did she not have a voice within whatever Spark Region she had? Sure, she may be kind of mean, but even the most infamous psychics in history had been known to have Sophia's voice as well. It was definitely not about morality if Sophia refused to guide you. So why then?*

Shee'vra would have to store that thought for later, as another wave of baddies were on the way. But as she let out another burst of wind, she saw through a window Louiz running by on all fours. *Where is he going?*

~ * ~

Balra could not bear this anymore. Urthona was working overtime. Now she was summoning copies of the guy Shèng Xià killed at the entrance, throwing cars and rubble around, granting herself as much durability as possible, checking the location of all enemies, as well as turning each reflective surface muddy to trap the girl in the mirror. All this going on at the same time was crushing her brain as if it were in a vise. Thank Sophia, her headband was keeping her balanced.

As she could see from her scrying, nothing was working. All opposition was mowing down her creations. At first, she only thought those twelve students showed up, but now more were coming in every minute. Veteran psychics. It was then that she realized that the field of normalcy she had once made was now utterly useless, as everyone within the city knew what was going on by now. Some one-eyed brute was punching through hordes of Jacques. A green-skinned mummy was not only healing wounds with his bandages, but also using them to entangle her manifestations. A middle-aged woman with butterfly wings was growing carnivorous plants around the area. And that was only the first three adults who showed up. Others were making blizzards, creating shadows, summoning animals with music, slicing up foes with pendulums, drowning foes in electrified water, pummeling enemies as a warthog beast, spreading pure dread among the Jacques, dissolving opposition as a giant pink ooze, and even more spark powers that hurt her head just thinking about.

Though mud was smeared on every mirror that appeared, Balra still had to deal with Caradoc and Basil. Both boys were extremely fast and anything she threw at them was dodged. When she created swords in the sky to smite them down, Basil dashed away at high speeds while Caradoc dodged, swerved, and parried each one of the swords with his own blades. Caradoc then jumped off from a car Basil made float onto the side of a building. Using his defiance of gravity to aid him, he then sprang diagonally downwards toward her at high velocity, ready to cut her down with both blades.

With her durable body, Balra moved her arm to block the Blades of Barsoom. Sparks flew from the slashes hitting what was essentially steel but, before Balra could counterattack, Caradoc leaped twenty feet back. Just when she thought the attack was a failure, she noticed that her forearm was cut. The wound was not too deep but proved that she was far from invincible as her green blood could attest.

Needing to wipe him out, Balra created a green ball of energy that expanded bigger and bigger. The energy grew to her size at first, but that would be too easy to dodge. She then added more aeon to make it as big as an elephant, though it still didn't feel like it would be impossible to avoid. To achieve maximum results, she increased the size of the destructive globe of green energy to that of the museum itself. She didn't recall ever using an attack this powerful so she didn't know how many foes she would kill with this, perhaps about five blocks. Though to minimize damage, she willed Urthona to ignore civilians and allies as well as to repair any damage to property immediately after the explosion. That should be enough, right?

"YOU'RE FREAKING NUTS!" Caradoc knew when to fold. He jumped leaps and bounds to get away. "Everybody get out while you can!" All the psychics took his warning and began to rush to what they hoped would be safety.

"Finally," Balra said to herself. "None of these pests will get in the way of the Lefty Gang ever again. They must pay for their meddling." She got ready to let loose the ball of destruction. "Whatever the gang wishes."

As she focused on throwing the blast to the floor to annihilate all the psychics, she felt beefy arms reach around her body. She felt herself getting lifted into the air, making all her effort of finishing this with one big attack pointless.

"You may be a goddess on the ground!" Basil stated to her as she struggled in his iron grip. "But you are powerless the moment you and the earth part ways!"

He was right. All around her, Balra's creations spontaneously ended. The Jacques vaporized in silent flashes; her flesh became as durable as a frail girl, and the colossal orb of destruction she manifested poofed out of existence, hurting nobody. Worse still, the mud on the reflective surfaces disappeared. As she tried to fight her way free, Bianca Narkissos stepped out of a mirror wall.

"It is finished, Enitharmon Loz." She walked up to her with an obsidian dagger at the ready. "It's obvious that you are under someone's control."

Enitharmon refused to answer. She always had mixed feelings of not being on the ground. Though it made her utterly worthless as a psychic, it was also somewhat of a sanctuary. Before she was given her headband, Enith had no idea how to even control herself. If she didn't keep her emotions in check, Urthona would go out of control. When enraged, aeon burst around her destructively, caused fires and shattered stone. When depressed, it would rain even when inside. When scared, she wouldn't even be able to do anything else until she felt better. When hysterical, Urthona become nigh impossible to control. Even when she was fine she had to concentrate on not warping reality too much. Like what if she got a criminal psychic's powers wrong or if she drastically imagined herself dying.

She remembered people she recalled as parental figures were not able to handle it when she got her spark at age six. They had absolutely no choice but to tether her up above the floor, never able to truly be free. The fact that her eyes were green as well as her blood also disturbed them, making her known by anyone who knew her as "The Green Child." Luckily, psychics eventually found her and took her to Aeon Sophia Academy to learn to control her unfathomable abilities.

But even within the primal elemental world of earth that was her Spark Region, she heard no voice to guide her. They said there was supposed to be a voice to help her control herself. Why was there nobody?

It didn't help that being suspended in the air for years atrophied her muscles, making her unable to compete with the other students in gym.

So even if she just used a Sarkic collar, she was simply a weak and sickly girl. She was either worthless or a danger to everyone around her.

But then she was brought into Heron Squad and…the three-eyed hand once again flashed inside her head. *What was I thinking about again?* But that didn't matter. What mattered was the Lefty Gang's mission.

Her pupils constricted as her voice lowered drastically. "I am Balra. I must do whatever they wish."

Bianca shook her head, her deductions correct. "I had a feeling you were under control from some other psychic." She stepped closer to her, knife at the ready. "I need to liberate you." As princess of Titlacuan, she knew she had been destined to make difficult decisions since she was born. This would be just one among many she must make.

Grabbing Enith's headband, Bianca severed the headwear with her weapon. With that complete, the pale princess dropped the cloth behind her. "It has been done. I have now destroyed the thing that has been controlling your mind. You are free now, Enitharmon." Desiderio was most likely going to be worried for her upon learning all of this, but hopefully the worst had passed. "Put her down, Basil. It's finished."

Though he paused for a moment, the wrestler did as he was told and put the former puppet of the Lefty Gang back on her two feet. Immediately upon freedom, she rushed to Bianca to take the headband back. Panic began to brew inside her head as she quickly used Urthona to mend her restraining device. The captain in front of her simply grabbed it out of her hands.

"Enough with this!" Bianca demanded harshly, though with traces of confusion. "Why do you need this so badly?" *If this is not some kind of mind controlling device of some sort, then what is it? It's much too important to just simply be an accessory. But what purpose does this serve?*

"Give it back!" Enitharmon demanded in a panic. "I need it! I NEED IT!" Green energy once again began to radiate under her. "I need it for control! Give it back!" She was beginning to lose it as more lime green energy began to surround her body. "GIVE! IT! BAAAAACK!"

"We're out!" Basil grabbed his captain and ran as fast as he could. He just barely managed to dodge a distressingly quick explosion of energy centering on the panicking girl. Any later and he would have lost his captain.

Enith began to freak out and scream louder as Urthona began to destabilize more and more. The bursts of energy shot out from her further and further as she went to her knees in utter pain. "MAKE IT STOP! MAKE IT STOP! MAKEITSTOPMAKEITSTOPMAKEITSTOP!"

Licks of energy randomly tried to hit Basil and Bianca, destroying all in their path. But before they could be disintegrated, Caradoc grabbed them both and jumped on top of a building with the two.

"What the hell is happening to her?" he demanded, fearing what was to come next. "Is this going to destroy everything?"

In a safe enough distance, the heir to Titlacuan looked on in utter horror at what her actions created. "This is all my fault." She could only look on, as the explosive energy got stronger and stronger.

She was not the only one. All the other psychics escaped as quickly as possible, but each one looked in horror at the sight of a spark seemingly destroying itself. Each one watched from their relative safety as the energy expanded to become as big as an entire city block.

Looking toward her side, Bianca saw the terrified expression of Desiderio. He pushed by his peers and superiors and rushed toward the green light in a desperate attempt to save his friend. Gaizka and Ludmila tried to pursue him but Mastema blocked them with his wings.

"What, are you just going to let him die?!" Gaizka roared out at him. "Going in there is suicide!"

"Are you so emotionally impaired you don't even blink when we throw our lives away?" Ludmila questioned angrily. "We need to bring him to his senses!"

Mastema tried his best not to look fazed by the accusations against him. He turned to look at his fellow captains. Hanako and Vural reluctantly watched on as Desiderio was throwing his life away while Alexandru gave him a look that showed that he understood Mastema's reasoning. Desi was emotionally compromised and would not be stopped. Trying to follow him would only end with more casualties. Even now, due to his flying eye spies being destroyed the moment he got too close, he could not gather information on what was occurring inside the museum or within the courtyard.

Mastema looked upon his angel and saw her looking at the site of Enitharmon, trying to appear poised. He could never blame her. Bianca was right in front of her when this all happened. Perhaps she blamed herself for the destruction.

Mastema reluctantly spoke up to the others. "Please forgive me for my…inaction. I feel that we have no choice but to let him go. Trying to pursue him would only…hamper him now." He delicately tried to find the right words. "Even now, there's an off chance that Winona Samhain and Ercan Ao'Si…could also be dead…along with anyone inside." He tried to refrain from looking at Ercan's worried mother. "But I'm more than confident that Desiderio can stop her. His spark allows him to go against impossible odds with a chance of victory. For us…there is a zero percent chance of success, but for him, there's always an opportunity to tip the scales in his favor. Believe me, all of you… he shall never disappoint us." He looked on as the lone figure moved toward Enitharmon, not yet vaporized. "Even now he surprises me… and he will surprise you."

After taking a breath from speaking more than usual, he saw up in the air a gigantic peacock. Landing near the cluster of psychics, the bird had on its back Mayil, Zivot, Cyrille, Xiu, Julia, and Yun. Cyrille and Yun were out cold, though Yun was the one most in need of medical attention.

Rina rushed toward Julia, visibly distressed. She shook her as she spoke. "Where are Ercan and Shee'vra? Are they alright?"

Julia hated to be the one having to answer a worrying mother, but she had little choice. "I-I don't know, Mrs. Ao'Si. Last time Xiu saw Ercan or Shee'vra was in the Barbar Exhibit the Lefty Gang wanted to raid so badly."

Xiu nodded in confirmation. "This man with a cane and fedora wanted the pauldrons for some crazy reason. I took Yun away to get healed and Ercan stayed to fight him off. That's also where I saw Shee'vra last." She looked down in shame. "Maybe I should have gone back to help them."

Rina placed a hand on the Qian girl's head. "Don't beat yourself over what-if's. You did the right thing helping Yun. My children wouldn't want you to think what you have done is wrong."

Up in the sky toward the group were two figures. Actually, more like one figure along with many smaller ones. A closer look showed that it was Shee'vra and Winona flying toward them. The moment Shee'vra touched the ground, she rushed to hug her mom.

"Oh, I'm so glad you're okay, Shee'vra!" Rina said as mother embraced her daughter. "I don't know what would happen if I lost you."

Shee'vra looked around to find her brother. "…Where's Ercan?" Rina didn't answer, so she deduced where he was. "He's still facing him then." Though she was supposed to be a tough psychic, she couldn't help but open the waterworks. The thought of her brother's death was just too much.

"Why are all you guys so worried anyway?" All eyes turned on Winona, aghast at her lack of sympathy. "Most of us know for a fact that Ercan is doing his damnedest to stay alive. He's not dumb. He can avoid all that aeon no problem. The only hassle is going to be the guy he has to fight, and I hate to say it, but he has a chance." She grumbled under her breath, remembering her humiliating defeat. "Mark my words. He'll survive to see the new morning. Nobody needs a seer to know that."

Though the witch's comments were insensitive at best, Rina and Shee'vra could tell that this was Winona being "nice." Every psychic there had no choice but to watch how this all played out.

Zuo felt like a twenty-year-old again. As he and Ercan fought, he moved about with great speed and agility. He loved not having to feel his bones rub up on one another like hormonal teenagers. He'd honestly never felt stronger in his life. In fact, not even the view of flashing green lights brought down his high.

But Zuo knew better than to get comfortable. The entire mission had been compromised and more psychics were coming by the minute. The kid was also extremely annoying with his chains. Sure, it was hurting Ercan every time he tried to tie up one of his limbs, but Zuo was unlucky enough to face somebody else with quick recovery skills. As long as he wielded the Odin spark and kept him at spear length, it would only be a matter of time until Zuo claimed victory, though the fact that his hat was ruined was an irritation.

He sliced off chains pulling his right arm. "Don't you have homework or something to do tomorrow?" Zuo dodged another attempt to bind him. "If so, you should just go home already. Don't want to get yelled at by the teacher." Ercan jumped behind an ancient shield to avoid another eye laser. "In my youth back in Qian Ye, missed homework would get my ass smacked red with a ruler. Now I might just be a total bastard, but I'm pretty sure everybody has contemplated once or twice just murdering a teacher you didn't like."

Ercan was in no mood for this guy's ramblings. "Shut up already!" He created three hooked skinny chains around his feet to trip up the Lefty Gangster. The mark's effects pulled at his leg and tore at his calf, but he persevered and tackled Zuo to the ground in order to rip those pauldrons off of him.

As Ercan reeled from pain on his back from Cain's backlash, Zuo created a katar in his off hand. A stab to the gut ought to get this pest off. "Anyone ever tell you to listen to your elders?"

"Quit speaking!" Ercan shot a spear tipped chain out of his mouth to pierce Zuo's hand. Even though he made him drop the punching dagger, he couldn't help but cry out as his hand got a new hole in it.

But the moment Ercan tried to pry a shoulder pad off him, Zuo punched him square in the face. He then grabbed Gungnir and got back to his feet. "Fine, fine. If you're not going to show me respect, I won't give you any either!" He kicked the redhead in the teeth. "Damn, it feels like an orgasm and a half wearing these things! I feel so refreshed!" He pinned him down and shot a laser into the teenager's shoulder. "I can just *taste* why my boss wants these relics of the empire! The power he lusts for!" He aimed Gungnir toward the boy's heart. "But you know what? Maybe I'll just keep this power to myself. Those lazy jackasses don't deserve it. I stole them, I get them!"

Despite not knowing him and giving an awful first impression, it was obvious to Ercan that this guy was not himself at the moment. Rather than remaining calm, yet trying to get under people's skin for attack purposes, Zuo had now full on gotten drunk with power. *Must have been a side effect of those pauldrons.* In life, Barbar was supposedly quite a cocky boisterous prick to his enemies. Perhaps the pauldrons were channeling that personality into Zuo.

Ercan grabbed Gungnir with his bare hands and shot two hook chains from his feet. Getting both hooks under the shoulder pads, he bent his legs in order to pry the source of his power with force. If Zuo moved forward, the pauldrons would get stripped from him. But if he moved back, Zuo would fall over once again.

The power drunkard chose the latter. Landing onto the ground, Ercan jumped up and took his chance to try to tie him up. But Zuo would have none of it, manifesting a dagger in his shoe to stab into Ercan's thigh. Before he could persevere from the pain, the purple-eyed master of chains felt Gungnir stab through his chest and out his back. He limply froze in place as he struggled to even breathe.

"You almost had me there, chum," Zuo taunted his critically wounded foe. "But not strong enough." He twisted his spear inside Ercan, causing him to pitifully gasp. "Looks like that Xiu bitch or what's-her-name isn't going to be 'avenged' and neither is my dumbass nephew." Zuo just found himself spewing more and more shit out of his mouth, not unlike P.J. "You know how old Yun was before he learned to read signs? Six! What a dumbshit!" He shook his head at the pathetic display of a bleeding-out adolescent. "But you have too much on your mind right now to hear me, don't you? Not many can still be standing after getting stabbed in the heart I give you that."

But as he was listening intently to Ercan's slowed breathing, something perplexed Zuo. His enhanced senses picked up another thumping sound. He'd got the bastard's heart so what was the big idea? Unless…

Does this guy…have two hearts for some twisted reason? What human has that? He shrugged after losing interest. "Well no matter." Not like having two hearts is going to save him. Tipping Ercan over, he summoned Gungnir back into his hand ready to stab him again. "Time to die alone!"

But before he could even land the finishing blow, the noises and lights outside stopped. It shouldn't have been such a big deal, but it just felt off. Ignoring Ercan for a bit, he strolled about the room trying to hear what had just happened. As he moved closer to the doorway, he heard cracking and smashing, alongside explosive noises. He figured that another psychic was on his way, one that utterly disregarded museum property. But rather than stay and fight, Zuo figured he needed to leave quickly. It didn't matter whether or not he wanted to fight, he could no longer waste any more time philandering with pesky kids. Perhaps if he could make it back to base, he could even just kill the boss and take over. He always did hate some of the rules anyway. Shèng Xià would be twice the leader Reliquit ever was.

As he got ready to leave, he saw Ercan up and ready to try to tie him up again. Zuo spat on the floor in disgust, having seriously misjudged that healing factor of this kid. "Your regenerative properties sure are better than mine. But seriously, just screw off already! I'm tired of your little S&M games!" Ercan's face began to pale as his violet eyes dilated. "What? You're stepping down already? God, you're a pussy!"

The moment he finished his sentence, the smashing sounds grew way too loud for him to just not care anymore. Turning back, he saw green energy flailing about like solar flares on the sun with no consistency at all. It seemed that the overwhelming energy was destroying the entire museum wing by wing. Probably already turned a third of the building to shreds, pebbles, and splinters.

Zuo had to run away, but that damn kid followed him. As they ran, the walls around them began to break down, and licks of energy just missed them as the green came closer and closer. Still, Ercan wouldn't let him get away.

Though focused on chasing down Zuo, inside, Ercan was terrified for his life. He may have been lucky and able to handle something like a spear to the heart, but pure energy like this would kill him in a snap. It would also get rid of the killer of Xiu's entire tribe. But even with having pure aeon chasing him down, he felt followed.

As if fate pulled the rug from under him, a wave of aeon energy hit both his legs, vaporizing them nigh instantly. There was not even pain left, the nerves were just gone. It would be a hassle but such a wound would take time to heal. Time for Zuo to escape.

After traversing several hallways, Zuo ran as fast as his body would allow him, his Valknut catching the eye of the woman overloading with power. Of course, it was Enitharmon. Either somebody must have convinced her the headband was a placebo or it got broken. Whatever it was, she was screaming her lungs out as she spasmed on the ground. He took aim with his new eye as he twirled Gungnir in his hands, ready to break a record in javelin throwing.

Sorry doll. Have to put you down now. Nothing personable. Consider this mercy.

~ * ~

All of Enitharmon's pathetic muscles were going insane. They constantly contracted and relaxed on their own accord in different areas at different intervals. Breathing became extremely difficult as she lay on her back, convulsing in pain. Her stress and panic had created an amorphous mass of lime green aeon that destroyed everything it swiped at. She wanted to stop herself from wrecking everything but, without her headband, she no longer had any control of Urthona.

She forced herself to bite down on her tongue to stop herself from screaming so much. She flopped onto her stomach and tried her hardest to get to her knees. But her seizure made any progress next to impossible.

She moved her head to the side, looking through her aeon at the destruction of the museum. Hopefully she didn't destroy the pauldrons or kill Shèng Xià. That would not be what Reliquit wished. But as she tried to narrow her eyes to see, she saw a bright pink light within the green. Was it another psychic perhaps? She didn't recall any of the members she came here with having a spark that could do that. In front of this pink light, magenta rings began to manifest closer and closer toward her, weaving around her destructive energy. Suddenly, one ring appeared right in front of her. Looking through worn eyes, she saw that they were inscribed with various runes she couldn't decipher. Curious, she somehow managed to find the will to almost stand up to see it, the green energy beginning to subside as she focused on this odd creation. Checking out the other rings, she saw a bolt of pink energy flowing through each and every ring, curving around to hit each one and accelerating faster with each ring entered.

It was so sudden. One moment she found herself on her two feet, regaining something resembling control. The next, she was pinned to what remained of a wall with an energy spear through her stomach. All the aeon around her disappeared within a millisecond upon getting hit. Her mind just felt so clear now. All there was now was this feeling that everything was beginning to grow dark. She was always told that this was what happened when at death's door, but she never expected it to feel so warm.

Green liquids came out of her mouth, both kinds to her distaste. But that was death for her. She was never really pretty, and it was only natural that she would die in an ugly fashion. But just before she shut her eyes, she stepped away from the warm embrace of sleep once she heard footsteps approaching her.

"Enitharmon!"

Another person who somehow knew her name. Typical. Moving her head toward the masculine voice's general direction, she saw this stunning Titlacua man. Somehow, he managed to go halfway through her destructive spasms with not even a scratch on him. How could he do that? Yet somehow this guy seemed familiar to her. Suddenly within her mind, a hand with three eyes bled from its ocular orifices then shattered to pieces.

She knew this handsome teenager. This was Desiderio Garza, her former captain of Heron Squad. Her other teammates/friends were Dunkeen, Petra and Draghignazzo. They were always so supportive of her, though sometimes it hurt being both the eldest yet the least in control of her power. Sometimes, she just felt so babied. But Desi and the others were always kind to her no matter what.

Once she graduated, she left to work in the Psychic Division of Sorchos. It was never a pleasant place to be, but maybe, just maybe she could find a way to fix that at least a little. But then she and a few cops found a secret base and next thing she knew, some guy with eyes in his hands grabbed her face. Since then, everything just felt like a fever dream with occasional lucidity that was yanked away by those eyes within her mind.

What she had done had finally dawned upon her. Tears began to fall down her face in an absolutely unappealing manner. She muttered to her former captain as if to plead for forgiveness. "I'm sorry! I'm sorry! Why did they make me do this?"

Desiderio had no idea what she was talking about but was more than willing to console her. He held her hand in both of his, trying to keep her calm. "Shhhh. Please keep it together." He ignored the rain that began to fall due to his friend's mood. "I'm not mad at you. I can never be. You were just unfortunate. I promise none of this will happen again."

Though her eyes were still filled with tears, she forced herself to weakly smile for him. He always knew how to calm her down on her worst days. To think just now she realized how much she missed him. "I missed you, Desi. How are Dunkeen, Petra, and Drag doing?" Though those three always bickered amongst one another over trivial matters, they were still her family. Why did she leave them?

"They're alive and well," Desi tried to comfort her, trying to keep his smile on. "Dunkeen still rambles on about crap, Petra's still deliberately getting a C in her classes, and Draghignazzo is working on his comedy routines. Between you and me, Drag still needs a lot of practice." He forced himself to chuckle at his lame attempts at humor. "Come on, just heal yourself already. Please."

"That's good." Enith said to her first crush she ever had. "I hope to see them soon. I hope they won't be too mad."

"They won't be. I can assure you that. They miss you and are worried sick. After all this is over, you should move back to Bythos. We can all live in an apartment together and such. We'd be like one of those corny sitcoms you used to love so much."

Gradually but surely, Enitharmon began to slide off the spear that pierced through her as if it didn't exist. "That sounds absolutely perfect. I can't wait." She needed to say something gravely important to her captain. "But before we leave, I need to tell you something…" She looked toward the remains of the museum and gasped in horror as she saw that pink light once again.

Desiderio didn't see what was about to come. "You mean who did this to you, right? Wh-WOAH!" Green energy pushed him ten feet away.

"THREE EYES ONE HAND!"

Immediately upon shouting those words, Enitharmon was engulfed by a large beam of pink energy that utterly wiped her off the face of the planet, all but her left hand at least. The sight ingrained itself into his memories to last for decades to come. Ever since he'd become a student at the academy, his teachers always told him about the dangers of the world around them and that no matter what, he would one day have to see his friends die in front of him. Such is the life of a psychic.

Reluctantly looking down upon her open palm, he saw that there were three eyes inside her palm. *Three eyes one hand. Three eyes one hand.* He etched those words and this picture into his mind. Whoever was responsible for Enitharmon's pain was going to wish they would not survive his wrath.

Odin's End

Even though Ult'Tan Ao'Si should be concentrating on his court cases, he couldn't keep his eyes off the CV. News of a massive battle occurring at the Sephirot was on all of the channels. A copter from above displayed psychics of all ages fighting off these guys in green suits that wore masks and had a combo-platter of powers. His focus to his work only got worse once explosive green light energy stuff began to explode and spew about in a chaotic mess. The library and museum was in ruins. Even if what was going on in the news was distracting everyone in the office, nobody dared to try to turn it off or change the channel.

Some of the other lawyers at Celestine Firm resided near the area and were worried for their families and homes. Though he knew none of this would reach his house, he too feared for his family. Though coming back to his wife and kids were the highlights of his week, he knew he would never get used to them diving into danger.

It was hard to be the only hylic in the family. Sure, he never needed to risk his life, but now his entire family had to. Every time Rina or Ercan would embark on some mission near or far, he just had to wait and pray to Sophia they came back in one piece. They would always convey to him that they were fine, but who knew what could happen within ten minutes when you were in the field against criminals and wild animals?

It used to be just his wife and son, but now his baby girl was a psychic. Now he had a third person to always fear for. He once thought that maybe one day she would grow up and find a nice cushy job as an orthodontist or theatrical agent or some other non-threatening job with a good salary. He'd even saved up a lot of money for when she was to eventually go to college. But now, that was a moot point. Now he must pray for Shee'vra too.

Taking a sip of the coffee that had long gone cold, he forced himself to at least try to get his work done. All he needed to do was convince himself that if he could finish reading the file on these two gang members that Shee'vra had told him about, he could then start writing up a case for them. Then maybe, just *maybe* he could manage to go back home to his family before sunrise. He may not be able to grow giant Venus flytraps with fairy seeds, create chains on his body, or control the air, but he still had the power that any father worth their salt must have—being able to financially support his family.

"I'm back, Mr. Ao'Si." The office intern came to his desk. "I got you your barbeque chicken wrap with potato wedges and fresh *Innuk Springs* bottled water, sir."

"Thanks, Connor," Ult'Tan said graciously to the newest worker on the floor.

Connor McDooley placed his dinner on the only part of his desk without documents and files. "Forgive me if this is insulting, but you seem to be a little out of it, sir."

He wasn't wrong. "Well, have you heard what's going on at the other side of the city?" He pointed at the ongoing news without looking away from his notes.

"What's going on toda—oh." Rina had told him that one of her old squad mate's sons had just finished high school and wanted an internship while he was in college. So he convinced his boss to let him in. He was a little slow on the uptake though. How could Connor not know what was going on at a time like this?

"Sir."

"Yes?" Ult'Tan really didn't want to see what was going on anymore.

"This girl around my age just got vaporized from some kind of giant pink beam."

Sometimes, Ult'Tan wondered if life would be less horrifying without people that could vaporize anyone whenever they felt like it. He just wanted to get his work done on time. "Why are you telling me this, Connor? I have work to do."

"Sorry, sir," Connor hastily apologized, feeling that he had committed some sort of transgression. "But at the museum remains, the spear wielding maniac that just killed that woman is oblivious to some red headed high-schooler just under him. This teen seems to be restoring his lost legs and getting ready to propel himself via a chain up toward whom I assume is supposed to be the bad guy. Hope my dad kicks his ass, pardon the language."

That sounded just like his son. Peeling his eyes away from work once more, he saw on screen Ercan in torn clothes pulling himself up toward this Qian man with really odd pauldrons. The guy with this weird pink eye seemed annoyed about his son confronting him. They were definitely going to fight if they weren't already.

"Kick his ass, Ercan. I know you can do it."

Zuo's Valknut felt like it was about to burst from his skull as he covered his eye. Turns out that making a laser large enough to disintegrate an entire bus was not a practical use for his new power. At least not yet. Balra pushed that other guy away from her at the last second though. It turned out she was much too sentimental to kill any witnesses. Who knew?

But at this point, everybody was going to know what happened tonight. September 16th would become the day everyone learned the marvelous power of the Eight Relics of Kadosh. No point in killing anyone else really. But something inside his heart really wanted him to.

Quell the rebels. Quell the rebels. Quell the rebels.

That mantra repeated nonstop inside his head. It was surreal to hear such things inside your head and have it not be your own voice. Plus he was pretty sure he wasn't insane. Was he?

But as he tried to resist the temptation to impale that Titlacua kid through the stomach, he realized that somewhere deep in his heart he wanted the grieving little nance to die. But before he could get Gungnir ready for round two, he saw that annoying scarlet shithead climb up from the floor below through a hole. The kid seemed to be running out of endurance though, so that was a plus.

Ercan felt that at least two thirds of his aeon had been used up. All these injuries had been mounting up on his healing factor and draining his energy. He could have spent some time to recharge his aeon score, but that would give Zuo time to escape. He would not allow that to happen.

Zuo just groaned at having to fight him again. "You're a real wart on my ass, you know that?"

Ercan didn't even reply, merely launching three bike chains at him from the back of his right hand, each one ending in a needle. Zuo was far from impressed, grabbing all three of them in his off hand.

"That was honestly pathetic," He told Ercan upfront. "I thought you'd do a *little* bit better. This is just sad at this point."

He should not have tempted the universe by saying "point." Just after mocking the obstacle in his path, many small spikes no bigger than thorns protruded from each chain, digging into his flesh. Zuo saw how Ercan ignored the grisly mutilating of his left forearm as he yanked at the chains binding them together.

Zuo resisted, the spines digging deeper into his flesh. "Have you lost it? Do you realize the sheer agony this is causing you?" Ercan's left arm looked like it was about to fall off.

Ercan gritted his teeth as his forearm held on by a sliver of flesh. "I don't care anymore." Another tug and he was now missing a hand. "I can heal this. You can heal that. But what you've done to Xiu will never be healed and never be forgiven." With a whip of the chains, all three of the links lit on fire.

The flames burned within Zuo's arm, grilling his flesh until it was black. Zuo screamed, in more agony than he'd had in a while. Despite being able to heal from wounds real fast, he never truly got used to abusing it. Most of the time, Cain was enough deterrent to ward off any attacks. But this kid just took the power of swift rejuvenation and ran with it, mastering the art of regeneration. And for some reason, Ercan's flesh didn't burn, to both of their surprise.

"How are you not set alight by now?!"

He didn't truly think about having an answer for that question. Ercan looked at the chains coming out of his arm and saw that the flames were touching his flesh. Chances were the fire even seeped under his skin, but still he didn't feel a thing. "Well then, I guess I'm immune to fire." It made a little sense. Maybe. Huge convenience. Then again, that didn't stop him from losing a limb again.

Stopping the bleeding in his arm for now, he focused on trying to get those pauldrons off Zuo. Shooting a meat hook from the stump of his arm, Ercan aimed to rip a shoulder pad right off. Zuo countered with a whirling of Gungnir,

Next was the hard part. Zuo needed to get rid of the fire chains. They were utter torture in his flesh. Even cutting them away from their creator might not put out the fire. There was only one sure way. Cutting off his arm with his spear. For most spears, this would be stupid to impossible. For Gungnir though, the tip might as well have been a sword, an unnaturally sharp one too. With one swipe, his arm was gone and he was free. Ercan tried to tackle him onto the ground before he could ready his weapon. Though he tried to chain him down, Zuo resorted to further desperate measures.

Though his magic eye still pulsated from overuse, Zuo had little choice but to use it. As he was being tied down, he used a more dangerous technique of the Valknut—one that was only suited for up close and personal situations—one that would place much strain on him.

"Time to become broken all over."

With that, Zuo's eye glowed brighter than ever. Before Ercan could react, he was sent flying back by a magenta force that emanated all around Zuo. Upon hitting the ground, Ercan felt that his limbs and ribs had become jelly from the sheer force. As he once again wallowed in his own blood, Ercan saw the effect the attack had on Odin's user.

The eye with runes on it swelled up. Upon reaching the size of a baseball, it abruptly burst like a water balloon. Along with blood, light blue juices seeped from the wound. Like any rational to semi-rational man, Zuo hollered at the top of his lungs.

"AAAAAAHHH! MY EYE! MY NEW EYE!" The pain was utterly staggering. "IT HURTS SO BAD! GUUUUH!" He'd been screaming a while before he managed to realize that he also had a spark that granted him a way to heal such a wound. After using Cain to restore his eye and arm, Zuo regained some of his composure, though he made sure not to be so reckless with the Valknut again.

At this point, Ercan had also healed and gotten up. Round three was ready to happen. Still reeling from having an eye burst in its socket, Zuo pointed his spear at the redheaded hero. "Something tells me we're both running low on aeon by now. You more so than me, though. Seriously, how much have you healed yourself today? Is your aeon three thousand or something? You must have plenty to waste."

"I have five thousand actually," Ercan responded with a grin, trying to psyche him out. *Hope he bought that I'm only half empty. Truth is, I might just only have about ten percent left.*

Zuo didn't show any surprise. He was much too tired for that. Instead he just got into action. Not even uttering a word of dialogue, Zuo launched a charging attack. *If I can just stab right through his skull, he will die instantly. That five thousand aeon won't be worth shit then.*

But something stopped his spear mid-thrust. He even saw the very tip of Gungnir's point fall and hit the ground. That shouldn't have been possible. Gungnir was made from energy. But it somehow broke? The culprit for this was right in front of him.

"Desi?" Ercan could not believe he was here. "H-how did you even manage to get here?" Knowing how Diomedes worked, there were two theories. One was that he simply sliced and destroyed any wave of aeon coming at him in defiance to all logic. Two was that he used his aeon equalization ability to absorb the aeon into himself without any harm and helped to balance Enitharmon out. He could have done both.

He would never receive an answer though. Desiderio just stood there silently in between them, glaring at Enitharmon's killer like a lion stares down a hyena that killed one of his cubs. "Why did you do it?"

Zuo seemed utterly dumbfounded by what he thought was a stupid question. "Did you honestly not see what she was doing? She could have killed us all."

Before Zuo could make an attack, Desiderio severed Gungnir into four pieces. Ercan was amazed at his peer's skill with the blade.

"Then why did you kill her when she got back in control of herself?" Desi questioned, not buying his excuses. "You had no reason for your actions, murderer."

Too many people had been calling him that lately. It was getting tiring. "Because she would have talked! Happy you have an answer now?"

Zuo tried to blast Desi through his head with his brand new Valknut. Desi deflected the easily choreographed attack into the sky with his rapier. For some reason, his eye swelled once again to the point of bursting.

Desiderio stared down as Zuo writhed in pain again. "Ever since our weapons locked, I have equalized our aeon. You only had about a quarter left. Mine is just forty-three. If you know your aeon score and some math, you should guess how weak you are right now," he pointed his rapier at his throat, "though I am very tempted to not give you that time."

"Wait!" Ercan put a hand out in front of the superior captain. "You see the mark on his chest? Whenever he gets hit, you'll get hurt far more. If you slit his throat or pierce his heart, you're as good as dead." Desi was usually an upbeat pervert; it was chilling to see him so dead serious. "I know what he did will never be forgiven, but killing him would only kill you. Don't let everyone lose you too. Enitharmon would never have wanted that."

Desiderio felt like that indigo mark was the most cowardly spark he'd ever heard of. A spark that allowed the user to deter retaliation without punishment. "Then what would you have me do? He killed a Heron without even hesitating." Enith saving him at the last second was still fresh within his mind. His father always said it wasn't masculine to cry, but he couldn't help but shed a few tears. "What would you have me do?"

Ercan knew exactly what to do. The same thing he promised to Xiu. "Then I'll fight in your place. All you need to do is help me get those pauldrons off of him." Ercan rattled his chains. "Then I can take him in alive. Got it?"

Before Desi could give a proper answer, Zuo got back up once again. His eye had healed for the second time. "You little shits. There's no way I'm going to just let you take me alive." He recreated Gungnir and twirled it. "Fight me again!"

Zuo must have been desperate by now. He fought like a cornered cobra against a mongoose. Ercan and Desiderio were forced to fight defensively. Zuo needed to keep midrange at the moment. Too close and the swashbuckler got him. Too far and he got restrained. As the three fought, Zuo noticed that some of the psychics who ran from the area were beginning to come back. Now there was no escape.

Feeling cornered, he scrambled inside his head to figure out a possible exit to this situation. But he just couldn't find one. A voice inside his head offered its advice. It told him that it was all over at this point, but it could also become the end of everyone in the entire vicinity. Its words were shockingly tempting to Zuo, who felt odd that he seemed so compliant with this proposition. The words "Blast them all" rang so loudly within his head that it would be criminal not to try.

He stomped his foot and aeon enveloped his entire body in magenta energy. His inner thoughts made him want to speak out with as much ham as possible. The world would remember him forever. "THIS IS WHERE YOU THINK IT ENDS, HUH?!" Zuo shouted out in defiance. "WELL IT WON'T BE! BARBAR HAD ONE MORE TRICK UP HIS SLEEVE!" Both his Valknut and Gungnir began to flash wildly and increase in size. "ALL OF YOU HAVE JUST PUT YOURSELVES IN THE GRAVE! I'M GOING TO BLOW THE HELL UP!" Panic entered Ercan and Desi's hearts. Desiderio tried to cut the pauldrons off of him, but Zuo grabbed Desi's hand. "EITHER WE ALL DIE OR ONE OF YOU KILL ME! WHO'S GONNA BE THE MARTYR, HUH!? WHO!? WHOOOOOOOO!?" The voice of Barbar wanted Zuo to laugh into the sky. "COME KILL ME, COWAAAARDS!"

~ * ~

Nine Years Ago

Zuo Xuanzang wandered the Winter Turtle District's alleyways. He'd left Jakaire in the motel to sleep for the night. The last few days had been harsh for her. It had been harsh for both of them. She'd just lost her family and he was now a wanted man. It turned out that killing your own country's soldiers and going AWOL was treason. Who knew?

Normally they would have snuck out of the country by now, but he needed to see somebody first. He passed by city folk selling commodities such as drugs, bootlegs, weapons, alcohol, their own bodies, and their skills in murder. Finally, Zuo found the bar he was looking for: The Wasted Panda. He could tell because of the neon Panda that staggered about as it took swigs out of a bottle.

Listening from the outside, the place seemed to be full of patrons chatting about random crap. The moment he pushed the doors open though, everybody in the bar from the town drunk to the dirty cop looked at him and froze up. To think his mere presence inspired so much terror. I mean he was just a lanky man with a cane. I guess that happens when you become part of a bar fight that ended with two dead,

440

three comatose, and somebody losing a jaw.

But he was here for one reason and one reason only. "Where's Xing?" A guy missing an eye pointed at a disheveled drunk sitting on a stool, his face on the counter and a bottle of booze in his hand. "Thank you, pal." He tipped his fedora at him and headed toward the drunkard. He poked him with his cane and he only grumbled in response. Having no time for this, he grabbed the man's head by his hair.

"Ow, ow, ow, ooooow. I told you I'd pay in a bit." Xing found himself face to face with his older brother. "Oh…it's just you. You had me worried there for a bit. Do you mind if you pay for my drink? I'm a little bit short."

Every time he did this it infuriated Zuo to no end. Rather than even try to work to support his wife and son, all he did was live off of welfare and waste any money he got his hands on for cheap liquor. "Fine." He slammed forty-two paz onto the counter. "You need to come with me, though. It's of upmost importance, brother." He made it sound as much of a demand as possible.

Xing groaned but knew it was next to impossible to deny his brother. "Fine, fine. Just let me get on my two feet." The moment he tried to walk, he staggered about. Zuo merely grabbed somebody's water and splashed it all over his brother's face. "GAAH! COLD! The Hell was that for?"

"Come. With. Me." Zuo exited The Wasted Panda, his brother reluctantly following suit.

The siblings walked without speaking for what seemed to be at least three miles. Soon enough, they came upon a broken bridge that nobody was around.

"So why do you want me here so badly that you couldn't just tell me before we took a hike?"

Zuo immediately got to business. "I'm leaving Qian Ye."

Xing could hardly register what his brother was saying. "What? Why?" It dawned on him what this must be. "You've deserted haven't you? Wasted your comfy psychic life over a mere disagreement, huh? Coward."

He tried to keep himself in check from such an accusation, but it was harder than Zuo thought it would be. "Tai Xun had me and others murder an innocent tribe from the Eversnow Mountains. Did you just expect me to just not care?”

“What does it matter?” Xing said coldly. “I heard about the tribe you just killed. They were Demiurge cultists. They murdered our leader in cold blood. And you have the nerve to abandon your country?”

Zuo shook his head. “None of that is true. There were no altars, no sacrifices, nothing of the sort. They did *nothing* to us and we slaughtered them in the middle of the night.” He felt it was useless to try justifying himself, so he moved on to the next important subject. “Because of all this crap, I won’t be able to support you, your wife, or your son. I demand as your elder brother that you find a job pronto.”

Xing groaned in frustration. “Really? But all the jobs here are shit.”

“I know that you don’t have the opportunities as some others out there. But you have a responsibility to your family to support them. Any job would do at this point, just anything but wallowing around!” He became as stern as he could. “And if I ever hear that you’ve been hitting them again, I’ll be sure to come back—fugitive status be damned.”

Xing spat onto the ground. “Why do you insist on butting into my life?”

“Because I’m the one keeping your family afloat.” If their parents were around, they would consider Xing a disgrace. “The least you can do is treat your wife and son as something other than a burden.” If he didn’t intend to marry, then he should not have gotten somebody pregnant.

“Dammit!” Xing stomped his foot. “Do you realize how weak I feel right about now?”

“Don’t care.” *Here he goes again.*

“Do you have any idea what it’s like to be a lower class hylic?” Xing questioned his brother. “I have no opportunities whatsoever. You, at least, can get missions and shit to score big money. All I get is the scraps. Do you realize how lucky you are to be a psychic? Hell I’d kill a kitten to get a spark, *any* spark. I hate being a hylic so freaking much!”

Zuo had for a long time known about Xing’s envy for psychics of all kinds. Something gave him the feeling that he became so frustrated by his lack of spark over the years that he began taking his anger out on his family. Zuo had seen the bruises and black eyes he inflicted on his nephew and sister-in-law and had had enough of it. It was time for an ultimatum.

"Stop drinking, get a job, and stop hurting Mei and Yun. This is your last warning."

Xing was not intimidated by his notorious brother. Perhaps it was the alcohol still in his system. "Or *what?*"

He had warned him. He'd put up with his crap for years now. But brother or not, Zuo was not leaving this man with what remained of his family. He created a knife in his hand. "Fine, then."

Grabbing Xing by the head, he stabbed him straight in the throat. Xing struggled for a little bit, gagging on his own blood, but Zuo did not let go. Eventually the struggling slowed, and then his brother became motionless. Zuo had read in his Spark Region that some people in the old world used to believe that Cain was the first human who ever committed murder. The first victim was his younger brother Abel. This felt oddly fitting, though Zuo wondered if Cain ever felt an ounce of guilt in his hundreds of years of life. He felt it already. His brother may have been what many would call an asshole, but Zuo knew he'd still committed the most unforgivable of familial sins.

But he did the deed and now he must live with his decision. He dumped Xing's body into the river and slowly walked back to the motel. Hopefully, Jakaire was still asleep. Didn't want her to be worrying about him, or worse, looking for him. They were ditching Qian Ye tomorrow and any speed bumps on the way could seriously hurt their chances.

The energy around Zuo became more and more intense as the explosion became imminent. Ercan had to do something to save himself and Desi. But what? Zuo was going to blow up any second and there was no way to escape in time. *So…this is how it's ending then?*

Ercan felt a calming chill come onto him as he created a spear point at the end of his chain. His hand trembled as it aimed for Zuo's throat. He saw that the other psychics were still rushing toward them a block away. *They won't stop. They won't. If I don't do something, we all die. I… have no choice. Please forgive me, Shee'vra.*

There was one thing the symbol of Aeon Sophia Academy never told them—the sword meant courage, but also sacrifice. This was a cruel end, but if it were to save psychics more skilled than him, he would do it all again.

But before his weapon could pierce his foe, a bloody clawed hand shot out of Zuo's chest. As Zuo gasped, all of the magenta energy that was being stored disappeared. Ercan and Desiderio saw that right behind the man was a familiar hyena badger beastman.

Louiz gasped in his attempt to speak. His lungs and heart were destroyed and he no longer even had a chest anymore. He could have just escaped; he'd considered it for a good while now. But seeing what those pauldrons could do first hand, his guilt would take over his very being. These artifacts were most definitely not meant to be used by anyone. If somebody managed to round all of them up, nothing would be the same anymore.

Did Louiz regret his decision? Yes, he did. There was no way he would survive. But even now he debated whether or not he even wanted to survive this night. His life would be over either way. If he lived, he would be sent to Prisoner's Perch. He might have a reduced sentence for helping preserve the pauldrons, revealing what he knew about The Lefty Gang, and perhaps good behavior. But counting the stuff he'd done, he would still be behind bars for years to come. Even after prison, where would he go? He couldn't go back to Dorado; they thought he was a fraud. Bythos (and probably all of Enotita) would treat him like a crook that only got out for being a snitch. Even if he got a job working as a mercenary or guardian, he would still inevitably have to sleep with one eye open. The Lefty Gang would never forgive him for his treachery.

Perhaps this was his best option. Perhaps he was just scared of what was to come. Fear of what would happen in the future. Fear of what his old fiancé would think of him when she learned what he'd been doing over these years. Maybe…the world didn't need him. But the world needed these kids. They had their whole lives ahead of them. He did not. Perhaps he could give these two some parting words at least.

"Don't…waste this." Louiz fell over, his hand leaving Zuo's body. As it all went dark, he became human for the last time. But at least he saw that those two boys wouldn't let this opportunity fade.

Ercan ripped off one pauldron with a hook and Desiderio cut the straps of the other. The last thing Louiz heard was the clanking of metal as they threw the artifact right behind their shoulders. *At least I did something of…*

Zuo gasped and struggled to look back at the corpse of Izquierda.

That traitor. I had this in my hands. Coward got himself killed so he could stop me from blowing up. Something dawned on him. *Wait. Why did I even think of blowing myself up? I would die. I might be old, but I don't want to die.* He looked down to see the gaping hole in his chest. *Oh holy dear Sophie frickadoodle! I've got to heal this!*

Ercan looked on as Zuo went to his knees and began to heal his colossal injury. With the situation no longer as dire, both he and Desi had the same idea. Let the guy restore himself back to health. At this point, he was no longer much of a threat. Odin was gone.

Once the hole in his chest was closed and a new heart created, Zuo got back to his feet. "Why the hell did you not bother to chain me up when you had the chance?" He was completely open; it was a perfect chance to disable him completely.

Ercan went behind Zuo. "One of the things we learn in Aeon Sophia Academy is mercy."

"If we'd just pinned you down, you wouldn't have been able to concentrate on restoring your heart," Desiderio explained as he kept his distance. "It wouldn't have been very honorable to let you just die like that. We academy kids at least *try* to have a sense of decency." *Though maybe someone like Winona or Gaizka would have their minions rip you in two.*

"The least you could do is not resist," Ercan said as he created a pair of handcuffs. "It's the least you could do after all the trouble you've caused."

Zuo let out a deep sigh. "Fine." He was all out of aeon at this point so it was no use struggling. "But I'll never reveal anything." As he put his hands behind his head, he winced in pain as he once again felt his bones rub together as usual. It was done. The Mark of Cain faded away as Zuo admitted defeat.

Victory for Now

The lack of casualties among the students and the authorities were nothing short of a miracle, though that could not be said about the library, museum, and a good chunk of the block. It was like something out of a disaster flick. Some of the professional psychics went in to check out what had happened after the green aeon subsided but insisted that no students come with them.

"Great Grasshopper of the Ground. Look at this damage." Vural looked at the remains of a once popular tourist destination. "What was around for decades, gone in mere minutes." The power of sparks were never anything to laugh at (most of them anyway) but some sparks could shake the will of even the most resolute psychics.

Mastema was personally unfazed. "We'll…worry about this in a while. It's nothing my grandfather cannot deal with himself." He noticed Bianca was looking quite down on herself. She usually had a stoic expression, but genuine sadness was rare to see. "Is something the matter, Bianca?"

Bianca seemed wracked with guilt. "I feel like I caused this devastation. If I hadn't tampered with Enith's headband, she may not have gone berserk like she did." She shook her head as she looked at the perfectly mundane piece of wool. "Somebody must have convinced her that it would help her control herself. If only I'd known."

"Nobody could have just guessed what it did," Hanako tried to reassure her. "I also assumed the headband was somehow responsible.

Maybe." Truthfully, she was just trying to make her friend feel better. She had been much too frightened to really think much about it.

Mastema placed a hand on the princess's shoulder. "You did what you thought was right. Nobody should ever blame you for that."

"Yeah. If anything, it should be my fault," Basil told his captain. "I'm the one who put her down when I had her in my grip. If anything, I messed up more."

Caradoc nodded in affirmation. Sadly, it was truly Basil's moment of mercy that caused the decimation of an entire block. No sugarcoating it. "It may be your fault. But let's face it, we're taught mercy in school. But realistically, sometimes mercy can just make things worse."

Basil died a little inside. "That's a dark way to put it."

"I'm sorry. But sometimes that's just how it is." Caradoc felt safe enough at this point to have his scimitars disappear. "No matter what, there will never be a perfect answer. We just need to follow what we believe would make things better. Then again, you did prevent her from lobbing a big ball of energy that could level the city."

Though the captains and her two squadmates spoke amongst themselves, Bianca still couldn't shake the feeling that both Enith and Desiderio could be dead because of her. If she couldn't save two people, how would she be able to protect Titlacuan? What sort of worthless Shrivatsa would she become?

"Fear not," Mastema said to her. "I feel that Desi…managed to reach her in time. Her aeon is no longer around, so I assume…he must have brought her back to her senses. With Enitharmon on our side… the Lefty Gang won't stand a chance." He chose not to add the off chance that the large influx of green aeon was gone because Enith was killed. She had enough on her mind as it was.

Off to the side, Winona looked through the eyes of one of her crows. She inspected what was going on around the battleground. As she scanned the area, she saw that Ercan and Desi were victorious.

"Pardon me, but what do you see, exactly?" Alexandru was savvy enough to know when she was spying on others.

"The two won," Winona replied dismissively, "though they might have been blown up if it weren't for this…one guy sacrificing himself to give them time to remove the relic."

Ludmila was a bit confused. "What relic, exactly?" She kept her armor on; still not sure whether she would need it. "And how would an item grant powers?

Winona groaned. "You guys are so nosy. Somehow, the shady guy who Ercan was fighting had some kind of weird spark that was connected to the Pauldrons of Kadosh."

"You mean Emperor's Barbar's shoulder gear?" Gaizka chimed in. "I did a report on that guy last year. Real battle-maniac. Gotta admire the guy. Was this gangster shit-stain using Gungnir?"

Winona went to school, so she among hundreds of millions of other people knew what Gungnir was. "Yeah, that Lefty Gang guy was wielding it for a good chunk of the time." She was usually dismissive of this kind of stuff, but she felt the need to tread lightly on her next few words. "It seemed that he used Gungnir to kill Enitharmon. That's why the green energy is all gone." She chose not to mention her being annihilated by a pink beam of energy. Her death was horrible enough to mention already. *I'll let Desi tell them if he feels the need to.*

Though the three seniors never really knew much about Enitharmon, they all knew that she died before her time. If only they knew who had done this to her. Alexandru would destroy his mind, Ludmila would beat the organs out of him, and Gaizka would tear the villain in half with his bare hands. Even Winona was dreading the day she met face to face with whoever had controlled Enith.

But at least tonight was behind them. They would all live at least. The captains found enough comfort in that knowledge.

Shee'vra did not pay much attention to the captains as they talked. She was mostly just focused on what was happening to her brother. The last time she saw him, he was about to face off with someone who had just activated some magic shoulder pads that gave him a new spark. She wasn't the only one concerned either. *Xiu must be beating herself up about letting him fight her fights. If…the worst happens…I don't want to think about it.* She turned back to see Mayil and Julia restoring Cyrille and Yun back to health.

"That should do it for now," Julia remarked, sounding tired. "Let's just wake them up. Worst comes to worst, we're going to need them."

"Agreed, Lady Themelia." Mayil snapped his fingers once and Cyrille was awake. "Welcome back, Master."

The bag over his head tore as Cyrille once again turned into a Basilisk. "Thank you so much, Mayil and Zivot! What would I do without you two?"

"Have different bodyguards?" Julia replied to a question not directed at her. Julia merely smacked Yun back from unconsciousness.

On instinct, Yun checked to see if his stomach was still intact. No pain, but he felt his cheeks sting as his eyes opened. "You know, Jules, you could have just asked me to wake up." He saw that it was still night time and he was lying in the middle of the road. He jumped back up. "Where's Zuo?"

Zivot slowly began to answer him. "Ercan Ao'Si felt the need to—"

"Ercan is faced off against that monster." Xiu did not care what relation he had to Yun, he would always be vile in her books. Even now, she had just learned that bastard's name. "Zuo is not getting out of this. He'd better not."

Yun felt uneasy immediately, remembering what hitting his uncle once did to him. "He's there alone? We should do something at least! He could die!" He stared forward to see the sheer devastation that had occurred. "What…what happened?"

"Massive bursts of pure aeon decimated the entire block," Mayil solemnly answered him. "I had to fly you and the others out by the skin of my teeth." He bowed his head. "I'm sorry, but I had no time to find Ercan as well."

Noxious liquids began to pour out of Cyrille's tear ducts. "So Ercan's gone forever?" He began to bawl in a way that did not suit his age, with everyone stepping away to avoid his noxious tears.

"Seriously, Cyrille? Stop crying." Xiu was in no mood to see people cry. It was making her eyes puffy too. "I'm sure Ercan and Desi are just fine. Probably beat that Zuo guy's ass by now." This was beginning to sound like wishful thinking. "Figured out a way to sneak around his weird markings. I mean Ercan may not be captain material but he's The Unbreakable. He can't just die before he even graduates." She made sure nobody saw the tears welling in her eyes. "I'm not the only one that thinks that's right?"

Julia ignored the crying of the chicken and gave Xiu a concrete answer. "If I didn't know better, I'd think you're going to miss him."

It was no time for any teasing, though. "It isn't right. But let's face it; none of us know the full potential of our sparks yet. That could mean two things. One is that Ercan was overwhelmed before he could master his true potential. The other is that what he knows now was enough to save himself."

Yun tried to reassure Xiu. "I can bet you a crap ton of paz that both he and Desi are still kicking. They may be a bit beat up, but nothing too serious." He would like to think that his uncle would at the very least try to hold back against his friends, though that was unlikely. He spoke to Shee'vra. "If you say that those bronze shoulder pads were what gave Zuo new abilities, that means all Ercan had got to do is take them off him, which would be a cinch with Desiderio's help. Then all Ercan had to do was pin him down, withstand the pain, and chain him up."

"You make it sound really easy, actually." Shee'vra began to feel a bit better, though Xiu didn't seem very convinced. "Maybe a little too easy."

Mayil interrupted the mourning. "I see that the old psychics are back. I feel this is good news."

Cyrille stopped bawling for a second. "Good…news?"

"Yes, Master Cyrille." Zivot repeated what Mayil said. "It seems that the adults are back, and somebody appears to be wrapped up in Mr. Jahikah's bandages. If I could make a fair guess, I would say that the criminals have been captured." She felt the chilly wind upon her back, regretting that she was still wearing nothing but pajamas.

True to their word, Aluja Jahikah was walking ahead of the group with Zuo wrapped in tight bandages. The criminal had a Sarkic collar around his neck. Each one felt relief, feeling that it was all officially over.

Mr. Jahikah acknowledged their existence. "If you're looking for your friends, they're just behind us." He didn't look at any of them as he continued to walk on by with Zuo marching in front of him.

Just behind those two was Mr. McDooley, audibly cracking his neck. "I guess you squirts are wondering what went down, huh?"

"Yes."

The cyclops ignored Cyrille answering his rhetorical question. "Well Ercan and Desi managed to stop the Lefty Gang guy that just passed by you seven. He's the only member of the gang we could find alive though." His one eye squinted. "It seems that five of them are dead, though Ercan reported that there was supposed to be eight members in total. I honestly try hard not to condone killing your opposition, but I have a feeling that you all must have had little choice."

Monoceros was carrying a stretcher along with a few other psychics that carried three corpses. Cyrille and his guards recognized Sinister's hunting vest, and Xiu glared at what remained of Ezker. Julia knew there was nothing left of Kairieji to even carry. Shee'vra and Yun could not help but feel pity of sorts once they saw Louiz's dead body.

"But we'll be contacting any known family members of these folks and finding out where to bury them." Monoceros proceeded to move on. "I don't know any of these guys, but hopefully they had some loved ones out there. Shame they have to learn about any possible secrets the hard way."

Watching the older psychics walk off, Yun made the bold decision to follow them. "I'm sorry, guys, but I need to speak with my uncle right now."

As she saw her fellow disciple follow the professionals to speak to Zuo, Xiu contemplated whether to follow or not. That killer seriously deserved a dislocated jaw for all he put her through and this was probably her only chance. At the very least she could insult him about his choices in life. But then again, Yun probably had that covered anyway. No point in dwelling on the piece of trash. Perhaps she could congratulate Ercan and Desiderio for taking down her parents' killer. But she felt that at a moment like this, there were too many people around. She wanted a more private conversation.

"Hey, Sheev." She got Ercan's sister's attention. "Tell him I said thanks and I'll see him tomorrow in class."

Though the request was sort of out of the blue, Shee'vra had no reason to refuse. "Alright, Xiu." She and Cyrille ran toward the general direction of the captain of Rooster Squad. "See you tomorrow for training!"

"Sure, sure." Xiu began to wander off back home. It was time for her to leave anyway. The day had been extremely stressful, and she needed her beauty sleep anyway. Perhaps tomorrow she could find the right words to thank both of them.

"You have the right idea," Julia said to her, sounding completely tired. "I want to get to sleep ASAP also, though I do admit that on days like this I feel bad about voting you out of the squad." She gave a rare contented grin. "You ever miss being a Rooster?"

Xiu had an answer for that. "In this moment of time, I feel honored to be both a Rooster and a Heron." They were both amazing birds in their own ways, both magnificent and having their own sort of grace to them.

"Real cheesy of you to say, Xiu," Julia remarked dryly. "Kind of lame actually. Popular girls like you shouldn't say such things."

"Whatever, nerd." Xiu would never understand why she would always casually say things like that. So unladylike. "And take a shower. You smell."

"Up yours, bitch." Julia playfully flipped her off. They smiled as they both went opposite directions back to their homes.

Mayil and Zivot watched the whole thing, stunned. "Are such insults truly healthy for friendships?"

Mayil gave an unsure shrug. "I don't really understand either. Thank Sophia, Master does not speak to others in such a crude manner."

Ercan walked alongside Desiderio and his mother. Desi seemed to be in no mood to speak. In fact, he seemed utterly devastated as the captain of Heron Squad held and stared at Enitharmon's hand. Ercan observed that there were three eyes sketched onto her palm. Not being able to recall that Enith had any such markings, perhaps this was a warning of sorts. A clue for what was behind all of this.

As Ercan focused on the hand, his mom spoke to him sternly. "What you did was extremely stupid." In her hands was the relic the Lefty Gang wanted so badly.

"I-I am sorry, mother. I felt that if I just ran away, things would have gotten much worse," he hated it when he was scolded, "though it doesn't excuse me for putting others at risk." Now that all this was over, he felt deeply concerned about what had happened to his friends. "But is everyone alright? Please tell me nobody died because I made a situation worse."

"All of your schoolmates are just fine, as are the BPD. Some are a little more banged up than others, but nothing life threatening or career ending." Rina looked directly at the kid she was raising as her own. "Each one fought extremely bravely for this city and, thanks to them, the civilians managed to evacuate the premises before everything went south." She sighed like any concerned mother. "I just wish you had managed to keep Shee'vra out of this mess. She's not ready for this kind of action." Though knowing her daughter, chances were Shee'vra would have still tried to help her squad despite the dangers. "As her older brother, you need to keep a sharp eye on her progress. I hope I can trust you with that."

Ercan paused for a moment but answered with honesty. "Of course. I'll find new ways to hone Shee'vra's skills no matter what." Lucky for him, he wouldn't be alone in that endeavor. Xiu would be teaching her Chin Na as well, and he was sure that the others would pitch in to help her be at her best.

"Relieved to hear that," his mom replied to him. "Though I am honestly extremely tempted to ground you, I'll resist the urge. You did what you thought was right and stopped them from stealing an important relic."

Though he felt a weight leave his shoulder when he was told that he would not be grounded for his rash actions, there were other concerns he had. "But the museum and library are utterly destroyed—priceless artifacts gone forever. I can't shake the feeling that it could have been avoided."

"Don't worry about that, son," Rina assured him with a serene smile. "Raziel will handle the mess. In a few minutes, it will be like nothing was ever destroyed." That was a good enough answer for Ercan. Rina then grew wings and began to fly up. "I'll be going home now to make sure I don't embarrass you in front your friends."

As she left, Ercan walked alongside Desiderio, who began to softly speak up. "You know I am truly envious you have a mother like that. Mine just married a man thirty years her elder in order to live rich, then left me to nannies to attend parties and cruise trips. Yours just seems so well adjusted, satisfied with her life, supportive of her children and actually loving the man she married. You have it so easy."

"I've been told that before." Ercan took no offense to that comment. "And it's true. I have had it easy over these years. But now, I feel that life is just going to get harder and harder from here on out. For all of us."

"I won't disagree with that," Desiderio said somberly. "If you must know though, Xiu will be just fine in my squad. I suggest you don't perseverate about whether or not she's fitting in."

"Good to know that. Thanks." He looked at his completely ruined clothes. His sleeves were completely torn; his pants were now shorts, and various rips were everywhere. "Man, I do wish that I looked presentable, though. I look like some kind of retro caveman." At least he still had his medallion intact.

The two of them came across their classmates waiting for them, receiving a warm greeting that they questioned if they truly deserved. Gaizka, Hanako, Vural, Ludmila, and Alexandru all applauded for them. Winona merely scoffed as if she was right about something super predictable and became a murder of crows to fly away home.

"You two look like you've seen a ghost," Gaizka commented to them. "But you both kicked ass. Kudos." He heartily patted both their backs.

Hanako was overjoyed to see her peers alive, a petite smile across her face. "You two were amazing! I wish I had the courage to stand up against a Lefty enforcer!" The group hardly ever heard her speak up in joy. She truly sounded lovely when she raised her volume.

Vural would be grinning if it were not for the fact that he had mandibles. "You guys were kickass. Wish the adults had let me come too." He looked away in frustration, his scarf blowing in the wind. "Then this would have ended twice as fast."

"I was told by your sister what that man could do," Ludmila lauded Ercan. "It seemed that you were perfect for the job."

As the four huddled around Ercan, Alexandru seemed to be the only one of the five to notice that Desiderio seemed to be looking quite blue. Once he saw Enith's hand, he personally chatted with the grieving captain. "I'm sorry Desi. If only I could have done something to prevent it."

"It's fine," Desiderio lied through his teeth. "It just goes to show how dangerous the life of a psychic is. McDooley is correct and will always be. None of us are going to die of old age."

That ruined the overall uplifting mood. But the dhampyr did have a retort. "Perhaps so. But that won't prevent us from trying to live our lives to the fullest. You of all people should know that. You dance, you drink, and you have relations with exotic members of the opposite sex. You live a life that most of us no doubt envy. But like the rest of us, you're going to have obstacles." Alexandru did not look his peer in the eyes. "I'm not hypnotizing you when I give you this advice, so either take it or leave it. Enitharmon would not have wanted you to just break down over her death. She would want you to remain who you truly are; improve even. Try to at least uphold her wishes for you and your squad."

"Perhaps that is what she would want." Desi put Enith's hand in his pocket, not caring about how gross such a thing was. He would have to give her remains to the authorities later as evidence. He noticed Bianca was also looking a bit down. "Princess, you're the only one of us who has yet to vote for Ercan's trial. What are you leaning toward, in or out? To be honest, I voted against him." Seeing what the redhead had done today, he was beginning to regret his decision.

Bianca tried to get out of her funk and address one of her subjects. "I have yet to truly think much about it. I feel like I should address him when he is not as overwhelmed." The three of them looked on as Ercan was greeted and hugged by his overjoyed sister and a chicken man. Even Caradoc and Basil were in on the celebrating, with Basil bringing a chunk of the students into a bear hug. "Hopefully that won't be too long from now. I need to speak to him."

"I guess," Alexandru replied without much thought. "To be honest, this whole election thing is kind of juvenile anyway. I am personally more worried about the fact that an entire city block is missing, though that might just be me. I don't know."

"It's not odd to think that." The spiffy man in purple nearly jumped when he noticed Mastema behind him. "But your worries are… unnecessary." He stared upwards.

All the students and even the older psychics checked above them to see Enotita's Guardian Angel and current Dhvaja Raziel Mattatron. His six wings radiated so brightly it made it seem as if it was daytime. The superintendent of Aeon Sophia Academy stared down at the wreckage in mourning.

"This night, lives have been lost, both innocent and guilty! But this land will not become ruins as long as I am still walking! As guardian of Enotita, I use my power to heal this city's wounds!" He threw his flaming sword into the ground. "With the power of Shamsiel, I restore my sanctuary back to its glory."

In that instant, everyone watched in wonderment at how the street and buildings began to repair themselves. Artifacts were restored, cars went back to mint condition, and gargoyles were put back in place. Within half a minute, it was as if nothing had even touched the area. But Raziel still spoke to any who would listen.

"Though our sanctuary is preserved, we must still remember the lives of those who are no longer with us!" With that, Bythos's Guardian Angel left as soon as he had come.

"Your grandfather sure is amazing," Bianca complimented Mastema, "to be able to just fix landmarks as casually as taking a walk."

"Indeed," the younger angel replied. "He is my greatest role model. I must strive to find a way…to live up to him." How he would be able to live up to his family name would be a question he would have to figure out another day. "I have observed that the line to Ercan is smaller. Now's your chance…to speak with him if you must."

Bianca gave a tired sigh. "We all might as well get this over with. Ercan!"

"Yeah, Bianca?" Ercan was quick to acknowledge the superior psychic. "What do you need?"

"I'll cut to chase. This is about your trial," Bianca said with all seriousness.

Ercan was shocked she was bringing this up now. "Really? Can't this wait until tomorrow or something?"

At that moment, he got a text from his crystalcell. It was a miracle it hadn't broken during everything that had happened tonight. Checking the message, it came from his father, saying *Saw it all on the news. Proud of my kids*. Ercan looked at his sister, who also must have gotten a similar text.

"It's rude to check your phone in the middle of a conversation," Bianca felt the need to remind him. Once she had his attention again, she continued. "We have the results of eight of the nine voters. Four voted for you to keep your captain position, four wanted it stripped from you." She kept her no-nonsense demeanor as she spoke. "After our battle, I initially thought to vote against you. But seeing how you defeated a major threat with no permanent harm to your teammates, I changed my mind." She offered a hand to shake. "Congratulations, Ercan Ao'Si. You are still a captain. I expect to see you tomorrow."

Ercan was overjoyed at the news, but deep inside felt that this wasn't right. During his time as captain, he had made many blunders. He had led many losses, made easily avoidable mistakes, and refused to blame himself for Rooster Squad's issues for the longest time. This last week had made him question whether his crusade to retain his position was even worth it at this point. His responsibilities would only become greater and greater and, if he wasn't sure he could handle it, the safest thing to do would be to simply turn it down. Keeping his position carelessly might just risk everyone. But who would replace him?

Julia Themelia seemed to be the most likely candidate. She was easily the most intelligent in the entire squad and the most cool-headed. She had also shown the versatile uses of Thoth more than once. But she also had stated to not want the position at all. Perhaps if she were pressured into the position she would begrudgingly accept, though it never seemed to be a wise idea to force somebody into leadership. She would probably half-ass the paperwork too.

Yun Xuanzang was another option. He was easily the strongest, fastest, and most durable in the entire group once he turned into a monkey. Martial arts were also a bonus. Downsides were that he might be too impulsive and easily duped. Sadly, even Ercan had to admit that his best friend was not exactly super bright. Probably wouldn't exactly care much for paperwork either. Damn, that paperwork was a nightmare sometimes. It would become night terrors for Yun.

Then there was the newest member; his little sister, Shee'vra. Though she was the sweetest girl he knew, signing her up in such an elite position boasted the most problems. She was still extremely green in the psychic ways and most definitely would subconsciously hold back even if her life was on the line. Besides, making her captain could paint a huge target on her back for any possible enemies. But perhaps when he finally graduated, she would have the skills to captain her own squad. Besides, he would feel bad about dumping the paperwork responsibility onto her.

So that left the rooster of Rooster Squad. Ercan tried to think of any qualities that could disqualify Cyrille Coq DeRoche. He didn't have a single malicious bone in his body, very protective and did not look down on anyone. Though he was a bit out there, he had surprisingly decent grades. One time he'd asked him how he possibly got a ninety-seven percent on a geometry test and Cyrille replied, "It would be inconsiderate not to listen to the teachers and try my hardest because they are trying their hardest with us." Though he wasn't exactly the most durable psychic in school, he was a good swordsman and the Basilisk spark was pretty much a win the moment it made any contact. He also essentially had his own little squad anyway with Zivot and Mayil.

In fact, there were only two downsides to such a decision. One was that a reptilian rooster with weird chameleon eyes would possibly creep out some people; the other was that Ercan felt a little ashamed that he was throwing his captain responsibility onto him, though he did recall that Cyrille had occasionally mentioned that some of his family members had mocked him for working under a "commoner." Perhaps this was an opportunity to make some of the more elitist DeRoches eat their words. Besides, maybe some people would find a toothy beaked scaly chicken oddly endearing. Cyrille would also definitely never skimp out on the paperwork anyway. Ercan would make it his responsibility to keep the work small.

He took a deep breath and saw that the rooster was still shedding toxic tears of joy into a handkerchief. It was time for Ercan to give an answer. "Cyrille." From Bianca's reaction, she seemed to pick up on what he was about to say.

"What do you need, hero of the day?" Cyrille was anxious to know. "Did you have some revelation of the events to come or perhaps you need a handkerchief to happy cry. Sadly, I have already coated my hanky in poisonous tears and toxic mucus so I cannot give it to you." He put his hazardous piece of white and green cloth back into his pocket. "But if you want my opinion on the current events, I will have to say it will be uphill from here."

"I want you to be captain of Rooster Squad."

Cyrille's comb lowered for a bit, trying to absorb that simple proposition. "Me? Why? Do you feel as if you didn't earn it?"

Ercan shook his head. "Maybe, maybe not. I don't really know myself. But I feel like Rooster Squad would be better off with an actual rooster as its captain. Besides, isn't the DeRoche family meant to be all about caring for those under them? You qualify more in that department than me any day."

Bianca seemed perfectly okay with this idea. She asked a fellow noble upright, "What shall it be, Cyrille? Do you wish to become a captain? If you don't want it, nobody will blame you." *Except perhaps some of his less savory family members, but to Hell with them.* "This is your choice and yours alone."

Cyrille still seemed a bit nervous about all this occurring at once. "Are you all sure? What if people start to think the concept of Squad Captains is just an excuse for upper class psychics to be above psychics with humbler backgrounds? I'd feel terrible if you were all slandered because of me."

Always thinking of others before himself, I see. Bianca tried to reassure him. "Do not care what others say about the rest of us. Just follow what you want—not Ercan, not me—you."

Cyrille shivered nervously as he saw everybody all looking at him expectantly. Even with his background, he felt so pressured at the moment. But if they all had so much faith in him, he would resolve never to fail any of them.

The first thing he did was cluck nervously, causing everyone to look at him weirdly. But taking a long breath, he found his inner warrior— the inner steel that each man and maiden kept inside them for when they were about to do something that would change their life. With as much willpower as he could muster, he answered everyone.

"I accept your proposition, Ercan Ao'Si. I shall lead Rooster Squad to glory and, in the next games, I vow that we are going to be at least fourth place. I solemnly swear it."

Now that everyone had high hopes for him, Cyrille had better live up to them.

~ * ~

Yun hastily followed where Mr. Jahikah was taking his uncle. He had to speak to him before he was put behind bars. "Zuo!"

His mummy teacher stopped in his tracks, allowing the monkey to catch up. Zuo was not exactly ready to speak with him, though. "So, I guess you're here to disparage me for my life choices, right?"

He was not exactly wrong. "Well yes. But I just need to know something."

"Why I did it? Well you probably heard about what I did to the Altahn tribe by now right?" Zuo showed no pride in his actions.

Yun's eyes narrowed at his uncle just at the thought of him murdering Xiu's parents. "I do."

"I think about what I did all the time. I consider it a blessing whenever I don't have a night pondering about what I've done." He refused to look at Xing's child all grown up. "I listened to my superiors and slaughtered them like cattle, but I could not even follow my country one hundred percent. Sometimes I wonder if sparing her was a good idea."

"How could you even think that?" Yun called him out. "Why would you even reconsider not killing a child?"

Zuo remained unfazed. "Maybe I never did grant her mercy. You know her better than me. Do you think she's as happy as she was before the massacre? Do you think she takes pride in the fact that she is the last member of the Altahni bloodline? Do you see other Qian with green eyes these days? Maybe I should have just put her out of her misery."

Yun couldn't answer even one of those questions. He did still have questions for Zuo, though. "Then why the Lefty Gang? You must have known their reputation."

"I adopted a young girl by the name of Jakaire Mara. Her family was murdered in the event that ignited the war. She was a psychic too, with a spark not unlike mine. It felt like fate wanted me to support her." Now he turned around, not to look at Yun but at the corpses of his comrades. "When you're a fugitive, you tend to have few options. I managed to find a connection to the gang and they offered to pay handsomely." Zuo was previously told of Jakaire's fate. "But she's gone now. You don't need to worry."

Yun got the message quickly. He did not need to say anything. Zuo continued the conversation for the both of them. "When I wore that shoulder armor and spoke those words, I felt something…off. Like my soul wasn't the only soul I had. As if something lived inside me and changed me." He hoped Yun knew what he was talking about. "The Artifact of Kadosh altered who I was. Not one hundred percent, but enough to make me…not feel like me. And for some reason I feel that the Lefty Gang knows this and still wants them." He felt that he was beginning to sound insane. "If Barbar was actually manipulating my thought process, then how would having more than one relic work? It would be pure chaos within your very essence. Y-you would lose yourself completely! How can something like them exist?" Even reading the book Cianfa gave him did nothing to quell his thoughts of all of this. Reading the book was surreal enough, but Zuo could rationalize that from being a unique spark or something. Experiencing it was something else entirely. He needed to give his nephew a warning.

The police car drove up to put the Lefty Gang member away for a long time. "Tell them not to speak the words and awaken the artifacts. All eight of them together would redefine the world as we know it."

Yun could not help but believe what his uncle was saying. Even when he was young, he never recalled Zuo lying to him once. Honestly, that just made the words he spoke all the worse. He spoke a solemn last few words. "This is goodbye for now. Maybe I'll consider visiting you if you request it. But for now, I need to get home."

Zuo understood. "Sure thing. Must have been a long night for you. A long life in fact." He watched as his nephew climbed up a building to avoid the streets.

Aluja heard the entire conversation and now Zuo was speaking to his old compatriot. "I have personally experienced death during a time way before the Demiurge itself, and yet I don't remember any of it. But I know there was something after. Ever since Sophia woke me up and brought me back to life, I tried to remember bits and pieces of it. But nothing." The mummy shook his head, trying to remember for the five thousandth time. "It's as if some force doesn't want me to remember what came after."

"Do you think I'm going to the bad place when I die?" Zuo asked as he was put in the backseat of the car. "Do you think both of us are?"

"I cannot say for certain, old friend." Aluja told him with shame. "What we did that night will affect how we are judged, no matter what we do now. But perhaps our efforts to better ourselves will hopefully save our souls." He began to sound openly worried. "It's hard to wake up every morning and come to class when one of your students is Altahni."

"Does she know about you yet?"

"No," Aluja confided in him. "She has no idea what I've done to her. But once she does figure it out, I will not blame her if she tries to kill me." He stared off into space. "I might sound like a coward who refuses to accept karma, but I feel that death from her hands would hurt her more than it would heal her. I won't resist if she tries it, but I pray she will learn mercy the day she figures out the atrocity I have committed."

The police closed the car door. Zuo waved goodbye through his cuffs. "I'll pray for your soul if you pray for mine."

Aluja gazed on as the cops drove away to take Zuo to the precinct. No doubt he would be declared guilty and sent to Prisoner's Perch. This would probably be the last time they would see one another. Perhaps the next time they met would be in Hell, or whatever afterlife the corrupted souls went to.

Monoceros was finished with bringing the bodies to professionals and walked toward his old squad buddy. "What's eating you?"

~ * ~

"I'm coming in, honey!"

Cianfa smashed through the nice and fancy condo door at the top of the most elite building in all of Sorchos. Several guards lay dead at his feet, all in a bloody mess. Azi Dahaka made it all too easy to rip them to pieces and crush their bones. The moment that Cianfa made it inside, he heard a woman screaming.

"Please! Don't come any closer!"

Was he really going to listen to some hylic female's pleas? No, of course not! "You know, I jussssst sssslaughtered all of yours and your hubby's bodyguardssss Mrsss. Sssswaine. The leassst I could do isssss finisssh the job." Those guards were all kenoma trash, utterly worthless for anything.

Cianfa tracked where the fearful sobbing was. Upstairs in what he could hypothesize was the bedroom. He called up to his target. "Come on, lady! You sssshould be thanking me! I'm doing thisss sssshithole of a city a favor!" He took his time going up each step, making sure she heard each creaking noise. "I jusssst persssonally dealt with a lot of the crime in Sssorchoss. I put a lot of criminal organizationssss in complete disssarray for your husband'sss city. If I needed to attempt to count the number of ssssscum I have executed perssssonally, I would ssssay about…around four…sssseventy wassstes of ssspace."

He made it to the top of the stairs, reveling in her terror. "But then I realized from a couple of hoity-toity mob bosssssesss that they were under the protection of one Mayor Marcussss Sssswaine. He and a few copssss were being paid to turn a blind eye to their dealingsss." The demon in physical form rolled his eyes, not be able to resist a chuckle. "Now I was never a politician, but I have a feeling that getting bribesss

as ever, but nothing contact lenses could not fix.

He flicked off a bit of dust from his shoulder. "I sure do miss the piercings." Cianfa reminisced about how he'd looked back in the day. "Gave me much more character." He wished he could have his nose piercing, tongue piercing, navel piecing, and nipple piercings, among "other" areas. But his boss insisted he have those removed, for they stood out too much. At least he got to keep the long dark green earrings he'd had since he was fourteen.

He felt the crystalcell in his jacket pocket vibrating. Checking it, his phone had been blowing up with messages since the last time he turned back. He answered it. "Greetings, Reliquit, you seem to really want to talk to me. Any problems?" He listened to his superior. "Now, now let's get the bad news over with." The voice on the other line seemed quite irritated. Cianfa could not really find himself giving a steaming shit. "Tragedy, real tragedy. Five Lefties dead and one arrested." He'd expected at least one casualty anyway. All he needed was results. "So, Shèng Xià was the one arrested. That's a shock. I was betting for him to be the one to escape. So who made it out and did they get the Artifact of Kadosh?...Really? Vinstri and Kushoto? Well, typical. A thief's blood is always yellow. But did they get Barbar's relic?"

He waited for a little bit until Reliquit gave an answer. "They actually did it? Well color me impressed. Almost tempted to thank them. I underestimated those sons of bitches. How soon do you think you'll meet them?" He received an approximate answer. "Three days seems like a good guess. Though I recommend that you have them pass the relic down to me, 'cause let's face it, I'm the only one who knows who you truly are *boss*." Without him, Reliquit was a sitting duck and he knew it. "I am going to see you in a few days. Tata."

He hung up the phone and was ready to get out of Sorchos. He'd caused some mayhem and was satisfied for now. Tragically, it seemed that Zuo may have left his book behind in Bythos. Very irresponsible. Hopefully Vinstri and Kushoto could get it back to him.

The police should be coming soon; he had to hide his appearance. Once again activating his demon dragon form, he was on his way out the door. As he left the master bedroom, he heard the crying of an infant. Piquing his interest, he took a little detour. The room was painted pink, making Cianfa assume the baby was female. To his right was a crib with little stars and stuff circling above the child. As he would expect, the infant was bawling its eyes out.

"You must have a pretty delayed reaction there, little skipper." Cianfa said words no infant would ever really understand. "You just woke up now?" His mere presence made the baby girl just cry harder than ever. "Hmmm? Well I guess I am pretty ugly in this form. But I need to be ugly for a little bit more."

To Cianfa, there was never really a point to killing an infant. Any infant could grow up to become a psychic, whether weak or powerful. In fact, he liked to assume that most children had the opportunity to transcend from being a mere kenoma into a pleroma, though his patience ended at fourteen years. After that, those hylics were fair game.

He gently took the baby in his arms, which must have instinctively known not to resist. "Don't worry; I'm not going to eat you." He wrapped the baby in a pink blanket. "I'm going to take you to a new home." Cianfa tried his best to ignore the crying.

He left the room to go to the balcony. Opening the sliding door, he manifested his wings onto his back at the edge of the building. "You better become a psychic by puberty. Or I *will* find you again." He flew above the buildings, infant in his arms.

The Demon Dragon would never be seen in Sorchos again.

Life Goes On

It had been five days since the incident at the Sephirot Museum. The Lefty Gang had gotten much too ambitious for its own good. Something had to be done about it. Raziel Mattatron organized an emergency conference with the other Ashtamangala. So now inside one room, were the most important psychics in the world—some of them doubling as the most powerful men and women in the world, period.

As the host of this meeting, Raziel was the first to speak. "I thank all of you for being here today. I understand that all of you are constantly busy with your own agendas so I appreciate that you've all spared some time to discuss this issue." He read from a document containing information gathered from both those involved and witnesses. "Last Wednesday, the museum was broken into by what is claimed to be eight members of the Lefty Gang. Luckily, a student from Aeon Sophia Academy was able to alert others of the break-in. The aftermath left five Lefties dead, one arrested and two remain missing. Though there were no civilian casualties due to the impeccable timing of Bytho's psychics along with our brightest students, there have been some deaths. Five professors and twelve guards who worked at the museum are dead along with one registered psychic named Jacque Jax Jackson. Moment of silence for the fallen."

Respectful silence filled the room. Soon after, it was back to business. The fourth Chatraratna Tharama Nejem was first to speak up. "On behalf of Sirochko, I express our condolences, though I feel that this meeting is wholly unnecessary if the problem is merely taking place in Enotita." The battle-scarred woman had no arms. In their place, she had many bright yellow flares that ended in hands. Somehow, the solar energy was able to manipulate a pen for taking notes.

Raziel cleared his throat. "Sorry, I should have been much clearer, Incarnate Tharama. The reason I brought all of you here is very much classified." Tharama paid close attention, watching with her remaining eye. "Are you all ready for the information I'm about to disclose?"

An elegant man with blue skin sat, legs crossed. "Must we all keep secrets from the people?" Vinda Caima lamented to his peers. "All this does is strain the trust of those we're meant to guide." Naya Jivana's Sankha had a reputation for never keeping anything confidential from his citizens. Then again, Vinda never really had the burden of keeping secrets. All Sankhas were more hermits than rulers that existed more to give spiritual advice than rule a nation.

"I'm afraid that secrecy is imperative at the moment," Raziel told the second youngest member of the group. "Any possible leaking of this information would only make things worse." He wasted no more time. "The Artifacts of Kadosh possess…unexplainable magical properties."

The rest of the Ashtamangala seemed more than surprised. The eldest one amongst them, the first and third Padma named Meinrad von Morgen, spoke up from his mechanical body. "To be frank with all of you, I've known that fact for over a century now." He wheezed through his breathing apparatus. "Though it is not 'magic' in the unexplainable sense. More like a spark that created a legend that allowed other sparks to follow in its footsteps. A spark that could make legends come true and become reality you could say," Meinrad told them as he waved his artificial hands, creating blue energy that became the word "Ouranos" in clear words. "Hundreds of years ago, Beatrice the Inquisitive made the first relic, the amulet that has been entrusted to the nation of Odandir."

Odandir's representative slouched back in his chair and affectionately pointed both fingers at his elder. "Thanks for the shout-out, Metal-Bro! As you all know me, I-X-N, got that shit covered, yo!" All but Meinrad himself groaned at the fact that this "fly" buzz cut-blond guy actually managed to become an Ashtamangala. "Ain't no reason to worry 'bout me gramps! Got it covered."

The Artificial Wizard felt no offense. Even during the fall of the

Protogenoi Empire, he was already a great-grandfather. "I thank you for being wholly dedicated to protecting your national treasure, Fourth Dharmachakra Irene Xavier Norbert."

I-X-N cringed upon hearing the name his mother gave him, but tried to respect his elder. "Yeaaaah, sure, no probs. It's all good up in Oh-dand-deer!"

A stocky woman in her fifties could hardly handle I-X-N's noise for much longer. "I *sure* am glad that an artifact is in your hands. Surely *you* would not do anything foolish to lose it." Kiara Salera, Titlacuan's Fourth Shrivatsa, had to listen to Irene's boom box spit out obscene garbage as they waited for Raziel. The patience of the Briny Lady was finite after all, though her detractors referred to her as "The Salty Lady," "But Meinrad, if you knew about the properties of the Kadosh Artifacts, why didn't you tell any of us for all of these years?"

Though more machine than man, Meinrad still depended on his brain to remember any possible reasons. Being a hundred-and-sixty-three, he had a lot of memories to sort through. "I'm not sure, exactly. I always did so much research back in the old Protogenoi days, and in those days I had bigger issues to worry about than what I thought were some silly old relics—" He had a bit of a coughing fit. "Forgive me, I must get my respirator upgraded. It keeps slipping my mind to get a new one. If only I could create a spell that allowed me to no longer need air. If I haven't found one already that is…I think I…I feel I have gone off subject again." His mechanical staff lit up as he activated his Merlin spark to explore the vault of his mind. "Oh, why yes. This is my reasoning. If I need to make a long tale short, I simply chose to not tell anybody out of fear of the knowledge being exploited. I guess somebody figured it out anyway."

Kiara was dumbfounded by her elder's forgetfulness. "Were you not the one who gave each nation one of the relics to guard when the empire fell?" She should sympathize with how a man on mechanical life support would have a faulty memory, but she would think such important information would have been a priority.

"I honestly gave those as gifts. I think I was meant to tell you what they were for…but you could guess by now that I did not." Meinrad's artificial lights for eyes faded in shame.

"At this stage, it doesn't matter when we learned this information, it is that we know it now," Raziel told the other seven, specifically Kiara. "With this information, we now know that we need to keep all of our artifacts locked up where no one will get their hands on them."

Tharama raised a solar hand with all seriousness. "How exactly did Barbar's pauldrons get activated? I feel the need to know in order to understand what to do with Danake the Explorer's Bracers."

"I'm glad that you asked," Raziel acknowledged the Chatraratna's question. "According to those who saw Zuo Xuanzang activate the Odin spark firsthand, he just wore the relic and chanted several sentences. Sadly, they cannot recall what he said due to stress from the events."

Seichi's representative, Kiyoshi Mizuchi, sneered at the lack of information. "Tch! Teenage psychics these days. Hormonal cowards that care more about living to fornicate another day than gaining information to benefit their nations." There was nothing but disgust in The Unknown Beast of the Six Heavens' tone. He looked toward the fifth Bumpa of Qian Ye. "They cannot even fully handle one treasonous defector from your nation, Linlung."

Linlung Kadru, the fifth Bumpa, was unlike any of the others. The others were at least shaped like a human, but the empress of Qian Ye used her spark to change her very form into that of a snake—a huge one with the bright jade scales of a boa. Three feet wide and over thirty feet long, she dwarfed every other person in the room. She didn't even have any limbs or other physical traits that could be somewhat anthropomorphic. She looked exactly like an animal that could coincidently speak. The only calling card of her humanity was a gold and red band around where a neck would be, as serpents had no use for any clothing, not even royal ones.

"Zuo Xuanzang was no coward, Emperor." Her voice was regal and dignified, her body coiled but alert. "He merely did not believe in Tai Xun's actions. For that I cannot blame him. Tai Xun's reign as Bumpa was regretful for all of Qian Ye. His paranoia took over his very soul." She kept a stern expression, but her voice shook a bit. "Thousands of Qian residents lost loved ones for completely avoidable reasons. For me, I personally lost my husband, Baraz, and my three sons, Kian, Ning, and Tao, bless their souls. If you lost what I have lost during the last war, you would not say that Zuo was a coward; you would pat him on the back, Kiyoshi. I condemn his affiliations with the gang, but I shall not blame him for deserting his country."

Vinda ardently defended the teenagers. "It is quite unfair to treat mere beginners as if they were on our level. They still have so much to learn about themselves that it would be cruel to just assume that they all could have our discipline. Our generations are from two worlds that could not be more different." He placed a hand on his bare chest just under his three beaded necklaces. "Disparaging them for not focusing on their survival would only result in the loss of potentially bright stars that could usher in a golden age."

Kiyoshi rolled his eyes at the blue man's words. "Big words for an Ashtamangala who would rather wait for karma to find its prey than actually do anything proactive."

I-X-N came to Vinda's defense. "Hey, step off, old fart! Quit acting like you know everything!"

"Are you implying that old is disgusting?" Kiara leered at the Dharmachakra.

"Of course Irene is not saying that," Meinrad answered her from under his large green cloak. "He is merely implying that Kiyoshi here is old-fashioned and not nearly as…liberal as the younger generation. He was just spouting words to insult him."

"I would have gone with the fact that his mustache looks like two thin catfish whiskers." Tharama said to I-X-N, enjoying how red Kiyoshi's face was getting.

Kiyoshi slammed his fist onto the table, causing it to crack. "I will not have my mustache insulted by a cripple!" It took precision and effort to get his mustache waxed just right. Any insults would bring his wrath.

Tharama pointed her solar arms toward her offender. "You know a Seichin took my arms during the war. He's now dead."

Everyone began to realize how south this meeting was going. Raziel needed to do something quick. Kiyoshi and Tharama were the most aggressive of the eight and a fight in the peace room would be both devastating and a huge blow to the council's reputation. In that moment, Raziel decided to stand up and let his shining wings do the talking for him. He stared each member down with his pure gold eyes.

"Do not start a diplomatic incident. We still have so much to talk about." He spoke in a calm and collected manner with a tone that showed strength and resolve. With some hesitation, the representatives of Sirochko and Seichi sat back in their seats. Immediately after, Raziel once again became jovial as if nothing happened. "Now back to the subject at hand, I think we should all come up with strategies to counter the Lefty Gang. Any suggestions, ideas, proposals?"

"We cannot leave them out in public places." Linlung suggested, seemingly oblivious that her words seemed like a backhanded insult to Raziel. At this point, everyone now knew how dumb it was to leave the artifacts in a museum.

Raziel took it in stride. "Great idea, Lady Kadru. Any other plans?"

The entire rest of the meeting was just the eight discussing strategies to counteract the potential theft of any of the relics. Now that they were aware of what they needed to do, they had to find a way to keep them safe, away from overly ambitious and destructive hands.

At SAIS Hall of Alumni, all of Heron Squad paid their respects to their fallen comrade. Desiderio placed green cymbidium orchids under Enitharmon Loz's portrait, her favorite. In inconsolable tears, Draghignazzo placed the green rubber chicken she always adored that he gave to her as a parting gift. For once, Dunkeen kept his mouth shut, placing a little stone figure of the deceased down as tribute. Petra was next, putting down a stuffed animal, Enith's favorite—an iguana. What remained of her body had been previously sent over to the authorities.

Xiu Lang admittedly had no idea what Enitharmon was really like when she was not brainwashed, but she felt the need to also come to the small funeral. Not knowing any preferences, she merely settled with placing an emblem of Sophia down. The moment of silence continued until Desiderio spoke up.

"Enitharmon Loz was a better person than she could ever imagine herself to be. She inspired all of us to strive to become better; whether it be to keep our grades up or to match her skills. Unfortunately, Sophia felt it was necessary to grant her a spark unlike any other—one so unstable that it took a toll on her physical and mental health. I thank this Academy for at least being the first people in her life willing to aid her, and I thank the students here for being willing to befriend her."

Xiu could not help but feel guilt. Never once had she even considered befriending Enith. She had always creeped her out and she'd thought of her as unstable to be around. It made her feel like a total asshole. Desi continued his speech.

"The color green, which we all knew her for, has many great meanings. It symbolizes the growth of character, a fresh start, emotional endurance, safety, and the natural world. Let us not have our dear friend's death be in vain. We must move on in this frightening world with our heads held high. Enith would want us to live our lives to the fullest and not let her memory weigh us down. But though we may have lost her, may her spirit watch over us and protect us. Hail Sophia."

"H-hail Sop-Sophia," Draghignazzo managed to say through his tears. Petra consoled the distraught demon.

"Hail Sophia." Petra looked down, trying not to cry. Her hand balled up into a fist, wanting so badly to strike down whoever was responsible.

Dunkeen said the shortest sentence he'd ever uttered. "Hail Sophia."

Shame enveloped Xiu as she stood at the picture of someone she never gave the chance to become a friend. She knew it was her duty to help Heron Squad get through this pain. She couldn't even challenge her parent's killer, but she had to become stronger if she was to ever be useful to any of them. It was her turn to say the two words.

"Hail Sophia."

School was to start in five minutes. They all needed to get their books and stuff, though chances were none of them were going to be able to pay much attention today, just like the last two school days. But they must bring their spirits up and not let their loss interfere with their learning any longer.

"I guess we all need to get going now," their captain told his squad mates as he made himself smile. "School is starting. See you all at the captain's initiation ceremony." Desiderio made his way to The Stage for McDooley's next lesson.

As the other four made their way out of the SAIS, Xiu tried to speak to the mourning group. "I'm sorry."

Drag stopped sobbing for a second. "For what?"

"For not knowing Enitharmon at all. From what you all said, she seemed like such a great human being. There isn't that many out there and I completely ignored one in this very school. I can't replace her in any way, but I hope you will all give me a chance I don't deserve to prove myself to the squad." Xiu knew they were aware of the reasons for her transfer to their squad. She just hoped they would not hold it against her.

Dunkeen answered her as he opened the door for everyone. "Of course all of us would. We all have our own issues to deal with. Every squad does. You think Sparrow Squad is a hundred percent perfect? Of course not, they just keep their personal problems out of their missions. We know you may not have been transferred here on your own volition, but I choose to give you the benefit of the doubt that you will not weigh us Herons down."

"Thank you, Dunkeen," was all Xiu could say.

"I'm sure that Enith would not mind you as a replacement." Draghignazzo blew into a tissue. "I need to respect her wishes."

Petra had a lot on her mind, so she just quickly said a few words. "Sure fine, just don't screw up and shit like that." She then hopped ahead of the group to class.

Xiu had had a lot of thoughts flooding her mind during the last five days. She'd remained fairly quiet since Wednesday. The only contact she really made with any of Rooster Squad was with Shee'vra's training and living with Yun. She never really spoke to any of the others. She felt horrible for having them fight her own fights but also knew that she needed to thank them. But how?

~ * ~

"See you after school, Sheev." Ercan waved back to his sister as she went into the sophomore classroom.

He walked down the halls with a merry step in his feet. It seemed that after the fiasco with Zuo, he and the rest of Rooster Squad had become a whole lot cooler in the public opinion, both in and out of school. Despite the fact that he gave up his title as Squad Captain, his self-esteem was higher than ever before.

But something was still concerning him. He had learned something about Xiu that, chances were, she told few others. The fact that a nation could just order their psychics to exterminate their own citizens was a chilling thought. Just the other night, he dreamt about getting eaten by the mutated Tai Xun that P.J had become. Each time he had that dream, he would be sure to check that his stomach was still intact. Though worse than mere nightmares, he was worried about Xiu as well. She hadn't really talked to him since she'd had to leave it to him to fight Zuo. Even sitting next to her in class barely made her speak to him, just lost in her own thoughts. Did she feel like he pitied her or something? He was sure she would hate it if he actually did.

Damn. Is she mad at me again? I just can't read her at all. Taking a right in the hallway, he ended up bumping into somebody by accident. "Crap! I'm really sorry!" As he tried to pick up the dropped books, he noticed that Xiu was right in front of him.

"Ercan?!" She seemed surprised to see him for a moment before composing herself. "I mean really you should know at this point to watch where you're going." This was her chance to say it. She got her nerves under control. "I know we haven't exactly been on speaking terms but..." Why was this harder than it needed to be? Why did she have all this excess pride? To make a compromise to herself, she spat it out quick. "ThanksIguessforhelpingmelastweek." No eye contact was made at all as she snagged her biology textbook from him.

"Huh?" He did not exactly get most of that, but hearing "last week" gave him a clue. "Wait, are you thanking me for last week?"

"Yes, I am thanking you!" She seemed almost exasperated. "And you better not have told anyone about that dream world crap!" She couldn't even hear the name P.J without feeling nauseous anymore. "Or about what *that man* did to me."

Ercan was quick to put her thoughts at ease. "No, not at all. Not even to Jules or Cyrille. And I doubt Sheev is going to blab about... that night to anybody." It was a bit confusing, though. "Though at this point, why do you insist for it to be a secret?"

She dreaded that question, but felt that she must answer him. Owed him that much at least. Checking the halls and seeing nobody, she began, "Because...the Altahn tribe never actually existed according to Qian Ye." A twinge of anger ignited inside her. "We were nomads native to the mountains, not considered important enough for most history books. Us 'primitives' were only remembered when it was convenient to the nation. Hell, none of us even actually had legal citizenship. And the only time they truly acknowledged us as Qian..." her eyes looked down to the floor, "...was to get rid of us. Even now, whenever anything Altahni is ever so rarely mentioned, it's to slander us more as sick cultists of The Demiurge." Ercan heard a slight sniffle.

But before Xiu could actually begin to form tears in her eyes, she felt Ercan's arms embrace her. She had not received a real heartfelt hug like this in years. Not since her parents. Her other father figure, Yeren, always kept his distance from his disciples and she usually preferred her personal space anyway. But this feeling reminded her how warm a human body actually was.

"You were not and will never be truly alone," Ercan comforted her. "You have Yeren, Yun, Hong, Caradoc, Sheev, Cyrille, Jules, Desi, Petra, Drag, Dunkeen, Shiro, Vasanti, Sabelle, and me. How many people is that?"

Xiu was seeing it now. "A lot." She truly had only been trapped once on her own against the world. In those dark caves with the Manticore. After that, she was found by Yeren and from then on had always had someone to support her. So why did she get so pigheaded and ignore most of them? "A lot of people."

"And I bet that even more in school would stand by you," Ercan added in as her head rested on his shoulder. "I also want you to remember something. The Altahn Tribe are not dead yet. You're still alive and kicking, right?

"Right." She did not dare wrap her arms around him in turn.

"Then there's still hope to clear your people's name. I am sure Empress Linlung would be reasonable enough to hear what you have to say. Then I'm sure the slander against your tribe will be brushed away by anyone with a brain."

"Sounds stupid, honestly." She would have preferred that he gave her a more optimistic percentage, but that would do just fine. She was just glad he was there for her. "But at least writing one letter won't waste my time too much. Maybe she'll get it; maybe she'll be a bitch and ignore it. I should try at least, though."

"Hey, you two." They both saw Gustave walking by. "Either get a room or get to class. We're all late."

Xiu hastily pushed Ercan away from her. "There is nothing between us if you must know." She tried to hide her blushing.

"Yeah, we're just mending fences here," Ercan told Gustave sincerely. "We're just friends once again."

The upright false gharial was amused by Xiu's almost distraught reaction to the F-word. *Well I'll be. A lovely young lady like her just got friend-zoned.* He turned his head from the two. "Whatever you guys say. See you both in class."

With the croc gone, Ercan turned back to Xiu. "I hope you feel better now. I'll be around if you need me." He followed Gustave through the hallway.

Xiu watched him turn the corner with her heart beating. Those damned feelings returned once again. *Why the hell is he so nice to me? I yell at him, snark at him, flat out avoid him, and he still tries to do what's best for me.* She couldn't just brush it off as him merely staying on her good side because he thought she was hot either. She'd just heard that he said they were just friends with total honesty. Maybe training Shee'vra helped his perception of her. Or perhaps…he was interested in someone else already.

She was tempted to do one of two things to the redhead. Either hit him over the head and call him out on how oblivious he was or just embrace Ercan with a kiss like in those guilty pleasure flicks she loved so much. Either way, her…like for him would be quite upfront.

But she chose the third choice and simply said nothing as his footsteps faded away. She shook her head to regain her thoughts. "I am such an idiot. I'm here to become a psychic warrior, not to go on dates." She was a strong, independent woman who needed no man in her life, to quote a line from a magazine. "Shit, at this point, maybe even Mr. Jahikah is on his way to class. I have to beat him to the door." Being considered late for Mr. Jahikah's class was just embarrassing to anyone in the Academy.

As she ran with her books in tow, the men's bathroom door creaked open. The green mummy felt the coast was clear now. Aluja had heard everything Xiu and Ercan said. "Hopefully Linlung will listen." Perhaps if he used his contacts in Qian Ye, maybe he could request that the fifth Bumpa could meet with the last Altahn. That would be the least he could do for her for the despair he'd brought her.

During lunch period, Zivot was once again helping Yun sharpen his scholarly skills. There was a test coming up and, if Yun failed, she would have failed Cyrille. They were working on chemistry at the moment.

Though Zivot had seen signs of improvement (as in H20 was two hydrogen plus one oxygen equaled water), he was lost in thought.

"Is something on your mind?" Zivot feigned ignorance, knowing exactly what he was thinking about. One does not just let go of the fact that your uncle was a Lefty Gang member that got arrested a week ago.

Yun was reluctant to answer, but gave in. "Yeah, it's more or less the uncle thing still." He put his pencil down in contemplation. "I mean, I know Uncle Zuo did all that stuff to Xiu, abandoned his country and joined a criminal empire, but even then, he didn't act like some malicious prick about it at all. It just makes me think he was just desperate to escape his old life."

She was not exactly in a position to give him any advice at all. So she just said whatever words of wisdom she'd read in a book once. "Well I heard from somewhere that when you have nothing else to lose and your final destination is Hell, you stop caring about how you pay the bills."

Yun looked at her weirdly. "Did you just quote the fourth chapter of *My Country Is Not My Country?*" It seemed he had been up to date on literature class at least.

"Just a coincidence," Zivot tried to hide her lack of originality. Cyrille was ten times better at cheering people up. She tried to find a way to change the subject. "So I have wondered this for a while, but what's up with Hong and that book?"

She pointed at the bluish salamander man with the glowing eyes sitting just above everyone else on what appeared to be thin air. In Hong's hands was a gigantic book that had a flesh-colored cover that was most definitely not paperback. He seemed utterly oblivious that a lot of people were staring at him.

"Oh, him?" Yun looked up at his long time peer. "That's supposedly a book full of ancient and forbidden secrets of the universe. No, I don't know how he can casually read it like that. Probably would make my mind melt." Yun shuddered at the thought of the things Hong knew but never told anyone. He'd told him, Xiu, and Caradoc about another dream this morning, one containing black snakes swimming in brine.

As the two got distracted watching Hong lounge about just under the ceiling, Winona entered the library. The woman in black seemed to be heading straight for the amphibian for some reason. She looked up toward Hong and addressed him. "Hong Hai Long. I need to have a word with you."

Yun was visibly worried, wondering what Hong could have possibly done to her to catch her ire. But Winona didn't exactly seem angry with him, just serious. Hong did not exactly seem to hear her, so Winona sent a crow to whisper into his ear hole.

"I will not ask again."

Hong got the message, made his tome disappear into thin air and turned off his ocular glowing. He then landed face first onto the floor, getting up limberly with his limited amount of bones. "What, exactly, are you calling me for? Need me for something…" He seemed to be struggling to remember this person's name.

"Winona. And I need to ask you two questions. First, can you hear Sophia?"

Yun, Zivot, and some other students watched as Hong contemplated for a few seconds before quickly shaking his head, causing slime to sprinkle onto the floor. "I'm afraid that I've never heard our savior within the catacombs of the region in my soul."

The idea that Sophia did not guide everybody in his or her Spark Regions was alien to Yun. He had never heard of any psychic not even being able to be guided by her voice. Why hadn't Hong ever told his fellow disciples or the rest of Kingfisher Squad?

Winona's black eyes narrowed as if she realized her theory was true. Other than that, she seemed unfazed. "So I guess you learned how to use Tsathoggua by yourself?"

Hong seemed to actually be quite interested in this conversation. Usually if he wasn't invested in talking to someone, he would just slink away without saying a word. Honestly, he could be sort of rude like that. But now he spoke as if they had something in common. "Yes and no, Winona. My Spark Region is a slimy underground tomb with glyphs of things I feel are better left not described. Through interpreting these pictures, it seemed the walls wanted me to imagine a large book for my two eyes only." He summoned his gigantic book yet again, making a thud on the floor. "This book I can summon is the Liber Ivonis." He opened the book to reveal that all the pages were blank. "Your mortal mind cannot see or comprehend the words within, but when my eyes transcend mortal coils…" His eyes flashed red as his voice deepened.

"…I can see many things within. The most mundane things are how to use my spark to perfection without even visiting my region within. More advanced things are concepts that I really shouldn't speak of to virginal ears. I see what shall not be seen and hear what must never be heard. I believe the world I can tap into is not of Sophia, but of something else." The entire library was trembling, other than Hong and Winona. After his little tirade, Hong turned his weird-vision off and dismissed his book with the wave of his hand. "Do you have a similar problem?" he asked with a child-like grin as if this was all fun and games.

Winona took her time to absorb the information given to her before she replied. "Since I got The Morrigan spark at age four, I have never once heard any voice within my Spark Region. I had to learn everything about what is essentially three different sparks inscribed on large standing stones scattered about a gray battlefield by myself. Even now, I feel like I have so many more abilities to master." She felt a sense of self-satisfaction for being able to learn so much without somebody holding her hand the whole way through. "Now that I know we have something in common, I propose another question to you. Do you think Ercan is unable to hear Sophia as well?"

Ignoring Yun's gasp, Hong answered, puzzled. "What would make you think that? I always just assumed that it only happened if you're born with inhuman qualities like you and me." He pointed at her feather-hair and his salamander body. "We are both born of human mothers, but for some reason, were born the way we are." He had a realization. "Though then again, Ercan has those unnatural purple eyes and Enitharmon bled green blood. Both have non-human qualities like us, if more minor, and both possess extremely high aeon scores just like us." Hong momentarily stopped talking as he realized something, something not right at all. "I need to speak to you in private!"

Taking her hand and escorting her to an empty library aisle, he abruptly summoned his book back for a third time and flipped through the pages quickly in a panic. He whispered ominously to her. "This could be nightmarish to comprehend, but I don't feel that our parents were both fully human. And I do not mean that they had a shapeshifting spark or willingly had themselves transformed by somebody else. I feel that there's a loose possibility that we might just be only three fourths human."

"Be clearer," Winona demanded, a part of her not wanting to understand what this whack job was saying to her. "Are you implying that we're pneumatics? That's impossible; those beings have not been around since the beginning of the empire. Sophia's body is gone. She has no way of reproducing with mortals. And even if she did, wouldn't you think a child of Sophia would be much stronger than us?"

Hong's face showed nothing but dread. "Who's to say that our grandparent was Sophia? Mayhaps an archon still wanders this world, making half-archon children every once in a while, and those pure pneumatics are mating with regular human beings to create us impure ones. Our archon blood may be quite diluted, but we still show signs of the archon taint."

This was a heavier discussion than Winona had imagined it would be. It had been a while since she actually felt utter terror like this. "This is…huge. We need to tell somebody about this. An archon lurking about today is…world shattering."

Hong shook his head in mellow acceptance. "I feel that we should let sleeping dogs lie for now. Right now, this archon is hiding among us. If we discover it, I feel that like a cornered rat it would try to attack anything in desperation to preserve its life. There's also the fact that we know nothing about this being. It's obviously hiding, but has also been mingling with humanity. That could imply that it can appear like a normal man or woman. If people knew that somebody of unknown gender could possibly be an archon in disguise, many of the nations would go into a paranoid witch-hunt. Some might even accuse others of hiding or protecting an accused archon. Just knowing that this being exists would sow utter chaos. It might even want that."

Winona was disgusted by the fact that an archon, a servant of the Demiurge, was free and roaming the earth and they could do so little about it, especially when it was theorized that it could reproduce with humans. "So what, are you just going to stick your head in the ground and allow this thing to bide its time for revenge?"

"No," Hong told her with a sullen expression. "I feel that I must use Liber Ivonis to look into this deeper. It will be hard and straining, but I promise you that I will find a way to make what I read comprehensible for you."

Winona felt that Hong had a valid point of keeping this covert from everyone else. She couldn't help but feel thankful for being offered such a deal from a non-captain. "I guess I have to be grateful for the offer. So thanks for entrusting me with this information." She began to walk off. "I'll be in contact with you." On the way out, Yun stood up curious as a monkey. "Step out of my way. I have things I need to do."

Not wanting to piss her off, Yun moved aside and allowed her to leave. Once Hong came back to the tables, he immediately questioned him with concern. "One moment, you two are talking about how you guys couldn't hear Sophia inside you. Next moment, you speak to her in private. What's up with that, man?" He felt it might have been better not to know, but he hated how Hong had so many secrets he could never tell anyone.

Surprisingly, he actually did get an answer from Hong. "I merely checked my book and looked up both of our parentage. Turns out we may just share a similar bloodline." It wasn't the main subject, but from what he read, it was no lie either. "She did not take it well."

"Oh, alright." Yun dropped the subject, wondering how two people who looked nothing alike could be possibly related. He just got back to work with Zivot. "See you at Cyrille's initiation."

Hong felt no need to stay in the library anymore and slipped out. He always hated how he could never tell his friends the whole truth. But he didn't want them to panic. When it came to his visions and readings, for every honest answer he had given, he had to speak fifteen lies. The universe was much too horrifying for man. So bleak. So empty. But not empty enough.

~ * ~

Julia sat on the staircase with her crystalcell at her ear. She waited for her father to answer. As always, he was quick to pick up.

"Happy noontime, Jules! Need to talk to your best friend?"

She couldn't help but cringe at how embarrassing a parent could be, despite being on a different continent. "Yeah. Hey, Dad. Look, I've been wondering about something for a bit now."

"Speak from the heart, light of my life!"

Julia waited for a squid-headed student to pass by to speak into the cell. "Well, I've been thinking about how Cyrille could always be so upbeat about his situation. We both have the fact that as psychics, we're denied our birthrights. But rather than be bitter, he still has a perfectly sunny disposition. And let's not beat around the bush here, the DeRoches make us look middle class in comparison. He should be way more resentful about this."

Her father paused to think about this for a moment. "Well…maybe he never really wanted to take over the family legacy. I know I would be more than willing to give it to you if not for laws and such. That or he simply never really thought about it."

She didn't disagree with that last statement. "That could be true. Cyrille is a bit odd like that. But he isn't stupid either. He must have considered it at least once. How is it possible for one guy to be so chipper about such a thing?" Julia honestly could not understand him.

"Well perhaps…he thinks there are things more important to him than birthright," her father guessed. "It's not like the law is going to change anytime soon, so he might as well not perseverate on a hopeless cause. Sorry to put it like that."

"No, no. It's fine. It is really dumb to focus on this all the time. Sorry." Julia honestly couldn't help but apologize.

"No need to say sorry, Jules. I know you're a very bright young woman and you would be ideal in being my successor. But psychic-hylic laws are just so lopsided. The psychics get the cool and not so cool powers, while hylics get the majority of the jobs. Sometimes I wonder if it's ever possible for true equality." She knew her father was probably thinking how great-gramps Merle must think of the world now.

"Me too…" she checked around for any footsteps, "…daddy. Thanks for speaking to me. But I have to go now. Class is starting soon."

"No problem, Jules. Hope to see you next month. Love you."

"Loveyoutoo." Julia hung up the phone and decided to get to gym class. Mr. Terrelli made late students run way too many laps for her muscles to handle.

But after school was Cyrille's inauguration for Captain of Rooster Squad. That should be interesting. *Good thing Ercan didn't choose me. Paperwork sucks.*

⌐ * ⌐

For the first time ever, Ms. Yamauchi allowed Shee'vra to use The Stage with the rest of her class. She was wearing her chainmail shirt and had Cloudstabber in her hands. It was to be a free-for-all with all twelve psychics of the sophomore class competing. Once she opened her eyes, Shee'vra found herself at a late night carnival. With her spark, she flew into the air smoother than she ever had.

Inspecting the landscape, she witnessed all of her classmates ready to duke it out. Vural swam in the dirt, Vasanti dashed about the arena at vehicle speeds, Alberto roared as the dinosaur stomped on bumper cars, Amund swished about as a swarm of swords, Jorun flew on top of her majestic Pegasus, Sanjay lurked behind the concession stand, ready to ambush unsuspecting prey, Saif extended his blade to twice the swordfish-person's size, Tommy dived into a puddle of blood, Draghignazzo flapped his batwings and shot out boiling pitch, Caradoc defied earth's gravity, and Hilbert found a high spot on the observation wheel to aim his lightning rifle.

These past couple days were some of the most exciting she'd had ever had. That may or may not have been a good thing, but she was going to remember these times in thirty or so years. She had learned more about Sylph in her Spark Region and Xiu had been giving her more pointers.

She shot Cloudstabber at Sanjay down below, which bounced off of his steel skin. Leaving the big masked guy for somebody else, she focused on the air instead. The Pegasus rider and a hundred blades headed straight toward her. Not too long ago, she would have been terrified. But now, she had no fear. Whether that was due to knowing this was all a simulation, she couldn't tell. But Jorun and Amund were in for it now. Nothing personal.

Putting her arbalest away, she spread both of her arms apart and held her hands partially open. Just like she practiced within her Spark Region, Shee'vra quickly twirled. Her hands seemed to scoop the air around her as she turned about. Just when sword and lance were about to hit their mark, waves of strong winds stopped both students midair. With one final swipe of both hands, a massive gust encircled her. Jorun and Amund had no chance to not get sent flying.

It worked. Shee'vra felt so proud that the move she'd spent the last few days practicing bore fruit. She may not have her brother's massive aeon score, Julia's smarts, Cyrille's poisons, or Yun's strength and agility, but she would find a niche in Rooster Squad even if it was the last thing she did.

Her little celebration didn't exactly last long. Being a sitting duck in the air allowed Hilbert to snipe her with massive watts of electricity. The art of being a psychic required baby steps.

~ * ~

"So how do I look, Mayil?"

"You do realize you are just wearing the same tux you wear four times a week, right, Master Cyrille?" Mayil questioned his superior's sense of fashion, but chose not to delve into it.

"Nonsense," Cyrille playfully brushed it off. "People love the tuxedo. And why would I not wear my best clothes for such a momentous occasion?"

Mayil had no retort, merely tightening his master's bowtie. "You look like the most bedazzling green chicken man I'll ever see." He opened the doors to the auditorium for him. "Now, enough grooming, they're waiting for you."

"Wish me luck out there." Cyrille politely dismissed Mayil for the moment and walked through the door. Looking at the seats in front of him, he heard what seemed to be every single psychic at the Academy applauding for him. Looking out at the crowd, he saw his teacher McDooley, Zivot sitting with the rest of her squad mates, Xiu sitting with her girl posse, and Hong staring into space as he clapped. He knew that the rest of Rooster Squad would be here without a doubt. Even Julia was there and for once not sleeping in her seat. If he were being honest, this big of a crowd made him feel a bit nervous. But Cyrille was a DeRoche, it was either learn how to cope with crowds or bring shame to his family. Besides, from here on, stage fright would one day be the least of his problems.

He moved toward the captains/future peers awaiting him at a long table. They all seemed to be glad to see him, though Winona seemed to have something on her mind as she was looking down at the table in contemplation. Desiderio grinned and applauded, but his eyes just didn't show any joy whatsoever. Cyrille hoped those two would eventually be relieved of their stress.

As he made it to the center of the stage, Ercan stood next to him and spoke to the audience, microphone in hand. "As some of you may know, I have chosen to resign from my position as captain of Rooster

Squad. I will still be in the squad, but now I'll be the one taking orders—from none other than Cyrille Coq DeRoche." Hardly anybody clapped, already knowing this information. "But anyway. Cyrille, do you swear to put your squad mates above yourself, engage the other captains in teamwork tactics on Mondays, and sacrifice your time and energy to the paperwork that is mandatory for every mission?" As the audience (even the teachers) groaned at paperwork, Ercan held a book in front of the reptilian rooster. The book had the academy symbol emblazoned upon the cover.

Like any teenager about to take a big responsibility, Cyrille hesitated for a moment as the room went silent. His hand shook above the tome, his talons almost scratching the surface. The pride of the DeRoche's won over, though, as he took the microphone from Ercan. Cyrille placed his palm upon the doorstopper of a book, raising his free hand as he made the oath.

"As leader of Rooster Squad, I shall show courage in the face of adversity, obey my superiors with upmost loyalty, show wisdom and insight in difficult situations, show mercy to my enemies when they are defenseless and, last but not least, keep my squad together in unity. This is the way of Aeon Sophia Academy and shall be the way of the psychic for generations to come."

He gave the microphone back to Ercan, who energetically spoke to the crowd. "It is now set in stone! Cyrille Coq DeRoche is officially the new captain of Rooster Squad!"

The auditorium was in a joyous uproar. It got to the point that Ercan was positive that if he was becoming captain, he wouldn't be cheered on nearly as much. Guess a lot of people really liked Cyrille. He watched as Cyrille happily took the tenth captain seat right next to Hanako, who seemed delighted to have him next to her. Ercan spoke to the audience one last time. "And now, here is Mastema Mattatron with important tips on making a squad for grades nine and under."

He tossed the mic to Mastema and took a seat in the audience next to his sister. Mastema caught it with one hand, looked at his cue cards and stood up to speak. The audience got much less excited, knowing what to expect from a speech from him.

"Greetings, all potential squad candidates." Mastema didn't take his eyes off of his notes. "You all might be wondering to yourself... how are squads truly made? Well, you see, it is actually a very complicated step-by-step process to analyze each individual spark of each potential psychic. The ones who do this work are the teachers of the Academy. And it is their duty to…"

Most of the sophomore and above students had already blocked out Mastema's words at this point. They knew he was just being an envoy for his grandfather, but did he have to be as boring when it came to speeches as Raziel was?

Shee'vra whispered to her brother. "Now that you're one of us, what are you going to do now?"

Ercan seemed really relaxed about all of this. "Well that's easy—get better at being a psychic. Somehow I feel like we all still have a lot to learn, and just because I'm no longer captain, that doesn't give me an excuse to slack off. Last week was hard for sure, but I can bet that it's just uphill from here."

"Any students from grades ten and up are free to vacate the premises if desired."

The moment Mastema finished that sentence, all the older non-captain psychics quickly began to leave. The rest of Rooster Squad also began to get up to follow the crowds. Ercan had an idea of where to go.

"So does anyone feel like going to the Chokmall?" He still needed to get a new scarlet outfit since the last one had been torn to pieces. Now he only had three plus the one for The Stage. "I'm sure everyone else is going."

"Sure thing," Shee'vra replied. Even though he was no longer her captain, Ercan would always be her big brother and she would follow him when needed.

Yun also seemed to brighten up at the idea. "Well, I do like the food court there, so why not. Chances are a lot of us are going to the exact same place, though. Prepare for lines."

Julia was blunter. "Anywhere but here is good."

All of the squads left the auditorium in a mass exodus. Some were going to hang out for a bit, others were off to train on The Stage or in the gym, and some were just going to go back to their dorm rooms to study or sleep. The smart ones were not going to take their time at the Academy for granted, for in the world outside lurked dangerous foes around every corner.

~ * ~

It had been less than a week in Prisoner's Perch and Zuo already had a visitor. Having no idea who it could possibly be, he accepted the visit. He sat in a chair in front of a desk with a large glass that represented the limbo between freedom and imprisonment. At least the orange outfits he had to wear didn't chafe too much. *Can't say the same thing about my collar, though.*

The buzzer buzzed as the visitor's door opened. Whoever wanted to see him tripped flat on his face, not watching his step. Not even the guards could help but snicker a bit as this clumsy idiot hastily picked up his papers. As the guy who wanted to see him got up, Zuo didn't recognize him at all. This young adult male wore a suit that made it obvious that he couldn't tie a tie at all. Scrutinizing his features, he noticed that this klutz was a redhead, though not at all like that Ercan kid's scarlet. This guy's hair was more orange, like the color of fire. His eyes also seemed to have that burning orange color as he took a seat in front of him.

Zuo was the first one to pick up the phone and speak. "So are you a Lefty or what?"

This mysterious man with orange hair quickly shook his head in fervent denial. "No, no! Not at all! I have absolutely no connections to that organization!" He tried to compose himself. "But anyway, Zuo, I think it would be considerate of me to introduce myself. My name is Sanshoo Kihaku. Father is Seichin, mother Enotitan." He bumped his hand on the glass when he tried to shake hands, forgetting about the barrier. "Ow! The glass here must be as tough a stone."

If this was the lawyer the county had given him, Zuo was supremely unimpressed. "So what do you want with a crook like me? If you're my lawyer, I think I'll take my chances alone, thank you very much."

Sanshoo shook his head. "No, no, no! Of course I'm not here for that." His voice got quieter. "I'm here under my superior's orders to give you a chance to be free once more. You know, to work under us."

This aging psychic had no more patience for such shady crap. Zuo would rather just let himself pass on peacefully in prison than work for another shady organization. He'd already done his fair amount of atrocities. No need to add to the reasons Hell would delight in having his soul.

"Tell your boss I refuse."

Sanshoo seemed to have expected this at least a little, so he tried to persuade him. "Are you sure? My master can grant you hefty amounts of paz. More than Reliquit ever could."

"I said no," Zuo firmly stated. "Now get out."

With the unambiguous rejection, Sanshoo felt that this was a lost cause, at least for now. "Well, to be honest, I was never exactly the most persuasive one in my group. So maybe one day you'll change your mind. Hopefully soon enough." He slid some sort of small medallion under the glass. "Us psychics have a gift, Zuo. They are a symbol of our birthright. The world needs to remember that."

With those parting words, Sanshoo hung up the phone. As he walked through the door, he once again forgot to watch his step. As the guards got their chuckles for the day, Zuo observed what was on the medallion the messenger gave him.

It was made of what seemed to be platinum, with a symbol of a half-moon with an eye on it. The dark side of the moon and the eye were a deep purple. Looked quite expensive, but he had no need for it here. Zuo slid the trinket away and walked away, wondering what would be for dinner tonight.